This book is dedicated, in memoriam,
to the two finest men I have ever known:
my father, historian extraordinaire, Harold J. Jonas,
and my mentor, Dr. Edward K. Barsky
(among other things, Commander of the Medical Unit
for the whole of the International Brigade in Spain)

PRAISE FOR THE 15% SOLUTION

Reminiscent of *It Can Happen Here* and *The Iron Heel*, the novel by Steven Jonas, *The 15% Solution*, looks into the future to fix the present, warning us eloquently about the dangers of religious fascism in America—a threat at present firmly encapsulated in the new Republican Party. The author visualizes a gradual takeover of the American government by Christian zealots and their prompt annihilation of the American Constitution, all perfectly prefigured in these fanatics' own declarations. A number of American sociologists, historians and journalists have argued that American Christofascism is an old phenomenon in the United States, a nation born out of transplanted religious fervor. Chris Hedges, among others, has persuasively shown that religious authoritarianism first reared its head during the Great Depression, suggesting that the tendency is latent in American culture, and, like a dormant virus, can be detonated by profound social dislocations. In Steven Jonas' view, the demise of what remains of American democracy is a long announced political cataclysm, but, inexplicably, the alarms continue to fall on deaf ears. Packaged as fiction, this volume is a serious new effort to shake the population out of its lethargy before time for effective action runs out.

—Branford Perry
Blitz Reviews, The Greanville Post

***

This fictional history first published in 1996 (the current edition has some minor revisions, but is not updated from the original) supposes that by "2001" political forces that agreed with the most extreme right-wing religious positions will have managed to take over the US government ... and create, among other things, an Apartheid state called the "New American Republics." In "2023" following the conclusion of the Second Civil War, NAR is defeated and Constitutional democracy is finally restored in the Reunited States. This unique exposition of political thought is divided into three main sections, ending with "*What Might Have Been Done*" to prevent the national nightmare from occurring. A notable feature of the book is that virtually every supposed event, Constitutional amendment, Supreme Court decision, speech, or diary entry in it is based on statements and writings that were actually made by right-wing figures and organizations in the United States, or real events that have already occurred here and in other countries. The book is fully referenced to these real sources and events. This is a fascinating new book on the rise and fall of Fascist America.

—**Christian Coalition Watch News Service**
(cc.watch)

QUOTES

"For every problem there is one solution which is simple, neat, and wrong."

—H. L. Mencken

***

"Posterity: What the Founding Fathers wouldn't have talked about so glowingly if they had known we were going to be it."

—Jacob Brauda

Editor

Speakers Encyclopedia, Stories, Quotes, and Anecdotes

***

"The only thing necessary for the triumph of evil is for good men to do nothing."

—Edmund Burke

***

"We're on the verge of taking [the Republican Party] back as prelude to taking back our country as prelude to taking back the destiny of America, and when we get there, my friends, we will be obedient to one sovereign in America and that is the sovereign of God himself."

—Patrick Buchanan

(during the 1996 Republican primary elections campaign)

***

"What happens when the people you patronizingly encouraged because you thought they were engaged in style and metaphor, turn out to have meant exactly what they said."

–Adam Gopnik

The New Yorker, (May 8, 1995)

***

"Nah, it can't happen here."

–Doug Henwood

Left Business Observer, No. 53

***

"Suppose, then, that we amend the Constitution and acknowledge the existence and supremacy of God—what becomes of the supremacy of the people, and how is this amendment to be enforced? A constitution does not enforce itself. It must be carried out by appropriate legislation. Will it be a crime to deny the existence of this Constitutional God? Can the offender be proceeded against in criminal court? Can his lips be closed by the power of the state? Would not this be the inauguration of religious persecution? It probably will not be long until the churches will divide as sharply upon political, as upon theological questions; and when that day comes, if there are not liberals enough to hold the balance of power, this Government will be destroyed. The liberty of man is not safe in the hands of any church."

–Robert G. Ingersoll

(undated)

Steven Jonas

THE 15% SOLUTION

How the Republican Religious Right Took Control of the U.S., 1981-2022

A Futuristic Novel

Trepper & Katz Impact Books
A Division of Punto Press

New York

THE 15% SOLUTION:
How the Republican Religious Right Took Control of the U.S., 1981-2022
A Futuristic Novel

Revised and expanded edition published by
Trepper & Katz Impact Books, an imprint of Punto Press Publishing
P.O. Box 943, Brewster NY 10509-9998 USA

Contact: admin@puntopress.com

Library of Congress Control Number: 2013902427

ISBN: 978-0-9840263-4-0

Cover and book design and interior illustrations by Sarah Edgar

The 15% Solution is a work of fiction. Any resemblance of fictional persons to actual persons, living or dead, events or locales is entirely coincidental.

Printed and distributed worldwide by Lightning Source, Inc.

Political fiction | Historical fiction | Religious radicalism | American Christofascism | Tea Party | Republican Party | Religious Right | Fascism | Apartheid

***

Trepper & Katz impact Books pays homage to Leopold Trepper and Hillel Katz, two heroic fighters against fascism in World War Two. May their example guide those who, in every latitude, struggle today against great odds for world peace and social justice.

ACKNOWLEDGEMENT

To my dear friend and comrade, the Founder, Editor, and Publisher of Punto Press Publishing, Patrice Greanville, who has the same concerns for the future of the United States of America under its present political leadership that I do, and who has the guts to publish this book of warning, when no other publisher would, then or now. So many thanks to you, Patrice, for your faith in me, my ideas, and my writing. Many thanks as well to Barbara Havlena for her fine work in managing the project and editing the text and to Sarah Edgar for her equally fine work on the cover and book design and interior illutrations, as well as to their staff.

–SJ

August 28, 2012

Table of Contents

SECTION 3: CONCLUSION

APPENDICES

AUTHOR'S PREFACE

CONTENTS

I. The Origins of this Book

I BEGAN THINKING ABOUT what would eventually become the book you see before you in the mid-1980s, after the re-election of Ronald Reagan. The thinking process went on for quite a while, and both the story-line and the format (novel, non-fiction, some combination of both?) underwent numerous changes. Whatever form the book would eventually take, I was concerned that during the Presidencies of Ronald Reagan and George H.W. Bush the Republican Religious Right (RRR) was becoming ever more powerful. I began to think about what might happen were they to effectively take over full governmental power at the Federal, and widely, at the state levels. Being an academic, to support whatever form I might come up with, I began collecting material on positions that both governmental and non-governmental representatives of the RRR were then taking about the matter of what they would indeed do, were they to gain that effective control. I gathered it from a variety of sources: published articles, books, fund-raising letters, position papers, newspaper and magazine articles about them. Finally, in 1994, I came up with the outlines of a scenario that they might follow, and began writing this book.

I am a writer of non-fiction, not fiction. (Believe me there are major differences in skills between the two. I regard the latter as much more difficult than the former. Non-fiction writers simply need to be able to undertake description and analysis, sometimes simply reporting. We need to use references. However, we do not need to be able to write dialogue, describe scenes and settings in appropriate prose, or engage in character development.) Thus for this book, even though I decided that I would be writing primarily in the non-fiction style, at the same time I would be writing fiction in the sense that after a certain point I would be making up the plot-line, certainly introducing fictional characters. At the same time, while the story-line would be set in the then-future, it would be based on real policies and politics that real people on the Right were promoting in the 1980s and 90s.

And so I came up with what I describe as a "cross-over" book: *fictional non-fiction*, purportedly written by a future professor of political science, "Jonathan Westminster." (For more detail on him, please see IV, below "Historical Voices.") The book is a supposed retrospective on the (supposed) U.S. fascist period, published in 2048 on the (supposed) 25th anniversary of the re-establishment of U.S. Constitutional Democracy, July 4, 2048, following the (supposed) triumph of the Movement for the Restoration of Constitutional Democracy in the Second Civil War (2022).

To my mind the most important feature of this book is that what is projected to happen is, to the extent possible, based on what the Republican Religious Right had been telling us, prior to the time I wrote the book in 1994-1996, they would do if they were ever able to gain full control of the government. Indeed, they were telling us that as far back as the 1980s. But back in the 80s and 90s nobody wanted to listen. They are telling us much more loudly now: see the Republican National Platform, 2012. More people are listening and more people are getting very afraid of a future governed by the Republican Religious Right. Nevertheless, to date no real political opposition with power and money behind it has developed. One of the main points that I make in the book is that the fictional transformation of the Republican Party to the "Republican-Christian Alliance" (sound familiar?) and then on to the "American Christian Nation Party" takes place out in the open and nobody in a position of political power and political authority says boo to a goose.

I published the original version of this book in 1996 under my own imprint, the "Thomas Jefferson Press." The title of that version was *The 15% Solution: A Political History of American Fascism, 2001-22* under the pseudonym "Jonathan Westminster." In the book, the future-historical scenario is framed by a series of (fictional) documents: Presidential Inaugural addresses, Constitutional Amendments, Presidential Declarations, a Supreme Court decision, one treaty with a foreign power, several acts of Congress, and the Declaration of the Movement for the Restoration of Constitutional Democracy.

I wrote the book as a warning, to which no one in a position to do anything about the situation has yet taken heed. With the help of my good friend Patrice Greanville, the Publisher of Punto Press Publishing, I am issuing the warning again. It is still not too late. But some folks in some position of power are going to have to wake up to the real threats to our body politic presented to us by the modern Republican Religious Right. Someone is going to have to start naming names, taking identities, and stop pretending that the party that runs on religious- and race-based hate and makes liberal use of the Hitlerian Big Lie technique, is not a) qualitatively different from its predecessor and b) a real threat to U.S. Constitutional Democracy as we know it.

II. A Brief Overview of the Book

The book is a novelized chronicle of the rise and fall of a Fascist regime in the United States during the years 2001-2023. It is intended to present a barebones view of the events of the "Fascist Period," as it could have been seen contemporaneously to those events. Further, it attempts to show how the origins of each major step taken by Republican Religious Right during the Period, in most instances represented by a major document (as mentioned above), could be found either in what is by "Westminster" 's time called the U.S. pre-fascist "Transition Era," 1981-2001, or in events that took place in one or another of the fascist states that existed in other parts of the world between 1922 and 1945. The principal goals of this book are similar to those of its major forebears: Jack London's *The Iron Heel* and Sinclair Lewis' *It Can't Happen Here*, as if those authors had written those books with 20/20 hindsight.

As noted, many 20th century sources are used to explicate the then-stated goals of the Republican Religious Right, ranging, for example, from the 1992 Republican Party Platform, to fundraising letters written by the Reverend Jerry Falwell, to position papers of the litigatory arm of [the] Rev. Pat Robertson's "Christian Coalition" (the chief national political organization of the old Religious Right), called the "American Center for Law and Justice." All sources are referenced in the text either by the name of the principal author or, if none is listed, by the name of the publisher. The reference sources are listed at the end of each chapter.

This book does not deal with the projected outcomes of Republican Religious Rightist policies over which there was in the late 20th century considerable scientific controversy. Thus for the most part excluded are, for example, in the environmental arena (except for natural resources policy) the (even-then) predictable effects of global warming caused by human activity (1), the marked destruction of the ozone layer, and the sharp decline in biodiversity. Many of the predicted environmental disasters caused or significantly abetted by Republican Religious Rightist policies are as of 2012 indeed occurring or well on their way to occurring (2, 3, 4). However, the book does project a future "Resource Based Economy" (RBE) based on the ever-expanding power of the extractive industries (which has in fact, in the intervening years, exploded before our very eyes). However, in the late 20th century, the outcomes of those policies could not have been predicted with nearly the accuracy of those predictions that could then have been made of the political and economic outcomes for the country if Republican Religious Right took power.

Once in power at the Federal and state levels, the Republican Religious Right is then projected to have achieved virtually all of its stated goals in the political, social, and economic arenas, and then some. In the beginning at least, through the electoral process they did this entirely by legal/constitutional means. The predictably widening use of force and violence came later. And the more profound results of the takeover, such as the creation of the apartheid-based "New American Republics," came later too, but predictably as well. All of the political figures which "Westminster" cites with quotes from materials that existed as of 1996 or before, during the so-called "Transition Period," are real. Most importantly, virtually all of the speeches and writings supposedly made the Fascist leadership from 2000 onwards are based on material published by various representatives of the Republican Religious Right and their political allies between 1981 and 1996. And they are fully referenced.

A Note on Foreign Policy

Except for some allusions to the "Latin Wars," I did not deal with foreign policy issues in the book. It is long enough as it is (as is this new introduction). Therefore, I am not going to deal with the many obvious ones here. Suffice it to say that, in a reverse of this book possibly being a guidebook for the Republican Religious Right as they proceed with their domestic policies, the real foreign policies of the Bush Administration (and some of the Obama Administration as well [5]) would likely find a home in the State and Defense Departments of the fictional Republican-Christian Alliance.

Structure of the Book

This book has three sections. Section I sets the stage. Chapter 1, "Prelude to Fascism," is an essay written in 1995 by "Dino

Louis," a fictional political analyst of the time. (For a brief biography of "Mr. Louis," see "The Historical Voices," below.) Several late 20th century analytical and prescriptive essays or notes for essays by "Mr. Louis," concerning major sociopolitical issues of the Transition Era are included in the book in Appendices II – VI. Chapter 2 presents an overview of the book and its historical scenario in outline.

Section II, the book's longest, features for the most part selected (fictional) historical documents which I designed to mark major events of the Fascist Period. Annotating, highlighting, and punctuating each of the documents are writings by four selected (fictional) observers/participants of the time (as noted, for their brief biographies, see just below). These personages provide comments/perspectives/reflections from several different points of view. The bulk of the text, however, is provided by "Westminster" in his "Author's Commentaries" and "Author's Notes."

Section II presents a retrospective chapter (20) by "Westminster" considering "What Could Have Been Done" to prevent the national nightmare from ever occurring.

The Cast of Characters

On the names. "Jonathan Westminster" is a mid-21st century Professor of Political Science at the (fictional) New State University of New York at Middletown. The name "Jonathan Westminster" is a play on the name Jack London, author of *The Iron Heel*, a prescient book published in 1908 foretelling of the advent of fascism in the capitalist world, before it first appeared as distinct political ideology in Hungary in 1920. The name "Dino Louis" (see also just below) is a play on the name Sinclair Lewis, author of *It Can't Happen Here* (the old Sinclair Oil company had a dinosaur—the source of oil, get it?—as its symbol). In his 1935 volume, Lewis speculated on the electoral institution of fascism in the United States following the election of 1936. The name "Alex Poughton" (see below) is a play on the name Alexis De Tocqueville, the 19th century

French author of *Democracy in America* (tocque/puff, ville/town). The authors of the 21st century publications cited in various reference lists are of course fictional, as are their books. Their names are plays on those of various 20th century jazz musicians, primarily African-American.

The selected writings appearing throughout the book are by the following five (fictional) historical figures, as they would have been described by Westminster:

- **Dino Louis.** A well-known, well-respected, and well-employed freelance sports journalist, Louis engaged in political analysis on the side. From time to time he made attempts to draw attention to his political work, but was never successful in so doing. Louis disappeared in 2001. It is not known whether he was able to successfully emigrate. Many who could afford it did in that year before foreign travel for American citizens was restricted as it had been during the McCarthy Era of the 1950s. (In that case he may just have maintained a low profile abroad to avoid detection by the International Death Squads.) Or he may have been caught and "disappeared" in the old CIA-inspired Latin American style of the 1970s and 1980s by a pre-Helmsmen (see Chapter 10) Domestic Death Squad. In any case, he had sent copies of the essays reproduced here to his friend Alex Poughton in London, as they were written. Those copies, preserved in Poughton's library, are used here with his (fictional) permission. (In fact, all of the writings of "Dino Louis" regardless of the date given them in the book, were done in 1995 or before. They refer to true events with true references.)
- **Alex Poughton.** The pencil-thin English journalist Alex Poughton sported a pencil-thin mustache and bore a striking resemblance to the well-known English actor of the second half of the twentieth century, David Niven. Poughton chronicled the Fascist Period for the *London Sunday Times* under the head "American Democracy." Staying in political tune with the owner of his newspaper, Poughton's writings were generally favorable to the Fascist regime. Thus he was

able to remain in and travel freely throughout the country (as a whole before 2011 and in the White Republic after that date).

However, published here are not his public puff pieces but private letters that he sent home by diplomatic pouch (through his connections in the British Embassy) from time to time. They present a rather different picture of American reality. The "Karl" to whom these letters were written has never been identified. Thus the originals are lost. But along with the Louis essays, copies were preserved in Poughton's English library and are used here with permission.

• **Curley Oakwood.** At 6'5" tall, weighing in at 320 lbs., his shaved head was always slightly aglow with sweat when bathed in the glow of television lights. He was the dominant electronic media figure of the Fascist Period. Presented here are transcripts of broadcasts he made during that time, until he went off the air the day before New Washington fell in 2023. A high-school dropout with a great radio voice, a great deal of personal hate and resentment of anyone he regarded as "different," and a great ability to absorb quickly and regurgitate faithfully the intensive political coaching he received daily throughout his career from his Right Wing Reactionary political mentors, Oakwood began his career at the age 25 in 1997.

Late in the Transition Era, he had succeeded one Rush Limbaugh as the dominant Right Wing presence on the contemporary mediums of "talk radio" and "talk television." He proceeded to go beyond Limbaugh, taking his one-time mentor's often subtle expressions of hatred and anger that were beginning to wear thin and become too subtle for many of Limbaugh's 20 million listeners to follow, to a much more open form.

Imitating the example of lesser-light reactionaries who had begun to appear mainly on local talk radio in the mid-1990s, Oakwood made it abundantly clear to everyone listening just how hateful and angry he was. In that time of mounting frustration and rage for so many in the country, open hate just began to play much better than any even slightly veiled version.

(Radio station KFSO in San Francisco, was one of the first to begin the "open hate" trend, early in 1995.) Oakwood went on to become the leading public, non-governmental voice of the American Fascists for their whole time in power. Unrepentant until the end, in 2026 at the age of 54 he was publicly hanged for the crime of "a principal leader of American Fascism." It was an unusual role to play for a media figure that remained in media. But it was one he had sought, and in the eyes of the forces whose interests he doggedly and faithfully served, he served them well.

• "Short, blond, and perky," according to a contemporary's description, **Constance "Connie" Conroy** was a White House press officer who, unwittingly mirroring Fouché's legendary ability to survive different regimes, managed to maintain her post through every twist and turn of the intense political infighting which characterized the Fascist Period. Her commentaries reproduced in this book are brief excerpts from a set of non-system, secret notes she kept throughout the time on an ancient personal computer called a "PC."

Conroy had first arrived in the White House under the "Last Republican," President Carnathon Pine (despite his age some say literally, others figuratively), shortly after his accession to the Presidency in 2001. She stayed on in the White House until the end of the Fascist Period. By pure chance, her old computer fell intact into the hands of the Constitutionalist forces during the conquest of New Washington. Fortunately for us, a technician of the Movement for the Restoration of Constitutional Democracy figured out how to work it. Conroy's notes, incomplete as they are, have provided the only "inside look" available to historians of the period. Following the lead of American Republican Religious Rightists in government ever since the then-famous "White House Tapes" incident which forced the resignation of President Richard Nixon in 1973, all of the official written and computer records of the whole Fascist Period located in New Washington were destroyed by the Fascists in the frantic weeks just before the city fell.

Conroy was Isolated for five years following the end of the Second Civil War. After her release she married a retired Constitutionalist press officer, and is still alive as of this writing. As readers will be aware, since the written record is so sparse, any writings of former Fascists, whether private or public, are by law in the public domain and so permission to reproduce is not required.

• **Parthenon "Pudge" Pomeroy**, the owner of a gasoline station in northern New Jersey, was an archetypal supporter and beneficiary of American Fascism. Accounting for his strange given name were the facts that his parents had been traveling in Greece the summer he was conceived, and liked alliteration. His childhood nickname had been considered to parsimoniously describe his appearance. People viewing at the same time adult and childhood photographs of him often remarked how much like 'himself' he looked at an early age. Well over age during the Second Civil War, he was forced to work for the Army of the New American Republics as a human pack animal (ironically for a man in his business, petroleum no longer being available for the mere transportation of supplies). He was killed during the Battle for the Liberation of New York in 2022. A diary kept by him from the year 2003, when he took over the family gasoline station from his father at the age 38, was found on his person. He had no known survivors.

And so concludes "Westminster's" description of the cast of characters.

III. The Modern U.S. Republican Party

As it happened, I was one of those political observers who, after the election of 1980, said "oh well, we'll have to live through four years of Reagan. The electorate will see through him immediately and surely the Democratic Party will be able to mount an effective opposition to him and his policies. Let's hope he won't do too much damage. Then we can get the Democrats back in in 1984." Little did I know how effective

Reagan and the Right-wing Republican machine would be at mobilizing various social prejudices for political purposes. So doing in turn enabled them to fairly easily pull the "economic wool" over the eyes of too many white working-class Americans, who became aptly known as "Reagan Democrats." This assured his easy re-election in 1984, although the ineffectiveness of Walter Mondale as the Democratic candidate and of the Democratic Party as a party certainly helped.

So what did Reagan do? First, he clearly indicated that he was going to follow Richard Nixon's "Southern [let's-use-racism-to-our-advantage] Strategy." For example, Reagan began his primary campaign in 1980 by giving a speech at Philadelphia, Mississippi. It had been the site of the famous murder of the three young civil rights workers, James Cheney, Andrew Goodman (who happened to be a son of a close friend of my mother's), and Michael Schwerner, in the "Freedom Summer" of 1964. Already in his primary campaign of 1976 Reagan had taken to describing welfare recipients as "Welfare Queens" from Chicago's South Side (an African-American neighborhood). This despite the fact that majority of persons receiving Aid to Mothers with Dependent Children (formal name of the law) were white. Further, in 1979 his campaign was already at work to mobilize the right-wing Christian vote for him (6).

Although the Christian Temperance Movement was one of the early supporters of the nascent Republican Party in the 1850s, and the Republicans had led the battle for Prohibition partly because of that alliance, the Reagan campaign's move marked the first time in the modern U.S. that religion and religious prejudice against all so-called "non-believers" was mobilized for political purposes. "Non-believers" for the Christian Right means persons of whatever religious or non-religious belief who do not happen to agree with their stance on a variety of social and political matters. That stance is usually based on their interpretation of selected passages of Biblical text as found in one particular English translation of the Bible, the "King James Version." (It should be noted that that translation was actually the product of the work of 52 selected academics, scholars and theologians in early 17th century England.) By the mid-80s, turning the emerging AIDS crisis to political use, the Reaganite Republicans had added homophobia to their own rapidly developing arsenal of hate politics.

Over the time from Reagan, through G. H.W. Bush to Bill Clinton, I observed what the Republican Party was doing and becoming. European history has provided a useful background for understanding the implications of those developments. Religious anti-Semitism had been developed in the Roman Catholic Church starting as early as the Fourth Century, C.E. Political anti-Semitism, that is the use of anti-Semitism specifically both for party/electoral political purposes and for political mass mobilization, was developed in Europe in the late 19th century. We know well what political anti-Semitism eventually led to on that continent.

On this continent racism, the White Supremacy Hypothesis, and anti-Native American prejudice had been used politically on the territory of what became the United States since well before there was a United States, beginning with the institution of slavery in 1619. But here was, in modern times, a political party that was attempting to mobilize additional prejudices and hatreds, such as homophobia, for political purposes. And they were doing it in a political context where no one and certainly no political party (namely the Democrats) of any influence was challenging them on that fact. And so I considered a variety of possible scenarios of what might happen if they kept going, unchallenged by any opposition that focused on what they were really doing and what they were really after. Of course the true Reaganite political/economic agenda had not changed much since right-wing capitalists had begun challenging the New Deal, from the time of its inception in 1930s (7). But just as at the time of this present writing, that was hardly an agenda that they could run and expect to win with.

The Right-Wing Republican economic agenda, then as now, included such items as: increasing the share of both national income and national wealth going to the super-rich (the distance, in dollars and political power between the "merely rich"—usually millionaires—and the super-rich—multi-billionaire class—is enormous, as to almost constitute a social divide between the two wings of the privileged); increasing the burden of state and local taxation, especially regressive taxation, on everyone else; priming the economic pump (if any priming were to be done) with increased military, but not much-needed national domestic, spending; cutting government aid to education at all levels; destroying the middle class's safety net, including programs such as Social Security, Medicare, Medicaid, and so on; punishing the poor for being poor by eliminating programs aimed at overcoming or compensating for poverty; ravaging the environment for the benefit of both extractive industries and property developers; breaking what was left of the American trade union movement for the benefit of corporate profits; encouraging the concentration of industrial ownership and the decline of competition, leading to the contraction of the so-called "free market" for goods and services; encouraging the export of capital; reducing to the greatest extent possible the regulation of the extractive industries, the financial markets, and the workplace. The preceding should not be read as exculpating the Democrats, who, on far too many occasions, simply did nothing to stop the Republicans or actively collaborated with them, albeit more surreptitiously and behind a curtain of demagogic populism, in pushing for exactly the same economic and military goals.

And so, from the time of Reagan the Republican Party turned to a focus on what are politely called the "Social Issues," but which are correctly called the "Issues of Personal Prejudice": those of racism, religious discrimination and authoritarianism (in the matter of abortion rights), homophobia, and more recently, Islamophobia (8). Other than that of racism, they are in fact correctly termed the "Religious Issues."

Some Lessons from History Elsewhere

For an historical perspective on the matter from outside the United States, I looked at where the political use of prejudice and hate, particularly of anti-Semitism (not in play [yet] in the United States, for obvious reasons), took the German Nazi Party (which represented the same economic interests that the Republican Party represents) and Germany. (One should note that there have been a wide variety of fascist governments appearing in countries around the world, most recently in Latin America in the 1970s [e.g., Chile, Argentina, and Brazil], since the first of them arose in Hungary in 1920, under Admiral Horthy. None of them ever ran on as virulent a form of anti-Semitism as Nazi Germany did.) Then, over time, I began to put the pieces together to project where the use of the several prejudices mobilized for political purposes, in defense of the same economic interest, might take the Republican Party in this country, in the absence, of course, of a real opposition to them. For example, see "The Second Final Solution," described in Chapter 18. If you think that that projection is far-fetched, in North Carolina in 2012 a man described as a "pastor," one Charles Worley, seriously proposed rounding up all "lesbians, queers and homosexuals," and depositing them in an open camp surrounded by an electrified fence, and except for air-dropping food, leaving them there to die (9, 10). When he delivered his proposal as part of a sermon in his church he received a standing ovation from his congregation.

Now in Germany, there was, on paper, a real opposition to the Nazis. But the Communist Party of Germany (KPD) and the Socialist Party of Germany (SPD) — a variant of early social democracy — were at each other's throats almost as much as they were opposed to the Nazis. The former, under the thumb of Josef Stalin's Communist International, spent much of its time attacking the "social fascists" of the latter, believing that "after Hitler, our turn would come" (11). There were also centrist parties opposed to the Nazis. But given the Socialist/Communist split in Germany, no united front ever developed. In the United States, however, the task for the Right was even easier.

Any meaningful truly left-wing political presence was destroyed by a combination of McCarthy-ite "anti-Communism" and the continuing assault on the never-too-strong-anyway U.S. labor movement following the passage of the Taft-Hartley Act in 1947. Then in the 1980s, whatever had been left of the very modest New Dealist left-wing influence in the Democratic Party was destroyed by its takeover by the "Republican-lite" Democratic Leadership Council, otherwise known as "DINO's," Democrats In Name Only. One need only look at the record of President Bill Clinton. For example, he destroyed most of what was left of the welfare system at the time, opened the floodgates for the export of U.S. capital, provided for the concentration of ownership of the print and electronic media, in his first State of the Union Address announced that "the era of big government was over" (a very Reaganite sentiment), and went to war in the former Yugoslavia (the first major war fought under the pretext of "humane intervention") without asking for Congressional approval, as required under the Constitution.

Turning back to the German lessons-of-history, Hitler still would have faced real, substantive opposition from both the Communist Party of Germany and the Socialist Party of Germany, despite the fact that they were never able to form a United Front against him. That is, if they had they been given a chance to get organized. However, from the day (January 30, 1933) he was appointed Chancellor of the Germany by the then President of the Weimar Republic, former Field-Marshall Paul von Hindenburg (known as the "first Hindenburg Disaster," the second being the one that four years later overcame the hydrogen-filled airship of the same name at Lakehurst, NJ), he used force to secure his control of the German government. Within 24 hours of taking power, the Nazis began rounding up Communists and imprisoning them in the first concentration camps. Given that the DLC-Democrats offered no real opposition and in some cases a good deal of support for the real goals of the Republican Religious Right, I figured that nothing like what had happened in Germany would be necessary for the latter as they began to take power here.

Nevertheless, I knew that, given their true economic and political program, which would necessarily lead to increasing economic and social misery for an ever-increasing number of Americans, in order to remain in power, the Republican Religious Right would eventually have to impose some version of fascism here. And so, after pondering the problem off and on for a number of years, I came up with the scenario of this book. "The 15% Solution" was actually a real, named Christian Rightist/Republican electoral strategy designed in the early 1990s to take over the political system with a minority of eligible voters voting. As described in detail in Chapter 2, I surmised that the Republican Religious Right, given the lack of any meaningful opposition, would triumph at the polls and thus take power electorally. (In the real world, in alliance with its current economic right-wing twin, the carefully manufactured "Tea Party," is currently in the process of doing just that.) They would not need to use oppressive force to stay in power until some years had passed. They would essentially use the U.S. Constitution and Constitutional processes to take over the system and eventually destroy the remnants of Constitutional democracy, already drastically diminished through bipartisan complicity.

The Republican Party and the "Rightward Imperative"

An essential element of this process is what can be called the "Right-Wing Imperative." Consider that in the 2012 Republican primaries a candidate for his party's nomination known as 'moderate' would propose to abolish Medicare. In boasting about it, this candidate said: "I'll end Medicare faster than Newt Gingrich." He also supported the proposed Mississippi Constitutional "Personhood" amendment to ensconce in that state's Constitution a particular religious belief as to when life begins (turned down by the voters of Mississippi!) Yes, that was Mitt Romney, who continued to have all sorts of trouble cozying up to the Republican Far Right, because of that awful label 'moderate' earned when he was Governor of Massachusetts.

Then there was the "traditional conservative" Rick Santorum who said (12): "As long as abortion is legal in this country ... we will never rest because that law does not comport with God's law." In other words, Santorum, as in that Mississippi "Personhood" Constitutional Amendment initiative that Romney supported, would put "God's law" above the *U.S.* Constitution. (Romney, it should be noted, believes that the Constitution was "divinely inspired.") None of the other Republican candidates pointed out either of two major features of Santorum's position. First, the central element of the Islamic "Sharia Law" that they all so eagerly pounce on, as if its institution were just around the corner in the United States, is that it proclaims that "God's law" is to stand above any civil constitution that happens to be in place in the country. Second, "God's law" in any country that is governed even in part by it means simply what some group of men happen to say it is, of course always citing some "holy book" (that just happens to have been written by men). But the Republican Party was by then so far to the Right that this position of Santorum's is not challenged within it (13). (See also "Rick Santorum's Most Outrageous Campaign Moments," *The Progress Report*, Jan. 5, 2012.)

Then there was another "conservative," Ron Paul. The bulk of the Republican establishment doesn't like him, because he would like to cut out virtually all of the US imperialistic overseas involvements, military and otherwise. That of course would lead to a major reduction in US military spending, but it would also end the cash cow that the war industry provides for its owners and their Congressional stooges in the US. It would also put an end to the central element of Cheneyism (14), the establishment of Orwellian Permanent War. It is this element of Paulism that attracts certain elements of the Left to him. But Paul also takes these positions, as *The Nation*'s Katha Pollitt has pointed out (15):

> "In a Ron Paul America, there would be no environmental protection, no Social Security, no Medicaid or Medicare, no help for the poor, no public education, … no anti-discrimination law, no Americans With Disabilities Act, no laws ensuring the safety of food or drugs or consumer products, no workers' rights, [no] Federal Aviation Authority and its pesky air traffic controllers."

On the other hand, this so-called "libertarian" would let the states criminalize any belief that life begins other than at the time of conception, and (quoting again from Pollitt) "he maintains his opposition to the 1964 Civil Rights Act and opposes restrictions on the 'freedom' of business owners to refuse service to blacks. … No wonder they love him over at Stormfront, a white-supremacist website with neo-Nazi tendencies."

In a rather remarkable way so-called "Libertarians"—chiefly by practicing ahistoricalism—have succeeded in selling themselves to a wide section of the electorate as "reasonable conservatives." But, in reality, in many areas, as Pollitt enumerates, they hold radical right-wing positions. Nobody in today's GOTP [Grand Old Tea Party] would get anywhere by challenging any of them. Today's GOP is a far cry from that of Dwight D. Eisenhower who said publicly that the New Deal reforms were accepted and acceptable public policy and that the only differences between Democrats and Republicans on them were how they should be implemented. But how did the Republican Party get from Ike to Mitt and Newt and Rick (either of them) and Ron? Through what I have already referred to as the Imperative of the Right-Wing Imperative (12). It started with Goldwater and has proceeded through Reagan and the Bushes down to the present day. They cannot put on the table what they are really in the game for, so they use something else, usually wrapped up in religious-based prejudices and racism.

Then we have this truly crazy Presidential electoral system in which truly tiny numbers of people in small states have an inordinate influence on who wins the Republican Presidential nomination. In 2012 little more than 200,000 generally far-right voters in Iowa determined who "won," Romney and Santorum with about 30,000 (!) each, and who "lost," all of the others. The Iowa caucuses are then followed by primaries in two more small states with right-wing Republican bases, New Hampshire and South Carolina, and then by Florida, which while not small also houses a right-wing Republican electorate. Thus to have a chance of winning the nomination, more and more the Republican candidates' pitches have to be pitched to the Right.

It was left for Norman Orenstein of the (formerly right-wing) U.S. "think tank," the American Enterprise Institute, no liberal he, to say, with Thomas Mann of the (no longer liberal) Brookings Institution, in their book *It's Even Worse than It Looks* (16): "[Today's Republican Party] is an insurgent outlier—ideologically extreme, contemptuous of the inherited social and economic policy regime; scornful of compromise; not persuaded by conventional understanding of facts, evidence, and science; and dismissive of the legitimacy of its political opposition."

Further Examples of the Religion-based Thinking of Leading Candidates for the Republican Presidential Nomination, 2012

Let's start with Newt Gingrich (17). In 1995 he proposed executing "drug smugglers." In 1994, before the election returns were in, he referred to the President and Mrs. [Bill] Clinton as "counter-culture [*sic*]." He said that he would seek to portray Clinton Democrats as the "enemy of normal people," and in a speech during the campaign he described America as a "battleground" between men of God, like himself, and the "secular anti-religious view of the left." He also blamed a tragic murder-suicide by a young mother in South Carolina on the "values" of the Democratic Party. In 1995, he said: "We are the only society in history that says that power comes from God to you … and if you don't tell the truth about the role of God and the centrality of God in America, you can't explain the rest of our civilization. I look forward to the day when a belief in God is once more at the center of the definition of being an American." Yes, folks, that was Newt, the self-styled "intellectual/historian" of the Republican Party.

In 1985 Gingrich addressed the issue of AIDS, which at that time appeared to be a disease that would affect only homosexuals. At one point he said: "AIDS is a real crisis. It is worth paying attention to, to study. It's something one ought to be looking at. … [For] AIDS will do more to direct America back to the cost of violating traditional values, and to make America aware of the danger of certain behavior than anything we've seen. For us [the GOP], it's a great rallying cry." Finally, in March, 2012, in discussing the possible imposition of (Islamic) Sharia Law in the United States [*sic*] that so many of his Republican colleagues seem to perceive as such a real threat, he said: "I am convinced that if we do not decisively win the struggle over the nature of America, by the time [my grandchildren] are my age they will be in a secular atheist country, potentially [one] dominated by radical Islamists." (How a man of his reputed intellectual stature can proclaim in one breath such a nonsensical contradiction is typical of the range of unchallenged imbecility that exists today in America's political culture. I, for one would like to know how radical Islamists, known for their deep religiosity, would dominate in a nation defined by Newt as "secular" and "atheist.")

Let's return to Rick Santorum (18, 19). Until Paul Ryan arrived on the national scene, he is the most like my fictional "Jefferson Davis Hague," (who, as the nominee of the "Republican-Christian Alliance" becomes President in "2004"). A major exception is that Santorum (and Ryan, it would appear) really believes the religious doctrines he pronounces while Hague doesn't believe the stuff at all. Hague just used it to get to the Presidency and then spouted it as necessary in order to remain unchallenged in office. If Mitt Romney does not win the Presidency in (the real) 2012, Ryan and Santorum will be quickly nominated, by the Fox "News" Channel at least, as the twin Republican "front-runners" for their party's nomination in 2016. (Fox "News" actually performed the same service for Romney in December, 2008.)

Santorum has referred to the science behind our understanding of global warming and the threats to humanity and indeed many of the Earth's species that it presents as "punk science." (Ryan also views global warming science as a hoax. He does receive major campaign contributions from the Kochs, et al.) He feels that we should continue to rely on fossil fuels and indeed would vastly expand the extraction of same regardless of the pollution of the air, water and ground that such extraction causes (see the book's "Resource Based Economy" [Chapter 14]). Santorum seems to be bothered by homosexuals and homosexuality to a rather extraordinary degree. He has compared homosexual intercourse to "bestiality," for example, and would outlaw it (see Chapter 11, "The Proclamation of Right." Then see Chapter 18, "The Second Final Solution.") In referring to the excesses of the French Revolution, he inferred that he believes in the "eternal values" upheld by the absolute monarchy that it overthrew.

On abortion policy, based on his religious belief about when life begins he is against it and wants it to be criminalized (see Chapter 7, "The Morality Amendment," which would put the contemporary "Personhood Amendment" also supported by Mitt Romney, almost word-for-word into the Constitution. Of course, Ryan does as well.) In the process he would of course criminalize the religious/secular belief of those of us who hold that life begins at the time of viability. He does not tell us if he would be for sending just the abortion providers to prison, or would he include those women who have them too (see also Chapter 7). He has not told us how he would go about paying for the massive increase in the size and scope of the criminal justice system that the criminalization of abortion in the way he contemplates it would entail. Finally, he has said that he would outlaw contraception, for it is "a license to do things in a sexual realm that is counter to how things are supposed to be."

Then we come again to Mitt Romney. Particularly interesting is his Mormon faith, discussed very little during the campaign, but which is the basic formative influence in his thinking about life and about the United States (20). For those concerned with the central political issue of the separation of church and state and the ever-expanding intrusion of religious doctrine into the law and politics (that is, the subject of this book at its core), this is a very serious matter. According to Frank Rich, "[Romney's] great passion [his Mormonism] is something he is determined to keep secret" (21). It is well-known that many Right-wing Christians refer to Mormonism as a cult, with the evidence contained in the Book of Mormon (22) (see also 23) to the contrary notwithstanding, "not Christian." (In fact, he is simply not their kind of Christian.) But such complaints generally don't make it to the national stage.

A *New York Times* article about Romney, "Mormonism and his Personal Mormonism," also deserves mention (24). The information contained in it, drawn from friends, colleagues and fellow Mormon activists (and he is, or at least has been, a Mormon activist), quoted by name, raised some serious concerns. In historical Mormonism, the church and state were fully integrated in the person of Brigham Young. Of course, it has not been, on paper at least, since 1890 when Utah made its deal to join the Union. But the important point was, where did Romney stand on this question? As of this writing (August, 2012) he had not answered it directly. But what he did say in the vicinity of the question must give pause for thought to those of us concerned with maintaining that separation.

His Liberty University Commencement Address (25) of 2012 contained such phrases as: "Marriage is the relationship between one man and one woman," a definition that is derived from religious texts (and of course a definition to which the Mormon Church did not adhere until 1890. Further, at least one of Romney's grandfathers had five wives, one of whom was presumably one of his grandmothers. Very interesting in light of his definition of marriage.) And, he said, "but from the beginning, this nation trusted in God, not man." And "there is no greater force for good in the nation than Christian conscience in action." Rhetorically at least, he believes that the United States was chosen by God to play a special role in history, and that our Constitution was "divinely inspired." He has also professed the view that "America is the [Biblical] Promised Land." Finally, Romney prays frequently, feels that he has a direct connection to "God," and indeed engages in conversations with "God," asking for guidance in making decisions, even about matters of investment. Now, one would have no objection to Tevye talking with "God" in "Fiddler on the Roof." But for someone who would be President of the United States the questions do arise: what is the nature of these conversations; how often do they occur; what influence do "God's" answers have on his decision-making; does "God" accept the principle of the separation of church and state and if so, how does Romney find that his conversations with "God" are consistent with this principle.

Other Republicans and the "Supremacy of God"

As it happens, these references to "God" and his/her/its influence on the affairs of state are not confined to major Republican candidates for their party's nomination for the Presidency in 2012. For example, in 1996 Patrick Buchanan said: "We're on the verge of taking [the Republican Party] back as prelude to taking back our country as prelude to taking back the destiny of America, and when we get there, my friends, we will be obedient to one sovereign America and that is the sovereign of God himself" (26). But that's Pat Buchanan. Is there a higher authority on the role of the Higher Authority?

How about one of George W. Bush's two favorite Supreme

Court Justices, Antonin Scalia, considered by many to be the representative exemplar for the Republican Religious Right? Beginning with a quote from St. Paul as his thoughts are represented in the New Testament, Scalia had this to say about the subject (27):

> " 'For there is no power but of God [St. Paul is said to have said]; the powers that be are ordained of God. … The Lord repaid — did justice — through his minister, the state. …' "[This was the consensus] of Christian or religious thought regarding the powers of the state. … That consensus has been upset, I think, by the emergence of democracy. … The reaction of people of faith to *this tendency of democracy to obscure the divine authority behind government should not be resignation to it, but the resolution to combat it as effectively as possible* [emphasis added]."

Justice Scalia is still fighting the dyed-in-the-wool religionists' battle against The Enlightenment which, ironically enough, was the inspiration of the Founding Fathers of the United States. Further, Scalia has said on more than one occasion that he thinks that there is some divine "authority" standing above the Constitution (28). His soul mate Clarence Thomas does too. Scalia could have written the book's "33rd Amendment" himself.

Of course there is no mention of such an authority, God or otherwise, standing above its precepts and proscripts in the Constitution itself, and it was written by the Founding Fathers to be the supreme law of the land. But Scalia is in a position to interpret the document and say "what it really means." So much for the Doctrine of Original Intent. Too bad I didn't have the above quote from Scalia at the time I wrote the book. I would have made it the rallying cry of the Republican-Christian Alliance as they proceeded to use the Constitutional amendment process to destroy the Constitution and convert the United States into a "Christian Nation."

Finally on this point, like Mitt Romney, President George W. Bush has been quoted as claiming something that Jefferson Davis Hague never did, even at the height of his powers: that he acts under the direct instructions of God. The quote came from what the leading Israeli daily *Haaretz* (29) stated was the transcript of the conversation of a meeting between Bush and the Prime Ministers of Israel and the Palestinian Authority, Ariel Sharon and Mahmoud Abbas on June 25, 2003. No denial of its validity ever came from the White House. And so:

> "God told me to strike at al-Qaida and I struck them, and then He instructed me to strike at Saddam, which I did, and now I am determined to solve the problem of the Middle East. If you help me, I will act, and if not, the elections will come and I will have to focus on them."

Bush did not claim, however, that he was acting under divine instruction in dealing with the Israel/Palestine conflict. Nor did he claim that God had already told him that He would be on his side in the upcoming elections.

And so, it happens that references to the "Supremacy of God" litter the speeches of the leaders of the Republican-Christian Alliance in the book, just as they litter the thought and the speeches of the leadership of the 21st century Republican Party and its peripheral formations in reality. In the book's scenario the concept actually makes it into the Constitution (the "33rd Amendment," see Chapter 9) and then helps to pave the way for their eventual formal declaration of the United States as a "Christian Nation" (a long-time goal of such Christian Right leaders as David Barton [30]). That "God is supreme" is a theory of government (theocracy, in one form or another) that the Christian Right has publicly subscribed to for quite some time now.

An Increasing Focus on Homophobia

Homophobia and its political consequences are very important in the ideology and subsequent policies of the Republican-

Christian Alliance of the book. First, as noted, in "2005" the Alliance puts into the Constitution (!) the notion that homosexual behavior is a matter of choice (Chapter 7). In "2009" the President, under his emergency powers, declares homosexuality to be a crime (Chapter 11). Finally, in "2020," with an active rebellion underway, the regime begins the "Second Final Solution," in which that "scourge upon society" on which all the people's troubles are blamed, are now to be arrested and sent to passive extermination camps (Chapter 18).

How far-fetched is this scenario? Well, at some time during the first two years of the G.W. Bush Administration, when Trent Lott was Senate Minority Leader, he said words to the effect that homosexuality is a sin and therefore evil, *because the Bible says so.* This man was the third-ranking leader of the Republican government at the time. A 2003 Bush nominee for the 11th Circuit Court of Appeals, the Attorney General of Alabama Bill Pryor, in a brief to the U.S. Supreme Court, at one time compared homosexuality with necrophilia, bestiality, incest and pedophilia. In April, 2003, Rick Santorum, when he was the third highest ranking Republican in the United States Senate, compared homosexuality to bigamy, polygamy, incest and adultery. President Bush's response to this statement was that he (Bush) was tolerant of a range of views on social questions. That range apparently didn't include the view not held by Sen. Santorum that homosexuality, regardless of origin, is a perfectly legitimate lifestyle, protected by the Constitutional right to privacy (declared by the Supreme Court in "Griswold" to be found under the Ninth Amendment). More recently, former Wisconsin Rep. Mark Neumann allowed that "If I was elected God for a day homosexuality wouldn't be permitted" (31). Mr. Neumann was a Republican candidate for the Senate from his state in 2012.

The Creation of the "American Faith Party"

Which leads us to what Howard Fineman, in 2012 a liberal (hardly radical) commentator for MSNBC and Editorial

Director of the *AOL Huffington Post Media Group* would say the following in March 2012 (32):

> "The signs are numerous, but it's still easy to miss the big picture: that the GOP now is best understood as the American Faith Party (AFP) and its members as conservative Judeo-Christian-Mormon Republicans. The basement of St. Peter's is just one clubhouse. 'There has never been anything like it in our history,' said Princeton historian Sean Wilentz. 'God's Own Party' now really is just that.' …
>
> "The American Faith Party is a doctrinally schizophrenic coalition bound by faith in the power of biblical values to create a better country; by fear of federal power, especially that of the federal courts and President Barack Obama and his administration; and by fear of rising Islamic political power around the world.
>
> "The AFP unites Catholic traditionalists who especially revere the papal hierarchy; evangelical, fundamentalist and charismatic Protestants; some strands of Judaism, including those ultra-orthodox on social issues and Jews for whom an Israel with biblical borders and a capital in Jerusalem is a spiritual imperative, not just a matter of diplomatic balance in the Middle East; and Mormons, who ironically aren't regarded as Christians by most other members of the coalition. Romney, a devout Mormon, is their man.
>
> "The four still-standing Republican presidential candidates are all AFP members in good standing on most of the party's key agenda items. The GOP platform is sure to feature all of them, including opposition to [legal] abortion and gay marriage; measures to counter what Republicans regard as attacks on religious liberty

> [*sic*]; expressions of fear about the extent of federal power, especially from the courts, on social and medical issues; libertarian economic policies that limit regulation and taxes (for religious conservatives and economic libertarians share a common enemy: government); denunciations of Islamic political power; and support for Israel. (Ron Paul is a dissenter on the last two points.)
>
> "All the candidates, including Paul, adhere to the AFP's central operational tenet: that professing your own faith—once verboten in American politics—is a necessary precondition to being taken seriously.
>
> "In the American Faith Party, in other words, every day begins with a prayer breakfast, a public ritual that used to occur only once a year."

In this book, I refer to the next stage of the projected historical development of the Republican Party, going into the (projected) election of "2004," as the "Republican-Christian Alliance" (see Chapter 6). According to Mr. Fineman, it now exists in reality.

IV. Fascism and the Trajectory of the Republican Religious Right

Since the principal focus of this book is on how the Republican Religious Right would come to create fascism in the United States, I feel it is important to present the definition of fascism that I use here. The bulk of this section is taken from Appendix II, "The Nature of Fascism and Its Precursors," supposedly written by "Dino Louis" in "1998." At this time (2012) the word "fascist" is not used in certain left-wing circles. It is thought to be too over-used, too out-of-date, too devoid of meaning, too nasty, too emotional. At the same, it is hurled around by right-wingers to describe certain social polices promoted by *liberal* Democrats. In that case, it is highly misused by people who do not have the foggiest notion of what forms of government the word describes that actually existed over time.

In the book, I project that in "2048", were a real equivalent of "Jonathan Westminster" to be writing, when describing the economic and political system which existed throughout the period "2001-2023," first in the old United States and then in the apartheid-state the New American Republics (NAR, see Chapter 13: "White," "Negro," "Indian," and "Hispanic"), the words "fascist" and "fascism" would generally not be used.

However, it should be understood that with few exceptions the Republican Religious Right leadership and its successors in both the old United States and New American Republics would vehemently deny that they were fascists, and would strongly shy away from ever using the term to describe themselves or any of their activities. They would, of course, continue to use it to describe the Resistance. Perfect Orwellianism.

Even at the height of the projected NAR's racist oppression of the non-white peoples of the Second, Third, and Fourth Republics, and violent repression of dissent and resistance within the White Republic itself, even at the time of the most extreme concentration of power in the hands of the Executive Branch of the NAR and the substitution of the rule of men for the rule of law, and even with the perpetuation of one-party (American Christian Nation Party, the ACNP, the successor to the Republican Christian Alliance) government, in my projection the Right would pursue the fiction that it was following the precepts of Democracy and was the protector of traditional American freedoms.

Even after it would have used the Constitutional Amendment process in the most grotesque way to make the original U.S. Constitution a mere shadow of its original self, the Republican Religious Rightists would claim that they were doing nothing more than protecting the traditional "American way of life." And they shunned the use of the term "fascism" even at the risk of alienating some of their projected strongest, and most violent, supporters from the traditional U.S. Far Right, groups and organizations that proudly labeled themselves "Fascist" and "Nazi."

But the ACNP leadership would persist in this policy to the very end. It was the natural outgrowth of a fashion broadly used by Republican Religious Right during the Transition Era, of racists claiming they were not racists, anti-Semites claiming they were not anti-Semitic, misogynists claiming they were not anti-female, xenophobes claiming they were not xenophobic, Islamophobes claiming they were not Islamophobic, and homophobes claiming they were not homophobic. Mindspeak again.

It was a peculiar tactic bred of a time just before the commencement of the projected Transition Era in 1980 when in fact prejudice of most kinds was considered by most people to be nasty stuff. The tactic, as we can see today, has served a very useful purpose for the Republican Religious Rightists because many of their opponents were drawn into useless, distracting, no-win "yes-you-are, no-I'm-not" arguments, rather than discussing and exposing the true policies and desired social outcomes advocated by the Right-Wing forces, regardless of how they characterized themselves. In "Westminster" 's time, the phrase "if it looks like a duck, walks like a duck, and quacks like a duck, it's a duck" would most certainly characterize the approach of most historians to the study of the period 1981-2022.

And so, here is a working description of fascism as "Westminster" would most likely understand it (drawn from the book's Appendix II).

V. A Definition of Fascism

Fascism is a political, social, and economic system that has the following baker's dozen plus one of major defining characteristics:

1. There is complete executive branch control of government policy and action. There is no independent judicial or legislative branch of government.

2. There is no Constitution recognized by all political forces as having an authority beyond that claimed, stated, and exerted by the government in power, to which that government is subject. The rule of men, not law, is supreme.

3. There is only one political party, and no mass organizations of any kind other than those approved by the government are permitted.

4. Government establishes and enforces the rules of "right" thinking, "right" action, and "right" religious devotion.

5. Racism, homophobia, misogynism, and national chauvinism are major factors in national politics and policy-making. Religious authoritarianism may be part of the package.

6. There is no recognition of inherent personal rights. Only the government can grant "rights." Any "rights" granted by the government may be diminished or removed by it from any individual or group at any time without prior notice, explanation, or judicial review. Thus, there is no presumed freedom of speech, press, religion, or even belief, automatically accompanying citizenship. There are no inherent or presumed protections against any violations of personal liberty committed by law enforcement or other government agencies.

7. Official and unofficial force, internal terror, and routine torture of captured opponents are major means of governmental control.

8. There are few or no employee rights or protections, including the right of workers to bargain collectively. Only government-approved labor unions or associations are permitted to exist, and that approval may be removed at any time, without prior notice.

9. All communications media are government-owned or otherwise government-controlled.

10. All entertainment, music, art, and organized sport are controlled by the government.

11. There may or may not be a single charismatic leader in charge of the government, i.e., a "dictator."

12. The economy is based on capitalism, with tight central control of the distribution of resources among the producers, and strict limitations on the free market for labor (as noted above).

13. The fascist takeover of the government of a major power always leads to foreign war, sooner or later.

14. Built as it is on terror, repression, and an ultimately fictional/delusional representation of historical, political, and economic reality, fascism is inherently unstable and always carries within it the seeds of its own destruction. To date, such seeds have always sprouted within a relatively short historical period of time. Retiring a deeply entrenched fascist regime is no easy task, however, as modern history has shown.

VI. Some Final Thoughts

Many books have been written about the Republican Religious Right in general and the Christian Right in particular, what they stand for, and how their ideology stands in complete contradiction to the fundamental principles of the U.S. Constitution and indeed our whole national multicultural, multiethnic, and multi-religious history and tradition. They range from Rob Boston's *Why the Religious Right is Wrong* to Sara Diamond's *Roads to Dominion*, to Frederick Carlson's *Eternal Hostility*, to Sean Faircloth's *Attack of the Theocrats!*

How the Religious Right Harms Us All —and What We Can Do About It.

This book is different. This book projects what things might actually look like, what actually might happen, should the Republican Religious Right take over, fully, and as I have said above, do exactly what they have already told us they would do were they to take full power (and are already doing to some extent with their partial power, especially at the state level). Think *Mein Kampf.* Hitler said exactly what he would do, were he to take power. Few other than his committed far rightists and his Storm Troopers paid any attention. It is actually scary to me as I re-read this book to see the number of events, speeches, doctrines, and policies that seemed so far-fetched when I originally wrote it and published it in the mid-90s actually happening, being made, and being implemented.

As "Jonathan Westminster" himself puts it (in "2048"):

> "Many books have been written about the Fascist Period. In fact, it has been estimated that if not for the chronic paper shortage, in the 25 years since the Restoration more books would have been written about both the Period and the Second Civil War than had been written about slavery and the First Civil War in the 100 years following the latter's conclusion. Many of these books have been devoted to detailed historical descriptions of the events, monumental and not so monumental, that took place during the time. Some of the more important ones are cited in the reference lists for this book.
>
> "However, as noted, this book has a rather different perspective from that of a conventional history book. I want people living now to know, not in detail about the depredations wreaked on our economy, polity, and society by the Fascists (although those are covered in outline), not about the defeats the Constitutionalist forces endured at first and the detailed story of their

eventual victory, not about the widespread environmental degradation at all levels that took place and from which we are still struggling to recover, but rather about how easily the forces of Republican Religious Right took over, how step by step they created Fascism by apparently legal means, how precious and at the time unappreciated our Constitutional Democracy was, and what must be done, even now, to defend it and eventually transcend it toward a far more real form of egalitarian power."

VII. References and Bibliography

1. Stevens, W.K., "Scientists Say Earth's Warming Could Set Off Wide Disruptions," *The New York Times*, September 18, 1995, p. 1.

2. Center for Biological Diversity, *Endangered Earth*, Winter, 2012.

3. Specter, M., "The Climate Fixers," *The New Yorker*, May 14, 2012

4. McKibben, B., "Global Warming's Terrifying New Math," *Rolling Stone*, July 19, 2012, http://www.rollingstone.com/politics/news/global-warmings-terrifying-new-math-20120719.

5. Lizza, R., "The Second Term: What Would Obama Do if Re-elected?" *The New Yorker*, June 18, 2012, p. 44.

6. Phillips-Fein, K., *Invisible Hands*, New York: WW Norton, 2009, p. 254.

7. ibid., Introduction.

8. *The Nation*, "Islamophobia: A Double Issue," July 2/9, 2012.

9. Turley, J., http://jonathanturley.org/2012/05/22/american-taliban-pastor-worley-and-how-to-solve-the-homosexual-problem/.

10. Cooper, A., "360," *CNN*, May 28, 2012.

11. *Wikipedia*, "Social Fascism," http://en.wikipedia.org/wiki/Social_fascism.

12. Jonas, S., "The Imperative of the Republicans' Rightward Imperative," Published on BuzzFlash@Truthout on Thu, 02/09/2012 [not copyright]. URL: http://blog.buzzflash.com/node/13269. (For the specific references in the quoted version here, see the column as published.)

13. *The Progress Report*, "Rick Santorum's Most Outrageous Campaign Moments," Jan. 5, 2012.)

14. Jonas, S. "The Triumph of Cheneyism," BuzzFlash@Truthout, 11/03/11 http://blog.buzzflash.com/node/13119.

15. Pollitt, K., "Ron Paul's Strange Bedfellows," *The Nation*, Jan. 23, 2012, www.thenation.com/article/165440/ron-pauls-strange-bedfellows

16. Rich, F., "Nuke 'Em," *New York* (Magazine). June 25 – July 2, 2012, p. 37.

17. Jonas, S. "Ask Newt Gingrich," Published on BuzzFlash@Truthout on Tue, 12/13/2011, URL: http://blog.buzzflash.com/node/13203. (For the specific references in the quoted version here, see the column as published.)

18. ibid., "Rick Santorum, Front-Runner–For 2016," Published on BuzzFlash@Truthout on Thu, 02/09/2012, URL: http://blog.buzzflash.com/node/13320. (For the specific references in the quoted version here, see the column as published.)

19. ibid., "Eleven Questions for Sen. Santorum," Published by BuzzFlash@Truthout on Fri, 02/24/2012, URL: http://blog.buzzflash.com/node/13344. This column also appeared on The Greanville Post, http://www.greanvillepost.com/2012/02/23/ask-senator-santorum/. (For the specific references in the quoted version here, see the column as published.)

20. ibid., "Mitt Romney's Issues (that He Doesn't Want Discussed), Published on BuzzFlash@Truthout on Thu, 05/24/2012, URL: http://blog.buzzflash.com/node/13515 (For the specific references in the quoted version here, see the column as published.)

21. Rich, Frank, "Who in God's Name is Mitt Romney?" *New York* (Magazine), Jan. 29, 2012.

22. The Book of Mormon, Salt Lake City, Utah: The Church of Jesus Christ of Latter Day Saints

23. Tarisco, V., "Former Mormon: What American Need to Know About Mormonism," Alternet.org, March 26, 2012.

24. Kantor, J., "Romney's Faith: Silent but Deep." *The New York Times*, May 19, 2012.

25. Mitt Romney Press, May 12, 2012.

26. Corn, D., "Buchanan Wins in New Hampshire," *The Nation*, 3/11/96.

27. Wilentz, S. "From Justice Scalia: A Chilling Vision of Religion's Authority in America," *The New York Times*, July 8, 2002, p. A19.

28. Chernus, Ira, "Scalia and a Supreme Being," *rd magazine: Politics*, February 13, 2008, http://www.religiondispatches.org/archive/politics/70/scalia_and_a_supreme_being.

29. Haaretz, " 'Road Map a Lifesaver for Us,' PM Abbas Tells Hamas," June 26, 2003, quoted in Floyd, C., "Global Eye --- Errand Boy," June 27, 2003, http://www.tmtmetropolis.ru. Haaretz also has its own website, on which this material appeared.

30. *Wikipedia*, "David Barton," en.wikipedia.org/wiki/David_Barton

31. Human Rights Campaign PAC, "If he were God, gays wouldn't exist," www.hrc.org, March 29, 2012.

32. Fineman, H., "Rise of Faith within GOP Has Created America's First Religious Party," http://www.huffingtonpost.com/2012/03/05/republican-party-religion-first-religious-party_n_1322132.html

Steven Jonas

THE 15% SOLUTION

How the Republican Religious Right Took Control of the U.S., 1981-2022

A Futuristic Novel

Section I:
Setting the Stage

CHAPTER 1

The United States in 1995: Setting the Stage for Fascism

Author's Note

The story of fascism in the old United States in my view begins with the accession to the Presidency of Carnathon Pine, The Last Republican, in the year "2001". And thus the drama as we will see it in some detail begins in earnest in the next Chapter, constructed around that personage's Inaugural Address. However, before dramas can proceed, the stage must be set. For this book, I have chosen to do that with an essay written by our friend Dino Louis in 1995. As you can see, Louis was never short on opinion and interpretation of facts. The bare facts he occasionally cites throughout the essay were taken primarily from a feature article that appeared in the then leading weekly printed newsmagazine *Time* early in that year (Hull, et al). I hope, dear reader, that you will find this essay helpful in understanding from whence fascism arose in our national ancestor.

IS THE STAGE BEING SET FOR FASCISM?
by Dino Louis, 1995

Politics Now

A spectre is haunting the United States of America. But it is not the spectre of communism. It is the spectre of fascism.

Elections '94. The Republicans win. The message is clear. Grinchism, developed by Newt Gingrich and his fellows as a meaner, harsher version of Reaganite-Bushism, is triumphant. The people have spoken. They and the Grinchites have clearly identified what's wrong with the country: government is too big, taxes are too high, the "undeserving poor" are "stealing bread from our table," people "different from us" have set out to destroy "our nation."

And on the "moral" side? Well, that slasher of national domestic spending Rep. John Kasich of Ohio, tells us (Nelson):

> "The American people in their guts, mothers and fathers across this country, know that over the last couple of decades we have removed the speed limits from the highways, the lines on the highways, the yes and the no, the black and the white and the rights and the wrongs. And Americans are beginning to say that ... culture has slipped and it's time once more to assert that Judeo-Christian tradition of rights and wrongs and values that guides our nation in the 21st Century."

The proposed solutions to these problems? Shrink government. Cut taxes. Slash government spending, especially on the poor. End tolerance, reinvigorate prejudice. On the "moral" side? Follow the Christian Coalition (Nelson) and outlaw freedom of choice in the outcome of pregnancy, require voluntary school prayer, make divorce more difficult (except for the leading Republican Presidential candidates), prohibit pornography (except for aspiring Republican Supreme Court nominees), ban sex education and contraception. And oh yes, above all free the "free market."

The "mainstream" Democratic response, enunciated by the Democratic Leadership Council and more or less followed along by the President? "Yes, for the most part, on the economic side, at least, you're right. Although we may disagree on some details of both problem analysis and program prescription, you are basically right. And we can be even more Republican than the Republicans. Just let us show you how."

But pause for a moment. Did "the people" as a whole really speak in the 1994 election? Well, no. The message of Reaction was supported by less than 20% of the eligible electorate. Not voting in droves were those who potentially benefit most from government intervention in the economy, and government protection of their rights in the society. It seems safe to assume that they didn't vote because even the Clinton Administration, with its emphasis on deficit cutting not growth stimulation, on being liked not aggressively protecting rights, did not seem to give them anything much to vote for in either intervention or protection.

And then consider, have the Grinchites identified the real problems the country faces? Well, no. Since Clinton was elected in 1992 the basic problem list has remained unchanged (Thurow): a declining industrial base; the export of manufacturing jobs, to be replaced, if at all, by lower paying service jobs; a continually deteriorating national infrastructure; serious problems in health services, education, and environmental protection and preservation; the ever-increasing gap between the have-a-lots and everyone else.

It is these problems, not some sudden changes in "Americans' morality," that are putting tremendous pressure on the American family, as Thurow has pointed out (1995):

> "Falling real wages have put the traditional American family into play, as the one-earner middle class family becomes extinct. ... 32 percent of all men between 25 and 34 years of age earn less than the amount necessary to keep a family of four above the poverty line. Mothers have to work longer hours if the family is to have its old standard of living.
>
> "Children exist, but no one takes care of them. Parents are spending 40 percent less time with their children than they did 30 years ago. More than two million children under the age of 13 have no adult supervision before or after school. Paying for day care would use up all or most of a mother's wages.
>
> "... Men have a strong economic incentive to bail out of family responsibilities since when they do so their

real standard of living rises 73 percent—although that of the family left behind falls 42 percent."

Added to these real economic and economy-based family pressures are resurgent racism and homophobia, the atmosphere of hate fed by a talk radio culture dominated by the Right Wing, and the new national chauvinism reflected in California's "Proposition 187."[1]

Will the DLC-lead me-too-ism effectively respond to this crisis? Well, no. It won't win elections. That was proven in 1994, when almost every me-too Democrat running in a closely contested election lost. As [postWorld War II President] Harry Truman once said, when someone wants to vote for a Republican, he'll pick the real thing over a pale imitation every time. But even more importantly, the DLC/Grinchite program simply cannot solve the basic problems the country faces because it doesn't face them. It deals with side issues like term limits and "shrinking government." It is an agenda of distraction, not focus.

Big problems require big solutions. It's not the *size* of government that's the problem. It's what government *does* with its size. It's not the number of terms of office that lead to a "non-responsive Congress," "devoted to the 'Special Interests'. " It's corporate campaign financing and the hidden system of lobbying. It's not the tax *burden* (one of the lowest in the industrialized world) that's the problem. It's what the tax revenues are spent on. It's not the poor that are dragging the country down. AFDC could be eliminated tomorrow and the total Federal saving would amount to less than 10% of the current deficit, less than 1% of the Federal budget. It's the declining industrial base, declining per capita income, and increasing true unemployment.

1. *Author's Note:* This latter item referred to a product of the old "Initiative and Referendum" system used most prominently in California. Once a tool of progressives, Initiative and Referendum became a leading anti-democratic tool of Right-Wing Reaction in both the Transition Era and the Fascist Period. I discuss it in some detail in Chapter 4.

And the whole so-called "moral" agenda, the fake "Contract on the American Family" of the Christian Coalition, could be enacted tomorrow and the economic problems that are the real factors making life ever tougher for evermore Americans would remain absolutely untouched. Much less personal freedom. No fewer, actually more, personal and family problems.

Atomization is Taking Over

The country thus seems to be falling apart. But at a time when people really need to pull together, under a constant barrage of Republican propaganda about "individual responsibility" and the ability of the "free market" to solve every conceivable problem, the people are pulling apart too. "Many Americans have stocked up on guns and walled in their communities," *Time* tells us in it's own "State of the Union" message (Hull, et al). "More than 700,000 children are educated at home." "Self-reliance" is spreading, and "in many cases Americans are acting out of long-term necessity, unable to depend on a life-long job or the pension that accompanies it."

"Many American families and businesses are being forced to privatize security and sanitation by default. Community associations, ranging from small condominiums to sprawling planned communities, have grown from 10,000 in 1970 to 150,000 in 1993 and now include 1 out of every 8 Americans." "Privatization of local services is, however, a lot less liberating for the millions of Americans who can't afford it."

The True Economic Perspective

In the face of all this, what is happening to wealth in America? Well, *family* income has gone up steadily since the Nixon years, but *per capita* income has declined. Why has the former risen while the latter has fallen? As pointed out above, *two-parent* employment, for the most part. Just one of the major family stressors that have arisen over the last 20 years. And while per capita income has declined, the concentration of wealth has increased.

Time again: "Over the past 20 years the very rich have improved their lot in life by getting richer. Half a million U.S. households (onehalf of 1% of the population) now owns 39% of all assets (stocks, bonds, cash, life insurance policies, paintings, jewelry, etc.). This makes the U.S. No. 1 among prosperous nations in the inequality of income. ... During the Reagan years ... the nation's net worth increased from $13.5 trillion to $20.2 trillion ... between 1983 and 1989, $3.9 trillion of the reward was captured by the top one-half of 1%." That's almost 60% of the *increase in wealth* going to that top 0.5%.

Or as Thurow put it (1995):

> "The tide rose (the real *per capita* gross domestic product went up 29 percent between 1973 and 1993), but 80 percent of the boats sank. Among men, the top 20 percent of the labor force has been winning all of the country's wage increases for more than two decades. ...
>
> "With the death of Communism and, later, market socialism as economic alternatives, capitalists have been able to employ more ruthless approaches to getting profits without worrying about political pressure. 'Survival of the fittest' capitalism is on the march. What economists call 'efficiency wages' (a company paying higher salaries than the minimum it needs to pay, so that it gets a skilled, cooperative, loyal work force) are disappearing to be replaced by a different form of motivation—the fear of losing one's job [and one's health insurance]."

I just wonder if Reagan's tax cuts for the wealthy and borrow-to-spend policies had anything to do with all these developments.

Some Social Issues

Let's take a look at some social problems, like crime for instance. The crime rate has actually been falling a bit over the last couple of years, while the nation rose to first place among developed nations for the proportion of its citizens incarcerated. But crime overall has risen dramatically during the period since the 1970s when all those prisons have been built. Why? They are irrelevant. There is an arrest in only about a fifth of all crimes, with only half of those leading to convictions in serious cases, and fewer than 50% of those leading to jail time (Lacayo).

Even while crime has been decreasing slightly in recent years, the fear of crime has risen markedly. Part of this is real. Murder is still a relatively rare event in this country, with a rate that has remained more or less unchanged since the 70s. But the proportion of murders committed by strangers has risen dramatically, while the homicide-solution rate dropped from 91% in 1965 to 66% in 1993.

And youth violence has increased markedly. What might the reasons be? Not enough prisons? Not long enough sentences? Well, the Director of the FBI, Louis Freeh, "recommends focusing on the increasing number of children brought up in 'no parent' homes." Dare I say there is some relationship between the latter and declining *per-capita*-income/rising-two-parent-employment, and rising one-parent-working/no-affordable-day-care-available for their preschool children?

However, at least part of the increasing fear of crime is definitely the work of politicians in both parties. For them a focus on crime and "being tough" on it wins elections (even if the advocated measures affect the crime rate not more than minimally). And then there are the media (primarily in the hands of major corporations like General Electric and major private right-wingers like Rupert Murdoch) for whom presenting crime, real, fictional, semi-real, and semi-fictional, in gorier and gorier detail, up-close and personal, makes money. Finally there are the demons of right-wing talk radio, who especially like to color crime black and brown.

What about education? Well, while, for example, our 13-year-olds rank 14th among the children of the developed countries in math performance, and does anyone know where Belgium is, it's estimated that less than half of the average of $5300.00

spent per pupil in this country goes to support classroom work. As to health care, costs continue to skyrocket, quality declines, health care corporation profits rise, and the critically required comprehensive reform is once again a dream that does not become reality, just as it has been every time it's been seriously proposed by a national leader, beginning with Teddy Roosevelt in his 1912 Bull Moose campaign.

In response to this situation, Americans turn to God, in massive numbers. 95% profess to be believers, distributed among about 1600 denominations (44% of them non-Christian). 40% of Americans profess to attend a religious institution regularly. With churches hardly hard to find, there is hardly "Christian persecution" going on, despite what the Religious Right would have us believe.

Democracy in Decline

In the face of all this, it seems that our democratic structures are beginning to crumble. According to John Gray, a fellow of Jesus College, Oxford University (England) (1995):

"In the United States the end of the cold war[2] has intensified a mood of political cynicism. American public opinion expects little from its democratic institutions, and if the experience of the last decade or so is any guide, even its modest expectations are likely to be disappointed. ...

"The mobility of capital has contributed significantly to the decline of the middle class and its distinctive culture. ... This may prove [to be] of decisive importance for democracy in the United States and in other Western democracies—namely the proletarianization, through rising debt, falling incomes and unrelenting job insecurity, of the traditional middle classes. The U.S. undoubtedly leads the field in replicating in a Western industrial economy the middle-class impotence that is an

2. *Author's Note:* The "Cold War" was a 45 year-long, primarily political, economic, diplomatic (but non-military) battle between the old U.S. and the old Soviet Union, that followed the end of World War II. The Cold War came to an end following the peaceful demise of the old Soviet Union as a nation-state.

endemic feature of many third world countries in Latin America and elsewhere. …

"In a worst case scenario, we may even glimpse a sort of Colombianization of the United States, in which failing political institutions become increasingly marginal in an ungovernable, criminalized and endemically violent society."

I could not have made the point better myself. But in the midst of all this, what does the winning party in the last election offer us? Why nothing other than the "Contract On," sorry, I mean the "Contract *For* America," alluded to above. Relevant to the problem list? Right up there with what we need? Problem-solutions provided by the Party of Business? Not quite!

For proof of that statement, here's the "Contract" in a nutshell (Kelly): a balanced federal budget by the year 2002; term limits for members of Congress; "tough" welfare "reform;" cut crime prevention, increase incarceration; carry out death sentences more quickly; permit the use of improperly seized evidence; restrict the use of U.S. troops in United Nations operations; prevent the use of money saved from military spending cuts for national domestic programs; cut the capital gains tax; raise the Social Security earnings limit; enact a 'loser pays' provision for civil litigation; cut Congressional staffing by a third and the number of Congressional committees; require Congress to apply to itself the laws it passes; require a three-fifths majority for tax hikes; and submit proposed Federal environmental regulations to risk-assessment and cost-benefit analysis.

Like the Christian Coalition's "Contract on the American Family" of which this "contract" was a precursor, what a prescription of irrelevance. Just put the real problem list against the "solution list" contained in either "Contract." Nothing on what really ails the country. Nothing on jobs, export of, and insecurity in. Nothing on the crumbling infrastructure. Nothing on health, nothing on education, nothing on the environment (except to make it easier for companies to poison it). Lots of focus on welfare, only a small chunk of Federal spending, but great politics because it's painted black (even though two-thirds of recipients aren't). The crime proposals focus on measures that just don't work and take money away from ones that either do or at least might. Balanced budget and term limits? How are they going to affect everyday life?

More tax cuts for the rich? In the 80s, cuts for them *didn't* lead to investment and jobs here at home—just to speculation, sometimes huge financial losses, export of capital, and that widening gap between rich and poor. Then there's the proposal for "reform" of the civil litigation system to address a problem that just doesn't exist: an "avalanche of tort litigation" *against* companies. In fact, the major increase in civil cases is in *contract* actions *between* companies (Kelder)—and so forth. And the Democrats right now have nothing much better.

And then there's the "moral" agenda, as noted not exactly designed to touch the declining industrial base and declining *per capita* incomes; the export of manufacturing jobs, to be replaced, if at all, by a less than equal number of lower-paying service jobs; and a continually deteriorating national infrastructure.

John Gray, in that last sentence I quoted from him, is right. And that "Colombian" state, that unstable, violent, insecure state, in a domestic environment of increasing racism and xenophobia, is a prescription for future, massive "civil unrest," followed by the imposition of a violent, oppressive, authoritarian governing structure to control it.

A spectre is haunting the United States of America. But it is not the spectre of communism. It is the spectre of fascism. Is anyone out there watching or listening? And if they are, are they seeing or hearing anything?

References:

Gray, J., "Does Democracy Have a Future?" *The New York Times Book Review*, January 22, 1995, p. 1.

Hull, J.D., et al, "The State of the Union," *Time*, January 30, 1995, p. 53.

Kelder, G., "What Speaker Newt's 'Contract on America' and Tort 'Reform' Mean for the Tobacco Control Movement," *Tobacco on Trial*, November/December, 1994, p. 3.

Kelly, M., "You Say You Want a Revolution," *The New Yorker*, November 21, 1994, p. 56.

Lacayo, R., "Lock 'Em Up!," *Time*, February 7, 1994.

Nelson, LE., "Contract Words, Deeds Divorced," *Newsday*, May 18, 1995, p. A 19.

Thurow, L.C., "Companies Merge; Families Break Up," *The New York Times,* September 3, 1995, News of the Week in Review.

CHAPTER 2
Fascism in America: An Overview

Author's Commentary:
How Fascism Came to the United States

Many lengthy books have been written on the tale of how fascism came to the old United States. In this chapter, I present a brief overview of the process. Some further description and analysis of the nature of fascism and its advent in the old U.S. is provided by a Dino Louis essay reproduced in Appendix II.

An ever-deepening economic decline occurred in the country in the latter part of the 20th century. The decline was not one that could be measured by the traditional yardstick of economic progress, the Gross Domestic Product (GDP). It continued to rise at a modest, non-inflation-producing pace, the latter maintained for the benefit of the wealthy by the monetary policies of the central bank (the "Federal Reserve"). But an increasing number of economists and other observers came to realize that the GDP did not tell all there was to tell about either the economy or the state of the nation (Cobb, et al).

As noted by Michael Lind, Dino Louis, Lester Thurow, and many other observers at the time, underneath the GDP climb, the poor were getting poorer and more numerous, the rich were getting richer, and everyone else was experiencing falling personal incomes and rising levels of personal and economic anxiety (DeParle; Phillips). Lind called attention to the underlying reasons for this state of affairs, such as a regressive taxation policy and the export of capital (1995).

Lind also noted that not only were the rich getting richer, but they were going out of their way to publicly deny the facts of the rising gap between the rich and everyone else, to create the illusion that it was not happening, and to create the impression that the causes of the economic malaise affecting almost everybody but them was caused by anything but them and their policies. The "anything" could be anything from people of color to immigrants to the poor to the feminists to homosexuals to environmentalists to the United Nations Organization to the "New World Order" to "international bankers" (read "Jews").

In fact, as noted by Dino Louis, in a process driven at its base by underinvestment at home and a concomitant export of capital abroad, the economy was rotting upwards from its foundations, with declining personal incomes, increasing job insecurity, the disaccumulation of labor from capital, and deindustrialization. The rotting process was accelerated by the existence of a huge, ever-growing government debt, created in large part during the 1980s by the policies of Presidents Ronald Reagan and George Bush.

Reaganite policy, in fact, had within a five-year period from 1981 changed the financial posture of the country from that of the world's leading creditor nation to that of the world's leading debtor nation. This borrowing was undertaken to finance a vast expansion of the U.S. military, at a time when the nation was ostensibly at peace, and large tax cuts for the wealthy and the large corporations (McIntyre). It produced a floridly growing economy at the time, for which the Reaganites took credit, but that was the product of nothing but old-fashioned Keynesian[1] government pump-priming, although through a very narrow spigot that dropped the largess almost entirely upon the military-industrial complex.

Thus for many years leading up to this time, American society had been characterized by economic and social conditions which might have led to civil and/or labor unrest.

---

1. *Author's Note:* John Maynard Keynes was an early twentieth century British economist who believed that in a capitalist state active government intervention was necessary for the maintenance of a healthy economy.

But many people were easily distracted from the realities of life and the true causes of their problems by the above-mentioned strategies of diversion. They also included a domestic "anti-communist crusade" (against a virtually nonexistent Communist Party), and the foreign "Cold War" against the old Soviet Union (designed not to "contain" it, as advertised, but to destroy it, which happened). As noted, the diversionary strategies also included such elements as manufactured racism and xenophobia.

A Transition Era poet and philosopher described the latter strategy well (Morrison):

> "Let us be reminded that before there is a final solution, there must be a first solution, a second one, even a third. The move toward a final solution is not a jump. It takes one step, then another, then another. Something, perhaps, like this:
>
> 1. Construct an internal enemy, as both focus and diversion.
> 2. Isolate and demonize the enemy by unleashing and protecting the utterance of covert and coded name-calling and verbal abuse. Employ *ad hominem* attacks as legitimate charges against that enemy.
> 3. Enlist and create sources and distributors of information who are willing to reinforce the demonizing process because it is profitable, because it grants power and because it works.
> 4. Palisade all art forms; monitor, discredit or expel those that challenge or destabilize processes of demonization and deification.
> 5. Subvert and malign all representatives of sympathizers with this constructed enemy.
> 6. Solicit, from among the enemy, collaborators who agree with and can sanitize the dispossession process.

7. Pathologize the enemy in scholarly and popular mediums; recycle, for example, scientific racism and the myths of racial superiority in order to naturalize the pathology.
8. Criminalize the enemy. Then prepare, budget for, and rationalize the building of holding areas for the enemy—especially its males and absolutely its children.
9. Reward mindlessness and apathy with monumentalized entertainments and with little pleasures, tiny seductions: a few minutes on television, a few lines in the press; a little pseudo-success; the illusion of power and influence; a little fun, a little style, a little consequence.
10. Maintain, at all costs, silence.

In 1995 racism may wear a new dress, buy a new pair of boots, but neither it nor its succubus twin fascism is new or can make anything new. It can only reproduce the environment that supports its own health: fear, denial and an atmosphere in which its victims have lost the will to fight."

In this analysis, Morrison retrospectively described the development of German Nazism in the 1930s based on the then-coming War Against the Jews (Davidowicz). She also chillingly and accurately prophesied the coming of fascism to America in the early 21st century through the War Against the Peoples of Color, as the process described in this book might be called, leading ultimately and inevitably to the establishment of the New American Republics.

By the time the turn of the 21st century was reached, the economic decline affecting all sectors of society other than the truly wealthy was quickening, and social unrest was doing the same. Then it was found by the wealthy and their political allies that the divisive/distractive strategies which had worked so well for so many years to keep a relative civil peace began to fail in meeting that objective. This process led to increasingly violent outbursts on the part of increasing numbers of people from all walks of life. And some of those outbursts began to focus on such matters as the widening gap between rich and poor, the loss of employment security, and the overall decline in the standard of living for most people.

The economic and political decisionmakers of the society thus gradually came to view it as a necessity that significant levels of force and repression be used, or at least made ready, to prevent the occurrence of full-fledged rebellion. Hence the final development of the fascist state in the old U.S. But it had to be realized, if at all possible, by democratic means.

Why so? Because the democratic tradition was strong in the United States of America. The tradition, and the basic American concept, "it's a free country," had been encouraged by the operations of the political system from the time of the nation's founding as the world's first democracy, however limited at the time, in 1789. "Free speech" and "freedom from government oppression" were slogans even of major elements of the Far Right, the foot soldiers of which would eventually and ironically become the agents of repression on the street and in the camps for the national decision makers.

However, no country had ever previously become fascist by majority vote of the whole electorate. Even in the Nazi Germany of the 1930s and 40s (where the fascists had taken power by constitutional means), the highest proportion of a free vote that the National Socialist (Nazi) Party had ever received was 37% (of a high voter turnout).

Just as in pre-World War II Germany, in the old U.S. it is unlikely that fascism, if openly put to a vote, could ever have attracted a majority of the eligible voters. But given the realities of voting patterns, that was not necessary for the constitutional installation of fascism. In the old U.S., even in Presidential elections, any voter turnout over 50% was considered good. And so, in the late 20th century a strategy was developed by

Right-Wing Reaction through which fascism could be brought to the old U.S. by Constitutional means, if not true majority vote. It was called "The 15% Solution."

"The 15% Solution"

"The 15% Solution" was an electoral strategy developed by the leading political organ of the Religious Right, the so-called "Christian Coalition" (ADL).[2] The "Christian Coalition" was an unabashed, unapologetic, and outspoken representative of that authoritarian thinking (see also Dino Louis' discussion of the nature of fascism in Appendix II) which under their influence was so prominently represented in the politics of the Republican Party, beginning at their 1992 National Convention. The strategy was designed to win elections even when the Coalition's supporters comprised a distinct minority of the eligible electorate. As an early Christian Coalition Executive Director, Ralph Reed, once said (Harkin): "I paint my face and travel at night. You don't know it's over until you're in a body bag."

Although in later public statements, the Christian Coalition made attempts to cover up or even disavow the strategy, according to its 1991 National Field Director, it was formulated in the following way (Rodgers):

> "In a Presidential election, when more voters turn out than [in] any other election you normally see, only 15% of eligible voters determine the outcomes of that

---

2. *Author's Note:* There is no indication or evidence that the Christian Coalition, Ralph Reed, the Rev. Pat Robertson, or any other member or leader of the organization, or any of the other historical personages mentioned in this chapter, such as Kirk Fordyce, David Duke, Paul Weyrich, George F. Allen, David Barton, or R.J. Rushdooney, would have supported or approved of any of the events that subsequently occurred in the United States or the New American Republics, would have associated themselves in any way with any individuals or political grouping which brought fascism or any similar system to the United States, or that they supported the development of any kind of fascist or otherwise authoritarian state in the country or its successors.

election. … Of all adults 18 and over, eligible to vote, only about 60 or 65% are actually registered to vote. It might even be less than that, and it is less than that in many states. …

"Of those registered to vote, in a good turnout only 50% actually vote. [Thus,] only 30% of those *eligible* actually vote. … 15% of adults eligible to vote determine the outcome in a *high turnout* election. That happens once every four years. … In low turnout elections, city council, state legislature, county commissions, the percentage who [*sic*] determines who wins *can be as low as 6 or 7%. We don't have to worry about convincing a majority of Americans to agree with us.* Most of them are staying home and watching 'Roseanne' " [emphasis added. *Author's Note:* "Roseanne" was a popular television program of that time.]

As one of the most influential leaders of the Religious Right, Paul Weyrich, succinctly put it (*Freedom Writer*, Nov., 1994): "We don't want everyone to vote. Quite frankly, our leverage goes up as the voting population goes down."

Elected allies of the Christian Coalition worked to make this wish a reality. For example, a Governor of Virginia, George F. Allen, elected in 1992 with open Christian Coalition support, attempted by the use of the veto to prevent implementation of Federal legislation designed to make it easier for people to register to vote (*NYT*).

By the national election of 1994, Right-Wing Reaction was well on its way to achieving its goal. Only about 38% of eligible voters voted. That turnout was part of the process that came to be referred to as the "Incredible Shrinking Electorate." With slightly more than half of those voting choosing the old Republican Party's Congressional candidates that year, the Party achieved a major turnaround in Congressional representation and took control of that body.

Many of the new representatives were supported by the

Christian Coalition and its allies. In an odd representation of reality, most media and political figures represented that victory as one reflecting the views of the "American people" as a whole. In fact, the Republican victory was achieved by garnering the support of less than 20% of the eligible voters. "The 15% Solution" was well within sight.

The political posture adopted by the opposition Democrats played a significant role in the creation of the Incredible Shrinking Electorate. They gave the majority of increasingly disaffected people nothing to come out to the polls for but either a warmed-over imitation of Republican Party policies, or a set of well-intentioned but ineffective alternatives.

The minority of eligible voters who actually supported Republican, and later, Republican-Christian Alliance, policies turned out and voted for them. Those who wanted something significantly different, consistent with the liberal tradition of the Democratic Party, not finding it on the ballot, just stayed home. Implementation of "The 15% Solution" proceeded apace. It was eventually used by the Right-Wing Reactionaries to impose their will on the majority of the people. And just like their German Nazi predecessors, once they gained power through Constitutional means, they maintained it largely through anything but.

The Apogee of American Fascism

The apogee of fascism in America is generally considered to have been reached around 2017. By that year, while the old Constitution (see Appendix I) was still technically in force, the old United States of America had for six years already been existing as that *apartheid* nation called the New American Republics. The NAR was designed along the lines of plans for racial separation which had been developed by such late 20th century Right-Wing Republican leaders as David Duke of Louisiana (Patriquin). It was the entirely predictable result of the American Right-Wing Reactionary movement that had at its core an ideology of black, (genetically-based), inferiority

(Herrnstein and Murray), and explicit or implicit White Supremacy.

There were still two years to go before the Latin Wars in the Fourth Republic would begin to turn sour and the formal Restoration Declaration would be issued by the National Leadership Council of the Movement for the Restoration of Constitutional Democracy in the old United States.

The sole legal political party of the NAR was the American Christian Nation Party (ACNP). In 2008, President Jefferson Davis Hague had formed it out of the Republican-Christian Alliance, successor to the old Republican Party. In rhetoric at least, the NAR was a "Christian Nation," achieving a goal of many leaders of Right-Wing Reaction in the old U.S. from a wide variety of backgrounds, such as the Rev. Pat Robertson, the head of the Christian Coalition, a onetime Governor of the state of Mississippi, Kirk Fordyce, and R.J. Rushdooney, a leader of Christian Reconstructionism and the Christian Coalition's more secretive 20th century counterpart, the Coalition on Revival.

Rushdooney, a very influential if not very well-known leader of the Christian Right, for example "advocated total Christian theocracy and [once] wrote 'Democracy is the great love of the failures and cowards of life' " (*Freedom Writer*, Jan., 1995, p. 1). Of the legal theory of Christian Reconstructionism, the basis for the Supremacy Amendment (see Chapter 9), one David Barton said (Schollenberger): "Whatever is Christian is legal. Whatever isn't Christian is illegal."

The NAR consisted of four "Republics." The "White Republic" controlled most of the territory of the old United States, as well as that of the four western Provinces of the old Canada.[3] The "Black Republic," in some ways like the Black "Bantustans" of pre-liberation South Africa in the 20th century, was a series

3. *Author's Note:* In 2017, the Legitimation Treaty between the New American Republics (NAR) and the Republic of Quebec (Republique Quebecoise, or RQ in French) was signed. It formalized the dismemberment of Canada and the northwest expansion of the White Republic of the NAR.

of disconnected, walled-off, "provinces" consisting of selected, old, predominantly black "inner cities," carved out of the old U.S. All blacks in the country not already living in what became the collective territory of the republic had been forcibly moved and confined to one "province" or another.

Similarly, the "Red Republic" was based on a set of walled-off former Indian Reservations to the west of the Mississippi, to which all Native Americans had been moved and confined. Fourth was to have been the Hispanic Republic, consisting of all the nations of Latin America, to which, coincidentally, all persons of Hispanic (Latino) origin living in the old U.S. were to have been deported. Full deportation was never achieved by the NAR government, just as full control of Latin America was never achieved either. But a "Killer Fence" (see Chapter 15) had been constructed along the length of the old U.S.-Mexican border, and the Fourth Republic was on the books.

How did all of this come to pass legislatively, one might ask? In brief, through the use of "The 15% Solution" Right-Wing Reaction had by the national election of 2004 taken full control of the Congress and the Executive Branch at the Federal level, and of more than 38 state governments. (The assent of 38 state legislatures was required for the ratification of any Constitutional Amendment.)

And where, one might also ask, was the Federal Supreme Court in all of this? Well, it had not reviewed actions of the other two branches of the Federal government for their constitutionality since it had handed down the *Anderson* Decision in 2003. In that decision (see Chapter 5), based on the strict Borkian[4] interpretation of the Doctrine of Original

4. *Author's Note:* Robert Bork was the leading Right-Wing Reactionary jurist of the Transition Era. Among those of the time, he held the almost singular view that if a policy, right, or procedure wasn't explicitly stated in the original Constitution it simply wasn't there, no way, no how, and anything else was unconstitutional, including certain undesirable amendments. This singular jurisprudence underlay the Supreme Court's decision in *Anderson v. Board of Education* (see Chapter 5).

Intent, the Court removed from itself the power to review the actions of the other two branches of the Federal government for their Constitutionality. The Court was thus out of the picture. *Anderson* was the most far-reaching Supreme Court decision in U.S. history since "Dred Scott" of 1857. In one sense, *Anderson* set the stage for the Second Civil War just as Dred Scott had set the stage for the First.

The Social Profile of the NAR

The very existence of the New American Republics in 2017 was the at least partly predictable result of policies that the American Christian Nation Party and its predecessors had been advocating and at times implementing for many years leading up to the NAR's creation in 2011. The social profile of the White Republic was fully predictable. It was just what Right-Wing Reaction had told the American people it would impose upon them if it ever got complete power. These changes were achieved largely through a series of Constitutional amendments which the Right-Wing Reactionary dominated national and state legislatures were able to adopt with ease in the first decade of the 21st century, even before the establishment of the NAR (see Chapters 4, 7, 8, 9 and 12).

Freedom of speech was a thing of the past, except on paper. "Christian Thinking," as defined by the ACNP and based on the "Innerant Bible," as interpreted by the ACNP, was the only way of thinking acceptable throughout the White Republic. People not accepting "Christian Thinking" who did not keep their thoughts to themselves were subject to a wide variety of penalties, from loss of employment (a practice previewed in the old United States by the so-called "black-listing" practice of the "McCarthy Era" of the 1950s) to confinement in a "drug rehabilitation" camp.

Freedom of the press and the media in general was also a thing of the past. Although all media outlets, newspapers, radio, television, and political virtual reality were privately owned, they were all licensed and no one who was not known to be an absolute supporter of ACNP policy could get a license. Freedom of choice in the outcome of pregnancy had long since vanished. The public school system that had been developed in the old United States since the early 19th century had ceased to exist, replaced by a combination of public and private religious schools and home-based education. Sex education and the provision of contraceptives were banned. Homosexuality had been made a crime. The old "welfare" system had been terminated completely, and the principal remaining achievement of the "New Deal" of the President Franklin Delano Roosevelt (1933-1945), the Social Security System, had been dismantled by a process Right-Wing Reaction called "Privatization."

The 16th Amendment (providing for a Federal income tax) had been repealed. Subject to Congressional review, the President had been given the power to rule by proclamation in "times of national emergency" (very similar to the "Enabling Act" passed by the German Reichstag [parliament] in the early days of the Hitlerian Chancellorship which gave him, through the democratic process, the authority to rule by decree [Shirer]).

By Constitutional amendment as well, the "Laws of God" were established as superior to those of the Constitution. (Although at the time of the Supremacy Amendment's ratification there had been some controversy about just what the phrase "Laws of God" meant, as noted, upon the creation of the NAR the ACNP proclaimed that thenceforth it would make all such determinations.) The 13th, 14th, and 15th amendments to the old Constitution had been repealed, under the Borkist theory of "Original Intent."

Economically, as a result of the previously noted under-investment in both the private and public sectors, manufacturing, the basis of American world-wide economic dominance for most of the second half of the 20th century, had declined to a very low level. However, all limitations on lumbering and coal mining had been eliminated, in order to establish what the ACNP called a "Resource Based Economy." That had made the takeover of the four Western Canadian Provinces with their largely untapped coal and timber reserves essential, and had at the same time reduced the NAR to the status of what in the 20th century had been called a "Third World," raw materials exporting, country, although one operating at a very high level.

But a one-party, theocratic state, based on a racist theory of human existence, with a continually declining standard of living, and a significant number of oppressed people under its thumb, even if it came to power by democratic means, cannot maintain that power without the use of brute force. The history of all other such countries demonstrated that fact. Thus there was a national police force called "The Helmsmen," "those with their hands on the helm of the ship of God's state."

The Helmsmen enforced ACNP rule and rules, legally and extra-legally (although there were no legal means to combat their extra-legal use of force). Having both a public and a secret face, it had much in common with the Schutzstaffel (SS) of the old Nazi Germany. A series of camps, under the control of the Helmsmen (as the "Concentration Camps" of Nazi Germany had been under the control of the SS), were located on closed former military bases. They had been originally established by one of the first acts of "The Last Republican," President Carnathon Pine (2001-2004), as part of the "Real Drug War" he had announced in his Inaugural Address of 2001 (see the next Chapter).

Well before 2017, the camps had been adapted to the broader purpose of confining, in not too pleasant surroundings, opponents of the regime. (The camps were, however, not nearly as unpleasant as the extermination camp for "homosexuals" which would be set up in 2020 as part of the "Second Final Solution" [see Chapter 18].) As noted, the Mexican border had long since been closed with a pro-active, at times seemingly life-like, "Killer Fence." More advanced versions of the "Killer Fence" were used to completely isolate the "Provinces" of both the Black and Red Republics.

And that, in brief, is a picture of the NAR in 2017. This book will fill in that picture, will add color, depth, and focus to it, by tracing the history of the Fascist Period[5] through a description and analysis of the documents which shaped it, and by hearing the voices of a few of those who lived it. In brief here is presented an overview of that documentary history.

The Documentary Trail of American Fascism

2001: The Inauguration of President Pine, the Last Republican, and the Declaration of the Real Drug War.

2002: The "Preserve America" (30th) Amendment to the Constitution. It provided that henceforth no person could become a citizen of the United States unless at least one parent were a citizen of the United States.

2003: The Supreme Court decision in *Anderson v. the United States*. It reversed the early landmark decisions by the Court of Chief Justice John Marshall, from *Marbury v. Madison* (1801) to *McColluch v. Maryland* (1823), which had originally established the Supreme Court's power to review and void on Constitutional grounds Executive and Legislative branch actions, a power nowhere to be explicitly found in the Constitution.

2004: The First Inaugural Address of President Jefferson Davis Hague (delivered from the National Cathedral on Christmas Day). He had won the Presidency as the candidate of the new RepublicanChristian Alliance.

2005: The Morality (31st) Amendment to the Constitution. It outlawed abortion under any circumstances; prohibited any teaching in any educational institution on any matters

5. *Author's Note:* This book focuses on the Fascist Period, 2001-2022. I am well aware that some historians do not consider that the Fascist Period began until President Hague formally converted the Republican Christian Alliance into the American Christian Nation Party at the end of 2008. But since the laying of the electoral, legislative, and judicial groundwork for the generally peaceful, on-paper "democratic" conversion to fascism was clearly begun during the Pine Presidency, I subscribe to the view that the Fascist Period did indeed commence at the earlier time. Thus the presentation of documents begins with that year.

concerning sexual functioning; declared homosexuality to be a matter of choice and denied any civil rights protections to homosexual persons; prohibited all forms of Federal, state, or local government funded outdoor relief for the poor; and repealed the 16th Amendment (which had established the income tax).

2006: The Balancing (32nd) Amendment to the Constitution. It required a balanced Federal budget, with no provisions for exceptions; required a two-thirds vote of the membership of each House of Congress for the approval of any tax increase; established a line-item veto; repealed the Fourth Amendment (prohibiting unreasonable search and seizure); and gave the President the power to declare "special emergencies" during which he could rule by decree.

2007: The Supremacy (33rd) Amendment to the Constitution. It gave the President and/or the Congress the power to declare the Laws of God as superior to those of the Constitution. It bound all judges, Federal and state, to abide by the terms of the amendment. It allowed the establishment of religious tests for any elected or appointed government official. Finally, it guaranteed organized prayer in the public schools.

2008: Hague's Second Inaugural. He announced the planned conversion of the Republican-Christian Alliance into the American Christian Nation Party.

2009: The Proclamation of Right of 2009. It made homosexuality a crime.

2010: The Original Intention (34th) Amendment to the Constitution. It repealed the 13th, 14th, and 15th Amendments to the Constitution (that had, respectively, abolished slavery, among other things applied the due process guarantee of the 5th Amendment to the states, and guaranteed the right to vote to former slaves and other persons of color).

2011: The Declaration of Peace. On July 4 of that year, it established the New American Republics (NAR).

2013: The Natural Resources Access Act. Among other things, it terminated the National Parks and National Forests systems.

2015: The National Plan for Social Peace. It was intended, among other things, to deal with the many social and legal problems not solved and/or created by the Fascist Period Constitutional Amendments.

2017: The Legitimation Treaty of 2017. This tri-partite Treaty, between the NAR, the rump Canadian government based in the Maritime Provinces, and the Republic of Quebec (RQ), recognized the independence of the RQ, the annexation of the Western Canadian provinces to the White Republic of the NAR, and the partition of the former Canadian Province of Ontario between the NAR and the RQ.

2019: The Restoration Declaration. The first formal statement by the new National Leadership Council of the Movement for the Restoration of Constitutional Democracy, which for the first time joined together previously unconnected resistance movements in the Four Republics.

2020: The Second Final Solution (the Second Holocaust). It was a secret program, purportedly designed to exterminate the remaining homosexual population in the NAR. However, its real purpose was to exterminate, without involving the local messiness created by the Death Squads, any opponents of the regime it could find.

2021-2023: The intervention by the East Asian Confederation in 2021, the successful conclusion of the Second Civil War in 2022, and the Restoration of Constitutional Democracy in 2023. Restoration formally dissolved the NAR (in the process formally liberating the Latin American countries), recognized the establishment of the Federal Republic of Canada within the former Canadian boundaries, including Quebec, with the re-establishment of the former U.S.-Canadian border, and created the Re-United States of America. The new

Constitution, based in many ways on the old but in many ways different too, featured strengthened protections for individual freedom and liberty, and strengthened governmental powers for intervention in the operations of the economy.

References:

ADL: AntiDefamation League, *The Religious Right: The Assault on Tolerance & Pluralism in America*, New York: 1994, pp. 3139.

Cobb, C., Halstead, T., and Rowe, J., "If the GDP Is Up, Why Is America Down?" *The Atlantic Monthly*, October, 1995, p. 59.

Davidowicz, L.S., *The War Against the Jews*, 19331945, New York: Holt, Rinehart, and Winston, 1975

.

DeParle, J., "Census Sees Falling Income and More Poor," *The New York Times,* October 7, 1994.

Freedom Writer, "Church Organization is key to Coalition's success," November, 1994, p. 2.

Freedom Writer, "Profile Chalcedon," January, 1995, p. 1.

Freedom Writer, "Concerned About Concerned Women of America," January, 1995, p. 3.

Harkin, T., Fundraising letter, Washington, DC: July, 1995.

Herrnstein, R.J. and Murray, C., *The Bell Curve*, New York: The Free Press, 1994.

Lind, M., "To Have And Have Not," *Harper's Magazine*, June, 1995, p. 35.

McIntyre, R.S., "The Populist Tax Act of 1989," *The Nation*, April 2, 1988, p. 445.

Morrison, T., "Racism and Fascism," *The Nation*, May 29, 1995, p. 760.

NYT: The New York Times, "U.S. Countersues Virginia Over Motor Voter Law," July 9, 1995.

Patriquin, R., "Duke Plan calls for dividing America," *Shreveport Journal*, February 7, 1989.

Phillips, K., *The Politics of Rich and Poor*, New York: Random House, 1990.

Rodgers, G., "Turning Out the Christian Vote in 1992," Christian Coalition Conference held at Regent University, Virginia Beach, VA, Nov. 1516, 1991 (partial transcript, p. 16).

Schollenberger, J., "Concerned About Concerned Women for America," *Freedom Writer*, January, 1995, p. 3.

Shirer, W.L., *The Rise and Fall of the Third Reich*, New York: Simon and Schuster, 1960, pp. 198-200.

Section II:
The History

CHAPTER 3
2001: The Real Drug War

Author's Commentary

The year 2000 marked the election of President Carnathon Pine, who came to be known as the Last Republican. A former Republican Senate majority leader, he was known for his sharp tongue, his war-damaged leg, and over the course of a long and not otherwise distinguished career, his exquisite attention to politics rather than policy and governance. At age 74, he was the oldest man ever to be elected President.

He had run on a platform of "if not her, then me," "everything they do is wrong," and, referring to the series of natural disasters which had befallen America annually since Hurricane Andrew of 1992 and the Great Floods of 1993, "God is punishing America for its sinful ways." This theme had become increasingly popular for Right-Wing Reactionaries since the mid-90s. For example, in 1993 Christian Coalition leader Pat Robertson said this about the flooding in the midwest of the old U.S. (*Right-Wing Watch*):

> "I just grieve to see this happening and we have to pray for them [the victims]. But ... the Bible makes it very clear. When you take God out of your life, and the Supreme Court clearly mandated God out, ... and [when you] have a President ... who is opening the floodgates of homosexuality and opening as best he is able the floodgates of this horror of abortion, ... [then] the Bible says that the blood of the innocents will cry out against us and the land will be cleansed and the only way it will be cleansed is through the blood of others ... So don't be

surprised if you see natural disasters (700 Club, July 2, 1993)."

For the focus of their Year 2000 campaign, the Right-Wing Reactionaries took off from the Republican 1996 Presidential election platform. That platform itself was much like the 1992 Platform (Bond), which had essentially been written by the Christian Coalition. However, by the Year 2000, the Republican Party, now the untrammeled promoter of Right-Wing Reaction in the old U.S., had become even more blatant and in essence honest about what they were really about.

And so, in addition to their themes of the 90s, they organized variously around such additional ones as: increasingly unvarnished racism and xenophobia expressed in such slogans as "you *know* who is stealing your jobs, sucking up your taxes, and attacking you in the streets—and we do too, trust us—we'll take care of them," "the U.S. is a Christian nation," "the Bible is our fount of natural law," "taxes are inherently unAmerican and unGodly," "the free market way is the only *moral* way," and "poverty is the fault of the poor, and no one else."

This last position was utterly central to Right-Wing Reactionary thinking. Its adoption was essential if the "poor" were to be characterized and maintained as the "enemy" of "hard-working" Americans. (Of course, by constant Right-Wing Reactionary propaganda contrary to the facts, in the minds of many the word "poor" was made synonymous with the word "black.")

But said straight out like that, it had a judgmental, some said "cruel," sound to it. A formulation designed to deal with that problem that became popular had first been uttered by one Michael Forbes, a Right-Wing Reactionary member of the famous "Freshman Class" of the 104th Congress. Shortly after his first election to the House of Representatives from the First District of Long Island, NY he said (Henneberger): "We don't have *actual* poverty. We have *behavioral* poverty. Very few people out there go to bed hungry [emphasis added]."

This original thought, and others like it, comprised an

internally consistent ideology. Never mind that in some cases this ideology, as reflected in the Right-Wing campaign themes of 1992, 1996, and the Year 2000 seemed to many outside observers to be in conflict with the facts and an understanding of reality that had been built up over decades.

Even more importantly for the future of the country, this ideology was in conflict with the basic, fundamentally American precepts of the Declaration of Independence, and the Constitution from the Preamble through the Bill of Rights (see Appendices I and VII). But no opponents of the Right-Wing Reaction in general or the Republican Party in particular ever made anything out of that finding or even seemed to recognize it.

The centrists, liberals, and progressives had been split, between the Democratic Party and a variety of "third parties of the left." They agreed on little except that Right-Wing Reaction was a bad idea. Neither the Democrats nor the third parties presented any coherent program for rescuing the continuously declining economy. And no major political organization, Democratic Party or otherwise, at the time recognized, publicly at least, the danger that the growing power of Right-Wing Reaction in general and the Religious Right in particular presented to the maintenance of Constitutional democracy in the United States.

Thus the opposition to Right-Wing Reaction failed to organize around the obvious theme, one with which they might well have been able to mobilize large numbers of Americans, especially nonvoters, to turn back the Right-Wing tide: "only the Declaration of Independence and the Constitution represent true American values, and only adherence to those values will preserve Constitutional democracy and the United States as we know it."

For the Democrats, not only was there was no comprehensive national strategy. Instead, as the Bush Republicans had done in the election of 1992, for example, all the Democrats offered was "we can do better than we have done—we deserve one more chance."

And the so-called "left" was not much of an improvement. They offered neither a comprehensive national strategy nor a specific program for the defense of Constitutional democracy. Rather, they presented a laundry list of complaints about both major parties; vague, wornout slogans like "no justice, no peace," and "the people, united, shall never be defeated"; and, in no particular order, a laundry list of specific "fix-it" programs from "jobs for all" to "affordable housing for all," all of which would cost much money. But they offered no politically viable program for raising it, saying only "tax the rich and cut military and prison spending."

In this environment, "The 15% Solution" worked to perfection. With neither the Democratic Party or the left-wing third parties offering viable, politically attractive and salable alternatives to either then-present policy or the longer-term Right-Wing Reactionary threat, voter turnout for a Presidential election fell to an alltime low in the year 2000: 39% of registered voters, representing 28% of the eligible voters. Former Senator Pine won the Presidency with 53% of that vote, amounting to precisely 15% of those eligible, just as the original "Solution" had called for. With similar voting outcomes, the 15% Solution also lead to the election of increased Republican majorities in both Houses of Congress.

Further, by this time almost all of the sitting Republicans had the endorsement of the Christian Coalition and openly espoused its political agenda. That agenda, first presented in summary form in 1995 in a document called the "Contract on the American Family" (PFAW; Porteous) featured the so-called "morality" issues, for example: terminating freedom of choice in the outcome of pregnancy, mandating prayer in the schools, government support of religious schools, banning sex education, denying the civil rights of homosexuals, and so forth. At the same time, its writers were giving almost equal billing to the primary interests of their major backers: further tax cuts, evermore deregulation of private economic activity, ever-freer rein to the reign of the profit-driven "free market."

In late 1994, with the prospect at that time of a Republican takeover of the Congress, the Coalition had briefly abandoned its primary focus on the "morality" agenda to concentrate on Right-Wing economic issues, such as tax cuts for the wealthy (DNC, 2/13/95). (It is fascinating that in his speech to the Republican National Convention in 1992, Pat Robertson had actually used the word "taxes" more than he had used the word "God.")

But after the election of the Republican Congress in 1994, in the runup to the 1996 Presidential elections that began in early 1995, the Coalition made it clear that "morality" (in its sense of the term) would always come before economics (Edsall). Since the Coalition controlled the core vote for the Republican Party, and showed that it could wield that control very effectively, every serious Republican Presidential candidate from 1995 onwards put Christian Coalition-type "morality" first, even if he or she didn't really believe it. Thus Pine's heavy emphasis on the matter in the year 2000. (Knowing that Pine wasn't *really* one of theirs, his Christian Coalition supporters often referred to him in a term they had also used for Bob Dole: "transitional President" [Judis].)

Actually, that sort of maneuvering for Right-Wing favor was nothing new for Republicans. In 1980, George H.W. Bush was offered the Vice Presidential nomination by the former Governor of California, Ronald Reagan, a determined opponent of freedom of choice in the outcome of pregnancy. Bush and his wife had been life-long supporters of an organization called Planned Parenthood. It provided sex education and elective pregnancy-termination services across the country. But Bush switched overnight to being an outspoken opponent of freedom of choice. And during his term as President the majority of his vetoes, the highest number ever recorded by a one-term President, were related to that issue.

Just like President George H.W. Bush, his Republican contemporary by age, Carnathon Pine had no real policy alternatives for governing the country and no concerted plan to turn the economy around other than “cut taxes and end government regulation, interference, and red tape.” This approach had already been tried under both Bush’s predecessor, Reagan, and his successor, the Bill Clinton/Newton Gingrich tandem. (Newton Gingrich was the first Republican Speaker of the House of Representatives in the 90s.) It was, however, not a solution to, but a major cause of, problems. But no one seemed to recognize that fact, or if they did, make much of it.

Although not a true believer himself, Pine had leaned heavily on the Religious Right for support. Thus in his speeches he spent much time talking about “moral decay,” “turning away from God,” the “failure of the family,” and (referring to the then still-legal medical procedure elective termination of pregnancy before the time of fetal viability) the “slaughter of innocent children in the womb,” as the primary causes of the problems the country faced. As has been pointed out previously, they were, of course, nothing of the kind. But given the weak opposition he faced, Pine was able to use the “moral decline” theme with great effectiveness.

The solution to the national problems that he proposed was “moral restoration as the savior of the nation.” Although the slogan had a nice rhyming ring to it, it unfortunately had nothing real to offer in the way of problem-solving. Pine sought to get around that problem by focusing the “strategy” on one or two well-defined areas of human behavior. A prominent one for him was the use of the so-called “illegal drugs,” primarily marijuana, heroin, and cocaine.

All of the “recreational drugs,” whether “legal” or “illegal,” were non-medicinal chemical substances used to achieve various desired alterations of the conscious state. (Such drugs often caused undesirable short- and long-term outcomes as well.) They ranged from alcohol through tobacco to cocaine. (As is well-known, today only those few of such substances that are relatively safe, unlike tobacco and alcohol, are widely used. The use of no psychoactive recreational drugs is promoted or advertised, of course, and all are sold only on a non-profit basis.)

Some saw the issue of the use of the "illegal" drugs as a moral one, while others viewed it as one of the public's health (alcohol and tobacco use being responsible for over 25% of all deaths at the time). But moral or health issue, following a traditional old politically-based American practice, government attempted to deal with the problem through the use of the *criminal* law. (Today, of course, this approach just makes no sense.) Thus, in the old United States all drug use was illegal, at least for some persons. However, the laws were enforced differently for different drugs and different types of person (Jonas). That reality created serious problems of its own, beyond those created by the action of the recreational drugs on those individuals using them.

For example, the sale of tobacco and alcohol to underage persons was seldom the focus of criminal prosecution, the non-prescription sale and use of prescription psychoactive drugs, also "illegal," almost never. However, in that national program called the "Drug War," violations of the laws concerning the possession, distribution, sale, and use of the named "illegals"—marijuana, heroin, and cocaine—were heavily enforced—for certain persons. Blacks and Hispanics were much more likely than whites to be punished for violating such laws.

Although the "War on Drugs" had little effect on drug use, it did wreak havoc on the minority communities in which it was waged, and filled the prisons with (mainly minority) non-violent drug offenders (Mauer and Huling). And it was very useful politically. Like President Bush, President Pine knew that. And so he set out to resurrect a strategy that had lain virtually dormant for the decade of the 90s. Mobilizing the "moral imperatives," Pine resolved to revitalize the "Drug War" by declaring "The Real Drug War."

"The Real Drug War" no more solved the problem of drug use/abuse as it was defined by Right-Wing Reaction than did the original "Drug War," prosecuted with varying degrees of vigor by Republican Presidents from Nixon through Bush (Jonas). But the idea was very effective politically, just as its predecessor had been. It created an enemy, and that enemy could conveniently be defined as black (even though the overwhelming majority of the users of illegal drugs were white).

More importantly, as we shall see, the "Real Drug War" was very significant in laying down the physical and psychological foundation for the coming Fascist Period. Pine felt that the drug issue would be so useful to him politically and institutionally that he devoted virtually his whole Inaugural Address to it. We present the complete text of that address here.

The Inaugural Address of President Carnathon Pine, Jan. 20, 2001

> Mr. Chief Justice, Madam Speaker, friends, my fellow Americans. It is both a privilege and a burden for me to appear before you in my new role today. A privilege because no one can aspire to a higher office than the Presidency of our great, God-blessed, land. A burden, because after all of my years in the Senate, many of them spent criticizing Presidents for doing this and not doing that, I now have to try to do what I said all along they ought to be doing but weren't.
>
> But in all seriousness, it is a burden because I take over this awesome responsibility at a time when our moral stock as a nation has sunk so low that it is hard to imagine it sinking any lower. The problems of the economy, overstated by some, are real. The problems in health care, in education, in getting the poor to bear some responsibility for their own situation, in dealing with our still-ballooning Federal deficit are real too. But underlying all of these is the fact that as a nation we have turned away from God. We have turned our back on Him.
>
> Of course I subscribe to our Constitutionally mandated protections of religious freedom. All of our cherished freedoms are built on provisions of the Constitution

such as those protections. But does that mean that there is an impenetrable wall of separation between church and state? Does that mean that we must shun God in any public place or ceremony? Does that mean that we must exclude religion from the public square? I don't believe for a moment that it does. And I pledge that this Administration will do everything in its power to restore God to His rightful place in our public life, within Constitutional limits, of course.

And as we restore God to His rightful place in our public life, we must restore Him to His rightful place in our private lives as well. For only by doing so can we recover from the depths of moral degeneracy into which we have plunged by turning our backs on Him.

Everywhere we turn we see evidence of this, from the glorification by our liberal-dominated media of the sexual act to the promotion of homosexuality as a preferred way of life. Some say that the series of natural disasters that has plagued our great land since Hurricane Andrew of 1992 is God's way of telling us that we must reform before it is too late.

But perhaps there is no symbol of our moral decay more prominent than the use of drugs. So powerfully do I feel this to be true, that it is to the use of illegal drugs and what the Pine Administration will do about it to which I will devote the rest of my address to you today.

Although these poisonous drugs, chief among them marijuana, heroin, and cocaine, have been illegal for many years, some of our people persist in their use. Thus these people fall into what some would call a double sin: the sin of use and the sin of violating the law. As our great and revered first Drug Czar, Dr. William Bennett, said way back in 1989 (Weinraub): "We identify the chief and seminal wrong here as drug use. Drug use, we say, is simply *morally* wrong."

President George Bush saw the problem with simple clarity (Pear): "People think the problem in our world is crack, or suicide, or babies having babies. Those are symptoms. The disease is *moral emptiness*."

But in this case the immoral act of taking is compounded by the fact that that taking is a crime. And so the taking of illegal drugs, to say nothing of their importation, distribution, and sale, must all be treated as all crime should be. As once again Dr. Bennett said, oh so long ago (Massing): "Those who use, sell, and traffic in drugs must be confronted, and must suffer consequences. ... We must build more prisons. There must be more jails."

So, as our nation descends into the slime of moral turpitude, it becomes apparent that symbolic of that descent is the double sin of drug taking. To destroy the sin and redeem ourselves from it calls for nothing short of War.

Now we have had drug wars in the past. In fact President Bush and the revered Dr. Bennett did their best to launch a truly effective one. But as we have seen so many times, they were thwarted in their efforts by the liberal do-gooders and do-nothings. Well, I am announcing today, as the first priority of this Administration, The Real War on Drugs. We are going to do it, and this time we are going to do it right.

During the election campaign we promised you a Federal budget, in balance, now, that will also deliver an across the board 10% tax cut. That was our number one promise. But as our first order of business, even before we submit that budget, we are going to send to the Congress our program for The Real War on Drugs. Once and for all, we are going to solve this problem. We are going to win this war. We are going to begin the long and arduous process of rescuing our nation from sin, and we are going to begin it right now.

The Real War on Drugs has three distinct arms.

1. Interdiction. The lily-livered ones of the last eight years suspended this operation telling us that it could never be done right. Well, it simply never was done right. We are going to do whatever it takes to stop the growing of drugs in whichever countries persist in growing them to poison our young people.

First, if it proves necessary, we will not hesitate to use our own military forces to destroy those drugs at their source. Second, as proposed not too long ago by the Great One, Newt Gingrich, we are going to enact the death penalty for drug smugglers. As Mr. Newt once said (*NYT*): "The first time we execute 27 or 30 or 35 people at one time, and they go around Colombia and France and Thailand and Mexico and they say, 'Hi, would you like to carry some drugs into the U.S.?' the price of carrying drugs will have gone up dramatically."

Furthermore, as proposed by the same fount of wisdom, we are going to modify the provisions these vermin will find waiting for them when they enter our criminal justice system: "They'd have one chance to appeal. They wouldn't have 10 years of playing games with the system."

2. Street-supply reduction. The lily-livered ones of the last eight years de-emphasized the arrest and incarceration of the snakes and gutter rats who sell and use drugs on the street. They told us that the effort was futile, that when one was sent to jail, another would always appear. They told us too that the filling of our jails and prisons with non-violent drug offenders just didn't make sense, especially since it cost so much to build the prison beds we needed, and overcrowding kept violent, non-drug, criminals on the street.

Well the other side was right—and it was wrong, unfortunately dead wrong. Mandatory sentencing for even nonviolent drug offenders is necessary if the message on drug use is to be clear. At the same time, that practice does take up space in prisons which should be reserved for those violent wretches who prey so mercilessly upon on our citizenry.

And so, on abandoned military bases which are crying out for use, we are finally going to establish the chain of drug offender camps that Dr. Bennett and many other right-thinking people have been calling for, for so long. These camps are for punishment, yes, and well-deserved punishment for the crime of drugs too. But in the new spirit of redemption which is sweeping across our land, moral rehabilitation of these lost souls will be high on the agenda of the camps' educational program. In fact, the camps will be called "Moral Rehabilitation Centers."

3. Finally, we are going to formalize in legislation the "drug exception" to our valued and traditional American protection of civil liberties, that "drug exception" which the Supreme Court, even when it was of that now-discredited liberal persuasion, has been developing so assiduously in case law over so many years.

I should note that, determined to make our great country once again safe for right-thinking Americans, our predecessors in the 104th Congress attempted to significantly weaken the so-called "exclusionary rule" that had let so many criminals go scot-free.[1] Like them, we cannot and will not allow slavish devotion to the discredited liberal interpretation of the Fourth Amendment to the Constitution to interfere with our efforts to once again make our streets safe for the true Americans among us.

Thus, once and for all we are going to put the "drug

1. *Author's Note:* Actually, in the mid-90s a defendant's claim of violation of the "exclusionary rule" by police lead to the failure of the prosecution's case in only from 0.6% to 5% of the criminal cases of the time (Seelye).

exception" to the Fourth Amendment into the law. And if those liberal opponents of everything that is right and good about God's America somehow succeed in getting that just law overturned in the courts, we will amend the Constitution as necessary.[2]

4. Now, we have every confidence that these measures, none of them extreme, all of them measured to the need, will work. But if by some chance they do not, we will go further. I want everyone within the borders of our great country and beyond who is any way connected with trafficking in or using the poisonous drugs of which we speak to be very clear about what I am about to say.

If the need arises, we will give very serious consideration to implementing a proposal that our esteemed colleague, Paul Weyrich, made back in 1990 when he spoke to Washington's University Club on this subject (Stan). At that time he "advised Congress to declare an official war on drugs, so that drug users and dealers, once apprehended, could be denied their right of *habeas corpus* and held as prisoners of war, allowing for their indeterminate incarceration under the provisions of the Geneva Convention."

My friends, I am making The Real Drug War my first order of business, even as we begin the mammoth job of reordering the disorder that has been dumped on our country during the last eight years. I will be making the Real Drug War my first order of business with the Congress because this drug problem is indeed the most serious one our country faces today.

We can solve it, we must solve it, and we will solve it, with God's help and with His blessing. And God's blessing we shall receive because He will know that in

2. *Author's Note:* The whole of the Fourth Amendment protecting all persons in the United States from from search and seizure without probable cause and a warrant, was eventually repealed, by a provision of the "Balancing Amendment" to the Constitution ratified in 2006 (see Chapter 8).

fighting the mortal sin of drug use we are doing the Lord's work. We can only hope that the Lord will see this effort as the first step we are taking on the long road to national redemption.

Good night, and may the God of Christ Bless you.

Author's Note

It may interest the reader to know that as far as "Drug War" strategy was concerned, there was not a single original thought in the Pine speech. (As we will see, this was a phenomenon that characterized both the thinking and the speeches of most of the fascist leadership throughout the Period.) All of his program components could be found in all or in part in the work of such leading Right-Wing Reactionaries and "Drug Warriors" as the ones to which he referred, Newton Gingrich and William Bennett, and less well-known ones such as Peter Bensinger, Robert Bonner, Herbert Kleber, David Musto, William Olson, and John Walters (Schumer).

The Supreme Court's "drug exception" mentioned by Pine is discussed by Alex Poughton in his letter reproduced below. Also as mentioned by Pine, in 1995 the House of Representatives had passed a bill which would have significantly undercut the provisions of the Fourth Amendment to the Constitution by allowing warrantless searches in certain circumstances (Seelye). Due to various legislative and judicial developments over the years, the measure had never been fully implemented. Of course, as noted the controversy was ultimately brought to closure by repeal of the Fourth Amendment in its entirety in 2006.

Following is the first of the series of letters by the English journalist Alex Poughton that appear throughout this book. You may recall from the Preface that for the *London Sunday Times*, throughout the Fascist Period Poughton reported on it under the heading "American Democracy." Consistent with the politics of the paper's owner, Poughton's published pieces tended to be puffier than penetrating presentation and analysis.

His private views however, contained in letters to a mysterious "Karl" and preserved in his library, were something else again. And so we turn to the first of those reproduced in this book, written shortly after the Pine Inaugural. For a journalist, Poughton reveals a fairly sophisticated understanding of the drug issue, among others.

An Alex Poughton letter

February 13, 2001

Dear Karl,

First let me note the quite remarkable fact that in his Inaugural Pine addressed in no way, even from the Right-Wing Reactionary perspective he personifies, the real problems facing the country: the declining standard of living for most Americans; the increasing economic and personal insecurity, both present and future, and the declining standard of health care and education for most Americans; de-industrialization and the gradual crumbling of the public infrastructure; the evergrowing cancer of racism; the evergrowing intolerance for "difference." But then again, how could he, really? It is the policies of his party that either cause, abet, or exploit to the full for its own political purposes, all of them.

Turning to the side, thoroughly distractive, subject Pine did address, I know that you know my private fears about Pine's "Real War on Drugs," and I think, I hope, that you share many, if not most of them. I also know that you know that given complete Republican control of the three branches of the American Federal government (capped off by a "filibuster-proof" majority in the U.S. Senate) there is little hope of stopping the Right-Wing onslaught, on drugs and everything else.

As you know only too well, I cannot write about any of my true views and feelings on these matters in my column and hope to keep my job. Thus, as we have discussed, I have decided to commit some of my true thoughts to paper from time to time, in private to you, to have them on the written, if unpublished, record, at least.

It is strange but I suppose highly appropriate that Pine should choose to start off what is bound to be the most Right-Wing Presidency ever in the U.S. with a renewed "War on Drugs." Of course, his "War" will be no more successful in reducing the use of those drugs against which it is aimed, marijuana, heroin, and cocaine, than the Bush-Bennett, Reagan, Rockefeller, or Nixon versions were over the previous 30 years. And of course like its predecessors, it fails to address those two "legal" drugs, tobacco and alcohol, which not only cause the vast majority of drug-use related illness and death in the U.S., but also, through their use by kids, *lead to almost all use of the "illegals" in the first place.*

(But heaven help the Right-Wing Reactionaries if they were ever to go after the real drug demons in the United States, the tobacco and alcohol industries. The Republicans actually go out of their way to protect those devils incarnate. They have to. They get too much in the way of campaign contributions and other goodies not to.)

But, again like its predecessors, the "Real Drug War" is in any case not designed to deal with the real drug problem. Like that of its predecessors, its primary purpose will be to reinforce political racism by framing the "drug problem" as a black one, when in reality 75% of illegal drug use is among non-blacks. And it will be useful for continuing to maintain a high level of drug-trade, not drug-use-related, violence in the black communities. Among other things at this time, this violence will sap the strength from a black community which might otherwise be prepared to offer real resistance to the oncoming fascist regime which as you know I see getting ever closer.

It amazes me, although I suppose it shouldn't, that Pine is turning back to programs that failed and failed badly the last time around: "massive interdiction" and "supply-side strategies." Of course, it is the new ones he has added that have me the most worried. First, the wild Gingrichian proposal for dealing with "drug smugglers." Then, the open suspension of civil liberties for drug dealers/users on the "drug exception" developed over the years by the Supreme Court. Remember that fine paper by our mutual friend Steve Wisotsky (1992)? Steve pointed out that over the years Supreme Court justices from left (William O. Douglas) to right (Antonin Scalia) have been prepared to abrogate the Fourth Amendment when it came to drugs. Well, this now has become national policy. Mark my word, as they say, it ain't going to end here.

Then, the building of that string of camps advocated so many times over the years by so many "Drug Warriors." Now, added to all of this is the new emphasis on (forced) "moral rehabilitation" under which the Right will finally get its chain of camps, on those abandoned Army bases, just like Phil Gramm proposed back in the '96 campaign (Berke).

Among other things this program will revive local employment which had been eliminated by the "liberal campaign against the military," and further build support for the "Real War on Drugs." In this way it will be very similar to the role played by prison construction in rural and semi-rural areas in the 1980s and 1990s, creating that which what is left of the opposition now calls the "prison-industrial complex" (Davis). Of course, you know what I think those camps (and all that wonderful local employment) are really going to be ultimately used for.[3]

I know, I know, I'm nothing but an alarmist. As so many say, "the genius of America is that somehow it always rights itself at the last moment." Well, my friend, not this time, I'm afraid.

By the way, where are those so-called "libertarians" of the Cato Institute now that we need them? I'll tell you where. As

3. *Author's Note:* In the Transition Era, the "camps solution" was proposed by many observers for many problems. And it was not the Right-Wing reactionaries alone who climbed on this bandwagon. President Bill Clinton endorsed the idea of "boot camps" for dealing with youthful offenders of all types. A centrist columnist of the time, one Pete Hamill, proposed that to solve the problem of homelessness then plaguing the big cities, camps should be set for them in which both conventional education and "moral instruction" would be provided (Hamill).

in 1995, after the Republicans first took control of Congress, so caught up are they in the "free-market capitalism/anti-government/anti-government regulation (of business)" act that Pine is going through, that just as the Milton Friedmans have always done, they are willing to overlook "a few limitations on civil liberties" in exchange for the enshrinement of the myth of the "free market."

"Few limitations," my foot. Civil liberties in the US are going, going, soon-to-be-gone, my friend, the soon-to-be-gone American Civil Liberties Union to the contrary notwithstanding. But the "libertarians" will have their "free market," which failed to work when Reagan gave it to them, and their "freedom from government red tape," which will just lead to ever more degradation of the environment, more white collar crime, more bankruptcy, and so on and so forth. But once again, as is my wont as you know, I digress.

Thanks for bearing with me. I hope, hope, hope, that I'm wrong about where this country is headed, but sadly I don't think I am.

All the best,
Sincerely, Alex

References:

Berke, R.L., "Amid Placards and Texas Pomp, Gramm Makes it Official," *The New York Times*, Feb. 25, 1995.

Bond, R.N., The Republican Platform, 1992, Washington, DC: Republican National Committee, 1992.

Davis, M., "Hell Factories in the Field," *The Nation*, February 20, 1995, p. 229.

DNC: Democratic National Committee, The DNC Briefing, "Republican Agenda," Feb. 13, 1995, p. 1.

Edsall, T.B., "Christian Coalition Threatens GOP," *The Washington Post*, Feb. 1, 1995.

Hamill, P., "Send Them to Camp," *New York* (Magazine), Sept. 15, 1993.

Henneberger, M., "You Must Go Home Again," *The New York Times*, February 8, 1995, p. B1.

Jonas, S., "The Drug War: Myth, Reality, and Politics," *Connecticut Law Review*, 27, No. 2, 1995, pp. 623 637.

Judis, J.B., "Camp Bob," *The New Republic*, December 11, 1995, p. 15.

Massing, M., "The Two William Bennetts," *The New York Review of Books*, March 1, 1990, p. 29.

Mauer, M. and Huling, T., *Young Black Americans and the Criminal Justice System*, Washington, DC: The Sentencing Project, 1995.

NYT: The New York Times, "Gingrich Suggests Tough Drug Measure," August 27, 1995.

Pear, R., "Bush Pushes for Senator and Against Congress," *The New York Times*, Sept. 13, 1991.

PFAW: People for the American Way, *Analysis of Christian Coalition Contract*, Washington, DC: June, 1995.

Porteus, S., "Contract on the American Family," *Freedom Writer*, June, 1995, p. 3.

Schumer, C., "The 1993 National Summit on U.S. Drug Policy," Thurgood Marshall Federal Judiciary Building, Washington, DC, May 7, 1993.

Seelye, K.Q., "House Approves Easing of Rules on U.S. Searches," *The New York Times*, February 9, 1995, p. A1.

Stan, A.M., "Power Preying," *Mother Jones*, Nov./Dec., 1995, p. 34.

Weinraub, B., "President Offers Strategy," *The New York Times*, Sept. 6, 1989, pp. 1, B7.

Wisotsky, S., "A Society of Suspects: The War on Drugs and Civil Liberties," *Policy Analysis* (Cato Institute, Washington, DC), No. 180, October 2, 1992.

Right-Wing Watch, "Quotables," Vol. 3, No. 12, Sept., 1993, p. 2.

CHAPTER 4
2002: The Preserve America Amendment (30th)

The 30th Amendment to the Constitution of the United States (2002): Commencing on the day following ratification of this amendment, no person not at that time a citizen of the United States may in the future become a citizen unless at least one parent of that person is a citizen of the United States.

Author's Commentary

The 30th Amendment to the Constitution of the United States was the third of a series of Amendments proposed by Right-Wing Reaction to pass the Congress and be ratified by the states since the Republican Party had taken over the Congress following the 1994 election. The 28th, the Balanced Budget Amendment (with loopholes), had been ratified in 1999. The 29th, the Federal Congressional Terms Limits Amendment, was ratified in the year 2000.

The 27th Amendment, which prevented any Congressional pay raises from taking effect during the term of the Congress that adopted them, and had its origins back in the Federalist Period, had been ratified on May 7, 1992. Previous to its adoption, the Constitution had not been amended since 1971. But starting in 1999, the pace of amending quickened markedly, and that pace would not noticeably slacken over the next eight years. The then on-coming flood of Right-Wing Reaction-sponsored Amendments would, in the first decade of the 21st century, alter the Constitution of the old U.S. almost beyond recognition.

The Ratification Process

The 30th was the first Amendment passed under the Presidency of the Last Republican, Carnathon Pine. It is noteworthy that while there had been some struggle over ratification of the 28th and 29th amendments, there was virtually none over ratification of the 30th. It took less than 13 months from the time the amendment was introduced in the 107th Congress during the first week of its first session in January, 2001, until it was ratified by the 38th state to do so, Iowa, on February 2, 2002. In fact, ten state legislatures had "ratified" the amendment (*de jure* indicating that they *would* ratify if it passed both Houses of Congress) even before the final language had been worked out and it was passed by an overwhelming vote in both Houses of Congress.

(This jumping the gun followed a practice initiated by the several states, for example New Jersey and Alabama, which had "ratified" the Balanced Budget Amendment [with loopholes], back in 1995, before the final vote in the Congress. Ironically, the Amendment did fail to pass the Senate that year, by one vote.)

Picking Up the Pace

Given the deliberate pace with which any proposals to change the Restored Constitution of our Re-United States are considered in our own time, the reader might find most peculiar the rush with which the venerable document that had stood the old U.S. in such good stead for 200 years was altered to fit the prevailing political prejudices of the time. But given the political realities of the Transition Era, this "speed-up" should come as no surprise. For just as "The 15% Solution" had provided the Right-Wing Reactionaries with a hammerlock on control of the U.S. Congress, so it gave them the same level of control on the legislatures of most of the states.

By 2002 the Right-Wing Reactionaries had achieved a two-thirds majority in both houses of the legislatures of 40 states. (Needed for ratification of any Amendment under the old Constitution was the affirmation of 38 states.) Only in Hawaii, Massachusetts, Minnesota, Nebraska (the one state with a unicameral, non-partisan legislature), New Mexico, New York,

Oregon, Vermont, West Virginia, and Wisconsin had the Right-Wing onslaught failed to achieve complete legislative control. In all of the other states, the inter-related, self-reinforcing combination of steadily declining voter turnout and no effective, distinctive electoral opposition offering real alternatives to Right-Wing Reaction had inexorably lead to its victory, as discussed in the previous chapter. This was the same combination of phenomenae that had accomplished the same end at the national level.

The Origins of the 30th Amendment

The expressed underlying purpose of the 30th Amendment was to end all immigration, legal or illegal, into the United States. This was clear from the several years run-up to its Congressional introduction (fulfilling a campaign promise made by President Pine). There had been much agitation and controversy over the role immigrants, of both the legal and illegal variety, played in creating and perpetuating the problems faced by the old U.S. in the 1990s. The character of the public reasoning offered in support of a measure designed to shut the door to potential immigrants to the world's leading nation of immigrants was well illustrated by the title given to the Amendment by its supporters: "The Preserve America Amendment."

The campaign had been up and running for some time. For example, in the mid-1990s an organization known as the Federation for American Immigration Reform (FAIR) called for a "Moratorium on Immigration" (c. 1994). The ultra-Right-Wing Republican Patrick Buchanan picked up the proposal in announcing his Presidential candidacy in 1995 (Berke). (Presaging the development of the Killer Fence, Buchanan also proposed at that time considering "defending the border" with National Guard troops and building a wall along it [Wright]. One question at that time was would Buchanan view potential illegal immigrants in the same light as an invading Army, and give his National Guard border guardians orders to shoot to kill.)

In 1995, an English immigrant, one Peter Brimelow, published a book called *Alien Nation: Common Sense About America's Immigration Disaster* (New York: Random House). Despite his own immigrant status, reflecting well the Right-Wing Reactionary propaganda on immigration of the time, he said (Lind):

> "The United States faces the direct equivalent of being abandoned by the imperial umpire: the breaking of … the racial hegemony of white Americans. … The contradictions of a society as deeply divided as the United States must now inexorably become, as a result of the post-1965 influx, will lead to conflict, repression, and perhaps, ultimately to a threat thought extinct in America politics for more than a hundred years: secession."

(In this last thought, Brimelow eerily presaged the reverse secession of the New American Republics to come.)

In its proposal, FAIR did not distinguish between legal and illegal immigration. And unlike Buchanan, they did not reveal just how they proposed to halt either variety in practical terms. But that did not stop them from blaming virtually every national problem, from unemployment, through lack of affordable housing, to the crisis in the health care and educational systems, on immigration, and by implication on the immigrants themselves. FAIR then went on to call for that "halt." However, by implication once again, they guaranteed that the nation's problems would somehow be magically solved if immigration were somehow stopped.

The "Open Door" Tradition

In 1883, the poet Emma Lazarus penned the sonnet that included the famous phrase (*The World Book*):

> "Give me your tired, your poor, your huddled masses yearning to breathe free, the wretched refuse of your teeming shore. Send these, the homeless, tempest-tost to me, I lift my lamp beside the golden door."

In 1903, it was inscribed on a tablet set to adorn the base of the Statue of Liberty in New York harbor.

In 1940, the liberal President Franklin Delano Roosevelt had addressed an organization known as the Daughters of the American Revolution. Xenophobic, isolationist, Right-Wing and inherently "anti-foreigner," it consisted of descendants of families that had been in the old United States since at least the time of the American Revolution. Roosevelt, who could trace his American roots back to 17th century Dutch settlers in Nieuw Amsterdam, opened his address with the greeting: "Fellow immigrants." A collision of the souls of Lazarus and Roosevelt spinning in their graves after observing the anti-immigrant movement of the Transition Era would have been something to behold.

Initiative and Referendum and Proposition 187

By the mid-1990s, the FAIR brand of agitation had lead, for example, to the passage of "Proposition 187" in the state of California in 1994, by the process of "Initiative and Referendum" (I&R)[1]. Some observers have noted the close parallel between

1. *Author's Note:* Interestingly, "Initiative and Referendum" originally had been created by progressive forces in a number of western states of the old U.S. in the late 19th/early 20th centuries. Citizens' groups able to collect enough signatures on a petition could directly place before the electorate legislative proposals and in some states constitutional amendments, thereby bypassing the legislative process.

I&R was originally designed as a counterbalance to the power of legislatures that at the time in many of those states were in the pockets of the railroad and/or mining industries. Ironically, just prior to and during the Transition Era, the process became a powerful tool of Right-Wing Reaction. This happened even as both the national and state legislatures were once again coming to be in the pockets of Right-Wing Reaction as well, through the process of special interest lobbying and campaign contribution.

Through the I&R process, to achieve ends it could not achieve in legislatures with significant liberal representation, Right-Wing Reaction could manipulate the direct electoral process with simplistic appeals to raw emotion and utter self-interest, supported by virtually unlimited budgets for political advertising.

In our own time, it is recognized that the true strength of traditional American democracy lies in its representative and necessarily deliberative nature, as envisioned by the Founding Fathers in general and James Madison in particular. ➤

the adoption of Proposition 187 in California in 1994 and the subsequent rapid rise of the anti-immigrant movement nationally, and the adoption of the property tax-limiting Proposition 13 in the same state in 1977 and the subsequent rise of the national "anti-tax" movement. Both propositions are now considered to have been major factors in the eventual rise of American Fascism (Terry and McGhee).

The Nature of Proposition 187

California's Proposition 187 prohibited the provision to immigrants who had not legally entered the country and state of a wide range of social services, from health care to education. It was eventually declared unconstitutional by the Supreme Court. (It later reappeared in a somewhat different form, before a radically different Court, and achieved approval). The Republican governor of California at the time, one "Pete" Wilson, had hitherto been considered a so-called "moderate" Republican. His use of this clearly Right-Wing Reactionary issue to help him come from way behind to achieve a landslide victory in the 1994 California gubernatorial election campaign, gave the issue respectability and a certain cachet (Maharidge).

Wilson had not always held to the position he took in 1994. In 1986, as a United States Senator beholden to powerful California farm interests, Wilson had made sure that the national immigration reform legislation of that year, aimed at illegal immigration as well, still made it possible for those interests to hire the illegal immigrant labor they needed to bring in their crops cheaply (Apple). But as Governor, he apparently realized that by opposing illegal immigration and making it a major issue, he could attract a large number of votes, whether or not the interests of his rich farmer backers were affected or not. (For more on this aspect of the issue, see the Dino Louis essay quoted at the end of this chapter.)

In part for that reason, and in part because of the specific abuses the process allowed to be perpetrated during the Transition Era, as every informed reader of this book will know, I&R is not permitted to the states by our present Constitution.

Indirection and Proposition 187

The choice of indirection employed by the framers of Proposition 187 to achieve the supposedly desired outcome, an end to illegal immigration, was an interesting one. The expressed theory behind the Proposition was, "cut off social services, and those people won't come." In nature, it was just like the standard Right-Wing Reactionary justification for significantly reducing the provision of welfare benefits during the Transition Era: "cut out welfare for single mothers and the illegitimacy rate will go down."

This kind of rationale connected a government social support program to an individual behavior. The linkage seemed utterly logical to the critic of both the support program and the behavior. But the same linkage rarely if ever made it into the mind of the program beneficiary/engager-in-the-behavior. The proponents of the existence of the linkages in fact were never able to cite databased proof to support the validity of either the "social services-are-linked-to-immigration" or the "welfare-is-linked-to-illegitimacy" theories, but that didn't stop them from using a position that sure sounded good in the political arena.

And in the political arena, it was likely that in reality the whole strategy of indirection was a highly cynical one on Wilson's part. He was smart enough to know that most immigrants who came illegally to California were seeking work, not social services, even education for their children. Thus he was smart enough to probably know that the flow of illegals to the farms of his rich backers would not be dried up if Proposition 187 were implemented (and he may well have privately told them that as well). But, as noted, it sounded good, it reinforced other Right-Wing Reactionary dogma, and it did win elections.

Following this position, indirection was at the core of the 30th Amendment. It didn't ban immigration directly; it just said that no immigrant could ever become a citizen, thus permanently making immigrants to the old U.S. permanently "different." Of course, immigrants had been made "different" before. For example, during the Transition Era, even legal immigrants had been made into a "different" category by the Right-Wing Reactionaries of the 104th Congress. They proposed that legal immigrants, who had Social Security numbers, worked legally, and paid taxes (just as many illegal immigrants did, it happened), be denied access to welfare and other social services. These were all measures aimed at creating a "politics of difference."

The "Politics of 'Difference' "

The politics of difference was standard Republican fare throughout the Transition Era. In his then-famous speech to the Republican National Convention in 1992, the prominent Right-Wing Reactionary Patrick Buchanan had said (1992):

> "There is a religious war going on in this country. It is a cultural war, as critical to the kind of nation we shall be as the Cold War itself, for this war is for the soul of America. And in that struggle ... Clinton and Clinton are on the other side, and George Bush is on our side ... we must take back our cities, and take back our culture, and take back our country."

When another of the men-in-a-perpetual-rage of the time, Senator Phil Gramm of Texas, announced his candidacy for the Republican nomination for President in 1995, baldly borrowing from Buchanan (without acknowledgment) he said (Page):

> "Our job is not finished. We are one victory away from reversing the course of American history. We're one victory away from getting our money back and our freedom back and our country back. And that victory is a victory over Bill Clinton in 1996."

Just who were the "we" and the implied "them," the nature of the "religious war," just what is the "soul of America," just what "culture" is being referred to, just what was meant by "freedom" and "country," and just exactly how a victory over Bill (and Hillary) Clinton would accomplish the undefined aims, were all left unelucidated in such speeches. But presumably the followers of Buchanan and Gramm, who would later become the stalwarts for Jefferson Davis Hague, "knew" whom and what they meant.

A liberal newspaper columnist of the time, Anna Quindlen, described this strategy as the "cult of otherness." She said (1994):

> "Otherness posits that there are large groups of people with whom you have nothing in common, not even a discernible shared humanity. Not only are these groups profoundly different from you, they are also, covertly, somehow less: less worthy, less moral, less good.
>
> "The sense of otherness is the single most pernicious force in American discourse. Its not-like-us ethos makes so much bigotry possible: racism, sexism, homophobia. …
>
> "[Newton] Gingrich began milking the politics of exclusion long before the [1994] election returns were in when he dismissed the President and Mrs. [Bill] Clinton as 'counter-culture.' Meeting with a group of lobbyists, natch, he said he would seek to portray Clinton Democrats as the 'enemy of normal people.' In a speech several weeks ago, he described America as a 'battleground' between men of God, like him, and the 'secular antireligious view of the left.'"

The politics of difference had been previously brought to its highest pitch by the German Nazis, who thoroughly demonized the Jews before they proceeded to exterminate all they could lay their hands on (Davidowicz). What was the function then of the politics of difference in the old U.S.? Over the next 15 years from 1995 it became increasingly and appallingly clear: to generate, reinforce, and morally justify xenophobia, racism, misogyny, homophobia, and widespread bigotry and suspicion, all vital for paving the road to that full Fascist takeover that was eventually achieved in 2011.

But while as noted above immigrants had been differentiated before, the 30th Amendment way to do it was something new. This differentiation would be in the Constitution. It would aim to accomplish its ends by indirection, just as did Proposition 187 and the "anti-illegitimacy" provisions of welfare "reform." And its being in the Constitution very quickly lead to some consequences that even some of its most ardent supporters had not envisioned.

For example, except for those few who were children of citizens, since now no non-citizen immigrants already living in the country had any future prospective Constitutional protections, it opened the floodgates for legislation enacting ever more punitive laws for dealing with illegal immigrants. It also lead to the enactment of laws establishing "special" (and most precarious) status for persons who had been legal immigrants before enactment of the Amendment, but who could now never become citizens, even if they had lived in the country for 30 years.

Even before passage of the 30th Amendment, anti-immigrant agitation had led to a variety of repressive measures. Back in 1995, Newton Gingrich, Speaker of the House or no, had called for "sealing" the Mexican-U.S. border with guards to prevent illegal immigration (*Newsday*). The implementation of that policy had led to the rapid expansion of the U.S. Border Patrol, even in a time of sharp cutbacks in Federal government spending in almost every arena. The ever-increasing strengthening of the Patrol eventually made it into a self-contained armed force, fully equipped with heavy weapons and its own air force and navy.

But this move too had unintended consequences. The costs of border guarding and imprisoning detainees mounted very quickly. And so the next step was building a wall all along the Mexican border, a move certain Right-Wing Reactionaries of the Patrick Buchanan stripe had been calling for for years. The first short sections of a passive fence, equipped with infrared, electronic, and radio devices had gone up in 1994 (Nathan). By 1999, a 1500 mile fence was in place. But it was not absolutely impassable. The Killer Fence would come later (see Chapter 15).

And now, for a contemporary view of the situation during the 1994 election campaign, we turn to an essay written by Dino Louis less a month before Election Day of that year. Crafted in a pop style, and thus obviously intended for a popular audience, whether it was ever published is not known.

Pete Wilson's Politics: Illegal Immigration and Etc.
by Dino Louis, 1994

Illegal immigration and California politics. Pete Wilson is stoking and using anti-illegal immigration fever to ride to re-election (Maharidge). He was originally well behind Kathleen Brown, when he was being forced to run on his record and the state of the California economy. But now he is laying it on thick about how much illegal immigrants cost California, in education, health, welfare costs, and so on and so forth.

Well, those data are actually murky. There is simply no evidence that anyone comes here to get on welfare and get health care (both negatives), although they may come for the education. But they do pay taxes. Those with fake social security numbers even pay income taxes, through withholding. And employers love illegal immigrants: they are cheap labor and make no trouble. It's notable that the 1986 law [*Author's Note:* which put penalties on employers hiring illegal immigrants] has never been enforced and Pete Wilson is not screaming for its enforcement either.

Even Ben Wattenberg, certainly no liberal, citing facts published by the Urban Institute[2] said that: most illegals don't cross the Rio Grande[3] but simply overstay tourist visas; only a third of

2. *Author's Note:* Actually Louis was being kind; Wattenberg was a well-known right-of-center columnist of the time; the Urban Institute was an African-American-sponsored research and advocacy agency.

3. *Author's Note:* The Rio Grande then constituted a significant stretch of the border with Mexico.

total immigration is accounted for by illegals; creating as well as "taking" them, immigrants have no net effect on the number of jobs; while the *number* of foreign-born people living here is at its highest level ever, the *percentage* of resident foreign-born people is just slightly more than half of what it was a century ago; total tax receipts paid to all governments by immigrants outweigh the total amount spent by all governments on them; immigrants, legal and illegal, use less welfare per capita than native-born Americans; foreign-speaking present immigrants learn English at about the same rate as their predecessors.

But the Right wants us to forget the facts, or, preferably, never know them. In fact, the Right goes out of its way to suppress the facts. It is just so useful for them to exploit the illegals politically. Limbaugh[4] was on the air a week ago complaining that any supporter of the new anti-illegal immigrant Proposition is being labeled a racist.

Well, maybe they aren't racists. But anti-immigration fever has long history in California, usually with a racist basis: for example, against the Chinese and the Japanese, the latter prejudice of course leading to the imprisonment of American citizens of Japanese descent during World War II for no other reason than that they were of Japanese descent. In 1882, reflecting widely-held attitudes, California had enacted the Exclusion Act, aimed expressly at Chinese immigrants (originally brought in by white businessmen to provide cheap labor first for the gold mines and then for railway construction).

Facing an ever-increasing influx of "Okies"[5] during the Great Depression, anti-immigrant fever in California was directed

4. *Author's Note:* The leading Transition Era Right-Wing Reactionary radio talk show host, Rush Limbaugh, was Curley Oakwood's role model.

5. *Author's Note:* "Okie" was the vernacular term applied to persons from the state of Oklahoma and its region fleeing the collapse of the farm economy there due to a combination of Great Depression-related farm mortgage foreclosures and a drought of several years duration that had produced a condition called the "Dust Bowl."

against other whites. But still, they were whites who were "different." The whole campaign certainly feeds right into the Limbaugh view of the illegals and their supporters as people who want nothing but a hand-out. That they just happen to be of Central American/Mexican Indian descent for the most part surely must be coincidental.

This anti-immigrant message sounds very much like the one the little mustached man delivered 70 years ago. "Whatever's wrong with our 'country/state,' it's someone else's fault. It's those 'Jews/ furriners,' they're the trouble." Shakespeare once said something like, "the fault is not in the stars, but in ourselves." But people like Pete Wilson and Adolf Hitler don't look at themselves. Wilson's only been in politics in California and Washington since 1966. But it's not his fault.

Watch this well. Despite his pledges to the contrary, Pete Wilson will likely be running for President in 1996[6]. This is the kind of campaign we have to look forward to: a message that stresses questions and problems, rather than answers and solutions. Above all, it stresses the identification and labeling of an "enemy," not us, never us, either explicitly or implicitly, someone to blame, an abstraction, and based on no data. And oh yes, just like he is doing in California, he'll run the whole thing on television: no legitimate questions; no legitimate answers. All neat and tidy. All modern Republican politics.

A Parthenon Pomeroy Diary Entry (February 3, 2002)

We did it, we did it. We're finally going to keep the Spics out, and throw out the towel-heads, and the slopes, and the slant-eyes, and the West Indian cinder faces too. Wow! 15 years of hard work. We're going to save our country, our freedom, our American way of life. I can't believe it. But I'd better believe it. I do believe it. This is going to fix things up all right. Jobs for

6. *Author's Note:* Wilson entered the race for the Republican Presidential nomination in 1995, generated little enthusiasm and less money, and promptly withdrew.

everyone. Tax cuts, more tax cuts. No more little messy forin [*sic*] kids in the schools, speaking giberish [*sic*]. This is what we need to get America to where it ought to be, to what it can be, to what it always was and will be again. Good bye, coons! Thanks, God, and thanks, Pat, too.

References:

Apple. R.W., "MediaWise Governor Runs a Smooth Race in California," *The New York Times*, Oct. 24, 1994, p. 1.

Berke, R.L., "A New Quest By Buchanan for President," *The New York Times*, March 21, 1995.

Buchanan, P., "Republican National Convention: Remarks," Washington, DC: Republican National Committee, August 17, 1992.

Davidowicz, L.S., *The War Against the Jews: 1933-45*, New York: Holt, Rinehart, and Winston, 1975, Part I.

FAIR: "Official Petition to Place a Moratorium on Immigration to the United States," Washington, DC: c. Summer, 1994.

Lind, M., "American by Invitation," *The New Yorker*, April 24, 1995, p. 107.

Maharidge, D., "California schemer," *Mother Jones*, Nov./Dec., 1995, p. 52.

Nathan, D., "El Paso Under Blockade," *The Nation*, Feb. 28, 1994, p. 268.

Newsday, Nation Briefs: "Gingrich: Seal Border," Feb. 6, 1995.

Page, S., "His Stetson's in the Ring," *Newsday*, Feb. 25, 1995.

Quindlen, A., "The Politics of Meanness," *The New York Times*, Nov. 11, 1994.

Terry, S., and McGhee, B., *California Leading*, 19771997, New Francisco, CA: The Press of the New California Historical Society, 2038.

The World Book Encyclopedia, "SoSz Volume 18," Chicago, IL: World Book-Childcraft International, Inc., 1981, p. 689.

Wright, R., "Who's Really to Blame?" *Time*, Nov. 6, 1995, p. 33.

CHAPTER 5
2003: *Anderson v. Board of Education*

Summary of the Decision *(Supreme Court Bulletin)*
"Supreme Court Has No Constitutional Review Authority"
Anderson v. Board of Education, Certiorari to United States Court of Appeals for the Third Circuit.
No. 10111. Argued October 31, 2002—Decided May 13, 2003.

Petitioner, a parent acting on behalf of her minor child, brought a civil action against the Board of Education of the state of New Jersey seeking to prevent it from enforcing a law passed during the 2001 session of the State Legislature mandating voluntary prayer in the public schools of that state. Both the trial and appeals courts in the state of New Jersey found for the respondent. Petitioner appealed to the Supreme Court. Without arguing the merits, respondent filed a brief claiming that under 28 U.S.C., Chap. 81, para. 1260, generally known as the "Helms Amendment[1]," the U.S. Supreme Court did not have jurisdiction in this case.

---

1. *Author's Note:* The "Helms Amendment," offered in Congress a number of times from the early 1980s onwards by Senator Jesse Helms (R-NC) (Cox) and his ideological successors, was finally passed by the 107th Congress in 2001. The language was unchanged from that version offered by Senator Helms in 1991 as S. 77: "Sec. (a) This section may be cited as the 'Voluntary School Prayer Act'. (b) (1) Chapter 81 of title 28, United States Code, is amended by adding at the end thereof the following new section: #1260. Appellate jurisdiction: limitations '(a) Notwithstanding the provisions of sections 1253, 1254, and 1257 of this chapter and in accordance with Section 2 of Article III of the Constitution, the Supreme Court shall not have jurisdiction to review, by appeal, writ of certiorari, or otherwise, any case arising out of any State statute, ordinance, rule, regulation, practice, or any part thereof, or arising out of any act interpreting, applying, enforcing, or effecting any State statute (and etc.) which relates to voluntary prayer, Bible reading, or religious meetings in public schools or public buildings ...' " ➤

Held: Under the cited section of the U.S. Code, the Supreme Court has no jurisdiction to review appeals of state school prayer statutes. Further, there can be found in the Constitution of the United States no grant of authority to the Supreme Court to review the action of any other branch of the Federal Government or any branch of any state government for its "constitutionality."

(a) Article 3, Section 2 of the Constitution defines the authority of the Federal judicial power: "The judicial power shall extend to all cases, in law and equity, arising under this constitution, the laws of the United States, and treaties made, or which shall be made under their authority; to all cases affecting ambassadors, other public ministers and consuls; to all cases of admiralty and maritime jurisdiction; to controversies to which the United States shall be a party; to controversies between two or more states."

(b) It is clear that the plain language of this article supports the holding of the Court. Under the Doctrine of Original Intent, by which the Constitution should always be interpreted, it is clear that the Constitution means only what it says, not what any individual judge or group of judges collectively think that it ought to say or would like it to say. It thus becomes clear that the series of decisions handed down by Chief Justice John Marshall and his colleagues in the first quarter of the 19th century which established the theory of Supreme Court "judicial review" for "constitutionality" were based on faulty legal reasoning.

(c) In the first of these cases, *Marbury v. Madison*, the Court invalidated an "Act of Congress giving the Court jurisdiction to hear original applications for writs of mandamus, because in such cases the Constitution limits the Supreme Court to appellate jurisdiction" (Cox). While that opinion may be valid, nowhere does the Constitution give the Court the power to apply it with the force of law. Rather, as in Great Britain, the

There is no indication or evidence that Senator Jesse Helms would have supported the specifics of the Supreme Court's decision in *Anderson v. Board of Education* or any of the actions taken pursuant to it by any branch of the U.S. government or any successor.

legislative branch, through the will of the majority, is the only appropriate judge of the "constitutionality" of its own acts. In his written opinion, the Chief Justice stated that if "the courts lacked the power to give sting to constitutional safeguards … , the Legislative and Executive Branches might too often override the Constitution" (Cox). That may well be true. But if the Founding Fathers had wanted to give the Federal judiciary that "protective" function, they would have clearly written it into the Constitution. Chief Justice Marshall was reading into the Constitution words that he wanted to see—but were not there.

(d) In *Martin v. Hunter's Lessee*, Justice Joseph Story expanded the Supreme Court's review powers to include decisions made by the State courts (Cox). Like Chief Justice Marshall, Justice Story was reading into Article 3, Section 2 of the Constitution what he wanted to see there. In *Cohens v. Virginia*, Chief Justice Marshall affirmed Justice Story's conclusion in *Martin*, using the same faulty reasoning (Cox).

(e) Finally, in *McCulloch v. Maryland*, Chief Justice Marshall not only reaffirmed the Court's review authority, unstated in the Constitution, but found in it other "implied powers," giving the Congress authority to undertake actions not otherwise specified by the Constitution (in this case renewing the charter of the United States Bank which it had originally established in 1791) (Cox).

(f) After extensive review of the opinions and reasoning in the decisions made in the aforementioned cases, careful review of the language of the Constitution itself, and a consideration of the available evidence on Original Intent, the Court was able to find no basis for the conclusions on "implied powers" that Chief Justice Marshall and his colleagues drew in those decisions referable to the authority of either the Supreme Court or the Congress. Thus, the Court held, the precedents established by those cases and all their successors down through the years were based on faulty reasoning and a reading of the Constitution not in accord with the Doctrine of Original Intent. Thus those faulty precedents must be abandoned. Since the specifics of *Marbury*, *Martin*, *Cohens*, and *McCulloch* had long since become moot, the Court chose not to reverse those decisions. However, it did reverse the holdings made in those cases that the Supreme Court had any power to review the actions of the Federal Executive and Legislative branches or any State courts for their "constitutionality."

11 F. 11th 111, Affirmed. Chief Justice Steps delivered the opinion of the Court; seven justices joining, one dissenting.

Author's Commentary

Anderson v. United States was the most significant decision handed down by the Supreme Court in the old United States since *Marbury v. Madison*, referred to in the decision summary reproduced above. In that case, Chief Justice John Marshall had established the power of the Supreme Court to review actions of the two other branches of the Federal government. As correctly noted by Chief Justice Steps that power is nowhere clearly granted to it by the Constitution itself. Nevertheless, Marshall said, if the Supreme Court found such actions to be unconstitutional, they were null and void. His reasoning went as follows (Cox):

> "The Constitution is either a superior paramount law, unchangeable by ordinary means, or it is on a level with ordinary legislative acts, and, like other acts, is alterable when the legislature shall please to alter it. If the former part of the alternative be true, then a legislative act contrary to the Constitution is not law; if the latter part be true, then written constitutions are absurd attempts, on the part of the people, to limit a power in its own nature illimitable."

Marshall, of course, held that the "former alternative" was true, its truth found in the fact of the Constitution itself. He then drew the defensible conclusion that the body given the power to adjudicate disputes arising under the Constitution, and Article 3 Section 2 surely did that, indeed had the power to review the actions of the other two governmental branches for their constitutionality. That authority was extended to the appellate review of state court decisions having constitutional implications under the defensible conclusion that by ratifying the Constitution in the first place, the states had ceded to the United States that appellate jurisdiction, which is clearly contained in Article 3 Section 2 (see the decision in *Cohens*).

Once the Court under Marshall's leadership had made those judgments, the full American power structure quickly came to agree with him. The Jeffersonians did make several modest attempts to undermine the independence and authority of the Supreme Court, but failed and ultimately gave up. From that time onwards, American jurisprudence came to be firmly established in the legal structure that Chief Justice Marshall had constructed on the Constitution's base, as he interpreted it.

One very important principle set forth by Marshall, and subsequently accepted by all parties to American government down to the Transition Era, was that the Constitution was a document that meant more than it explicitly said, that was open to interpretation, and held within itself "implications." And by implication that meant the Constitution was a document that could grow and change with changing times and circumstances, that it was indeed designed to grow and change with changing times and circumstances.

During the Transition Era there came to be propounded what the *Supreme Court Bulletin*'s summary of *Anderson* refers to as the "Doctrine of Original Intent." One of its early protagonists was one Edwin Meese, the most prominent of President Ronald Reagan's several Attorneys General. A former local prosecutor with no background in Constitutional law, a lawyer who once was supposed to have said that if the police arrested someone that was evidence enough he or she was guilty, Meese held that if it wasn't in the Constitution, in clear language, it didn't exist. (Meese later became the head of the National Council on Policy, the highly secretive coordinating body for a wide range of Reactionary Republican and Christian Rightist organizations during the run-up to fascism.)

A more cerebral proponent of the Doctrine was one Robert Bork. He had two principal claims to fame. One was that as the third-ranking Justice Department official in 1973, on the orders of President Richard M. Nixon he fired a supposedly independent prosecutor during the scandal that eventually came to be known by the name "Watergate" and that eventually led to Nixon's resignation as President. (Bork's two superiors at the time both resigned rather than carry out an order which indeed was later found to be unlawful.)

The other was that he was the most celebrated failed Supreme Court nominee in the history of the old U.S. And his nomination failed precisely because he held to Constitutional theories that were completely at odds with those held by almost everyone else at the time considered to be an authority on the matter. But his time eventually came. The Court did adopt the theory he espoused so eloquently in so many legal papers and articles. Summarizing the theory, Bork held that (1993):

> " … principles not originally understood to be in the Constitution [have no constitutional validity]. Where the Constitution is silent, [a Supreme Court] Justice has no [legislative review] authority. To act against legislation without authority is to engage in civil disobedience from the bench and to perpetrate limited coups d'état that overthrow the American form of government."

By implication, of course, Bork was attacking Marshall, because what he found in the Constitution was certainly not *originally* understood to be there (assuming that "originally" in this context means "when the Constitution was written"). And by so doing, Bork was in the front of a movement to deny 200 years of American jurisprudence. His, in essence, was the thinking behind *Anderson.*

It is interesting that Bork's theory of Original Intent would appear to have much in common with the theory of "Biblical Inerrantism" that was all the rage among the Religious Right during the Transition Era and provided a major piece of the foundation of the thinking that lead to American Fascism. But that's another story, one we will get to later.

A spirited attack on the theory of Original Intent had been offered a few years before Bork wrote the article cited above by Judge Irving R. Kaufman, a Federal Circuit Court of Appeals judge (1987):

> "I regard reliance on original intent to be a largely specious mode of interpretation. I often find it instructive to consult the Framers when I am called upon to interpret the Constitution, but it is the beginning of my inquiry, not the end. For not only is the quest for 'intent' fraught with obstacles of a practical nature—notably that the Framers plainly never foresaw most of the problems that bedevil the courts today—it may also be more undemocratic than competing methods of construing the Constitution.
>
> "If the search for 'intent' sums up the constitutional enterprise, then current generations are bound not merely by general language but by specific conceptions frozen in time by men long dead. …
>
> "*The open-textured nature of most of the vital clauses of the Constitution signifies that the drafters expected future generations to adapt the language to modern circumstances, not conduct judicial autopsies into the minds of the Framers.* When the Founding Fathers talked about due process, equal protection and freedom of speech and religion, they were embracing general principles, not specific solutions [emphasis added]."

Kaufman here is of course defending the expansive approach to Constitutional interpretation that lead to the broadening of protections for individual rights that so enraged Right-Wing Reactionaries in the latter half of the 20th century and lead eventually to *Anderson*.

It is ironic that in his younger days Kaufman was the judge who presided over the trial of Ethel and Julius Rosenberg, accused of being atomic weapons spies, convicted, and eventually executed. Many people around the world thought the trial and the subsequent failed appeals process were possibly rigged and certainly major miscarriages of justice. Both Ethel and Julius were political progressives and he was an active member of the Communist Party. Ethel was almost certainly not a spy, and if Julius was, he was apparently engaged only in stealing industrial, not atomic weapons, secrets.

The trial and execution of the Rosenbergs, it was revealed later, featured unprecedented collusion between the Federal Bureau of Investigation, the Federal Department of Justice, and the Courts, including both Judge Kaufman and the Supreme Court (Meeropol; Schneir and Schneir; Wexley). But it was a major feature of the so-called "McCarthy Period" (1945-60). During that time of so-called "anti-Communist hysteria," individual rights for many left-wing Americans were harshly suppressed. Punishment, most often in the form of political and judicial harassment and loss of employment, not imprisonment or death, was meted out simply for having, holding to, and expressing unpopular ideas, not for engaging in any even faintly illegal activity.

As an echo in a way of McCarthyism, in *Anderson* a group of Right-Wing Reactionary justices overturned the whole U.S. legal tradition from the time of the founding and organization of the Republic because they didn't like the outcomes that tradition had produced. With the Court out of the way, by its own hand no less, Right-Wing Reaction had succeeded in emasculating the powers of one of the three protectors of American constitutional democracy, the Courts, the media, and the Congress, on which it had set its sights during the Transition Era (see Appendix III). Thus *Anderson* significantly accelerated the development of fascism in the old U.S. But who ever said that the Court was not always truly a political institution (Rodell)?

A Parthenon Pomeroy Diary Entry (May 15, 2003)

We did it, we did it. We've finally got the Supreme Court out of our hair. And those old fogeys handled the comb themselves. The people are going to rule now. Wow! 15 years of hard work to change that damned Court. We're going to save our country, our freedom, our American way of life. I can't believe it. But I'd better believe it. I do believe it. This is going to fix things up all right. Jobs for everyone. Cut taxes to the bone. And we can get the coons out of the schools, get sex out of the schools, get those faggots out of the schools, get prayer back in, where it belongs. Yowy kazowy. This is what we need to get America back to where it ought to be, to what it can be, to what it always was and always will be. Thanks, God, and thanks, Pat, too.

References:

Bork, R., "The Senate's Power Grab," *The New York Times*, June 23, 1993.

Cox, A., *The Court and the Constitution,* Boston, MA: Houghton Mifflin, 1987, pp. 58, 59, 63, 66, 75, 342, 360.

Kaufman, I.R., "No Way to Interpret the Constitution," *The New York Times*, Jan. 2, 1987.

Meeropol, R., "Critique with Mort Mecloskey," WUSBFM, 90.1, Stony Brook, NY, October 30, 1995.

Rodell, F., *Nine Men: A Political History of the Supreme Court from 1790 to 1955*, New York: Random House, 1955.

Schneir, W. and Schneir, M., *Invitation to an Inquest*, New York: Doubleday, 1965.

Supreme Court Bulletin (Windham, NH), "Supreme Court Has No Constitutional Review Authority," Vol. 24, No. 8, June 2003, p. 3.

Wexley, J., *The Judgment of Ethel and Julius Rosenberg*, New York: Cameron and Kahn, 1955.

CHAPTER 6
2004: The First Hague Inaugural Address

The First Inaugural Address of President Jefferson Davis Hague, December 25, 2004[1]

Mr. President, Mr. Chief Justice, Mr. Speaker, my fellow Americans under God. I stand here before you today, on the birthday of our Lord Jesus Christ, in all humility awaiting my time to do His bidding. And I can tell you that his bidding now is to fight the good fight, for the Lord, and for you the American people under God.

For there is a religious war going on in this country. And we, the Americans of God, must win it. We must take back our cities, and take back our culture, and take back our country [Buchanan]. To do this, we must return to our Christian roots. If we do not, we will continue to legalize sodomy, slaughter innocent babies, destroy the minds of our children, squander our resources, and yes, sink into oblivion [Robertson].

We are in an eternal battle. The battle is between right and wrong, between truth and lies, between life and death. And if we ever forget what it is about, if we think we are in a battle for electing people to hold office,

1. *Author's Note:* There is no indication or evidence that any of the historical figures quoted in the Hague First Inaugural Address or elsewhere in this chapter, among whom are Patrick Buchanan, M.G. Robertson, Paul Weyrich, Keith Fournier, Gary Bauer, Jerry Falwell, and Newton Gingrich, would have supported or associated themselves in any way with any of the actual positions or actions that Jefferson Davis Hague or any members of his government or political parties took, at that time or in the future.

simply controlling political parties, then we will not accomplish what we are meant to achieve. We need to hold to our principles, and stick to them regardless.

The real enemy is the secular humanist mindset which seeks to destroy everything that is good in this society. The fight that we are fighting, the battle we have joined, is one that encompasses our entire life span. Remember, you have God. You have your families; you have your community, your church community, your neighborhood, and all the things you are concerned about. They have only power. That's all that matters to them. They will fight with everything that's in them to keep that power [Weyrich].

Today we face what I believe is an even greater threat to our lives. The enemy is more insidious, more chameleon-like than a Hitler. *And this enemy is even more deadly.* The enemy is lethal and must be stopped [Fournier].

So far from having ended, the cold war has increased in intensity, as sector after sector of American life has been ruthlessly corrupted by the liberal ethos. Now that the other 'Cold War' is over, the real cold war has begun [Kristol, quoted in Starr].

Yes, we are engaged in a social, political, and cultural civil war. There is a lot of talk in America about pluralism. But you can't have a society whose highest value is merely live and let live. The bottom line is somebody's values will prevail. Somebody is going to win this civil war. And the winner gets the right to teach our children what to believe about things like life and death, love and sex, and freedom and slavery.

As I have travelled the length and breadth of this great God-given land of ours, I have often run into skeptics. They say, "Well, J.D., if there is a civil war going on, where are the two sides?" And my explanation is that on one side there are men and women like Americans under God. People who believe that God is. And believing that God is, they are required, they are obligated to take the positions they take on a whole host of issues. And on the other side of this great conflict there are people at very significant positions in our culture who begin their thinking with the belief that God isn't. They are our enemy [Bauer].

Yes, it is time to take America back, from the liberal politicians who are attempting to erase every evidence of God from public life, from government officials who hide their radical, anti-Christian bigotry behind a twisted view of "the separation of church and state," from gay and lesbian radicals who not only claim the right to lead their Godless lifestyle, but demand that we support this abominable behavior, from the radical feminists whose "right to choose" has caused the murder of millions of innocent unborn little babies, from the militant left which is the fount of all evil—take her back from every group or individual that refuses to recognize our beloved nation for what it truly is—*a nation under God!* [Falwell]

We are the only society in history that says that power comes from God to you … and if you don't tell the truth about the role of God and the centrality of God in America, you can't explain the rest of our civilization. I look forward to the day when a belief in God is once more at the center of the definition of being an American [Gingrich, 1].

As to the future, if you think about the notion that the great challenge of our lifetime is first to imagine a future that is worth spending our lives getting to, and then, because of the technologies and the capabilities we have today, to get it up to sort of a virtual state, although that's done in terms of actual levels of sophistication, all that's done in your mind.

And that takes leadership. Most studies of leadership argue that leaders actually are acting out past decisions. The problem when you get certainty with great leaders is that they have already thoroughly envisioned the achievement, and now it is just a matter of implementation. And so it is very different. And so in a sense, virtuality [*sic*] at the mental level is something I think you find in leadership over historical periods. But in addition, we are not in a new place; it is just becoming harder and harder to avoid the place where we are [Gingrich, 2].

In fighting this fight to avoid this place, we face an increasingly militant, radical, socialist left. And this is how we are going to win the war against this left. We will use the same strategy General Douglas MacArthur employed against the Japanese in the Pacific in World War II: bypass their strongholds, then surround them, isolate them, bombard them, then blast the individuals out of their power bunkers with hand-to-hand combat. The battle for Iwo Jima[2] was not pleasant, but our troops won it. The battle to regain the soul of America won't be pleasant either, but we will win it [Robertson].

Yes, with your help and God's blessing we will win it. Thank you and good night.

A Connie Conroy Note (December 27, 2004)

We did it! We pulled it off! We got the Prez a good speech, a great speech, if I may say so myself. And after all those drafts he didn't like at all, too. Trying, honestly, honestly, to come up with a new way to say the same old thing he had been saying over and over in the campaign. And so what did we do? We went back to some tried and true stuff from our "Patron Saints," (if I may say so, revealing my Catholic background—don't let any of the true Fundy Ministers hear me saying anything like that!): Pat Buchanan, Pat Robertson, Gary Bauer, Jerry Falwell, the Newt Man.[3]

2. *Author's Note:* Named for the island on which it took place, "Iwo Jima" marked the penultimate major battle of the Pacific War in 1945.

3. *Author's Note:* In her Note Conroy did not identify which sections of the speech were based on the words of which of the "patron saints." But with some ➤

Just took some of their best stuff, threw it together, nobody was the wiser, especially the Prez, and presto! The best speech money couldn't begin to buy. And I'll tell you, after old Carney, I think that this young guy is going to be fun!

Author's Commentary
The Hague Heritage

On Tuesday, November 2, 2004, Jefferson Davis (J.D.) Hague was elected as the 45th President of the old United States. He was a great-grandnephew of the preWorld War II Mayor of Jersey City, NJ, Frank Hague, a man who once said (Peter):

> "You hear about constitutional rights, free speech and the free press. Every time I hear these words I say to myself, 'That man is a Red, that man is a Communist!' You never hear a real American talk like that."

J.D.'s father, "Big Daddy Hague," was a truck driver who sported the old Confederate States of America flag on the radiator of his 22 wheeler's tractor, and carried a loaded sawed-off double-barreled shotgun underneath the passenger seat. It was there, Big Daddy would confide in friends, "to protect myself from the niggers." His choice of name for his second-born son came as no surprise to his friends, especially since his first-born son "Nat" had been named after Confederate General Nathan B. Forrest. This man's principal claim to fame was that a year after the end of the First Civil War he had founded the virulently anti-black terrorist organization known as the Ku Klux Klan.

Big Daddy happened to be a passionate reader. His taste in books ranged from those carried in the Paladin Press catalog (1991, focusing on guns, explosives, and survivalism) to those

detective work and using the process of elimination, it has been possible to determine with a fair degree of certainty just who was responsible for what. The putative sub-authors are named in the text in [ ], and the putative sources are listed under their names in the reference list at the end of the chapter.

carried in the National Vanguard Books catalog (1993, featuring anti-Semitism, racism, glorification of Hitler's Germany, and children's books).

J.D.'s mother had been an active and vocal member of the movement to harass and assault elective pregnancy termination clinics, their staffs and patients. She had joined the first Northern New Jersey chapter of the militant, violence-inducing anti-freedom-of-choice organization called "Operation Rescue" when it was founded in the mid-1980s. She had been arrested many times for screaming at staff and patients alike "up close and personal," attempting to physically block clinic entrances, and on suspicion of participation in anti-clinic vandalism.

One of President Pine's first acts in 2001 had been to order the end to enforcement of the Freedom of Access to Clinic Entrances (FACE) Act, a Federal law passed by the 103rd Congress that had offered some protection to the clinics. (In ordering the non-enforcement of existing legislation that he didn't like, Pine was following a well-known Right-Wing pattern. For example, former 1996 Republican Presidential candidate Phil Gramm had declared that if he were elected President, one of his first acts would be to end enforcement, on his own authority, of Federal affirmative action (equal rights in employment) law [Page].)

J.D.'s mother was one of the first in the nation to publicly take advantage of the new Pine policy. She went on to become a national leader of the violence-centered movement spawned by Operation Rescue and its many mutations. Aided by Pine's Executive Order and the subsequent repeal of the FACE Act by the 107th Congress, by the middle of the Pine Presidency, the movement had succeeded in driving out of business most of the open elective pregnancy-termination centers around the country, even though the procedure was technically still legal.

The Development of the Republican-Christian Alliance

Hague was the candidate of the newly-formed Republican-Christian Alliance (R-CA). The R-CA had been created at the quadrennial Republican National Convention held in Indianapolis, IN in the second week of August, 2004. It was the final recognition of a reality that had been developing since the Republican National Convention held in Houston, TX August 16-20, 1992 had adopted a platform largely written by representatives of the Christian Coalition (RNC). Over the intervening 12 years, the dominant and driving force in the Republican Party had become ever-increasingly the Religious Right, led by its dominant political arm, the Christian Coalition.

It is interesting to note briefly the parallels between the development of the Republican Party in the last decade before the First Civil War and of the Republican-Christian Alliance in the second decade before the Second (Marsden). In the 1850s, the "Anti-Masons," an evangelical political party opposed to "free thinking" as well as slavery, lead the movement which divided the old Whig Party into two. Subsequently, the Anti-Masons/"Northern Whigs" evolved into the new Republican Party.

In the case of both the latter and the R-CA, a movement that began with moral preaching eventually married itself to political power. It was ironic, of course, that the Republican Party of the Transition Era, the R-CA, and its successor, the American Christian Nation Party (ACNP), would eventually undo much of what the original Republican Party had accomplished when under President Abraham Lincoln it had lead the nation into war over the twin issues of preserving the Union and ending Negro slavery.

The ACNP would, by creating the New American Republics in 2011, break up the Union, and institute enforced, absolute, racial segregation that to some represented a form of slavery. Prior to the formation of the NAR, although the action had no practical application, it happened that they had, for the symbolic reason of adhering to the "Doctrine of Original Intent" concerning the Constitution, in 2010 among other things repealed the XIIIth Amendment (which had abolished slavery).

It was at the 13th annual "Road To Victory" national meeting of the Christian Coalition held at Regent University in Virginia Beach, VA in November, 2003 that Jefferson Davis Hague had gained the Coalition's "highest moral evaluation." (Right up to the adoption of the Supremacy Amendment in 2007, the Coalition was always careful to do nothing to jeopardize its tax-exempt standing. The adoption of the Amendment had, among other things, lead to the passage of Federal legislation guaranteeing "approved" churches tax exemption regardless of what activities they undertook. Before that time, however, the Coalition never "endorsed" candidates [*Freedom Writer*]. It simply "recognized their moral value.") Once having achieved the Coalition's top rating, Hague had the Republican-Christian Alliance Presidential nomination well in hand.

The Political Background of Jefferson Davis Hague

Given Jefferson Davis Hague's background, it would come as no surprise that as President, he would live up to the heritage implied by both his given and surnames, and then some. At age 34 in 1994, Hague had been elected to the House of Representatives from a district in Northern New Jersey. He thus became a member of that year's so-called "Freshman Class" of Right-Wing Reactionary Republicans. A salesman of heavy-duty truck rigs of the type his father drove, typical of many in the "Freshman Class" before his election he had had no experience in government at any level. He saw government in general and the Federal government in particular as enemies to be subdued, not as a set of institutions there to be made to work for the benefit of all the people, operating under a Constitution that gave the Federal government a broad mandate and responsibility to work on behalf of the public good.

He was from the beginning vocal and vigorous in promoting the whole Right-Wing Reactionary agenda: end welfare, cut taxes, emasculate government regulation and "interference in the free market" with a special emphasis on gutting environmental regulation, significantly reduce legal protections and recourse for both consumers and organized labor, introduce Congressional term limits, and so forth. (That he was especially vocal on the term limits issue is highly ironic in the light of his own later history.) He was also at the cutting edge of developing the new political racism that began with the Republican anti-affirmative action campaign first featured in the 1996 elections.

He finely honed the line of assaulting "preferences, quotas, and special privileges for special interests," while proclaiming all the while that he was "no racist," and simply wanted a "colorblind society" (Wilkins). He also was one of the first to develop the strategy by which the Republicans were able to maintain support for affirmative action programs benefiting (white) women while attacking those benefiting all persons of color. This tack proved very useful electorally for the Republicans.

Like many of his Right-Wing Reactionary cohorts supported by the Christian Coalition he had never been particularly religious himself. For example, he had never attended church on a regular basis. (That inconsistency was nothing new for Right-Wing Reaction. Its patron saint, Ronald Reagan, himself attended church infrequently.) It is not even clear that Hague believed in a God conscious of his own person, a key tenet of the New American Religion (Bloom). Nevertheless, throughout his tenure in the House he spent an increasing amount of time developing his "pro-Christian" position and allegiances. As indicated, this proved very useful to him in the Presidential primaries of 2004.

From 1995 on, he attached himself closely, both physically and ideologically, to Newton Gingrich, the Right-Wing Reactionary Speaker of the House. And Hague quickly rose through the ranks of the House leadership, despite his young age. By the time the 108th Congress convened on Monday, January 3, 2003, he had become Chairman of the increasingly powerful House American Morality Committee (HAMC). It was created at the behest of the Religious Right by the 106th

Congress. The HAMC had been formed to investigate the "moral decline" of America and propose ways and means to deal with it.

The HAMC

In many ways, the HAMC was like its ideological predecessor, the old House Un-American Activities Committee (HUAC, 1938-1975). The HAMC spent a great deal of time defining groups that supposedly constituted "moral enemies of the American Way of Life." It then spent a great deal of time "investigating" supposed members of these supposed groups. A major means for doing this was to conduct highly publicized hearings into the private lives of American citizens, especially prominent ones, who did not buy into the ideology the HAMC represented.

Unlike the HUAC, which focused on political issues, as its name indicated the HAMC focused on "moral" ones. It was especially interested in "sexual morality," sex and sexual identity being almost a matter of obsession for many a Right-Wing Reactionary. Also unlike the HUAC, which never in its entire tenure proposed even one piece of legislation, much less secured its passage, the House American Morality Committee was very busy in both regards.

The HAMC became the most public proponent of the position that private morality should be the subject of the public law, especially the criminal law, the position held so strongly by the Religious Right during the Transition Era (see Appendix IV for a theoretical discussion on this subject by Dino Louis).

The HAMC held the legislating of "moral behavior" to be its highest responsibility. Hague's vigorous and very public efforts in leading this crusade were central in getting him the 2004 Republican Presidential nomination. He in turn, publicly at least, held the passage of the 31st and 33rd Amendments to the Constitution, (the Morality and Supremacy Amendments respectively [see Chapters seven and nine]), to be the most important achievements of his first term.

The Elections of 2004

By 2004, "The 15% Solution" was in full operation for the electoral benefit of Right-Wing Reaction. The Democratic Party had still not recovered from its Transition Era, Democratic Leadership Council-inspired, "me-too" stupor. The left, such as it was, was never able to develop a solidly American ideology and program that went beyond a Christmas tree ornament package with individual proposed solutions to individual problems, having nothing to tie anything together into a consistent, politically salable, comprehensive philosophical and programmatic package.

Thus, with no viable alternatives to the continuation of Right-Wing Reactionary policies offered by the R-CA, voter turnout remained abysmally low. Hague waltzed in with 55% of the vote, and the Republican Party gained solid two-thirds-plus, "Amendment-guarantee," majorities in both Houses of Congress. As had been the case from 1994 onwards, even though the number of voters choosing the Republicans hovered around 15% of the total number eligible to vote (thus "The 15% Solution"), the victory was hailed by the media as a "landslide."

The First Hague Inaugural

President Hague's First Inaugural Address was delivered from the National Cathedral on Christmas Day, 2004. Under President Pine, Inauguration Day had been moved from January 20th to that date. The move accomplished the dual purpose of having the new President in place before the new Congress would convene on Monday January 3, 2005, and making a strong Republican nod in the direction of the Religious Right, even before the formalization of the R-CA. The National Cathedral had been taken over several years earlier by the New American Religion (Bloom), the rapidly growing religious arm of the political Religious Right.

The text of the Hague speech contained a peculiar amalgam of styles. On occasion it was quite explicit but in one place it was quite opaque. For a speech that definitively announced to the world that the new U.S. President fully intended to carry out his campaign promises, it had a somewhat jumbled nature and was quite short. However, the latter characteristic was quite common in Hague addresses (and quite the opposite of the usual style of dictators from Mussolini and Hitler through Stalin to Castro, a role Hague would later fill).

Historians of our time generally consider Hague's trademark brevity to be a nod, conscious or unconscious, in the direction of recognizing that a short attention span was characteristic of most of his followers. For many years, historians have been split on what, even in the context of understandable brevity, accounted for the strange nature of the text of his first Inaugural. Indeed, the controversy of the "why and how" raged hot and heavy in certain quarters until it was settled by the recent discovery of the "Connie Conroy Note" which answered the question (see above): the speech was a cut-and-paste job using various Right-Wing Reactionary texts from the late Transition Era.

An Alex Poughton letter

December 31, 2004

Dear Karl,

I am writing you on this last day of this dismal year before I dismally go into my cups and hopefully pass out before the cheers of the faithful echo around Washington welcoming in what they expect to be a glorious New Year. Glorious for the faithful, perhaps. But for this increasingly benighted country, I don't think so.

What a speech! First, my suspicion is that few of its words were original. I know I heard several of the most famous 90s quotes from Buchanan and Robertson, without attribution, of course. And towards the end there was something that sounded just like Gingrich. But plagiarism is a detail in the context of the politics of the thing. Hague and his new "Republican-Christian Alliance" are just evermore deeply into the "Politics of Mythology."

You will recall that that strategy was introduced first in the 1980s by Reagan with the use of, for example, mythical "Welfare Queens" and fake quotes from Lincoln (Mitgang). But it was really developed intensively in the 1990s by such people as the Republican ideologue Bill Kristol and the controllers of Rush Limbaugh: inventing some thing, some force, some trend in society, some supposed social policy that really doesn't exist, then getting people to believe that it does, and finally making it into "The Enemy."[4]

The latter was crystallized in this speech by the short section referring to the "enemy's" "insidious, chameleon-like" nature. That "enemy" is never clearly identified, but presumably the faithful know precisely to whom the reference is being made.

In the 90s, for example, Kristol and his ilk constantly harped on the "Counter-Culture" of the 60s and its impact on American values, in the 90s. They conveniently neglected to define it, of course—its major social features happened to have been the promotion of peace, love, and community (Vitello). (They liked to focus on the "sexual revolution" which supposedly accompanied it, but then these guys are all sex-obsessed anyway.)

They conveniently neglected to point out that there never was a national political leader who ever came close to adopting the "Counter-Culture" as representing his basic values, so it never received that kind of *imprimatur*. But for the Right-Wing Reactionaries, that lacuna in their logic was just an inconvenient detail.

They also conveniently ignored the fact that the "Counter-Culture" was marginal to most of the lives of many Americans even when it was a somewhat prominent feature of American life back in the 1960s. And they most conveniently ignored

4. *Author's Note:* Poughton could also have referred to the use, starting in the 1980s, by Right-Wing Reaction with help from the Right-Wing Democrats, of the Immigration (see Chapter 4) and Welfare (see Chapter 7) issues as if they were truly significant causes of the major problems facing the country, which they were not, to promote distraction and hate.

the impact on American life of the Reaganite ideology of "every man for himself and the devil take the hindmost"[5].

That ideology, of course, was very influential in the historical period just prior to Kristol's first rise to prominence in the mid-Transition Era. And because it was associated with a very popular national leader, and was backed up by his social, political, and economic policies, it happened to have had a much more widespread and extremely deleterious impact on American life than did the "counter-culture." The Reaganite ideology of the 80s was also the centerpiece of the Limbaugh ideology of the 90s, disguised as "self-responsibility" (both harking back to Herbert Hoover's pre-Great Depression "rugged individualism"). But Kristol and Limbaugh, and the other promoters of the Politics of Mythology just ignored the historical facts.

Proceeding along these historical lines, in March, 1994, for example, Kristol's ideological soulmates at the old Wall Street Journal wrote an editorial that actually blamed the murder that month of Dr. David Gunn, the first victim of the violent wing of the forced birthing movement, on the "permissiveness" of the 1960s! Talk of "The Politics of Mythology!"

Then there was Limbaugh himself continuing in the spring of 1995 to rail against the Congress as the fount of all evil. He did this even after Congress had come under Right-Wing Republican control. Back then, despite the power of Bob Dole and Newton Gingrich and the success of Right-Wing Republicanism in the Congress, Limbaugh was already beginning to call for the election of a "strong leader in the White House," to solve the country's problems, because "Congress couldn't do it." The Politics of Mythology again.

Or take the Religious Right and the Politics of Mythology. For years they regularly railed against the "secular humanists" as the most dangerous enemy of everything that was right

5. *Author's Note:* See also the quote from Michael Levin that appears in Chapter 7 (below), p. 102.

about America. In the mid-90s, I know for sure, the leading organization so-labeled by the Religious Right, the American Humanist Association, had all of 5400 full members. Hague took pains to single out the "secular humanists" in his speech, and no one has heard of the American Humanist Association for quite some time now.

In that tradition of creating supposedly powerful enemies where there are none, in his speech Hague talked about:

- A "militant left" when no active left, militant or otherwise, exists in this country—and hasn't for decades—proposing to "bombard" and "blast" them, to boot.
- "Radical feminism," when it had been marginalized long before 2004.
- The "promotion of homosexuality by homosexuals," never a feature of the Gay culture, a culture that has for the most part tucked itself well-back-into-the closet in the face of the manufactured hate-filled homophobic public atmosphere of 2004.
- The claimed "anti-Christian bigotry" of anyone who dares to simply *disagree* with so-called "Christian" *policies.*
- And so on and so forth.

But those who rise to power by generating an ever-rising tide of hate and fear need to keep the supposed enemies front and center. And just as in the 90s, if they aren't here in fact, they have to be invented.

As usual, thanks for bearing with me. You are familiar with the nice things I must say about this place in my regular columns. You are my only outlet for what I know to be the truth.

All the best,
Sincerely, Alex

A Parthenon Pomeroy Diary Entry (December 26, 2004)
We did it, we did it. We've finally got the President we need. Wow! 15 years of hard work to get someone who is on our side.

He's going to save our country, our freedom, our American way of life. I can't believe it. But I'd better believe it. I do believe it.

This is going to fix things up all right. Jobs for everyone. Cut taxes to the bone. And we can get the coons out of the schools, get sex out of the schools, get those faggots out of the schools, get prayer back in, where it belongs. Really keep those damned foreners [*sic*] out. This is what we need to get America to where it ought to be, to what it can be, to what it always was and always will be. Thanks, God, and thanks, Pat, too.

References:

Bauer, G., "Speech," Christian Coalition Road to Victory Conference, Regent University, Virginia Beach, VA, 1991.

Bloom, H., "New Heyday of Gnostic Heresies," *The New York Times*, April 26, 1992, p. 19 (see also Bloom's *The American Religion: The Emergence of the Post-Christian Nation)*.

Buchanan, P., "Speech," Republican National Convention, 1992.

Falwell, J., Fundraising letter, May, 1993.

Fournier, K., Fundraising letter, American Center for Law and Justice (Virginia Beach, VA), April, 1995.

Freedom Writer, "Stealth? Deception? You decide," April, 1994, p. 7.

Gingrich, N., 1, quoted in a fundraising letter, American Humanist Association (Amherst, NY), Summer, 1995.

Gingrich, N., 2, quoted in Kelly, M., "Rip It Up," *The New Yorker*, Jan. 23, 1995.

Marsden, G., "The Religious Right: A Historical Overview," Chap. 1 in Cromartie, M., Ed., *No Longer Exiles*, Washington, DC: Ethics and Public Policy Center, 1993, p. 4.

Mitgang, H., "Reagan's 'Lincoln Quotation' Disputed," *The New York Times,* August 19, 1992.

National Vanguard Books, *Catalog No. 15*, PO Box 330, Hillsboro, WV 24946, 1993.

Paladin Press, Catalog Vol. 21, No. 2, PO Box 1307, Boulder, CO 80306, 1991.

Page, S., "His Stetson's in the Ring," *Newsday*, Feb. 25, 1995.

Peter, L.J., *Peter's Quotations: Ideas for Our Time*, New York: Morrow, 1977, p. 46.

RNC: Republican National Committee, *The Republican Platform: 1992,* Washington, DC: August 17, 1992.

Robertson, P., quoted in fundraising letter of the ACLU, 1993, *Freedom Watch*, March/April, 1994, Vol. 3, No. 2, and *Right-Wing Watch*, Vol. 2, No. 11, Sept., 1992.

Starr, P., "Nothing Neo: Neo-conservatism: The Autobiography of an Idea by Irving Kristol," *The New Republic*, December 4, 1995, 35.

Vitello, P., "No Sign of Counterculture," *Newsday*, December 6, 1994, p. A8.

Weyrich, P., quoted in "The rights and wrongs of the religious right," *Freedom Writer*, Oct. 6, 1995, p. 6.

Wilkins, R., "The Case for Affirmative Action," *The Nation*, March 27, 1995, p. 409.

CHAPTER 7

2005: The Morality Amendment (31st)

The 31st Amendment to the Constitution of the United States (2005):

Section 1. Life begins at the moment of conception; the unborn child has a fundamental individual right to life which cannot be infringed by any person, or public or private agency or organization; the fifth and fourteenth amendments to this Constitution apply equally to all persons, born and unborn; any artificial interference with unborn life is murder [p. 22].

Section 2. No educational institution may teach any approach to any aspect of human sexuality, outside of marriage, other than abstinence [p. 10].

Section 3. Engaging in sexual relations with persons of the same sex is a matter of choice; no provision of this Constitution may be deemed to provide preferential status in the civil or criminal law at the Federal, state, or local level to any person or group of persons based on their chosen sexual preference [p. 16].

Section 4. Neither the Federal government nor any state or local government may make any provision for support, financial or otherwise, of persons not supporting themselves, outside of an institution expressly provided for that purpose.

Section 5. The 16th Amendment is repealed. Within five years of ratification of this Amendment, Congress is required to repeal any and all statutes providing for the levy of either individual or corporate income taxes.

[The bracketed page numbers in the text of the Amendment above refer to the planks in the 1992 Republican Party Platform (RNC)[1] that specifically turned up in the Amendment.]

Author's Commentary

Although the changes made in the national ethic by the 31st Amendment to the Constitution of the United States were nothing short of revolutionary, their eventual adoption, given the electoral success of "The 15% Solution" should have come as no surprise to anyone. For example, in one form or another, as noted, most of the concepts embodied in it, as well as a good deal of the specific language had appeared in the 1992 Republican Party Platform.

The 31st Amendment speaks volumes about the nature, thoughts, and goals of those who governed both the old U.S. and its successor state the NAR for most of the time from the beginning of the Transition Era through the end of the Fascist Period. With the 32nd (Balancing) and 33rd (Supremacy) Amendments, the 31st formed a "triple play" that had as much impact on the development of the nation subsequent to their adoption as the 13th (outlawing slavery), 14th (extending the due process guarantees of the 5th Amendment to the states), and 15th (voting rights for former slaves) Amendments had had in their time following the end of the First Civil War. Volumes have been written on the origins, implementation, and outcomes of the 31st Amendment alone. Offered here are a few comments on certain aspects of the Amendment that appear to be particularly important.

1. *Author's Note:* There is no indication or evidence that either the Republican National Committee or any of the historical figures quoted or mentioned in this chapter, including but not limited to J. Danforth Quayle, Robert Dornan, Michael Levin, and the Rev. Pat Robertson would have necessarily or actually supported or associated themselves in any way with any of the provisions of the 31st Amendment to the Constitution of the United States or any of the actions subsequently taken pursuant to it by the United States or any successor regimes.

The Failure of the Religious Message

The 31st Amendment is primarily about certain content matters of personal thought and conduct that the Religious Right considered to be within the purview of religion, that is human sexuality. Given that content, it is fascinating that Right-Wing Reaction also "threw in" the banning of any non-institutional "welfare" payments and repeal of the income tax. The given rationale for so doing was that both the provision of "welfare" outside of institutions for the "truly destitute" and the income tax were both "immoral" and so belonged with the other "morality" elements of the Amendment.

Some historians believe that the Right-Wing Reactionaries were simply in a big hurry to get their highest tax and fiscal priorities through the Constitutional Amendment process, and so chose the "tack-on" method of doing so. Certainly, as did the Rev. Pat Robertson in his speech to the 1992 Republican National Convention, so this Amendment gave almost equal time to both the Religious Right's version of "God's word" and tax matters.

The Religious Right always considered the matter of what constitutes appropriate sexual conduct for human beings a religious issue, not one of personal belief and predilection. This Amendment says in very bold type that the Religious Right in the United States simply failed, and failed miserably, to get its message on sexual conduct across to the American people, and by so doing induce desired behavior changes.

The 31st Amendment was adopted about 35 years after the time of the so-called "sexual revolution" of the 60s and the *Roe v. Wade* decision of the Supreme Court[2]. During that period, the Religious Right, of both the Fundamentalist and Catholic varieties, had been thundering one message on sexual conduct and its outcomes at the American people:

---

2. *Author's Note:* That decision held that the states could not interfere in any significant nonmedical way with freedom of choice in the outcome of pregnancy, until the fetus had reached the developmental stage of viability outside the uterus.

- Life begins at the moment of conception.
- Once pregnant, a woman has no say in the matter of what happens to the pregnancy.
- Elective termination of pregnancy even before the time of fetal viability is murder.
- Premarital sexual relations constitute a sin.
- Sex education other than that which teaches abstinence before marriage is inherently evil.
- Having sexual relations with a person of the same sex is one of the worst sins imaginable.

And the given rationale for all of these positions? They should be adhered to either because certain sections of that book known as the Bible says so or because "the Church's teachings" (according to the Pope in Rome) say so.

During the Transition Era, Americans reported themselves as highly religious, Bible-believing, heavily Christian, and regularly church-going (Ostling). Indeed, the country was covered with tens of thousands of churches of all religious denominations, but mostly Christian. In many, although certainly not all of them, the message preached was the one summarized above.

Especially since the late 1980s, with the explosion of Right-Wing Reactionary political and religious radio programming across the country, this particular version of the message had been thundered at the American people 24 hours a day, 7 days a week. And it had had little impact on behavior. It was a "lousy sell," as they say in the retailing business.

Some Americans followed the precepts, of course. But in most cases where they did, it was not because as adults they had first practiced one way and then had been persuaded to change their minds. Rather it was because they had been religiously trained in that way of thinking from childhood. But most people who had not been so religiously trained simply did not accept the arguments of the Religious Right on sexual behavior or the rights of women or personal morality/responsibility or when life begins.

The Religious Right failed at salesmanship, they failed at persuasion, they failed at education. For example, the Catholic Church taught that both the use of artificial birth control methods and divorce were sins the commission of which required that the committer be cut off from any official Church relationships and functions (a process called "excommunication"). Yet millions of American Catholics routinely ignored Church teachings on both matters. Even elective termination of pregnancy was known to be fairly widely practiced among Catholics.

But even though the Church could not convince *its own members* to follow its "moral" teachings in all cases, it still wanted to use the force of law in an attempt to force *everyone* to do so (see also Appendix IV, "On Morality and the Uses of the Law" by Dino Louis.) In thus turning to the law, and the criminal law at that, in an attempt to achieve what it could not achieve through education, persuasion, and/or preaching, both the Catholic Church and the Right-Wing Fundamentalist churches revealed the fundamental weakness of their theological message. But their political message was clear: "If we cannot get what we want through the power of preaching and persuasion, we are going to get it through the power of the law."

In the late Transition Era, when the Religious Right was not able to have freedom of choice in the outcome of pregnancy criminalized by means of the democratic process, some of its members held that they were justified in committing crimes themselves, including murder, to enforce their point of view. For example, consider the "Defensive Action Declaration" (*Freedom Writer*):

> "We, the undersigned, declare the justice of taking all godly action necessary to defend innocent human life including the use of force. We proclaim that whatever force is legitimate to defend the life of a born child is legitimate to defend the life of an unborn child. We assert that if Michael Griffin did in fact kill [Dr.] David Gunn, his use of lethal force was justifiable provided it

> was carried out for the purpose of defending the lives of unborn children. Therefore, he ought to be acquitted of the charges against him."

But now, with a Congress and the requisite number of state legislatures dominated by representatives of the Religious Right, elected by a distinct minority of the eligible voters, a philosophy and ideology that the American people could not be persuaded to adopt voluntarily was imposed upon them. Those who would have used criminal means to achieve their goals now had the force of law on their side. "The 15% Solution" had struck again.

The Implementation of the Forced Birthing Policy

There were some amusing as well as terrifying practical outcomes of the adoption of this Amendment and its subsequent legislative implementation. For example, Section 1 was interpreted by Federal Courts dominated by Right-Wing Reactionary judges to ban the use of artificial contraceptives, as well as freedom of choice in the outcome of pregnancy.

Some religious zealots to the right even of the Christian Coalition wanted to ban the use of the rhythm method of contraception too. They argued that in the eyes of God, there was no difference between mechanical contraception and contraception based on counting days in the woman's menstrual cycle. Both made possible sexual intercourse for mere pleasure rather than solely for procreation, the former being a highly undesirable outcome in their eyes. While from the theological point of view they were clearly in the right, they eventually lost the argument to a political reality: there were, in the absence of an institutionalized State of violence (then yet to come), limits on what behavior changes could be imposed on a population widely resistant to them.

As noted in the previous chapter, violence encouraged by Federal policy had by 2005 driven out of operation virtually all public centers for elective pregnancy termination (EPT), even though it was legal right up to the time of the adoption of the 31st Amendment. And because it was legal, private (although increasingly secretive) elective pregnancy termination services had still been provided in many parts of the country until the adoption of the 31st.

The provision of these services had been greatly facilitated by the appearance on the market in the late 90s of several different pharmaceutical methods of elective pregnancy termination. The most well-known of them was a Franco-German preparation called "RU-486." Of course, with the adoption of the 31st Amendment, the provision of surgically-based elective pregnancy termination dropped off even further than it already had with the increasing availability of drug-based procedures.

Even before the Amendment was ratified on Monday, June 13, 2005, by the 38th state to do so, Delaware, the development of an illegal black market in pregnancy termination drugs was well underway. In response to that development, the Law began to gear up too. For the supporters of the 31st knew that if 30 years of attempted persuasion had not worked on the American people (and it had not: the elective pregnancy termination rate varied little during that time), force would indeed be needed.

A statute adopted by the state of Louisiana in 1991 aimed at ending freedom of choice in the outcome of pregnancy had provided for the death penalty for performers of elective pregnancy termination. That law was declared unconstitutional at the time. On the first day of its session in 2005, the Louisiana state legislature reenacted it, providing that it would take effect on one minute after midnight of the day after the 38th state ratified the 31st Amendment. The Louisiana statute became the model for similar state laws around the country.

A leading Transition Era opponent of freedom of choice in the outcome of pregnancy, Randall Terry, referring to providers of elective pregnancy termination services, had once said (Abramsky): "When I, or people like me are running the country, you'd better flee, because we will find you, we will try you, and we'll execute you." In terms of the legislation adopted by many (eventually all) states, his words proved prophetic.

But catching the providers of elective pregnancy termination services proved difficult, especially since most such terminations were now drug-induced. Thus the law enforcement effort soon turned on women having elective pregnancy terminations, even though the mainstream supporters of illegalization over the years had often declared that no such thing would ever happen.

Striking parallels between the old "War on Drugs" and what came to be known as the "War for the Preservation of Life" shortly appeared. For example, while underground laboratories to produce the elective pregnancy termination drugs domestically were quickly established, a good deal of the supply was smuggled in from abroad. Thus, a massive Government "interdiction campaign" was quickly geared up to try to "stop the manufacture of the killer agents at their source," and "to close our borders to the lethal substances."

However, the drugs in question occupied little space and thus were easy to conceal, while not cheap were not exorbitantly priced, and were in great demand. Thus, just like the campaign against the importation of cocaine and heroin, drugs with similar physical and economic characteristics, this effort failed miserably to achieve its objective, at a similarly great cost.

The historical parallels were striking. In prosecuting the 1989 iteration of the "Drug War" that had been going on under Republican Presidents since Richard Nixon (picked up once again of course by President Carnathon Pine [see Chapter 3]), President George Bush and his "Drug Czar," Dr. William Bennett, had decided that going after drug traffickers alone wasn't doing the trick. They then turned on mere drug users, under a doctrine they called "User Responsibility" (Bennett).

That sort of thing became part of the "Life Preservation War" as well. "Interdiction" didn't work any better for the small-volume pregnancy termination drugs than it did for the small-volume recreational drugs such as cocaine and heroin.

Since in most cases, the elective pregnancy terminations were by now drug-induced, the health care providers of the drugs were hard to find, and the EPT drug importers/wholesalers proved as elusive as the "illicit drug traffickers" had. And so, as noted, the anti-choice drive turned on the women themselves in a massive way, with results for the nation's criminal justice system that could have been anticipated. They were not, of course, because the promoters of the Life Preservation War naively expected it to work for them without much enforcement. It did not.

There were still an estimated 1.5 million elective pregnancy terminations being performed each year. The regular law enforcement agencies already had their hands full with conventional crime. And so, just as there were special Federal illegal drug police in an agency of the Department of Justice (DOJ) called the Drug Enforcement Administration (DEA), there came to be a special Federal "Life Preservation Police," also part of the DOJ. And because the criminal justice system was already overburdened, there came to be "Life Preservation" courts, prosecutors, judges, and "Life Preservation" prisons too, as well as defense attorneys specialized in representing persons accused under the "Life Preservation" statutes.

The operation soon became immense, even though it has been estimated that at its height only one in 15 of the women electing to terminate their pregnancies each year were caught and convicted (Van Ronk). Although the death penalty for elective pregnancy termination associated crime was on the books, it was little used, except for providers. On the average, patients convicted under the law were sentenced to terms of only five years in prison.

Nevertheless, in an overcrowded and ever-expanding national prison system, by the end of the first five years of the program, an extra 500,000 prison beds had had to have been built. That increased the total national prison bed complement by one-third to a total of two million. (It had been over just one million in 1994 [Holmes].) The cost of building those beds was $50 billion in 1995 dollars, with an annual maintenance cost of $20 billion, to say nothing of the myriad other costs of law enforcement in support of the statutes.

Perhaps the saddest thing that came out of all this is that as far as is known, even over time the 31st Amendment's very expensive criminal law enforcement program did not drop the EPT rate much at all. Although there are no hard numbers available, of course, it probably went up, as the anti-sex education and anti-contraception provisions of the 31st Amendment took hold. That is, the rate went up until the governmental system of organized violent repression that became the hallmark of the New American Republics came into being following the NAR's establishment in 2011. But that is another story.

On Homophobia

On the content of the 31st's Section 3, in the 1992 Presidential election campaign, Vice President J. Danforth Quayle, a then-important leader of Right-Wing Reaction, declared that homosexuality was "more of a choice than a biological situation," and "I think it is a wrong choice. It is wrong" (DeWitt). The language of the 31st itself reflected a 1992 Amendment to the Colorado state Constitution, passed in a referendum by the voters, subsequently overturned by the courts. "Amendment 2" would have mandated that neither the state of Colorado nor any locality therein could pass any law, regulation, or ordinance which mandated a "protected status based on homosexual, lesbian, or bisexual orientation."

Reflecting on the power of homophobia as a unifying political force for Right-Wing Reaction in the later stages of the U.S. Transition Period, it is interesting to note, for example, the 1992 declaration by the Rev. Pat Robertson on this matter (*Right-Wing Watch*):

> "As an issue in American politics, abortion is no longer current. The people of America overwhelmingly think that the slaughter of unborn babies is a good thing and

> they want no restraint on it. The 'gay issue' is, however, most promising."

Although subsequent developments proved that denial of freedom of choice in the outcome of pregnancy would once again become a strong political rallying point for the forces of Right-Wing Reaction, as Robertson cynically predicted, homophobia did as well.

In 1995, for example, Rep. Robert Dornan, a Right-Wing Reactionary from Southern California introduced a bill (104th Congress, H.R. 862) requiring that "no Federal funds may be used directly or indirectly to promote, condone, accept, or celebrate homosexuality, lesbianism, or bisexuality." Required for implementation of this bill would have been a permanent investigatory bureaucracy assigned the task of ferreting the defined evil wherever it might be found (PFAW). (For a brief description of the ultimate outcome of the political promotion of homophobia, see Chapter 18.)

For politicians who were continually screaming about "getting the government off your back" when it came, say to helping the poor or protecting the environment, this sort of thing made it clear that they were not interested in "getting the government off your back" in general. Rather, they wanted to do so in certain arenas such as taxation of the wealthy and land and resource exploitation for private profit. When it came to personal freedom, the drive was exactly in the opposite direction, as illustrated so starkly by the "Life Preservation War." (See also Appendix V.)

On the Philosophy of "Welfare"

Underlying the banning of "outdoor relief" and the repeal of the income tax was the Right-Wing Reactionary concept of "self-responsibility." An excellent summary of the latter from the late Transition Era was written by a City University of New York philosophy professor, Michael Levin, best known for his views on the "genetic inferiority" of blacks (Levin):

"Welfare rests on a logical fallacy and a myth. The fallacy is what logicians call composition, reasoning from properties of the parts of a whole to properties of the whole. I am responsible for my children, you for yours; in this sense we are all responsible for our children. But then this 'we' is surreptitiously interpreted to mean all of us collectively, so that 'our' children suddenly become all children together. Suddenly America must take care of 'its' children, and then, only a little less suddenly, everyone who can pay is paying for everybody's children.

"Reinforcing this fallacy is the myth that we Are All In This Together, that we all share each other's fate. We don't. We are separate persons, families, clans and groups, pursuing our various ends. We can and should cooperate, and sometimes, not always, offer help in adversity. But we are all individually responsible for our fates, a responsibility that cannot be undone by forcing some people to pay for the heedlessness of others."

That, among other things, the Preamble to the old U.S. Constitution established promoting the "general Welfare" as one of the primary duties of the Federal government apparently meant nothing to Professor Levin. His personal predilections were in the opposite direction, and that, for him, was that. Interestingly enough, although through the amendment process the Republican-Christian Alliance essentially destroyed the essential nature of the old U.S. Constitution, they never did amend the Preamble. They just pretended it wasn't there, as had most Presidents, Republican and Democratic alike, from the time of Richard Nixon.

On Amending the Constitution, and the Specifics of "Welfare": An Alex Poughton letter

March 17, 2005

Dear Karl,

I'm feeling a bit greener than usual today. And even though

that green, the green of nausea, not of celebration, has nothing to do with either St. Patrick or the United Republic of Ireland, perhaps it is why I'm writing you on this particular day, to, my friend, continue with the analysis I started in last week's letter on the 31st Amendment to the Constitution of the United States. Last week, I took on the church. This week I'm taking on the state.

But first off, I should note that the speed with which that formerly durable document known as the Constitution of the United States can now be amended is just incredible. To say nothing of the fact that the amendment process increasingly is being used to deal with issues that are rather more legislative than constitutional. Of course, the Administration, the Congress, and more than three-quarters of the State legislatures are firmly in the control of the Republican-Christian Alliance. Thus procedurally, it's a piece of cake. But still, the process boggles the mind.

This Amendment was fully prepared and ready to go when the 109th Congress convened on Monday, January 3, 2005. It was given perfunctory hearings in both houses on the Tuesday and Wednesday of that week. Following a pattern that had been gradually introduced under House Speaker Newton Gingrich back in 1995, opponents in each House were permitted a total of 30 minutes for their testimony.

I recall that when in 1995 the Republicans were gutting two huge Federal programs providing limited health care cost coverage for certain persons, called "Medicare/Medicaid," there was but one day of Congressional hearings in each House before the legislation was rammed through. This was at a time when many days of hearings were consumed with Republicans trying to nail Presidential assistants on precisely when one talked to another about the processing of some Presidential papers that were all eventually turned over to Congressional investigators anyway, part of the so-called "Whitewater Affair" with which the Republicans had so fiercely harassed President Clinton (and his wife) during his entire time in office.

Since the outcome of the voting on the Amendment in the Congress was a foregone conclusion, it really didn't matter how much or how little time opponents were given anyway. No report of even a peep of opposition appeared anywhere in the now well-cowed American media. Three days after its introduction, on Thursday, January 6, the Amendment was passed with majorities well over the two-thirds required in each House. It is now being estimated that ratification by the states will be accomplished in the shortest time on record for any amendment. The 30th Amendment (to remind you, the one that virtually banned legal immigration) was bad enough. Many thought that it was perhaps just a legislative idiosyncrasy. Now we can see clearly that it was not.

It is ironic that the Right in this country has clearly begun the step by step use of the Constitutional Amendment procedure as the primary means by which they will destroy the essential nature of the U.S. Constitution as it has been known for 200 years: a Constitution that on the one hand provides for the distribution of governmental power fairly evenly among three branches of government that, among other things, "check and balance" each other, and on the other hand provides a broad range of guarantees of individual freedom and liberty to each and every American. In this way, the Right is mimicking the German Nazis in their efforts to keep their program for the destruction of constitutional democracy perfectly "legal" (Deighton).

Turning to one other matter, the way the so-called "welfare system" is treated by this Amendment is another prime example of the use of the Politics of Mythology I discussed in my letter to you of December 31, 2004 [see Chapter 6]. Broadly, since the 1990s the Right in this country has been declaiming against the "Welfare State." They asserted either that the country simply couldn't afford it, or that its existence was somehow the engine of national decline, or that it was thoroughly immoral, or some combination of all three. Well, as someone coming from the country that was one of the inventors of the modern welfare state (although ours is in a bit of mess itself right now), first I have to ask, "What 'Welfare State'?"

Measured against the Euro-Japanese model, it's a myth, an absolute myth that one exists here, or ever has, even at the heights of either Franklin Roosevelt's New Deal or Lyndon Johnson's Great Society. Like "it's a colorblind society," that claim is just another part of the Politics of Mythology that the Republicans and their reactionary Democratic allies have spun for the last 15 years.

Just consider. There is/are: no comprehensive health care system or even provision of national health insurance; very skimpy support payments to the poor (and they are now being eliminated entirely); no childrens' allowances (except tiny ones provided through the taxation system for employed workers making above certain minimum incomes—the poor don't get them); skimpy and limited unemployment benefits; no national workers' health promotion/disease and injury prevention program; no comprehensive child day care system; no government-supported paid sick/disability leave; no free higher education with paid student allowances *en suite*; no new public housing (there has been none since the time of Reagan); no pension guarantees; few protections for unionized workers (the few of them who are left), and so on and so forth. By no stretch of the imagination is or was there ever a "welfare state" here.

And then more narrowly to "welfare" (support payments for the poor) itself. The way the Right talks about it, you would think it is *the* anchor dragging the country down. Although most of the people on the system are either children or their single mothers, the Republicans characterize welfare recipients as "lazy, shiftless, irresponsible, feeders at the public trough." They blame the welfare *system*, not the socio-economic factors that force people onto it, for everything from "high taxes" to the high illegitimacy rate.

Well, as you know, the people of this country have just about the lowest collective taxation rate of any industrialized country (which is one reason why they don't have a "welfare state," of course) (USBOC, Table No. 1376). As for the high illegitimacy rate, any single woman who would have another child just to get the measly $67.00 [in 1995 dollars] extra per month (Corn) would need to have her head examined. But then again, these Right-Wingers themselves are so money-motivated that they probably can't understand anyone who isn't.

And in any case, a very perceptive Transition Era liberal newspaper columnist (a rare bird, indeed), Robert Reno, once pointed out that the U.S. illegitimacy rate skyrocketed during a time when "median state payments under Aid to Families with Dependent Children have, adjusted for inflation, *fallen* 45 percent in the last 25 years [emphasis added]" (1995). Some incentive!

The Right claims that "welfare fosters dependency." Thus, they claim that ending it will end this awful state that envelops vast numbers of people. Well, back in the mid-90s "half of welfare recipients quit the dole within a year, 70 percent within two" (Corn). The system is supporting hordes of utterly dependent teenage moms, they tell us. Well, less than 1.2 percent of mothers on welfare are under 18. And as for the "welfare moms breeding like sows" image, "72 percent of families on welfare have only one or two children."

Some more numbers (Rosenbaum [a])? As of 1993 (more recent statistics are hard to come by since the Federal socio-economic and health data gathering systems were gradually shut down by Republicans beginning in 1995), 67% of the "money-grubbing, freeloading" recipients of Aid to Families With Dependent Children (AFDC) were, guess what? Children.

Despite the best efforts of the Right to paint the system and its beneficiaries black, fewer than 40% of them were black. The average family size of the "welfare monster" was 2.9 people. Almost half of the families going on welfare did so because of divorce or separation, but only 25% of poor mothers got child support money from the children's father.

The total amount of money spent at the Federal level? In 1995, after having dropped steadily in real terms for the preceding 25 years, it amounted to about 1% of the annual budget. If "welfare" had been wiped out at that time, as it is about to be wiped out now, so doing would have saved not more than six week's worth of the then annual budget *deficit*.

But do you want to know the most shocking figures of all? Fully *40%* of poor children in what was then the richest country in the world, were *not* on AFDC (Rosenbaum [a]). In 1992, there were fully *six million* children under the age of six living in poverty, 26% of the age group, up from 3.5 million, 18% of the age group, in 1979 (just before the Reaganites came to power) (NCCP). *Poverty, not* welfare, now as then, is the problem of poorness here. It's just that the Right-Wing Reactionaries managed to wipe that issue off the political agenda when Reagan came to power and it has stayed off ever since.

That they were able to do that was as much a result of Democratic weakness as of Republican strength. As of 1995, the most recent year for which I could get figures, the general public's position on *poverty* (not *welfare*) went as follows (LBO):

- 86% of Americans felt somewhat or very concerned about poverty. 84% agreed, 48% strongly, that "society has a *moral* obligation to try to alleviate poverty."
- Over half believed the official poverty line was too low.
- 75% thought that reducing poverty would reduce crime.
- About 80% thought that poverty was not, as the reactionaries put it, part of an unchangeable "culture," that government *could* change things, and "has a responsibility to try to do away with poverty."

But no politicians were brave enough to follow that line. And the line has now led to the abolition of welfare, except for the camps. Some welfare. Well, that tells the tale, doesn't it? Until it's time for the next tale, then, hopefully with a bit less verbosity, I remain,

Your Friend,
Alex

A Curley Oakwood Radio Broadcast Transcript, June 14, 2005, Excerpt

Oh God, can you just hear the liberal nigger lovers moaning and groaning. "Oh no, oh no, our blessed welfare is dead. What will we do? How will we ever bring it back? How are we ever going to get anyone to vote for us ever again? And all those poor people. How they will suffer. They won't be able to grub food from the white folks table, take the clothes off those evil peoples' backs."

Well folks, that's just too bad. We *feel* your pain. But we're going to let you moan and groan anyway. You've had it coming to for a long, long, time. Feel sorry for the poor? Hah! Those free-loading, money-grubbers have no one to blame but themselves. If they can't survive, that's their problem, not ours.

Just remember, if a "poh' folk" can't take responsibility for himself, why should you and I have to take responsibility for him. I'll tell you what. You want to know the truth? And you know we always tell the truth here. *Here* is where you get the truth. Unvarnished. With all the rough edges. But the *truth*!

Now people don't like to hear me say this, and I really shouldn't say it because some people's feelings will be hurt, but I have to say it because it's the truth and if nothing else you know that I am compelled, just compelled, to speak the truth. So I am going to let you in on the God's honest truth. Well, I'll *let you in on it,* that is, if you haven't been listening before, because I have saying this truth for a long, long time.

Poverty, my friends, is nothing but sin. It's just immoral, folks. That's why the end of any responsibility for paying to support, paying to reward, paying to maintain the sinners belongs in the "Morality Amendment."

If you are poor you must be punished. Now I have to tell you. I'm no expert on this. I can't tell you which came first, the chicken or the egg. I can't tell you for sure whether it's that if you are poor you are sinful and God punishes you by keeping you poor, or whether if you are sinful, God punishes you by making you poor. But either way it's your fault and not my responsibility. And so finally, bloodsuckers, you're on your own!

You know years ago one of my idols, Bob Grant,[3] said that the good folks of this country were "shackled" with the welfare system, and that no one would *ever* be able to mount the "political courage" to get rid of it. Well, on this one I know you would feel good, real good, to be proven wrong, old buddy. We did it. With help from guys like you who got the ball rolling oh so long ago, we did it[4].

A Parthenon Pomeroy Diary Entry (June 19, 2005)

We did it, we did it. We're finally going to get sex straight in this country, and stop the baby killing hellocost [*sic*] at the same time. We finally got what we really need, and now the country will get on the right track. And that dammed immoral, unfair, income tax too. Bill Buckley started on this one back in the 50s. I think. And we finally got there. Thanks, Bill.

This is going to fix things up all right. Taxes are gone. The faggots have to go back in their holes, where they can get in their holes to their heart's content, for all I care. It's only going to lead them straight to hell. And no more creeps on welfare. This is what we need to get America to where it ought to be, to what it can be, to what it always was and always will be. Thanks, God, and thanks, Pat, too.

Author's Commentary

Pudge's happiness at the demise of the income tax would not be too long-lived. That measure had been sold to those Americans who were still players in the political process as

3. *Author's Note:* Bob Grant was one of the original talk radio racist hate-mongers, starting back in the 1970s. Oakwood is referring to excerpts from a Grant show originally broadcast on WABC AM radio in New York City on March 30, 1995.

4. *Author's Note:* For a Dino Louis commentary on the relationship between poverty and sin, and how Right-Wing Reaction used their position on the matter, see Appendix V, "On Poverty, Sin, Regulation, and Freedom."

"the end of taxation." Of course, it was nothing of the kind (Kinsley). It was simply the end of any kind of *progressive* taxation, namely that those who make more have the responsibility to pay somewhat more, in order to ease the burden on everyone.

The Federal government still needed money, even if most of it by now was going to support the ever-present military establishment, the ever-growing criminal law enforcement complex, and interest payments on the national debt. And so, a (regressive) national Value Added (sales) Tax was quickly enacted. And local property taxes became evermore burdensome.

These developments had been previewed towards the end of the Transition Era. For example, following the Republican Congressional sweep of Congress in the 1994 elections, the Chairmanship of the House Ways and Means (tax origination) Committee fell to one Bill Archer of Texas. Coming from one of the six most affluent Congressional districts in the country, one that was once represented by former President George H. W. Bush, Archer's constituents were typically "bankers and oil company executives" (Rosenbaum [b]). And his tax policies reflected their interests.

For example, Archer once said that his longterm goal was to "tear out the income tax by its roots and discard it and replace it with a new form of taxation" (Rosenbaum [b]). He noted that he would prefer a flat 15 to 20% sales tax to the income tax (as would, of course, his wealthy backers for whom tax payments would thus become a much smaller proportion of their total expenditures).

Pudge eventually got what Archer preferred. Pudge's real tax burden went up, while that for the wealthy went down even further. However, he didn't even notice. Doing the Right thing just felt so good.

References:

Abramsky, S., "Taxpayers' Revolt?" *In These Times*, January 22, 1996, p. 10.

Bennett, W.J., "Introduction," *National Drug Control Strategy*, Washington, DC: The White House, Sept., 1989.

Corn, D., "Clinton & Co.: ProLife Support," *The Nation*, February 27, 1995, p. 261.

Deighton, L., *Winter,* "1933 1938," New York: Ballantine Books, 1987.

DeWitt, K., "Quayle Contends Homosexuality Is a Matter of Choice, Not Biology," *The New York Times*, Sept. 14, 1992.

Holmes, S.A., "The Boom in Jails Is Locking Up Lot of Loot," *The New York Times*, News of the Week in Review, Nov. 6, 1994.

Kinsley, M., "The Flat Tax Society," *The New Yorker*, May 1, 1995.

LBO: *Left Business Observer*, "Public Not Hostile to Welfare," No. 67, December 22, 1995, p. 7.

Levin, M., "End Welfare, but Not for the Old Reasons," *Newsday*, January 26, 1995.

NCCP: National Center for Children in Poverty, "Young Children in Poverty: A Statistical Update," New York: Columbia School of Public Health, 1995.

Ostling, R.N., "The Church Search," *Time*, April 5, 1993, p. 44.

PFAW: *People for the American Way News*, "On Capitol Hill," Summer, 1995, p. 8.

Reno, R., "Shoot Wounded Under Banner of Welfare Reform," *Newsday*, February 24, 1995.

Right-Wing Watch, Vol. 3, No. 3, Dec. 1992.

RNC: Republican National Committee, *The Republican Platform: 1992*, Washington, DC: August 17, 1992.

Rosenbaum, D., "Notebook: Welfare: Who Gets it? How Much Does it Cost?" *The New York Times*, March 23, 1995 (a).

Rosenbaum, D., "A Zeal for Tax Cuts Now Has Power Too," *The New York Times,* April 3, 1995 (b).

USBOC: US Bureau of the Census, *Statistical Abstract of the United States, 1994*, Washington, DC, 1994

Van Ronk, D., *The War on Choice: 1981-2021*, New York: The Scattered Home Press, 2029.

CHAPTER 8
2006: The Balancing Amendment (32nd)

The 32nd Amendment to the Constitution of the United States (2006):

Section 1. Commencing on the first day of the next fiscal year following the date of ratification of this Amendment, separate Federal budget accounts shall be established for the maintenance of the national defense, for the payment of interest on the national debt, and for the general operations of the Federal government.

Section 2. The 28th Amendment to the Constitution of the United States is hereby repealed.

Section 3. Commencing on the first day of the next fiscal year following the date of ratification of this Amendment, any budget adopted by the Congress under which funds are appropriated for the support of any general operations, activity, or functions of the Federal government must show a surplus of income over expenditures of at least one dollar.

Section 4. No tax, fee, or other charge levied for the purpose of supporting any general operations, activities, or functions of the Federal government may be increased without the approval of two thirds of the members of each House of Congress.

Section 5. Every item in the Federal budget for the support of general operations shall be considered to have been presented separately to the President and be subject to the procedural provisions of Article 1, Section 7, of this Constitution.

Section 6. In addition to the powers enumerated in Article 2, Sections 2 and 3 of this Constitution, the President shall have the authority to declare a "special national emergency." To take effect, any such declaration must be approved by a simple majority of the members voting of each House of Congress. During any such special national emergency, the President shall have the authority to rule by decree for a period of sixty days. This authority may be renewed by the President unless it is rescinded by a vote of two thirds of the membership of each House of Congress. Any Presidential decree made under the provisions of this Amendment may be nullified by a vote of two thirds of the membership of each House of Congress.

Section 7. The Fourth Amendment to the Constitution of the United States is hereby repealed.[1]

A Curley Oakwood Radio Broadcast Transcript, October 13, 2006

Well my friends, ladies and gentlemen, now we've really got the liberal nigger lovers where we want them. No more excuses. Just a lot of sobbing. That imperious congress is finally going to have to toe the line. We've got a balanced budget amendment that's going to work this time, not like that old, wimpy, good-for-nothing liberal monstrosity, the 28th. We've got the line item veto in the Constitution, where it belongs. Congress is just going to have to stop, stop, stop spending *your* money on things *you* don't want it spent on and let you start spending it

1. *Author's Note:* The Fourth Amendment to the old U.S. Constitution read: "The right of the people to be secure in their persons, houses, papers, and effects, against unreasonable searches and seizures, shall not be violated, and no warrants shall issue but upon probable cause, supported by oath or affirmation, and particularly describing the place to be searched, and the persons or things to be seized."

the way you know best. Yes, you *do* know best how to spend your money and Congress *doesn't.*

You know, my friends, they just don't get it, do they? But now they're going to have to get it, because now it's right there in the Constitution, large as life, for everyone to see. Just think. No more government handouts. No more anybody who feels the urge taking your money out of your pocket, no more Democrats lining up the votes of the lazy good-for-nothing bums by giving them something for nothing. Yes, this is a great, great day for the American people.

Author's Commentary

This was classic Oakwood, echoing his Transition Era Right-Wing talk radio mentors, using distortion and outright lies to paint a mythical picture of a political reality that was almost the complete opposite of that which he was describing:

- Bashing Congress as an institution when it was thoroughly under the control of his own party (and had been for quite some time).
- Bashing by implication a welfare system that even in its heyday had never taken up any significant percentage of Federal spending, but under the 31st Amendment to the Constitution adopted the previous year did not even exist.
- Putting responsibility for the first "balanced budget" amendment on the "liberals," when the liberal forces at the time, within and outside the Congress, had strongly opposed it.
- Claiming that the Democrats offered to provide handouts in return for votes and had always done so, when for the most part people on welfare didn't vote anyway and never had done so, official Democratic Party support for welfare had been virtually non-existent for 15 years, and now, with no welfare system would not have had that reason to vote Democratic even if the latter had supported it.

On this last point, at best the old welfare system had provided support for only the most meager of living standards. Perhaps if during the Transition Era the Democrats had been able to do something significant for the poor, like establishing and implementing a broad, comprehensive plan to eliminate poverty, as we have done in the Re-United States, they would not have become the permanent minority they did. But that's another story.

Note that Oakwood doesn't even mention either Section 6 or Section 7 of the 32nd Amendment, establishing Presidential emergency powers and repealing the 4th amendment, although he must have known how significant they were. He was also probably aware that this time around in the amending process the real goal of Hague and the R-CA was getting those items, not the "balancing" ones, into the Constitution. But the Hagueites didn't want to publicly acknowledge what was really at stake.

In hindsight, the Hagueites were obviously out to destroy the basis of Constitutional democracy in the old United States, and use the Constitution itself to accomplish that end. But during pre-dictatorship times, when they still had to be concerned with such matters, in public relations terms it was much better for them to use a "stealth" approach than try to confront the issue directly. And so, as Oakwood and all of his ilk did, so much the better to focus on false "Imperial Congress" and money themes than on what their real agenda was.

A Connie Conroy Note (January 12, 2006)

Brilliant, brilliant, brilliant. I've got to say, this President is just brilliant. He knows that as our enemies continue to conspire to pull us down, to pull our nation down, to pull our people down, he is, he's got to be, the bulwark against this. And as much as we've got that Congress in our pocket now, as old George H.W. used to say, "Who needs Congress?" so now we've finally got a way around them, even when we've got them.

But did the President directly go after the power he needs?

Nosiree bob (or is it Bob?) He used the old misdirection play he learned so well from Newton. He went right back to the tricks of the 104th and its great, great "Freshman Class" that gave him his start. He actually mentioned just the other day what he called the "tax-cut-to-put-money-back-in-your-pocket" ploy.[2]

He told me that what his guys really wanted was to get that money back into the pockets of the rich. "After all," he said, "remember Newton's First Law of Politics: Reward Your Friends." And it was the rich guys who sent the famous "Freshman Class" there. But under Newton's leadership the tax cut was made to sound like it was for everyone. And the poor old Dems. They just didn't know how to handle it.[3]

So with this one J.D. concentrated on selling a "no-loopholes" BBA and the line item veto, to "balance things out" between that dirty old Congress (even if it's our dirty old Congress now) and "the people's President." He just kind of slid in the decree power (still "checked and balanced," naturally), with the "well, if you're going to balance things out, might as well

2. *Author's Note:* The "tax-cut-for-you"-when-it-was-anything-but tactic Conroy refers to itself harked all the way back to the 1978 "Proposition 13" tax cut in California (Brinkley). That one was sold to the voters as a "tax cut for everyone" but in reality provided most of the reductions to business. It saved business money indeed. But it was a major factor in the decline of California that occurred over the succeeding two decades. For example, in 1978, when Proposition 13 had passed, California's schools were among the nation's best (Blumenthal, 1995). By 1995, money starved by the property taxation strictures of Prop. 13, they ranked among the worst.

3. *Author's Note:* There was ammunition. But the Democrats didn't use it. Many of their leaders were wedded to a "your taxes are too high" fiction themselves. For example, the 1995 tax cut proposed by the Republicans would have provided the average American taxpayer with–68 cents per day (Rosenbaum). This was at the cost of significant reductions in the two partial national programs for paying for some of the costs of health services, "Medicare" for the elderly and "Medicaid" for the disabled and the poor, environmental protection, public health services, veterans' benefits, occupational safety and health protection, Federal recreational activities, and virtually every other direct and indirect service provided by the Federal government other than the military and prisons.

do this too" argument. And repealing the Fourth? Well, that one was "for balance" also—"balancing things out for the people and against the criminals."

Naturally, everyone knows that that balanced budget and line item veto shit are nothing more than that, shit. We control the Congress and the White House, and that doesn't look like it's going to change any time soon, particularly given that the Democrats, what's left of them, look to be on life-support. The Congress does what we tell them to. So who needs a line-item veto, anyway?

As for that balanced budget crap. We haven't had one in years. And we won't get one any time soon, either. That's because the "balancing" requirement applies only to the "other" expenditures, not defense or interest payments, the two largest items. But it looks good, right there in the Constitution, with no loopholes, heh, heh. But ruling by decree and the end to that "unreasonable search and seizure" crap. Now we've really got something.

Prez sez he's going to be careful with the decree power. He probably won't use it just yet. He'll see how things are going, but he may actually wait until Term II. But no Fourth? Now we're really going to be able to go after those Connie bastards.

An Alex Poughton Letter

October 31, 2006

Dear Karl,

Halloween is an appropriate day to be writing you about what is going on here now. It's scary. The basis for dictatorship has been established, right in the Constitution, no less. And no one seems to know it, or least they don't acknowledge it publicly. "It's just part of the balancing act" my "White House sources" say as I make the rounds preparing my next puff (or is it Pough) piece on this place. As for repealing the Fourth Amendment, they just mumble something about "maintaining a balance in internal security." Well, I really don't think that allowing the police to ride roughshod over one's person and property just because they think it's a good idea is the way to accomplish that.

You can't tell from government propaganda that there is any unrest or even unhappiness here, because they just tell you all the time how terrific everything is. After all, the major media here have been owned by large manufacturing or entertainment corporations for quite some time, and they just follow the government line (or do they make it?)

I can't find out anything directly because it's been a couple of years since even "friendly" foreign journalists like me could freely go anywhere and talk with anyone. And you have a hard time telling anything from economic or social data because there is so little of it available.

You may know that David Stockman, Ronald Reagan's first Budget Director once said that he would like to vastly reduce government data publishing because that would deprive the liberals of ammunition. Well, they've finally done it. There either is no data, or it's based on "optimistic" projections, like that old "dynamic budgeting" ploy the Republicans used in '95 to try to sell the country once again on that "supply-side" economics nonsense that cutting taxes for the wealthy would actually increase government revenues.

Well I suppose it's because, data aside, there may well be something negative going on here. After all, if everything is so terrific, why do they need to possibly destroy basic civil liberties as well as establish the basis for a Presidential dictatorship? On the first of those points, I recently came across a statement that Winston Churchill made when he was Home Secretary way back in 1910 (Lewis):

"The mood and temper of the public in regard to the treatment of crime and criminals is one of the most unfailing tests of the civilization of any country. A calm dispassionate recognition of the rights of the accused, and even of the convicted criminal, against the state—a constant heart-searching by all charged with the duty of punishment. ... These are the symbols which ... mark and measure the stored up strength of a nation, and are a sign and proof of the living virtue in it."

So much for the thought of a true conservative, compared with those of this reactionary rabble.

On the second point, even with access by the domestic media and ourselves both tightly controlled, you do hear stuff, the reasons why a dictatorship might just be in the cards. Like real incomes continuing to fall, as they were 10 years ago, and for 20 years before that (Thurow). With the decline of American manufacturing that began back in the Reagan Presidency likely to be continuing, there's no reason to believe that that isn't the case.

Like real unemployment climbing—and even in the 90s when reliable numbers were available, because of the way they counted (Sklar) real unemployment could have been up to three times the reported figure. Like the widening of the longstanding gap between the rich and everyone else (Cassidy), both poor and "middle class." An author of the mid-90s called the process "Colombianization"[4]. There is no data, but if what one sees on the street truly represents reality, it's happening.

You hear stuff like increasing numbers of people going to bed hungry, and perhaps starvation becoming a real factor (with the absolute end of welfare, food purchase assistance, and so on). Certainly despite the best efforts of the police to sweep the streets clean, the number of beggars you see around in the major cities is increasing. And you hear stories about street sweeps being made and beggars and the homeless being sent to those camps that were set up on abandoned army bases under President Pine's "Real Drug War." But no one can get close to the camps, so who knows.

Certainly the R-CA and most especially its Oakwood style cohorts try to maintain racial tensions and homophobia and xenophobia in the old Republican style to distract people from what's really going on. As then Arkansas Governor Bill Clinton

4. *Author's Note:* See Chapter 1.

said when he announced for the Democratic Presidential nomination back in 1991:

"For 12 years, Republicans have tried to divide us—race against race—so we get mad at each other and not at them. They want us to look at each other across a racial divide so we don't turn and look to the White House and ask, why are all of our incomes going down, why are all of us losing jobs? Why are we losing our future?"

(Too bad he never followed through politically on those thoughts.)

On the other side of the struggle, you do hear stories too of occasional joint black-white-Hispanic labor protests. The private sector trade unions are almost gone, and many states have banned public employee unions entirely. But some workers, I hear, are beginning to realize one way or another what's really been done to them.

"Labor unrest." I wonder if that's the real reason why Hague rammed through the decree power now. Well, only time will tell.

Keep well.

Your friend,
Alex

A Parthenon Pomeroy Diary Entry (June 19, 2005)

We did it, we did it. We're finally going to get on the right track in this country. Now our President is going to have real power. That's what we really need. One man can make a difference. And that meddling Congress can't stop him unless it really wants to. This is going to fix things up all right. This is what we need to get America to where it ought to be, to what it can be, to what it always was and always will be. Thanks, God, and thanks, Pat, too.

Author's Commentary

The 32nd Amendment was a catchall along the lines of the "Morality Amendment" (the 31st). Like the latter, the 32nd placed into the Constitution a number of *desiderata* of Right-

Wing Reaction harking back to the Transition Era (HRC; RNC) i.e., its Sections 1 through 5 and 7. Of course, in historical terms, Section 6 was the 32nd's most significant element for them, and it was new. It ultimately made it possible for Right-Wing Reaction to use the Constitution to destroy Constitutional government in the old U.S.

Legislating by Amending

The Hagueites put the most political emphasis upon the provisions of the 32nd designed to force the Congress to balance the Federal budget. In this regard, the 32nd was following the Right-Wing penchant for attempting to solve what were essentially legislative problems through the medium of a Constitutional amendment. For example, historians now generally consider that Sections 2, 3, and 4 of the 31st Amendment (respectively prohibiting sex education, constitutionalizing anti-homosexual discrimination, and restricting welfare maintenance solely to persons institutionalized for the purpose) had more of a legislative than constitutional nature.

By doing this kind of detailed work in the Constitution, Right-Wing Reaction was following a pattern that it increasingly adhered to beginning with the adoption of the first Balanced Budget Amendment in 1999. Following legislative procedures, the Congress could have adopted a balanced budget any time it wanted to. And any President could have proposed one too. But those who declaimed the loudest about the importance of balancing the budget did nothing but make things worse.

In the 12 years of the Republican Presidencies of Ronald Reagan and George Bush from 1981, neither one ever submitted a balanced budget or anything close to it to the Congress, although both were strong, vocal supporters of the Balanced Budget Amendment. During the Reagan-Bush years the national debt quadrupled, from $1 trillion to $4 trillion (Brinkley). The actions of Reagan and Bush lead directly to this situation. They just talked the talk; they did not walk the walk.

In fact, over those 12 years the Congress, primarily under

the control of the then so-called "tax and spend" Democrats, adopted budgets totaling only about $100 billion (in 1992 dollars) more than the proposed budgets submitted by the supposedly "fiscally responsible" reactionary Republicans in the White House—an $8 billion per year drop in the $1 trillion average annual Federal budget buckets of the time.

Right-Wing Reaction and the Balanced Budget Amendment

Why then did Right-Wing Reaction so vigorously support a Balanced Budget Amendment during the Transition Era? Common at the time was the view that it was just typical right-wing simplistic, "sound bite" politics that sounded good while meaning little. One modern view holds that it was part of the pattern of not trusting and wanting to stifle the democratic process that became evermore part of the Right-Wing Reactionary strategy of the time (Hopkins) (see also Appendix III).

Certainly Right-Wing Reaction's other prime Amendment of the 90s, Congressional Terms Limits, was the epitome of anti-democratic thinking (see also Appendix III). The private thinking of the Right-Wing Reactionaries on this issue may well have gone: "If legislative matters are put into the Constitution while we control the amendment process, it will be that much tougher for them to change things back if and when we ever lose that control."

It is known that that kind of thinking lay behind the creation of the huge Federal debt by the Reaganites in the 1980s (Brinkley; Stockman): to tie the hands of any future "social spenders" by increasing the Federal annual deficits and total debt. Ironically, it was a Democratic Congressional leadership in the early 1980s that bought into the "supply-side" fiction that the government could simultaneously cut taxes, sustain services, and reduce the deficit, if not the national debt that allowed the debacle to occur (Blumenthal, 1993; Brinkley).

It didn't work that way, and the Federal budget would over the years become ever more burdened with ever-increasing interest payments to wealthy bondholders. As one wag of the time put it, the Republicans cut the taxes of the rich and then paid them to loan the government the money it needed to run its operations, operations the rich should have been paying taxes to support all along (*The Nation*).

The Balanced Budget Amendment

The theory behind the Balanced Budget Amendment had been that without it an "undisciplined Congress" would never pass a balanced budget, and that "Republican Discipline," through the Constitution, was required if that laudable goal were to be achieved. (The Reagan-Bush unbalancing act referred to above was seldom mentioned.) In actuality, the original Balanced Budget Amendment had had other goals: political gimmickry; protecting the rich and the large corporations from income tax increases (a threat now of course eliminated by the repeal of the 16th Amendment that was part of the 31st Amendment); and continuing the attack on the Congress as an institutional cause of national problems, even though it was firmly in the hands of the R-CA.

The 28th Amendment, itself intended to force the balancing of the Federal budget, had been passed by the 105th Congress, one in which the old Democratic Party minority still had significant representation in each House of Congress. Whether for that reason or not, the 28th Amendment had had in it what the Right-Wing Reactionaries considered to be "significant loopholes." And in practice, it had proved to have significant loopholes.

Some Outcomes of the 32nd

With the ratification of the 32nd, the Right-Wing Reactionaries had what they considered to be an "ironclad" version, with no loopholes—except for "national defense" and interest payments on the national debt. Once again the exceptions, even if they were Right-Wing Reactionary exceptions, formed the kicker. They were put in for both ideological and practical reasons.

Since the early 1990s, as Bill Clinton had discovered to his chagrin early on in his Presidency, military spending had been specially protected when it came time for the annual Federal budget slashing exercises that both the Congress and Presidents from Clinton onwards undertook. And the national debt service was untouchable anyway.

Nevertheless, with the 32nd, Right-Wing Reaction insisted on ensconcing in the Constitution the special status of military spending, "to show the American people and the world that the United States would never back down from any military threat." In the context of ensconcing military spending, Right-Wing Reaction had to ensconce debt service spending as well, to make sure that both domestic and foreign debt holders would sleep easily at night.

Subsequent events, however, demonstrated that no matter what Constitutional/legislative twists and turns Right-Wing Reaction followed, since the "balanced" requirement applied only to the "general operations" part of Federal government activity (see Section 3), the actual budgetary outcome changed little. There still was a real annual budget deficit, only it was only for military and debt service spending.

As they had throughout the Transition Era, Right-Wing Reaction of course continued to be unwilling to levy the taxes on those who could afford to pay, to meet even the minimal requirements of a government that had very few national domestic programs left. This was the case despite the fact that overall the taxation level in the old U.S. was at the very low end of the range for industrialized nations (Reno). This unwillingness applied especially to those individuals and corporations that could afford pay.

"Slashing the Federal payroll/getting rid of those excess bureaucrats" (at a time when the number of Federal non-military/non-criminal justice employees had reached its lowest level since the days of Calvin Coolidge) became ever more difficult. Favorite Transition Era Federal targets of Right-Wing Reaction, like the Departments of Education, Commerce,

Labor, Housing and Urban Development, and Energy, and most of their programs had long since been eliminated.

In fact, as noted above, since discretionary non-military spending had already reached such a low level, following the passage of this Amendment, to get the "other operations" section of the Federal budget into actual balance, financial support for the Federal criminal justice system was by legislation moved to the "national defense" budget. The "correctional-industrial complex" as it had been described in 1995 by Barry Krisberg, President of the National Council on Crime and Delinquency (Butterfield), had become the equal of its big brother, the old "military-industrial complex."

This development would have major sociopolitical ramifications in subsequent years. In the present time, given the level of expenditure on it, it meant that the real, overall Federal budget would remain in deficit. In practice, then, this Balanced Budget Amendment had as much or little impact as had its predecessor (or had any Federal attempts to force the adoption of a balanced budget, dating from the "Gramm-Rudman-Hollings" Act of the 1980s [Reno].)

The Line Item Veto

The line item veto was an example of the closing-the-barn-door-after-the-horse-had-fled exercise Right-Wing Reaction often engaged in during the Transition Era and early Fascist Period. Such a measure had been enacted into law by the 104th Congress. Once the R-CA had taken control of both the White House and the Congress, it had little meaning and had been little used. But by putting the measure into the Constitution, its sponsors were able to show their ideological purity.

For many years, the theory behind the line item veto had been that the "checks and balances" of the Constitution gave the Congress "too much power" and "tied the hands of the President." In actuality, the measure was simply another step down the road towards the concentration of all governmental power in the hands of the Executive Branch. In fact, if it hadn't been for Sections 6 and 7 of the 32nd Amendment, the measure could have been seen simply as part of a stepwise progression towards that end. Benjamin Franklin had foreseen the whole thing, many years before. He once said (Lind): "The Executive will always be increasing here, as elsewhere, till it ends in a monarchy."

The Concentration of Power

Sections 6 and 7 of the 32nd made single steps into huge leaps. The basis for the creation of a dictatorship was now established. And of course, the national government under the R-CA would need it to deal with the increasing level of national unrest alluded to in the Poughton letter, and dealt with in great detail by other modern historians of the Fascist Period (see esp. Gillespie).

With the Balanced Budget Amendment and the line item veto receiving all the play in a media now firmly under the thumb of the R-CA, as Conroy readily admitted into the privacy of her illegal computer's memory, Section 6 was essentially "snuck in," as an additional method for "correcting the imbalance between the Branches."

Except in certain limited circumstances, the decree power was indeed not used by President Hague for another five years. But as noted, this provision of the Constitution itself, legally adopted by Federal and state governments that happened to be put into place by the medium of the "The 15% Solution," would be used to destroy Constitutional democracy in the old United States. By the time that happened, repeal of the Fourth Amendment and its aftermath had already effectively destroyed the most important offspring of Constitutional Democracy, civil liberties.

The Outcomes of Repeal of the 4th Amendment

As predicted by Conroy, the power to search and seize without judicial limitation was used right away. But for the most part it was not used against garden variety criminals. As with all other data from the Fascist Period, criminal justice data are very skimpy. But apparently rates for arrests (in about 20% of crimes) and convictions (in about 50% of arrests) had changed little since the mid-90s (Lacayo).

The small proportion of cases getting to court in which a claimed illegal search was even a factor in trial outcomes, in the Transition Era 0.55% (Seelye), probably hadn't changed either. But now Right-Wing Reaction could go after its *political* enemies with a vengeance. And with increasing vigor, they did. The populations of the camps apparently exploded, with the influx of the poor on the one hand, and political prisoners on the other.

In that regard, it is interesting to note Conroy's early use of the term "Connie." It was an epithet the Hagueites used to describe their enemies. Sounding like the old 20th century epithet "Commie," one which by Conroy's time meant nothing to most people, "Connie" was employed to refer to someone who supported the old Constitution before the R-CA had amended it literally to death. And through the likes of Oakwood, "Connie" was quickly made into a dirty word, much as Rush Limbaugh and his cohorts had managed to do with the previously quite innocuous term "liberal" back in the 90s.

Eventually, under the New American Republics the forces of Constitutional democracy adopted the term "Connie" for themselves, so that in the Second Civil War in their own vernacular the two sides were the "Connies" (for "Constitutionalists") and the "Fundys" (for "Fundamentalists").

Strangely enough, even the Hagueites felt that there were some limits on how far they could go in strangling Constitutional democracy by Constitutional means. Back in 1995, one of the icons of Right-Wing Reaction, the political columnist George Will, had actually proposed to abolish the secret ballot for voting (Will). He said:

> "What should be the practice for people morally sturdy enough to deserve democracy—oral voting. … Abolish secret voting, have every voter call out his or her choice

> in an unquavering voice and have the choice recorded for public inspection. You probably will have a smaller electorate, but also a hardier, better one."

When the 32nd came up for consideration, there was some sentiment for sticking this one in too. But the Hagueite inner circle decided that even for them it was a bit too much. It was dropped. In another five years, the whole matter had become moot anyway.

The German Nazi leader Adolf Hitler established his dictatorship by constitutional means through the Enabling Act (Davidowicz). Jefferson Davis Hague established his, eventually, by means of the Balancing Amendment. Interestingly, Hitler had had to decree the end of civil liberties in his country. Hague's forces achieved that end too through the Constitutional amendment process. "The 15% Solution" had once again struck at the heart of everything that had once made the old U.S. a very unique place in the world.

References:

Blumenthal, S., "The Sorcerer's Apprentices," *The New Yorker,* July 19, 1993.

Blumenthal, S., "The Pete Principle," *The New Yorker*, October 30, 1995.

Butterfield, F., "Political Gains by Prison Guards," *The New York Times*, Nov. 7, 1995.

Brinkley, A., "Reagan's Revenge," *The New York Times Magazine*, June 19, 1994, p. 36.

Cassidy, J., "Who Killed the Middle Class?" *The New Yorker,* Oct. 16, 1995, p. 113.

Clinton, W.J., "Announcement Speech," Little Rock, AK: October 3, 1995.

Davidowicz, L.S., *The War Against the Jews: 1933-45*, New York: Holt, Rinehart, and Winston, 1975, Part I, p. 51.

Gillespie, D., National Decline, *Labor Unrest and the Rise Fascist Power in the Old United States, 2001-2011*, New York: The Freedom Press, 2042.

Hopkins, L., *The Decline of Democracy in the Transition Era*, New York: The Freedom Press, 2034.

Lacayo, R., "Lock 'Em Up!," *Time*, Feb. 7, 1994, p. 50.

Lewis, A., "'A Culture of Rights,'" *The New York Times*, June 9, 1995.

Lind, M., "The Out-of-Control Presidency," *The New Republic*, August 14, 1995, p. 18.

HRC, House Republican Conference, *Contract With America*, Washington, DC: September 27, 1994.

Reno, R., "One 'Historic' Budget Accord After Another," *Newsday*, November 1, 1995.

RNC, Republican National Committee, *The Republican Platform, 1992*, Washington, DC: August 17, 1992, pp. 39, 40.

Rosenbaum, D.E., "What Politicians Aren't Saying: A Tax Cut measured in Pennies," *The New York Times*, November 8, 1995.

Seelye, K.Q., "House Approves Easing of Rules on U.S. Searches," *The New York Times*, Feb. 9, 1995, p. A1.

Sklar, H., "Back to the Raw Deal," *Z Magazine*, Nov., 1995, p. 19.

Stockman, D., cited in "Balancing the Budget," *National Rainbow Coalition JaxFax*, Vol. III, Issue 10, March 9, 1995.

Thurow, L.C., "Companies Merge; Families Break Up," *The New York Times*, September 3, 1995.

The Nation, "Unbalancing the Economy," March 13, 1995, p. 329.

Will, G., "Let every voter stand up and be counted," *New York Post*, October 26, 1995.

CHAPTER 9

2007: The Supremacy Amendment (33rd)

The 33rd Amendment to the Constitution of the United States (2007):

Section 1. Article 6 of this Constitution in its entirety is amended to read as follows:

> This constitution, and the laws of the United States which shall be made pursuant thereto shall be the supreme law of the land, except when the President, or the Congress by a majority vote of both houses, shall declare the Law of God to be superior to it. Article 1 section 7 of this constitution shall apply to any Congressional decision in this matter. Congress may overturn a Presidential decision in this matter by a two-thirds vote in both houses.
>
> All Federal judges and the judges in every state shall be bound by the provisions of this amendment, any thing in the constitution or laws of any state to the contrary notwithstanding. No Federal or state court may judge any act or action taken under this Amendment for its constitutionality.
>
> The senators and representatives before-mentioned, and the members of the several state legislatures, and all executive and judicial officers, both of the United States and of the several states, shall be bound by oath or affirmation, to support this constitution; religious tests may be required as a qualification to any office or public trust under the United States.

Section 2. Neither Congress, nor any Federal court, nor any state or local government or other agency supported by tax revenues may prohibit organized or voluntary prayer or other reasonable religious devotion in any public educational institution.

Author's Commentary[1]

First, the 33rd Amendment, generally referred to as the "Supremacy Amendment," set some unspecified "Law of God" above the law of the Constitution. While the latter was written down in the original document and in many Supreme Court decisions made pursuant to it, the specification of just what "God's Law"was, was left to the President and the Congress.

The Amendment also extended the substance of the Supreme Court's decision in *Anderson v. United States*, permitting both "organized" and "voluntary" prayer in schools. (Incorporating a "school prayer amendment" into the Constitution had been part of the old Republican Party's national platform as least far back as 1992 [RNC]). And, it permitted the establishment by the Federal government and the states of religious tests for office.

Further, the Amendment was almost as important for what it removed from the Constitution as for what it added. In redoing Article 6 of the Constitution, the 33rd deleted the clause of the original that referred to the pre-Constitution debts of the predecessor governments of the United States, assuming them as obligations.

That specific matter had long since become moot. But the

1. *Author's Note:* There is no indication or evidence that any of the historical figures or organizations quoted in this chapter, some mentioned elsewhere, additionally including but not limited to Don Feder, Bob Weiner, the Rev. Tim LaHaye, and the US Taxpayers Party would necessarily have supported or associated themselves in any way with the "Supremacy Amendment" or any of the actual positions or actions that Jefferson Davis Hague or any members of his government or political parties took pursuant to it, at that time or in the future.

deletion gave certain people pause for thought as to what the American government's attitude towards some or all of its debts might be at some time in the future. Section 4 of the 14th Amendment had specifically declared debts of the 19th century Confederate States of America not to be debts of the United States. Was something similar brewing here? Future events would prove the concerns about the attitude of future U.S. and successor governments towards past debt to be quite valid.

The primary purpose of the Amendment, however, was to place into the Constitution the concept that there was some freestanding, encoded, "Law of God" (sometimes referred to as "Natural Law") that could somehow be defined by the President and/or the Congress, standing above the Constitution. The campaign for the adoption of the concept as a part of the foundation of the American legal system went well back into the Transition Era.

For example, the first black Right-Wing Reactionary Supreme Court Justice, Clarence Thomas, when justifying his rejection of the very modest Transition Era attempts to rectify institutionalized racial discrimination against blacks in employment and educational opportunity, called "affirmative action," said that "God's law" compelled him to do it (White). And he specified the God-concept he was thinking of too: "You cannot embrace racism to deal with racism. It's not Christian."

On the Separation of Church and State

The prohibition of religious tests for candidacy for public offices had been a vital component of the "wall of separation between church and state" that was a central feature of the old U.S. Constitution. Eliminating that wall or trying to prove that it never existed in the first place was a major goal of Right-Wing Reaction, finally achieved by the adoption of the 33rd Amendment. As the Rev. Pat Robertson had said in November, 1993 (Foxman):

> "They have kept us in submission because they have talked about separation of church and state[2]. There is no such thing in the Constitution. It's a lie of the left, and we're not going to take it anymore."

In 1993 also, a group called "Concerned Women of America" had articulated this position thusly (Glasser): "Christian values should dominate our government. Politicians who do not use the Bible to guide their public and private lives do not belong in office."

Early in the history of the Republic (and in one instance, quite well into it) certain states had imposed religious testing for candidacy for office (Menendez). For example, despite the fact that the Maryland state Constitution, adopted in 1776, acknowledged the "duty of every man to worship God in such manner as he thinks most acceptable," in that State candidates for public office were required to declare "a belief in the Christian religion."

It was not until 1826, following a lengthy campaign by a Scottish Presbyterian immigrant named Thomas Kennedy for what his opponents called the "Jew bill," that Jews were permitted to stand for election in Maryland. New Hampshire, known during the Transition Era as one of the bastions of Right-Wing Reaction in the Northeast, did not remove its last religious test provision until 1968!

The "Cultural Civil War"

Having a free, open, debate on such subjects as the nature of the family and what constitutes healthy sexual behavior, with the possibility that in a pluralistic society there could be more than one "right" answer, was beyond the ken of the Religious Right. To them, there was only one possible right answer to

2. *Author's Note:* For an excellent summary of both the Right-Wing Reactionary position on the issue of separation of church and state and the Constitutionalist response to it, see Transition Era works by Boston (1993) and the Anti-Defamation League (ADL).

such questions, and they already had it. For Right-Wing Reaction, establishing the supremacy of "God's Law" was essential to winning what they viewed as the "cultural civil war" in which they saw the country engaged. Presented here are some of the voices of Right-Wing Reaction from the Transition Era on the subject.

On the battle between "religion" and "anti-religion," listen to Newton Gingrich, the famous Speaker of the House from 1995 onwards and patron of J.D. Hague (Blumenthal):

> "[There is a] battleground about the nature of the American future [between the God-fearing and the godless]. I do have a vision of an America in which a belief in the Creator is once again at the center of defining being an American, and that is a radically different vision of America than the secular anti-religious view of the left. … Frankly, history is an on-going rebuke to secular left-wing values. They can't afford to teach history, because it would destroy the core vision of a hedonistic, existentialist America in which there is no past and there is no future."

Don Feder, a syndicated columnist, self-described "Jewish Conservative," in fact a leading figure of co-opted Jewish Right-Wing Reaction, said (1994):

> "A cultural civil war is raging across our nation. Arrayed on one side is society's cultural elite (those who command the nation's idea generators): the professoriate, the media (news and entertainment), most elected officials, the bureaucracy, corporate America (when it deigns to take sides), the mainline Protestant churches, as well as most foundations.
>
> "On the other side are a handful of family activists [*sic*], social conservatives, a definite minority in academia, a few embattled officeholders, and iconoclastic

> commentators. Engagements are fought in editorial pages, in high school and college classrooms, and legislative hearing rooms, as well as on TV/radio talk shows. Territory is gained or lost at polling places. The prize is the soul of Middle America.
>
> "The outcome of this debate will determine whether the paganizing of America will proceed apace or, as a society, we will rediscover traditional values."

Feder's "traditional values" had nothing to do with those of the Declaration of Independence, the Constitution, or the Bill of Rights, such as freedom of thought, freedom to worship or not worship, and tolerance of difference. Rather he was a follower of those on the Religious Right, as highlighted for example by Gingrich and Robertson, who would for everyone prescribe certain ways of thinking, acting, and being, and proscribe others. Events showed that, whether to their surprise or not, Gingrich, Robertson, Feder and their cohorts would win the "cultural civil war" Feder described.

At the start of the "cultural battle" Right-Wing Reaction was far stronger than the "left." The latter, in various stages of disarray continuously from the time of the civil rights and anti-Vietnam War struggles of the 1960s, was far weaker than people like Feder ever admitted. (It is possible, but unlikely, that the mouthpieces of Right-Wing Reaction were in fact as paranoid as they so often sounded and thus really were incapable of knowing that they held most of the cards). But with the ratification of the Supremacy Amendment, Right-Wing Reaction had achieved the final destruction of the Constitutional barriers separating church and state that had existed whether Robertson thought they were real or not. That destruction had been a principal goal of Right-Wing Reaction from early in the Transition Era.

(Of course subsequently, when it became clear to the American people as a whole that the victory of Right-Wing Reaction in the "cultural civil war" meant the end to traditional American Constitutional democracy, a Second [military] Civil War would be fought. From that War, as readers of this book know well, the forces of traditional American Constitutional government would ultimately emerge victorious.)

On the "Law of God"

On the specifics of the supremacy of "God's Law" over that of man, listen once again to Pat Robertson (1991):

> "According to the word of God, we will not have universal peace, we will not have equity … until the world gives God's people in their midst the place that is due them, which is the head and not the tail … We will see the standard of Biblical values raised over this land … [T]hose who have mocked you and cursed you and cast your people out as evil will be put down."

And to Bob Weiner, President, Marantha Campus Ministries (1991):

> "The Bible says we are to rule. If you don't rule and I don't rule, the atheists, the humanists, and the agnostics are going to rule. We should be that head of our school board. We should be the leaders of our nation. We should be the editors of our newspapers. We should be taking over every area of life."

And to the Rev. Tim LaHaye of the American Coalition for Traditional Values (Buchanan): "The problem with America is … we do not have enough of God's ministers running the country."

Keith Fournier, the Executive Director of the Christian Coalition's "American Center for Law and Justice," said it a bit more eloquently, but the meaning was the same (1995):

> "The way of the Christian Church recognizes the God-given unalienable rights to life, liberty, and property. A

> way that has in fact given birth to true economic liberty and a free enterprise system that is tempered by compassion and infused with an understanding of social responsibility. … The way of the church is set in radical contradiction and prophetic distinction to the way of the individual or the way of the state. … It holds the state responsible to a higher law."

The little-known "guru" of the Religious arm of Right-Wing Reaction, a close colleague of the Reverends Pat Robertson and Jerry Falwell, was one R.J. Rushdooney (Boston, 1988). Rushdooney was the leader of "Christian Reconstructionism," a movement whose theology was based on "theonomy," literally "God's law." Thus Christian Reconstructionism was a religion, or religious theory, focused almost entirely on state power and its use.

Rushdooney pulled no punches in advocating a modern theocracy (Boston):

> "Only God is the Lord or sovereign. The modern state claims sovereignty therefore sets itself up in the place of God. The sovereign is the source of law and for us only God can be the ultimate source of law, not any human agency."

And:

> "The Christian must realize that pluralism is a myth. God and his law must rule all nations."

Finally, a late-Transition Era Right-Wing political party, the U.S. Taxpayers Party, had this to say in the Preamble to its National Platform (Abramsky):

> "[We ask for] the blessing of the Lord God as Creator, Preserver and Ruler of the Universe and of this Nation,

[and know that the U.S. Constitution] is rooted in Biblical law."

On "Inerrancy"

Now, according to Rushdooney, just what is "God's law" and who were supposed to deliver the message to the people? Why a book called the Bible, that he and many other Right-Wing Reactionary religious figures of the time described as "inerrant." "Inerrant" meant to them that Biblical statements were to be taken literally and that whatever it says is right, correct, and true, that is, according to their interpretations, of course. Further, in the view of Rushdooney and his ilk, these Biblical statements were to be controlling of all human behavior.

One problem for the Inerrantists was that there were a fair number of different translations of the original Hebrew and Greek Biblical texts, in some cases carrying widely different meanings (Niebuhr). The Right-Wing Religious types generally felt that the King James Version of the Bible was the authoritative one, apparently because it conformed to their male-centered, authoritarian view of the world and the "word of God" (Williams). However, that there were numerous translations of the Bible, meant that while they were able to cite the "word of God" on many issues, they never were able to come up with the Word of God on just what, exactly, *in English*, were *the words of God*, on many issues.

That detail seemed to trouble them not, however. As the field manual of the Free Militia, a paramilitary group that closely associated itself with the Religious Right said (TFW): "The Bible is word for word the word of God. Therefore it is completely true and without any errors. This is what we mean by inerrancy." But even given that there might be some agreement on exactly which translation of the Bible was "God's translation," who would tell the people just what the "inerrant" meaning of any given statement in the Bible is? Why those who claim to know—like Rushdooney, for example.

Compounding all of this, the Religious Right would have

imposed their position on all human beings, whether or not believers in the Bible. However, the Supremacy Amendment was as far as they were able to get. Try as they might, the primacy of *Biblical* Law, as they interpreted it, was one concept the Religious Right was never able to get into the Constitution. J.D. Hague was not about to give up control of the country's civil and criminal legal system to "a bunch of fucking preachers," as he was known to refer to them privately.

In any case, the Bible's text is not unambiguous. It is, rather, in many places quite ambiguous, self-contradictory, and widely open to interpretation (as well as inaccurate historically) (Fox). Nevertheless, according to the promoters of the theory of "inerrancy," what the Bible "inerrantly" says and means is just what, and only what, the human claimant that it is inerrant says that it says and means.

However, even among the supporters and promoters of the theory of "Biblical inerrancy," there were many, sometimes fierce, internal debates as to just what the Bible "inerrantly" meant. For example, a strongly anti-Semitic Right-Wing Reactionary preacher of the Transition Era, one Pastor Peter J. Peters (1994), held up the "inerrant" Bible as the complete justification for his doctrine. At the same time, the Right-Wing Reactionary Reverends Pat Robertson and Jerry Falwell, certainly claiming to be anything but anti-Semitic, also cited the "inerrant" Bible to support their doctrines.

As was often his wont, Dino Louis came at the subject of "inerrancy" from a perspective not shared by too many others. A short, previously unpublished essay of his from 1997 on one aspect of the subject is presented here.

On "Inerrancy," Creationism, and Evolution
By Dino Louis

Inerrancy: "the Bible means what it says, and that's it." Further, according to its promoters, "inerrancy" means that the Bible is literally "the word of the Lord." In use, however, "inerrancy" means no more and no less than: "the Bible says what I say it means, that's it, and that's that." In this light comes consideration of the question of whether or not creationism rather than, or at least next to, evolution science, should be taught in the schools[3].

There is nothing inconsistent between the theory of evolution and belief in God. Many supporters of evolution theory do believe in God. They hold simply that evolution is the means God has used and uses to create life and control its progress through history and changing conditions on Earth. From their perspective, the Bible, even if it is the word of God, and some believing evolutionists hold that it is, is not to be taken literally from anyone's perspective.

For example, in 1994 an organization called the Lexington (KY) Alliance of Religious Leaders issued the following statement (Scott):

"As religious leaders we share a deep faith in God who created heaven and earth and all that is in them, and take with utmost seriousness the Biblical witness to this God who is our creator. However, we find no incompatibility between the God of creation and a theory of evolution which uses universally verifiable data to explain the probable process by which life developed into its present form."

For the Fundamentalists the problem with this kind of thinking is that evolution science is completely inconsistent with the theory of "inerrancy." For if the story of Creation is just a story, or an allegory, or even a moral but non-literal presentation of evolution science, then everything and anything in the Bible could be just a story or an allegory or a moral but non-literal presentation.

If that is the case, if the Bible is not "inerrant" in the sense that it should not or need not be taken literally in anyone's

3. *Author's Note:* "Creationism" held that the Biblical fable that some unknown and unknowable being called "God" created the world in seven days about six thousand years ago should be taken literally. Further, it held that the story should be taught in the schools as fact, and that on its basis, evolution science should be held to be completely without validity.

interpretation, the whole basis of American Fundamentalism and the politico-theological basis of the Religious Right crumbles instantly.

First of all, the Bible becomes open to interpretation by anyone, not just those religious figures who claim that their interpretation reflects "inerrancy." Second of all, if that is the case, what justification can there be for putting any one religious figure's moral views into laws that become binding on everyone whether they are believers or not?

The usual justification given for doing so is: "the Bible says it's so, so we must put the force of law behind it." But in the absence of "inerrancy," that justification falls apart. Third of all, if the Bible is open to interpretation by anyone, and if all or part of the Bible may just be a collection of stories/allegories, why should it be accorded the status of "Natural Law" and placed above the Constitution as controlling human behavior?

The Bible is, of course, nothing more, or less, than a collection of stories, myths, fables, genealogical tables, wise sayings, moral instructions from one perspective or another, insightful observations on human existence and the human comedy, helpful hints for healthy living, helpful guides to civil life, some history—both real and fanciful, prejudices of the literate classes, and old-time civil and criminal law dressed up in religious trappings. In both the Old and New Testaments, great parts are based on recollection and oral tradition, e.g., the first description of the life of Christ (what is called the "Passion of Christ" by believers) wasn't written down until approximately 100 years after his death.

The Bible is an interesting and sometimes useful book that has benefited from an extraordinarily successful marketing program over the centuries. But the claim that its story about Creation must be taught in the schools as an equal of evolution science is not based on the utility of the Creation story to help people understand anything. Rather, it is based on the necessity of being taught as reflecting reality, if "inerrancy" is to be established for all the other parts of the Bible.

For if the "inerrancy" of even this one section of the Bible can be brought into question, then the "inerrancy" of any other section could be brought into question as well. And that is why the campaign to gain educational legitimization of the Creation story, to go so far as to even label this religious fable itself as "science," is so important to the Religious Right. [End of the Louis essay.]

The Catholic View of the "Law of God"

As a final authority on the proposition that the "Law of God" stands supreme to any law of man (including the old United States Constitution), its supporters could quote the Roman Catholic Pope John Paul II. In a "Papal Encyclical"[4] supporting the position that there is no such thing as freedom of choice in the outcome of pregnancy, he said (Keeler):

> "Therefore, by the authority which Christ conferred upon Peter and his Successors, and in communion with the Bishops of the Catholic Church, I confirm that the direct and voluntary killing of an innocent human being is always gravely immoral[5]. No circumstance, no purpose, no law whatsoever can ever make licit an act which is intrinsically illicit, since it is contrary to the Law of God."

And why is such "an act" "contrary to the Law of God" in the Pope's eyes? Because, using the circular reasoning common among the Right-Wing Religious leaders of the time, he knew for sure (in some way or another that he did not share with his readers) that it was, and because he said so.

And so, to the direction of its future by this kind of thinking was the old United States condemned. The campaign to sunder

4. *Author's Note:* Statement of highest Church authority.

5. *Author's Note:* Referring here to the antiquated religious concept held by some at the time that there is some such entity as an "unborn" or "pre-born" child.

the Constitutional separation of church and state in the old U.S. had commenced in earnest at the beginning of the Transition Era. That campaign finally realized its objective in full with the adoption of the 33rd Amendment.

On Separation of Church and State, Revisited

Some think it odd that perhaps the best counter to the arguments of Right-Wing Reaction on the matter was given some 20 years before the beginning of the Transition Era by the first Catholic President of the old United States, John Fitzgerald Kennedy (1960):

> "I believe in an America where the separation of church and state is absolute—where no Catholic prelate would tell the President, should he be a Catholic, how to act, and no Protestant minister should tell his parishioners for whom to vote; where no church or church school is granted any public funds or political preference, and where no man is denied public office merely because his religion differs from the President who might appoint him or the people who might elect him.
>
> "I believe in an America that is officially neither Catholic, Protestant, nor Jewish; where no public official either requests or accepts instruction on public policy from the pope, the National Council of Churches, or any other ecclesiastical source; where no religious body seeks to impose its will directly or indirectly upon the general populace or the public acts of its officials; and where religious liberty is so indivisible that an act against one church is treated as an act against all.
>
> "For, while this year it may be a Catholic against whom the finger of suspicion is pointed, in other years it has been, and may someday be again, a Jew—or a Quaker—or a Unitarian—or a Baptist[6]. It was Virginia's

6. *Author's Note:* Ironically, the Baptists would become one of the leading sects among those of the Religious Right.

harassment of Baptist preachers, for example, that helped lead to Jefferson's Statute of Religious Freedom. Today, I may be the victim, but tomorrow it may be you, until the whole fabric of our harmonious society is ripped at a time of great national peril.

"Finally, I believe in an America where religious intolerance will someday end; where all men and all churches are treated as equal; where every man has the same right to attend or not attend the church of his choice; where there is no Catholic vote, no anti-Catholic vote, no bloc voting of any kind; and where Catholics, Protestants, and Jews, at both the lay and pastoral level, will refrain from those attitudes of disdain and division which have so often marred their works in the past, and promote instead the American ideal of brotherhood."

Amen.

References:

Abramsky, S., "Taxpayers Revolt?" *In These Times*, January 22, 1996, p. 10.

ADL: Anti-Defamation League, *The Religious Right: The Assault on Tolerance & Pluralism*, New York: 1994.

Blumenthal, S., "The Newt Testament," *The New Yorker*, November 21, 1994, p. 7.

Boston, R., "Thy Kingdom Come," *Church & State*, Sept., 1988, p. 6.

Boston, R., *Why the Religious Right is Wrong about Separation of Church and State*, Buffalo, NY: Prometheus Books, 1993.

Buchanan, J., "In the Name of God," *People for the American Way Quarterly Report*, Fall, 1984, p. 3.

Feder, D., "The Paganizing of America," *Law and Justice* (ACLJ), Vol. 3, No. 1, 1994.

Fournier, K.A., "The Third Way," *Law and Justice*, Vol. 4, No. 3, 1995.

Fox, R.L., *The Unauthorized Version*, New York: Knopf, 1991.

Foxman, A.H., Fund-raising letter, New York: Anti-Defamation League, Jan., 1994.

TFW: *Freedom Writer,* "Biblical inspiration and authority," June, 1995, p. 3.

Glasser, I., letter to "ACLU Guardians of Liberty," Sept. 29, 1993.

Keeler, B., "Papal Creed," *Newsday*, March 31, 1995.

Kennedy, J.F., "On the Separation of Church and State," Greater Houston (Texas) Ministerial Association, September 12, 1960.

Menendez, A.J., "No Religious Test, Part Two: States' Rights, Religious Wrongs," *Church & State*, May, 1987, p. 8.

Niebuhr, G., "'In Other Words': Bible's Evolving Language," *The New York Times*, December 23, 1995, p. 1.

Peters, P.J., "The Religious Racket in America," Vol. III, "Thoughts on Love," Vol. IV, *Scriptures for America*, (LaPorte, CO) 1994.

RNC, Republican National Committee, The Republican Platform, 1992, Washington, DC: August 17, 1992, p. 10.

Robertson, P., "Benediction," "Road to Victory" Christian Coalition Conference, November, 1991.

Scott, E.C., "Creationism: The Growing Threat," *Freedom Writer*, September, 1994, p. 1.

Weiner, B., interview, KFCB, California, quoted in Wipfler, W., "The Religious Right: Sanctification of a Political Agenda," 1991.

White, R., "Protest Target: Judge's House," *Newsday*, September 12, 1995.

Williams, A., "Re-Authoring a Better Bible?" *Jerry Falwell's National Liberty Journal*, January, 1996.

CHAPTER 10
2008: The Second Hague Inaugural Address

The Second Inaugural Address of President Jefferson Davis Hague[1] December 25, 2008

My fellow Americans under God. I stand here before you on the birthday of our Lord Jesus Christ, anticipating in all humility the opportunity you have so graciously given me to continue to do His bidding as your President. And I can tell you that His bidding now is to continue to fight the good fight, for the Lord, and for you the American people under God.

In fighting this fight, to the best of my ability, blessed by both our Lord Jesus Christ and you, the American people under God, I am both pleased and privileged to be able to announce today the first step we of the Second Hague Administration have taken to do just that. We have converted our nation's leading political party, the

1. *Author's Note:* There is no indication or evidence that the Christian Coalition, Keith Fournier, R.J. Rushdooney, Thomas P. Monaghan, the Rev. Pat Robertson, Kirk Fordyce, Randall Terry, the Rev. Jerry Falwell, Mr. Robert Flood, Mrs. Cheryl Gillaspie, Mr. Robert Simonds, Focus on the Family, or any other organization, or any of the other historical personages mentioned in the "Hague Second Inaugural," elsewhere in this chapter or elsewhere in this book in a similar manner, would have supported or approved of any of the thoughts, positions, or actions taken by Jefferson Davis Hague or any member, employee, or associate of his government, either of the U.S. or the NAR, or of any of the events that occurred in the United States or the New American Republics subsequent to the delivery of the Hague Second Inaugural Address and the implementation of the policies carried out pursuant to it.

Republican-Christian Alliance, the party of God-fearing people that has put you in complete control of the government here in Washington, into a brand new entity.

This is an historic decision, comparable to the one that established the original Republican Party back in the mid-19th century. For all of us, Christian and pagan American alike, it will usher in a glorious new era of peace and harmony under the blessings of our Lord and his only son whose birthday we celebrate today, Jesus Christ.

Reflecting the spirit of our times, and the best of all American traditions, we have named our new party the American Christian Nation Party. For yes, in truth, declaring and carrying out Christian policies is the only way that we will be able to continue to fight the good fight to rescue our beloved country from the forces of sin, Godlessness, and liberalism[2] that continue to drag her down.

For inspiration in this never ending struggle, I have turned often to the great Keith Fournier, who sat at the

2. *Author's Note:* "Liberalism," however one wanted to define it, had long since lost whatever force it once had to influence the direction the country was taking. Nevertheless, it and its supporters, the "liberal nigger lovers" as Curley Oakwood liked to call them, were still blamed by the Right-Wing Reactionaries for virtually all of the ills of the time they cared to identify. As noted previously, during the Transition Era Right-Wing Reaction had used something they called "The Counter-Culture" in much the same way.

Right-Wing Reaction's common political strategy, described previously, was to first demonize and then blame "the other" for whatever troubles they wished to focus the public's attention on. At the same time, as we have noted previously, they neither defined precisely what they were talking about as "the enemy" nor proved in any way that whatever or whomever the identified enemy was had in fact caused the harms Right-Wing Reaction identified with it.

Whatever the "Counter-Culture" really was or had been, by the time of the Reagan Presidency it had lost whatever national influence it had had. However, absent people and absent movements both find it difficult to either defend or promote themselves. That was the case for both the "Counter-Culture" and the "liberals" during the times they were, respectively, the leading targets for Right-Wing Reaction. But my, what convenient targets they did provide.

right hand of our beloved Rev. Pat Robertson, as the Executive Director of the American Center for Law and Justice. As he said (1994):

> "The challenge I have as a Christian is to bring people to Jesus Christ, to a personal decision to accept Him as Savior and Lord, to bring them to personal repentance and conversion. But for me that is only the beginning. That salvation must be sustained, nourished, and deepened. It must also lead to personal transformation and holiness through implantation into Christ's Body, the church. The church is not an option, an extra we can accept or reject. It is the ark, the ship of God, and her mission is to help rescue and restore the drowning. This has always been her primary mission. The church exists to evangelize and disciple toward personal and corporate transformation, a mission entrusted to her by her Head, Master and Lord, the evangel Himself, Jesus Christ."[3]

To our friends who are not Christians we say first, join us, for the Christian Way is the Godly Way. But for those Americans who choose to continue to exercise their right as an American to freely practice the religion of their choosing, a right we fiercely defend, we say ally with us, to carry out the work of the Lord. And let me make it very clear that no one has anything to fear from our new party or the new policies we will be carrying out, as long as he is a loyal American, devoted to God.

3. *Author's Note:* At the time Fournier wrote this passage, the "church" he was referring to was the Catholic Church, a fact omitted from the quoted passage. But by the time Hague was quoting the text, the dominant Christian Church in the old U.S., supported by most members of the old Religious Right, Catholic, Protestant, or Jewish, was that of the homogeneous, but definitely Far Right, New American Religion.

But let me also make it very clear that woe be to him who is Godless, or worships a false God, or does not accept the Holy Bible as the inerrant word of our Lord God and his only son Jesus Christ. For upon him will fall the wrath of God—and our wrath too. Let that be known[4]. For as the great R.J. Rushdooney has said (Sloan):

> "Every social order institutes its own program of separation or segregation. A particular faith and morality is given privileged status and all else is separated for progressive elimination. ... Every faith is an exclusive way of life; none is more dangerous than that which maintains the illusion of tolerance."

Let me now turn to sharing with you the genesis of our brand new American Christian Nation Party. It sprang from the God-inspired minds of the forefathers of our movement[5]. And it is the thinking of some of them, both great and small, that I would like to share with you now.

To set the stage as it were, I will first turn to the writings of Thomas P. Monaghan, a Senior Counsel of the American Center for Law and Justice (1994):

> "In human existence there is only one moral order. This is an order that, through the grace of God, has been revealed to all human beings. The Lord gives us reason and faith so that at all times and in all places we are called to the good, which is ultimately God Himself. We all—Christians,

4. *Author's Note:* As a past chairman of the House American Morality Committee (see Chapter 6), Hague would speak with special feeling on this point.

5. *Author's Note:* Hague was referring here not to the traditional "forefathers" from the time of the founding of the nation, but rather to prominent Transition Era figures representing Right-Wing Reaction, especially of the religious variety.

> pagans, and others—have this law engraved on our hearts, … The choice before us today is what it has always been: Christ or Caesar. Caesar can never give the human heart that for which it hungers. Christ can."

And how in our country, with our valued Constitution, do we reconcile Caesar and Christ? The Rev. Pat himself told us (ACLU, 1992):

> "The Constitution of the United States is a marvelous document for self-government by *Christian* people [emphasis added]. But the minute you turn the document into the hands of non-Christian people and atheist people, they can use it to destroy the very foundation of our society."

And the Rev. Pat told us how Christian governmental control is to be achieved and maintained (*Freedom Writer*, Feb. 1995):

> "Christians founded this nation, they built this nation, and for three hundred years they governed this nation. We can govern again. That's why I founded the Christian Coalition. … The mission of the Christian Coalition is simple: to mobilize Christians one precinct at a time, until once again we are the head and not the tail, and at the top rather than the bottom of our political system."[6]

And finally the Rev. Pat, in 1993 speaking at his Regent University law school, predicted that what we

6. *Author's Note:* Some extensive sleuthing found Robertson originally making this statement on a 1990 Christian Coalition recruiting video called "America at the Crossroads." The nascent campaign Robertson was describing lead directly to the development of "The 15% Solution." The creation of the ACNP can be seen as the eventual, logical, outcome of the whole process.

have now achieved would indeed be achieved by us (Clarkson):

> "One day, if we read the Bible correctly, we will rule and reign along with our sovereign, Jesus Christ."

But let me refer to other of our forefathers besides the good Reverend Pat. Being just plain forthright about it, the 1990s Republican Governor Kirk Fordice of Mississippi put it thusly (Berke, 1992):

> "The United States of America is a Christian nation … the less we emphasize the Christian religion the further we fall into the abyss of poor character and chaos …"

And our revered Randall Terry, the founder of Operation Rescue, the prototype of those many organizations which now militantly protect and defend God's Way, said back in August, 1993 (Foxman):

> "Our goal is a Christian nation. We have a biblical duty, we are called by God, to conquer this country. We don't want equal time. We don't want pluralism."

And he said further (Porteous):

> "You better believe that I want to build a Christian nation, because the only other option is a pagan nation. … A Christian nation would be defined as 'We acknowledge God in our body politic, in our communities, that the God of the Bible is our God, and we acknowledge that His law is supreme.' "

The great Rev. Jerry Falwell, writing in 1993 under the headline "America is a Christian Nation!":

> "Our pledge of allegiance declares we are 'one nation under God.' Our currency states 'In God We Trust.' The Declaration of Independence says we have a God-given right to 'life, liberty and the pursuit of happiness.'[7] "
>
> "Yet today, we find our religious heritage under attack. Ungodly forces in society seem intent on removing God from every area of public life. ... But despite what the Supreme Court and radical liberal activists may say, AMERICA IS A CHRISTIAN NATION!"

Mr. Robert Flood of that God-serving organization "Focus on the Family" said in 1992 (*Freedom Watch*):

> "The Constitution was designed to perpetuate a Christian order."

Mrs. Cheryl Gillaspie, a right-thinking Councilwoman from that font of Right Thinking, Colorado Springs, CO[8], said in a November, 1994 speech to the local chapter of the Christian Coalition (*Freedom Watch*):

7. *Author's Note:* Neither the Pledge nor the currency said precisely which or whose God was being referred to. The Declaration mentions God but once, in the context of Nature, but emphasizes "our Creator," a rather different concept, popular with the Deists who wrote and signed the document. But that didn't stop Falwell from making a leap of faith from "Creator" to "God" to a "Christian God" to a "Christian God with the characteristics I, Jerry Falwell, attribute to Him." And it was a "him," you can be sure.

8. *Author's Note:* Colorado Springs was a central focus of Right-Wing Reactionary activity in the old U.S. For example, it was the home of the organization that in 1992 put together the famous homophobic "Amendment 2" that became the prototype for much of the homophobic legislation that spread nationally over the following two decades (see the next chapter.) Colorado Springs was also home to the courageous early Constitutionalist organization, the "Citizens' Project."

> "There is no validity to the doctrine of separation of Church and State ... America was established as a Christian nation by believing Christians."

Mr. Robert Simonds, president of Citizens for Excellence in Education tells us (*Freedom Watch*):

> "Government and true Christianity are inseparable! There can be no morality (right or wrong) without the Bible—man's only reliable book on right and wrong. Christians can properly apply Bible principles to government, because they are the ones who read the Bible."

And finally, my friends, in an early version of Focus on the Family's Community Impact Curriculum, we are told (*Freedom Watch*):

> "[T]his was really a Christian nation and, as far as its founders were concerned, to try separating Christianity from government is virtually impossible and would result in unthinkable damage to the nation and its people."

It is this thinking and these thinkers and their successors that have provided the foundation of our new Party. But I want to tell you that our Party has not been formed with Christian leadership alone. The ACNP provides nothing if it does not provide a "Big Tent"[9] to accommodate many differing views on how we can best move our nation forward.

9. *Author's Note:* During the Transition Era, some members of the old Republican Party had developed the "Big Tent" concept in an attempt to keep both pro- and anti-freedom-of-choice-in-the-outcome-of-pregnancy but otherwise reactionary elements in the party. That attempt ultimately proved to be in vain, as the "Rightward Imperative" (see below) took effect. This second Big Tent strategy of Hague's was much more successful.

Thus I am pleased to announce that we have been joined by and welcome as integral parts of our new Party, among others The Order, the Ku Klux Klan, the Leadership Coalitions for America, the Skinheads Factions, the Militias, Jews for Christ and Tradition, the Aryan Nations, the Men of Liberty, the Posse Comitatus, the Armed Survivalists, and Christian Identity.

The Republican-Christian Alliance has been strong, and it has brought us a long way. But we have yet a long way to go, and it is the American Christian Nation Party that will get us there. In closing, my friends and fellow Christian Americans, let us join together in pledging allegiance to our new Christian flag[10]:

> "I pledge allegiance to the Christian flag, and to the Saviour, for whose Kingdom it stands, one Saviour, crucified, risen, and coming again[11], with life and liberty for all who believe."

Thank you my friends, God bless the God-fearing, and good night.

---

10. *Author's Note:* The "Christian flag" at this time was the old U.S. flag with a Christian cross emblazoned on the field of red and white stripes. At a January, 1994 training conference for Religious Right activists called "Reclaiming America," looking at such a flag, a former Vice President of the old U.S., J. Danforth Quayle, lead the crowd in reciting the Pledge with which Hague concluded his speech (Blumenthal).

11. *Author's Note:* The apocalyptic concept of the "Second Coming" of Jesus Christ, based on the Book of Revelation and part of the theology of many an evangelical preacher like Jerry Falwell and Pat Robertson, had begun to make its appearance in the rhetoric of Republican political candidates late in the Transition Era. For example, Senator Phil Gramm, a Far Right candidate for the 1996 Republican Presidential nomination, said in a 1995 fundraising letter (Niebuhr): "I ask you to fight tirelessly and when you are too tired to go on, remember that there is only one person who has ever lived whose values we would be willing to see imposed on America. And when He comes back, He's not going to need Government's help to get the job done."

A Connie Conroy Note (December 27, 2008)

We did it again! Maybe not as sintilating [*sic*] as the first time around, but we did it. We produced a great speech, at the last minute, again. Boy it's great to have those quotes to go to. I hope there are some left we can use next time. This time it was a brilliant stroke too to recognize that we were using that old stuff by name. No more charges of plajarism [*sic*] from those sticklers among us.

And I like the way we slipped in those old Far Right groups at the end. Boy, some of them are really crazy! But we need them. Things are starting to get a bit rough out there. Sometimes we've just got to have some unofficial "off the shelf"[12] muscle to get things done we just can't ask the cops or the FBI or the Federal marshals to do. Those other guys can do it and sometimes do do it for us. Better to have them inside than out.

Interesting. Some people have already noticed that the Prez specifically didn't mention the American Nazi Party, which has been growing by leaps and bounds over the last few years. Well, for the record, that's for our Jews. I'm not sure what the final answer is going to be on the Jew Question. But for now anti-Semitism is officially out, no matter what the bastards do.

The Prez sez that "our Jews" have been too important to us and our growth to chuck them out now. He says that's why we won't have anything to do with the Nazis or with the swastika[13]. Not only the Nazis but several of the groups in our new coalition use it as their symbol. Well, our Jew allies understandably don't like it. Also, and not too many people know this, the Nazi swastika is simply the reverse of an old American Indian symbol that meant good luck. Well, we

12. *Author's Note:* "Off the shelf" is a term the arch Right-Wing Reactionary William Casey, President Ronald Reagan's first Director of the Central Intelligence Agency, used to describe an extra-legal right-wing foreign insurgency instigation and support group he had put together during his tenure at the CIA.

13. *Author's Note:* The swastika or *hakenkreutz* ("crooked cross" in German) was the symbol of the German Nazi Party between 1933 and 1945.

certainly wouldn't want to be associated in any way with a symbol used by one of the inferior races.

Anyway, the Prez sez we are officially *not* anti-Semitic. Naturally, from time to time we do have some flare-ups of that stuff on the street. But they almost always involve liberal nigger-lover Renegade Jews, not Real Jews[14]. So nothing to worry about there. Our Jews stay with us, and with a wink and a nod[15] we let the boys have their fun.

The Prez does acknowledge, privately and publicly, that many outstanding Jewish thinkers made very important contributions to the political doctrines underlying our system of government. He likes especially to hark back to a Right-Wing Jew organization called "Toward Tradition" (1994), formed during the election of '94 that created the famous "Freshman Class" of which he is so proud.

Anyway, big win, great speech, if I do say so myself. Onwards and upwards!

Author's Commentary

And thus on a fateful Thursday, President Jefferson Davis Hague delivered his Second Inaugural Address from the National Cathedral in Washington, DC. Although it would indelibly set the future course of the nation under his leadership (which would last until the final overthrow of the NAR), one wouldn't have known that fact from the speech. Departing

14. *Author's Note:* The Hagueites commonly referred to that tiny, but very visible, vocal, and influential minority of the American Jewish community that supported Right-Wing Reaction as "Real Jews." Their leading organization by this time, "Jews for Christ and Tradition," was officially welcomed into the ACNP coalition by Hague in his speech. The traditionally Constitutionalist Jewish community, representing a majority of American Jews, was referred to as "the Renegade Jews."

15. *Author's Note:* The phrase "a wink and a nod" came from the practice President Reagan had used to give his approval for "unofficial" governmental activities of questionable legality without committing anything to paper, and oftentimes not saying anything directly at all to those on the operational level, even privately.

from a Presidential tradition, Hague did not address the major problems faced by the country at that time, even to the limited extent he had in his first Inaugural.

That critical problem list included:

- A standard of living that still continued to fall for most Americans, and a gap in both income and wealth between the very rich and everyone else that still continued to widen. Both patterns, as noted on several previous occasions, had been established during the Transition Era (Bradsher; Thurow; and see Chapter 1). They were firmly entrenched by R-CA Federal tax, fiscal, and regulatory policies of the early Fascist Period, policies that echoed that of the infamous 1994 Republican "Contract on America" (HRC).
- The continuing decline of manufacturing in America, caused by continuing "globalization," a cosmetic term that really meant the export of capital and the jobs that accompanied it.

  The massive economic and social impact of the decline in manufacturing was left untouched by what had been touted to replace it: the old Tofflerian "Third Wave/ Information Age." That was a notion that somehow the *processing* of an intangible, "information," could replace the *production* of tangible goods and services as the regular, reliable, adequate source of income for any significant number of people.

  Further, the now long-discredited notion held that somehow the processing of information could meet real, tangible needs of everyday life of the people for goods and services. For everything from survival to the full enjoyment of life, people need food, clothing, shelter, transportation, health care and education, entertainment, cultural activities, athletics, and so on, not *information* about them. In the real world, where needs for tangibles are tangible, the "Third Wave" notion simply didn't work. But it had made for good political theater.

- The virtual disappearance of governmental investment in "infrastructure:" roads, bridges, tunnels, railways, and airports; public health care facilities, schools, colleges, universities, and research institutions; water supply and sewage disposal systems; flood control, irrigation networks, and other waterway maintenance projects; the air traffic control system, national parks and forests and wilderness areas (soon to disappear entirely); seashore maintenance and coastal navigation systems; and the like.

  What remained for the most part was only that which had been "privatized" and then survived. The result was a very spotty system. To be sure, the rich and others living in the growing number of walled communities guarded by private armed forces did well (Egan). And, as noted in Chapter 8, the prison system flourished, continuing a pattern established in California in 1995-96 when for the first time spending on the state prison system had exceeded that on the state's two university systems (Butterfield). The prison system had been "privatized" to a significant degree, and provided huge profits for those connected to the new Prison/Industrial Complex (see also Chapter 3).
- The continuing growth of interpersonal violence accompanying the repeal of any limits on gun ownership that had occurred early in the Pine Presidency.
- The public and political prominence of public and personal racism, homophobia, misogyny, and xenophobia, and their continued exploitation by the forces of Right-Wing Reaction.
- The constantly spreading personal alienation and destruction of the basic interpersonal fabric of society resulting from the incessant promotion by Right-Wing Reaction of the philosophy of "every man for himself and the devil take the hindmost," otherwise known as "self-responsibility" (see Chapter 7 for an excellent Transition Era summary of this philosophy by the Right-Wing philosopher Michael Levin).

- The failure of any of the measures adopted through the Constitutional Amendment process since the ratification of the 28th (the first Balanced Budget Amendment) to materially affect in a positive way any of the underlying economic or social problems faced by the old United States.

  Because they in no way addressed those underlying economic or social problems, to summarize, primary among them being capital disinvestment, the disaccumulation of labor from capital (Judis) as a result of technological change (Wright), and institutionalized racism, the "solutions" could not have been expected to work. Nor were they intended to.

  In fact, as often noted, they were often intended to do nothing more than distract the American people from what the real problems of the society were. In that, this consciously planned and carefully executed strategy had from the beginning of the Transition Era been very successful for Right-Wing Reaction, in both increasing the wealth of the wealthy and maintaining its own political power.

  The primary tangible outcome of the "solutions" for the most part was either to cause problems in the first place or seriously aggravate them, that is if the negative outcomes were not ones actually desired by Right-Wing Reaction. (For more on this subject, see the Alex Poughton letter at the end of this chapter.)

In his address, Hague did not outline his plans for the conduct of his Second Term (most likely because at that time, as events would show, it was in Hague's best interests to keep them secret). In any case, like his political forebears, such as his original patron former House of Representatives Republican Speaker Newton Gingrich and former Senate Republican Minority then Majority Leader Bob Dole, Hague's strengths were in politics and power, not policy. Thus it is understandable that Hague devoted the bulk of his speech to announcing the conversion of the Republican-Christian Alliance into the American Christian Nation Party, and giving his rationale for so doing.

Hague and the "Christian Nation" Concept

In analyzing and understanding the Hague approach to that issue, it is important to note that neither in this speech nor elsewhere did he ever *officially* declare or decree the U.S. to be a "Christian Nation." Note too that as noted above the quotes from "The 15% Solution's" Godfather Pat Robertson that Hague chose to include, themselves never referred directly to the concept but only alluded to it. In fact, Robertson was usually quite careful not to use the words directly, even though most of his followers and most of his allies had the "Christianizing of America" right at the top of their agenda, and just "knew" that Pat did too. But not using the phrase gave the Reverend Reaganesque "deniability."

Following this pattern, Ralph Reed, Jr., the first Executive Director of Robertson's Christian Coalition, during the Transition Era periodically had tried to obscure its true agenda. For example, addressing a group of national Jewish leaders in 1995, he said "that it was a 'blatant wrong' for some on the religious right to talk of the United States as a 'Christian Nation'" (Niebuhr). Reed "also said his group was committed to the separation of church and state" (*Time*).

One wonders how Reed would have reconciled that claim with the statements his boss, Robertson, had previously made, quoted by Hague in his Second Inaugural. Contemporary observers raised the question (Rich). But there is no record of Reed ever having been able to achieve such a reconciliation. Nor is there any evidence that Reed ever disavowed statements like one the activist Mrs. Gillaspie made to a Christian Coalition chapter, quoted by Hague. In reality Reed was just "blowing smoke," as they used to say back then. But the smoke helped to keep the Right-Wing Reactionary Jews on board. As Conroy noted, in 2009 that was still a vital interest of the Hagueites.

Following this pattern of obscurantism, even the New American Republics would not be officially designated a "Christian Nation." In practice, of course, both the NAR and the old U.S. under Hague and the Republican-Christian Alliance were "Christian Nations" as the term was understood by those who had promoted the notion during the Transition Era, and their ideological successors. But by never saying so in so many words, and never making "Christian Nationhood" official policy, Hague was always able to deny that that was indeed the case, a politically useful maneuver.

The same "misdirection play" was later used to deal with the question of whether or not the New American Republics was a fascist state. Certainly the NAR was by definition a fascist state (see Appendix II). Nevertheless, the ACNP which founded it and became its only legal political party officially continued to deny that it was. This "being-but-denying" approach followed the pattern established by the old Republican Party during the Transition Era, discussed by Dino Louis in Appendix II, p. 372. As Louis so eloquently said: "If it looks like a duck, walks like a duck, and quacks like a duck, it's a duck."

The "Rightward Imperative"

The "Rightward Imperative" I mentioned in an "Author's Note" to the Hague Address (see p.154) described a pattern of a constant rightward policy shift that could be observed in the old Republican Party during the Transition Era, and then in the R-CA/ACNP during the pre-NAR Fascist Period. First on economic issues, then on social ones, so-called "moderates" were read or ridden out of the Republican Party, unless they radically moved their positions to the Right on both economic and social issues. For example, the Republican Senate Majority Leader Robert Dole of Kansas did that in the run up to the 1996 Presidential election (Kramer) (see below).

It became *de rigeur* in the 1980s to recite the mantra of "tax cuts/balanced budget amendment/free market" that would have horrified old-line "moderate" Republicans like Nelson

Rockefeller, former Governor of New York and Jacob Javits, former Senator from New York. Even former President Richard Nixon and George H.W. Bush, before he became Ronald Reagan's Vice President, had problems with certain sections of that agenda.

Then came the 90s mantra of "ban abortion/prayer in the schools/no civil rights for homosexuals." This was designed specifically to appeal to the growing Religious Right and the Rev. Pat's Christian Coalition. They formed the core vote of an ever-rightward moving Republican Party, they were the constituency which made "The 15% Solution" possible. They had to be kept in tow.

During the Transition Era the Rightward Imperative was perhaps best personified by Senator Dole (mentioned above). He had been a Nixon Republican, tough on rhetoric in practice but relatively progressive on domestic issues (Berke, 1995). He had, for example, introduced the Nixon health care reform plan in the Senate in 1973, a plan that had much in common with the (Pres. Bill) Clinton Health Plan that Dole played a major role in defeating, primarily for political reasons, in 1994.

For most of his career, Dole had downplayed the Right-Wing Reactionary "social issues" such as banning freedom of choice in the outcome of pregnancy, requiring voluntary prayer in the schools, and introducing censorship into the entertainment industry. In 1995-96, running for President in a Republican Party already well under the spell of the Christian Coalition, he quite suddenly became a supporter of their position on these matters and related ones. He was being realistic. As he said (Berke, 1995): "Any survey research you or I have seen shows that these are the issues that [far-right Republican] primary voters care about or are motivated by."

The Stirring of Political Violence

Once "The 15% Solution" had succeeded, during the pre-NAR Fascist Period Right-Wing Reaction found that its policies did not indeed solve problems, as noted above. It also found that there was, therefore, an increasing amount of labor and racial unrest. Too, there was potential political trouble, as various groups tried to reinvigorate the still Democratic Leadership Council led Democratic Party or set up some left alternative to it. Political violence, unofficial to be sure, increasingly became the order of the day. The Rightward Imperative continued to operate.

Political violence was to be intensified by the formal establishment in 2009 of the force known as the Helmsmen. This was part of the campaign to promote and enforce the Proclamation of Right (see the next chapter). An important prototype for the Helmsmen was the German Nazi dictator Adolf Hitler's *Sturmabteilung* (SA), the Storm Troopers. The SA was a private army of thugs used primarily to terrorize the center and left opposition before Hitler's official takeover of the German government in 1933.

Preparing the way for the formation of the Helmsmen, a number of the groups that Hague welcomed into the official American Christian Nation Party at the time of its founding had armed wings. While uncoordinated to be sure, for the R-CA in its later stages and the ACNP in its early one they generally served the purpose that the SA had for Hitler in pre-Nazi Germany. Faced with increasing although unfocused resistance, the Hagueites needed armed support for repressive purposes. By officially recognizing and indeed embracing them, the successors of the old Republican Party were just continuing at a different level the Rightward Imperative it had experienced for the previous three decades.

The Exclusion of Anti-Semitism

As discussed by Conroy, the exclusion of anti-Semitism at least from the public ideology of the ACNP if not at the street level, was regarded as essential by the leadership. (It is interesting to note, however, the perhaps unconscious anti-Semitism that slipped into Conroy's prose.) But Right-Wing forces had changed their positions on various religions a number of times throughout U.S. history.

For example, during the 20 years prior to the First Civil War, there had existed a far-Right-Wing party popularly known as the "Know-Nothings." Officially (and ironically in light of the ethnic group to which the name came to be applied in the latter half of the 20th century), the party was called the Native American Party. Its colloquial name came into use because its members refused to publicly answer questions about what they stood for. This party was violently xenophobic, focusing especially on Irish-Catholic immigrants fleeing the Irish Potato Famine of the 1840s.

During one of its periodic resurgences, in the 1920s, the traditionally anti-black racist Ku Klux Klan was also virulently anti-Catholic. It focused especially on relatively recent Catholic arrivals from Italy as well as on Catholic Americans of Irish descent. By the 21st century, however, the ultimate political achievement of Right-Wing Reaction, the American Christian Nation Party, would itself be led by an American Catholic of Irish descent.

On the other side of the coin, in one of the more striking ironies of American history, what some historians consider the best speech ever on the issue of the separation of church and state, the one I quoted from at length at the end of the last chapter, was given by a great American of Irish descent, the first and only Catholic President of pre-fascist times, John Fitzgerald Kennedy.

An Alex Poughton letter

December 31, 2008

Dear Karl,

You may recall that I wrote to you just four years ago this date, commenting on Hague's First Inaugural. I don't know which address, the first or the second, will be considered more depressing by future historians. But I am depressed enough thinking that this poor benighted country has another four years of this guy to endure[16]. The formation of this new

16. *Author's Note:* Poughton had no way of knowing that the country would have coming many more than four more years of Hague.

"American Christian Nation Party" comes as something of a shock, although I suppose using the retrospectroscope you could have seen it coming. The good news? Hague straddled on the "Christian Nation" issue itself. The bad news? The official welcoming into the party of the goon elements that have been unofficially been providing Hague and his men with street-muscle for a few years now.

The worst news, I suppose, is that Hague had to form the party at all. He wouldn't have done it if things had been going well here. Noticeable by its absence in his speech is any consideration of the myriad current problems this country faces. Noticeable also by its absence is any presentation, even in the most general terms, of policies he intends to follow to try to deal with them. And he's got to have something in mind, because everything major they've tried so far, each of course supposed to "solve the problem" and "set the country on the right track" hasn't worked. (He could have talked about that too, but somehow I don't think he would have.)

And so, going back with these guys to the 90s, the first Balanced Budget Amendment was supposed to do it; then Term Limits; then the "Real War on Drugs" (the subject of my very first letter to you); then ending that "burdensome immigration" with the Preserve America Amendment; then getting that "meddlesome" Supreme Court out of the way with *Anderson v. Board of Education*; then putting into the Constitution the definition of "when life begins," what can and cannot be taught to kids about sex, a full legal sanction for homophobia, and outlawing freedom of choice in the outcome of pregnancy; then ending any form of "welfare;" then repealing the income tax, having another go at trying to get to a balanced budget by amending the Constitution, making any tax increases virtually impossible, and ensconcing the line item veto; then giving the President decree powers (which he has yet to use) and ending the Constitutional prohibition on unreasonable search and seizure (that one, I hear, is being widely used—but even there, to deal with the apparently rising unrest, they have been rumored to be making use of these unofficial "militias"); then making the "Law of God" supreme, and finally Constitutionally putting God "back in the schools" (although he, or she, has firmly been there since *Anderson v. Board of Education*).

And of course, nothing "did it" because none of these policies addressed any of the underlying problems of this country, that I wrote to you about earlier this year during the election campaign. (And ah yes, the election campaign. The Democrats still didn't get it. They still haven't learned that "me too" doesn't work. And the real left? "Oy," as my Jewish friends are wont to say.)

So anyway, Hague needed some new distraction, and the formation of the ACNP is it. We'll see what comes next, but I cannot imagine it will be anything good. At the rate he's going, it could be a full-blown police state.

Well, enough gloom and doom for now.

Your friend,
Alex

A Parthenon Pomeroy Diary Entry (January 1, 2009)
We did it, we did it. We're finally going to get on the right track in this country. We've finally got the Party we need. And we're going to have a party. We've got some muscle, if you know what I mean. Now we're going to really be able to deal with the niggers, and the spics, and the faggots, and the yids (I don't care what the President says about them, a Jew is a yid and a yid is a yid). We've always known God is on our side. And now we've told Him so. This is going to fix things up all right. This is what we need to get America to where it ought to be, to what it can be, to what it always was and always will be. Thanks, God, and thanks, Pat, too.

References:

ACLU: American Civil Liberties Union fundraising letter, quoting Rev. Pat Robertson, 1992.

Berke, R.L., "Religion Issue Stirs Noise in G.O.P. Governors' 'Tent,'" *The New York Times*, Nov. 18, 1992.

Berke, R.L., "Dole Works on Expansion Of a Conservative Resume," *The New York Times*, April 12, 1995.
Blumenthal, S., "Christian Soldiers," *The New Yorker*, July 18, 1994, p. 31.

Bradsher, K., "Gap in Wealth In U.S. Called Widest in West," *The New York Times*, April 17, 1995.

Butterfield, F., "New Prisons Cast Shadow Over Higher Education," *The New York Times*, April 17, 1995.

Clarkson, F., "Neither a Juggernaut Nor a Joke," *Freedom Writer*, October/ November, 1993.

Egan, T., "Many Seek Security in Private Communities," *The New York Times*, Sept. 3, 1995, p. 1.

Falwell, J., "America is a Christian Nation!," *Drawing Closer*, Vol. 1, No. 7, 1993.

Foxman, A.H., Fundraising letter, New York: Anti-Defamation League, Jan., 1994.

Freedom Watch, "Exploring the Myth and Reality of 'Christian America'," Vol. 4, No. 3, March, 1995.

Freedom Writer, "Reed Masks Coalition's True Agenda," Feb. 1995, p. 3.

HRC, House Republican Conference, *Contract With America*, Washington, DC: September 27, 1994.

Fournier, K.A., *A House United?*, Colorado Springs, CO: Navpress, 1994, p. 33.

Judis, J.B., "The Jobless recovery," *The New Republic*, March 15, 1995, p. 20.

Kramer, M., "Will the Real Bob Dole Please Stand Up?" *Time*, November 30, 1995, p. 59.

Monaghan, T.P., "Nosophobia," *Law and Justice* (American Center for Law and Justice) Vol. 3, No. 1, 1994.

Niebuhr, G., "Gramm, on Stump, Invokes the Second Coming of Christ," *The New York Times*, September 20, 1995.

Porteous, S., "OR founder calls for a 'Christian nation,' " *Freedom Writer*, Sept., 1995, p. 1.

Rich, F., "Bait and Switch, II," *The New York Times*, April 6, 1995.

Sloan, J., "A hidden agenda?" *Freedom Writer*, April, 1995, p. 1.

Thurow, L. C., "Companies Merge; Families Break Up," *The New York Times*, September 3, 1995.

Time, "Chronicles: An Olive Branch," April 17, 1995, p. 16.

Toward Tradition, "Should Jews Fear the 'Christian Right'?" (an advertisement), *The New York Times*, August 2, 1994.

Wright, R., "Who's Really to Blame?" *Time*, November 6, 1995, p. 33.

CHAPTER 11
2009: The Proclamation of Right

Presidential Decree No. 1: The Proclamation of Right (Easter Sunday, March 29, 2009)[1]

"Section 3 of the 31st Amendment to the Constitution of the United States has established that the human aberration homosexuality is a matter of choice. Homosexuality and its associated behaviors, pedophilia, sadism, and masochism, are all abnormal, wrong, unnatural, and perverse, as well as sins against God. They are to be discouraged, avoided, and yes, condemned.

"Despite the measures taken pursuant to Section 3 of the 31st Amendment, in the eyes of God and every right-thinking American, homosexuality and its associated perversions still constitute a plague upon our land and people. Therefore, pursuant to the powers vested in me by Section 6 of the 32nd Amendment to the Constitution, I hereby decree a special national emergency in order to deal appropriately with this plague.

"As of this holy day, in homage to our almighty God, in recognition of His declaration that homosexuality is

1. *Author's Note:* There is no indication or evidence that J. Danforth Quayle, the Rev. Pat Robertson, the Rev. Jerry Falwell, Newton Gingrich, Pastor Peter J. Peters, Keith Fournier, John Eldridge, the Christian Coalition, or any of the other historical personages or organizations mentioned in this chapter or elsewhere in this book in a similar manner, would necessarily have supported or approved in any way of the Jefferson Davis Hague's "Proclamation of Right," or any of its predecessor or successor laws, regulations, policies, or procedures, or of any of the events that occurred in the United States or the New American Republics at any time in the future, subsequent to his announcement of it and the implementation of the policies carried out pursuant to it.

> the worst kind of perversion, I hereby declare that homosexuality, in action or thought, is a crime. The Congress and the legislatures of each state are hereby empowered to enforce this Proclamation in any manner of their choosing. They will be supported by the power of the Federal government to the full extent of the law."

Author's Commentary

Much of the defining language of President Hague's statement was drawn directly from that of an Amendment to the Constitution of Oregon, a state in which the Constitution could be amended through the process of Initiative and Referendum (see Chapter 4). First proposed in 1992, adoption of the Amendment was defeated by the voters in that year, but eventually passed, in 1998. The Amendment read (Egan):

> "**Section 1.** This state shall not recognize any categorical provision such as 'sexual orientation,' 'sexual preference,' and similar phrases that includes homosexuality. Quotas [*sic*], minority status, affirmative action, or any similar concepts, shall not apply to these forms of conduct, nor shall government promote these behaviors.
>
> "**Section 2.** State, regional and local governments and their properties and monies shall not be used to promote, encourage, or facilitate homosexuality, pedophilia, sadism or masochism.
>
> "**Section 3.** State, regional, and local governments and their departments, agencies and other entities, including specifically the State Department of Higher Education and the public schools, shall assist in setting a standard for Oregon's youth that recognizes homosexuality, pedophilia, sadism and masochism as abnormal, wrong, unnatural and perverse and that these behaviors are to be discouraged and avoided.

"**Section 4.** It shall be considered that it is the intent of the people in enacting this section that if any part thereof is held unconstitutional, the remaining parts shall be held in force."

Homophobia in the Law

Restrictions had been placed on public and private homosexual behavior and "thought" by Federal and state legislation written pursuant to Section 3 of the 31st (Morality) Amendment. (That Amendment you may recall, following the precepts of former Vice President J. Danforth Quayle [De Witt] and other Right-Wing Reactionaries of the Transition Era, declared that homosexuality was a matter of choice [see also Chapter 7].) Some of that legislation was modeled on the provisions of the Oregon measure as well as that of a similar one known as "Colorado Amendment 2," which first made its appearance in that same year.

However, all of this, the President told the people, was not considered to be "enough" to deal with the "threat." Thus, according to Hague, issuance under the Presidential decree power of the Proclamation of Right was absolutely necessary if morality, and by implication the Republic itself, were to be saved and redeemed in the eyes of the Lord.

After Hague issued the Proclamation of Right, some states enacted legislation placing homosexuals entirely outside the protection of the law, and disenfranchising them. A forerunner of this action was the enactment of the "Nuremberg Laws" against the Jews by the Nazi German Reichstag on September 15, 1935, that eliminated most civil rights and liberties protections for Jews living in Nazi Germany). As Professor Lucy Dawidowicz once wrote (1975):

"These laws legitimated racist anti-Semitism and turned the 'purity of German blood' into a legal category. They forbade marriage and extramarital relations between Jews and [other] Germans and disenfranchised those

> 'subjects' or 'nationals' of Germany who were not of 'German' blood."

Details of just how the determinations of "homosexual" were to be made, by whom, and with what appeals procedures, were not included in any of these statutes. That followed the pattern of the "homo-quarantine" (they meant "isolation") proposals that were made by some Far Rightists during the Transition Era for dealing with the AIDS problem: no details on who, where, by whom, for how long, at what cost, to be paid for by whom, and so forth. These details had also been ignored in the Colorado and Oregon Amendments and their campaigns. In practice, the legislation passed pursuant to the Hague decree was enforced with what might be politely called "rough justice," usually meted out by the Helmsmen (see below).

The Politics of Mythology

It is a fascinating commentary on the projection and use by Right-Wing Reaction of what Alex Poughton referred to as the "Politics of Mythology" (see Chapter 6) that in both the old Oregon initiative and the very first Presidential decree issued by Hague, homosexuality was directly linked with "pedophilia, sadism, and masochism." It was well known at the time of the first introduction of the Oregon measure that the vast majority of sex abusers of children of either gender were heterosexual males, 60 percent of them family members of the abused child, and fewer than 5 percent of them strangers to the victim (Groth).

Further, there was no evidence to show that (presumably sexual, but otherwise undefined) "sadism and masochism" were any more widely associated with the sexual practices of homosexuals than with those of heterosexuals. But once again, in the 90s it was considered unfair to confuse Right-Wing Reactionaries with facts. Both at that time and later, if the Right-Wing Reactionaries in question were homophobic, racist, misogynist, or otherwise xenophobic, and also possibly prone to violence, it was considered unwise to do so as well.

The Politics of Homophobia

As detailed earlier in this book (see Chapters 4, 6, and 7), homophobia had been a major element in the Republican-Christian Alliance's drive to virtually complete control of the government both at the Federal and state levels. I have previously cited the statement by the Rev. Pat Robertson commenting on tactics and strategy used in the 1992 elections (*Right-Wing Watch*): "As an issue in American politics, abortion is no longer current. … The 'gay issue,' however, proved promising."

In 1995, in a fundraising letter (June, 1995), the Reverend Jerry Falwell posed the question: "Has America become 'One Nation Under Gays?'" He then went on to tell his readers that "the radical gay agenda is destroying America!" And what precisely was that country-destroying agenda?

> "**Homosexual Demand #1:** Passage of a Gay Civil Rights Law.
> "**Homosexual Demand #2:** Massive increase in spending for AIDS research and patient care.
> "**Homosexual Demand #3:** An end to 'family' related discrimination against gays, lesbians, etc.
> "**Homosexual Demand #4:** Acceptance and promotion of the gay lifestyle within the educational system."

And that was it, not underinvestment, the "free market" and its necessarily accompanying greed run wild, or institutionalized and political racism, but those four elements of some imaginary national homosexual manifesto. They were "destroying America." One could imagine none of those things being done (and they weren't), and the country still being in a pretty bad way (it was). But that didn't stop Falwell or his colleagues in Right-Wing Reaction from using the arguments over and over again. After all, they thought it was good politics, if nothing else.

As early as 1985, at a conference entitled "How to Win an Election," the future patron of Jefferson Davis Hague, Newton Gingrich, spoke about Acquired Immune Deficiency Syndrome.

"AIDS," as it was known, was a painfully debilitating condition that almost invariably lead to death. It was later shown that in many of its victims AIDS was associated with a wide variety of diseases that generally weakened the immune system, some of which diseases were sexually transmitted. However, it had been quite incorrectly thought for quite some time that the appearance of AIDS had some special linkage to homosexuality. (The homophobes never abandoned that view.)

In any case, in 1985 when Gingrich addressed the issue AIDS presented as a serious public health threat, one that was poorly understood. An increasing number of people, many of them happening to be homosexual, were suffering terribly from the condition. At that time, addressing a Right-Wing Reactionary political planning conference, the future speaker of the House of Representatives had this to say about it (The Freedom Writer): "AIDS is a real crisis. It is worth paying attention to, to study. It's something you ought to be looking at."

"Ah ha," you might say, "your arch Right-Wing Reactionary is showing concern about AIDS and its victims, and thinks something should be done to deal with it." Well—no. Our "Mr. Newt" as the Right-Wing Reactionary political flack Rush Limbaugh inexplicably liked to call him, was not showing concern about this new disease and its victims. Rather he was showing concern about the potential to exploit this growing health and health care problem for Right-Wing political purposes. For he had gone on to say:

"AIDS will do more to direct America [*sic*] back to the cost of violating traditional values, and to make America [*sic*] aware of the danger of certain behaviors than anything we've seen. *For us, it's a great rallying cry* [emphasis added]."

As noted in Chapters 4 (see esp. the quote from Quindlen) and 9, and illustrated here by Robertson, Falwell and Gingrich, an important part of the Right-Wing Reactionary strategy was the "Politics of Difference," the development of "enemies," the use of, as Sklar termed it (1995), the "Snake Oil of Scapegoating." The purpose was to provide a focus for rage and a distractor of anger that might otherwise be turned by the American people on the true causes of their dissatisfaction with their lot.

Accomplishing this end proved to be a challenge towards the middle of the Transition Era, following the collapse of the old Soviet Union in 1989. The "Commies,"[2] both domestic and foreign, had provided a convenient enemy for over 40 years. But memories of them were rapidly becoming extinct, especially among a U.S. population that had so little appreciation for or understanding of history. Anti-black racism was a constant, of course. But homophobia proved very useful.

The phenomenon of homophobia was in fact perfect for Right-Wing Reactionary political exploitation. It went much deeper into the unconscious of many people than either anti-communism or choice control in the outcome of pregnancy did. It appealed to the sexual drive, issues of sexual identity, sexual insecurity, the fascination with the ultimate sexual symbol, the gun, especially the pistol. (In Right-Wing Reactionary propaganda, homophobia and fear of "gun control" were often closely linked.) These were all issues that psychologically drove the Right-Wing masses in the old U.S.

"The Helmsmen"

As mentioned briefly in the last chapter, early in 2009, appropriately enough on Friday the 13th of February in that year, Hague established an armed force called "The Helmsmen," HM for short. Neither of the military nor of the Federal, state, or local police, the HM was an arm of Hague's new American Christian Nation Party. They were described as "those with their hands on the helm of the ship of God's state."

In this, as noted in the last chapter, in composition, role,

2. *Author's Note:* "Commie" was a 20th century pejorative vernacular term applied to a wide variety of persons, ranging from members of the tiny Communist Party/USA, through almost any citizen of the old Soviet Union, to many political progressives, whether Communist or communist or neither, both at home and abroad.

and function the HM had much in common with Adolf Hitler's "Brown Shirts," the SA (*Sturmabteilung*), as they existed before the establishment of the national German government called the Third Reich. They also had much in common with Benito Mussolini's Black Shirts in Italy before the establishment of the fascist state there in 1922. The HM would also quickly come to have much in common with the Latin American "Death Squads" of the latter half of the 20th century.

Following the establishment of the New American Republics in 2011, the HM would come to combine the functions of the SA, its successor in Germany, the SS (*Schutzstaffel*, the "Black Shirts"), and the Gestapo (*Geheime Staatspolizei*, Secret State Police), as well as the Death Squads. However, in all of its activities, just as the SS was attached directly to the German Nazi Party, not to any branch the German government, the HM would be attached directly to the ACNP.

Therefore, in addition to a wide variety of responsibilities for forceful political repression, it was also charged with carrying out a variety of "moral policing" duties on behalf of the Party. Since this was the case, of the secret police/public state terrorist organizations known throughout the world, the HM was perhaps, ironically, most similar to the Muslim fundamentalist Iranian "Komitehs." They too combined a supposed "moral" regulatory function with their main role as physically violent political repressors.

There was an interesting historical circle connecting the Helmsmen with the Komitehs. In 1953 in Iran, a coup had overthrown a popularly elected Premier, Muhammed Mussadegh. It was engineered by the old U.S. Central Intelligence Agency (CIA) and lead on the ground by one Kermit Roosevelt, a son of the 26th President of the United States, Theodore Roosevelt. The CIA replaced Mussadegh with a man who had been an open admirer of Adolf Hitler, Muhammed Reza Shah Pahlevi. He was the son of a former Army officer who himself had taken power from the previous ruler in a coup in 1921.

The "Shah," as he called himself, needed a secret police for political repression, and the CIA created and trained one for him. It was known as Savak. It was also known as one of the most brutal secret police forces in a world of many highly brutal such organizations (many of them trained by the CIA).

In 1979, the Shah's regime was overthrown by an even more repressive one, that of the Islamic Fundamentalist Ayatollah Khomenei. The Savak essentially remained in place for the Fundamentalist regime, which simply converted it into the Komitehs. In the waning days of the old U.S., a group of top-ranking officers of the Komitehs, considered to be expert in combining the "moral policing" and secret police functions, came over to help train the first core group of Helmsmen. They were returning the CIA's "favor," as it were.

The membership of the HM was originally drawn from the ranks of the armed wings of the various Far Right groupings that Hague had drawn into the ACNP. As far back as 1994, Randall Terry, founder of the militant anti-freedom-of-choice-in-the-outcome-of-pregnancy organization Operation Rescue, had established a "leadership institute" to train "a cadre of people who are militant, who are fierce, who are unmerciful" (Stark). He said at the time that "the battle for America's soul" would produce "turmoil and disruption that will make the civil war look civil." In that he was prescient.

Some of the men and women first recruited to the HM already had significant experience in political violence. This stemmed, for example from the days in which they had destroyed most of the public elective pregnancy termination clinics and had intimidated or murdered enough legal abortion providers to drive the rest, qualified and unqualified, underground. Homophobic violence, of course, was featured by these groups as well. From the perspective of its creators, the HM would get off to a good start.

The HM also attracted many members to its ranks from the well-established Right-Wing Militia movement (ADL). It had experienced virtually unfettered growth from the time late Transition Era Republican leadership had sanctioned its "anti-

(Federal)-government" philosophy (although, of course, "not its methods") (*Newsday*). That growth had been accelerated by the repeal by 2003 of all state laws (which had never been enforced in any case) that banned private militias and armies.

A Curley Oakwood Radio Broadcast Transcript (March 30, 2009)

Thank God, my friends, thank God, my friends, my friends—Thank God! For through the mouth of Brother Hague, He has spoken. And He has spoken on our beloved and God-blessed nation's greatest problem: the plague of faggots! Oops, sorry. I guess I'm just not being politically correct[3] there. I meant to say the plague of fairies.

We are finally going to get some action, some real action,

---

3. *Author's Note:* The term "politically correct" was a leftover from Transition Era Right-Wing Reactionary attack vocabulary. Oakwood and a few others still used it, although the Right-Wing Reactionary state and Federal governments had long since removed any public or private attempts to limit what was then called "hate speech." "Hate speech" was the term used to characterize the increasingly violent and virulent personal verbal attacks upon individuals and groups related to skin color, ethnicity, sexual orientation, and the like, that had taken place with increasing frequency towards the end of the Transition Era.

The Right-Wing Reactionaries of the Era had applied the term "political correctness" in a derogatory fashion to any attempts by liberals and progressives to cause a general or specific moderation of such attacks. Those attempts, it should be noted, were circumscribed and had had a limited ameliorating effect at best. By the early Fascist Period they had generally come to an end, under a relentless Right-Wing Reactionary onslaught spuriously based on "defending the First Amendment."

Not unexpectedly, the Right-Wing Reactionaries trotted out the First only to defend hate speech, not any other kinds of unpopular speech, such as that of critics of the old Viet Nam War. (Consistent with the concept of freedom of speech, much hate speech could have been circumscribed by invoking the old English common law intentional tort of assault: creating in another the apprehension of imminent physical harm. But the liberals never seem to have made use of that concept, one that is ensconced in our Constitution, of course.)

Be all this as it may, Oakwood and his ilk still went after the long gone challengers of hate speech years later, using the "politically correct" label, just as during the late Transition Era Limbaugh and his ilk had gone after the long defunct "Counter Culture" even though likewise at its peak the latter had had a limited influence on the nation as a whole.

going on here. Now my friends, it's not as if this hasn't been called for a long time. It has. Why way back in the 90s, the good old Rev. Jerry [Falwell] said (1993):

> "The battle lines are now drawn. If the gay agenda for America succeeds ... you as a Christian will lose many of your rights. Our churches will be under attack. *We will no longer be one nation under God.* There is no middle ground. For Christians, there can be no peaceful coexistence with those Sodomites whom God has given over to a reprobate mind. IF THE GAYS AND LESBIANS WIN THIS STRUGGLE ... AMERICA WILL BE ON A ONE WAY STREET TO SODOM AND GOMORRAH. ... I am not going to sit back and let our precious nation be swept away by this demonic assault on our Christian values."

At about the same time, the eminent Keith Fournier, the Executive Director of the Rev. Pat's American Center for Law and Justice said (1994):

> "There's nothing compassionate or socially desirable in tolerating, much less legislating, immorality, and yet we are coming to believe there is. We have bought the lie of the militant homosexual community—namely it is 'compassionate' to elevate a *disordered appetite* to a civil right [emphasis added]."

And finally, ladies and gentlemen, permit me to sum up with a trenchant quote from the wellrenowned John Eldridge of Focus on the Family (*Freedom Writer*):

> "I would not say this in other cultural contexts[4], but the gay agenda has all the elements of that which is truly

4. *Author's Note:* Eldridge was speaking, it has turned out, at a secret meeting of anti-homosexual-rights groups in the Glen Eyrie Castle outside of Colorado Springs, CO, held in the spring of 1994.

evil. It is deceptive at every turn. It is destroying the souls and lives of those who embrace it."

Well, at that time Mr. Eldridge felt he couldn't say what was in his heart, in "other cultural contexts," meaning that outside world dominated by the liberal nigger loving media and the cultural elite, if you know who I mean—are you listening Hollywood? But he could have now, and the President has said it for him.

Well, Mr. President. Now that you've said it, I hope you'll show some *cojones* (see, I'm multilingual—no ethnic bias here) and do something about it.

And while I'm at it, ladies and gentlemen, let me just mention, let me just comment briefly, on the President's best tool (if I may use that term) for doing something about it, if you know what I mean. I am referring of course to our new arm of discipline, The Helmsmen.

The Helmsmen are the People's Guides. They make sure that the Ship of State is always held on the course designed for it by the President and the Party. We value our freedom and we know how to handle it. But at the same time, we know that there are still plenty of secret liberal nigger lovers, faggots, blacks, spics, and other weak-minded people who they influence around. They remember the bad old days when you could say and think just about anything you wanted. And they'll abuse that freedom if left to their own devices.

We know that all men, even the best members of the Party, need guidance; that without it we all will descend directly into sin. So we have the Helmsmen, on the street, in our homes whenever with God's guidance they see the need, in all public places. They are always on the lookout to uphold and defend our nation's bedrock values of God, Church, and Family.

I have a message for you, my friends, and for all of our courageous Helmsmen, who are all my friends. The Helmsmen have a job to do, and they are going to do it. And my oh my, is our country going to be a better place for it. God bless each and every God-fearing American. Good night.

A Connie Conroy Note (February 14, 2009)

Some people think that the Helmsmen were named for the late Senator Jesse Helms. To be sure, we owe a great deal of our thinking to him. It was a national tragedy that he died before he could see the greatest that his type of thinking has produced for our country. He was one of the few men in the old nigger loving liberal Congress who knew which end was up, that, for example, if there was a national holiday for Martin Luther Coon, the U.S. of A. didn't have long to go. And as it turned out, he was right. The Prez sez that if he had lived, he would have had a very important seat in our government. But it's just coincidence that the Helmsmen are called what they are.

Oh yes. Wish I had a Valentine today.

An Alex Poughton letter

August 18, 2009

Dear Karl,

Curiouser and curiouser. Funny things are happening in the follow up to Hague's anti-gay decree. The homosexual population here has long since either gone to ground or, if they could afford it, moved to another country, if they could find one that would take them. Yet Hague chose to go after them, by making their sexual orientation, defined as "choice" in the U.S. Constitution of all places, a crime, of all things.

Then, however, he takes no steps to officially enforce this new "law" at the Federal level, although his new "Helmsmen" are rumored to be having an "unofficial" go at it. Neither do very many of the states move to enforce it, although some move quickly to deprive any homosexuals who would dare to let it be known that they are such of any civil rights.

So the general opinion in the diplomatic and foreign journalist community is that with the number of closet gays in the Government and the military, if there were to be a real crackdown, it could be very embarrassing. Or that Hague is just sucking up to the Religious Right and showing how devoted to "God's Way" he really is, at least in word if not in deed. Or perhaps it's both.

You know that for years the Religious Right has made a big deal about what a sin, sin, sin homosexuality is. The Bible tells us it's bad, bad, bad, you know, so it must be so, so they tell us. Apropos of that position, although it means nothing here now, I came across an interesting piece written by a liberal churchman in the mid-90s. His view of what the Bible really has to say on the issue was rather at odds with the usual Right-Wing presentation of it back then. I thought I would share a few quotes from the article with you (Gomes).

"Christians opposed to political and social equality for homosexuals nearly always appeal to the moral injunctions of the Bible, claiming that Scripture is very clear on the matter and citing verses that support their opinion. … They do not, however, necessarily see quite as clear a meaning in biblical passages on economic conduct, the burdens of wealth and the sin of greed.

"Nine biblical citations are customarily invoked as relating to homosexuality. Four (Deuteronomy 23:17, I Kings 14:24, I Kings 22:46 and II Kings 23:7) simply forbid [directly or by implication] prostitution, by men and women.

"Two others (Leviticus 18:1923 and 20:1016) are part of what Biblical scholars call the Holiness Code. The code explicitly bans homosexual acts. But it also prohibits eating raw meat, planting two different kinds of seed in the same field and wearing garments of two different kinds of yarn. Tattoos, adultery, [incest], and sexual intercourse during a woman's menstrual period are similarly outlawed.

"There is no mention of homosexuality in the four Gospels of the New Testament. The moral teachings of Jesus are not concerned with the subject.

"Three references from St. Paul are frequently cited (Romans 1:262:1, I Corinthians 6:911, and I Timothy 1:10). But St. Paul was concerned with homosexuality only because in Greco-Roman culture it represented a secular sensuality that was contrary to the Jewish-Christian spiritual idealism. He was against lust and sensuality in anyone, including heterosexuals. …

"And lest we forget Sodom and Gomorrah, recall that the story is not about sexual perversion and homosexual practice. It is about inhospitality, according to Luke 10:1013, and failure to care for the poor, according to Ezekiel 16:4950: 'Behold, this was the iniquity of thy sister Sodom, pride, fullness of bread, and abundance of idleness was in her and in her daughters, neither did she strengthen the hand of the poor and the needy.' To suggest that Sodom and Gomorrah is about homosexual sex is an analysis of about as much worth as suggesting that the story of Jonah and the whale is a treatise on fishing."

As you know, Karl, I'm no biblical scholar. And certainly the "inerrancy boys" read what Prof. Gomes read and saw the stuff quite differently. But that really is the point, isn't it? The Bible is open to interpretation. The Fundamentalists are ministers, some of them Baptists. But Prof. Gomes was a Baptist minister too.

There is nothing I can find, even in the Bible, that says that one Baptist minister is any more qualified to give the final word on what the Word is and means than any other Baptist minister. But of course, that kind of reasoning wouldn't stop even one preacher who claims that the Bible is "inerrant" from doing so, and proclaiming that he (and it is usually a "he") knows for sure just what it "inerrantly" means.

Well, theology and Bible interpretation aside, there's one other curious thing about this whole thing I want to mention. (I do go on so, don't I?) In the grand scheme of things that are going on here, one has to wonder why Hague chose this one as the issue on which to issue his first decree, after having had the decree power for three years or so, what with there being so few identifiable gays and lesbians left here.

I wonder if this was really just sort of a dry run. Try out the technical features of the clause. See how the Congress and what's left of "public opinion" reacts. Well, in the event, all that stuff went very smoothly for Hague. And he relinquished his decree power in less than 60 days. But I just wonder if there isn't something bigger coming[5] .

All the best,
Alex

References:

ADL: Anti-Defamation League, *Beyond the Bombing: The Militia Menace Grows*, New York: 1995.

Bradsher, K., "Gap in Wealth In U.S. Called Widest in West," *The New York Times*, April 17, 1995.

Dawidowicz, L.S., *The War Against the Jews*, New York: Holt, Rinehart and Winston, 1975, p. 63.

De Witt, K., "Quayle Contends Homosexuality Is a Matter of Choice, Not Biology," *The New York Times*, September, 14, 1992.

Egan, T., "Oregon Measure Asks State to Repress Homosexuality," *The New York Times*, August 16, 1992.

Falwell, J., Fundraising letter: "WARNING: DO NOT ALLOW CHILDREN TO VIEW THE CONTENTS OF THE ENCLOSED SEALED ENVELOPE" [*Author's Note:* which contained photos of males kissing in public, women uncovering their upper bodies in public, and mild crossdressers], Spring, 1993.

Falwell, J., Fundraising letter: "Has America Become One Nation Under Gays?" June, 1995.

Fournier, K.A., "Appetite of Civil Right," *Law and Justice*, Vol. 3, No. One, 1994, p. 1.

Freedom Writer, "Inside Glen Eyrie Castle," August, 1994, p. 1.

Gomes, P.J., "Homophobic? ReRead Your Bible," *The New York Times*, August 17, 1992.

5. *Author's Note:* Poughton was right. There would be "something bigger coming," two years down the road. Hague was sparing in his use of the decree power under the old U.S. Constitution. But the next time he used it would spell the end of that document in all but name.

Groth, A.N., cited in Meehan, B.T., and Graves, B., "OCA [Oregon Citizens Alliance] stirs emotions with its 2nd flier," *The Oregonian*, September 25, 1992.

Newsday, "Gingrich: Fear of Feds is Genuine," May 8, 1995, p. A5.

Right-Wing Watch, "Getting Ready for '94 and '96," December, 1992, Vol. 3, No. 3.

Sklar, H., "The Snake Oil of Scapegoating," *Z Magazine*, May, 1995, p. 49.

Stark, K., "Call It Pro-Death," *The Nation*, August 22, 29, 1994, p. 183.

Freedom Writer, "Newt Set Strategy For Religious Right–10 Years Ago!" February, 1995, p. 19.

CHAPTER 12
2010: The Original Intent Amendment (34th)

The 34th Amendment to the Constitution of the United States (2010)[1]:

> **Section 1.** The thirteenth, fourteenth, and fifteenth amendments to the Constitution of the United States are hereby repealed.

A Connie Conroy Note (April 13, 2010)

Man oh man. What a performance! The Prez has set a speed record for this one. Introduced in the Congress on Opening Day, Tuesday, January 5, 2010, and a little more than three months later—bang, we got it through the states, and almost unanimously. The only holdouts? Hawaii (too many slant-eyes), New York (too many Renegade Yids), Massachusetts (too many Kennedy-Catholics), and Vermont (who knows?). We'll have to do something about them.

Anyway, you gotta love the way the Prez sold this one. "Back to Original Intent," he said. "We just have to be consistent," he said. "I know the liberals" (he meant "liberal nigger lovers" but he does go out of his way to be nice, this man) "are not

1. *Author's Note:* There is no indication or evidence that Clarence Carson, Robert Bork, Brent Johnson, Patrick Buchanan, or any of the other historical personages or organizations mentioned or alluded to in this chapter or elsewhere in this book in a similar manner, would necessarily have supported or approved in any way of the repeal of the 13th, 14th and 15th Amendments, or any of the successor laws, regulations, policies, or procedures enacted pursuant to that repeal, or of any of the events that subsequently occurred in the United States or the New American Republics at any time in the future, subsequent to that repeal and the implementation of the policies carried out pursuant to it.

going to be happy. But God, and our Party, and the American people have not been happy about what the liberals have been doing to our country since 1865.

"They have put the Federal government between the people and the Constitution, between the people and their true voice, the state governments, and they started it by sneaking these amendments we're now getting rid of through Congress, when half the country wasn't even represented there. So we are going to put things back, we are going to set things right, we are going back to the Original Intent of the original Founding Fathers. And we are going to set this country on the path of righteousness once again."

That is what he said. That is what President Jefferson Davis Hague said[2].

It's all so simple. That stuff in the 13th, 14th, and 15th Amendments was anything but in the original Constitution. Slavery was in the original constitution. Now, by God, no one (well almost no-one) has any intent to go back to slavery. It just doesn't work very well. And nobody needs field hands today anyway (heh, heh). But we have to be consistent, the Prez sez. Oh yes, the Prez sez: Original Intent is our guide. I remember Clarence B. Carson's description of his great historical work, *Basic American Government*, discussing this very issue (NLJ):

> "It would be considerable fraud to do a book on American government which talked as if the Constitution were still

---

2. *Author's Note:* At perhaps the height of irony, and surely not knowing whom she was quoting, Conroy intoned the words "This is what he said." That was a famous line given the voice of the narrator in the 20th century American composer Aaron Copeland's cantata "A Lincoln Portrait." Amazing. Abraham Lincoln freed the slaves. A man named for the leader of the enslaving forces puts through a Constitutional amendment that reverses Lincoln's greatest achievement, and one of the man's minions refers to his words in words that had been previously reserved for praise of Lincoln.

In doing this however, Conroy was unwittingly following the example set during the Transition Era by certain Right-Wing Reactionaries such as Ronald Reagan and Newton Gingrich, of attempting to take over the legacies of great liberal American historical figures such as Jefferson, Lincoln, and Franklin Roosevelt, and pretend that Right-Wing Reaction was simply following in their tradition, which by its own definitions it was not.

> being substantially observed, that pretended that when presidents took the oath of office they intended to observe the bounds set by the Constitution, that Congressmen recited their pledges with the same intent, and that federal judges were still construing the Constitution as it was written. In sum, any book on American government worthy of the name ought to make clear how remote from the Constitution the government has become."

Well, *this* President intends to observe and is observing the bounds set by the *original* Constitution, and thank God, we've got a 2/3's-plus majority of Congressmen who do the same. Since we passed the 28th back in '99, we've been headed nowhere else but right back to the Original Intent of the thing, what the Founding Fathers were aiming for. And what had the liberal nigger lovers done since 1865, from the conclusion of that unconstitutional civil war (NLJ)? Taken us right the opposite way.

Take the 28th, our first effort. Well, it didn't work very well. It didn't get the budget balanced. But we tried. And we've done better with all the ones we got passed since. Getting back the Constitution to the way it oughta be: America for us. We put morality first. Then we really balanced things, and got rid of the income tax (no Original Intent anywhere in that dead letter). Then we put God in first place, just like the Founding Fathers said (Falwell). So now we're just being consistent.

And who needs those amendments, anyway? The 13th? Slavery's a dead letter. That reference to abolition in the Constitution just puts off so many of our core white supporters around the country. We don't need it, so good riddance to it.

The 14th?[3] A lot of the trouble started when they extended

3. *Author's Note:* Repeal of the 14th Amendment was high on the list of demands of many a Right-Wing Reactionary Organization during the Transition Era. For example, one Linda Thompson, who termed herself the "acting adjutant general" of the "Unorganized Militia of the United States," called for repeal not only of the 14th, but also the 16th and 17th Amendments (Heard). (The 16th, of course, went out with enactment of the 31st. The issue of the 17th would become moot with the establishment of the New American Republics in 2011.)

due process to the states, as the boys used to say back in the 90s. It's there in the 5th, and if you ask me, one mention in the Constitution is enough for that troublemaker of a clause. Section 2 of the 14th, that roundabout, really unfair, way they tried to secure the vote for the niggers, was never used anyway. So we've just gotten rid of some clutter. Section 3, the one that put in political penalties against former Confederate officials, was put to bed by a 2/3rds vote of each House of Congress in 1898, so it's moot. Section 4, on Confederate debt, is moot too. No reason not to toss them all out.

And as for the 15th, that direct guarantee of votes for niggers, just like with Section 2 of the 14th, the liberal nigger lovers back then were as lily-livered as they are now: it was never enforced either. Funny, if it had been, the liberal nigger lovers never would have needed their precious Civil Rights Acts of the 1960s.

So that's that. Our people asked for a pure Constitution. And we gave it to them. It is just as pure now as the driven snow.

Author's Commentary
Consistency, "Original Intent," and the Politics of Mythology

According to Conroy, all of this was done simply for the sake of consistency, and following the "Doctrine of Original Intent" (Reynolds). In so saying, Conroy illustrated that self-contradictory thinking to which so many Right-Wing Reactionaries of her time were in thrall. It is very difficult for observers from our era, even conservative ones, to understand it. Even during the Transition Era most authorities on the Constitution of any stripe other than Far Right-Wing Reactionary did not give it any credence at all. Recall, for example, the writing of Federal Appeals Court Judge Irving R. Kaufman, certainly no liberal, that rather neatly disposed of the Doctrine (see Chapter 5).

For the most part, all of the Right-Wing Reactionary amendments to the old U.S. Constitution Conroy cites were self-evidently not at all consistent with the Doctrine of Original

Intent, as that doctrine was put forth by its own supporters. Virtually no basis for any of the provisions of the Amendments from 28 onwards could be found anywhere in the original document (see Appendix I), either explicitly or implicitly.

However, almost all of the themes played out in those amendments can be found in the 1992 Republican National Platform and other similar political documents from the late Transition Era (see, for example, Chapter 7). Yet the supporters of all those provisions that on their face were contrary to those of the original document were the selfsame champions of the Doctrine of Original Intent.

As examples that little in the Right-Wing Reactionary agenda reflected Original Intent as they themselves stated it, consider:

- The Founding Fathers had discussed requiring a balanced budget and setting Congressional term limits and had rejected both ideas.
- A ban on immigration never crossed their minds, and given the nature of the country at the time, wouldn't have. The "naturalization" process wasn't mentioned until the adoption of the 14th.
- Legislating, and even worse, constitutionalizing certain views on morality was contrary to both the spirit and the words of the Jefferson/Madison Bill of Rights, while repeal of the Fourth Amendment was absolutely contrary to its letter.
- As for Presidential decree powers, that is precisely the type of concentration of sovereign power typical of the monarchical system of government the American Revolution had been undertaken to free the former colonies from. Further, the whole complex system of "checks and balances" was designed to prevent such a concentration of power from happening in the future.
- And finally, putting the "Law of God" (as defined by some men, of course) above that of the Constitution itself defeated the very purpose of having a Constitution in the first place.

Thus if there were consistency in the Right-Wing Reactionary approach to these issues at the time, it is hard to discern it from this historical distance. It appears in fact that during the Transition Era and early Fascist Period the only occasions on which the Right-Wing Reactionaries invoked the "Doctrine of Original Intent" was when they were battling against some Supreme Court interpretation of the Constitution that served to protect an individual right or liberty.

When they themselves were battling to limit individual rights and liberties, as for example on the issues of freedom of choice in the outcome of pregnancy, sexual identity/ preference, relationship between church and state, or freedom from unreasonable search and seizure, the matter of Original Intent never seemed to come up, with one exception.

When Right-Wing Reaction wanted to deny the possible existence of an individual right, liberty, or freedom that wasn't specifically mentioned in the Constitution, they always conveniently ignored one provision that clearly is: the Ninth Amendment. It states: "The enumeration in the constitution of certain rights shall not be construed to deny or disparage others retained by the people." But once again, Right-Wing Reactionaries were never much for letting facts get in the way of ideology.

Nevertheless, the themes of "Original Intent" and "consistency," repeated over and over again by the Right-Wing Reactionaries from the Transition Era onwards, were what the Hagueites used to sell the 34th Amendment. In fact the public relations name they gave to the Amendment was "Original Intent."

In their sales campaign (to the extent they needed to sell anything political in a setting in which they were virtually unchallenged), the Hagueites went back to the theory that the Supreme Court had used in *Anderson v. Board of Education*. (That was the case in which the Court had removed from itself the power to review actions of the other two branches of the Federal government for their constitutionality [see Chapter 5].)

You may recall that the primary Transition Era exponent of the Doctrine was one Judge Robert Bork (1993) (see also

Chapter 5). His position can be paraphrased in one sentence: "Principles not originally understood to be and not clearly stated in the Constitution have no constitutional validity." It is certainly true that none of the principles stated in the 13th, 14th, or 15th Amendments were "originally understood to be," much less "clearly stated" in the Constitution. And so—out! But as illustrated above, none of the Right-Wing Reactionary amendments could be "understood to be" part of the original thinking behind the Constitution nor "clearly stated" in it either.

It was just that, as pointed above, almost all of them were advocated as part of the Republican Party's own national platform, at least from 1992 onwards. But such inconsistencies had bothered neither the Republicans, nor the Hagueites. It was all part of the "Politics of Mythology" as Alex Poughton liked to call it.

The Right-Wing Reactionary Historical Theory behind the Amendment

In historical terms, this Amendment represented a frontal assault on the whole political basis for the structure of the country since the conclusion of the First Civil War. Indeed, the ratification day for the 34th was arranged by the Hague government to be on Monday, April 12, 2010. That day was the 149th anniversary of the commencement of the First Civil War, when Southern rebel forces shelled the Federal Fort Sumter in Charleston (SC) harbor.

As has been noted, in the late Transition Era it was in vogue among the Right-Wing Reactionaries to blame everything that was wrong in the country not only on the (ill-defined) "liberals" and the by-then dead 1960s "Counter-Culture" of 30 years before, but also on President Franklin Delano Roosevelt and his "New Deal" of 60 years before. The Hagueites simply took this kind of thinking one step further back in time.

The Right-Wing Reactionary trend towards dating the beginning of the country's modern troubles back to 1865 had begun in the late Transition Era and had come to full flower in the early Fascist Period. It blamed everything that was wrong in the country not only on the Transition Era's favorite 20th century targets, but also on the First Reconstruction era policies of the Radical Republicans 1865-1876. (The latter were related only in name to their late 20th century descendants.) It was the three amendments repealed by the 34th that epitomized the First Reconstruction.

Thinkers such as Brent Johnson (1995) claimed that "citizenship" as conceived of by the Founding Fathers lay with the states, not the nation. This reflected the thinking of John C. Calhoun (1782-1850), chief ideologue of slavery (Niven). He held that within the United States, sovereignty lay entirely with the State governments, and thus that citizenship was entirely State, not Federal, in nature.

Calhoun's ideological descendants went on to claim that it was only the 14th amendment that created national citizenship, and that had by so doing somehow set the "Federal government between the people and the states." In this view, the Federal government had limited legitimacy on the one hand, and vast responsibility as the cause of any difficulties faced by the nation on the other.

Supporters of this view then went on to trace the origin of all the then-current problems of the old United States to the adoption of the 14th amendment. They put forth the notion that citizenship should arise from each person's relationship to a state government, not to the Federal government. It was on this basis that they advocated repeal of the 14th. It was then an easy leap to include the 13th and 15th as targets for repeal as well, "for the sake of consistency."

In undertaking such advocacy, such thinkers ignored the fact that the old U.S. Constitution was designed specifically to develop a national government, that both the Preamble and a number of its operative clauses (e.g., Article I, Section 8), gave the national government broad responsibilities and powers, some of them preemptive, that by joining the union the states specifically gave up certain elements of their sovereignty, and that while the original Constitution did not define "citizenship" per se, the Preamble begins "We the people of the United States," and the body does refer to "citizen(s) of the United States" Article II, Section 1.

But be all that as it may, in summary the "Doctrine of Original Intent" seemed to provide an historical rationale for undermining both the foundations of the power of the Federal government (except for the Executive Branch when under the control of Right-Wing Reaction, of course), and the Constitutional protection of individual rights, freedoms, and liberties. It thus attracted a grand following among the Right-Wing Reactionaries.

The True Political Motives for the Amendment

1. Promotion of racism

As far as can be discerned from the present historical distance, as Conroy stated, the reinstitution of slavery was not among the intentions of the promoters of the 34th (Calloway). But the Amendment was nevertheless clearly intended to exacerbate racism. First and foremost, there was its content, including the gratuitous repeal of the 13th Amendment. There were also the details. For example, the choice of the anniversary of the First Civil War's commencement as the date for the final ratification of this amendment could hardly have been coincidental.

As has been noted before, using code words and coded signals, especially on the race issue, was an old Right-Wing Reactionary tactic dating from the Transition Era. Listen, for example, to one of the patron saints of Right-Wing Reaction, Patrick Buchanan, talking in 1993 about the First Civil War (EXTRA! Update): "The War Between the States[4] was about

4. *Author's Note:* Buchanan was here using here the phraseology of the unreconstructed adherents of the Confederacy and slavery. The term "The War Between the States" was one of the most powerful of the many code words/terms that Right-Wing Reaction used from the beginning of the Transition Era onwards to signal to its constituency where it "really stood" on the race question. By using such using expressions, rather than the explicitly racist language of such later spokesmen as Curley Oakwood, Right-Wing Reactionaries of the Transition Era were able to "plausibly deny" that they were engaging in racism. In our time, most historians simply apply the Dino Louis Duck Rule, and easily determine what was what and who was who.

independence, about self-determination, about the right of a people to break free of a government to which they could no longer give allegiance."

This statement of Buchanan's could be interpreted as giving legitimacy to both secession and slavery, in the name of "fighting for freedom" (a strange juxtaposition, to be sure). But when in response to his statement the first black female United States Senator, Carol Moseley-Braun of Illinois, noted simply that the Confederacy he was celebrating was built on slavery, Buchanan responded that she was just "putting on an act."

Buchanan's formulation on the nature of the War was contrary to the position taken by most pre and post-Fascist Period historians from President Lincoln (see his Second Inaugural Address) onwards down to our own time. In that view, the First Civil War was primarily fought over the institution of slavery and the desire of the Southern states to extend it into the territories, without limitation.

Buchanan appeared to present the slaveholders' position on the War, and by implication their justification of slavery: that blacks constituted an "inferior race." In reversing the Constitutional sequelae of the Civil War, the 34th Amendment put back into the Constitution the original formulation that a black person was the equivalent of three-fifths of a white, the baldest kind of racist concept.

The motivation for this? To maintain its power, Right-Wing Reaction needed to maintain the "Politics of Difference" (Sklar; see Chapter 4). The homophobia regenerated by the previous year's Proclamation of Right was already wearing thin because there just weren't enough homosexual persons left out in the open to make any kind of believable enemy. But there were still plenty of blacks. It was a Right-Wing Reactionary political tradition to blame the country's troubles on the blacks. The passage of the 34th helped to recycle the hate, for the nth time in American history. It would prove very important for that reason in the next year. It would also prove important then for a legal reason.

2. The End of Due Process and Equal Protection, and Expansion of the Camp System

Conroy summarized the content of the 13th, 14th, and 15th Amendments pretty well. But whether intentionally or not, she left out a couple of important details about the 14th, details that had made major contributions to the development and maintenance of civil liberties in the old U.S. In addition to applying the due process clause to the states, the 14th defined citizenship and required the states to provide "equal protection of the law" for "any person within its jurisdiction."

The purposes and uses of the camp system created by President Pine's "Real Drug War" had long since been expanded beyond their original focus. The first major expansion was for enforcing the Constitutional ban on elective pregnancy termination following ratification of the Morality (31st) Amendment in 2005.

Since the beginning of Hague's second term in 2008, especially following repeal of the 4th Amendment that had been part of the 32nd Amendment of 2006, the camp system increasingly had been used to incarcerate certain political enemies of the Hague regime. Many were simply murdered by the Helmsmen (HM) or their less well-organized but equally violent unofficial precursors in their "Death Squad" incarnation.

Other opponents could be charged with a conventional crime, be convicted, and placed in the ever-burgeoning conventional prison system. That "crime" was usually "drug possession." Convictions were readily obtained using police-sourced "evidence," the collection and presentation of which had not been subject to 4th Amendment protections since the late Transition Era. But still other opponents were neither murdered nor confined to the conventional prison system on spurious charges and convictions. They were simply picked up by the HM and sent to the camps, much as the SS had simply picked up persons and sent them to the camps in Nazi Germany.

Forever having difficulty writing original material, the Hagueites borrowed the language of the directive that established this latter function for the camps from that of the Bosnian Serbs back in the First Bosnian Civil War of 1991-95 when they established their own camps for punitive action against Bosnian Muslims and other opponents in their territory (Gutman):

> "Local citizens are to identify and expose ringleaders and operatives of enemy and other destructive operations; the security services are to arrest subversives, criminals, and the like; they may detain certain persons in certain places, employing political isolation, in combination with other measures and procedures, including physical liquidation."

By 2010 too, the camps were becoming "home" to an increasing number of people whose "crime" was simply that they were poor. The Morality Amendment had terminated public welfare at the Federal, state, and local levels. For a time, voluntary agencies had been able to cope with some of the load. But they were now being overwhelmed.

Similar to the response to the much smaller numbers of homeless persons who had appeared following the welfare and mental health system "reforms" of the 80s and 90s, cries went up, encouraged by Right-Wing Reaction and their minions, to "get those irresponsible good-for-nothings off the streets" (where they were increasingly accumulating). Where to put them? The camps, for them functioning somewhat like the old 19th century poorhouse/workhouse system, of course.

But there were these two legal impediments to all this arbitrary imprisonment (even though the Hagueites never referred to the camps as "prisons"): the "due process" clauses of the 5th and 14th Amendments, and the "equal protection" clause of the latter. Access to the courts was difficult, of course, especially for the poor, for both economic and political reasons. But occasionally a poor person or a political prisoner made it through to that venue. The result was occasionally embarrassing or inconvenient for the regime.

By 2010, all the camps had been put under the administrative control of the HM, just as Hitler from the beginning of the Third Reich had placed control of his camps with the SS. But the HM was a Federal agency, so 5th Amendment protections, in theory at least, applied. The Federal due process clause impediment to arbitrary arrest and imprisonment was dealt with by transferring all HM functions, including the camps, to the states. That meant that the Federal courts would simply no longer be involved with such matters.

Of course, state control of the HM was on paper only. The Federal government financed their operations completely, advised the States on who was to be in charge, and provided "Federal oversight" of the program, to make sure that "the Federal taxpayers' dollars were being spent wisely." Thus, while there was the occasional bureaucratic foul-up, the Hagueites maintained real control of the HM. But for the record, Hague could maintain that "the peoples' voices," the governments of the States, were running it.

The 5th Amendment could have been repealed, of course, but to allow completely unfettered exploitation of natural resources the Hagueites needed to maintain its "just compensation" clause (see Chapter 14). Therefore, they just left the 5th Amendment in place and made the due process clause functionally inoperative in reference to the HM. Then, with the 34th, the requirements for *state* due process and equal protection were simply wiped out. The HM, technically under state control, could operate without any judicial impedimenta. All nice and legal, just as on paper it had been in Nazi Germany (Deighton).

Although there is still some controversy among historians on this question, it is likely that Hague's primary motive for passage of the 34th Amendment was repeal of these two critical civil liberties clauses of the 14th, that is, due process and equal protection of the law. At any rate, removing the 14th Amendment from the Constitution played a very important role in the process that lead to the formation of the New American Republics, as we will see in the next chapter.

An Alex Poughton Letter

April 19, 2010

Dear Karl,

Today is "Patriot's Day" in the state of Massachusetts (one of only four states not to ratify the 34th Amendment, about which I presume you have heard by now). Although the true meaning of the event has been lost on most people (as for the rest, the day is redolent with irony), they still commemorate the 1775 Revolutionary War Battle of Lexington on this day here.

They're still running the Boston Marathon too, for the 114th time today. I'm up here to cover the "social aspects" of it for the *Sunday Times*. "Social aspects," ha! I'm not allowed to mention that there haven't been any foreign runners allowed in it for four years, or that because of that, the men's winner likely will be someone who doesn't get below 2:15, while the winner in a rapidly dwindling women's field (the result of the repeal of all Federal requirements for equal treatment of women's sports a few years ago) probably won't break 2:35.

It's all getting to be so hollow. God, I wonder what the Adams cousins would think if they came back today. Or Crispus Attucks. Or Paul Revere. Or the men who died at Breed's Hill.

It's all so sad. I still think that despite the public face the Hague regime (I just can't bring myself privately to call them a "government" or "Administration" anymore) puts on things, the majority of Americans really don't approve of what is happening to their country, a la Germany at the time the Nazis took over. That is a guess, of course, and perhaps a wishful one. But I think it's true. Everyone except the ACNP *actives* is just so apathetic.

This whole business just kind of crept up on the Americans. And it's all been legal, of course. The Right won all these elections with ever-dwindling voter turnouts, but they won them. The Democrats were just so concerned with "me-tooing" all over the place, and the left could never get out of its own way. So, as I've said before, there was just no significant opposition.

And then the Right just changed the Constitution in ways they had, for the most part, told everyone they would do if they ever got power. And they wrote the laws they told everyone, for the most part, they would write. And now they've got the "HM" to put entirely "legal" force and violence behind the whole thing.

And they are loading up the racist cannon again. I wonder what's coming next. I don't think anything could surprise me, but you never know.

All the best,
Alex

References:

Barton, D., *The Myth of Separation*, Aledo, TX: Wallbuilder Press, 1993.

Bork, R.H., "The Senate's Power Grab," *The New York Times*, June, 23, 1993.

Calloway, C., *The 34th Amendment: Motives Real and Imagined*, New York: The Scattered Home Press, 2043.

Deighton, L., *Winter*, "1933 1938," New York: Ballantine Books, 1987.

EXTRA! Update, "News Briefs: The Noble South," October, 1993, p. 2, quoting from a P. Buchanan article that appeared in the *New York Post* on July 28, 1993.

Falwell, J., "The United States of America: Still One Nation Under God," Faith Partners, Old Time Gospel Hour, Lynchburg, VA, 1994.

Gutman, R., "Federal Army Tied to Bosnia Crimes," *Newsday*, November 1, 1995.

Heard, A., "The Road to Oklahoma City," *The New Republic*, May 15, 1995, p. 15.

Johnson, B., "Freedom Bound promotional material," Nevada City, California Republic USA: 1995.

Niven, J., "Secession," in Foner, E., and Garraty, J.A., Eds., T*he Reader's Companion to American History*, Boston, MA: Houghton Mifflin Co., 1991.

NLJ: National Liberty Journal, "Conservative Book Club advertisement for *Basic American Government*, by Clarence B. Carson, April, 1995, p. 16.

Reynolds, W.B., "Power to the People," *The New York Times Magazine*, September 13, 1987.

Sklar, H., "The Snake Oil of Scapegoating," *Z Magazine, May*, 1995, p. 49.

CHAPTER 13

2011: The Declaration of Peace and the Establishment of The New American Republics

Presidential Decree No. 2: The Declaration of Peace (Monday, July 4, 2011)[1]

My fellow citizens. For many years, following in the footsteps of our great Republican forebears, the most perceptive leaders of our movement have been telling us that ours is a nation at war with itself, that we have been engaged in a civil war without knowing it, that it is a civil war in which those of us who believe in God and the best of American values have been engaged in a struggle to defend those very values against the dark forces of evil.

Many of us have not wanted to believe those words. I must admit to you that I have not wanted to believe them myself. For we are traditionally a people of people of peace, a kind, gentle people, as our Lord Jesus Christ has taught us to be. And our Party has followed in that tradition. Every step we have taken in the decade we have been in power for the sake of the Lord has been aimed at amelioration of those conditions which have made some of our fellow countrymen less than happy.

1. *Author's Note:* There is no indication or evidence that Keith Fournier, Michael Levin, Charles Murray, Rupert Murdoch, William Kristol, Minister Louis Farrakhan, Minister Khallid Abdul Muhammed, Minister Conrad Muhammed, Timothy McVeigh, or any other individual or organization mentioned or alluded to in this chapter or elsewhere in this book in a similar manner, would have supported or approved in any way of the creation of the New American Republics, its structure or function, or of any of the events that subsequently occurred in them or elsewhere as a result of NAR policies and programs.

But now, my fellow citizens, it pains me to tell you that I have come to the conclusion that we have failed, and I have been wrong. I should assure you that we have not failed through any lack of effort on our part. Rather we have failed because the methods we have so far used to address the problem we face cannot solve it.

We are in a civil war[2] and those of us who believe in God and the American Way are losing. But I can tell you that with God's blessing neither I, your President, nor the American Christian Nation Party that I lead, are going to allow defeat to overtake us.

To solve any problem, you first must know its cause. Long and deep analysis, in consultation with the political and religious leaders of our Party, has lead me to conclude that the principal cause of all our troubles, for members of all the races of the United States—and it pains me to say this—is race-mixing. Having people of different races live together, go to school together, work

---

2. *Author's Note:* This was the standard rhetoric of Right-Wing Reaction going back to the Transition Era. No matter how much influence and then power they amassed, no matter how dominant they became in the political and cultural arenas (see Chapter 15), they always portrayed themselves as on the losing side, as the underdogs, as downtrodden and misunderstood (Dionne; Kristol; Porteous). At the same time they portrayed themselves as always righteous and destined by God to be ultimately victorious, if not before, then certainly at the Rapture foretold by the Biblical Book of Revelation.

For example, no matter how much Right-Wing Reactionary talk and religious radio and television there was, in their presentation of reality the "media" were always totally and unalterably "against us." No matter how many Christian churches there were to be found, in every corner of every community large and small across the nation, Christians, according to the leadership of the Religious Right, Protestant and Catholic alike (Fournier, 1995) were always being "persecuted" and "kept from the public square," that is if attempts were not being made to banish religion from American life altogether (Fournier, 1993).

They attained much influence and ultimately power, within the old Republican Party and its successors. They eventually took over the Federal government. But no matter. They always cast themselves as having to endlessly struggle to get any political attention at all, much less power, in a "hostile environment," just as Hague said at this time.

together, especially when one race has to bear financial and spiritual burdens created by the other races, simply does not work. I know that many of you will understand what I am saying, and will agree with what I am saying.

Years ago, the liberals who have done so much damage to America and the American way of life tried to convince us all that we live in what they called in their own peculiar way of speaking, a "multicultural society," that all the races in America had value and contributions to make, that there was no single, dominant, Right, way of thinking and doing for Americans.

They tried to change our educational system, our cultural institutions, our basic values. They even tried to rewrite our history. But we know better. There is a Right Way. It is the Christian, White Way. And the other ways are wrong.

The liberals succeeded in none of what they were after, thank the Lord. We know who settled this country. We know who this country belongs to. We know who God made this country for. He made it for us. And with us it will remain.

We also know that God made two kinds of men: smart ones, and not-so-smart ones. We know, from the work of those great scientists Arthur Jensen, Sir Cyril Burt, William Schockley, Michael Levin, Charles Murray, and Richard Herrnstein (Naureckas), that the Negro is simply the genetic inferior of the white man[3]. We know this too from the Word of God in the Bible. Both science and the Bible tell us that this is true. Need I say more? Can anyone doubt the truth of what I say?

We are the smart ones. As for the others, well, they are the ones who are not-so-smart. When you mix smart

3. *Author's Note:* Notes for an essay by Dino Louis (apparently never written) on the "science" underlying the theory of "black genetic inferiority" can be found in Appendix VI.

and not-so-smart, what do you get? Nothing good. You pull the smart down, but you don't raise the not-so-smart up. And that is what has happened here in our great nation. For all our efforts, we and our kind are still being pulled down, held back, and retarded, by them. And they have become utterly dependent on us. That is good neither for us nor for them. That is the source of the conflict which is so harmful to both us and them.

We tried, ladies and gentlemen, we tried to create a color blind society all these years (Raskin), a society in which no man would be given any advantage over any other man, by the law. You know we have tried. And you know how hard we have tried. But our efforts have been in vain. We have learned along the hard way that neither the white man nor the Negro can be happy if they try to live together.

And so my friends, finally, the solution has become clear. Racial separation is what we need, both to lift that unfair and unwanted burden off the white man's shoulders, and to give the Negro the chance to prove, to himself, to us, and to the world, that indeed if left alone, if given the chance, if removed from his dependency state, he can make it on his own, that, in the final analysis, he does not need the white man, any more than we want him.

As the great Alexander Stephens, Vice President of the Confederate States of America, once said (Cole): "Our new government is founded on the opposite idea of equality of the races. Its cornerstone rests upon the great truth that the Negro is not equal to the white man."

Therefore, on this 235th Anniversary of the original Declaration of Independence, I declare the independence from each other of the four major American races: we Whites, the Negroes, the Indians, and the Hispanics.

By the power vested in me by Section 6 of the 32nd Amendment to the Constitution of the United States, I hereby decree a Special National Emergency in the matter of race mixing. With this power, I hereby issue a Declaration of Peace between the races. I declare an end to this cultural civil war we have all been living with for the past two decades or more.

To achieve this Peace that we all desire from the very bottom of our hearts, I decree the establishment of a new structure for our national government, under the framework of our Constitution. Following the required Constitutional procedures, this decree has already been approved by each House of Congress[4]. The Congress has also voted to adjourn indefinitely, most generously giving me the authority to call it back into session the moment that proves necessary.

I call our new national structure The New American Republics, the NAR, under the Constitution of the United States. There will be four such Republics: the White Republic, the Negro Republic, the Indian Republic, and the Hispanic Republic.

---

4. *Author's Note:* Hague was being somewhat disingenuous here. He claimed he was acting under the provisions of the old U.S. Constitution. And technically he was. But, he had decreed nothing more nor less than the end of the old United States, hardly a routine matter, even if done "constitutionally."

Further, when the requisite simple majority of the members voting was recorded on the evening of July 3, there was barely a quorum in each House, and the Capitol was ringed by members of one of the elite Helmsmen units, the Hawks' Heads. Even some of the most loyal members of the ACNP delegation in the Congress had some doubts about what Hague was doing in this instance. Although there is no record of any public disapproval, apparently there was a significant amount of private disapproval. It was even said that the word "dictatorship" was bandied about. But mouths were either kept or forced to remain shut.

The National Emergency decreed by Hague ultimately came to an end only upon the occasion of the collapse of his regime at the end of the Second Civil War. But until that time, Hague maintained that what was in essence an internal coup d'état had all been undertaken "lawfully." To be sure, fully in accordance with the requirements of Section 6 of the 32nd Amendment, Hague renewed his declaration of National Emergency every 60 days for the balance of his rule, the last renewal coming just three days before the fall of New Washington on March 17, 2022.

Periodically, Hague called the Congress back from adjournment to enact specific pieces of legislation he wanted. It never did test its rescission authority under the 32nd.

The White Republic, as is our due and our just desserts [*sic*], shall consist of most of the territory of the contiguous 48 states. Certain urban areas shall constitute the territory of the Negro Republic. The Indian Republic shall consist of the territory of certain present Indian Reservations which lie to the west of the Mississippi River. The Hispanic Republic shall consist of certain territories south of the Rio Grand [sic] River which choose to join our new confederation.

I am pleased to note especially that we are finally making good on the pledge to our Indian friends that was contained in the Northwest Ordinance of 1787 (Campbell, p. 168):

> "The utmost good faith shall always be observed toward the Indians, their lands and property shall never be taken from them without their consent; and in their property, rights, and liberty, they shall never be invaded or disturbed, unless in just and lawful wars authorized by congress; but laws founded in justice and humanity shall from time to time be made, for preventing wrongs being done to them, and for preserving peace and friendship with them."[5]

For the duration of this National Emergency, I decree that the authority of the state legislatures is suspended. The state Governors, reporting to me, will rule directly[6].

5. *Author's Note:* The irony neither of the original statement nor of Hague's use of it need be commented upon.

6. *Author's Note:* As to the state governors, now ruling directly like he was, Hague made sure, in one way or another, that each was personally loyal to him. In the early days of the NAR, not all of the Governors were entirely on board. But there were three unexplained deaths among the Governors (two of them lukewarm in their support of Hague, the other, one of his most vigorous supporters). Things then quieted down.

Congress has endorsed that decree. The authority of the State legislatures shall be restored when the present National Emergency comes to an end. The territories of the Negro, Indian, and Hispanic Republics shall be self-governing[7]. Further, I decree the suspension of the 22nd Amendment to the Constitution of the United States and declare that next year I shall be standing once again as a candidate for the Presidency of the United States.

Ladies and gentlemen, my fellow American citizens under God. We face difficult times. Some would describe them as tough times. But as our great forebear, President Richard Milhous Nixon, once said: "When the going gets tough, the tough go shopping." No, I mean "the tough get going."

We are tough, you and I. And we are underway. Once we realized, finally, with the help of Almighty God and the spirit of his only Son, Jesus, just what is and who are holding our country back, the course we must follow, as painful as it may be for some, became clear. And that is the course upon which we are embarking today.

With your help, with your faith, with your trust in God, and with God's trust in us, we will, we shall, we must succeed. Thank you, God bless you, and good night.

A Curley Oakwood Radio Broadcast Transcript (July 5, 2011)

It is a glorious day, my friends, a glorious day. As we look back on what is truly American about the Glorious Fourth, our barbecues and parades, our speeches and our marching bands, our hearts swelling with the pride of true American patriots, ladies and gentlemen, across the fruited plain we can celebrate

7. *Author's Note*: In the beginning, the disparate units of the Negro and Indian Republics were "self-governing" in name only. Puppet governments much like those of the "Bantustans" of the old apartheid South Africa were established. The gradual displacement of those regimes would occur later (see Chapter 15).

this event, the founding of the New American Republics as the one, the one event above all the other great achievements of President Jefferson Davis Hague and the American Christian Nation Party that is going to move our country to God's City on the Hill[8].

As you know, when our beloved President first took office in 2004 our country was in a terrible mess: inflation, crime, the niggers, spics, and slant-eyes taking over everything, taxes on the honest white working man going out of sight, the Democrat liberal nigger lovers in Congress giving away your hard-earned dollars.

Since that time President Hague has labored long and hard to clean up the mess. While his efforts have met with considerable success, they have not met with as much success as he would like. The influence of the liberal nigger lovers, of the Democrat Party (may it not rest in peace), of the Counter-Culture elite, the New Deal, and the nigger-loving Old Reconstructionists, are still with us[9]. As the President so eloquently said, race mixing and all our attempts to build a truly colorblind society just haven't worked. Indeed, as our President has shown us, they can't work, because of the mental inferiority of the Negro.

8. *Author's Note*: "City on the Hill" was a meaningless phrase borrowed, without attribution, from the extensive collection of such rhetoric left behind by that Right-Wing Reactionary patron saint, Ronald Reagan.

9. *Author's Note*: It is fascinating that at this late date, the Right-Wing Reactionaries were still trying to blame everything on political organizations, policies, and movements that were long since dead. But in doing so they were simply following the previously noted pattern laid down during the Transition Era. As a 1995 advertising brochure for the Transition Era magazine *The Weekly Standard*, published by one of the arch Right-Wing Reactionaries of the time, Rupert Murdoch, and edited by another, William Kristol, said (1995): "From the New Deal ... to the Great Society ... affirmative action ... to the welfare system ... the deficit ... to defense cuts ... liberals have made America what it is today."

It is fascinating too to note that Oakwood had by now included the post-First Civil War Reconstruction leadership in the Pantheon of left and liberal historic devils supposedly responsible for all that was wrong with his contemporary America. He was careful to distinguish that leadership from the "*Christian* Reconstructionists" upon whom the Hagueites depended so much for their theology.

J.D. Hague and the American Christian Nation Party, blessed be they by God, had the guts to say out loud what everybody knows: the real cause of all our dissatisfaction, of our anger, of our frustration, is the Negro. We just must be separated from him.

And now in his infinite wisdom, guided by the hand of God, our Mr. Jeff has established the New American Republics. We are, if I may presume to borrow an old saying, going to be free at last. And in their own way, the niggers will be, too[10]. As for the Spics, they will be dealt with soon. But, and may I say it, may I, with your graceful permission, stick it in the liberal nigger lovers' craw—sorry about that, just really sorry about that. It is not too soon for the celebration to begin.

A Connie Conroy Note (July 7, 2011)

Well, well, well, the Prez has outdone himself this time. It's a biggie. There is even some whispering going on around the White House. Is he really going to get away with this one? After all, they say, he says it's all Constitutional, but what he

10. *Author's Note:* There was a certain element of black nationalist leadership which had survived from the Transition Era that was very happy with this turn of events: the so-called Black Separatists. They took their cue from certain Transition Era black separatist leaders. For example, Minister Conrad Muhammed of Minister Louis Farrakhan's Nation of Islam had once upon a time said that the old United States should set up separate black areas, and (1993): "[G]ive us the machines and tools we need, and give us 25 years to 'make it.' If we don't make it in 25 years, then you can come in and mow us down with machine guns".

The next year, Nation of Islam Minister Khallid Abdul Muhammed said (Rosenbaum): "We have a right to seek a nation of our own. White people have a nation. We have a right to freedom and independence. We don't want to rule you. That would be racist. We don't want to oppress you. We just want to be left alone."

And in 1995 the Nation of Islam said (Ness): "We want our people in America whose parents or grandparents were descendant from slaves, to be allowed to establish a separate state or territory of their own—either on this continent or elsewhere. We believe that our former slave masters are obligated to provide such land and that the area must be fertile and minerally rich."

The new black separatist leadership of course did not get the latter, but they did get power—for a brief period.

really has done is set up a new country and put himself in as, dare I say it, dictator.

Well, yeah. That's all true. But it's also true that it's all constitutional, the way we got the Constitution to be written. It's all legal. We won all those critical elections, local, state, and Federal, fair and square. We amended the Constitution fair and square too. If you look back, you can see how this brilliant guy got to here, one careful step at a time.

As for the country, is there anything else he could have done, really? Things are getting bad, really. Thank God we don't publish the numbers anymore, but unemployment continues to go up. The rich, who just love us, get ever richer, but there are more and more poor. Self-responsible or not, there are just more of them, of all colors. The camps are starting to fill up, I hear.

And so then what happens. Challenges to our authority. The HM tells us there's lots of challenges to our authority, sometimes more than they can handle under the current setup. Sometimes, even some niggers and spics have gotten together to make trouble with some renegade whites, and not old-fashioned liberal nigger lovers either, but supposedly our kind of whites. Complaining about jobs, or wages, or health care, or the condition of the roads, or prices of things, or about education for their kids. That's dangerous. Something had to be done. So the Prez did it.

Will it work? The geeks on the other side have forever accused us of playing what they call the "race card" whenever we get into trouble. Well you know something? We would never in a million years admit it, but they're right. And why not? It's worked hasn't it? Dick did it, and Ron did it, and our Jesse, and Newt, and Carney, and the Prez himself, like with last year's Original Intent Amendment. They all did it. And it's nothing to be ashamed of, if you've got God on your side. And we do have that. So now we're just playing the race card on a bit of a grander scale, that's all. It's going to work, I'm sure of it.

Race-mixing's the cause of all our troubles, the Prez sez, so ending it is the cure. And we're going to learn something from the old South Africa too, before it tragically went the other way 20 years ago. Well, the Prez sez, a group of retired ex-South African security officers he's brought in to help us design our new system have told him if he wants to make this set up work he must do one thing very differently from the way they did it.

They let blacks work in the white areas, even though they couldn't live in them. That, our South African friends tell us, was a critical factor in the downfall of the old regime. Some whites got kind of comfortable with blacks, seeing them around every day and all that. And blacks started to get educated and emboldened by being around whites and seeing that they could get along alright. So we're not going to make the same mistake. We're going to keep the races completely separate. The Niggers and the Redskins simply won't be able to get out of their Republics.

To do that trick, the Prez is talking about putting in some real hightech fences that he says have to be seen to be believed. Course we'll still be able to work the niggers all right. We're going to set up Enterprise Zones right on their borders. But nobody's going to be able to get out of, or into, them either.

The Prez did give me some fun stuff to work on for this one, like our new flag. It's a symbol everyone in the country, White or inferior, will understand the meaning of. It's based on the good old Stars and Bars of the CSA [*Author's Note:* Confederate States of America].[11] The colors are, of course, red, white, and blue. We just made a couple of little modifications.

Rather than having 11 stars, one for each of the old Confederate States, in each of the four arms of the "X" formed by the bars there is one star, each one standing for one of the four New American Republics, the three we've got now and the one we will have soon.

To symbolize our devotion to God in the NAR, at the center of the "X" we have placed the symbol of the agony, devotion,

11. *Author's Note:* Even during the Transition Era, it was noted that (Sack): "As a symbol of enduring racial tensions in the South [and elsewhere the observer might have noted], the Confederate battle flag is waving just as strongly as ever."

and sacrifice of our Lord, Jesus Christ. So we're connected in all ways to the very best of our past. The "X" in a square, with the Cross at its center, taken from the flag, has become the militant symbol of our Party[12].

Author's Commentary
Jefferson Davis Hague, the Constitution and Power: Repealing the Old Constitution

The Hagueites had just functionally repealed the Constitution of the old United States. Once they had consolidated their power, they also soon suspended the constitutions of each of the 50

---

12. *Author's Note:* There was a great deal of controversy over the choice of the NAR/ACNP symbol. It reflected the two main historical streams that had joined together form the ACNP. They were the Christian Right and the old Republican Party that during the Transition Era had become ever more "Southern-based" (Lind, a). But, reflecting the Rightward Imperative to which American Right-Wing Reaction had been subject for over two decades, the militant Far Right, represented by such groups as the Aryan Nations and the newly formed Militias for Christ, became more and more important in the American Christian Nation Party. This was especially so with the growth in the size, power, and authority of the Helmsmen.

Many of these militant Far Right groups used some variation of the old German Nazi Swastika as their symbol. They clamored for its adoption by the NAR, the ACNP, or at least the HM. But Hague was nothing if not astute. He realized early on that too many of his supporters had fathers or grandfathers who had fought in World War II against German Nazism.

In fact, many Right-Wing Reactionary leaders had managed a neat trick over the years. On the one hand, they were promoting fascist ideas, for example in the areas of controlling human behavior and political expression by legal means backed up by force. On the other, they often loudly declaimed that liberal opponents of, say, hate speech, were "behaving like Nazis." Also, while many non Far Right Hague supporters were anti-Semitic to a greater or lesser extent, they still linked the swastika and the Nazis with evil. Also, Hague knew how important Right-Wing Reactionary Jews had been to his success. He needed to be sure that he kept them on board.

Some of Hague's advisors tried to convince him that thinking that the German Nazis were evil was just liberal and/or Jewish propaganda (*The W.A.R. Eagle*). But he never bought that argument. Thus even though many of his policies were indistinguishable from those of Nazi Germany, just as mainstream Right-Wing Reaction had done during the Transition Era he stayed as far away from any symbolic or stated association with overt Nazism as he could.

states, again using the Presidential decree authority, in combination with, of all things, the Federal supremacy clause, a clause they had taken many whacks at in the cause of constitutional litigation during the Transition Era. They made much of the fact that they had done all this using constitutional means. Of course, in practice the NAR was no more Constitutionalist than the 20th century Soviet Union was Communist. But the whole process looked good on paper.

There was some scattered resistance following the promulgation of the Hague decree, and several thousand people, mainly non-whites, would be killed around the country during the upcoming "Relocations." This was mainly the result of HM activity, not any organized military actions. They were few and far between. In that wise, then, this coup was similar, for example, to the American-backed coup in Chile in 1973 that had overthrown the democratically elected government of Salvador Allende Gossens, and the earlier American-backed coup in Brazil that in 1964 had overthrown the democratically elected government of Joao Goulart.

But of course this coup was not against an elected President, but by one against the constitution under which he had been elected. That it was relatively bloodless was a measure of the demoralization and weakness of the opposition, a weakness Right-Wing Reaction had so carefully worked to nurture over the years. Despite the relative lack of military-level violence, however, with the "Declaration of Peace," on his own Jefferson Davis Hague had declared all-out war on all the non-white and some of the white inhabitants of the old United States.[13] Thus the coup was very violent in terms of individuals. As had happened in Germany both at the beginning and throughout the Hitlerite terror, many, many people were detained without

13. *Author's Note:* It should be noted that defining precisely what was meant by "non-white" would come to present some serious problems for Hague and his American Christian Nation Party, just as it had for the German Nazis and the South African apartheid racists. "Scientific racism" (see Appendix V) had glossed over that problem, but the Hagueites had to deal with it in practice. L. Armstrong's book (2042) is widely regarded as the best review on the subject.

charges, "investigated," and then confined to the camps for an indefinite term without trial. Within a short ten years, the bill for Hague's war on the American people would come due, and would be paid for with the blood of many Americans, of all colors, classes, and ethnic groups[14].

The concentration of power in the hands of the Federal Executive Branch was begun by the Republican Richard Nixon and amplified by the Republicans Ronald Reagan and George Bush (Lind, b). Brought to the next higher level by the Last Republican, President Carnathon Pine, under Jefferson Davis Hague, first of the Republican-Christian Alliance, now of the American Christian Nation Party, the process had been completed.

Military Considerations

As alluded to above, the physical creation of the NAR was done with surprising speed and efficiency, and met with little organized resistance. It was extremely well planned, in utter secrecy even though thousands of people were involved. This sort of thing was not unusual in the old U.S. For example, the old Federal Bureau of Investigation and the Central Intelligence Agency had managed to keep a great deal of their work secret even in a supposedly "open" society (see, e.g., Cook), even though they had many thousands of employees.

Militarily, Hague had firmly on his side the Helmsmen and most of those militias that had chosen to remain independent of the HM. Together this force totaled about 1.3 million men. In the military itself, there were many officers and enlisted men who were entirely sympathetic to the Hagueites, growing from the nuclei of Right-Wing Reactionary service people that

14. *Author's Note:* Many books have been written about the events surrounding the establishment of the New American Republics and the institution of outright fascism in the old U.S. In my view, the best of these is the recently published *The Domino Theory: American Fascism, Real and Imagined* by my colleague F. Domino here at the Middletown campus of the New State University of New York. For an alternative view, written closer in time to the Fascist Period by one who lived through it as an adult, see *The Rise and Decline of Fascism in the United States* by O. Gibbons.

had existed during the Transition Era (Gleick). Also, most of the white-dominated, thoroughly racist, local police forces came right over to the NAR.

From the Transition Era through the early Fascist Period, the American military had remained the most racially integrated major "corporation" in the old United States. However, during the six months prior to the issuance of the Declaration of Peace, the Hagueite forces within the military quietly established a series of all-white or nearly all-white elite units (such as the one the first suspect arrested in the infamous Oklahoma City bombing of 1995, Timothy McVeigh, had belonged to when he was in the Army [Gleick]).

The Hagueites had secretly transferred to these units the lion's share of heavy weapons, while quietly removing same from the units that had remained integrated, usually on the excuse of "for repairs, maintenance, or upgrading." By secret order of the Secretary of Defense, the Air Force and Navy had been placed under the control of "sympathetic" officers.

Thus those members of the mostly non-white units in the armed services who did try to resist the establishment of the NAR were for the most part easily disarmed, demobilized, and deported. These actions were carried out by the newly formed white units within the armed forces, the HM, and the militias. Given the preponderance of firepower on the Hagueite side, and the general rationality of the non-white troops, there were surprisingly few casualties on either side. Some of the demobilized non-white troops would become the armed forces for the NAR puppet governments in the Negro and Indian Republics. Others would eventually form the core of the future Resistance forces.

Hague in Charge

In this environment, by issuing his decrees and finding no significant or effective opposition to their implementation, Hague showed who was in charge of the country: himself. Not the Constitution, although he bowed vigorously in its direction, not the Congress, certainly not the courts, long since made irrelevant by *Anderson v. Board of Education* (see Chapter 5), and neither God nor the churchmen.

In regard of the latter, it is interesting to note that neither Hague nor the Congress had ever once used the "Law of God" powers granted to them by the Supremacy Amendment (see Chapter 9). For Hague, they looked good on paper. But attempting to invoke them would almost certainly have required consultation with theological authority, something Hague was absolutely loathe to do.

Hague was a careful user of power. The decree under which he established the New American Republics was only the second he had issued under the authority of the 32nd Amendment in the five years of its existence (the first having been the Proclamation of Right, criminalizing homosexuality). But he also liked to keep power to himself. While he had ridden the Christian Right's political might to what had become full authority over the nation, he had no intention of sharing any of it with that group he privately called, as previously noted, "those fucking preachers." Hague was in charge and he intended to remain in charge.

THE WHY AND THE WHAT

Constitutional Democracy

Why and What are the two critical questions to be answered in understanding this most momentous of events in the history of the old United States: its destruction by technically Constitutional means. What is the essence of Constitutional Democracy? Nothing more, or less, than the Rule of Law, embedded in a set of special laws called a constitution, designed among other things to preserve and enhance the democratic process.

By the mutual consent of the governed and the governors, a constitution is endowed with a high degree of permanence, although in order to deal with changing times and circumstances, it must be amendable. It is designed to stand above the less enduring law enacted by legislatures and laid down by the courts. Indeed, a constitution determines the broad guidelines within which legislative and judicial law is to be made. However, constitutions must be capable of change, both by interpretation and formal amendment. The experience of the old U.S. showed that, as has ours under our Restored Constitution. However, Right-Wing Reaction in the old U.S. also showed that a constitution can be used to destroy itself.

The NAR and the Constitution

Now then, what did Right-Wing Reaction, as personified by one Jefferson Davis Hague, do upon the establishment of the New American Republics? They substituted lock, stock, and barrel of the gun, the rule of men for the rule of law, while all the time claiming that everything they were doing was legal and Constitutional (just as Hitler and the German Nazis had done when they took over state power [Deighton]). And, to repeat, technically the Hagueites were right.

The preservation of real constitutional democracy requires the determined, continued, vigilant, principled, intelligent, alert, participation in that act of the masses of the people. There also must be a leadership devoted to the democratic process, dedicated to the preservation of constitutional democracy (as was the Leadership Council of our own Movement for the Restoration of Constitutional Democracy [see Chapter 19]), concerned with the economic and social interests of all the people of the country, and equipped to carry out its responsibilities. As noted, those conditions were not met in the old United States. In analyzing this national catastrophe, we shall first review why the Hagueites did what they did and then what in fact they did.

THE WHY

1. The Conditions. Life for most Americans continued to worsen during the second Hague Presidency, as noted by such observers as Conroy herself. Continuing the pattern established during the late Transition Era that continued as noted previously through the early fascist period, the gap between rich and poor widened further, and the standard of living for most Americans continued to decline, although the gap had become so large that the rate of decline was slowing. As deindustrialization/computerization/robotization reached a peak, both immediate employment opportunities and long term career prospects for many Americans became ever more grim. In response to all of this, there was increasing labor unrest, racial unrest, unrest among the ever increasing number of poor, accompanied and exaggerated by an increasing level of violence perpetrated by the Helmsmen.

2. The "Solutions". None of the "solutions to the nation's problems" introduced by the Republicans, the Republican-Christian Alliance, or the Hagueites over the years had ever worked. Consecutively, as noted by Alex Poughton in his letter of December 31, 2008 (see Chapter 10), it had been "if we just fix (*blank*), then the nation will be on the right track." They got what they wanted in the constitution and the law, from Congressional Term Limits through the outlawing of elective termination of pregnancy to repeal of the 14th Amendment. Each of these moves, or some magic combination of them together, was always supposed "to put things right," "to reverse half a century of liberal-inspired national decline," "to clean the evil out of the stables of the Lord." But the national course continued to spiral downhill just the same.

Why? Because, as previously noted, none of those remedies were aimed at the primary causes of the downward spiral: deindustrialization, the disaccumulation of labor around capital with computerization/robotization, export of capital, under-investment in national infrastructure, undertaxation of the wealthy and the large corporations, the resulting ever-rising gap between the rich and everyone else. Nor under a Right-Wing Reactionary regime could the remedies be expected to be aimed at the primary causes of the downward spiral.

The real problems just listed resulted from the policies of the economic interests which controlled and paid for the old

Republican Party (Nelson; Reno), the Republican-Christian Alliance, and the American Christian Nation Party in the first place. Right-Wing Reactionary governments were not about to do anything that would harm economic interests of those forces that controlled them. Indeed the "remedies" those governments implemented were designed precisely to distract the public from paying any attention to the real causes of national problems. However, as also previously noted, when the strategy that had been so successful for so long no longer worked, the only answer was the NAR and fascism (see Appendix II).

3. *The New Factor.* As noted, from the beginning of Hague's second term, Right-Wing Reaction considered the newly developing alliances between white and black workers to be quite dangerous. Most historians now agree that the murders back in the 1960s of the then two great black leaders, Martin Luther King, Jr. and Malcolm X, had occurred because they were beginning to introduce economic arguments into their political strategies, and beginning, just beginning at that early date, to appeal across the color line to similarly affected white workers.

With continually worsening living conditions under the Hague regime, this sort of thing was happening again, even without any national leadership. The potential for an effective black-white alliance was the real threat perceived by the ACNP and the economic forces they represented. And with whites evermore suffering economically from the economic policies of Right-Wing Reaction, in certain quarters the effectiveness of the traditional race card was beginning to wear thin.

After the First Civil War the former slaveholders in the South had worked very hard to forcefully repress the newly freed slaves and physically and psychologically separate them from their natural allies among the poor white farmers. That was one of the primary reasons for the institution of racial segregation in the post-First Civil War South of the old U.S.

Listen to a fictional reconstruction, considered to be historically accurate, of a speech given by an organizer for the Ku Klux Klan in the South during the First Reconstruction (Fast, 1947, pp. 93-94):

> "A few acts, a nigger put in his place, a rape scare, a lynching—those will come about naturally; and when they come the Klan can ride. … We strike—with force, force and terror; because force and terror are the only two things that can decide the issue. … The Klan will smash this thing that has arisen. … The nigger will be a slave, again, as he has been, as he is destined to be. Yes, he will fight—but he will not be organized for terror, for force, and we will be. Some white men will fight on his side; fear and the badge of a white skin will take care of that."

At this critical juncture in American history, Right-Wing Reaction needed to physically separate working-class whites and blacks, as well as reinforce white racism once again, so as to make resistance more difficult. The creation of the NAR accomplished this end. Right-Wing Reaction also very cleverly created a cover that conveniently served as a bone for both White and Black separatist supporters of the ACNP.

4. Support for Race Separation. Race separation had been on the agenda of certain elements of the Republican Right, usually surreptitiously, since the rise to prominence of the well-known Republican politician David Duke of Louisiana during the Transition Era (Lee; Patriquin). The "War Between the States" rhetoric of certain Republican figures of the late Transition Era was interpreted by some as a bow in the same direction. At the time of its formation, the ACNP had incorporated many Far Right organizations which were frankly racial separationist (Peterson; Reiss; Van Biema).

As one of them, the National Alliance, put it (Ness):

> "After the sickness of 'multiculturalism,' which is destroying America, Britain, and every other Aryan nation in which it is being promoted, has been swept away, we must again have a racially clean area of the earth for the further development of our people. We must have White schools, White residential neighborhoods and recreation areas, White workplaces, White farms and countryside. We must have no non-Whites in our living space, and we must have open space around us for expansion."

The ACNP had counted heavily on these groups in forming the Helmsmen, and for providing additional extra-"legal" armed assistance to the Helmsmen in the military actions undertaken in establishing the NAR. Formal separation met the demands of all of these groups and interests. So it had an internal political, as well as external political motivation. The Rightward Imperative continued to work its devilish influence on the descendant of the old Republican Party.

THE WHAT

The Physical Division of the Nation

The prime components of the Negro Republic were: the New York City boroughs of Brooklyn and The Bronx; Newark, NJ; the "North End" of Philadelphia, PA; the predominately black Wards, 1, 4, 5, 6, 7, and 8, of Washington, D.C.; Charleston, SC; the "Liberty City" section of Miami, FL; Atlanta, GA; Mobile, AL; Memphis, TN; Hattiesburg, MS; East St. Louis, IL; the "South Side" of Chicago, IL; Gary, IN; Detroit, MI; Omaha, NB; Beaumont, TX; the "South Central" and Watts sections of Los Angeles, CA; and Oakland, CA.

Certain rural areas of the South with high concentrations of blacks were also designated as part of the Negro Republic. All blacks not already living in a community so designated were within one month forcibly moved to the one nearest to their former home, in a violent and ruthless process that came to be known as the "Relocations." Certain other communities were later added to the Negro Republic. However, none were ever established in New England (with the exception of the "Paradise Ghetto" on Martha's Vineyard, MA, named after the infamous German Nazi show concentration camp, Theresienstadt [Davidowicz, p. 137]), the Rocky Mountain States, or the Pacific Northwest.

Within 24 hours of Hague's Declaration, in an operation that had been secretly and meticulously planned over several months, the designated areas had been temporarily enclosed with hundreds of miles of high voltage passive electrified fences. Within a few months following the Declaration of Peace, most of the permanent, early model, proactive, computer-controlled, "killer fence" walls that made physical separation virtually absolute were erected (see Chapter 15).

All whites living in designated non-White areas were of course relocated out of them, and were given substantial financial assistance to do so. Monetary assistance took the form of payments for old homes, moving costs, and rent for temporary living quarters in the locales to which they were moved, as well as low-interest loans to help defray the costs of new homes.

This assistance also took the form of property taken from blacks and Amerindians living in various parts of the country not included in the "Negro" or "Indian" "Republics," some of those individuals quite well-off, who had been "Relocated." This followed the pattern the German Nazis had employed for disposing of stolen Jewish property both in Germany before the commencement of World War II and in the occupied territories during it.

Amerindians living to the west of the Mississippi River outside the designated reservations, and all of those living east of the River, were forcibly relocated to the designated reservations and were not given any assistance of any kind (other than transportation), to do so. For many persons so displaced, the process recalled the many forced marches to which many Amerindians had been subjected during the mass relocations of the 19th century (Brown; Fast, 1953).

Since the "Hispanic Republic" consisted of territory not at the time under the control of the NAR, LatinoAmericans not classified as "black" or "Indian" could not be moved anywhere immediately. When the NAR eventually took control of some of the designated territory in Latin America, some Latino-Americans were deported. But complete Latino separation was never achieved. They thus ended up living in parts of each of the four "Republics."

Neither were the members of the large Asian minority that had lived in the old United States segregated, in this case by design. No "Republic" was ever established for persons of Asian ancestry. And thus the strong anti-Asian prejudices of some of the ACNP's most loyal, and violent, supporters, were never satisfied. Policy towards the Asian minority was in fact left purposely vague.

First of all, even though racist-minded Whites in their heads easily lumped all persons of Asian origin together, the group was highly heterogeneous, even more so than the Latino population. It consisted not only of persons of Chinese, Korean, and Japanese origin, but also of those with ancestry hailing from the Indian sub-Continent and its environs, Southeast Asia, and the Indonesian-Philippine Archipelago.

Second of all, in regard of the Sino-Japanese origin group, the last thing the Hague Administration wanted to do was antagonize its two major trading partners, China and Japan. Hague was counting on them to stay out of his hair. And they did so (until the concluding phase of the Second Civil War, as is well known).

The major Asian nations did utter pious phrases now and then about "violence and bloodshed," and the "suppression of civil liberties," much like the West had done, for example, for four years before forcing a settlement in response to the multilevel civil war in the former Yugoslavia 20 years before, and in response to China's suppression of its own "Democracy

Movement" in 1989. But trade is trade, and for the most part the race-based dismemberment of what had been the world's foremost democracy was treated by the Asian nations as an "internal matter."

Economic Considerations

There were important potential benefits for the economic decision makers behind the formation of the NAR. Part one was the creation of a separate, truly low-paid *domestic* work force, the low-paid worker energy for the U.S. economy having been originally generated by the North American Free Trade Agreement of 1994 and its successors, and on a grander scale the worldwide export of American capital, having long since been spent. Economically, the NAR created a captive and very cheap labor force, working in sometimes almost slave-like conditions in the "Enterprise Zones" mentioned by Conroy, known colloquially as "Kempsites" (see Chapter 15).

Part two of the new economic policy was the development of a new domestic physical energy policy, to produce and export fuels cheaper than the foreign petroleum upon which the country's economy was still dependent and which was now getting to be really expensive as the end of the supply hove into historical view (see Chapters 14 and 16).

And so, after a 30 year dusk, night descended upon the old United States.

An Alex Poughton letter

July 14, 2011

Dear Karl,

In my letter to you written on Massachusetts' Patriot's Day last year, I recall saying that I didn't think anything these jokers could do could surprise me. I was wrong. On the greatest of American holidays, the one that celebrates "all men are created equal" and "endowed by their Creator" (not God—Jefferson chose his word with care, I am sure), and "certain unalienable rights," and "it is to preserve these rights that governments are instituted among men" (I'm quoting from memory, so you'll excuse me if I've got a word wrong here or there), with a stroke of the pen (and a meticulously planned, apparently almost flawlessly executed military operation), the Hagueites take it all away.

These guys do so much that is ironic, using the Constitution to destroy it, talking about free speech when without limit they are using it only to verbally assault real and imagined enemies and promote hate. Now "Declaring Peace," while literally ripping the country apart. I wonder if they ever recognize just how ironic they are. At any rate, you might note the irony that I am writing you this letter about the final end of American freedom and liberty on the day that celebrates the beginning of it in France way back when, Bastille Day. Thank God it still exists there, as well as in the cool green hills of England.

So the fascism that you heard whispered about for the last 30 years is finally and fully here. "Nacht und Nebel," Night and Fog, the German Nazis decreed for the occupied territories in Europe (Shirer, pp. 957-58). It descended with a wallop, there. But here "the fog came in on little cat feet," as the American poet-historian Carl Sandburg once wrote. It just crept up on the American people bit by bit.

Almost 20 years after apartheid was finally interred in South Africa, it was resurrected (and I chose *that* word with care) in the United States. How did this happen? It all seemed so contrary to American traditions of freedom, liberty, and openness, so, well, Un-American.

The Politics of Mythology rampant. The Constitution and especially its Preamble, after all that is what the whole enterprise was *for*, forgotten. No Democrat worth his (or her) salt. The Left paralyzed. (I don't think it ever recovered from McCarthyism.) The labor movement moribund. (It never recovered from the old Taft-Hartley Act, its own "anti-Communism" and racism, mob influence, and government interference like the infamous state "Right-to-Work" laws and support for scab labor.)

Thus no effective opposition. An apathetic electorate with

no real alternatives to the Right to vote for. Just like what the old Christian Coalition worked on years ago: "The 15% Solution" [*Author's Note*: see Chapter 2]. They *said* that would be their road to power. They counted on a declining electorate to win. God, I can remember that Far Right guru Paul Weyrich saying back in 1994, "We don't want everyone to vote. Quite frankly, our leverage goes up as the voting population goes down" (*Freedom Writer*). They didn't.

I don't know if people like Weyrich and Robertson and the Christian Coalition leadership and so forth ever had anything like this outcome in mind, but electorally "The 15% Solution" worked. The Right won. This is what they got. The wind was seeded and the American people have reaped the whirlwind.

Now, of course, there seems to be mounting opposition. But, to use an old American expression, it's a day late and a dollar short. Precisely because there is mounting opposition, they've got fascism on their hands, and in their bedrooms, their schools, their laps, their heads. When they could vote with effect, they didn't. (Of course, they had nothing, really, to vote for.) But now if they say boo, it's off to the camps, in the company of your friendly Helmsman.

Looking back, you can see that the die was cast when Hague won his first term with the "Republican-Christian Alliance." That string of amendments. And their legislation, even with the Court out of the way after *Anderson*. And then the Helmsmen. When Pine was in, even with Right-Wing Republican control of the Congress, there was still a chance. At least they were still nominally Republicans. At least they *seemed* to play electoral politics by the rules. The election of 2004, that was the last chance for the preservation of constitutional democracy by Constitutional means here. And the Democrats blew it.

But looking back. Jesus God, what good will that do? The American people have to look ahead and figure a way out of this mess they got themselves into. I wonder how long it will take.

All the best,
Alex

A Parthenon Pomeroy Diary Entry (July 11, 2011)

Yes, yes, yes! This is it! We did it, we did it. We've finally got it right. No more niggers, no more spics, no more slant-eyes slanty looks. Wow! 25 years of hard work. We're going to save our country, our freedom, our American way of life. I can't believe it. But I'd [*sic*] better believe it. I do believe it. This is going to fix things up all right. Jobs for everyone. Tax cuts, more tax cuts. No more Niggers in the schools, speaking giberish [*sic*]. This is what we need to get America to where it ought to be, to what it can be, to what it always was and will be again.

Good bye, coons! Coon, coon, black baboon. Brutal worthless, thieving goon. Often high, thrives in jail, his welfare check is in the mail. Some 40 offspring have been had, not one will ever call him Dad[15].

Thanks, God, for blessing us with the *New American Republics!* And thanks, Pat, too.

References:

Armstrong, L., *Racial Assignment in the New American Republics*, Chicago, IL: University of Chicago Press, 2032.

Brown, D., *Bury My Heart at Wounded Knee*, New York: Holt, Rinehart, and Winston, 1970.

Campbell, J., *The Way of the Seeded Earth*, New York: Harper & Row, Publishers, 1989.

Cole, L., "The Crossroads of Our Being," *The Nation*, December 3, 1991.

Cook, F.J., *The FBI Nobody Knows*, New York; The Macmillan Co., 1964.

Cooper, A., Fundraising letter, Simon Wiesenthal Center (Los Angeles, CA), April, 1995.

15. *Author"s Note:* This rhyme was typical of the racist, anti-Semitic, homophobic, and violence-promoting hate propaganda that proliferated around the world towards the end of the Transition Era in the old U.S. It had been circulated widely on the first generation international computer network called "The Internet" (Cooper). Why Pomeroy chose to put this old racist rhyme (interestingly enough in a shortened version) into his diary is unclear.

Davidowicz, L.S., *The War Against the Jews*, New York: Holt, Rinehart, and Winston, 1975.

Deighton, L., *Winter*, "1933 1938," New York: Ballantine Books, 1987.

Dionne, E.J., "High Tide for Conservatives, But Some Fear What Follows," *The New York Times*, October 13, 1987.

Domino, F., *The Domino Theory: American Fascism, Real and Imagined*, Albany, NY: The New State University of New York Press, 2046.

Gibbons, O., *The Rise and Decline of Fascism in the United States*, New York: The Scattered Home Press, 2029.

Fast, H., *Freedom Road*, New York: The World Publishing Co., Tower Books Edition, 1947.

Fast, H., *The Last Frontier*, New York: The Blue Heron Press, 1953.

Fournier, K., *Religious Cleansing in the American Republic*, Washington, DC: Life, Liberty, and Family Publications, 1993.

Fournier, K., *A House United? Evangelicals and Catholics Together*, Virginia Beach, VA: Navpress/Liberty, Life and Family, 1995.

Freedom Writer, "Church Organization is key to Coalition's success," November, 1994, p. 2.

Gleick, E., "'Something big is going to happen'," *Time*, May 8, 1995, p. 50.

Kristol, I., "The New Face of American Politics," The Wall Street Journal, August 26, 1994.

Lee, M.A., "Friendly Fascism: National Media Give Duke a FaceLift," *FAIR: Extra!*, January/February, 1992, p. 6.

Lind, M., "The Southern Coup," *The New Republic*, June 19, 1995, p. 20 (a).

Lind, M., "The Out of Control Presidency," *The New Republic*, August 14, 1995, p., 18 (b).

Muhammed, C., "Curtis and Lisa Sliwa Show," WABCFM, at about 8:10 AM, September 1, 1993.

Naureckas, J., "Racism Resurgent," *FAIR: Extra!*, Jan./Feb., 1995.

Nelson, LE., "GOP Revolution: Calling All Fat Cats," *Newsday*, March 14, 1995.

Ness, E., "Dueling Bigotries: Nation of Islam vs. White Racists," *The New York Times* (News of the Week in Review), October 22, 1995.

Patriquin, R., "Duke plan calls for dividing America," *Shreveport Journal*, February 7, 1989.

Peterson, I., "White Supremacists Meet in Quest for Homeland," *The New York Times*, July 14, 1986.

Porteous, S., "Road to Victory '95," *Freedom Writer*, October, 1995.

Raskin, J.B., "Affirmative Action and Racial Reaction," *Z Magazine*, May, 1995, p. 33.

Reiss, T., "Home on the Range," *The New York Times*, May 26, 1995.

Reno, R., "GOP Is Liberal When It Comes To Aid for the Rich," *Newsday*, November 8, 1995.

Rosenbaum, A., "'Leave Us Alone,'" Statesman (SUNY at Stony Brook), May 13, 1993, p. 1.

Sack, K, "Symbol of the Old South Divides the New South," *The New York Times*, January 21, 1996.

Shirer, W.L., *The Rise and Fall of the Third Reich*, New York: Simon and Schuster, 1960.

The W.A.R. Eagle, Vol. 1, Issue # 1, Summer, 1993.

Van Biema, D., "When White Makes Right," *Time*, August 9, 1993, p. 40.

CHAPTER 14
2013: The Natural Resources Access Act

Author's Commentary

The Act terminated the National Parks and National Forests systems (as early as 1995 closing the national parks had been for instance advocated by Republican Congressman James Hansen of Utah [Sher]).[1] It turned the parks, forests, and other designated wilderness areas over to proprietary interests (a greed-gratifying process called "privatization" in those days); repealed the remnants of the Clean Air and Clean Water Acts, in the process finally shutting down completely the long-crippled Environmental Protection Administration.

Finally, it removed all remaining governmental regulations and limitations on oil exploration and production, lumbering, and mining on all lands that were part of the White Republic of the NAR (the old "Endangered Species Act" having already long since departed the legislative playing field). The Act's public premise, to the extent that a public premise was needed in a country governed by a dictatorship (see Chapter 15), was the further glorification of the "Free Market" as the ideal public policymaker and economic resource allocator.

1. *Author's Note:* There is no indication or evidence that James Hansen, Alan Gottlieb, Ron Arnold, any other member or associate of the "Wise Use Movement" or related organizations, John Kitzhaber, Pete Wilson, Tim LaHaye, Don Young, or any of the other historical personages or organizations mentioned or alluded to in this chapter or elsewhere in this book in a similar manner, would have supported or approved in any way of the passage of the "Natural Resources Access Act," or any of the regulations, policies, or procedures created or implemented pursuant to it in or by the New American Republics at any time in the future, subsequent to its passage and the implementation of the policies carried out pursuant to it.

The institution of the "Resource Based Economy" (RBE) (see below), that was both the motivation for and the result of policies instituted pursuant to this Act, as we know ultimately failed. We are still recovering from the massive environmental destruction caused by the RBE. The RBE experience did, however, offer the final proof, if any more were needed after the deindustrialization of the old U.S. that lead to its adoption, that the "Free Market" was indeed anything but the ideal public policy maker and economic resource allocator it was cracked up to be.

The Right-Wing Reactionary Environmental Agenda

With the passage of *The Natural Resources Access Act*, Right-Wing Reaction finally achieved in full the goals for environmental protection and energy policy they had set back in the mid-Transition Era. At that time, one of the leaders of what some called the environmental destruction movement, Ron Arnold, had put it succinctly (Stapleton): "Our goal is to destroy, to eradicate, the environmental movement."

The environmental goals of Right-Wing Reaction were laid out in more detail in, for example, *The Wise Use Agenda* (Gottlieb) and the 1992 Republican National Platform (pp. 46-56). Even the self-styled "environmental President" George Bush had proposed in 1992 to allow surface "strip mining" for coal in National Parks (Schneider). The so-called "Wise Use" agenda had included (Stapleton):

- Breaking up the National Park Service.
- Opening all national parks and wilderness areas to mineral and energy [resource] production.
- Clear cutting all ancient forests, using the bizarre argument that 'decaying and oxygen-using' old growth contributes to global warming.
- A major 20-year construction program to build [privately owned] lodging and concessions in national parks.
- A public land giveaway: redefining grazing rights to 'recognize

[that] these ranches are not public lands but split estate lands, co-owned by government and the rancher.'

- Gutting the Endangered Species Act.
- Constructing wilderness trails for offroad vehicles.
- Immediately developing petroleum resources in Alaska's pristine Arctic Wildlife Refuge (ANMWR).

Building on the record of legislative success of the "Wise Use" movement that had begun following the election of the 104th Congress in 1994, this Act of 2013 consolidated and codified the gains that Right-Wing Reaction had made under the Republicans, the Republican-Christian Alliance, and the American Christian Nation Party alike.

In the 104th Congress, in addition to many elements of the "Wise Use" agenda, the Right-Wing Reactionary environmental destruction shopping list was designed to (Lewis, [a]):

- Prevent the Environmental Protection Administration (EPA) from keeping possibly toxic fill out of lakes and rivers.
- Deprive the EPA of funds to keep raw sewage out of rivers and away from beaches.
- Cut by two-thirds, from 300,000 acres to 100,000 acres, the wetlands to be bought from farmers by the Agriculture Department for a preserve.
- Increase logging in the Tongas National Forest, a remarkable rain forest in Alaska.

Lewis went on to note that: " 'Congress has set up a virtual environmental exemption bazaar,' Gov. John Kitzhaber of Oregon (Democrat) said the other day, 'granting special interest after special interest exemption.' "

The "special interests" that Gov. Kitzhaber referred to were almost invariably major contributors to the campaign funds of the Republicans who championed these proposals in the Congress.

At the same time, at the state level, similar initiatives were being taken elsewhere (Schuchat):

- In California, Gov. Pete Wilson pushed for a bill to gut the state's Environmental Quality Act.
- Maine's Legislature slashed financing for the state's most important water quality program.
- The people of Arizona no longer have the right to sue a company for polluting private or public property.
- Oregon legislators have denied local communities the right to set stronger restrictions on pesticides than the state does, even though some towns' water supplies have been contaminated by state-sanctioned use of pesticides.
- In Wisconsin, lawmakers drastically cut back the state Department of Resources public advocate, an office that had acted as an environmental watchdog, and prohibited it from taking legal action against other state agencies.

Right-Wing Reactionary Environmental Rhetoric and Tactics

In carrying out their campaign, the environmental destructionist forces were not exactly tactful. Ron Arnold stated their substantive goals bluntly (Gleeson): "We want you to be able to exploit the environment for private gain, absolutely. And we want people to understand that is a noble goal."

Reflecting the "cultural, religious war" rhetoric of certain Right-Wing reactionary leaders of the time, Charles Cushman of the National Inholders Association (an organization of owners of private property lying within the boundaries of national parks, forests, and wilderness areas), said (Gleeson)

> "It's a holy war between fundamentally different religions ... The preservationsts [environmentalists] are worshipping trees and sacrificing people. ..."

Indeed the Religious Right itself weighed in on the issue,

invoking old Red-scare tactics. Listen to the well-known Fundamentalist Minister Tim LaHaye (Gleeson):

> "The phony environmental crisis is a socialist plot to create so much bureaucratic control of business in the name of saving the environment that it will cost billions of dollars and thousands of lost jobs during the next ten years."

But the Red-scare tactic was not the property only of the Religious Right of the time. Representative Don Young, Republican of Alaska, said (SCLDF):

> "If we lose the private land concept in this country, let us all become Communists. That is what communism is all about, that in the national interest we shall do what is right. But the basis of our democracy has been based upon the individual rights of that one person, not in the national goodness."

Personal attacks and threats were also part of the environmental destructionist arsenal during the Transition Era. For example (Helvarg):

> "On November 14, 1994, Ellen Gray, an organizer with the Pilchuk Audubon Society in Everett, WA, had just finished testifying at a County Council hearing in favor of a land use ordinance to protect local streams and wetlands when a man stood up in front of her with a noose and said, 'This is for you.'
>
> " 'We have a militia of 10,000,' another man told her, 'and if we can't beat you at the ballot box, we'll beat you with a bullet.' "

(It is fascinating to note, among other things in this statement, the rejection of constitutional democracy, whether by the threatened or actual use violence as in this case or other means, that was so common to so much of Right-Wing Reactionary thinking.)

What Had Been Done

In the almost two decades from the commencement of the 104th Congress in 1995, much had been accomplished in dismantling the series of environmental, wildlife, wilderness, natural resources, and commercial animal protections that had been enacted by the Congress, under both Republican and Democratic Presidents since the first term of Richard Nixon (1969-73). But, by and large, this dismantlement had been undertaken in piecemeal fashion.

The effort had left behind a hodgepodge of laws and programs, of partial repeals and draconian spending reductions, of full-throated rhetoric and half-hearted measures, primarily slanted in favor of resource exploitation and economic development, but with some throwbacks, quirks, and internal contradictions. As noted, the Natural Resources Access Act was intended to deal with such problems and establish a single, consistent national policy, not only on natural resources, but also on environmental protection, commercial and wild animals conservation and preservation, and undeveloped areas.

To do this, the Act set a single national standard to be applied to policy-making in all of these related arenas. As succinctly stated by "Wise Use Movement" leader Ron Arnold and Republican Congressman Don Young (quoted above), the new national standard held that the "free market" was to be the primary determinant of policy and that the fundamental right to be protected was that of private property ownership and its benefits to the owners. In supporting its position, the "Wise Use Movement" often quoted part of an opinion handed down as part of a 1972 Supreme Court decision (*The Private Sector*):

> "The dichotomy between personal liberties and property rights is a false one. Property does not have rights. People

> have rights. The right to enjoy property without unlawful deprivation, no less than the right to speak or the right to travel, is in truth, a 'personal' right, whether the property in question be a welfare check, a home, or a savings account. In fact, a fundamental interdependence exists between the personal right to liberty and the personal right in property. Neither could have meaning without the other."

For a movement that had little concern with the personal rights of, say, thought, expression, and protection against arbitrary search and seizure, it was odd that Right-Wing Reaction showed so much concern for this one personal right in particular. But then again, a money value can be placed on property. One cannot be placed on liberty and freedom.

Why At That Time?

As previously noted, over the previous 25 years the economic decision makers of the old U.S. had consciously implemented the policy of diminishing public and private investment in productive resources, coupled with economywide computerization/robotization and disaccumulation of labor around productive resources. The resultant deindustrialization had led to the then current state of affairs, privately recognized even by the Right-Wing Reactionaries as a problem.

They did not regret the outcomes of their economic policies for a moment, because those outcomes had led to huge profits and a highly luxurious lifestyle for themselves. But they recognized that as a natural result, the economy could less and less be supported by industrial production of goods and services. More and more, continued prosperity for themselves would require the unfettered harvesting and production of agricultural products and natural resources for export. Thus, to the greatest extent possible, any remaining limitations (and there were not too many) on environmental exploitation needed to be removed, regardless of any immediate or longer term negative consequences.

During the Transition Era, many scientists and liberal policymakers had predicted that following the Right-Wing Reactionary economic, energy, and environmental policies of the time would in the old U.S. eventually lead to a gradual decline to Third World Nationhood, albeit a heavily armed and fairly wealthy one (see Chapter 1). And that is precisely what happened. To this major reconstruction of the economic base of the country, the Hagueites gave that grand sounding name "Resource Based Economy." We will return to a consideration of its nature.

Let us turn now to the brief speech President Jefferson Davis Hague made in presenting the legislation to the Congress which he had called back into session for the single purpose of considering (and of course passing) it.

Speech by Jefferson Davis Hague, upon the Introduction of the Natural Resource Access Act, made on Arbor Day, Monday, April 15, 2013[2]

> Americans are becoming outraged to discover that their home is no longer the land of hope and optimism, the one nation in the world where anything might be possible.
>
> Something is wrong, dreadfully wrong. Our nation's strength is being sapped. Somebody, as our English

2. *Author's Note:* The reader may recall that President Hague had trouble finding writers who could prepare original speeches. For example, as Connie Conroy revealed (see Chapter 6), his First Inaugural was drawn largely from the work of Transition Era Right-Wing Reactionary leaders. It has been discovered that this Arbor Day speech was based in large measure (with a great deal of cutting, some direct quotation, a good deal of paraphrase), on the writings of two leaders of the Transition Era Right-Wing Reactionary "Wise Use" movement, Ron Arnold and Alan Gottlieb, that appeared in their book *Trashing the Economy: How Runaway Environmentalism is Wrecking America*, Belleville, WA: Free Enterprise Press, 1993, pp. 1 74. There is no indication anywhere, however, that either Arnold or Gottlieb would have endorsed the Hagueite ideology or mode of government in any way.

friends would say, has put a spanner in America's works, and the assembly line is shutting down.

But who would do such a thing? And how did we let it happen? The answer is a stunner: the Spanner Crew is the old environmental movement. And by trusting our government too much, we let it happen.

In every act of 'environmental protection' there is an economic decision. For example: protecting old growth trees rather than allowing them to be converted into homes for people, banning offshore oil exploration in so-called "sensitive areas" while driving up the price of heating homes and driving cars, expanding a national park by knocking down homes and businesses, protecting so-called "wetlands" which aren't even wet most of the time.

Putting harsh restrictions on business was the way many of these laws worked: infringing on private property rights by confiscatory regulation, putting resource-rich Federal lands off limits to private enterprise, taking over private property for so-called "nature reserves."

The environmentalists have cost us money out-of-pocket, they have prevented economic growth, they controlled land use against development. They have destroyed private property rights on a massive scale.

But it is private property and property rights which have been one of the cornerstones of our historic prosperity.

Land is the fundamental source of that which keeps us alive. Industry is the fundamental instrument we have to get the materials out of the ground that can be made into the goods we need to survive and prosper. And what has the environmental movement done? Nothing but trash, bash, and try to stash industry away.

And so now, finally, we are going to get government out from between you and industry, out from between industry and the good it can do for you, out of the way of industry so that it can concentrate on doing what it does best, making life better and better for each and every one of us.

As we accomplish this good for the American people on what used to be income tax day and is now National Arbor Day[3], please recall which Party it is that has substituted trees for taxes for you.

Thank you. And please, do plant a tree today.

Oakwood Transcript (April 16, 2013)

Well good afternoon ladies and gentlemen here in the East, and good morning to those of you still residing out on the Left Coast. Did you hear the President's speech yesterday? I mean, did you hear it? You didn't? Well you should have.

Ah the sound of chain saws and the smell of two-cycle fuel exhaust in the morning. Could anything be better? They make a true outdoorsman's heart beat faster. And that's what Mr. Jeff's speech did for me.

Let me tell you. He gave it to those environmental wackos, whatever's left of them. Boy have they done a job on this country. You know, people really forgot how rich in natural resources the American Continent really is. Or they knew, but wouldn't let us exploit our God-given natural wealth the way God meant for us to exploit it. After all, if He hadn't meant for us to use it, He wouldn't have put it here for us in the first place, would He?

But those liberal nigger lover enviro-fascists just kept holding us back. You couldn't drill here, couldn't mine there, couldn't burn that kind of fuel here, couldn't cut down those trees there. They just stood in the way of development and progress. And of course, they prevented us from building any decent nuclear energy capacity at all.

3. *Author's Note:* It is not known whether or not Hague was struck by the irony of his making such a speech as this on Arbor Day. It was formerly a locally determined holiday celebrating tree planting. Hague happened to have made it into a national holiday celebrating an act that would bring about, among other things, the wholesale slaughter of trees on the North American continent.

Well, the coming end of the towel-heads' oil has taught us all a good lesson. Soon there's not gonna be no more oil from there, as they say. The Japs and the Euros have been able to meet some of their need because with the divvying up of Russia between them, they have taken over the Russkies' oil.

But where does that leave us? Nowhere. So we have to turn to ourselves. And when we get back to 54-40 we'll be in even better shape.[4] Between the Canucks and us there's coal, timber, oil, and natural gas aplenty. And now with this new Act, there will be no more restrictions on mining, drilling, lumbering, anywhere. We just did away with them. The free market, self-responsibility, people making their own decisions about cutting down a tree or saving an owl. That's the American Way.

And, of course, we're going nuclear again. But this time we're doing it the smart way. We're putting our new plants just inside the borders of the Nigger and Redskin Republics, wrapped around by Protective Fences, of course. So there's no danger to the White race if there's an accident every now and again. And I have to admit, since we're honest over here, that they do happen. And we dump the nuclear wastes in those Republics too, right along with all the rest of garbage.[5] After all, garbage loves garbage, doesn't it? But we are letting those lesser lights have some light from the plants—if they can pay for it.

But, you tell me, there are always those yammerers about the future. Well, we're using sulfured coal again—there's plenty of it, and we wouldn't want it to go to waste now, would we? And we're letting cars burn just about anything. And we're getting along just great.

---

4. *Author's Note:* The "54-40" reference is to a mid-19th century slogan of settlers in the U.S. Northwest, "54-40 or fight." It encapsulated a territorial goal of the time which, if achieved, would have incorporated into the United States much of what later became the four Western Provinces of Canada (Chernow and Vallasi). Subsequent events would see that goal achieved for the NAR (see Chapter 16).

5. *Author's Note:* "Racial dumping" of toxic wastes had been widely practiced in the old U.S. for many years (In Brief).

We've finally learned we just don't have to worry about the future. It will take care of itself. It's that kind of liberal nigger lover environmental wacko thinking that got us into trouble in the first place. Just look at how prosperous we are now. And this new Act is going to make us even more prosperous. Just you wait.

Author's Commentary
On the Hague Speech

The Hague speech was remarkable for what it didn't say as well as for what it did say. First as to the latter. This speech was a classic Right-Wing Reactionary diversionary tactic dating from the Transition Era. By this time, they had used it so many times that they probably no longer realized what they were doing. (When they started using it, as far back as the pre-Transition Era politics of President Richard Nixon, it was apparent that they knew precisely what they were doing, and did it consciously.)

It was the old formula. Identify a problem (in this case loss of jobs specifically in the energy and natural resources sectors, and more generally in the economy as a whole). Create an enemy, one that is easily identifiable from your side. Make sure that the identified enemy is in no way related to the real causes of the identified problem so that no linkages can be made. (In this instance, the real causes were national investment and energy policies generally, and private timber and coal industry practices in particular.)

If the identified enemy is nonexistent, weak, or long gone from the scene, even better. Then it cannot defend itself against your attacks and is ill-equipped to identify and educate people about the real causes of the problem(s). In this case, the problems were real enough, and highly threatening to the whole fabric of the economy. But the supposed cause identified by Hague, the "environmental movement," had long since departed the scene.

The environmental movement was one of the earliest victims of the late Transition Era Right-Wing Reactionary policy of "defunding the Left" by arranging to end the Federal income tax deductibility of voluntary monetary contributions to it. At the same time, the policy severely limited the ability of all sorts of voluntary agencies such as the American Red Cross and the Boy Scouts even to speak out on public issues (Crowley; Lewis, [b]). Of course, with the repeal of the income tax, all tax deductibility disappeared anyway, and the rich who benefited from the effective tax reduction were highly unlikely to be contributors to organizations devoted to protecting the environment.

The operation of the "free market" in timber and energy policy had led, for example, to the destruction of thousands of square miles of forest and range land (through strip mining for coal). That process was already well underway by the mid-Transition Era (see, for example, Egan). That was why the NAR, in developing the RBE, would have to expand into the as yet unspoiled wilds of Western Canada (see below, and Chapter 16).

Overfishing had led directly to the destruction of the food fish populations of the Georges and Grand Banks off the eastern coast of the U.S. and Canada. It was certainly feasible to achieve sustainable use of these renewable resources through careful management and planning (Rosenberg, et al). That was never done; it would have been a Young-like "Communist plot" and "interference with the free market."

Further on fishing, it was over harvesting and the destruction of the Western rivers by damming and the despoliation of the land by timber overcutting leading to soil erosion and its consequences that virtually destroyed the salmon industry in the Northeastern Pacific Ocean. Nevertheless, according to Hague and his forebears it was the "enviro-fascists" who did all the damage. Little had been done to correct that false message when it first made its appearance during the Transition Era. With control of the media completely in Hagueite hands, it was of course impossible to do anything about it in 2013.

As to Hague's point about the environmental movement and job loss, many more jobs had been lost because of industry policies and practices than because of environmental regulation and protection. For example, in the timber industry, most job loss occurred because of clear-cutting and the closure of private lumber mills as industry sales and marketing practices changed (Durning; Egan; Johnson; Linden). "Interference" from the environmental protection movement was not a primary cause of job loss.

In fact, it had already been shown in the 90s that environmental protection could actually create jobs in areas that private timber companies had already overharvested (Glick; Seagar). At the same time, in the then two principal economic rivals of the old U.S., Germany and Japan, "environmental protection [was seen] as an opportunity for economic development, not a barrier to growth" (Moore). Much of the advantage that they quickly achieved in the field of environmental preservation technology was based on methods and systems that had been originally developed in the old U.S., but never exploited there, either by government or private industry.

On the Oakwood Transcript

Note the casual prejudice ("the towel-heads' oil") that was so much a part of the Oakwood presentation. Note, too, the casual manner in which he alluded to the end of the oil supply from the Middle East, something that had been warned against by energy supply experts for decades. However, profits, not prudence, had ruled the utilization of those reserves.

In the 1970s the oil-rich countries surrounding the Persian Gulf had nationalized their own petroleum reserves. Subsequently, the only way the large American oil companies which had previously owned the stuff could make money was by acting as the middleman and selling large quantities of it on the retail market. The more oil they sold, the more money they made. But they could no longer make money simply by owning the oil reserves and seeing their value rise over time.

The oil companies wanted nothing to interfere with their short-term profit-making potential, so they made sure that any oil conservation or conversion programs were muzzled. Ironically, if they had owned the reserves, they might have been interested in conservation to make the petroleum-basis of the economies of the industrialized countries last longer into the future, when the resource would be more expensive.

In fact, the Reaganite destruction of the American domestic oil industry (in which many relatively small companies were factors) during the early Transition Era was prompted by the need the large oil companies had for maintaining American dependence on foreign supplies, sold in America at high profits, by those self same companies.

The Reaganites also virtually shut down the nascent industry in alternative energy sources, such as solar. These policies were all undertaken at the behest of Big Oil, major benefactors of the Reaganite Republicans. After President Clinton had overseen a modest restart in alternative energy resource research and development in 1993, the Republican-controlled 104th Congress moved smartly to shut it down.

The reference to the siting of both the nuclear power and the nuclear waste "disposal" industries on the borders of the Negro and Indian Republics needs no comment. As to the "don't worry about tomorrow" message, that was an old one for Right-Wing Reaction, dating back to the early Transition Era and President Ronald Reagan.

On the "Resource Based Economy"

Hague did not discuss the "Resource Based Economy" (RBE) in this speech. But it was the Natural Resources Access Act that led directly to its development. Indeed the Act was needed if the RBE were to be developed. With the continued relative decline in American industrial capacity, and the coming severe limitations on petroleum supplied from the Middle East, the economic decision-makers had determined that America would live on its natural resources, and eventually those of its neighbor to the north.

The aim was to make the NAR one of the two major energy sources for the industrialized world (the other being the now divided nation of Russia). The NAR would more and more meet its own energy needs from the unfettered use of nuclear power, now that plant siting and nuclear waste dumping were to be considered "No Problem."

Domestic petroleum reserves were fast disappearing, even from the Arctic areas and the continental shelf. However, with the reintroduction of the use of sulfured coal and the end of any restrictions on strip mining, the NAR's coal reserves were numbered in the several hundred years. Nevertheless, the NAR was using up its own trees rapidly, even with the new technologies that made energy extraction from them much more efficient. Thus the drive to take over Western Canada and its seemingly countless trees intensified. (It had coal, oil, and natural gas reserves too.) This policy had been advocated during the Transition Era by certain Right-Wing Reactionary figures such as Patrick Buchanan (c. 1989). (There is no indication, however, that Buchanan would have endorsed the specific policies followed by Hague and the NAR.)

Responding to the long-standing economic depression in Canada, and using the economic advantages afforded by the North American Free Trade Agreement of 1994 and other similar pacts with Canada, American resource capital had moved evermore strongly into the four Western Canadian provinces during the early Fascist Period. The larger and larger American economic presence supported the political drive. The latter eventually culminated in the dismemberment of Canada and the Legitimation Treaty of 2017 (see Chapter 16).

Thus the passage of the Natural Resources Access Act, which led to the massive despoliation of the environment from which we have yet to recover, was a pivotal event for the history of the whole of North America. It also marked a major step down the road towards worldwide environmental destruction and its consequences that Dino Louis had described in an unpublished commentary on the Earth Summit of 1992 held in Rio de Janeiro, Brazil. The essay had apparently been written at the request of a friend of Louis' who was an international authority on epidemiology. It responded to a general question the friend had posed: "What are the world's five major health problems, as you see them?" This brief essay is reproduced here.

Five Major Health Problems (Plus One)
by Dino Louis
June 8, 1992

In opening the Earth Summit of 1992 at Rio de Janeiro, Brazil, Maurice Strong of Canada, Summit coordinator, said (*New York Post*):

> "We have been the most successful species ever. ... We are now a species out of control. Our very success is leading to a dangerous future. ... The wasteful and destructive lifestyles of the rich cannot be maintained at the cost of the lives and the livelihoods of the poor and of nature. We are either going to save the whole world or none of it."

That's the number one health problem: the future of the human species, and perhaps of all life on Earth. That problem is also two, three, four, and five.

Another way to characterize the present situation is by listing the Four Horsemen of the Apocalypse:

- Pestilence
- Famine
- Flood
- War

One would only need to add one more Horseman that the conceivers of the Four could not have thought of: Overpopulation, the health problem which underlies and is a major factor in each of the first four.

(If overpopulation had been an even barely perceptible future occurrence at the time the original Horsemen were conceived of, there surely would have been Five of them to begin with. But human overpopulation was far beyond anyone's ken 2000 years ago. It has become possible only in our era, when dogma has failed to keep up with science.)

When done correctly, after description, the Public Health Method of problem solving moves on to causal analysis. Many books have been written on the present predicament facing life on earth, and it is a highly complicated one. But "the wasteful and destructive lifestyles of the rich" are certainly the most prominent of those causes. Major responsibility for the parlous state of the world does lie with the industrialized countries and the political, social, and economic policies they have followed over the last 300 years or so.

Currently, the major factors in the imminent environmental disasters that await us are:

- The heavy reliance on carbon dioxide-producing fossil fuels for energy, especially by the United States.
- The exploitation of natural resources around the world by the industrialized countries, without regard for the ultimate outcomes of that exploitation.
- The use of chloroflurocarbons for a variety of purposes, many of them frivolous.
- Destruction of the forests around the world for profit, as well as for fuel and the creation of arable land to support the rapidly burgeoning population.
- The active opposition to population control, for ideological/ political reasons on the part of the Eurocentric Roman Catholic Church, and for domestic political reasons by the Reaganite/Bushist Administration in the United States.
- Underlying all of the above is production for profit rather than use, which has produced the enormous human, biological, economic, solid, and toxic wastes that now burden us.

Solutions to the problems represented by the Four Horsemen Plus One require very significant political, economic, and social policy changes on the part of the industrialized countries, especially the United States, as was borne out on an almost daily basis during the Rio Summit. The solutions require policy changes on the part on the "developing" countries as well, but without action by the former, action by the latter will mean nothing.

Present policy changes agreed to by the industrialized countries, especially the United States, will make only minor alterations in the present downward course toward the Apocalypse. To change them significantly will require major political shifts in those countries. In my view, that is one of the most important tasks to which public health authorities in those countries should currently be lending a hand.

However, looming on the horizon is an even more serious threat to human existence than present industrialized country policy: the threatened takeover of the governments of a number of the industrialized countries, not in the least the United States, by far right-wing, authoritarian, sometimes theocratic, political parties. We have already experienced more than a whiff of what this would mean for the future of the world in the present Reaganite/Bushist policies that were most recently played out by the American approach to the Rio Summit.

The advent of such authoritarian governments would virtually ensure the end of civilization as we know it, if not of the human species itself, because of their known policies on: the use of petroleum and other fossil fuels, global warming, ozone depletion, population control, the use of force backed up by thermonuclear weapons to achieve political and economic objectives not obtainable by other means, and the belief of their religious Fundamentalist wings in the inevitability (to some of them the desirability) of the Apocalypse in any case. Thus, in my view, the number one health problem facing those of us living in the industrialized nations is changing the course our governments are taking and, for those of us living in countries threatened by authoritarian takeover, the fight to prevent that catastrophe from occurring.

Author's Comment

Unfortunately, in this essay Louis was nothing if not prescient.

References:

Arnold, R. and Gottlieb, *A. Trashing the Economy: How Runaway Environmentalism is Wrecking America*, Bellevue, WA: Free Enterprise Press, 1993. 1 74.

Buchanan, P., *Patrick J. Buchanan ... From the Right*, fundraising letter, c. 1989.

Chernow, B.A. and Vallasi, G.E., Eds., *The Columbia Encyclopedia, Fifth Edition*, "Oregon," New York: Columbia University Press, 1993, p. 2021.

Crowley, M., "Mistook Istook," *The New Republic*, November 27, 1995.

Durning, A.T., "Saving the Forests: What Will It Take?" *Worldwatch Paper* 117, December, 1993.

Egan, T., "A Land Deal Leaves Montana Heavily Logged and Hurting," *The New York Times*, October 9, 1993.

Gleeson, K., "Patriotic Games," *The ZPG Reporter*, November, 1992, Vol. 24, No. 5.

Glick, D., "Having Owls and Jobs Too," *National Wildlife*, August/September, 1995, p. 9.

Gottlieb, A.M., *The Wise Use Agenda*, Bellevue, WA: The Free Enterprise Press, 1989.

Helvarg, D., "The Anti-Enviro Connection," *The Nation*, May 22, 1995.

In Brief, "And Justice for All," Sierra Club Legal Defense Fund Newsletter, Summer 1993, p. 1.

Johnson, R., Sierra Club Northwest Office, Personal Communication, September 30, 1992.

Lewis, A., "On Another Planet?" *The New York Times*, September 29, 1995, (a).

Lewis, A., "A Menacing Vendetta" *The New York Times*, October 2, 1995, (b).

Linden, E., "The Green Factor," *Time*, October 12, 1992.

Moore, C., "Bush's Nonsense on Jobs and the Environment," *The New York Times*, September 25, 1992.

New York Post, "U.S. Likely Scapegoat as Earth Summit Gets Underway," June 4, 1992, p. 15.

Rosenberg, A.A., "Achieving Sustainable Use of Renewable Resources," *Science*, Vol. 262, November 5, 1993.

Schneider, K., "Bush StripMining Plan for Parks is Blocked," *The New York Times,* October 3, 1992.

Schuchat, S., "Unfit Stewards," *The New York Times*, September 20, 1995.

SCLDF: Sierra Club Legal Defense Fund, "Was the Election as Horrific as it Seemed?" *In Brief*, Winter 1994-95, p. 2.

Seager, S., "The Other Logging Dispute Rages in the Forest Primeval in New England," *The New York Times*, November 27, 1995.

Sher, V., "Lawless America?" *In Brief*, Summer, 1995.

Stapleton, R.M., "Greed vs. Green," *National Parks*, November/December, 1992, p. 32.

The Private Sector, "Governing," Vol. 8, No. 1, Spring, 1995, p. 3

CHAPTER 15

2015: The National Plan for Social Peace

Author's Commentary[1]

Sometime in the early 1990s, the Rev. Pat Robertson, leader of the Christian Coalition, said (Porteous): "We have enough votes to run this country, ... and when the people say, 'we've had enough,' we're going to take over!" As is well known to readers of this book, they did.

They did not, of course, ever get a majority of the eligible voters of the old U.S. to support them. And there is no indication that if Pat Robertson himself had succeeded electorally, the events described in this book would have occurred as they did. Nor is there any indication that Pat Robertson had any intent or interest in following the path down which success of "The 15% Solution" lead.

But with the unintended complicity of the majority opposition, Right-Wing Reaction was able to implement "The 15% Solution" and as surely as the sun rises in the East, early in this century they did "Take Over!" And what subsequently happened did indeed happen, possible wishes to the contrary of the founders of the movement notwithstanding.

Just this sort of thing had occurred in another great country,

1. *Author's Note:* There is no indication or evidence that David Barton, Michael Farris, Chuck Baker, Mary Matalin, Paul Weyrich, Phil Gramm, Bob Dole, the Bob Jones University, the National Rifle Association, Wayne R. LaPierre, G. Gordon Liddy, or any other historical personage or organization mentioned or alluded to in this chapter or elsewhere in this book in a similar manner, would have supported or approved in any way of any of the institutions, events, laws, policies, or procedures of the NAR, mentioned, discussed, or alluded to anywhere in this chapter, or supported, approved of, or applauded any of the events that occurred pursuant to any NAR policies described or alluded to in this chapter.

in the previous century. William Shirer, author of *The Rise and Fall of the Third Reich* (1960), observed (Porteous):

> "The cardinal error of the Germans who opposed Nazism was their failure to unite against it. ...But the 63% of the German people who [at one time or another] expressed their opposition to Hitler were much too divided and shortsighted to combine against a common danger which they must have known would overwhelm them unless they united, however, temporarily, to stamp it out."

In the old U.S., at the polls the anti-Rightist majority of eligible voters could have easily defeated the Christian Coalition-dominated old Republican Party and even its successor, the Republican-Christian Alliance. However, with no effective leadership, that anti-Rightist majority acted like the Shirer-described anti-fascist majority in pre-Nazi Germany. And a long national nightmare descended upon the country, just as it had upon Germany.

This chapter provides a partial picture of what life was like in the American fascist state, the New American Republics, when the Hague regime was at the height of its powers (see also Chapter 2. For a complete description, see, for example, the work by Ellington [2037].) The bulk of the chapter consists of the transcript of an interview conducted by Alex Poughton with the White House Press Officer Connie Conroy. Poughton at the time was wearing his public "friendly foreign journalist" hat.

The interview was held on the occasion in 2015 of the establishment of a new national holiday called National Social Peace Day. Observed on May 30, it replaced a holiday celebrated in the old U.S. called Memorial Day. The latter had since the late 19th century been a holiday honoring the dead of all the nation's wars. But the holiday, formerly called Decoration Day, had been originated just after the First Civil War to honor the dead of the Union (anti-slavery) side in that conflict.

The current change in the holiday was part of the Hagueites' efforts to expunge all "black references and influences" from the life of the White Republic of the NAR (see "culture" in the Poughton-Conroy interview that follows). It was also a political nod towards the "pro-Confederate" racists of the stripe of Hague's own father. (He, you may recall, was a truck driver who sported a Confederate States of America flag emblazoned on the radiator grill of his rig.) "Remove any vestige of the white supremacists' defeat" was the implied message here.

As to "National Social Peace Day" itself, it was established to recognize and celebrate Hague's new "National Plan for Social Peace." This was just another in the endless series of constitutional amendments, laws, proclamations, declarations, decrees (the major ones having been reviewed in this book), that Right-Wing Reaction had been trotting out since the Transition Era, with the claim that "this is now going to solve all our problems."

However, just like its predecessors, from the old Republican "Contract on America" through Carnathon Pine's "Real War on Drugs" to Jefferson Davis Hague's "Declaration of Peace" and the establishment of the NAR itself, the National Plan for Social Peace solved none of the problems the country faced. It could not, because like its predecessors, it was not aimed at the causes of those problems, that still could be summarized in one phrase: "underinvestment in productive resources."

Like its predecessors, this one, just a warmed-over version of the "Declaration of Peace," actually made matters worse, because it focused on repression throughout the NAR. Going back to the Transition Era, Right-Wing Reaction always looked first to the expansion of the criminal law and criminal law enforcement, as well as the military, as the solution to problems, both perceived and imagined. Often their proposals went no further.

The "new" plan had nothing to do with "Social Peace." It rather called for an increase in law enforcement in the White Republic itself, an upgrading of the Killer Fence system which surrounded the Black and Indian Republics, an expansion of the counterinsurgency efforts in the Fourth (Hispanic) Republic, further expansion of investment for the Resource-Based Economy in Canada, "improvements" in the racist/homophobic/xenophobic/misogynist propaganda machine, a redoubling of efforts to enforce the criminal laws governing what the Hagueites called "morality" (almost exclusively devoted to sexual matters, as had been the Right-Wing Reactionary pattern since the Transition Era), and so forth.

But it was easy for the Hagueites to convince their supporters that this was "something new," just as they had always done, because they certainly did everything they could to ensure that those folks' political/historical memories remained very short, just as they had always been able to do.

Following the transcript of the interview, which Poughton preserved in his library, are some further comments and explanation of my own on its specifics. The ground rules of these interviews, held on a periodic basis, were that Poughton could ask just about anything he wanted to, even "tough" questions (to show how "open" the Hague regime was), but could ask no followup questions.

Poughton-Conroy Interview, Monday, June 1, 2015

Q. Ms. Conroy, I want to thank you very much for granting me this interview. The NAR has many admirers in Great Britain, eager for the latest news on the progress you are making here. Since this latest initiative is called the National Plan for Social Peace, let's begin with a review of some of the social policies of the NAR.

A. Alex, it's always a delight to talk with you. So few members of the international media give us a fair shake. It's only through those few objective reporters like you that the world can get to see what we are really like.

Q. My pleasure. Let's turn first to the matter of religion. The NAR is led by the American Christian Nation Party. Yet the

NAR has yet to become, officially, a "Christian Nation." Can you tell us why not?

A. Our party and our nation are fully committed to the Christian principles on which our party is founded: Family, God, and Country. And we, and our predecessor party, the Republican-Christian Alliance, have enacted, and indeed have put into our Constitution the full Christian political and social agenda. I am sure I do not have to review it here for you, Alex.

But let me say briefly that in general, within certain limits, we follow the principle laid down by the great David Barton (Schollenberger): "Whatever is Christian is legal. Whatever isn't Christian is illegal." We do expect people to subscribe to Christian Thinking, as defined by our Party, and accept the Inerrancy of the Bible, as laid down by the Party.

At the same time, religious freedom is one of the most important traditions of our country. And we have many friends and supporters who are not Christian. We are sensitive to their sensitivities. Thus, while our government follows Christian principles, and Christianity has taken its rightful place in all aspects of public life, we have not made, and have no present intentions to make, the NAR officially a Christian nation.

Q. A major concern of the ACNP and especially its predecessors, the old Republican Party and the Republican-Christian Alliance, was with legalized pre-born baby killing.[2] That led, for example, to the passage back in 2005 of the Morality Amendment which made the practice illegal under any circumstance. That then led to the Life Preservation Police, the War for the Preservation of Life, the significant expansion of the penal system to enforce the law and so forth.

However, since the establishment of the NAR, you have followed a bipartite policy on this matter. The killing of the pre-born is illegal

2. *Author's Note:* Presumably just being diplomatic, Poughton used Right-Wing Reaction's term for the medical procedure that before the Fascist Period was called abortion and now is generally referred to as elective pregnancy termination (see also Chapter 7).

in the White Republic, and you still devote significant resources to enforcing those laws. Yet you have legalized the practice in the Negro and Indian Republics. Could you explain why?

A. Certainly. We think the way we deal with killing of the pre-born is indicative of the enlightenment that we have brought to America. We recognized that you couldn't have one policy on legalized pre-born baby killing for everybody. That's because contrary to what the liberal nigger lovers used to tell us, the colored races are not the equal of the Whites. That as you know, Alex, is the fundamental principle on which the NAR is founded.

So for us Whites legalized pre-born baby killing is baby killing, pure and simple. There's simply no two ways about it. It's something that civilized people don't do. It's God and man, not woman, who make babies. After all, without God and man there would be no babies, would there? No woman has the right to undo the work of God and man. Pre-born baby killing is a sin of the first water. And so, we are very strict on this matter when it comes to White people.

But the inferior races are another matter indeed. They just aren't human. God views them in a different way, more like the highly intelligent animals they are, so monkey-like, you know. So for them, pre-born baby killing is OK. When they kill one of their unborn offspring, they're not killing another human being, because they aren't human themselves. So we actually encourage the practice in the other Republics.

They are starting to get kind of crowded and we have to find ways to keep the population down. The space they've got is the space they get, and they do get a fixed amount of food each day too. If the population goes up, the food per person goes down. So we've trained some Negro and Redskin women on how to do pre-born baby killing and provide the procedure free at Pre-born Baby Killing Stations in the non-White Republics.

By the way, any non-White woman who gets pregnant after having one child must have the pre-born baby killed and then must be sterilized. We keep track of those things pretty well. No non-White family can get more than one child ration card.

Q. You have recently achieved complete abolition of the system of Public Education. All children are now educated in private schools or at home. Parents receive private tuition aid in the form of "education vouchers" (Schrag). Could you explain the advantages of this system?

A. The old public schools were places where young minds were polluted, where Christ was excluded, where our values were denigrated. As Michael Farris[3] once said (*NYT*, 8/18/93), the public schools were "godless monstrosities," "values-indoctrination centers," and a "multi-million dollar inculcation machine."

Teachers taught what they wanted to teach instead of what the parents wanted them to teach. As the revered Chuck Baker[4] once said about our children attending public school (*Freedom Watch*): "They're not learning facts, they're not learning things. They are being conditioned to cooperate with their neighbor." The worst of the public school teachers tried to get children to actually think for themselves. Can you imagine that? Can you imagine a child who is capable of thinking for himself? It's that sort of thinking which got this country into such trouble in the old days.

The only solution to this problem was to get rid of the public schools. Now our children are taught either by their parents in the home or in private schools where the teachers teach what's right and what they are told to teach. And the children learn what's right and what we want them to think.

Q. Since the establishment of the NAR, you have extensively reorganized your system of higher education. Could you comment on that?

A. There is quite a system of higher education in the White Republic, of which we are very proud. The major research

3. *Author's Note:* Michael Farris was the Republican candidate for Lieutenant Governor in Virginia in 1993.

4. *Author's Note:* Chuck Baker was a Right-Wing Reactionary radio talk show host in the 90s.

universities, which had been dying for quite some time anyway (Rich), are gone. They cost too much and they tended to breed free thinking. So we got rid of them, and all the socialistic pointy-heads who worked in them. We can do the scientific research we need to do in government operated laboratories.

But the religious-based institutions are thriving, as are the state colleges and the community colleges. The latter two all have Party boards to control faculty and curriculum. There is a precedent for that going all the way back to the late 20th century I know you'll be pleased to know. Those were the "Nassau Laws" of '97.[5]

Q. As is well known, all those activities popularly known as "culture" are closely monitored by the government here, much more so than in other countries. What advantages does that bring to the NAR?

A. First, we should make it clear that we are talking about culture in the White Republic. What goes on in the other Republics that *appears* to be the same is obviously not, because those inferior peoples are just not capable of anything approaching true culture.

Art is the great potential destroyer of minds and hearts. One of the two most important concepts in our art policy is "potential obscenity." We simply cannot allow anything that might produce sinful thoughts to be placed in the minds of our people, especially our vulnerable young. Every contemplated art work, regardless of who pays for it, whether painting, sculpture, literature, film, theatre, music or dance must be approved in advance by the Bureau of Moral Standards of the Department of Information. There must be no sexual references of any kind

5. *Author's Note:* These laws, eventually enacted in every state, empowered politically appointed community panels to eliminate portions of curriculae and fire faculty they didn't like at tax-supported institutions of higher learning. The movement to enact such laws had begun at the Nassau Community College of Nassau County, NY back in 1989, when a lay "taxpayer group" demanded the right to review curriculae for anything they deemed "controversial" (Ain). The first object of their inquiry had been a college-level sex education course.

in any work of art. There is just no way to refer to sex in public that is not obscene or potentially obscene.

The other primary principle of our art policy is that nothing with any Negro influence is allowed any longer to contaminate White minds. So, for example in popular music, there's no ragtime, no jazz, no blues, no swing, no rock and roll of any kind, certainly none of what they used to call "rap." Good God's Music[6] and White Country & Western are what our stations play now. And no radio or TV stations are permitted in the other Republics. Our stations take care of the needs of those people, if they pay the media tax.

While we are on the subject of Negro influence on American culture, naturally in the White Republic nonWhites are no longer permitted to be members of any professional sports teams at any level. And, returning purity to all of our sports, we have expunged all records of past non-White players from both the college and professional record books, and removed them from the various Halls of Fame. Negroes and others just got there because of special privileges, like affirmative action, being granted to them. They just never belonged. And so, they're gone.

And we changed the team names when we had to, too. For example, we got rid of those Indian names: the Cleveland Indians, the Atlanta Braves, and the Washington Redskins. I'm not much of a team sport fan myself (I like auto racing and going out with the boys on a honey hunt[7]), but I know that they've got new names.

---

6. *Author's Note:* Beginning in the early Transition Era, a genre of pleasant, "popular sounding" music, with texts based on Biblical or other religious themes, became well accepted in certain parts of the old U.S. Like Country & Western, without the stimulation of music coming from other cultures, it persisted pretty much unchanged throughout the Transition Era and the Fascist Period. Originally referred to by such names as "Biblical Pop," during the latter time it came to be called "God's Music," much to the benefit of its composers.

7. *Author's Note:* "Honey hunting" was a "sport" in which a young woman, usually one the hunters considered "attractive," taken against her will from a nearby Moral Rehabilitation Center, was stripped naked and set out on a secluded ➤

Q. If I may touch briefly on a touchy subject, you appear to have done away with the traditional American right of freedom of speech, even within the White Republic. Many of your critics cite that as one of the major flaws in your polity. How do you answer those critics?
A. First of all, we do have freedom of speech in the White Republic. That's a bedrock American right we value most highly. Of course we've done away with what the liberal nigger lovers called "freedom of speech" because that wasn't freedom; it was just licence. There was no responsibility attached to it. They thought that anyone could say whatever they wanted to without thinking of the consequences or how right-thinking people might react.

But that's just plain wrong. There's good speech and bad speech, right speech and wrong speech, moral speech and immoral speech. Good Americans have the free right to say anything they want to, just as long as it is good, right, and moral. As for the bad Americans, they don't handle free speech with any sense of responsibility at all. So they don't have it.

Q. You have made extensive changes in your legal system. Would you care to comment on them?
A. As is well known, we have done away with jury trials, except for party members in which case the juries are of their peers. Juries just got too cumbersome. Jury picking became a lawyers' art form. Juries just got in the way of justice. So did due process

---

"hunting ground," usually at night. She was then "hunted" by a group of men on horseback using hunting dogs, much in the fashion that foxhunters used to hunt foxes. When caught (the only ones not caught were those who died of wounds suffered while trying to elude the "hunters"), the woman was subjected at a minimum to gang rape.

This "sport" was started by wealthy ranchers and businessmen primarily in the South and Southwest during the Transition Era. For the most part, at that time they used paid prostitutes as their quarry. One gubernatorial candidate in a large Southwestern state was said to have lost his election, to a woman opponent, at least in part because he was alleged to have participated in "honey hunts" and never categorically denied the charge.

and *habeas corpus*. Too many criminals got away with murder because of them. So we got rid of all of them.

Q. There are widespread rumors that torture is widely used in your criminal justice system. Is there any truth to those rumors?
A. Absolutely not. Sometimes, in protecting the interests of the state and the people it is there to serve, it is necessary to use some physical force in questioning prisoners. But it is always done under medical supervision, and could never be defined as torture.

Q. Your government and its predecessors made and make much of the "crime problem," and tout your abilities to deal with it. Since the mid-1990s, your country, under whatever leadership, has had the highest incarceration rate in the industrialized world (Butterfield; Sklar). Now I know that you have not kept statistics on these matters for some years, but according to many reports, crime, especially violent crime, remains at a high level in the White Republic. Could you explain that?
A. We have a great record on crime. For example, we've been able to eliminate the crimes of child abuse, wife-beating, and sex abuse, at least in the White Republic, very simply. We just corrected the errors in the definition of what a crime is that had been foisted on us by the liberal nigger lovers. It was those intruding liberals who made what a man does inside the confines of his own family and his own home a crime.

We have restored man to his rightful place as the head of his family. Any man has the right to do what needs to be done to control his family, and, I might add, teach his children about sex in any way that he sees fit. So, those crimes are just gone.

Q. In the White Republic, you have recently introduced what you call the *Personal Identification System.*[8] Your government

8. *Author's Note:* The *Personal Identification System* (PIS) was to have been a massive outgrowth of the satellite-based Global Positioning System (GPS) for naval vessels that during the Transition Era had been refined and modified ➤

has said that it is for the purposes of personal safety. But questions are being raised abroad, suggesting that your government is now moving to attempt to control the movements of every resident of the White Republic. Is that true? Is the system intrusive? Is it to be used, as your critics claim, for monitoring, intelligence, and the control of personal movements?
A. Our critics claim many things. They always have. They always will. But they are just that, critics. And they will make up any story they want to, they will invent any libel, just to criticize. They have nothing better to do with their time, when in fact they should be doing time for their slanders. The PIS is a marvelous invention. It is designed to enhance the personal safety of each and every citizen of the White Republic, and that is what it will be used for.

Q. You have a bipartite weapons policy. Could you explain it for our readers?
A. In the old days, the right to own firearms was one of the basic rights that the old Republican Party and then the RCA set out to protect, against the attacks of the liberal nigger lovers. In the Second Amendment,[9] the Constitution clearly grants

---

for personal use in boating (Boat/US). The GPS was capable of taking an electronic signal sent by a transmitter on earth to the satellite system, thence back to an earth-bound receiver, and record the geographic position of the transmitter on a computerbased digital or graphic locator.

For the PIS, every person was supposed to swallow, or be forced to swallow if necessary, a device which biologically attached itself to the wall of the small intestine, just below the Ampulla of Vater. Powered by an eternal battery which was to recharge itself using the electron differential of intestinal fluid, the device was to emit a signal detectable by the satellite network. The system never even came close to being fully operational (see also "Author's Commentary").

9. *Author's Note:* The Second Amendment read: "A well regulated Militia, being necessary to the security of a free State, the right of the people to keep and bear Arms, shall not be infringed." The generally accepted modern interpretation, which is at odds with Conroy's, will be found in the text below in the "Author's Commentary." The Amendment, misinterpretation and misuse of which brought so much figurative and literal grief to the old U.S., was of course clarified in the Constitution of the Re-United States, Article VIII, Section 2 (see Appendix VII).

that right. And of course we have secured it in the New American Republics. For personal protection, Whites may own any kinds of individual firearms they want to, without restriction, up to and including machine guns and grenades.

None of the other races are permitted to own firearms, nor are any of those few liberal nigger lovers remaining in the White Republic. Any such person caught with a firearm will be deported to one of the colored Republics, sent directly to a Moral Rehabilitation Center (MRC), or be subject to trial and imprisonment. The penalty imposed depends upon the type and number of weapons we find in the possession of such snakes. Enforcing the firearms laws is an important function of the Helmsmen.

Q. You mentioned the Helmsmen. The institution of the Helmsmen is a touchy subject abroad. There are rumored to be "Death Squads." What are the functions of the Helmsmen, how are they controlled, and what is their relationship to the Independent Militias?
A. The Helmsmen are the Peoples' Guides. They know what's right; they know what's wrong; they know the Word of God. They are everywhere. Their job is to preserve peace and safety everywhere they are. Again, our great country is being libeled by ridiculous charges from self-interested parties or people who are frankly criminals. I can categorically deny the existence of any so-called "Death Squads."

The Independent Militias are simply groups of like-minded men who like to dress up like soldiers and get together for fun and games on the weekends, like the local militias did in the old days. They have very good relationships with the Helmsmen.

Q. Another touchy subject abroad is that matter of the "Protective Fences" that surround the units of the Negro and Indian Republics, and separates the Hispanic Republic from the White Republic along the old Mexican border. Some call them "Killer Fences." What is your response to that charge?

A. Again, there is so much distortion. The term "Killer Fence" is used only by our enemies. We consider it to be defamatory. These fences were set up to protect the inferior peoples, for their own good. There is nothing more or less to say about them.

Q. Turning to a completely different area of social policy, the NAR has recently abolished the old Social Security System. Could you explain how that undertaking is going to improve living conditions in your country?
A. Yes. Too many good White folks were putting too much money into Social Security that they weren't getting back. And anyway, people should be responsible for themselves. God will always provide for the righteous. So, without too much publicity, we have terminated the Social Security System. It follows welfare onto the scrap heap of history, where it belongs. After all, that was the idea of one of the worst liberal nigger lovers of them all, Franklin Delano Rosenfeld.

In ending Social Security, we ended a great social wrong. We gave the Whites back what they had put in. But we kept what the other races had put in, as payment for all of the welfare they got.[10] The assets came to close to $200 billion (USBOC). That money helped us to pay off our foreign creditors.

Now everyone knows in advance that they are on their own. God helps those who help themselves. If they can't make it, that's a sign that they are inferior (see Chapter 7 and Appendix V), which means that we either send them to an MRC or deport them to one of the other Republics.

Q. Along that line, on one aspect of your racial policy, I have recently come across the term "black Whites." Could you explain it for our readers?

---

10. *Author's Note:* A precedent for the confiscation of non-white contributions to Social Security can be found in the German Nazi confiscation of Jewish property during the 1930s, even before the onset of the Second World War.

A. Certainly. It's really very simple. Everyone can work, and everyone has the responsibility to work. We have no minimum wages, and since there is no such thing as unemployment, there is no such thing as unemployment insurance, of course. If a white is not working and has no other means of support, and claims therefore to be "poor," that simply means that they are lazy and irresponsible.

Those are characteristics of Negroes, not of White people. Such people are then declared to be de facto blacks. The Helmsmen round them up and send them off to various locations in the Negro Republic.

The rationale, as I said, is a simple one. If they don't work, they are not self-responsible. Since they are not self-responsible, they cannot be White, because by definition, all Whites are self-responsible. Therefore, such people must be black, and thus must be separated. Since self-responsibility is an inherited trait of Whites, these non-self-responsible, so-called "Whites" are obviously genetically inferior, and must be removed from good White society. Especially if they are of reproductive age, they cannot be allowed to continue to live in the White Republic and possibly end up poisoning the white gene pool.

Q. Miss Conroy, I want to thank you for being so generous with your time, and so forthright with your answers. I know that our readers will be most grateful to you for both.
A. Alex, it's has been a pleasure. As you know, you are welcome to talk with us any time.

Author's Commentary
The Opening
Poughton had as much access to the Hague regime as any journalist of the time. None, not even the lackeys of the regime-beholden domestic media, had access to any official more highly placed than Connie Conroy, who was still simply a White House press officer. The real powers in the regime held "the media," any part of it, in absolute contempt.

This attitude stemmed from the days when Right-Wing Reaction had portrayed "the media" as one of the prime enemies of the American people (see Appendix III). For example, during the 1992 Presidential campaign, a citizen sent a news clipping from *The New York Times*, considered by some to be the bastion of newspaper liberalism, to the campaign headquarters of then President George Bush. The clipping contained a news item that was mildly critical of "something the campaign said" (Barrett). The writer received the following response from the Bush campaign:

> "Thanks for taking the time to write me with your thoughts, and for the clippings. I should caution you against believing everything you read in the newspapers, particularly *The New York Times*. It is a reputable newspaper, but it is editorially LIBERAL and not read in places not under the influence of New York City. Sincerely, Mary Matalin."

Many of the high Hague officials were so indoctrinated by the political anti-media claptrap of the type that had been spewed by hate radio's Limbaughs, Liddys, and Grants in the "bad old days" (of the Transition Era) that they actually believed it to be true. (Just as they actually believed that blacks were the genetic inferior of whites. That belief would eventually play a significant role in their ultimate downfall.)

Poughton, as previously noted, paid for his access to the regime by writing frequent puff pieces for his paper, the *London Sunday Times*. In return he not only had access, but could travel fairly easily at least to those many areas of the country not closed entirely to foreigners. And he did last all the way through the fall of the NAR, one of the few foreign journalists to do so. So, he was "nice" to Conroy, and to the regime, and just recorded her answers to his questions as she gave them, without adding any comments.

Any guilt feelings he had about the role he played were

apparently assuaged by the letters he sent to "Karl," and by the fact that he steadily accumulated and preserved voluminous amounts of data/information about what was really going on in the NAR. Since so many official records were destroyed by the Hague regime when it fell, the Poughton library has been and continues to be of great use to modern historians.

On Religion

The NAR/ACNP policy on religion was remarkable. Hague, in essence, had his cake and ate it too. He was both President and head of the American Christian Nation Party. Regularly renewing the NAR-creating "emergency decree," under which, among other things, he had suspended elections, he was effectively President for life, or as long as he could hold onto power.

He owed everything to the Right-Wing Religious Politics that had first been perfected by the old Christian Coalition during the Transition Era. (There is no indication that the Christian Coalition or any of its leadership would have specifically approved of any Hagueite polices.) It was one possible outcome of the old Christian Coalition's "15% Solution" that put him where he was. The Supremacy Amendment, which put the "Law of God," in reality whatever Hague said it was, above the "Law of Man," at Hague's pleasure, was part of the Constitution. (As noted above, although Hague had that power, he had never used it, for reasons discussed just below.)

Hague had ridden to his current position on the strength of the "America is a Christian Nation" arguments he set forth in his Second Inaugural. "Christian Law," which like the "Law of God" was whatever Hague said it was, was paramount. Hague publicly accepted the "Inerrancy" of the Bible (see Chapter 9). Despite all of this, Hague refused the many entreaties of the Right-Wing Reactionary Christian ministry to officially declare the NAR a Christian Nation. Why?

Surely it was not for reasons of religious freedom, as Conroy disingenuously stated. As noted, there were no personal freedoms in the NAR, religious or otherwise. There were putative non-Christians who supported Hague, such as the political descendants of that sliver of American Jewry that during the Transition Era had allied itself with Right-Wing Reaction (Toward Tradition). However, that group had long since compromised any religious or ethical principles based in the Jewish tradition, or religion, it might have had.

No, the reason was a simple one. As previously noted, Hague had no intention of ever sharing power with those "fucking preachers." And that he would have had to do if he had declared the NAR a Christian Nation, officially. For if the NAR were officially a Christian Nation, who but the Christian religious leadership would have the primary responsibility for determining just what that meant, on all issues from great to small?

As more than one of those "fucking preachers" was known to have said over the years of the NAR, "you know, Reagan fucked us on the moral issues, now Hague has fucked us on sharing the power. The question now is, is God going to fuck those bastards when it comes to Judgment Day?"

The Religious Right had been through this abandonment process before. For example, on the "moral" issue of freedom of choice in the outcome of pregnancy, during the early Transition Era President Ronald Reagan vigorously opposed it in rhetoric. But in practical terms he did little in an attempt to legally deny it. Although not using the kind of language quoted above, leading Right-Wing Reactionary figures of the Transition Era such as Paul Weyrich (1993) referred to the Reaganite policy as a "blow" to the "Religious New Right."

On Elective Pregnancy Termination Policy

This policy was so patently racist (expected) and hypocritical (not necessarily expected, but not surprising either), that no further comment on the policy itself is necessary. One interesting fact. For all the anti-feminist, misogynist, anti-choice propaganda that was featured throughout the time of the NAR, and for all the repression, many women in the White Republic continued to have or attempted to have elective pregnancy terminations using the black market drugs that were readily available.

Even with the media fully under its control, its churches benefitting from the blessings of the state, public education replaced by church or homebound education, and so forth, many women still wanted to control their own patterns of reproduction. Thus the "War for the Preservation of Life" carried out by the "Life Preservation Police" had to continue unabated, and continued to keep the "Life Preservation Prisons" full. And the abortion rate remained high.

On the elective pregnancy termination (EPT) services that were provided in the non-White Republics, the "Pre-born Baby Killing Stations" were a myth. They did not exist, and did not have to exist for EPT to be readily available. The Right-Wing Reactionaries had simply never been able to come to terms with the fact that for many years virtually all elective pregnancy terminations had been accomplished by using drugs, not surgery (see Chapter 7).

EPTs were widely available, by choice of the pregnant woman, using drugs which were either smuggled into the non-White Republics or, in certain cases manufactured in them. Furthermore, Conroy was also unable to deal with the fact that the writ of the NAR extended very little in practical terms into the territories of the non-White Republics (see also Chapter 17).

First, the racism of the Hagueites was so ingrained in their thinking that they really could not conceive that non-Whites could effectively govern themselves. The Hagueites really thought that they were "animal-like," and that the best policy was to treat them with "benign neglect" because they couldn't possibly organize themselves to bring any harm to the Whites. Second, even if this proved to be the case, the Hagueites were sure that the Killer Fences and the Helmsmen Garrisons provided the Whites with complete control of and security from the non-White Republics (they did not; see below and Chapter 17).

Third, the Hagueites thought that their population/food

policy was effective, creating, if all else failed, the potential for semi-starvation as a means of control. It wasn't. The non-White populations did practice voluntary population control policies, based on sound family planning principles, which did not include forced sterilization. (The Hagueites were simply given reports that forced sterilization had been carried out, when it had not been.)

As to food, the Hagueite "this is the amount of food you get and that's that" policy had much in common with the old Republican "block grant," "welfare payments are fixed no matter how much misery there is," policy of the late Transition Era. However, at least in those Black Republic Sectors which had access to a significant water supply, local scientists were able to develop hydroponics, the growing of food in a water-based environment, to a high level of sophistication and efficiency. In many of the Indian Republic Sectors, traditional Amerindian agriculture and animal husbandry was reintroduced, emphasizing maize and the raising of bison (Goodstein).

On Culture

The censorial approach to culture was a natural extension of the Right-Wing Reactionary censorship movement of the 90s, and the constant attacks on the "mainstream media" and Hollywood, even by "mainstream" Republican politicians like Sen. Phil Gramm of Texas (Orin) and Sen. Bob Dole of Kansas. The racism of the NAR policy was the natural extension of the creation of an apartheid state in the first place. The exclusion of black culture or even any black cultural influences in the White Republic was a classical cut-off-your-nose to-spite-your-face Right-Wing Reactionary move. It echoed the banning of "degenerate" (read Jewish and left-wing/progressive) art by the German Nazis under Hitler and Goebbels (Hughes).

In the White Republic, radio and television featured either ACNP propaganda, hate, or blandness. In the non-White Republics, low-power FM radio, illegal to be sure, quickly developed to provide an alternative to the dominant media culture. Later, shortwave radio would provide the critical linkages between the various non-White Republics Sectors as first the revolts and then the Second Civil War got underway.

On Civil Liberties

Conroy ducked, dissembled, and distorted on her answer to this question. She was well schooled in the old racist Right-Wing Reactionary "racists-who-us-are-you-kidding?" ploy, and applied it to questions on civil liberties.

In the NAR, there were no civil liberties, in the constitutional sense, even though the old U.S. Constitution was technically still in force. The Fourth Amendment had been repealed some time before. The Hague Declaration of Peace, a national emergency, was still in effect. There were no elections. The Helmsmen ruled the streets (see below). Although the rule of law was still on the books, *de jure*, the rule of man had replaced it, *de facto*, as it had in every other fascist country from Japan of the 1930s and Spain of Franco's time (1939-75) to Uruguay and Argentina of the 1970s.

So when the Hagueites defined "freedom of speech" to exclude anyone declared to be a "liberal nigger lover" (and the declarer was usually a Helmsman acting on his own authority, often on the word of an informer), that arrangement defined just what "freedom of speech" really meant. "Good speech," "Christian," "moral," pro-ACNP/regime speech was accorded freedom; "bad speech" wasn't, under the watchful eye of your friendly Helmsman.

Hate speech, directed at blacks (even though there were none left in the White Republic), Latinos and Asians (there were still some of them around), homosexuals (none were visible, of course, since homosexuality had been made a crime), women, the aged, the handicapped, "foreigners," and so on and so forth, was perfectly "free." In fact, it was encouraged, just as it had been on Transition Era hate radio.

The Hagueites defended to the hilt the right of anyone to freely spew hate (just as long as it was right-wing hate) just as

Right-Wing Reaction had done back in the Transition Era. That Right-Wing Reaction defended free speech rights for no other kind of speech during either the Era or the Period never seemed to strike any on the Right as peculiar or contradictory.

On the Legal System

There was no "legal system" in the constitutional sense, because there was no "law" in the constitutional sense. Torture was widely used, and, for example, just as it had been in Argentina's "Dirty War" of the 1970s (Dorfman), it was done under "medical supervision." Its use was acknowledged within the NAR's "criminal justice system," if you could call it that. Employees of that system who might express some reservations about the practice, (and since the system was so large and employed so many people, there were bound to be objectors from time to time), were told that "torture purifies the soul."

Unlike in Nazi Germany, where Hitler quickly unified all police and secret police functions under the S.S., in the NAR, following the pattern of the old U.S., there were multiple and rival police-type jurisdictions and organizations: the traditional local and state police/prosecuting attorneys/courts/prison system; the National Intelligence Agency (NIA), created by merging the old Federal Bureau of Investigation (primarily but not exclusively focused on domestic matters) and Central Intelligence Agency (primarily but not exclusively focused on foreign matters); the ever on-going "War on Drugs" and the Drug Enforcement Administration; the ever on-going "War for the Preservation of Life," and its special courts, police, and prisons.

Looming over all of this was the Helmsmen (HM), which, like the German Nazi S.S., had its public and secret (Nazi Gestapo-like) branches. It had no courts or prosecutors, because it didn't need them; it had the power of arbitrary arrest and detention, "on God's Word." The HM had its own prison system, the Moral Rehabilitation Centers. And it could step into the actions of any of the other law enforcement agencies whenever and wherever it wanted to.

In addition to the HM, there were the "Independent Militias." They were the descendants of those of the old Transition Era and early Fascist period Right-Wing Reactionary local militias that did not choose to merge into the HM. (There is no indication, however, that any of the militias actually existing during the Transition Era would have performed in any of the ways herein described, either as part of the HM or independently.) The Independents were closely allied with the HM and often carried out its extra-dirty, extra-extra-legal functions. Almost all of both the International and the Domestic Death Squads were run out of Independent units rather than the HM *per se*.

In this complex but essentially arbitrary environment of criminal "law" enforcement, that jury trials and *habeas corpus* had been abolished meant nothing. Even though this complex, many-tentacled structure for repression was ridden with incessant bureaucratic, even occasionally violent, infighting, standing astride it was the HM, and all that that meant. The Atmosphere of Fear was all-pervasive in the nation.

On Crime

Conroy ducked the question on crime. And while Poughton must have strained to ask a followup on this one, he knew that if he broke the ground rules once, he would never have another interview with Conroy, whether she wanted to do one or not. (All interviews were monitored by the NIA.) The position on domestic violence was simply an extension of the "man is the master in his own home" thinking that was characteristic of Right-Wing Reaction.

Its modern version had its origins in the Transition Era. For example, during that time at Bob Jones University, a then unaccredited Right-Wing religious institution of higher education, female students were taught that sexual harassment of women by men, and indeed rape itself, was to be blamed on women who are either too "provocative" or "threatening" to men (Edwards).

Although much of the "law" enforcement effort in the White Republic focused on political repression, it is interesting to note that the very high level of incarceration had no more of a salutary effect on the commission of conventional crime than it had had in the old U.S. (Lacayo, 1994).

On the Personal Identification System

The PIS had as its goal to monitor the physical location of each and every person in the White Republic at all times. Thus it was to be the ultimate means of intrusion on individual freedom and liberty, not a system for "personal security." The goal was there, the system was proposed, the developmental work was done. The scientific principles on which it was based were quite sound.

But the technical operating problems of continuously keeping track of the movements of over 200,000,000 people proved impossible to solve. This was especially true for a regime that, because of its virtual destruction of the higher education system, had an ever dwindling supply of well-educated scientists, engineers, and computer specialists at its call.

In an echo of the old Reaganite "Star Wars" anti-missile system boondoggle, the Hagueites spent tens of billions of dollars trying to perfect the PIS before they eventually abandoned their attempts to put it into general use. A limited version of it was used by the central commands of the NIA and the Helmsmen to monitor the positions of their agents/members at all times.

Weapons policies

The private weapons policies of the NAR were developed for it by the All-American Rifle Association (AARA), a descendant of the Transition Era organization called the National Rifle Association (NRA). Theoretically a membership organization, the NRA had been in fact a political front and lobbying group for the gun manufacturers' and dealers' industry. Founded in the 19th Century, it became especially powerful beginning in the Transition Era, under the political patronage and protection of the Reaganites. During the Transition Era, the further the old Republican Party moved to the Right, and the more power the Party gained, the more powerful the NRA had become.

Its attitude towards guns and their private ownership was well summarized by this statement one Wayne R. LaPierre, NRA executive vice president, addressed to his membership during the late Transition Era (*NYT*, 5/8/95):

> " 'The Final War Has Begun. A document secretly delivered to me reveals frightening evidence that the full scale war to crush your gun rights has not only begun but is well underway. What's more, dozens of Federal gun ban bills suggest this final assault has begun—not just to ban all handguns or all semi-automatics, but to eliminate private firearms ownership completely and forever. I firmly believe the NRA has no alternative but to recognize the attack and counter with every resource we can muster.' "

The NRA, using both this kind of persuasion and its even more persuasive political muscle, managed to convince many people, and especially members of Congress to whom they made large campaign contributions, that only the second part of the Second Amendment was operative. Recall that the Second Amendment read: "A well regulated Militia, being necessary to the security of a free State, the right of the people to keep and bear Arms, shall not be infringed." The NRA managed to functionally block out from the public consciousness the terms and phrases "well regulated," "Militia," and "security of a free State."

On the old Constitutional issue of the true meaning of the old Second Amendment, modern historians now generally agree that:

- "Well regulated" meant "well regulated," not "unregulated."
- "Militia" referred to a "military organization" of a particular type, and that "as the U.S. Supreme Court observed as early

as 1886 'Military operation and military drill are subjects especially under the control of the *government* of every country' [emphasis added]" (Dees and Zelikow).

- The word "state" in the phrase "security of a free State" referred to a government entity, not any individual or group of individuals.

Therefore, it is now generally agreed that by its plain language, if read as a whole, the Second in no way conferred upon any individual the right to own one or more guns, free of regulation or control. Furthermore, they note that the old U.S. Supreme Court never interpreted the Second as doing anything of the kind. (This modern interpretation has informed weapons ownership policy in the Re-United States; see Article VIII, Section 2 of the Constitution of the Re-United States.)

Nevertheless, in the old U.S. it was neither the Supreme Court nor a literal reading of the Amendment that made gun policy. It was the NRA, backed as it was by a very profitable industry that wanted very much to stay that way and thus needed an ever expanding market. Thus in the old U.S., private gun ownership eventually became completely unlimited and completely unregulated. Such a policy was to the political advantage of Right-Wing Reaction, which gained major support from the gunners.

Once the NAR was established, however, the needs of Right-Wing Reaction *vis-a-vis* gun ownership changed. It then wanted to limit, to the extent possible, gun ownership by real or potential opponents of the Hague regime. And so did their gun policy change, as spelled out in the Conroy-Poughton interview. That is one reason why the NRA was replaced with the AARA.

Recognizing that the "unalienable right to own a gun" and any kind of gun you wanted at that, was a good thing only when most of the gunners were on your side politically, the AARA was right out in front with the Hagueites on the new policy. There was no apparent reason for the gun industry to have an interest in selling weapons to interests which, if they ever took power, would sharply curtail the business of that industry.

"Protective Fences"

What Conroy called "protective fences" were actually the deadly, computer-operated, proactive, "Killer Fences." They were able to seek out and destroy any living beings that approached within 100 yards of them. "Reach Out and Grab Someone" was the slogan its operators applied to the system. The technology was extremely complex (see, for example, Blake). Some of its forerunners were already under development during the Transition Era, although a "Killer Fence" was certainly not under consideration at that time (Lacayo, 1991; Nelson).

The fences featured such devices as skin pigment readers (color cinematography, computer-read for skin color); body temperature readers; distant DNA evaluators; remote human heartsound detectors, all hooked together by super-super computers, operating in the nanosecond range. Triple camera systems permitted pinpointing of victims, followed by ultrasound immobilization and killing by laser beams.

The idea of fencing to achieve national policy goals was not a new one to Right-Wing Reaction. During the Transition Era, Right-Wing Reactionary leaders had urged the construction of an electrified fence along the entire 2000 mile length of the Mexican border. That fence, a passive, low-tech apparatus, was intended simply to keep people out. But along the boundaries of the Sectors of the Black and Red Republics, the very high-tech Killer Fences were intended to keep people in. And until they began to fall into disrepair, for there were thousands of miles of them, and the inhabitants of the Black and Red Republics learned how to safely get around, through, under, and over them, they did keep people in.

"Black Whites"

Officially there was no unemployment in the White Republic.

Thus there was no unemployment insurance. There was no minimum wage either, and all labor unions had been shut down, replaced by government-sponsored "benevolent societies." Real wages and family incomes had just continued on the steady downward trend that had been established in the old U.S. even before the commencement of the Transition Era. However, there were also not enough jobs to go around for everyone who wanted to work, even for abysmally low wages. So how could there have been no unemployment?

The "black Whites" solution was developed to deal with this situation. It helped control the labor surplus, by shipping excess workers out of the White Republic. At the same time, it also helped to depress wages, by making sure that the incentive to work for low wages was high: if you didn't work, you got deported to a non-White Republic or sent to an MRC.

In a sense, this arrangement was like the old 19th century English poorhouse/workhouse system. That one was constructed on the theory of "less eligibility." To the person not working and who otherwise had no or insufficient income, for whatever reason—no available jobs, laziness, mental or physical illness, family problems, lack of skill or knowledge, whatever—the system said: "We will take care of you." "BUT," it also said, "you will live in a way that is 'less eligible' than anything you might find on the outside." That is, even the worst of independent living conditions would be better than that *designed for* the poorhouse or workhouse.

The Hagueites had no way of knowing that it happened that many of those whites deported to a non-White Republic ended up living better than they had in the White Republic, as long as they lived by the rules of their new "country." So secure were the Hagueites in their racist ideology, that they never bothered to look, and certainly couldn't have conceived of what happened happening. But that is another story (see Chapter 17).

Was the NAR Fascist?

The final question for this chapter: does all of this represent fascism? Was the New American Republics a fascist country, as claimed by this book? Neither the American Christian Nation Party nor the Hague regime ever used the terms fascist or Nazi to describe themselves, even though some of their constituents wished they would. But there were other Far Right constituents who thought, or at least pretended they thought, that Right-Wing Reaction was actually fighting fascism/ Nazism.

For example, during the Transition Era a strong adherent of the NRA compared "the behavior of our uncontrolled Federal agents to that of the Nazis in the Third Reich" (*NYT,* 5/8/95). Another referred to members of the Bureau of Alcohol, Tobacco, and Firearms conducting searches for illegal weaponry (and there was at the time a very limited list of weapons that were illegal) as "jack-booted, bucket-helmeted, [Federal] Government thugs."

This analogy was apparently intended to stir up negative images of German Nazi storm troopers, while claiming that opposition to gun control was the protection of American freedom at its most basic. At the same time, of course, it was the gunners who later formed the core of the HM. The ideology of most of the Transition Era militias was virtually the same as that of the German Nazis during the 1930s and the European neo-Nazis of their own time. Thus, Right-Wing Reaction revealed some curious contradictions.

Hague, by decree, had made himself President indefinitely, and had made Congress into his handmaiden. But the Hague regime constantly claimed that it was ruling under the U.S. Constitution and stood for "freedom and the American Way." So was the Hague Regime fascist or not? To be informed on that question, let us recall the Dino Louis Duck Rule: "If it looks like a duck, …, it's a duck." Then, more rigorously, let us apply the Dino Louis Transition Era definition of fascism, spelled out in his 1998 essay, "The Nature of Fascism and Its Precursors" (see Appendix II), to the condition in which the nation found itself in 2015.

A Definition of Fascism

Louis defined fascism as a political, social, and economic system that has the fourteen major defining characteristics (see that Appendix). We shall consider them ad seriatim, as they may be applied to the NAR under Jefferson Davis Hague and the ACNP. Just how did the Hague regime stack up against the Louis definition?

1. There was complete executive branch control of government policy and action. There was neither an independent judicial nor an independent legislative branch of government.
2. *De jure*, there was a constitution in force, and supposedly governing. However, *de facto*, the rule of man had been substituted for the rule of law.
3. Rival political parties to the ACNP still existed on paper, even a weak Democratic Party still parroting the old Democratic Leadership Council "we can be better Republicans than the Republicans" line. But there was only one political party that meant anything, no mass organizations of any kind other than those approved by the government were permitted, and in any case, elections had been suspended.
4. The ACNP and the government established and through the HM enforced the rules of "right" thinking, "right" action, and "right" religious devotion.
5. Racism, homophobia, misogynism, and national chauvinism were major factors in national politics and policy making, e.g. consider the structure of the NAR itself, the major place given to homophobia in national policy both before and after the founding of the NAR, the oppression of women by law, and the chauvinistic nature of both Latin and Canadian policy.
6. Again *de facto* there was no recognition of inherent personal rights, although they existed *de jure*. There was not even *presumed* freedom of the press. There were no inherent or presumed protections against any violations of personal

liberty committed by law enforcement or other government agencies.

7. Official and unofficial force, internal terror, and routine torture of captured opponents were major means of governmental control.
8. There were few employee rights or protections, although on paper workers still had the right to bargain collectively through the government authorized "benevolent societies."
9. All communications media were government-controlled, although in a "free market environment" not government-owned (see, for example, Sherrill, on the international media mogul of the Transition Era who served the interests of Right-Wing Reaction around the world, the Australian-born Rupert Murdoch).
10. All entertainment, music, art, and organized sport was operated under government censorship/control.
11. Hague was dominant in the government, close to being a dictator. Although he made frequent public appearance on television and in otherwise controlled settings and was generally popular among his own ideological constituents, he was not a charismatic leader in the Hitler/Mussolini mold. Thus he fell somewhere between that model and the rather faceless leaders of Japanese fascism.
12. The economy was based on capitalism, but ideologically bound to the "free market." So there was no "tight central control of the distribution of resources among the producers." In fact, the insistence by the economic decision makers who pulled Hague's strings on maintaining as free a market as possible did produce problems for Hague in war production when the Second Civil War got underway.
13. There was a foreign war, the "Latin Wars." But it was not of the World War II type, by any stretch of the imagination.
14. The NAR was inherently unstable and carried with it the seeds of its own destruction, as we shall see below. And they did sprout within a relatively short historical period of time, although it was much too long for most Americans

who had to live through it, and certainly for the many who did not survive it.

Although the NAR did not match the Louis definition in every detail, for the most part it did. The consensus of modern historians is that, yes, the ACNP was a fascist party, Hague was a fascist dictator, and the NAR itself was a fascist country.

References:

Ain, S., "College Defends Sex Education Materials," *The New York Times*, July 16, 1995.

Blake, E., *The "Killer Fence:" High Technology in the Service of High Level Oppression*, New New York: The Freedom Press, 2038.

Boat/US (Alexandria, VA), "The GPS/Loran Debate–Which is Best for Me?" *Catalog*, 1995, p. 24.

Butterfield, F., "More in U.S. Are in Prisons, Report Says," *The New York Times*, August 10, 1995.

Dees, M., Zelikow, P., "Shut Down America's Terrorist Training Camps," Southern Poverty Law Center, information letter attachment, May 3, 1995.

Dorfman, *A., Death and the Maiden*, (a play).

Edwards, L. "Worldly Lessons," *The New York Times*, May 30, 1993, "Style" section, p. 1.

Ellington, D., *The New American Republics: Fascism Rampant on a Field of Blood: 2011-2019*, New New York: The Freedom Press, 2037.

Freedom Watch, "When 'Reform' Becomes a Dirty Word," Vol. 3, No. 4, Jan/Feb, 1994.

Goodstein, C. "Buffalo comeback: Native Americans try restoring a spiritual economy based on bison," *The Amicus Journal*, Spring, 1995, p. 34.

Hughes, R., "Culture on the Nazi Pillory," *Time*, March 4, 1991.

Lacayo, R., "Nowhere To Hide," *Time*, November 11, 1991

.

Lacayo, R., "Lock 'Em Up!," *Time*, February 7, 1994.

Nelson, L.E., "A Gun Detector, High-Tech Style," *Newsday*, March 22, 1994.

NYT: The New York Times, "'Godless Monstrosity' in Political Debate," August 18, 1993.

NYT: The New York Times, "Bearing Arms, and Harsh Words," May 8, 1995.

Orin, D., "Sexplosive charge links Phil Gramm to skin flick," *New York Post*, May 18, 1995.

Porteous, S., Institute of First Amendment Studies, fundraising letter, May, 1995.

Rich, F., "The Unkindest Cut," *The New York Times*, May 21, 1995.

Schollenberger, J., "Concerned About Concerned Women for America," *Freedom Writer*, January, 1995, p. 3.

Schrag, P., "Bailing Out Public Education," *The Nation*, October 4, 1993, p. 351.

Sherrill, R., "Citizen Murdoch: Buying His Way to a Media Empire," *The Nation*, May 29, 1995, p. 749.

Shirer, W.L., *The Rise and Fall of the Third Reich*, New York: Simon and Schuster, 1960.

Sklar, H., "Reinforcing Racism with the War on Drugs," *Z Magazine*, December, 1995, p. 19.

Toward Tradition, "Should Jews Fear the Christian Right?" (an advertisement), *The New York Times*, August 2, 1994.

USBOC: U.S. Bureau of the Census, *Statistical Abstract of the United States, 1994* (114th Edition), Washington, D.C., 1994, Table 581, (projection).

Weyrich, P., "Comments: The Future," in Comartie, M., Ed., *No Longer Exiles*, Washington, DC: Ethics and Public Policy Center, 1993, p. 53.

CHAPTER 16
2017: The Legitimation Treaty

Author's Commentary[1]
"The Treaty of Comity"

"The Treaty of Comity Between the New American Republics and the Republic of Quebec (RQ)" served to affirm in their entirety a new set of territorial arrangements within and between the two countries made at the expense of a third, the former nation of Canada. The latter was for all intents and purposes dismembered. Signed and ratified by the NAR and the RQ in 2017, the treaty became effective on the second Monday in October (that year October 9), which happened to be Canadian Thanksgiving Day.

In making their new treaty effective on Canadian Thanksgiving Day, the North American fascists (for the RQ was, like the NAR, a fascist state) exhibited the same high sense of irony their ideological and historical forebears, the German Nazis, had. For instance, during the Second World War, the S.S. had hung over the gate to their principal extermination camp for Jews and other national minorities at Auschwitz, Poland a sign saying *Arbeit Macht Frei* ("Work Makes You Free").

1. *Author's Note:* There is no indication or evidence that Patrick Buchanan, Lucien Bouchard, any Quebec or other Canadian separationist/independence organization, the "Wise Use Movement" or any of its leadership, membership, or constituent organizations, or any other historical personage or organization mentioned or alluded to in this chapter or elsewhere in this book in a similar manner, would have supported or approved in any way of "The Treaty of Comity," or any of the institutions, events, laws, policies, or procedures created or carried out pursuant to it by the NAR or any Canadian or successor Canadian entity such as the "Republic of Quebec," mentioned, discussed, or alluded to anywhere in this chapter or subsequent ones.

The treaty quickly became known as the "Legitimation Treaty," for two reasons. First, it simply legitimized changes in national boundaries and determinations of sovereignty that had already been accomplished through economic power playing, treachery, and the force of arms, rather than diplomatic negotiation. Second, few people knew what the word "comity" meant.

Oddly enough, since the treaty had everything to with force, it had nothing to do with comity in any case. A dictionary definition from the pre-fascist period [Guralnik] of the word "comity" as applied to the relationship between nations indicates that it was a term implying grace and elegance: "the courtesy and respect of peaceful nations for each other's laws and institutions." Grace and elegance, however, were terms which could be applied neither to the two governments that made the treaty nor to what it meant for the nation of Canada. To use the word "comity" in the name of such a treaty, however, was entirely consistent with the respective claims of the NAR that it was not racist on the basis of skin color and the RQ that it was not anti-Semitic.

The Treaty's Historical Precursors

As to the economic and political events leading up to the dismemberment of Canada, from the NAR's perspective its "Resource Based Economy" underlay the territorial push northward in the West where the available untapped resources were. As previously noted, during the Transition Era certain Right-Wing Reactionaries such as Patrick Buchanan (1989) had advocated the annexation to the old U.S. of the four western provinces of Canada: Manitoba, Saskatchewan, Alberta, and British Columbia.

Annexation of all or part of Canada was not a new idea in the United States, however. Although nothing came of it at the time, it was one of the impetuses for the War of 1812 with Great Britain. In the early 1840s, when the "Oregon Territory" in the lower northwestern region of the North American continent was being opened up to European settlement, it was at first jointly controlled by the United States and Great Britain. The territory encompassed what eventually became the states of Oregon and Washington, and the Canadian provinces of British Columbia and parts of Alberta (Chernow and Vallasi).

Those settlers of the Oregon Territory with allegiance to the growing United States wanted to incorporate all of it, extending to latitude 54 deg. 40 min. N, into the old U.S. (Chernow and Vallasi). The territorial slogan of those settlers was "Fifty-Four Forty or Fight." The settlers with British allegiance did not like that idea at all. In 1846, the "Oregon Controversy" was settled with an agreement between the U.S. and Great Britain to fix at the 49th parallel the boundary between what would become the states of Minnesota, North Dakota, Montana, Idaho, and Washington and the four Western Canadian Provinces.

Just after the First U.S. Civil War a campaign for annexation of all of Canada was undertaken in the U.S. Congress. It held strong appeal to such men as General William Tecumseh Sherman (Fast), (who happened to be one of the early inventors of modern total war against civilian populations). That campaign was an important factor in the passage in 1867 by the British Parliament in London of the British North America Act that created the modern Canada (Taylor).

The 1867 Act unified the then separate British colonies of Upper Canada (Ontario), Lower Canada (Quebec), Nova Scotia, and New Brunswick into the "Dominion of Canada," which was then made part of the British Empire. ("Upper" and "Lower" refer to the provinces' relationship to the location of the headwaters, at the outlet of Lake Ontario, of the northward flowing St. Lawrence River. The terms do not refer to the provinces' north-south geographical relationship.) Over time, the four Western provinces and the two additional Maritime Provinces, Prince Edward Island and Newfoundland and Labrador, were added to the country (Jenson).

The way to the eventual annexation of the four Western provinces to the NAR was originally paved by the U.S.-Canada

Free Trade Agreement of 1988. It had provided a major easing for the entry of U.S. capital into the Canadian economy. The North American Free Trade Agreement of 1994 extended the process. This lead to the eventual domination of the Canadian economy by that of the U.S. A steady loss of manufacturing jobs from Canada to the U.S. and Mexico accompanied the implementation of NAFTA. Too, there was an associated decline of Canadian agriculture. During the time of the early Fascist Period in the old U.S., this combination of events lead to increasing social unrest in Canada, the kind of unrest that in the old U.S. had lead up to the founding of the NAR.

It happened also that there was a growing fundamentalist, religion-based, Right-Wing Reactionary political movement in Canada, paralleling that of the old U.S. (although some years behind in its historical development) (*Freedom Writer*). In addition, there was a long history of separatist struggle within Quebec, lead primarily by French-Canadian Right-Wing Reaction. As a late 20th century separationist leader, Lucien Bouchard, said in 1995 after the very close failure of a separationist referendum (Farnsworth, 1995):

> "Quebecers don't want to waste time with fuzzy ideas about recognizing Quebec's 'distinct society,' based on failed past attempts, with byzantine nuances only lawyers can draw. We want our own country, now."

The economic decline and resulting unrest lead the Canadian economic decision makers to desire the same kind of authoritarian government their counterparts did in the old U.S. They found strong political allies in the home-grown Canadian Religious Right, as well as in the traditionalist Catholic hierarchy in Quebec.

However, there were certain limitations on the ability of Right-Wing Reaction to undertake direct action in Canada. Racism (directed at blacks [Farnsworth, 1996] and Canadian Native Americans, and between the Francophones of Quebec and the Anglophones of the rest of Canada), homophobia, and xenophobia (especially directed at postWorld War II Asian immigrants), certainly existed there. But because of the demographics of the country, and a strong tradition of tolerance among certain sectors of the Canadian population, they did not constitute nearly the potent political forces they were in the old U.S.

In certain parts of English-speaking Canada, especially Saskatchewan and Ontario, the traditions of personal freedom were actually more ingrained than they were anywhere in the old U.S. There was a Charter of Rights and Freedoms in the British Constitution Act of 1982 which had established full independence from Great Britain for Canada (Canada). In many of its terms, that Charter was more explicit than the old U.S. Constitution's Bill of Rights. Under agreements reached in 1992, the Canadian Native American population had achieved a good deal of internal autonomy, especially in the old Northwest Territory. So the likelihood of the successful establishment of a fascist regime across all of Canada, as a result of internal action only, was not high. A different resolution was arrived at.

The Establishment of Fascism in Quebec

With covert military assistance from the NAR, in 2015 an armed fascist takeover in Quebec was accomplished. The fascist political entity in Quebec differed somewhat from its old U.S. counterparts, the Republican-Christian Alliance and the American Christian Nation Party. First, the Right-Wing Reactionaries in Quebec openly and unashamedly identified themselves with fascism, calling their party the Parti Fasciste Quebecoise (PFQ).

Second, they relied heavily on anti-Semitism for their ideology. They proudly traced their fascist roots back to France, the France of the pre-World War I anti-Semitic hysteria of the "Dreyfus Affair," the anti-Semitic/fascistic Action Francaise and Croix de Feu parties of the pre-World War II period, and the World War II Nazi-collaborationist Vichy regime. They also proudly traced their ancestry to the regime of the proto-fascist and anti-Semitic Maurice Le Noblet Duplessis, founder of the Union Nationale and Premier of Quebec Province from 1936-39 and 1944-59.

The decades-old threat of a Canada split both constitutionally and geographically by an independent Quebec was finally realized. As its days in existence anywhere were being numbered by the Canadian fascists and the NAR, the Federal government of Canada was forced to leave the Federal capital of Ottawa because of its physical proximity to the territory of the new nation of Quebec, just across the Ottawa River at Hull.

(The logical move was to Toronto, capital of the nation's most populous province, Ontario, and home of the perennially successful major league baseball team, the Toronto Blue Jays. The Canadian government, however, made an effort to diminish its identification with the liberal majority in Ontario, while still locating the new capital centrally. They also wanted to evoke the tradition of the old ties to England. Thus they chose a place that looked for all the world like an English provincial town. Appropriately named London, it lay in fertile Ontario farmland about 60 miles to the east of the important Great Lakes port located at the southern tip of Lake Huron, Sarnia. The ploy obviously did not work.)

Fascism in Western Canada

With the secession of Quebec, the pro-fascist forces in the four Western provinces recognized both their opportunity and their weaknesses. Due to the growing instability of the central government, the Western fascists knew that the time was ripe for the promotion of their cause. The Canadian Religious Right outside of Quebec was at its strongest in the West. While anti-Semitism was a non-factor in Western Canada, anti-Ontario and anti-French-Canadian/Quebec feelings had a long history. There had been independence/separationist sentiments in the region for decades, going all the way back to 1867. And the fascists worked hard to exacerbate them.

With the heavy dependence of the economy on the old U.S. and now the NAR, and with the need for forceful repression steadily growing because of increasing social unrest, simple independence was not a viable option for the Western provinces. However, there was another simple one, accomplishing the same end. In 2016, facing valiant but out-gunned local opposition, Canadian "freedom fighters" organized by the new Canadian Party of Fascism, massively assisted by "volunteer" units of Helmsmen "on vacation in the beautiful North" (with their heavy weapons, it happened), took over the four Western Provincial governments. They made a show of talking about confederation with their fascist counterparts in Quebec, but those two groups actually hated each other's guts, on religious grounds if nothing else. So the Western Canadian fascists formally "requested the cooperation" of the NAR. A de facto annexation of the four provinces by the NAR was arranged later in 2016.

The Dismemberment of Ontario

With an incredibly effective winter action early in 2017, a combined offensive of Canadian Party of Fascism forces from the west and RQ fascist forces from the east invaded Ontario. They both had air, heavy weapons, and significant logistics support from the NAR. The invaders quickly overran the Provincial defense forces. The RQ and the NAR then proceeded to divide Ontario between themselves, along the natural boundary provided by the Albany, Kenogami, and Aguasabon rivers, running from Terrace Bay on Lake Superior to Fort Albany and Kasechewan on James Bay, the southern projection of the Hudson Bay.

At the same time, the RQ annexed Labrador, the mainland portion of the Province of Newfoundland and Labrador, which had a 1400 mile common border with Quebec and was rich in natural resources and hydropower. The four Maritime provinces, New Brunswick, Nova Scotia, Newfoundland (shorn of Labrador), and Prince Edward Island were left intact as a rump "New Canada." It quickly became a "protectorate" of the RQ, similar in form to the "independent" Slovakia that had been created by the German Nazis after they had dismembered the Czech Republic in 1938. It was all of these geographical and political rearrangements that were recognized, by the regimes of the NAR and the RQ, at least, in the "Treaty of Comity" of 2017.

And what did the annexation bring to the NAR? It expanded its territory by more than one-third, adding over 1.4 million square miles of land to a country that just six years before had arbitrarily reduced its size by about 200,000 square miles for reasons of race. More importantly, it more than tripled the area of prime land open for timber harvesting, strip mining for coal, and subsurface mining for minerals.[2]

Natural Resource Policy

From the late Transition Era onwards, the Right-Wing Reactionary policies of "Wise Use" (Gottlieb), that is "private property rights above all else," had controlled natural resource use policy in the old U.S. (see Chapter 14). As predicted by the forces of environmental preservation and balance that at the end of the Transition Era had been overwhelmed by the forces of greed and environmental destruction, these Right-Wing Reactionary land and resource use policies had led to the gradual rape of the land. Following the passage of the Natural Resources Access Act in 2013, the process had intensified and quickened.

The clear-cutting of timber and the strip mining for coal, copper, and other minerals, had virtually destroyed the surface of the old U.S. Northwest. Rivers became clogged with silt,

2. *Author's Note:* For purposes of comparison, the important territorial figures were: Western Ontario: close to 300,000 sq. miles; Manitoba: 250,999 sq. miles; Saskatchewan, 251,699 sq. miles; Alberta, 255,285 sq. miles; British Columbia, 366,253 sq. miles; five province total: over 1,400,000 sq. miles. U.S. territory total: 3,623,420 sq. miles. Idaho, 83,564 sq. miles; Montana, 147,046 sq. miles; Oregon, 97,073 sq. miles; Washington, 68,139 sq. miles; four state total (these were the major timber states): 395,822.

and both wild and commercial animal life declined precipitously. The precious natural resource, wood, over which the fuss was ostensibly being made, renewable if care is taken with forest management as it is now, virtually disappeared.

But with its new Resource Based Economy, the NAR paid little attention to these considerations. Preservation of neither nature nor employment meant anything in the face of preservation of the "free market" and profits. Thus, access to new untouched areas for exploitation was essential. The Treaty confirmed the accomplishment of that end.

The annexation of the four Western Canadian provinces plus Western Ontario by the NAR opened up tens of millions of acres of virgin forest to lumbering. It also brought directly under NAR control the remaining oil and natural gas reserves of Alberta as well as the huge new subsoil coal fields discovered in the Canadian Plains between Brandon, Manitoba and Medicine Hat, Alberta. Fortunately, the area opened up in Western Canada to the completely unfettered ravages of the "free market in natural resources" was so vast that there were still large areas left untouched by the time the NAR fell in 2022.

Expansion South

At the same time all of this military and diplomatic activity was going on north of the old U.S., there was quite a bit of the same kind of activity going on to the south of the old U.S. as well. With the infusion of new natural resources to exploit, the NAR economy was suddenly booming. The realization of the "Fourth Republic," through expansion to the south backed by military force, was a real possibility.

In 2018, the Sixth Bankruptcy swept through Latin America. This time there would be no last minute "save the nations" deal by the NAR banks or the NAR Treasury or the NAR's National Monetary Board (the Presidentially-controlled central banking successor to the old independent Federal Reserve Board) or the Multinational Bank or the United States of Europe Central Bank or the Cooperative Bank of the East Asian Confederation.

The previous time around the Latin American nations had been forced to put up their territories as collateral for further loans. This time the NAR, and the other international powers for which the NAR acted as agent, foreclosed. The Fourth Republic of the NAR became a reality in 2019. (Ironically that was the same year that the finally united resistance forces within the three Republics that occupied the territory of the old U.S. issued the Restoration Declaration. The fight that would eventually lead to the overthrow of the NAR then began in earnest [see next chapter].)

There was a close-to-century-old tradition of fascism in many of the Latin American nations: Argentina under Peron in the 40s and 50s and later The Generals of the 1970s; Uruguay under it nameless fascist leadership of the latter time; Brazil for 20 years under the military dictatorship that with U.S. help overthrew the democratically elected Goulart Presidency in 1965; Chile under Pinochet in the 70s and 80s; Paraguay under Stroessner from the mid-50s to the mid-80s; Somoza in Nicaragua; The Generals in Guatemala. The fascist tradition had never died, and from its adherents the NAR received significant cooperation.

As with Canada, interest in the annexation of significant parts of Latin America by the *Norte Americanos* had gone back to the birth of the Republic. Thomas Jefferson thought that taking over Cuba from Spain would be a fine idea. That never occurred, but in the mid-19th century Texas, New Mexico (including what later became Arizona), and California were taken from Mexico. After the Spanish-American War of 1898, Puerto Rico was made into an American colony rather than being granted independence.

Early in the 20th century, the old U.S. under President Theodore Roosevelt created an artificial country, Panama, by forcefully separating its territory from Colombia. This was to make it possible to build an American controlled Panama Canal. Sovereignty over the land through which the canal had been cut, originally held by the old U.S., had been returned to the Panamanian government in the late 20th century, according to a treaty signed in the mid-70s.

(Under the Fourth Republic of the NAR, control of the Panama Canal reverted to the successor to the old U.S. government. That met a long time goal of Right-Wing Reaction. Blaming its existence on "the liberals," the Right-Wing Reactionaries had always called the Panama Canal Treaty "treason," even though it had been negotiated principally by Republicans.)

What happened to Latin America under the NAR was nothing new, in principle, just different in the form.

Latino Deportation

The deportation from the White Republic of the U.S. Latino population, whether U.S. citizen or not, got underway with a vengeance shortly after the creation of the Fourth Republic. Deportation of Latinos to their supposed "homeland" was simplified, since the "other side" of the Killer Fence along the old Mexican Border was now, technically at least, part of the same country. To the deporters, it mattered not that the families of many of the deportees had lived in the territory now controlled by the NAR for some generations.

Internal deportation of persons based on ethnicity had a long history in the old U.S., from the forcible movement of Native Americans many times during the 19th century, to the internment of American citizens of Japanese descent during World War II, to the forced mass movements of blacks and Native Americans which accompanied the founding of the NAR itself.

Revolts

These takeovers were accomplished primarily in a peaceful fashion, much as the original establishment of the NAR had been. In a short while, however, revolts against the NAR dominion in Latin America got underway. They began among the Quechua Indians in the Peruvian and Bolivian Andes, and spread rapidly, especially among the Indian-dominant sectors of the population. Quickly it became apparent that the supply and communications routes were simply too long for the NAR to maintain. But until that happened, for the first time in history, if only briefly, there was one government holding sway on the American Continent from the Strait of Bering through the Straits of Magellan to the tip of Terra Del Fuego.

As the Latino revolts spread, there were increasing demands on NAR White Republic military forces to prop up the NAR Fourth Republic "provincial governors." The existence of an expensive foreign military drag on the NAR was an important factor in its ultimate downfall. This marked the first foreign involvement of American troops since the end of the Somalian/United Nations and Balkan/North Atlantic Treaty Organization actions in the 1990s.

Overseas Involvement:
The Beginning of the End

Isolationism, not internationalism, had become the hallmark of Right-Wing Reactionary foreign policy from the end of the Cold War against the old Soviet Union on. Isolationism was in fact the traditional policy of Right-Wing Reaction, e.g., the refusal of a Republican-controlled Senate to join the League of Nations after World War I. The isolationist, sometimes anti-Semitic/pro-Nazi, "America Firsters" of the 1930s were primarily Right-Wing. The post-World War II Right-Wing internationalism was developed entirely to defeat the old Soviet Union. Then there was the increasing use of anti-UN/"New World Order" propaganda from Right-Wing Reaction during the Transition Era.

With the demise of the "Communist Threat" and the decline in the importance of Middle East oil to the U.S. economy, according to the Right-Wing Reactionaries there was no reason for the U.S. to maintain any military forces outside of the Western Hemisphere. Certainly, they said toward the end of the Transition Era that neither "humanitarian assistance" (in the case of the African nation of Somalia, for example), nor "protection of human rights" or "fighting the UN's battles," (in the case of Bosnia-Herzegovina in the European Balkans) (Kramer), were any of the U.S.' business. One of the first orders of foreign policy business when President Hague had taken office had been to withdraw from the United Nations entirely (leaving $4.5 billion in debt unpaid).

But "Protection of the Legitimacy of the Republic" as the Hagueites called it was quite something else again (sort of like fighting to protect Saudi oil reserves in the Gulf War of 1991, some wags said). So off the forces went to Latin America. And once again the American government was involved in an expensive overseas war. As in Vietnam, it could ill afford the monetary investment. But this time around, because minority troops were not available to it, and so much manpower was required to maintain repression at home, it couldn't afford the manpower either (see Chapter 17). Both deficiencies begin to take their toll fairly soon. The Latin Wars marked one of the major beginnings of the end for the NAR.

References:

Buchanan, P., *Patrick J. Buchanan ... From the Right*, fundraising letter, c. 1989.

Canada, "The Constitution Act, 1982; amended by Constitution Amendment Proclamation, 1983 (SI/84102)," Ottawa, Ontario: 1986.

Chernow, B.A. and Vallasi, G.E., Eds., *The Columbia Encyclopedia, Fifth Edition*, "Oregon," New York: Columbia University Press, 1993, p. 2021.

Farnsworth, C.H., "Ottawa Unity Plan Draws Fire From Both Quebec and West," *The New York Times*, December 1, 1995.

Farnsworth, C.H., "Canada's Justice System Faces Charges of Racism," *The New York Times*, January 28, 1996.

Fast, H., *The Last Frontier*, New York: Blue Heron Press, 1953, p. 91.

Freedom Writer, "Religious Right Hits Canada," Religious Right Update, February, 1994.

Gottlieb, A.M., *The Wise Use Agenda*, Bellevue, WA: The Free Enterprise Press, 1989.

Guralnik, D.B., Ed., *Webster's New World Dictionary*, New York: The World Publishing Co., 1970.

Jenson, J., "Canada," in Krieger, J., Ed., *The Oxford Companion to Politics of the World*, New York: Oxford University Press, 1993.

Kramer, M., "The Art of Selling Bosnia," *Time*, December 11, 1995, p. 56.

Taylor, G.D., "Canada-U.S. Relations," in Foner, E., and Garrity, J.A., Eds., The *Reader's Companion to American History*, Boston, MA: Houghton Mifflin, 1991.

CHAPTER 17
2019: The Restoration Declaration

The Restoration Declaration, July 4, 2019

Where We Come From

> "We the People of the United States, in Order to form a more perfect Union, establish Justice, insure domestic Tranquility, provide for the common defence, promote the general Welfare, and secure the Blessings of Liberty to ourselves and our posterity, do ordain and establish this Constitution for the United States of America."

This is the Preamble to the old Constitution of the United States of America, written in 1787. With the Preamble, the Founding Fathers said: we have formed a new nation that unlike its predecessor is more than simply a collection of separate states. With grace and elegance, in that one sentence the Founding Fathers of our great nation went on to lay out the responsibilities of the national government they had just designed. The government of this new nation, they said, was to take an active role in its economic and social affairs, for the benefit of all the people.

With the Bill of Rights, the first Ten Amendments to the Constitution, added four years later, the Founding Fathers said: this government is to actively protect the freedom of thought and action of the people, stay out of their private affairs, and promote personal liberty, to the greatest extent possible within the bounds of maintaining a civil and law-abiding society, and to the extent that one person's exercise of freedom does not unreasonably impinge upon the same freedom of others.

The Founding Fathers provided for a representative democratic government, with certain restrictions. Over time, using the amendment process wisely built into the document, many of those restrictions on democracy were removed. The processes of democracy and amendment are two of the principal guarantors of liberty, freedom, change, and progress.

But processes by themselves guarantee nothing. Processes must be used, they must be implemented, or they mean nothing. They can be used for the benefit of the people as a whole; they can be abused for the benefit of the few. It is the latter, tragically, that has happened in our great country over the past forty years. For many reasons, the interest of the majority of our nation's people in the democratic electoral process declined, allowing the special interests of Right-Wing Reaction, representing a minority of the people, to take over the government with the intent to operate it for the benefit of those special interests.

And they did so. Greed, selfishness, and making money for its own sake and for the sake of making money, exploiting and exhausting the resources with which Nature has blessed us, motivated Right-Wing Reaction. Then with their urging, planning, and plotting, the anti-human values of every-man-for-himself, and bigotry, and prejudice, and race-hating, and hating difference, took over. Finally, the Right-Wing Reactionaries, having successfully promoted an agenda of anger and rage among their constituents, used the Constitutional process of amendment to destroy both the spirit and the substance of the Constitution itself.

Oh they left the form, they very cleverly left the form. They can claim with justification that much of what they have done is lawful and carried out under the provisions of the Constitution.

But form does not function make. And the functions for which U.S. Constitutional government was designed have been discarded, abandoned, cast adrift, trampled upon. The responsibilities our national government is to undertake as set forth in the Preamble to the Constitution have been ignored and forgotten. The Bill of Rights has been altered until it is unrecognizable.

We the people of the United States had a more perfect union. We did not have a perfect union, but it was more perfect than most others. It has been destroyed by the forces of Right-Wing Reaction and Religious Fundamentalism, by unfettered "Free Market" capitalism, by racism and bigotry, by greed and selfishness. Democracy has been replaced by tyranny, liberty by race-based imprisonment, freedom by oppression.

Where We Are Going

With this Declaration of Restoration, we, the forces of the Movement to Restore Constitutional Democracy to the United States of America, pledge ourselves to accomplish this end by all means at our command, political, diplomatic, economic, and military. In so doing, we resolve to achieve the following goals:

1. The utter destruction of the illegitimate, fascistic, construct known as the "New American Republics."
2. The restoration of the United States of America, comprising the former contiguous 48 states, with the option of the overseas states and territories to return as they wish.
3. The restoration of the full territorial integrity of the bilingual nation of Canada.
4. The restoration of full sovereignty to the nations of Latin America.
5. For the United States of America itself, the restoration of Constitutional government as it stood before the adoption of the 28th Amendment. Central to this restoration is the renewal of our traditional American national commitment to freedom and liberty.

   Freedom we define as: a state of being characterized by the ability to positively express and act upon beliefs about the nature of human life and behavior, social and economic relationships, and political processes, without hindrance, except to the extent that such thoughts and actions might impinge upon the freedom of others.

Liberty we define as: a state of being characterized by the absence of arbitrary or unreasonable or non-judicial limitations on personal thoughts, beliefs, and actions maintained and employed by state power backed by the use of force.

6. In the restored United States of America, tolerance of difference will be respected and valued, while institutional, political, and governmental discrimination based on race, sex, sexual orientation, and religious belief or non-belief, will be outlawed; a positive campaign to wipe away from our national polity the bitter vestiges of racial, sexual, national, and other prejudice and discrimination will be undertaken and prosecuted until that end is achieved.
7. A new economic policy will be instituted, based on the following principles:

   a. The market for capital investment decisions will be socially based while the market for the production, distribution, and sale of goods and services will be privately based; b. Production for use will take precedence; c. The establishment of equality of economic opportunity, the elimination of poverty, and the maintenance of a reasonable differential in both income and wealth between the richest and poorest members of society, as is found in the world's other industrialized democracies, will be primary objectives of the national government; d. The restoration, renewal, and protection of the environment and the use of natural resources so as to support sustainable growth will be a fundamental principle guiding all economic activity.
8. For all the people presently living under the sway of the "New American Republics" and its continental allies, the creation of a life based on: healthy regard for the earth and the abundance it can provide to us all; recognition of the essentiality of interdependence and community to

individual and species survival; respect for the dignity and individuality of each human being and the importance of true multiculturalism to national survival; and faith in humankind and our ability, working together, to solve our problems and create a bright future for our children, their children, and their children's children on down through the ages, through the democratic process.

Why We Are Going There

On this day 233 years ago there blazed forth from the mind of Thomas Jefferson the brightest beacon of freedom and liberty for Americans. To describe at this time why we are going where we are going, we turn to the words he wrote in his first great work, the Declaration of Independence, modified suitably for our time and place.

It was the Declaration of Independence that originally set forth the national *purpose* of the new nation whose birth it announced: to demonstrate unequivocably that "all men are created equal, that they are endowed by their Creator with certain unalienable Rights, that among these are Life, Liberty, and the pursuit of Happiness."

And it was the Declaration of Independence that originally set forth the *purpose of the national government* that its signers hoped to establish upon these shores: "to secure these rights, Governments are instituted among men." No more and no less.

And so, taking our inspiration, and indeed borrowing much of the text as it was originally written by the great Thomas Jefferson over 240 years ago, we say:

When in the Course of human events, it becomes necessary for a people to rise up against its tyrannical government but a government that is nevertheless recognized by most of the world's great powers as legitimate, pledge to violently overthrow it, and to assume for themselves the sovereignty of the nation, a decent respect to the opinions of mankind and its legitimate governments requires that they should declare the causes that impel them to the rebellion.

We hold these truths to be self-evident, that all men are created equal, that they are endowed by their Creator with certain unalienable Rights that among these are: life, liberty, freedom of belief and expression, health, and economic security. —That to secure these rights, Governments are instituted among men, deriving their just powers from the consent of the governed, —That whenever any Form of Government becomes destructive of these ends, it is the Right of the People to alter or abolish it, and institute new Government, laying its foundation on such principles and organizing its powers in such form, as to them shall seem most likely to effect their Safety and Happiness.

When a long train of abuses and usurpations, pursuing invariably the same Object evinces a design to reduce them under absolute Despotism, it is their right, it is their duty, to throw off such Government, and to provide new Guards for their future security.

Such has been the patient suffering of these former United States; and such is now the necessity which constrains us to overthrow the present illegitimate Governmental regime. The history of the present President of the "New American Republics," his "American Christian Nation Party," the economic interests to which they are beholden, and their despotic allies elsewhere on the American continent, is a history of repeated injuries and usurpations, of widespread oppression and repression of the vilest and most violent kind, of the promotion of bigotry, prejudice, and hate so as to set people with otherwise common interests at each other's throats, of the violation of Mother Earth at the most egregious level, all having in direct object the establishment of an absolute Tyranny over the many peoples of the United States, of Canada, and of the nations of Latin America, for the promotion of private, monstrous personal gain for the very few.

We, therefore, the National Leadership Council of the Movement to Restore Constitutional Democracy to the United States of America, appealing to the Supreme Judge of the world for the rectitude of our intentions, do, in the Name, and by the authority of the good People of the former United States of America, solemnly publish and declare, That we are Absolved from all Allegiance to the illegitimate regime of the "New American Republics," that this political, economic, and social monstrosity should and will be totally dissolved and wiped off the face of the Earth; that traditional, North American, Constitutional representative democracy will be restored to our nation as we know it, and that the ethic for guiding human behavior, one person to another, as set forth by the Prophet Ezekiel so many centuries ago in Chapter 18 of his Book in the Bible, having been banished by the religious zealots of Right-Wing Reaction under the selective, destructive doctrine known as "Biblical inerrancy," shall be given a place of honor in our national consciousness.

And so it was said:

"5. But if a man be just, and do that which is lawful and right, ...

"7. And hath not oppressed any, but hath restored to the debtor his pledge, hath spoiled none by violence, hath given his bread to the hungry, and hath covered the naked with a garment;

"8. He that hath not given forth upon usury, neither hath taken any increase, that hath withdrawn his hand from iniquity, hath executed true judgment between man and man,

"9. Hath walked in my statutes, and hath kept my judgments, to deal truly; he is just, he shall surely live, saith the Lord God."

For the support of this Declaration, with the firm reliance on the Protection of Divine Providence, Nature, and the Human Spirit, we mutually pledge to each other and all the people for whom we speak, our Lives, our Fortunes, and our sacred Honor.

The National Leadership Council of the Movement for the Restoration of Constitutional Democracy in the United States of America

July 4, 2019

A Curley Oakwood Radio Broadcast Transcript (Friday, July 5, 2019)

My friends, did you hear, I mean, did you *hear* that pathetic, I mean that *pathetic* broadcast which emanated from who knows where (and when we find out where, that's going to be the end of that I can tell you), by those pathetic liberal nigger lovers, calling themselves who knows what, desecrating the sacred day of July 4, the day celebrating our Independence.

By the way, hope you all enjoyed your hot dogs and hamburgers and chips and beer on your good old American barbecue like I and the wife did down at the White House with President Jeff yesterday. Nothing like a good hot July 4, and the speeches, and the bands, and the parades to make me think back to what this country really stands for and make me proud to be a good White American.

And yes, speaking of President Jeff, if I told you what he told me he will do to those liberal nigger lovers when he gets his hands on them, well you wouldn't need any charcoal to fire up your next barbecue, I can tell you, if you know what I mean.

Yes, we do have a little trouble right now. Those bastards are making trouble. They just don't know their place. They will when we put them back in it, but they don't know it now. But they will, they will. I can't give you the details, but President Jeff told me that he is mobilizing our forces as we speak to take care of those little hot spots, right away. And he's going to make it good and hot for them, hotter than it was even yesterday, I can tell you that.

So, my friends, not to worry, do not worry. If you hear a little gunfire now and again, it's just our boys cleaning up some mess. But do keep your own stuff locked and loaded, so that you can have a little fun yourself—should the opportunity arise to use your rations—if you know what I mean.

Not that I think any of you or any loyal American would be the least bit attracted to the garbage we're hearing, but just remember what it was like before we ended race mixing back in 2011. The crime, and the drugs, and the welfare, and the taxes, and the abortions, and the faggots running around trying to take your good little boys off with them, and God cast out of everywhere, and Big Government, and the niggers with their hands out, and the liberals wanting to take from your hands and put it in theirs. They caused it all, and if they ever, and they will never, but if they ever get back to power, they will start it all over again.

And so my friends, if you hear anybody speaking even a bit kindly about the garbage the liberal nigger lovers are spewing, do let your local Helmsman know, won't you? Just a touch of Moral Rehabilitation should fix that person up just fine.

And do have a nice day, for Christ and country.

A Connie Conroy Note (Wednesday, July 10, 2019)
Jesus H. Christ, I wish Oakwood would learn to keep his mouth shut. We do have some trouble here, and I think it's real trouble this time. The Prez sez we have nothing to worry about. But a couple of the guys I know over at the NIA don't give me that picture. The goddamn liberals, and the goddamn niggers, and the goddam 'skins, and even a few goddamn spics and slopes, really seem to have gotten together on this thing.

Isolated outbreaks, OK. We've been dealing them for years. No problem. And it usually just ended up with a bit or more of that good old soul-purifying torture or the Death Squad routine.

But these guys seem to have communications, they seem to have a command structure, their attacks of the last few days seem to be coordinated, they seem to have enough supplies and ammunition at least for now, they seem to have picked their targets with care. They've even got a bunch of old Afghan War Stinger missiles, so our close-in air support has been limited. If they ever get hooked up with the goddamned Latin rebels, I don't want to think about it.

And how could they do this, anyway? We've been told for years that the niggers and the 'skins, and the spics are just too dumb, dumb enough anyway not to be able to do something like this, so we would never have to worry about it. Well, maybe they're all white/Niggers, but they're supposed to be mental misfits too. I don't know what's going on, but there is trouble in River City, right here in River City, and it ain't about a shortage of band instruments.

Of course, the guys in the know are keeping quiet about what they know, and I'm going to keep quiet about it too. I don't want to go off to some MRC for a little "re-education on account of doubt and disloyalty" now, do I? Thank God I've got this computer no one else knows about or could even get into if they did. So I can vent, as they used to say in the old days, and no one's the wiser.

But then Oakwood vents—in public. That goddamn name-dropper. All he was really interested in was letting his dear listeners know just how close to the Prez he is. But then he goes and gives these goddamn liberal nigger lover rebels *recognition*. He tells everyone that they exist and that they've done something big enough to catch his attention and mentions it on the most listened-to radio program in America. So he puts them down, so he feels good. But by mentioning them at all, he puts them up. Damn!

I know he's censor-exempt, but we're going to have to do something about this kind of stuff if he doesn't learn to keep his mouth shut. Oh what a pleasant job I have as "White House Press Officer" to try to do that. It's like trying to shoe a caterpillar in a shoe store that has only size 13 triple-E's left, and only three pair of them at that.

So I'll talk to Oakwood, and he'll rant and rave about how close to the Prez he is, and how the Prez wouldn't be where he is if Oakwood weren't where he is, and how he knows what he's doing, and I'll say "Great, Curley, but we're talking about security here. We don't want our people to think there's *anything* wrong, and we certainly don't want the liberal nigger lovers to think *they're* doing anything right." And as usual, I'll get nowhere with that fat, overblown windbag, but at least I'll be able to report back to the Prez that I tried.

An Alex Poughton Letter
Saturday, July 20, 2019
Dear Karl,

Well, well, well. It has been a busy week. The fat is really in the fire this time, I think. There have been outbreaks of resistance before, right from the start of things. But they've been sporadic, sometimes bordering on terrorism, often seeming to border on desperation. Nothing in more than one place at a time as far as I could tell, nothing coordinated, and no grand statement of purpose (I'll get back to that magnum opus in a bit).

The NAR has always been able to put any rebellions down hard, and fast. And they have claimed publicly that's that what they did this time. But privately I hear otherwise. My sources over at the NIA tell me it might not be so easy this time. They are sure they will win, but they are not quite sure when.

There is a bit of worry in the Pentagon, too, I'm told. The Latin Wars are not going so great. In fact, the farther south the action gets on the continent, the less well it is going, I hear. You know, the classical "over-extended supply lines" problem. Also the Pentagon is beginning to worry about finding the money to pay for the whole thing, and about manpower too.

In a population of about 200,000,000 that's bulging with aging "baby-boomers," they have got about 80,000,000 men and women between the ages of 18 and 45. With the NAR policy on the place of women, they are back to the World War II Women's Army Corps roles in the armed services, in other words very limited, and nothing near combat. So they have a pool of about 39,000,000 men to pull from for the serious military and paramilitary tasks.

Let's say half of those are necessary for civilian production. That leaves 18.5 million. The conventional prison system, plus the drug prisons and the "Life Preservation" prisons, and so forth, house about 4,000,000 people, three-quarters of them white, three-quarters of them men. They need about 1,500,000 people to guard them, guard the borders, staff all the various conventional police forces, and so forth. They have got about five million in the various branches of the Helmsmen, taking running the camps and all that into account, and another one million or so in the "Independent Militias" that do the real dirty work. Now we are down to nine million.

They already have three million men in the armed services, and my Pentagon sources tell me they're going to have to increase that soon to deal with what they euphemistically call the "Fourth Republic problem." The draft is back, as you know, and that's not good for civilian morale. And then they have to worry about those Whites who may be secretly siding with the rebels, and could be saboteurs or worse, within the armed forces. They are beginning to scrape the bottom of the manpower barrel, and this place is a garrison state already.

And then the two policy types in the White House who will talk to me off the record are also getting worried. Seems there are some problems with getting access to timber, and oil, and coal in the Western Provinces, and the East Asian Confederation is beginning to make some noises about the old-time trade imbalance which has never changed in kind but is now so monstrous in amount that no one even publishes the figures any more.

Seems some of the boys over on the other side of the peaceful sea are beginning to wonder if the Big Typhoon everyone has been quietly worrying about all these years is finally beginning to form in the form of, dare I say it, default on loan interest payments. Ouch!

And then into all of this comes this terribly earnest-sounding "Movement for the Restoration of Constitutional Democracy" (MRCD). Terribly earnest, and terribly well-organized too it seems. They have already gotten some stuff to me, indirectly. Given the tenor of my published stuff, I wonder how they knew I would be sympathetic, under cover(s). You didn't tip them off, did you? I may get to meet with an MRCD liaison officer soon. Got to be very careful about that. But the NAR is still letting me go pretty much wherever I please, and doesn't seem to have put a tail on me yet. I just have to make sure that I don't give them any reason to do so.

So back to this MRCD. Multiracial. All over the place. Well equipped. And long-winded. Have you seen their "Restoration Declaration" yet? I know they broadcast it round the world on shortwave. My God, those people can go on and on. And rewriting Jefferson too. Now that takes gall.

Well, at least they gave him credit, unlike Hague when he plagiarized some early stuff of that completely misnamed "The 'Wise Use' " movement for that major speech announcing the creation of the "Resource-Based Economy" (read Rape of the Environment Economy) back in 2013, or his First Inaugural when he stole without attribution from those old-time Right-Wingers of the 1990s. (At least when he filled his Second Inaugural with quotes from way back then too he gave the writers credit.)

But anyway, back to now, here are these guys "updating" Jefferson. It makes me think of the first Yiddish translation of Shakespeare that appeared back in the 19th century where it said on the title page, "Translated and Improved By" so-and-so. But if you are talking about freedom and liberty, who better to borrow from than Jefferson I suppose.

The politics of the "Restoration Declaration," as they call it, are very interesting, if you take a close look at it. Lots of compromises there, between the socialists and the social capitalists (no "free marketeers" in that group, I don't think), between the pure secularists, the enlightened religious types, and the spiritualists, between the revanchists and the peacemakers.

But they do seem solid on the matter of race and hate, the matter that in the end tore this country apart. Multiracial, multicultural, pluralistic, tolerant it will be, should they succeed, and that will be enforced. And they seem solid on their pledge to restore representative democracy, with those stated limits. I guess they agree with old Winnie[1] when he said something like, "Representative democracy is the worst system for governing—except for all the others."

1. *Author's Note:* Referring here to the great 20th century English political figure Winston Churchill, Prime Minister during World War II.

Anyway, I complain about how longwinded these new rebels are and I'm at the same thing again myself. More on their politics next time.

All the best,
Alex

Author's Commentary
The Organized Resistance Begins

From the time of the formation of the NAR in the year 2011[2] and the forced relocation of millions of people into living conditions that were for the most part very difficult, there had been armed opposition and resistance to the Hagueites, the ACNP, and the NAR. However, it had been scatter-shot, ill-planned, ill-equipped, and uncoordinated between the centers of resistance. In the presence of the Helmsmen, the National Intelligence Agency (NIA), and the other repressive forces of the NAR, organized resistance to the rule of the Hague regime was extremely dangerous and difficult.

But the human quest for self-determination never dies, especially in the historical context of the true American traditions of freedom and liberty. Furthermore, the NAR was a very large country. Additionally, as noted previously, the Latin Wars, just starting in earnest this same year of 2019, quickly caused great strains on the repressive, oppressive abilities of the NAR. Although their forces were vast, they could not be ubiquitous.

The Movement for the Restoration of Constitutional Democracy (MRCD) was formed in this environment. It was based primarily in the Negro and Indian Republics, but resistance units were found scattered throughout the White Republic as well. The formation of the MRCD was the result of the devotion of several years of very dangerous work. It cost

2. *Author's Note:* The recently published six volume opus by Joplin (2046) covers in great and very well done detail all of the events that we are able to only touch upon lightly, and many others of course. Starting the narrative with the formation of the NAR, it is now considered to be the definitive work on the Second Civil War.

many lives just to establish communications links between the many Sectors of the Black and Red Republics alone, as well as with the disparate White resistance groups. A unified command structure, the National Leadership Council, was eventually created. It was able to produce a common policy for armed and coordinated resistance. And it was able to collectively produce the Restoration Declaration.

There was one important characteristic of the Hague regime itself that aided the growth of the Resistance. Because of the thoroughly ingrained racism of the Hagueites, and their unshakeable conviction that blacks and Native Americans really were intellectually inferior species, they were convinced that "nothing very serious" in the way of resistance could ever be mounted by them (see the next section, below).

Thus the majority of direct repressive force, aside from maintaining the Killer Fence system, and attempting to control the supplies of food and water provided to the non-White Republics Sectors, was directed at the White resistance. There was very little physical White NAR presence inside the Sectors of the Negro and Indian Republics. There were the Helmsmen Garrisons placed at strategic locations throughout the Sectors. And punitive expeditions would occasionally sally forth from them. But in their very modern fortresses, the Helmsmen eventually became hostages, not controllers.

Arms in sufficient quantities were difficult for the MCRD to get, but if the Warsaw (Poland) Jewish Ghetto fighters of 1943 could get them to battle the German Nazis, so could the MRCD. There was no shortage of personal weapons. Despite the efforts of the Hagueites during the formative days of the NAR, there were hand guns and long guns everywhere. To the frustration of the Hagueites, this situation was the direct result of the complete lack of regulation of gun ownership that Right-Wing Reaction had implemented during the late Transition Era and early Fascist Period at the behest of its paymasters in the National Rifle Association and the gun industry.

Ammunition, medium and heavy weapons were a more

difficult matter for the MRCD. Some were captured from the NAR, both within the Sectors from the Helmsmen Garrisons and, when The Sieges got underway, from NAR army units outside. They were smuggled in by Resistance allies both at home and abroad. And they were bought on the black market from NAR armed units of all categories except the ultraracist Independent Militias.

As for manpower, although they made for a somewhat aging army, there were many ex-military service people ready, willing, and able to fight on the side of the MRCD. Aging, but ready, willing, and somewhat able too in the Black Sectors were members of Black gangs from the pre-NAR times. (The gangs had disappeared of their own volition or had been put out of business fairly early on by the internal governments within most of the Black Sectors.) Too, on the remote parts of their Sectors, many young Native Americans rediscovered their 19th century ancestors' martial abilities.

The first coordinated military actions of the MRCD occurred within days of the issuing of the Restoration Declaration. They achieved some level of success throughout the rest of 2019 and on into the winter of 2020. That success pushed the Hagueites to the 2nd Final Solution (see the next Chapter), which marked the beginning of the end for them.

Causes of White Unrest in the NAR

It is not known, and not knowable, whether the collapse of the NAR would have come about so quickly if the Resistance had been only from the Black and Red Republics (plus the Latin Wars, of course). But there was a significant element of resistance in the White Republic as well. (In the Black and Red Republics, able-bodied "black/Whites" who had not remained captive to Right-Wing Reactionary racist ideology joined the Resistance in droves.)

The causes of White unrest in the NAR were many. Primary among them, there were simply not enough jobs to go around for all the Whites, even with no minimum wage law, government propaganda to the contrary notwithstanding. First, the RBE was by nature heavily dependent on the export of energy resources and other raw materials, not the investment of capital in productive employment-generating enterprises. Second, in the service and remaining manufacturing sectors of the economy, computerization/robotization and the resultant disassociation of labor from capital, the old Tofflerian "Third Wave," had continued on apace. But in a "free market" economy there was not the least concern on the part of the economic decision-makers about consequences for employment opportunity of such an industrial policy, and of course no planning to deal with the problem.

The trend in declining individual purchasing power that had started back in the 1970s, discussed on many occasions in this book, had continued. Moderating the effect of that trend during the Transition Era was the changing role of women that had begun back in the enlightened time of the 1960s. Married women were liberated to go out to work if they so chose. This change lead to the institution of the two-income family, by choice.

As individual purchasing power fell over time, however, that institution became more pervasive, as many families found it financially necessary to have both adults working outside the home whether both wanted to or not. Thus both by reason of choice and of necessity the family standard of living had been maintained in many cases, although for many it was a struggle. Furthermore, with the onset of Reaganite economic policy early in the Transition Era, the export of manufacturing capital to low-wage countries and the willingness to import low-cost consumer goods even at the expense of an ever increasing trade deficit that had begun in earnest. That had ensured a continued flow of low-cost consumer goods to the American marketplace. That mitigated the decline in personal incomes to some extent.

However, with the accession to power of Hague and the ACNP the promotion by the regime of the Religious Right's view of the "traditional role for women" (that is bound to the home), discouraged many women from working. Also, in practical terms for the Hagueites, if fewer women were to work, there would be more jobs available in a dwindling job market for the Party's primary constituency, White males. But still, the Hagueite version of the German Nazi "Kinder, Kuche, und Kirche" policy for women caused much grumbling, even among some men. Further, the "black/Whites" policy of deporting to the non-White Republics unemployed Whites who could not make it financially, as their "punishment for being poor," was not well accepted by White males. Taken together, these policies eventually proved destabilizing for the Hague regime.

Strict Racial Separation: A Unique Feature of the NAR

What some called "American Apartheid" [lit., "apartness"] after its South African historical forebear (1948-1994) was actually much stricter than its namesake. In the NAR, racial separation was virtually absolute. With the establishment of the Negro and Indian Republics, there was virtually complete physical separation of those people deemed "White" from those deemed "black" or "red"[3]. That was something the South African racists never accomplished. Under strict South African

3. *Author's Note:* Deciding just who was what did present serious problems for the Hague regime, as we have noted before. The pigment scale for persons described by Murrayite racists (see Appendix VI) as "black" actually covered a very broad range. Very few people labeled by Murrayites as "black" actually had a "black" skin color in the sense that a native African is "black."

That fact itself had given the lie to the Murrayites early on: how can there be a "race" supposedly defined by skin color when what is labeled as such is in reality so heterogeneous by skin color? And how can that "race" be "inferior black" when the natural creation of that skin color spectrum meant much mixing of supposedly "superior" "white" genes with supposedly "inferior" "black" ones? In any case, as Kaufman and Cooper once said (1995): "Race is a social convention, not a biological concept." However, as was so often the case with Right-Wing Reactionary thinking of all sorts, such science never got in the way of Hagueite racist policy making. See Armstrong (2032) for a detailed discussion of the matter of racial assignment.

apartheid, blacks lived in completely separate areas, all public facilities were strictly segregated (a la the American South before the passage of the Civil Rights Act of 1964), and "race mixing" at any level was strictly prohibited. However, as unskilled and semi-skilled laborers, blacks were very much physically present in South African economic life, and as maids, nursemaids, gardeners, and so forth, in South African social life. None of that happened in the NAR. As we shall shortly see, that policy was a major element responsible for the subsequent downfall of the NAR and the ultimate end of American Apartheid.

It was not that the economic decision makers in the White Republic did not exploit non-White workers (and White ones as well, of course). But unlike the case in South Africa, the non-Whites didn't have to be physically brought or allowed out of the non-White Sectors areas in order to work for White owners. The old Right-Wing Reactionary concept of "Enterprise Zones" dating from the Transition Era (Drier) was rehabilitated.

Under this concept, during the Transition Era special industrial/manufacturing areas were supposed to be established in non-White neighborhoods. Through special tax reductions, zoning variations, exemptions from certain environmental and work rules, and so forth, industries would be encouraged to locate in them. For many reasons, the "Enterprise Zone" concept never worked in the old U.S. But under the highly restrictive conditions of the NAR, they did.

For reasons which are not clear, the zones were colloquially referred to as "Kempsites." It may have been an anti-Semitic jibe at the stereotypical "New York Yid" accent. Or the name may have been picked to differentiate these zones from the Moral Rehabilitation Centers, colloquially known as "The Camps."

Physically the Kempsites were always on the border of a non-White Republic Sector. They were surrounded on all sides by a Killer Fence, one side of which formed the outer boundary of the Sector in which it was located. This arrangement would later provide an excellent smuggling route for men and materiel to supply the MRCD.

Racism: the Driver of Policy

Racism had been a major feature of Right-Wing Reactionary Politics from the beginning of the Transition Era. But with the advent of the Fascist Period in 2001 and the advent of fullblown fascism in 2011, the racism of Right-Wing Reaction became harder and harder, stricter and stricter, harsher and harsher. There were no compromises, no allowances, no toleration of difference of any kind. To that extent, the racism of the Old South in the old U.S., that had at least allowed blacks their own institutions, if funded at an inferior level and if in the context of legal segregation of public facilities, seemed somewhat mild by comparison.

The Hagueites had become the complete ideological captives of the "scientific racism" of Jensen and Shockley, Murray and Herrnstein (see Appendix VI). They had also become the complete captives of the gutter racism of the American neo-fascist and neo-Nazi movements that had flourished since the 1960s (Ridgeway), the same gutter racists whom Hague had welcomed into the American Christian Nation Party when he formed it in 2008.

Certain earlier leaders of Right-Wing Reaction in the Republican Party and the Republican-Christian Alliance knew that "scientific racism" was nonsense and that gutter racism belonged in the gutter. They used both for political purposes anyway. But the NAR leadership really believed that the Blacks and the Native Americans were inferior, that they were both members of subhuman species, in the case of the Blacks (as "black" was defined by the Hagueites, given that the actual skin colors of persons assigned to this group ranged from very dark to very light), considered to be not much above the level of chimpanzees.

Therefore, by Hagueite ideology and dogma non-Whites were considered to be no threat to the established order in any way, as long as they were isolated. It was simply inconceivable to the White leadership that any Black or Native American, "inferior as they were," was possibly capable of doing any of the things that many of them eventually did. This is how the total racism of the NAR actually sowed the initial seeds of its own downfall.

In the old United States, it was the *politics* of the Republican Party in particular and Right-Wing Reaction in general that was built on racism. By the time the NAR was created, it was the *policy*, not just the politics, that was built on racism. That development had its parallel in Nazi Germany, where the *politically driven* propaganda of the 100 years preceding the founding of the anti-Semitic Third Reich was actually believed by the latter's leadership and thus became the basis for murderous policy (Davidowicz).

Therefore, the Hagueites developed no policies to protect against the eventuality of a revolt based in major part in the non-White Republics (other than the "Fourth," considered in a completely different light). The few voices within the NAR policy establishment that raised the issue of possible threats were simply dismissed as those of the "soft-headed," if not those of potential security risks.

The Self-Destructiveness of Racist Policy, In Practice

Although the comparison is not absolute, there are certain similarities between the self-destructiveness for the NAR of American Apartheid and the self-destructiveness for Nazi Germany of the "Final Solution," the plan adopted at a meeting in Wannsee, Prussia on January 20, 1942 to murder in its entirety European Jewry (Shirer, pp. 963-979).

If the extermination policy had not been adopted by Nazi Germany, it is highly likely that it would have lost World War II anyway. But there is a difference between unconditional surrender and a negotiated settlement. The diversion of resources that could have supported the German war effort, to pursue the Nazi policy of extermination of the Jews, was a major hindrance to that effort. This was especially so on the Eastern Front, where the major mass murder camps were located, and where the fighting was particularly ferocious, carried out over huge distances. And it was especially so towards the end of the war, when the Germans were running short of men, fuel, and equipment, on all fronts.

The Hitler/Himmler/Eichmann murderous obsession with exterminating European Jewry used precious manpower, fuel, rail transport, and some heavy equipment that could have otherwise been devoted to prosecution of the war. Thus, if not for the "Final Solution" and the material demands it made, the German Nazis might have been able to hold off the Allied forces long enough to be able to sue for a negotiated peace.

In the case of the NAR, it is highly likely that it too would have collapsed eventually. This would have been due in part to the inherent inability to govern over long periods of time that is a known historical characteristic of dictatorships in the industrialized world. It would also have been due to the fundamental instability of its economic system. (In these two regards, the NAR was much like the old Soviet Union, the 20th century rival of the old U.S., which collapsed largely of its own political and economic deadweight in the early 1990s. However, it should be noted that over time a significant factor in that collapse also was The Seventy-Five Years War, hot and cold, that was waged on the Soviet Union, from the time of its founding in 1917 until its final demise in 1992.) But if the Hagueites had not sold so short on the ability of non-White peoples to mount an effective resistance to horrible repression, the NAR might have (unfortunately) lasted much longer than it did, perhaps even to this very day.

Racism and the White Republic's Lack of Intelligence

Because of the policy of complete racial separation, the Hagueites were never able to put together a working intelligence system within the non-White Republics. Thus no intelligence worthy of the name was ever collected, and the regime truly did not know what was going on inside them. Neither were the Secret Police, either of the HM or the NIA variety, effective in the Black or Red Republics, for the same reason.

The Hagueites simply had no way to recruit spies in the non-White Republics. All Blacks and Native Americans had to live within the boundaries of the non-White Republics' Sectors. There were no separate areas where non-Whites sympathetic to the racists for one reason or another could go. This stood in contrast with, for example, the Zulu district in the old South Africa. It was home to the collaborationist Inkhata Freedom Party, and provided a sanctuary for its pro-apartheid regime spies and agents provocateurs, paid by the racist regime.

There were no well-off people in the Black and Red Republics. Anyone who had any extra money to spend immediately became suspect. Anyone who disappeared for any time at all, unless known to be a Resistance operative, was immediately suspect. Spies, when caught, were quickly executed. Thus the NAR was limited to high tech surveillance, and it proved not to be good enough.

The Black and Red Republics become High-Tech

In this regard, one major factor the Hagueites failed to recognize was that in most Sectors of the Negro Republic there were large numbers of highly trained professionals, academics, scientists, engineers, public and private sector executives and administrators, entrepreneurs, and military men and women. Although fewer in number, these occupations were represented in the Indian Republic as well.

The numbers in both Republics were augmented by Latinos in those occupations who had been deported to the contiguous non-White Republics, not south of the old Mexican border to the Hispanic Republic. (Of course, these occupations were also well-represented in the Hispanic Republic, but the Latin Wars and the people of the Fourth Republic played only a tangential role in the Second American Civil War.) Working together, these well-trained, well-educated folks were able, among many other things, to produce the following technological advances that greatly benefited the MRCD cause.

1. The electronic communications system among the Sectors. It was bi-partite. First, they developed a means of using the satellite uplinks for the Personal Information System (PIS) senders that were in the body of every member of the NAR security force. Using the old telegraphers' Morse Code, they were able to piggy-back onto the signal with one that was off by 0.0001 megahertz.

   Morse having been dropped by official agencies as an antiquated means of communication late in the Transition Era, no one in the NAR's NIA knew or could recognize the Code. When the electronic noise was picked up, it was just considered to be interference. (Since Morse Code and the telegraph had been one means of their repression in the 19th century, Native Americans took particular ironic pleasure from using Morse to help undermine the NAR.) Also developed was a highly sophisticated short-wave and Ham radio network, replete with codes, and so forth.
2. A technique for breaking through the Killer Fences was developed using automated signal-senders to overload the receptors in the Fences. Small sections were disabled for short periods of time to permit passage of men and materiel without setting off a general alarm. Once that was done, a regular messenger service between the Sectors was set up, as well as an "Underground Railway"[4] through the White Republic to the rump Canada (the Maritime Provinces).
3. There were significant advances made in the development of solar, tidal, and geothermal power sources.
4. In agriculture, as previously noted, hydroponics was brought to a very high level in the Black Republic, as was low-moisture agriculture in the Red Republic.
5. In both the Black and Red Republics (much more so in the latter than the former because of the availability of

4. *Author's Note:* The "Underground Railway" for guiding escaped slaves to Canada was a feature of the northern part of the old U.S. before the First Civil War.

space) there was widespread development of hemp agriculture. Hemp cultivation had a long tradition among Native Americans. For example, the name of the Tuscarora tribe is derived from the Iroquoian word *skaru'ren*, meaning in English "hemp gatherers" (Campbell, p. 241). The Tuscarora were active in hemp agriculture at least as far back as the early 18th century. They used the material both for its fibre and its medicinal properties.

Hemp is the source of marijuana, a mildly intoxicant recreational drug that was banned in the old U.S. in favor of the much more dangerous recreational drugs tobacco and alcohol. (There were many reasons accounting for this seemingly ludicrous policy of the old U.S. Chief among them was that the production of alcoholic beverages and tobacco products was highly profitable for their manufacturers. Marijuana, obtained from one of the hardiest weeds known to man, never could have been made to be nearly so profitable, since many users could simply grow their own.)

In the Indian Republic in particular, the use of alcohol, "The White Man's Poison" that had been employed so effectively to incapacitate Native Americans during the 19th century conquests, was widely frowned upon. The use of the less harmful marijuana met with more acceptance. It produced a relaxed, mellow state of intoxication, rather than the aggressive one associated with alcohol.

Much more important for the economic health of the non-white Republics, various parts of the hemp plant can also be used to make a wide variety of commercial products and uses up little of the Earth's own resources in its own growth (Rosenthal). In the Red Republic especially, hemp thus became a major source for paper and other formerly wood-based products, paint, varnish, soap, clothing, food, pharmaceuticals, building supplies, rope, and energy. As a late Transition Era treatment of the material noted (Chun):

> "Hemp is an environmentally friendly crop. It requires little water and no chemical fertilizers or pesticides. Beyond this, it does not drain the soil of nutrients and its deep root system prevents erosion. Hemp also yields four times more fibre per acre than trees do. ... Environmental considerations aside, hemp [makes] a superior fabric. ... Hemp looks and feels like its pedigreed cousin, linen. ... [I]n stress tests, hemp had eight times the tensile strength and four times the durability of cotton."

6. The most important technological advance in the non-White Republics was the re-creation of public primary, secondary, and higher education. As the stream of well-educated persons who could think for themselves, and not simply regurgitate by rote doctrines taught to them, was drying up in the White Republic, what started as a trickle of bright, question-asking problem solvers was on its way to becoming a flood of them in the non-White Republics.

The Second Civil War Begins

The Second Civil War did not begin with a single bang the way the First had. The latter commenced on April 12, 1861 with the firing of the first cannon shot against the Union's Fort Sumter in Charleston (SC) Harbor by the army of the Confederate States of America. In contrast, the Second Civil War "crept in on little cat feet" the way fascism itself had come to the old U.S. The Hague regime did not even realize that it was in a full-scale war until it was well underway in the spring of 2020.

No one on either side referred to the conflict as the "Second Civil War" until it was concluded with the ceremonial, unconditional surrender of the NAR forces on April 9, 2022. The MRCD arranged for that surrender to take place in the courthouse at Appomattox, VA, where at the end of the First Civil War, after fighting to defend the same basic, destructive doctrine of white supremacy, the Confederate General Robert E. Lee had surrendered to the Union Commander Ulysses S. Grant exactly 157 years before.

But the conflict was a Second Civil War and it was even more ferocious than the First. Hundreds of thousands of people were killed on both sides. (Because of the destruction wrought by The Sieges laid to Black Republic urban Sectors by the NAR forces, no accurate count of the deaths has ever been possible.) Broad swathes of territory all over the country were laid waste. Fortunately, neither nuclear or biological/chemical weapons were used by either side, for reasons still in dispute (see Chapter 19).

Like the First, the Second was fought for freedom and liberty and the restoration of Constitutional government throughout the land. But in the aftermath of the Second, unlike that of the First, the fruits of victory were not quickly discarded. Just the opposite occurred. In our ReUnited States of America, the seeds of liberty and freedom that were planted after the victory of the MRCD have been cultivated and replanted such that the trees that have grown from them are truly unshakeable.

References:

Armstrong, L., *Racial Assignment in the New American Republics*, Chicago, IL: University of Chicago Press, 2032.

Campbell, J., *Vol. II: The Way of the Seeded Earth*, New York: Harper and Row, 1989.

Chun, R., "World's Oldest Fabric Is Now Its Newest," *The New York Times*, June 25, 1995, p. 37.

Davidowicz, L.S., *The War Against the Jews: 1933-45*, New York: Holt, Rinehart and Winston, 1975.

Drier, P., "Bush to Cities: Drop Dead," *The Progressive*, July, 1992, p. 20.

Joplin, J., *The Second Civil War: From Start to Finish*, Six Vols., Cambridge, MA: The All-Ivy University Press, 2046.

Kaufman, J.S. and Cooper, R.S., "In Search of the Hypothesis," *Public Health Reports*, 110, 662, November/December, 1995.

Ridgeway, J., *Blood in the Face*, New York: Thunder's Mouth Press, 1990.

Rosenthal, E., *Hemp Today*, Oakland, CA: Quick American Archives, 1994.

Shirer, W.L., *The Rise and Fall of the Third Reich*, New York: Simon and Schuster, 1960.

CHAPTER 18

2020: The Second Final Solution

Author's Commentary

The Progress of the War[1]

Following the issuance of the Restoration Declaration on July 4, 2019, the Movement for the Restoration of Constitutional Democracy undertook a summer multifront offensive. It was somewhat effective. The MRCD forces demonstrated that they had a working communications and command and control system and could carry out complex, coordinated operations in up to a dozen locations at the same time. They showed that they were well supplied and well equipped, and from captured NAR materiel and other sources had the ability to make up supply and equipment losses fairly quickly.

They demonstrated that they were in regular communication with the commanders of the anti-Fascist forces in the Latin Wars and could coordinate actions with them when necessary. They were able to establish defensible lines around many of the urban Sectors of the Black Republic. An important military asset were the hostages they were able to make of the troops in the Helmsmen Garrisons inside the Black and Red Republic Sectors, either by physically capturing them or bottling them up and cutting their sources of supply.

They of course did not have air support in the urban Black Sectors, but they did have an ample supply of old 20th century Stinger handheld ground-to-air missile launchers and missiles.

1. *Author's Note:* As noted in the previous chapter, the recently published six volume history of the Second Civil War by Joplin (2046) covers in great and very well done detail all of the events that we are able to only touch lightly upon here, and many others as well, of course.

Those weapons had been widely used and very amply supplied by the US/CIA to the Rightists in the late 20th century Afghanistan civil war. Following the end of that war, there were a large number of them left over. Still, from 2019 on they were readily available on the worldwide armaments black market. A large number of these missiles had been painstakingly collected by the MRCD forces over a several year period before the Declaration of Restoration. Their use significantly diminished the effectiveness of Hagueite close-in air support in many urban Black Sectors.

In terms of an air-arm of its own, in several of the wide-open Red Sectors, the Native American forces of the MRCD were able to assemble small fleets of captured attack helicopters. They were effectively employed in "air guerrilla" operations. When not in use they were kept hidden in caves to protect them from Hagueite attacks.

However, despite these military achievements, in 2019 the MRCD forces were unable to make any significant territorial gains, nor were they able to make any one Black or Red Republic Sector secure enough to establish a base for a permanent provisional government. Yet they were able to tie up Hagueite forces, disrupt supply lines and communications, cost the Hagueites considerable sums of money, and inflict significant casualties on an already over-burdened military/ oppressor force. They were also able for the first time to mount and maintain a significant international diplomatic effort on behalf of the oppressed peoples of the NAR, of all Republics, colors, and ethnic groups.

International Developments

In that summer of 2019, the first international response from the Two Major Powers, the United States of Europe (USE) and the East Asian Confederation[2] (EAC), to the MRCD diplomatic

2. *Author's Note:* The East Asian Confederation consisted of Japan, Korea, China (including the formerly independent territory of Taiwan), the Philippines, the Federal Republic of IndoChina, Thailand, and Malaysia.

effort was one typical of its sort over the course of history. The violence was "officially condemned," as were the "atrocities on both sides." (There were few documented atrocities on the MRCD side, many on the Hagueite side, but the usual "balance" was achieved in this announcement.) "American Apartheid" had already been condemned some years before by what was left of the United Nations, but no formal actions against it had ever been taken. The Two Major Powers had never addressed the issue, and neither did they do so at this time.

The "good offices" of the Two Major Powers were offered to negotiate an end to the conflict. The offer was rejected by both sides. The Hagueites claimed, variously, that it was a "matter of no consequence," that the "disturbances would be brought under control soon," that such an offer constituted "meddling in the NAR's internal affairs," or, digging up some hoary language not much used in recent years, that such an offer was "part of an anti-Christian, socialist plot of the New World Order and the United Nations." The MRCD position was simple: the restoration of Constitutional democracy, freedom, and liberty, and the end to racist repression and division of the nation were not negotiable.

Trade between the NAR and the rest of the world had since the former's founding continued unabated. After all, with the decline in the supply of Middle East petroleum the NAR had become one of the world's two major suppliers of energy and other raw materials. (The other was the Siberian Region of Russia, now jointly administered by the Two Major Powers.) With the outbreak of the rebellion, a voluntary trade and cultural boycott movement that had been underway in a desultory manner for several years began to grow. Along with it there were increasing demands addressed to the United Nations and the Two Major Powers by liberal and left-wing governments and non-governmental organizations around the world to do something on behalf of democracy, Constitutionalism, and human rights, ranging from economic sanctions, to supplying arms to the Constitutionalist side, to armed intervention.

The first official international response to these developments was a classic: an embargo by the Two Major Powers on arms shipments to *all* units of the NAR. In practice, this "even-handed" move would have impact upon only the MRCD side. The Hagueites of course already had a highly developed military supply industry and had no need for imported arms. Thus on paper the arms embargo was like the one imposed by the Western democracies during the Spanish Civil War (1936-39).

In practice that embargo had deprived only the elected Republican government of Spain the weapons it needed to defend itself against the fascist rebels under Generalissimo Francisco Franco. The latter received all the weapons they needed from fascist Italy and Nazi Germany, both of which ignored the embargo. The Italian and German fascist government also sent on the order of 60,000 troops to fight alongside of the Spanish fascist forces. That effort, plus the effectiveness of the embargo on the Republican forces, doomed them to defeat from the start.

However, the embargo in the Second American Civil War turned out to be about as effective as a high-quality sieve, to the benefit primarily of the MRCD. No foreign nations were about to send ships across a minimum of 3000 miles of open ocean in an attempt to enforce it. The NAR had close to 5000 miles of ocean coastline, dotted with many harbors both great and small, especially on its Atlantic, Gulf of Mexico, and Northwest Pacific coasts.

Over the preceding ten years, with the diversion of military funding to support domestic repressive forces and the land-based units necessary to prosecute the Latin Wars, the Navy of the White Republic had been allowed to decline. In support of the Latin Wars that Navy was already stretched thin. Thus while the Hagueites themselves announced a blockade in an attempt to prevent arms from reaching the MRCD, it had little practical effect.

The Hague Regime Begins to Feel the Pressure

As a result of all this military, international, and diplomatic activity, even though none of it was perceived by the outside world as immediately destabilizing for the Hague regime, it felt threatened for the first time. As a result, on the military side, The Sieges of the principal Black Urban Sectors were begun in the fall of 2019. Although they had little military effect, the toll in human suffering was quite high.

On the politico-repressive side, early in the winter of 2020, planning was begun for the Second Final Solution, which would be yet another play on homophobia. It was implemented with the coming of spring in 2020. The Hagueites, like fascist bullies everywhere over the course of history, would be much more successful in carrying out actions against unarmed civilians than against opposing military forces of even somewhat equal military capability.

Homophobia in the Law During the Fascist Period

During the Transition Era, such Right-Wing Reactionary leaders as Pat Robertson and Newton Gingrich had seemed to look upon homophobia as a political tool with much apparent pleasure (see Chapters 7 and 11). Jefferson Davis Hague was about to gladly use it for political and repressive purposes for the third time during his reign. The outcome of this effort would be the deadliest of the three. (There is no evidence that any of the Transition Era Right-Wing Reactionary utilizers of homophobia would have approved of or condoned in any way the outcomes of its use under Hague.)

To briefly review Hague's use of homophobia, in 2005, during his first term, the Republican-Christian Alliance had enacted the 31st Amendment to the Constitution of the old U.S. (see Chapter 7). Section 3 of that Amendment stated:

> "Engaging in sexual relations with persons of the same sex is a matter of choice; no provision of this Constitution may be deemed to provide preferential status in the civil or criminal law at the Federal, state, or local level to any person or group of persons based on their chosen sexual preference."

Functionally, this act and the legislation written pursuant to it at the Federal, state, and local levels around the country had three principal outcomes: it lead to an explosion of public and private discrimination against persons based upon their sexual orientation; it legitimized homophobic violence and in many jurisdictions essentially decriminalized it; it drove to ground most homosexuals who were not already there.

Four years later, Hague had delivered his "Proclamation of Right," decreeing that homosexuality was a crime (see Chapter 11). In the Decree Hague said in part:

> "Homosexuality and its associated behaviors, pedophilia, sadism, and masochism are all abnormal, wrong, unnatural, and perverse, as well as sins against God. …Despite the measures taken pursuant to Section 3 of the 31st Amendment, in the eyes of God and every right thinking American, homosexuality and its associated perversions still constitute a plague upon our land and people. … As of this holy day, in homage to our almighty God, in recognition of His declaration that homosexuality is the worst kind of perversion, I hereby declare that homosexuality, in thought or action, is a crime."

Functionally, this decree and the legislation written pursuant to it at the Federal, state, and local levels around the country had three principal outcomes: it gave law enforcement officials a free hand to imprison or send to a Moral Rehabilitation Center (MRC) *anyone*, based upon their sexual orientation or their *suspected* sexual orientation; it thus completely terrorized the remaining sexually active homosexuals, of whom there were now very few; and it thus gave the forces of repression a very convenient "legal" method for imprisoning without trial anyone they could not imprison on other grounds: simply accuse the person of *thinking* homosexual thoughts.

This approach harked back to the anti-communist hysteria of the McCarthy Period (1946-60). As previously noted, during that time many people suffered both criminal and civil sanctions simply because they *thought* unpopular thoughts and took unpopular positions, not because they *did* anything unlawful. The only difference was that now, in aid of repression of opponents of the regime, it was sex, not politics that was the apparent indicator for action, even though in both cases politics was the ultimate motivator for the repressors.

The Presidential decree of 2009 resulted in the legalization of homophobic violence in the following sense. It was still technically a crime to assault (or worse) a homosexual, or someone the assailant claimed was a homosexual. However, from the time of the onset of organized violence against elective pregnancy termination clinics during the Transition Era, the pattern had been established of permitting private citizens to take the law into their own hands even to the extent of committing a crime by so doing, if the victim were perceived by Right-Wing Reaction as a "moral enemy" (Hill). Homophobic violence was just an extension of this pattern.

Since homosexuality was now a crime, persons convicted of engaging in it or even thinking about doing so, were subject to incarceration. However, the prisons were already very overcrowded, even after the massive Federal and state prison construction programs that had been commenced during the early Transition Era and continued unabated. Thus most homosexuals picked up under the Hague decree of 2009 were sent to an MRC.

(Since so many were incarcerated in them, the MRCs subsequently became just about the only loci in the NAR in which homosexuals could live without fear for their lives and engage in what for them were fairly normal sexual practices. A parallel in the days of the old Transition Era "Drug Wars" was the easy availability of drugs in prisons [Purdy].)

The establishment in 2009 of the new "legal" category "suspected homosexual" opened up a huge can of highly poisonous worms. This new construct contrasted sharply with the old racial one. In most cases, one could not be labeled a "suspected" Black, or Latino, or Native American, just as in Nazi Germany there had been no category for "suspected" Jew. In the eyes of the respective regimes, the person either was or wasn't a member of the named category, and in either case, for the racial assignment that was made some kind of positive proof, no matter how arbitrary or capricious, could be offered.

In the matter of "suspected homosexual," however, any person so labeled who claimed the assignment was not based on fact had to prove a negative: "I am not a homosexual," or even further, "I do not think homosexual thoughts." The regime did not have to prove a positive. It only had to produce a statement from someone, anyone, saying "I suspect so-and-so" of either being or thinking as a homosexual.

The imprisoning of homosexuals simply on the basis of their previously open homosexuality, a la Nazi Germany, represented one kind of horror. Imprisoning non-homosexuals on the grounds that they were indeed homosexuals, represented an even deeper horror (that is, if one can rank horrors). And then, in 2020, both the "homosexual" and the "suspected homosexual" labels came to be used to put people to their deaths, not just imprison them. For in that year the Hagueites implemented what came internally to be called the "Second Final Solution."

The Basis of the Second Final Solution[3]

The Second Final Solution (SFS) was a secret plan with a public face. The latter presented itself as a program aimed at rounding up the homosexual population remaining in the White Republic of the NAR. The SFS actually aimed to exterminate those persons, as well as anyone identified as an "enemy of

3. *Author's Note:* There is no indication or evidence that the Rev. Pat Robertson, Newton Gingrich, P.J. Hill, Pastor Peter J. Peters, or any other historical personage or organization mentioned or alluded to in this chapter or elsewhere in this book in a similar manner, would have supported or approved in any way of "The Second Final Solution," or any of the institutions, events, laws, policies, or procedures created or carried out in planning it or pursuant to it by the NAR, as mentioned, discussed, described, or alluded to anywhere in this chapter or subsequent ones.

Christ" or an "agent of the devil," that is, otherwise, any opponent of the Hague regime, what it stood for, and what it was doing, without the benefit of any kind of criminal justice procedure. The plan also avoided the local messiness created by the Death Squads.

The strategy was based in part on a Transition Era text by a "Christian Identity" minister known as Pastor Peter J. Peters entitled *The Death Penalty for Homosexuals* (1992). Peters cited several well-known excerpts from the Bible that taken literally call for the death penalty for persons committing homosexual acts. For example:

> "If a man also lie with mankind, as he lieth with a woman, both of them have committed an abomination: they shall surely be put to death; … (Leviticus 20:13)." (See the Poughton letter in Chapter 11 for a different interpretation of that same excerpt by a Baptist minister.)

The Reverend Pat Robertson took a position similar in certain ways to Peters'. During a television program broadcast on May 5, 1985 he said, in part (Porteus):

> "The [Biblical] wars of extermination have given a lot of people trouble unless they know what was going on. The people in the land of Palestine were very wicked. They were given over to idolatry; … they were having sex *men with men and women with women*; … and they were forsaking God. God told the Israelites to kill them all … [emphasis added].
>
> "And that seems to be a terrible thing to do. Is it? Or isn't it? … God saw that there was no cure for [what the people of Palestine were doing]. … [A]ll they would do is … pull the Israelites away from God, and prevent the truth of God from reaching the Earth. So God, in love, took away a small number that he might not have to take a large number."

(Pastor Peters, of course, accepted the Bible as the "Word of God," as did the Rev. Robertson. Interestingly enough, to support this position Peters cited a secular authority, a resolution actually passed by the Congress of the old U.S. in 1982 that began with the words [P.L. 97280]: "Whereas the Bible, the *Word of God*, has made a unique contribution in shaping the United States as a distinctive and blessed nation and people, ... [emphasis added].")

In contrast with Pastor Peters, others might say that the writers of the Leviticus text quoted above, and those of similar import, were, a) men, not God, and b) were men afflicted with a radical form of homophobia themselves. The question might be raised, why should people living three thousand or so years later in a completely different culture, environment, and socio-economic system pay any mind to the sayings of a sheep-herding homophobe living in a very constricted society?

Further, it might be said that such men were inveterate rule-makers for behaviors of which they did not approve for one reason or another, like homosexuality, incest, adultery, and eating pork or shellfish. In our time, few people follow their dietary rules, for good reason—they are no longer necessary to protect health. If that is so, maybe their other rules should be examined too, on a case-by-case basis, to see if they have any modern utility, rather than just accepting them on an arbitrary basis (see also Appendix V). Actually, the Christian "Inerrantists" had already done this. For while they fiercely advocated following Biblical rules on sexual behavior, they carefully did not recommend following the accompanying dietary laws, otherwise known as "keeping Kosher."

And finally, others might say, dietary rules or laws might have some public utility or effectiveness, and recommendations on what constitutes "moral" behavior might have some utility too. But attempting to legislate morality, especially with criminal penalties for non-compliance with such laws, has never been shown to be particularly effective over time in "improving morality." Rather, it has been shown to be very *demoral*izing to the population upon which it is imposed.

Nevertheless, it was the Peters view on what should be done to homosexuals, that is kill them, that eventually came to form the basis of the SFS. (It should be noted that there is no indication anywhere in the historical record that either Pastor Peters or the Rev. Robertson would have approved of or condoned the SFS.) It was set forth in a document named for the small Colorado town in which it was drawn up, *The LaPorte Protocol.*

The model for The LaPorte Protocol was the infamous Nazi German "Wannsee Protocol" which outlined the first "Final Solution" (Davidowicz, pp. 136-139). The latter lead to the virtual extermination of European Jewry. The former lead to the extermination of virtually all white homosexuals remaining in the NAR, as well as many non-homosexuals branded as such for one reason or another and shipped off to the designated extermination camp.

Why the Policy? Why at That Time?

For the Hague regime the SFS (publicly it was called "The Campaign for Sexual Cleansing") was a three-pronged strategy. First, with the war now underway in earnest not only in the Fourth Republic but almost in the backyards of many people in the White Republic, the Hagueites once again needed a Distraction. Second, although the level of repressive terror in the White Republic itself was already very high, the Hagueites figured they needed to crank it up a notch further since significant armed White resistance to American fascism seemed to be developing for the first time. Third, they needed a swift, efficient, low-cost way to get rid of their enemies. The prisons and the MRCs would no longer do and the Death Squads were coming to be of limited utility.

This situation stood on contrast with that of Nazi Germany in regard of the First Final Solution. It had a singular focus: exterminate the Jews of Europe. There was one reason for the policy: Hitler actually believed it to be necessary for the creation and ongoing security of the "Thousand-Year Reich." It did not have an external political purpose. Thus it was not publicly advertised to the German people.[4] In contrast, in the NAR, much was made of the new program, although there was a very serious attempt to keep its operational details secret.

The new Hagueite effort did have an external political purpose. "The Campaign for Sexual Cleansing" was on its face simply a reimplementation of the previously decreed criminalization of homosexuality. It was announced to the people of the White Republic as a renewed battle against the "ultimate evil." This action was to be taken, so the people were told, variously to: (a) "expunge sin from the society," (b) "punish sin," (c) round up the homosexuals "for their own protection," (d) isolate the "disease-causers from the normal people," (e) and "deliver the sinners from evil through redemption."

Whatever the reason, according to the public announcement all homosexuals were to be sent to camps for "re-education" and "purification of the soul." But, just as the creation of the hated "other" had been used by Right-Wing Reaction so many times in the past, once again the public campaign was intended to "supply an enemy."

Why Not Racism?

The Hagueites had come to realize that the old standby, racism, just wasn't working so well for them anymore. There were many reasons to account for this state of affairs, but one of them was a direct result of the Hagueites' own actions. One of the numerous outcomes of the policy of complete racial separation discussed in the last chapter was the decline of the political and

4. *Author's Note:* The German Nazi Minister of Propaganda, Josef Goebbels, was one of the three most powerful men in Nazi Germany after Hitler (the other two were Hermann Goering and Heinrich Himmler). He was the man who would have run the publicity campaign, if there had been one, promoting the Final Solution as the only solution. Himmler once said (Davidowicz, p. 139): "Beginning with Lublin, the Jews in the General gouvernement [Nazi occupied Poland] are now being evacuated eastward. The procedure is a pretty barbaric one and not to be described here more definitively. Not much will remain of the Jews." In all respects, the Nazi policy was kept secret, as quiet as possible.

social utility of racism as a means of control. Since racial separation was now virtually complete, in the White Republic racism could be reinforced only in general terms. There were no longer daily (if unrepresentative or distorted) examples of the "bad race"—people on welfare, drug users, the homeless (blacks were in fact a minority of each group, but portrayed as dominant in each)—examples who whites could see.

For 10 years most whites had not seen a Black except in an occasional chain gang (Cohen), had seen only an occasional un-deported Latino in the previous three years, had almost invariably looked past Native Americans in any case, and were taught by the regime that Asians were in a different racial category (NAR Asian policy being in a constant state of flux). Racism as a political weapon thus had come to have its limits.

Implementation of the "Campaign for Sexual Cleansing"
As noted, the regime did not publicly announce that according to the LaPorte Protocol it had decided in advance that there would be no "re-education" or "purification" carried out. And it did not announce that there would be no return for the affected persons. Death, pure and simple, was the object. And unlike in the Nazi death camps such as Auschwitz, death was accomplished simply. No attached slave labor factories. No gas chambers. No ovens. And there was only one camp. It was located in an area of Southeastern California about 100 miles southwest of Las Vegas, Nevada. By a cruel irony indeed, the place was called the Devil's Playground.

Bounded on the west by the Bristol Mountains and the east by the Providence Mountains (misnamed in this context), taking up part of the by then defunct East Mojave National Park, the regime simply ringed with a Killer Fence an area of desert 20 miles east to west and 40 miles north to south. The homosexuals and the "suspected" homosexuals were rounded up, taken to the area by truck along the old Interstate 15 to the north or 40 to the south, and deposited, left to die without food or water.

The NAR learned this technique of dealing with its enemies, real or imagined, from the old Saudi Arabian monarchy. When it caught significant opponents, including even high-ranking military officers and members of the very large Royal Family who had gone over to the opposition, they were simply taken out to the center of the vast Arabian desert, the Rub' al Khali (the Empty Quarter), and left there. Of course, the Saudi Muslims did this only on a very limited scale, to people it considered especially important enemies of the ruling clan. It was left to the Hagueites to apply it on a large scale, with little discrimination. Since it was a large scale operation, in the end the Hagueites found it impossible to maintain complete secrecy.

While there were few survivors of the Devil's Playground, as one might imagine, enough lived to convincingly tell the horrific tale. Almost all records were destroyed in the last days of the NAR, but a few were not. Most of the truck drivers were killed by Helmsmen, but a few survived to tell what they knew too. For some time there was a market in the bones of the dead from the camp, just as there had been a market for the dried bones of dead buffalo on the Great Plains in the 1870s. A few of the drivers of the "bone buggies" survived as well.

There is no way of estimating just how many people died in this camp. But given the level of homosexual repression that had been in place since the passage of the Morality Amendment in 2005, it is fair to say that many more of them were simply opponents of the regime at one level or another than were actual homosexuals.

Next Developments in the War

The next developments in the war were in part determined by the worldwide response to the developing horror of the SFS as the details leaked out. It was rather different from the response which had been accorded to discovery of the First. The German Nazis began perpetrating their horror in the summer of 1941 with the construction of the first *Vernichtungslager* ("annihilation camp") (Davidowicz, p. 135). Credible evidence of the Nazi mass murder campaign started coming out of Eastern Europe within months of its commencement (Wouk, Chapters 13, 14, 16, 18).

Nevertheless, it took several years for a world that did not want to know about it, and did not want to worry about what it might have to do to resettle several million European Jews, to recognize just what was going on. And still next to nothing was done about it other than a certain amount of handwringing.

In the case of the SFS, verifiable documentation, from satellite photos to personal reports, were already circulating widely around the world on the PlaNet by the summer of 2020. And this time, the world didn't have to figure out how to handle an unwanted load of refugees. To stop the slaughter, if that were the intent, the world simply had to figure out how to help the MRCD bring the war to a successful conclusion.

Pressure from people of good will around the world to do something about the Hagueite horror built very rapidly. It led to the imposition of the first economic sanctions on the NAR by the USE and the EAC in the fall of 2020. Just as economic sanctions had eventually played a positive role in bringing down South African Apartheid in the late 20th century, so too did they play such a role in bringing down American Apartheid, happily in a much shorter period of time, in the early 21st.

As the tide of history finally began to turn on Right-Wing Reaction in America, observers began to take note of that fact. Curley Oakwood, for one, did not much like what was going on.

A Curley Oakwood Radio Broadcast Transcript (Wednesday, April 1, 2020)

My friends, my friends, my friends. And you are all my friends, because I am one of the friendliest guys you will ever want to meet, and if you've already met me you already know that, and if you haven't, then anyone who has will tell you that you are in for a treat of the friendliest friendliness you can find anywhere. No foolin'.

Yes I have to tell you in all honesty, in all seriousness, that it is a treat to be me, and that's no foolin' either. And it's a treat to be White, and Christian, and live in God's White Republic of the New American Republics. For whatever anyone may tell you, and there are some naysayers out there, there are some doomsday prophets out there, and that's not God's Final Judgment I'm talking about, I'm not talking about that Glorious Day of Redemption which is yet to come, but about those doomsayers of the here and right now, of those treacherous, disloyal bums who would sell our wonderful country so short they couldn't see over the top of a blade of grass, about those nattering nabobs of negativism, as the blessed Bill Safire called them so many moons ago, whatever anyone may tell you, the White Republic and the whole of the NAR are at the top of their game right now.

There may be a few shortages here and there, and you may hear a bit of gunfire now and then, and your sons may be a bit more caught up in the military game than you'd like them to be, but this is it, life is good. The liberals are gone, the niggers are gone, the Skins are gone, the spics are going, and the slopes, well you just pay them no never mind. The liberal nigger lovers in Congress are in their place. They can't touch you. And, and, and—we are finally doing to the queers what we should have done to them long ago: get rid of them, get them out of our hair, out of schools, out of our way.

With our military, our HM, and our Independent Militias, let's not forget them, rolling the way they are, President Jeff is soon going to have everything under control. And we will be right back to where we oughta be. So be happy folks. You should be.

And if you aren't, I can tell you on very good authority—mine—that you have only yourself to blame. No foolin'. And by the way, if you do come across a nattering nabob of negativism, even if it's a friend or family member, do, as a loyal White American Christian, mention it to your local HM patrol, won't you? No foolin'.

A Connie Conroy Note (Wednesday, April 15, 2020)

Usta was they collected taxes on this day. That was before the glorious 31st [Amendment]. Now they collect them year round[5]. God what I am saying? I better make sure the HM never sees this, or it's off to a camp even for me.

And speaking about off to a camp, this latest move by the Prez is kicking up quite a ruckus among his "Gay Teammates," in and out of government. Some of those HM units are taking their job quite seriously. The Prez has told me to see to it that we work out some kind of system to protect our favorite gay guys and gals *before* they get picked up and someone has to intervene at the last moment. Getting a "friend" off one of those trucks once they're on has proved pretty difficult, I can tell you. And once they're through that gate, forget it!

So we have to work something out. Queer is queer, but when they work for us, when they follow good Christian principles, when they are Whiter than White, ah well, that's something else again. We can do it. I know we can.[6]

5. *Author's Note:* The national sales tax (NST) (CAST) that had been substituted for the income tax was, of course, collected every time one made a purchase. But not only, like all sales taxes, was the NST regressive. Repression is expensive and the demise of national domestic programs such as welfare, such as it had been in the Transition Era, saved very little money. Thus to raise its needed funds, and unable to tax incomes either personal or corporate, the regime had steadily raised the NST until it now stood at 30%.

6. *Author's Note:* The German Nazis under Hitler had an official anti-homosexual policy. Known homosexuals were forced to wear a pink triangle patch on their outer clothing, as Jews were forced to wear a patch with a black Star of David on a yellow field. Known homosexuals were among the first persons to be rounded up and sent to early concentration camps inside Germany. Yet there were numbers of known homosexuals who held high rank in the Nazi Party. It was rumored that Hermann Goering, Commander of the Luftwaffe (Air Force) and designated successor to Hitler, was among them. This too was the case in the NAR, and before it in the American Christian Nation Party, the Republican Christian Alliance, and the old Republican Party. Thus some few homosexuals allied themselves with the most reactionary elements of their time, elements that would discriminate against them and worse (as it later came to be), because of—what? Self hate? The desire to be accepted by those perceived to hold the power? Schizophrenic splitting? A true belief in the oppressive Right-Wing Reactionary economic theories. Or --- what? (Contin.) Whatever the reason, throughout history, in more than one country, both open and completely closeted homosexuals have served the interests of virulently homophobic Right-Wing Reactionary interests very well.

A Parthenon Pomeroy Diary Entry (Saturday, July 11, 2020)
I wonder what's going on. Things are supposed to be getting better, but now they seem to be getting worse. I don't want to be disloyal and the President assures us there's nothing to worry about it, and with the RBE, as he calls it, the economy's going to turn the corner any day now.

And we did do it. We got rid of the niggers, and we're getting rid of the spics, and they tell me that out west the 'skins are gone too, but who cares about them anyway. I know we worked hard. We've saved our country, our freedom, our American way of life. We cut taxes to the bone. We got God back in the schools. We've saved the unborn. We ended handouts to those with their hand out all the time. We got that liberal nigger-loving Congress out of the way. We put that goddamned Supreme Court in its place. Those back-stabbing liberal media are gone. We put Christ in His rightful place too, above us all.

And it's still not quite right. I know I'd better keep these thoughts to myself, or the HM will send me off to the camps too, just like they did Tony down the street for complaining at the local after he got drunk. Even with both my boys in uniform, I've got to worry about that. Well maybe President Jeff is right. Maybe once we get rid of all the queers, everything will be alright. I sure hope the President is right on that one.

But anyway, thanks, God, for blessing us with the New American Republics! And thanks Pat, too.

An Alex Poughton Letter
September 17, 2020
Dear Karl,

Just a quick note on something that strikes me as real funny. I know you've been hearing about this huge scandal here, the extermination camp out in California (that's not the funny thing—read on). I think the bastards are actually going to be forced to close it down soon. International pressure is actually accomplishing something!

So they're already desperately casting around for new

stereotypes to use to label the "enemy" (increasingly their own people!) One of the funniest ones I've come across is "Connie," the word they're using to describe the other side, you know, the "Constitutionalists." It's too bad for the Hagueites, but those "dirty words" to describe their enemies that the Right has loved to use for so long, like "liberal" or even "liberal nigger lover" have little meaning to most whites in the NAR now.

So they've come up with this new one, that, get this, rhymes with "Commie!" Ouch! Well you know, most people are kind of hazy on the time when there were Communist governments in the world and good old anti-communism was the staple of American foreign and domestic policy. But there is this sort of instinctive collective memory that somehow Commies are bad people. Well, "Connie" rhymes with "Commie," Commies were always bad, and so are the Constitutionalists, and so on and so forth. You know, even the propaganda machine of this Godforsaken "Christian Nation" is running down.

Will write more soon.

All the best,
Alex

References:

CAST: Citizens for an Alternative Tax System, "A National Retail Sales Tax," Manassas, VA: 1995.

Cohen, A., "Back on the Chain Gang," Time, May 15, 1995, p. 26.

Davidowicz, L.S., *The War Against the Jews: 1933-45*, New York: Holt, Rinehart and Winston, 1975.

Hill, P.J., "Defensive Action," Pensacola, FL: P.O. Box 2243, c. 1994.

Joplin, S., *The Second Civil War: From Start to Finish*, Six Vols., Cambridge, MA: The AllIvy University Press, 2046.

Peters, P.J., *The Death Penalty for Homosexuals*, LaPorte, CO: Scriptures for America, 1992.

Porteous, S., "Robertson on God's Love," *Freedom Writer*, December, 1995, p. 8.

P.L. (Public Law) 97280, *Joint Resolution: Authorizing and Requesting the President to proclaim 1983 as the "Year of the Bible"*, Washington, DC: U.S. Congress, October 4, 1982.

Purdy, M., "A State Tries to Rein In a Prison Awash in Drugs," *The New York Times*, October 30, 1995.

Shirer, W.L., *The Rise and Fall of the Third Reich*, New York: Simon and Schuster, 1960.

Wouk, H., *War and Remembrance*, Boston, MA: Little, Brown and Company, 1978.

CHAPTER 19

2021-2023: The Restoration of Constitutional Democracy in the United States of America

Author's Commentary: The Progress of the War

The Economic Sanctions

It was only after the revelation of the Second Final Solution that the United States of Europe (USE) and the East Asian Confederation (EAC), the Two Major Powers, first imposed economic sanctions on the NAR, in the fall of 2020. That they did so was not entirely a sign of altruism or dedication to the cause of freedom and liberty. For years the Two Major Powers had stood by idly as the Hagueites and the American Christian Nation Party had brought fascism to the old United States, and then extended it into Canada and Latin America. Once the NAR was established, both governments happily traded with it. As noted, it was one of the world's two principal suppliers of raw materials and fossil/biomass energy resources.

However, unlike the old U.S. and the NAR itself, both the USE and the EAC realized that the key to future economic security lay with renewable energy sources and that biomass, although renewable, had its limitations. So they had forged ahead with solar, geothermal, tidal, wind, and thermonuclear energy development. (There had been precedent for this. For example, by the mid-90s one of the principal members of the USE, France, was already supplying 75% of its electricity needs from nuclear power, an intermediate stage energy source between the polluting non-renewables and the non-polluting renewables.) Thus, by the time the Second U.S. Civil War broke out, the Two Major Powers were already well on their way to energy independence from the NAR and even from their own Siberian energy resources, making it easier for them to step away.

Further, there was the matter of the NAR's foreign trade debt. It dated from the time during the Transition Era when the old U.S. ran such huge negative trade balances with the old Japan and the old People's Republic of China. The annual amounts of the deficits had been reduced somewhat under the NAR as energy and raw material exports increased and the purchasing power of its citizens and subjects decreased, reducing imports. (Non-Whites, of course, had been virtually wiped out of the market for consumer goods.)

Nevertheless, the *total debt* continued to increase and questions were continually being raised about the ongoing ability of the Hague regime to meet its interest payments. The economic sanctions were strengthened by early winter 2021, as the international community became increasingly concerned not only with what was going on in North America but also with the very disruptive nature of the Latin Wars. The noose had begun to tighten around the Hague regime's neck.

The International Brigade

A new element increasing the pressure on the Hague regime appeared in the spring of 2021. At that time, the first units of the Edward K. Barsky[1] International Brigade arrived to fight

1. The Brigade was named in honor of an American surgeon who was the Commander of the Medical Unit for the International Brigade. (This book is dedicated in part to Dr. Barsky's memory.) During and after the Second World War (1939-45), Dr. Barsky headed an American organization called the Joint Anti-Fascist Refugee Committee (the "Spanish Committee" for short). It was established to provide assistance for refugees from Spanish fascism living all over the world, but especially in the south of France.

Shortly after the end of World War II, Dr. Barsky became a victim of what would soon become known as "McCarthyism" in the old U.S. As noted in Chapter 5, McCarthyism was an "anti-communist" political, economic, and social hysteria, aimed at repressing any left-wing activity in the country. It was named for an alcoholic junior Senator from Wisconsin, Joseph R. McCarthy, who was one of its two most prominent and vicious proponents. (The other was Representative, then Senator, then Vice President Richard M. Nixon of California, who would in 1974 become the only President of the old U.S. to resign the office rather than face almost certain impeachment for crimes against the Constitution committed while in it.)

McCarthyism gripped the old U.S. from 1947 through the end of the 1950s.➤

on the side of the forces of the MRCD. The original International Brigade was a volunteer military unit that had been organized for and served on the democratically elected Republican government's side in the Spanish Civil War (1936-39). It had been made up of people from over 40 nations around the world, including Germans and Italians who fought against the German Nazi and Italian fascist forces which had intervened on the side of the Spanish fascists under the future Spanish Fascist Dictator Franco (see previous chapter). The original International Brigade had defied the arms embargo established by the so-called "Western Democracies" (primarily the old United States, Great Britain, and France). In the end, it could do nothing to stem the fascist tide in Spain, but it established a glorious tradition. This new International Brigade, the "E K Bees" as they were called[2], constituted the first non-mercenary, non-governmental external military force to intervene in a civil war anywhere in the world since the one in Spain.

Its most prominent feature was that through a combination of legal action and socio-economic pressure left-wing citizens were made to pay a price for holding perfectly legal beliefs and taking perfectly legal actions that stood contrary to the prevailing right-wing views in the country, for refusing to disavow their beliefs, and/or before official bodies of one kind or another name others as "left-wing" or "disloyal" as well. The prices paid ranged from loss of livelihood and/or profession to going to prison.

Dr. Barsky had refused to reveal the names of contributors to his organization to the inquisitors of the notorious House Un-American Activities Committee. (This agency of repression was the historical predecessor of the House American Morality Committee that would, in the early Fascist Period, first bring Jefferson Davis Hague to national attention [see Chapter 6].)

Because of his refusal to "name names," along with several other prominent Americans such as the writer of progressive historical fiction Howard Fast, Dr. Barsky was cited for contempt of Congress. He was convicted and sentenced to six months in jail, of which he served four. Following his jail term, the New York State Board for Medicine suspended Dr. Barsky's medical license for two years, entirely for political reasons. After his license was restored, he returned to the practice of surgery, carrying on until his death in 1963.

2. *Author's Note:* The name was a play on the old "Seabees" of the United States Navy during World War II, the Naval Construction Battalions that built so many fortifications on islands and atolls across the Pacific Ocean during the amphibious campaigns against the Japanese Empire, 1942-45.

The first E K Bee forces were dispatched to three fronts. The Alaskan Force linked up with Inuit units to harry the last Hagueite forces as they pulled back from Alaska just before the spring thaw of 2021, the Hagueites having already decided that that northern outpost was no longer defensible. The Canadian Force established a freestanding front along the New Canada/New England border and also helped the forces of New Canada in their struggle against the Quebec fascists. The Southwestern Force, landing in Baja California of the old Mexico, was able to make its way through to the Navajo/Hopi Native American Sector in Arizona. Additional E K Bee units would arrive through the summer of 2021 in various locations.

The Summer of 2021

The Hagueite Sieges of selected Sectors were intensified. Newark, NJ, Atlanta, GA, and Gary, IN, were overrun and demolished. Much as happened following the Jewish Warsaw Ghetto Uprising against the German Nazi forces in April, 1943, those of their inhabitants and defenders not killed in the fighting were sent to camps. (The destinations did not include the Devil's Playground, already shut down in response to international pressure.)

At the same time there were the breakouts by the MRCD forces, at The Bronx, NY, Charleston, SC, Mobile, AL, Chicago, IL, Los Angeles, CA, and Oakland, CA (see below). In what came to be known as the Second Indian Wars, the MRCD forces also achieved a certain degree of success in the old Plains states and the Southwest. In Latin America, successive defeats of Hagueite forces holed up in the Andean city of Cuzco, Peru, the major Amazonian port, Manaus, and the Colombian port of Cali, plus the loss of control of the Panama Canal (the Pacific Locks of which the Hagueites dynamited before leaving), lead to the Hagueite Withdrawal To Mexico.

A major result of this stepped-up military pressure on the Hagueites was a further increase in the already high level of violent anti-civilian repression in the continental NAR. Hagueite atrocities featuring massacres, rape, and torture harking back to Nanking in 1937, Indonesia in the 1960s, Cambodia in the 1970s, East Timor in the 1980s, and Bosnia-Herzegovina in the 1990s became evermore commonplace. The HM and the Independent Militias were especially active in this regard. There is some evidence that these tactics were the result of official policy decisions, but it is not conclusive.

The Use of Weapons of Mass Destruction

As the Hagueite military position deteriorated in the summer of 2021, discussion of the possible use of nuclear and/or chemical/biological weapons was undertaken at the highest levels of the Hague regime. Potential use of the latter weapons group was quickly rejected for logistical reasons: it would simply be too hard to control the potential spread of toxic agents to areas of the White Republic adjacent to any selected targets.

To this day the question of why were nuclear weapons never used by the Hagueites has not been completely answered. There has been much speculation on it, however. (The best, most recent summary of both the available evidence and the discussions of it is by Beiderbecke and Goodman [2043].) Nuclear weapons, called the "Hammer of God" by the Hagueites, were clearly considered part of their military arsenal. It was also clear that since non-Whites were considered "inferior beings" and White opponents of the regime "agents of the devil himself," "minions of the anti-Christ," and/or "black/Whites" (see Chapter 15), there would have been no compunctions about using them against either group. But nuclear weapons were not used, and the reasons why remain shrouded in mystery.

Most NAR records were destroyed before the fall of New Washington at the end of March 2022. (Shredding of sensitive documents had been built into the Right-Wing Reactionary mentality since the days of the Nixon Watergate scandal in the 1970s, the Ronald Reagan/William Casey/Oliver North Iran-Contra scandal of the 1980s, and George Bush's departure from White House at the end of his Presidency in 1992.) But a few records and some recorded post-War recollections remain. The possible reasons for non-use may be summarized as follows.

First, there was a recognition by the (very few) wise heads within the NAR's *inner sanctum* of the very real dangers posed by the spread of radiation with damage to the NAR's own military capacity that would necessarily occur in the environs of any target area. Second, there were strong, although unsubstantiated, rumors that the MRCD had nuclear weapons too, and would retaliate with them if first attacked. (MRCD records that would speak to this issue are still held under the highest level of security classification.) Third, in certain quarters of the NAR leadership, there was fear of the certain negative reaction around the world, and what further pressure that might bring to bear on an NAR already beginning to suffer significantly from the effects of the economic sanctions.

Then there were the technical problems. Because of the precipitous decline in the number of trained nuclear scientists, engineers, and technicians available following the abolition of the public education system and the elimination of the non-religious universities, nuclear (as well as chemical/biological) weapons stockpiles had not been well maintained. Further, no new nuclear weapons had been produced since before the creation of the NAR. Thus, the Hagueite military could not be sure that a weapon would work, even if the attempt to use it were made. (That fear may have been justified. One nuclear weapon may well have been triggered by the NAR and failed to explode: just what the Beaumont [TX] Initiative was has never been fully explained.)

As to other possible reasons for non-use, not surprisingly there is no evidence that either moral or general environmental considerations played a part in the decision making process.

The Final Push

By late summer 2021, it was clear that the MRCD forces were gaining. Following the Oakland Breakout, they had captured San Francisco. With control of both sides of the Golden Gate, they were able to clear enough of the remains of the Golden Gate Bridge, blown up by the Hagueite forces as they left the area, to create a passable channel into San Francisco Bay.

Thus the MRCD was able to establish a base for a Provisional Government and a major port for the entry of supplies and equipment (by this time the international arms embargo generally existed only on paper). Shortly thereafter, following the respective Breakouts, the ports of Charleston, SC and Mobile, AL were opened for the MRCD forces as well. Nevertheless, although pressed on every front, the Hagueites held out. It was their default on interest payments on their very sizeable debt to the EAC that ultimately lead to their demise.

The East Asian Confederation had been considering military intervention for quite some time. Their supplies of raw materials had been significantly disrupted, and the remaining North American markets for their manufactured goods had virtually disappeared. There was also the increasing worldwide moral pressure to do something about a situation that created ever intensifying human misery in the Americas and threatened stability around the world. Further, the EAC secretly obtained an agreement from the MRCD National Leadership Council that should they prevail, the MRCD would honor the NAR's foreign debt obligation, on a renegotiated, long-term repayment schedule. When the NAR defaulted, the EAC decided to move.

On December 7, 2021, the EAC declared war on the White Republic of the NAR, launching a massive invasion through the Western Provinces of the former Canada. (The USE responded with a half-hearted cheer.) The assault came 80 years to the day after the surprise attack by the fascist Imperial Japanese forces on Pearl Harbor, HI that had precipitated the entry of the old U.S. into World War II. The Japanese element in the EAC High Command had insisted upon this date for launching the attack against the fascist, anti-democratic regime in North America. This would be a symbolic way, they said, of "making amends," in part at least, for that attack by the Japanese fascists on the democratic old United States so many years before.

The invasion was made possible by one of the great technical feats of military history (akin in its day to the Carthaginian general Hannibal transiting the Alps of Switzerland with elephants during the Second Punic War). The EAC army was in winter able to rapidly move huge amounts of men and equipment across vast stretches of difficult terrain in Alaska and the old Canada. In part they accomplished this feat by developing a whole new class of motorized transport vehicles modeled on the "foot fortresses" that appeared in the pre-Transition Era science fiction movie The *Return of the Jedi*, the third of the great filmmaker Stephen Spielberg's *Star Wars* trilogy.

Also, they were able to escape detection by the NAR's partially functioning satellite surveillance system. This was accomplished by the invention of "electronic ground camouflage." Among other things, this system was capable of disguising both visual and "down-looking" radar images as observed from above, and neutralizing heat emissions from internal combustion engine exhausts so that they could not be picked up by infrared sensors.

This operation was later compared to a grand maneuver of the Imperial Japanese Army undertaken in 1942 just after its entry into World War II. It managed to pass undetected 600 miles through some of the world's thickest jungle down the Malay Peninsula to attack from the rear the then-British outpost and military base at Singapore. The British military leadership of the time had said that such a feat need not even be contemplated, much less defended against, because there was absolutely no way it could be accomplished.

The Hagueite High Command said much the same thing about the threat of an EAC invasion from the north in winter. And they were just as wrong as the British generals had been. The Winter Campaign of 2022 lead eventually to the fall of New Washington in mid-March of that year, and the end of any effective Hagueite resistance shortly thereafter.

The Core Issues of the Second Civil War

The MRCD leadership knew that this Second Civil War had

been fought in part over the same issues that were at the core of the First: the theory of White Supremacy, the political use of racism, and the exploitation of man by man based on the color of one's skin. New were the major issues of the destruction of personal freedom and liberty for all citizens, the end of church/state separation, the re-imposition of second-class citizenship for women, and class-based oppression of all workers regardless of skin color.

Back in the 19th century, the battle of the First Civil War to abolish slavery had been won. But, the MRCD National Leadership Council knew, subsequently there had been fought an ongoing, undeclared, 150 years' war still on the race issue. It was not military but it was often violent, and always political. Over time, the forces of humanism had lost that war to the forces of racism. The final, tragic end came with the formation of the NAR itself.

The Leadership knew that in the aftermath of the Second Civil War, the victory over the forces of fascism and Right-Wing Religious authoritarianism, and the destruction of the racism that Right-Wing Reaction had so effectively used for so many years to maintain its control over the American people, would have to be consciously and completely secured this time around. That would take much attention and continuing effort (which has in fact been supplied over the succeeding years, with much success).

Symbolism

As part of that effort, the National Leadership Council knew the strong supporting role that symbolism could play in achieving long-term success. And so, the MRCD leadership arranged for the formal unconditional surrender of the NAR forces and the coincident absolute and complete dissolution of the NAR government to be held at the Appomattox, VA, Court House, on April 9, 2022. That was 187 years to the day after the Union commander Ulysses S. Grant had accepted the surrender of the Confederate Commander Robert E. Lee in the same place, marking the end of the First Civil War. And passing through Richmond, VA on their way to Appomattox, the MRCD forces took care to demolish every one of the equestrian statues of Confederate generals that had lined Richmond's Monument Avenue for so many years (Allen). Those egregious reminders of the horrors of slavery, not a noble institution in any way, were finally gone.

On the same day there was a ceremonial co-surrender by NAR forces to Native American forces. It was held at the Little Big Horn, Montana site of the defeat, on July 25-26, 1876, of U.S. Army troops under Gen. George Armstrong Custer, by Sioux/Cheyenne forces lead by Chief Sitting Bull. That action had been the last significant victory in the Native Americans' long-term losing struggle for self-determination against European settlers. (That struggle, as most readers of this book know, spanned close to three centuries. It would come to its final, bitter end 14 years after the victory at Little Big Horn with the massacre of non-combatant Native Americans by U.S. Army troops at Wounded Knee, S.D. [Brown].)

A Provisional Government was established by the MRCD National Leadership Council on the day of the Hagueite surrender. It ruled until Constitutional government on the territory of the contiguous 48 states of the old U.S. was restored a little over a year later, on July 4, 2023, with the name, the Re-United States of America. A Restored Constitution was duly promulgated after ratification by the reformed states. Although many important functional changes were made, in overall structure the new Constitution and the government for which it provided the authority were largely drawn on the original (see below and Appendix VII).

A new holiday to coincide with Independence Day was declared. It is called Restoration Day, in honor of the Restoration of Constitutional Democracy in the Re-United States of America, and the formal dissolution of the NAR. Restoration also recognized the renewal of the nation of Canada (restored to its former borders), the reestablishment of the U.S.-Canadian border, and, with certain changes made by the antifascist forces there, the reestablishment of the nations of Latin America.

The Restored and Revised Constitution

When the National Leadership Council of the Movement for the Restoration of Constitutional Democracy convened the Restoration Convention to write the document that would be the means to achieve their goals, they laid down several ground rules. Primary among them was that the drafters would start with the old Constitution as the foundation of their work. They would not attempt to create something entirely new. The old one had worked very well for two centuries, until the people and the Constitutionalist leadership had let down their guard against the forces of economic oligarchy (as the author Jack London had labeled them a century and a half before in his prescient book *The Iron Heel* [1907]) and religious authoritarianism.

Furthermore, no one was convinced that anything better than the political framework created by the Founding Fathers could be devised anyway. Federalism, the Separation of Powers, and the System of Checks and Balances were sound principles for effective government of a large nation. For years, the whole resistance movement had gathered its strength from the Restoration Declaration which focused on the Constitution. This was no time to scrap it. Thus the drafters simply had to put into it certain new provisions and principles that would permit the new government established under it to achieve the goals for the nation the MRCD had set forth in the Restoration Declaration. And that the drafters did. (The Constitution of the Re-United States of America is reproduced in Appendix VII.)

It is interesting to note that among those changes were not any specific measures designed to make it more difficult in the future to concentrate power in the Executive Branch, the occurrence that had ultimately lead to fascism. It was decided that the task of preventing the reoccurrence of fascism or anything like it is ultimately the responsibility of the people, actively participating in the democratic process, and an active, aware, and responsible pro-democracy, pro-Constitutionalist leadership.

It was strongly felt that attempting to prevent the reassertion of Executive Branch domination by the means of written clauses in a Constitution would be fruitless in any case. After all, the political success of "The 15% Solution" had showed precisely how Constitutional means could be used to destroy Constitutional democracy itself. If it happened before, it could happen again.

In addition, a significantly weakened Executive Branch would have made it even more difficult than it already was to solve the vast problems the nation faced in the wake of the NAR's economic, social, political, and physical destruction and desecration. Democracy cannot be legislated for any more than morality can. It requires the continued participation of an enlightened citizenship corresponding to the electorate. It also requires effective, informed, dedicated leadership. Fortunately, to this day, at least, we have been blessed with both.

The basic principles of the Restored Constitution are as follows:

1. The *structure* of the Federal government as originally designed is not changed. As noted, Federalism (the division of sovereignty between the Federal government and the states), the Separation of Powers, and the System of Checks and Balances among the three branches are all maintained.
2. The Federal government is an entity with *independent powers*, representing the people of the nation as a whole. An American citizen is a citizen of a nation, not of a separate state. These principles, all implied or stated only in ambiguous terms in the old Constitution, were made explicit in the restored one.
3. The Federal government has a major role to play in the social, economic and political life of the *nation as a whole*. This principle was also implied in the old Constitution and made explicit in the restored one. The restored Constitution makes it clear that the Federal government is to take an

active role in the economic affairs of the country. The impetus for this emphasis was the so-called "anti-government," so-called "free market" forces' miserable failure in all aspects of their stewardship of the economy through the Transition Era and the Fascist Period.

4. Finally, again as implied in the original, the Federal and state governments' abilities to interfere with and limit individual freedom and liberty, as long as the expression of those rights on balance harms no one else, is severely limited. At the same time, reflecting the Jeffersonian principle so clearly stated by him in the original Declaration of Independence with the statement "it is to secure these rights [of "life, liberty, and the pursuit of happiness"] that governments are instituted among men," under the restored Constitution the government has the obligation to actively protect individual freedoms and liberties and defend their expression, again with the caveat, as long as the expression of those rights on balance harms no one else. Just what that "balance" in each and every case was, was to be left to the courts to decide.

Some of the Details

Although the overall structure remained unchanged, many detailed changes were made. For example, the Electoral College system for the election of the President was replaced with direct, popular election, the Senate was enlarged to one-third the size of the House of Representatives and the seats were allotted to the states roughly in proportion to their population (rather than the arbitrary two each) with a provision for cumulative voting, and the old First Amendment was significantly expanded. As noted, the full text (with extensive "Author's Notes" dealing with most of the changes) is reproduced in Appendix VII. For quick reference, many of those changes are summarized below, not necessarily in order of importance, but in order of how they appear in the document.

The *Preamble*, largely ignored by politicians of all stripes in the old United States, was explicitly incorporated into the sections of the reestablished Constitution that described the legislative, executive, and judicial branches of the Federal government. Further, it was significantly expanded, to wit:

> "We the people of the Re-United States, with faith in our humanity and ability to work together within the democratic process, in order to form a more perfect Union, banish the disease of racism, create respect for the dignity and individuality of each human being, establish justice, implement true multi-culturalism, insure domestic tranquility, promote the general welfare, protect our environment, provide for the common defence, recognize the essentiality of interdependence and community to individual and species survival, and secure the blessings of freedom and liberty to ourselves and our posterity, do ordain and re-establish this Constitution for the United States of America."

Article I, among other things, clearly established the Federal government's authority over the composition of the State and local governments. It also removed from anyone with any official connection to the old NAR regime eligibility for participation in the restored Constitutional government, except in very special circumstances. As elsewhere in the Constitution, with the creation of the system of direct election for President/Vice President, the former reference to "electors" was deleted.

The old political practice of "gerrymandering" electoral districts to fit political needs, named after an early nineteenth century governor of Massachusetts, Elbridge Gerry, was prohibited. The old national "Election Day," the first Tuesday in November, was retained by specification.

The Senate as a separate, longer-term, hopefully more deliberative institution was preserved, but representation by State in it was made proportional to population. With the adoption of cumulative voting for Senatorial candidates, some provision for proportional representation was made. The reinstitution of the old "filibuster rule" in the Senate, under which a minority could prevent a matter even from coming to a vote, and the enactment of any "3/5ths" rule for categories of legislation like tax increases that were so favored by Right-Wing Reaction during the late Transition Era, or any similar anti-democratic measures, were prohibited.

The practice of buying the votes of Senators and Representatives through the medium of political campaign contributions had accelerated during the Transition Era. Various attempts to institute "campaign finance" and "lobbying" reforms all failed before the onset of the Fascist Period, while the practices at which such reform attempts were aimed played a major role in the onset of fascism. Thus the reforms were put directly into the new Constitution.

Many changes were made to Article I, Section 8, the one that describes the functions of the Congress. The broad outlines of a new economic policy, called by some the "Guided Free Market" and other "Social Capitalism," were spelled out. The provision for the income tax was incorporated directly. As in all other industrialized countries, the national government was given an explicit role in supporting of the arts and the sciences.

Full Federal representation for the residents of the Capitol district, without also creating the complex intergovernmental relations problems that outright statehood would have created, was provided for. The institution of Federal land ownership was placed in the Constitution. Finally, the Congress was given the authority and responsibility to implement one of the most important elements of the Preamble: "banish racism."

In Section 9, the authority of the restored Constitution was explicitly extended to cover the actions of government at all levels, and a non-discrimination clause, reinforced by various provisions of the new *Article VIII* covering Rights and Liberties, was added.

In *Article II*, as noted a system of direct election for the President/Vice President was created. In *Article III* the power and authority of judicial review of the Constitutionality of actions of the other two branches of the Federal government, and of the actions of all branches of the State and local governments, was explicitly given to the Supreme Court. All actions taken by the Supreme Court of the old U.S. before it had handed down its decision in *Anderson v. Board of Education* (2003, see Chapter 5) removing from itself the judicial review power, were held to be valid as precedent for the new Court. But Supreme Court decisions from that date forward were made invalid as precedent for the new Court.

A legal category of "Crimes Against the Constitution" was to be defined by Congress, limited to acts performed by officers and employees of the NAR.

In *Article V*, as previously noted, even though fascism had been first brought to the old United States by entirely legal means, especially through the process of Constitutional amendment, the authors of the new Constitution were willing to put every one of its provisions at risk of future amendment. They thus put their faith in the renewal of the democratic process in the Re-United States as the primary bulwark against any future "Constitutional" reimposition of fascism. That faith has so far been fully rewarded.

In *Article VI*, all debts contracted and engagements entered into, by the old United States of America as well as by the regime of the "New American Republics," before the adoption of the Constitution, were declared to be valid against the Re-United States. This provision recognized the obligation undertaken by the Movement for the Restoration of Constitutional Democracy's National Leadership Council to the East Asian Confederation, as a consideration to the latter for their intervention in the Second Civil War on the side of the MRCD.

All of the Amendments to the old Constitution after the XXVIIth were simply ignored and thus made moot, except one. The old "Supremacy Amendment" (see Chapter 9) that had enabled the placement of the "Law of God" above the Constitution itself was explicitly revoked. The "no religious test" provision of the old Constitution was reinstated.

The new *Article VIII* covered Rights and Liberties. In any cases of conflict with the old Bill of Rights, the original First Ten Amendments to the Constitution, the latter were amended to conform with the new, expanded list. Further, an attempt was made to remove ambiguities from the Bill of Rights, which became Sections 1-10 of this Article.

In Section 1, what had been the original "First Amendment" of the old Constitution, the "Wall of Separation" between Church and State implicit in it was made explicit. To prevent the exploitation of the right of free speech by the forces of hate, hatred, and division, as happened to an increasing extent during the Transition Era and of course the Fascist Period, a free speech limitation based on the English Common Law Intentional Tort of Assault was added.

The subsequent language in this Section is taken from language of the "Declaration of Rights" of the Treaty of Paris (1990) adopted by an international organization of the time called the Conference on Security and Cooperation in Europe (Bush, G.H.W.; "Charter of Paris"). Some of the language is redundant with that found in other Sections of this Article, but in the shadow of the horrors of American fascism and its prelude, the drafters wanted to be certain that the basic rights and freedoms would be clearly protected by the Constitution.

Section 2 of *Article VIII* clarified the original intent of the old Constitution that indeed the Second Amendment applied strictly to state militias, not the private ownership of firearms, and also explicitly provided for government-regulated ownership of same. Section 5 combined the major provisions of the old Vth and XIVth Amendments, and qualified that highly contentious promoter of selfishness, the old "takings clause." Section 8 prohibited the use of the death penalty by any level of government jurisdiction, with one, political, exception. The IXth and Xth Amendments, important defenders of individual rights and freedoms, were retained unchanged.

The language of the old "Equal Rights Amendment" for women, that in the early Transition Era had failed ratification by one state following an intense campaign against it by Right-Wing Reaction was inserted. Section 12 established freedom of choice in the outcome of pregnancy as a Constitutional right, and established a government obligation to protect its exercise. Section 13 made it unconstitutional to discriminate on the basis of gender preference, identity, or orientation in any public accommodation, facility, or institution, public or private employment, or educational institution receiving public support.

The Civil Rights Act that had been made part of the old Constitution by the XVth Amendment, but never enforced until the passage of the legislative Civil and Voting Rights Acts of the Johnson Era, was retained. Finally, the Restoration Convention chose not to enact term limits of any kind, concluding that no matter how couched and for what purpose, they were anti-democratic. Thus the XXIInd (Presidential term limit) Amendment was left out.

This then constituted the restoration of Constitutional democracy in the Re-United States of America, the work concluded on the fifth day of May in the Year of our Lord two thousand and twenty three.

References:

Allen, M., "Home of Dixie Generals Bungles Salute to Ashe," *The New York Times*, January 4, 1996, p. A14.

Beiderbecke, B., and Goodman, B., *Nuclear Weapons and the Second Civil War: To Use or Not to Use; That Was the Question*, Los Alamos, NM: Lost Horizon Press, 2043.

Brown, D., *Bury My Heart at Wounded Knee*, New York; Holt, Rinehart, and Winston, 1970.

Bush, G.H.W., "CSCE: Putting Principle into Practice," *U.S. Dept. of State Dispatch*, Vol. 1, No. 13, Nov. 26, 1990.

"Charter of Paris," signed, November 21, 1990; excerpts printed, *The New York Times*, Nov. 22, 1991; U.S. Dept. of State, "CSCE at a Glance: Fact Sheet," September, 1990.

London, J., *The Iron Heel*, reprinted, Chicago, IL: Chicago Review Press, 1980, first published, 1907.

Section III:
Conclusion

CHAPTER 20
What Might Have Been Done: An Effective Opposition and Progressive Attack Politics

Author's Commentary

Introduction

Hindsight is almost always 20/20. From the vantage point of 2048, it is easy to look back 50 years and lay out "what might have been." And I must admit to you, dear reader, that I cannot resist doing just that. In this chapter, I present for your consideration some approaches to the development of liberal/progressive political processes that might have been effective in protecting, preserving, and expanding Constitutional democracy in the old U.S. during the Transition Era, thus preventing the onset of fascism.

Factors in the Onset of Fascism in the Old U.S.: A Review

The Causes of Rising Unrest

Towards the end of the Transition Era (1981-2001), as noted on several previous occasions, the country faced increasing, and increasingly severe, economic difficulties (Wright). They were characterized by steadily declining real wages, real personal incomes, and job security, steadily increasing public and private debt, a steadily widening gap in both wealth and income between the rich and everyone else, steadily increasing permanent un- and under-employment concentrated in certain portions of the population. There were many causes of this state of affairs. It is now understood that the central element, the most important cause of this state of affairs, was the disordered public and private investment policy resulting from the use of the so-called "free market" to determine capital investment decisions.

Unrest and the Right-Wing Reactionary Response

This economic situation led to rising unrest in many sectors of the population. Some focused on the real causes of the problems. But many others were searching for easy, simplistic solutions to the national dilemma. Right-Wing Reaction was only too happy to supply such generalizations and non-answers as: "it's because of a decline in moral values."

The trend in simplisticism then was aggravated by the increasingly vigorous exploitation by Right-Wing Reaction for political purposes of religion and religious prejudice, racism, and xenophobia. The common denominator of the several approaches was blaming "The Other" for the nation's difficulties (Wright). Eventually, however, these measures failed to adequately damp down the unrest.

The Political Destruction of Constitutional Democracy

The forces of Right-Wing Reaction then had to move to a second stage: the political destruction of Constitutional democracy. Since the beginning of the Transition Era, Right-Wing Reaction had been gradually but inexorably destroying by political means the bulwarks of Constitutional democracy: the Courts, the Congress, and the media. Under the NAR, they were physically destroyed or neutralized, and the organized use of broad-based repression and force was broadly employed as well, of course.

During the Transition Era, Right-Wing Reactionary political leadership did its best to undermine the Constitutional concept of the "United States," as well as destroy the concept of a Constitutionally-based national government with broad authority and responsibility. This was directly contrary to the word and meaning of the Preamble to the Constitution. It states clearly that there is a nation, that there is a national government, and what its purposes are:

> "We the people of the *United States*, in order to form a more perfect Union, establish Justice, insure domestic tranquility, provide for the common defence, promote

> the general Welfare, and secure the Blessings of Liberty to ourselves and our Posterity, do ordain and establish this Constitution for the *United States of America.*"

Pretending that it didn't, or perhaps not knowing that such a statement begins the Constitutional text, leading Transition Era Right-Wing figures tried to very significantly narrow the scope of the national government. For example, Richard Armey, the House of Representatives Republican Majority Leader in the 104th Congress, when asked about the functions of the Federal government, said (Sanger):

> "Defend our shores, build a system of justice and construct some infrastructure."

At about the same time, the Republican Speaker of the House Newton Gingrich put it more broadly (Kelly):

> "It [the Federal government] is powerful in foreign policy, it's powerful in keeping the dollar stable, it's powerful in stopping all drugs from coming into the country, it's powerful in doing those things we give to the central government. And then it says, you know, frankly: 'You've got a lot of things to do back home. Don't even call me. I don't want to know. There's no reason I have to pay attention.'"

Well, there was a reason to "pay attention." It was called the Preamble to the Constitution. But few people of the time were aware of it or its import. And the positions taken by the likes of Armey and Gingrich made it more certain that ever fewer people would know what the responsibility and authority of the Federal government, *under the Constitution*, was.

One way to insure the death of something is to ignore it. A sign on the wall of my dentist's office says, "Ignore your teeth, and they will just go away." The Right-Wing Reactionary attack on the Constitution was both active and passive. It succeeded all too well. (It must be noted that there is no evidence that either Mr. Armey or Mr. Gingrich would have approved of what eventually happened in fact to Constitutional democracy in the United States.)

No Effective Political Opposition

While this process was occurring, in many sectors of the population an abiding faith was maintained that Democratic *forms*, without content, would protect the American way of life. We know now that while democracy is the principal political weapon for the defense of Constitutional government and the rule of law against fascism, as a process it cannot stand by itself. It can be effective in that regard only if used in the promotion of a concrete ideology and a comprehensive political and economic program that stands in contrast to those of the fascists. That did not happen. Thus there was no effective political opposition to the eventual fascist takeover. (Note, however, as in the case of Nazi Germany, the existence of an Opposition, even a strong one, is no guarantee that the fascists will not take power in any case if the conditions for such a takeover are right.)

Furthermore, many people simply did not believe that Right-Wing Reaction would do what it said they would do if they took power—but it did. (The same thing had happened in 20th century Germany. In Adolf Hitler's prophetic book *Mein Kampf* he laid out exactly what he would do if he took power, including the extermination of European Jewry. Few took him seriously.)

The Failure of Opposition Leadership

As the process of fascist development proceeded, liberals of whatever party tended to "take a balanced view" and see "two sides of every question" until it was much too late to organize against the onslaught. As early as the 1992 Republican National Convention, the Right-Wing Reactionaries had declared that there was a "war on for power and control of the American spirit." The Democrats and other liberals failed to grasp just what they meant ("it's *our* way or the highway"), until it was too late.

Even within social groupings that would appear to have been natural opponents of Right-Wing Reaction, for example the Jews and the blacks, there were major splits. Although most Jews were liberals or progressives, Right-wing, so-called "neo-conservative" (known in the vernacular of the time as "self-hating") Jews were among the most vocal supporters of Right-Wing Reaction. Black leadership was split as well. As surprising as it may seem, during the late Transition Era and the early Fascist Period certain blacks in government, academic, and religious circles carried out some of the most important Right-Wing Reactionary work in promoting both anti-black racism and black anti-Semitism, as well as the general Right-Wing Reactionary line.

At the other end of the spectrum, there were multiple, small left-wing "third parties." But they could never get together and sometimes spent much more time and energy fighting each other and the Democratic Party than fighting the common enemy. Finally, a major factor in the relatively easy success of the Right-Wing Reactionaries was the gradual destruction of the American labor movement.

Post-Second Civil War historians have traced that process back to the day after the passage in 1938 of the Wagner Act, that for the first time legalized collective bargaining in the old U.S. The American economic decision-makers just never accepted their loss in that one. They kept fighting until that defeat was turned into victory. American labor, which decades before had been robbed of any effective leadership by Federal labor legislation known as the Taft-Hartley Law, offered little in the way of effective opposition to the fascist takeover.

Thus the majority liberal and progressive forces failed to:

- Recognize that they indeed held a majority of the electorate if they only would and could mobilize it.

- Recognize the clear and present danger to the future of Constitutional democracy and the maintenance of true Americanism that the Right-Wing Reactionaries represented.
- Develop a comprehensive, consistent, progressive, broad-based, socially-conscious truly American, politically-salable ideology to put up against the Bible-based, fundamentalist ideology and Right-Wing anti-social individualism upon which Right-Wing Reaction were fundamentally based, to fight for the preservation and expansion of American Constitutional democracy.

But, as noted, the liberal and progressive forces did nothing along these lines. The Right-Wing Reactionaries of course developed, and implemented, "The 15% Solution." It worked. They won. And the rest, as they say, is history. (Again, it should be noted that there is no evidence that any of the original conceivers of the "The 15% Solution" would have sanctioned any of the policies developed under it or approved of any of the outcomes that occurred following its electoral success.)

The Importance of the Past and the Future

To implement fascism, both the past and the future must be wiped from public consciousness. I once saw a cartoon entitled "Diary of a Cat." It illustrated several entries in such a diary. The first was, "*Today.* Today I got some food in a bowl. It was great! I slept some too." The next was, "*Today*. Played with yarn. Got some food in a bowl. Had a good nap." And next, "*Today*. Slept, food, yarn. Fun!" And so forth. The cartoonist knew that cats live entirely in the present. For them there is no past, no future, no calendar. Only now, only *today.*

One of the features that distinguishes humans from all of the other animals is that we have pasts and futures that we know and are aware of, or at least can be. We have the *ability* to learn from the past and apply that learning to formulating our conduct for the future. However, not all of us use, or can use, that ability. In that, some of us are quite animal-like. As one Joe Klein, a political writer for the old *New York* magazine, noted (1991):

> "The essential failing of the Reagan-Bush years has been a near-total lack of interest in the future."

He might have added:

> "Since learning from the past is necessary to support an interest in the future, there has been no interest in the past and its lessons either."

For the Right-Wing Reactionaries, life came in discrete time parcels. Like the cat in the cartoon, they lived day by day, only in "Today." And of course they made policy on that basis. They generally did what seemed to work at the time, to achieve some political gain or secure short term profits for one or another of their special economic interest support groups. There was no public attention to, and no apparent political interest in or concern with, the long-term negative outcomes of any policy. But in the pay of a major sector of the economic decision-maker group, they plowed ahead.

What Happened in Nazi Germany

We have seen from the history recounted briefly in this book that in the old U.S. the progression to fascism did not occur by great revolutionary leaps. Rather, there was a step by almost imperceptible step progression to it. And although, by looking backwards we can see that that progression was inexorable from the late Transition Era onwards to the founding of the NAR, to most observers at the time it appeared to be anything but.

The primary lesson to be learned from the pre-fascist American experience with the development of fascism was that its prevention would have required early action. In this case that action would have centered on the early disruption of the progression of "The 15% Solution" itself. As in Nazi Germany, once it gained power through Constitutional means, the Right-Wing Reactionary coalition that instituted fascism in the old U.S. never relinquished that power until it was defeated militarily.

Recall that the German Nazis had come to power in 1933 in the first instance by democratic means. It happened that within 24 hours of Adolf Hitler's accession to the German Chancellorship, his police and para-military forces had begun moving to secure that power indefinitely, by the suppression of democratic processes, suspension of individual rights and liberties, and the use of terror. But the initial accession to power was constitutional and non-violent.

Unlike the Nazi Germans, in major part because there was no significant or effective opposition, the American fascists did not need to use force widely at the beginning of their reign. They were able to rely on electoral victories and seemingly Constitutional government until they had been in power for a number of years. Of course, by that time conditions had deteriorated so much that they had no choice but to turn to the violent repression and terror that became so characteristic of the NAR.

American Neo-Exceptionalism and Historical Exactism

Those persons who during the Transition Era warned of the possible development of fascism in the old U.S. had to deal with two common schools of thought both labeling such voices as nothing but alarmist. One school was what we now call "American neo-exceptionalism." It said that what happened in those countries that became fascist during the pre-World War II period was unique to those countries, primarily the result of the accession to power of persons with twisted characters.

The other school of thought was "historical exactism." It said that what happened during the pre-World War II fascist period, while not uniquely "German," or "Italian," or "Japanese," was uniquely a product of the circumstances of the time, and that they could not recur. Both theories were interpreted to mean "it can't happen here."

Both arguments needed to be countered. But the subject was a delicate one. Politically it had to be treated with great care. The old U.S. was not a "nation of innocence." For example, slavery had existed in it followed by legal discrimination against persons of color in the states of the former Confederacy and social discrimination against them throughout the country; virtually complete suppression of the Native American political economy and cultures had been carried out; Japanese-American citizens, accused of nothing more than being of Japanese descent, had been arbitrarily imprisoned during World War II without the benefit of judicial proceedings of any sort; terror aerial bombing against civilian targets in foreign wars had been developed to its highest degree of sophistication; in foreign countries with democratically-elected governments that adopted policies considered inimical to U.S. economic and political interests, those governments were routinely overthrown.

Despite these facts, many Americans persisted in the belief that nothing bad like fascism could come to pass in the old U.S. But of course it did. Among many other things, no one in the Opposition had ever figured out before it was too late how to counter either Neo-Exceptionalism or Historical Exactism in a politically effective way. Admittedly, it would have been difficult.

Developing an Effective Political Opposition

The Dual-Track Approach to Opposition Development

A political strategy that might have been effective in preventing the onslaught of fascism was following a dual track approach to developing the Opposition. The necessary measures of attempting to convert the Democratic Party to a liberal/progressive party and developing a single left-wing third party should not have been seen as mutually exclusive. Both goals should have been pursued, as long as the focus of attack was the common enemy, Right-wing Reaction, not each other. Unfortunately, as noted, the latter pattern was a trap liberals and progressives of various stripes often fell into.

Controlling the Agenda

Assuming that a political candidate is intelligent, well-qualified, personally attractive, a good speaker, has good name-recognition, and is comfortable in the rough and tumble of electoral politics, the most important element in winning the Presidency in the poltico-electronic age that marked the old U.S. in the second half of the 20th century was control of the political agenda. Some of the many real problems faced by the country during the Transition Era were the result of historical forces beyond anyone's control. However, many of them were the result of disastrous Right-Wing Reactionary policies. For obvious reasons, the Right-Wing Reactionaries wanted to retain control of the political agenda.

What Republican Goals Really Were

Just imagine running for political office, even during the Right-Wing Reactionary-dominated Transition Era, on a platform that included such planks as:

- Providing more income to the rich.
- Increasing the burden of state and local taxation, especially regressive taxation.
- Priming the economic pump with increased military but not needed national domestic spending.
- Creating the highest real interest rates in history.
- Cutting aid to education at all levels.
- Punishing the poor for being poor by eliminating programs aimed at overcoming or compensating for poverty.
- Ravaging the environment for the benefit of developers' profits.

- Breaking what was left of the American trade union movement for the benefit of corporate profits.
- Encouraging concentration of industrial ownership and the decline of competition: the contraction of the free market for goods and services.
- Encouraging the export of capital.
- Exacerbating racial antagonisms for political gain.
- Undermining the Bill of Rights, especially on freedom of speech, freedom of religion, and right to privacy issues.

Now, that would be a winner, wouldn't it? Well, based upon twelve years of Reaganite/Bushism (1981-93) and the Grinchism of the "Contract on America" (1994-5), it was clear to anyone who cared to look past the smokescreens that that was what the Republican platform really was. But the Democrats were never able to cast a clear, bright focus on that agenda and keep it there. Nor were they able to paint a clear picture of what the real problems faced by the country were, how Republican policies did nothing but make them worse, and how a comprehensive liberal/progressive political and economic program could solve them.

The Negatives of Reaganite Economic Policies

By the mid-90s, the Right-Wing Reactionaries were pretending the Reagan Era never happened, even though the Presidency had been in their hands for all but four years from 1969 to 1993 (and some observers felt, given the performance of President Jimmy Carter, 1977-81, all of those years). They consistently traced all of the country's economic problems back to the so-called Great Society of Lyndon Johnson (never more than partially-implemented) and even more ludicrously to the New Deal of President Franklin Roosevelt, a set of policies that happened to have rescued American capitalism from itself. The Republicans never talked about, and why should they have, the facts of "Reaganomics."

- The tax cuts for the rich did not produce the projected increases in national revenues predicted by the economic theories of the so-called "Supply-Siders," properly-labeled "Voodoo Economics" by none other than the man who would later become Reagan's most loyal acolyte, Vice-President under Reagan, then President, George H.W. Bush. Actually, those cuts produced quite the opposite effect.
- The so-called "Reagan boom" was the product of Federal deficit spending on a scale never even closely equaled in the past by either party, the deficit spending, however, being pumped into the non-productive (but highly profitable) military sector. This policy left the country with a huge national debt, the interest payments for which put an enormous burden on the Federal budget (probably the result of Republican intent), and an annual Federal deficit problem highly resistant to solution other than by the draconian methods eventually adopted.
- Partly because of Federal fiscal policy and partly because of the active encouragement of deindustrialization and the export of capital by Reaganite policies, within three years of accession to office the Reaganites had converted the U.S. from the world's largest creditor nation to the world's largest debtor nation, putting an enormous private debt service burden on the economy to accompany the public debt service one.
- For these and other reasons such as its energy policy (that, as noted, encouraged increasing dependence on foreign oil, to benefit the large international oil companies), "Reaganomics" also lead to an explosion in the U.S. balance of payments deficit. Reaganomics also created the highest true interest rates seen in the U.S. for a very long time. Finally, Reaganomics and Reaganite deregulation were responsible for the most expensive scandal ever in the American economy: the Savings and Loan disaster.

And the Democrats let them get away with all this.

The Need to Frontally Attack Racism and its Political Usage
Racism, usually unspoken but well-symbolized by them, was the bedrock of Republican politics. The Democrats should have exposed the Republicans for using the issue politically, and developing ways to show white people how they were being used by it. President Bill Clinton began this line of attack during his first campaign. In the speech with which he declared for the Democratic nomination for the Presidency on October 3, 1991, he said (1991):

> "For 12 years, Republicans have tried to divide us—race against race—so we get mad at each other and not at them. They want us to look at each other across a racial divide so we don't turn and look to the White House and ask, why are all of our incomes going down, why are all of us losing jobs? Why are we losing our future?"

Clinton unfortunately did not continue with this line of attack during his Presidency. But these words are an example of what could have been done. The argument "racism hurts everyone, first in the pocketbook (excess costs in the criminal justice system), and here's how," could have been exploited by the Democrats as well.

Progressive Attack Politics
"Progressive Attack Politics," related to what he called the Local Problems Bank, was a strategy developed by Dino Louis during the mid-Transition Era. But he was never able to successfully promote it. (Perhaps the reason it never "sold" was the acronym. "PAP" is just not a good one.) It was a proposed progressive response to Right-Wing Reactionary "negative campaigning." The latter was a sophisticated version of traditional American negative campaigning, which had been part of the American political scene since the Adams-Jefferson election of 1800.

Traditional negative campaigning attacked the person of the opponent, from the charge that Grover Cleveland had fathered an illegitimate child to the quiet, but persistent reference to Franklin Delano Roosevelt as nothing but a sick cripple. The Right-Wing Reactionary variety did engage in traditional American political negative crudities on occasion, slinging some old-fashioned mud, especially "manufactured" mud. For example, in the 1988 Presidential campaign Republican political operatives spread completely unsubstantiated rumors that the Democratic Presidential candidate, Massachusetts Governor Michael Dukakis, had been treated by a psychotherapist and that his wife Kitty had burned a flag. But the stuff that really worked for the Republicans was very much issue-oriented, on their mythological issues.

They played to and exacerbated racism, "gut-feelings," and empty "patriotism" (as in "revere the flag"). This was not negative campaigning as much as it is *distractive* campaigning. One of the early practitioners of the art, President Ronald Reagan, had actually been for things, like the touchy-feely saying "it's morning in America" and "standing tall in the saddle," or the misleading "cut your taxes," "build up our defenses," and "get the government off your back." Newton Gingrich's Contract on America (see Chapter 1) was for such things too (many of the same things that Reagan went for).

What was really going on here? The touchy-feelies were irrelevant to the real problems facing the nation. And as pointed out in Chapter 1, most of the Right-Wing Reactionary program components, whether Reaganite or Grinchite, were irrelevant to solving the real problems the country faced, from underinvestment to racism. In fact, the use of the term "negative campaigning" to describe this strategy that was so central to Transition Era Republican politics was itself a distractor. The term "negative campaigning" was used to get the focus of the debate that arose on its use away from the real objective of the strategy. That objective was not primarily to attack the person of the opponent, even though it might have seemed so. Rather, it was to get the focus of the political debate off what was really important, and especially off the Republican record.

Progressive Attack Politics, according to Louis, was not to be negative campaigning. It was not to engage in *ad hominem* attacks. When it criticized specific Republican policies, the critique was always to be accompanied by a positive recommendation for meeting an identified challenge/need. Just as the objective of distractive campaigning was to get on the offensive and stay there, so was that the objective of Progressive Attack Politics. Elections cannot be won while on the defensive.

There was also a generalized basis for attack, which could have been used against all distractive campaign elements put forward by the other side, simply revealing them for what they were: attempts to distract the electorate from the real problems at hand, and their causes. Further, the charge could have been laid on that distractive campaigning was nothing but a sign of weakness, designed to deflect the voters' attention from the real campaign issues.

To be effective, Progressive Attack Politics needed a large data-base, just like the Local Problems Bank did. A major share of campaign resources would had to have been put into issues, positions, and historical research. A sophisticated, cross-referenced computer-based positions/data files library that could have been accessed at secure terminals all across the country would have to have been developed. This would have been expensive, but absolutely essential to the success of progressive attack politics. It could easily and cost-effectively been linked to the development of the Local Problems Bank as well.

Language

An important element of Progressive Attack Politics would have been the careful, planned use of language. The Republicans were very successful in this regard. For example, they managed to turn the rather benign, gentle term "liberal" into a dirty word by clever references to it as the "L" word (cf. "the 'F' word"). Newton Gingrich once put together an extensive guide to using the language for political purposes, to bash his liberal opponents (*EXTRA! Update*). The liberals could have done the same thing.

The term we now use to describe the Reaganite/Bushists, the Grinchites, the Hagueites and the other fascists, "Right-Wing Reactionaries," could have been used with effectiveness back then too. For too long the rightists got away with labeling themselves with the rather comfortable word "conservative." They were often not the least bit conservative, for example when it came to the environment, or maintaining the U.S. position as the world's leading industrial power, or conserving progress in civil rights, or in maintaining civil liberties or legal precedent. Some other examples? Rather than "defense spending," "military spending" should have been used. Similarly, the term "national domestic spending" might have been substituted for "social spending." The latter has a soft, "socialistic," dirty-word sound; the former has the toughness of "national." "Personally Sensitive," P.S., could have been substituted for the phrase "Politically Correct," P.C. so prostituted by the Right-Wing Reactionaries. "Social issues" should have been called what they really were: "religious issues."

When progressives did from time to time attack the Republicans for their proto-fascist policies and fascist tendencies, in the political climate of the time it might have been helpful to substitute the cooler word "authoritarian" for the hot-button word fascist, if only so that the Republicans could not make an issue out of the use of the word, thus once again avoiding debate on substantive issues.

The Restructuring and Redirection of the Democratic Party
Finally, desperately needed was a carefully planned and consistent electoral strategy, which in turn eventually would have required a restructuring of the Democratic Party. In essence, Democrats needed to act like Democrats, not like Republicans. To do so would have been good government and also would have been good politics. The Democratic Party

would once again have been appealing to its primary constituencies. For example, in late 1995, Senator Edward Kennedy sent a memorandum to the Senate Minority Leader, Thomas Daschle (1995). Senator Kennedy had polled his "key supporters" on vital issues then facing the nation. Almost unanimously they: rejected seeking a "middle ground" with the radical right-wing Republican legislative agenda of the time, advocating rather a strong political education campaign on what the real issues and positions were; supported denial of further tax cuts for the wealthy in favor of maintaining the integrity of the Medicare program (tax-based partial payment for health services for the elderly); rejected compromise of basic, traditional Democratic principles, in favor of fighting the Republicans on matters of principle, even if it meant taking the blame for legislative "gridlock."

The Democratic Party needed to institutionalize a lesson that it was learning the hard way through the elections of the mid-90s: it could no longer rely on the set of policies and political practices advocated by the reactionary Democratic Leadership Council (DLC). This set was nothing more than a pale imitation of the race-based "Southern Strategy" originally developed for the Republican Party by one of the founding modern Right-Wing Reactionaries, former Senator from Arizona and Republican presidential candidate in 1964, Barry Goldwater. It was brought to full maturity by Richard Nixon and Ronald Reagan (Lind, [a]). By the late 1980s, the DLC was trying to develop a Democratic version of it that might have best been called the "Alienated White Male Strategy," AWMAS.

A good many white males in the country had good reasons to feel alienated from the Federal government and the political process. Primarily, they had been economically abandoned by that process which began with the export of capital and deindustrialization, augmented by the wide-spread but little talked about computer revolution. However, the AWMAS did nothing for white men, other than maintain their alienation. For the AWMAS was a code term for running a campaign designed to appeal to the classic "Southern white male," (read "xenophobic, chauvinist, homophobic, militaristic, racist"), now, fed by Right-Wing Reactionary propaganda, found all over the country.

The DLC's attempt to develop a modern, sophisticated, Democratic-coded AWMAS was couched in terms of a "return to traditional values." It turned out the values referred to were not those of the Declaration of Independence and the Constitution. Rather they were the Americanized version of Hitler's "Kinder, Kuche, und Kirche" so beloved by the Right-Wing Reactionaries. The AWMAS strategy was based on The Politics of Difference rather than the truly American Politics of Inclusion.

Translated, this version of "traditional values" meant reliance primarily on jingoistic false patriotism; support for the military and military spending without a clear definition of goals, role, and function; "dedication to family" while using the term "family" primarily to deal with issues of sex and intra-family male power; "fiscal responsibility" without detailing just who benefits from the pro-rich policies carried out under that rubric. Most important was the strong underlying, although unstated, theme of racism. The original Southern Strategy had worked well for the Republicans since 1968, primarily because when certain Democrats were not ineffectually trying to use it themselves, the national Democratic Party came up with nothing effective to counter it.

There were three reasons why the AWMAS should have been abandoned by the Democrats and no attempt to develop a Democratic version of it made. First, and most important, it caved into racism, the most serious, divisive, demoralizing, and money-wasting national domestic issue faced by the old U.S. during the Transition Era. Second, since its original version, the "Southern Strategy," clearly was the property of the Republican Party, the AWMAS could not possibly work for Democrats, whatever it was called. Third, the results of many state and local elections showed that the voters would only infrequently elect a Democratic candidate who adopted it and the motto: "Let's try to out-Republican the Republicans." As noted before, why should voters who wanted to elect a Republican choose anything other than the real thing? Fourth, even if it could work, the voting margins in the South were too wide to be overcome by such a strategy.

But in any case, why should the Democrats have developed a strategy which appealed to the worst, rather than the best, instincts of any voting group? Why in the South, for instance, should the Democratic Party not have attempted to revive the Post-First Civil War alliance between blacks and white workers/small farmers? This was the alliance that so terrified the Southern white power structure that it created the Ku Klux Klan, Jim Crow, and institutional racism to break it up and keep the two groups permanently apart. The trying to be all things to all people strategy of the recent Presidential campaigns did not work either. It was time for something new, the Politics of Inclusion.

Primarily it was necessary for the Democratic Party to focus on policies not aimed at winning back the racist "Reagan Democrats" all over the country. But rather the focus needed to be on developing policies that would appeal to those millions of eligible voters so alienated by a political process and government that simply did not respond to their needs. Such large worker and minority populations could have been expected to respond to a strong anti-racism cast. It would have aimed at the old core of progressive Democrats who could see how they had been betrayed, the minorities, as well as the large untapped pool of then non-voters who would have voted for a real progressive alternative if they saw one.

As part of this whole progressive strategy, the Democrats needed to return to old-fashioned "shoe-leather" politics. One of the reasons they strayed further and further to the Right during the Transition Era is that as television-based political campaigning became more and more expensive, they became more and more beholden to corporate-based political campaign contributions (Ferguson). In a little-noticed election campaign in Baltimore in 1995, the black Mayor, one Kurt Schmoke, running an underdog, underfinanced campaign for a third term, went back to political techniques of an earlier era (Janofsky). They worked. To wit:

> "Rather than bombard voters in the modern mode of clever sound bites[1] in television commercials, Mr. Gibson [the campaign director] said the campaign decided to sell Mr. Schmoke's accomplishments through more low-tech means, including a 155-page book called 'Reasons to be Proud,' a tabloid called 'Baltimore Progress' that reviewed the Mayor's contribution to each of 50 areas of the city, Kurt Schmoke trading cards and a flier of voting recommendations that Mr. Gibson called 'the wordiest Election Day ballot I've ever seen.'
> "'We had to combat the image The Sun was presenting, that the city was going to hell in a hand basket,' Mr. Gibson said. 'I've been doing campaigns since 1968, and I've never run anything like this before, anything so information intensive. *I think people appreciated our appeals to their intelligence* [emphasis added].'"

No further comment is required.

Finally, Democrats needed to welcome and indeed encourage the defection of their own reactionaries from their Congressional delegation to that of the Republican Party. The attitude should have been: good riddance to bad rubbish. The Democrats *needed* to down-size, dropping its own reactionary baggage that put such a drag on progressive policy development.

For example, Right-Wing, health care industry funded, Democrats were a major factor in the 1994 defeat of a modest

1. *Author's Note:* "Sound-bite" was the term given to a very brief, one to three sentence explication of some political thought, that fit the very short time-requirements of the standard television news broadcast of the time.

reform called the "Clinton Health Plan." The Democrats could have been liberated to become a truly liberal/progressive party. (In this instance, following the Grinchite/Republican example, but going the other way.) This process should have been accompanied by active attempts to recruit the few remaining liberal Republicans in the Congress.

Conclusion

So here we are in 2048. Ah yes, hindsight is always 20/20. But it does seem, from the perspective of close to 70 years, that what needed to be done was so obvious that it should have been done. But, what was the number one "but?" That in the 1980s and 90s, gathered around the Democratic Leadership Council and the leadership of President "Bill" (as they called him back then) Clinton most of the elements of the Democratic Party of the time really represented the same economic and political interests that the Republican Party did, that is before the Republican Party started going off the deep end in responding to the Rightward Imperative. By the time the majority of the people in the nation realized what was happening, which way the Republican Party now firmly under the control of the Radical Religious Right and beneath them the Corporate State that made sure that they stayed in control of the Party and its policies, was now firmly in control of the state apparatus of government, national, state and local, it was too late.

And so the story that has been told in this book. It is to be hoped that should our great nation ever face such a threat again that the lessons of the past would this time have been learned and the "cowboys," as the Rampant Capitalists of the time of "The 15% Solution" were sometimes called, would be turned back at the pass.

References:

Ailes, R., *You are the Message*, Homewood, IL: Dow Jones-Irwin, 1988, p. 19.

Atwater, L., with Brewster, T., "Lee Atwater's Last Campaign," Life, Feb., 1991, p. 58.

Bennett, G., *Crimewarps*, New York: Anchor Books, (2nd revised edition): 1989, sections III and V.

Birnbaum, N., "Uncertain Trumpet," *The Nation*, Feb. 18, 1991, p. 201.

BOC: Bureau of the Census, *Statistical Abstract*, 1994, Washington, DC: 1994.

Brinkley, A., "Bush Surrenders at Home," *The New York Times*, Jan. 29, 1991.

Brown, L., et al, *State of the World, 1991*, New York: W.W. Norton, 1991, (see also *State of the World, 1984-90*).

Carnegie Foundation for the Advancement of Teaching, *An Imperiled Generation: Saving Urban Schools*, Princeton, NJ, 1988.

Clinton, W.J., "Announcement Speech," Little Rock, AK: October 3, 1991.

CCMC: Committee on the Costs of Medical Care, *Medical Care for the American People*, Chicago: University of Chicago Press, 1932. Reprinted, Washington, D.C.: USDHEW, 1970.

Dilulio, Jr., J.J., "Mission Possible: Reform the Penal System," *Newsday*, Feb. 29, 1991, p. 87.

Dowd, M., "Bush Sees Threat to Flow of Ideas on U.S. Campuses," *The New York Times*, May 5, 1991, p. 1.

DPC: Democratic Policy Commission, New Choices in a Changing America, Washington, DC: Democratic National Committee, 1986.

Feldman, D.L., "Let the Small-Time Drug Peddlers Go," *The New York Times*, Feb. 23, 1991.

Ferguson, T., "GOP $$$ Talked; Did the Voters Listen?" *The Nation*, Dec. 26, 1994, p. 792.

Finder, A., "How New Yorkers Feel Budget Squeeze," *The New York Times*, November 3, 1995.

Goldstein, P.J., "Most Drug-Related Murders Result from Crack Sales, not Use," *The Drug Policy Letter*, March/April, 1990, p. 6.

Gordon, D., *Steering a New Course*, Cambridge, MA: Union of Concerned Scientists, 1991.

Greenwald, J., "Time to Choose," *Time*, April 29, 1991, p. 54.

Henwood, D., "Setting the Tone," *Left Business Observer*, No. 40, Sept. 14, 1990.

Hertzberg, H., "Comment: Stoned Again," *The New Yorker*, January 8, 1996).

Hicks, J.P., "Crisis Puts a Shine on Coal, the Plentiful Standby," *International Herald Tribune*, Aug. 27, 1990.

Hilts, P.J., "Bush Enters Malpractice Debate With Plan to Limit Court Awards," *The New York Times*, May 13, 1991.

James, G., "New York Killings Set a Record, While Other Crimes Fell in 1990," *The New York Times*, April 23, 1991, p. A1.

Jamieson, K.H., "Lies Televised: Negative Campaigning and the 1988 Election." *The National Voter*, April-May, 1989, p. 10.

Johnston, D., "Bush, Pushing His Bill on Crime, Bends Again on Gun Control Law," *The New York Times*, April 19, 1991.

Jonas, S., "Solving the Drug Problem: A Public Health Approach to the Reduction of the Use and Abuse of Both Legal and Illegal Recreational Drugs," *Hofstra Law Review*, Vol. 18, No. 3, Spring 1990, p. 751.

Jonas, S., "Health Care Financing and Cost Containment," Chapter 7 in *An Introduction to the U.S. Health Care System*, New York: Springer Publishing, Co., 1991.

Jonas, S., "Commentary on Drug Legalization," *Connecticut Law Review*, Vol. 27, No. 2, Winter, 1995, p. 623.

Kelly, M., "Commentary," *The New Yorker*, January 23, 1995.

Kennedy, E.M., "Memorandum: Legislative Strategy," Washington, DC: October 25, 1995.

Klein, J., "Sex, Lies, and Ozone Depletion," *New York* Magazine, April 22, 1991, p. 14.

Lacayo, R., "Back to the Beat," *Time*, April 1, 1991 (no foolin'), p. 22.

Leven, D.C., "Prisons Are Clearly Not the Answer to Crime," *The New York Times*, (letter), April 19, 1990, p. A25.

Lind, M., "The Southern Coup," *The New Republic*, June 19, 1995, p. 20 (a).

Lind, M., *The Next American Nation*, New York: The Free Press, 1995.

Lynn, F., "Criticism is Harsh as Nominees Clash in Race for Mayor," *The New York Times*, Sept. 14, 1989, pp. A1, B3.

Lynn, F., "With Koch Out, Giuliani Tailors Appeal to the Right," *The New York Times*, Sept. 20, 1989, p. A1, (a).

Malcolm, A.H., "More and More, Prison is America's Answer to Crime," *The New York Times*, (News of the Week in Review), Nov. 26, 1989, p. 1.

Malcolm, A.H., "Steering Inmates to Jobs By Innovative Training," *The New York Times*, Jan. 19, 1991.

Marist Poll, "People Willing to Pay Taxes, Dump Quayle," Poughkeepsie, NY: Mar. 11, 1991.

McCabe, E., "The Campaign You Never Saw," *New York* Magazine, Dec. 12, 1988, p. 33.

McGinniss, J.M., and Foege, W.H., "Actual Causes of Death in the United States," *Journal of the American Medical Association*, November 10, 1993, p. 2207.

Meddis, S., "Drugs fuel 3% rise in crime rate," *USA Today*, April 9, 1990, p. A1.

Morrow, L., "Rough Justice," *Time*, April 1, 1991 (no foolin'), p. 16.

Nelson, F.H., *International Comparison of Public Spending on Education*, Washington, DC: American Federation of Teachers, Feb., 1991.

Newsday, "Schwarzkopf a Hit on Hill," May 9, 1991, p. 7.

The New York Times, "Study Shows Racial Imbalance in Who Is Punished," Feb. 26, 1990.

The New York Times, "Malpractice Victims: Ignored," May, 16, 1991, p. A22.

The New York Times, "Exxon Chief in Speech," Mar. 6, 1991.

Pear, R., "President Submits Spending Package of $1.45 Trillion," *The New York Times*, Feb. 5, 1991.

Pope, C., "The Politics of Plunder," *Sierra*, Nov/Dec 1988, p. 49.

Prevention Report, "Violence and Abuse in the United States," Feb. 1991, p. 1.

Reel, B., "The Last Little Whorehouse in Queens?" *Newsday*, April 26, 1991.

Reno, R., "Did You Miss It? The Government Has Shut Down," *Newsday*, November 17, 1995.

Rothenberg, A.I., "Assembly Line Justice Threatens the Whole System," *Los Angeles Times*, March 13, 1990.

Sanger, D.E., "Republicans Want to Renew Vision of Reagan (Then Redo His Math)," *The New York Times*, January 15, 1995.

Saul, S., "'90 Expected To Set Record For Murders," *Newsday*, Dec. 10, 1990.

Schneider, K., "Bush's Energy Plan Emphasizes Gains in Output Over Efficiency," *The New York Times*, Feb. 9, 1991.

Shapiro, B., "The Wrong Choice," *The Nation*, May 20, 1991, p. 652.

Shenson, D., et al, "Jails and Prisons: The New Asylums?" *American Journal of Public Health*, 80, 655, 1990.

Sherrill, R., "The Looting Decade," *The Nation*, Nov. 19, 1990.

Sierra, "Positive Energy," March/April 1991, p. 37.

Sirica, J., "Bush's No. 1 Concern: The War," *Newsday*, Jan. 29, 1991.

Sirica, J., "Debate Rolling Down Highway," *Newsday*, May 13, 1991.

Smith, P., CNN, at about 9:30PM, Feb. 8, 1991.

Smith, R., "NY's Prison Boom," *Newsday*, Oct. 8. 1990, p. 5.

Smolowe, J., "Race and the Death Penalty," *Time*, April 29, 1991, p. 68.

AFTERWORD BY THE AUTHOR
(Steven Jonas)

Introduction

And so, dear reader, it is now once again I, Dr. Steven Jonas, (not Jonathan Westminster) who is, as in the New Introduction to the book, communicating with you. We have come to the end of a complicated tale, part politics, part history, part historical projection. For me, the saddest part of the whole enterprise, of the republication of the book now, 17 or so years after its first publication, is that so many of the events and policies that were described as having happened from the perspective of "Jonathan Westminster's 2048", have actually come to pass.

This is not because I was particularly brilliant or made things up out of whole cloth. I simply read a lot of what the Republican Religious Right was already telling us in the 1980s-90s they would do if they ever took full power. And then I projected that information into what I considered to be a likely future political/historical reality of the United States.

And so, policies of the real Republican Religious Right, ranging from the criminalization of the abortion procedure to the destruction of the National Park and Forest Services, by now long on the table, would come to be implemented. As for projected technological developments, a fence with certain computer-aided detectors has been built along long stretches of the Mexican border. (As for the NAR's "Killer Fence," one has actually been created in Israel, although as of 2012 it had not yet been deployed [1]). Then consider the "Second Final Solution," presented in Chapter 18.

Although based on a projection of the Nazi German "Final

Solution" codified at the Wannsee Conference on January 20, 1942, for the Jews and other identity groups, even I thought that it was a pretty wild idea. You can imagine my particular horror when in 2012 a US "pastor" actually proposed doing to the homosexual population what I had projected *might* happen if the Republican Religious Right took power (2). And so on and so forth for the issues and policies of the Republican Religious Right that I chose to deal with in the book.

But there were two major issues that I did not deal with in the book. One is the nature of capitalism and the capitalists who provide the underlying support for the Republican Religious Right, whose interests the RRR so vigorously protect and project. The other is the matter of human-caused global warming and the climate change secondary to it that is already occurring. I think that it is safe to say that if it weren't for capitalism we wouldn't be facing the catastrophic future, due to climate change, that we presently do. I did not deal with the first, a) because the book was already getting long enough and b) because back in 1996 I really wanted to keep the principal focus of the book on what was happening to the Republican Party and how they would contrive to use the Constitution to destroy U.S. Constitutional Democracy (*already far more a formal democracy than a substantive one*), under some form of capitalism. I did not deal with the second, again for reasons of length but also because back then so much less was known about the problem, in particular about how quickly it would progress if no radical and immediate measures to limit carbon emissions were taken. But I cannot, in 2012, leave the book without dealing *ever so briefly* with both subjects, which I shall do here.

What is Capitalism?

Man is unique among the species on Earth, animal and plant, in that in order to survive, its members must convert elements that they find in their environment, animal, vegetable and mineral, into other elements. Thus foodstuffs become food, a sheep's wool becomes clothing, and petroleum becomes the stuff of heating homes. It is true that certain species do some sort of conversion on a limited basis: beavers build dams, birds build nests, prairie dogs and rabbits dig tunnels. But for the most part, when they do those things, they do them on a limited basis and (except for birds' nests) collectively. No individual "owns" the dam or the tunnel in the same way that a member of our species "owns" a house, or a farm, or a factory.

But for man, with the exception of very (what we term) primitive societies, as Friedrich Engels informed us in *The Origin of the Family, Private Property, and the State*, the conversion process for just about everything is essential to survival for both individuals and the species. Whoever owns or controls it thus holds the keys to survival for all. Karl Marx (and perhaps others before him) called the components of the conversion process for changing environmental elements into usable goods and services, the "means of production."

We don't know for sure, but it is likely that in the early days of human society the means of production were owned collectively. But sometime back in the dawn of the history of modern *Homo sapiens* things changed. Ownership of the means of production, whether it be simply of the farms from which food was grown or the mines from which the stuff of the early metal tools and weapons was dug, or the boats and pack animals through which early trade was carried out, came to rest in private hands, ultimately very few private hands. Some people owned the means of production; many more did not. The owners then came to employ the non-owners, either as slaves or for payment of one sort of another, to do the physical labor necessary to support the conversion processes.

Over time, the non-owners would produce excess product, beyond what the owners could consume themselves or they would allow their non-owners to consume. For quite some time, the owners would use these excesses simply to build ever-grander abodes and accoutrements, expand their property through purchase from other owners, raise armies to engage in conquest for similar purposes, or defend themselves against like-minded other owners. But then something changed. Beginning in Western Europe, during the 16th century (and in certain cases even before), some owners began investing their surpluses not in land or war or fancier castles, art work, and clothing. With the discoveries (that is discoveries for Western Europeans, for surely the people who lived in the other lands already knew they were there), rather, they began to invest the surpluses in trading and expanding trade. In the process they discovered that they could accumulate rather larger surpluses than their forebears had under feudalism and before that, in the slave societies. And so, mercantile capitalism came into being: the investment, either directly or indirectly, in trade and benefiting grandly (that is accumulating surpluses) from it.

We all know what happened next. With an expanding capital base arising from trade, and with the technological explosion that both accompanied and fueled the early industrial revolution, came industrial capitalism. The owners of the means of production employed those who weren't. They converted the surplus labor power of the non-owners into what we know as "profit." As Karl Marx demonstrated (at great length, in *Capital*), the seeking of profit and ever-expanding profits at that, became the sole goal of industrial capitalism and the capitalists, disputations of this fact by the capitalists and their representatives in the political system and the media to the contrary notwithstanding. With rare exceptions, the owners of the means of production are in business first and foremost to make profits for themselves. Anything else, such as technological advancement to produce increased profits, which might, and in many instances did, benefit relatively large numbers of people, was purely coincidental. Any "sharing of the wealth," in the form of higher wages or "social benefits" granted by the owners' state apparatus, usually came as the result of pressure applied in one way or another by the non-owners.

Ownership of the means of production, which, we must recall, had been the key to survival of the human species from its beginnings, came to be evermore concentrated. From time to time the non-owners would attempt to organize to achieve one or more ends: more sharing of the fruits of their labor power through the formation of labor organizations; the development of political parties, strategies and tactics to promote their interests at the governmental policy level; in a few cases completely dispossessing the owning class, at least for some period of time. But by and large capitalism, in one form or another, has remained in control of human society around the globe. Although there were threats to its hegemony from revolutionary Russia and China in the last century, those threats have long since dissipated. The Russian experiment eventually succumbed to what someday will be called The Seventy-Five Years' War Against the Soviet Union. The Chinese experiment succumbed to a very cleverly managed, mostly non-violent, internal counter-revolution, which did, however, manage to produce a mixed capitalist/somewhat-socialist economy.

Capitalism in the United States

In the United States, over time the capitalist class proved to be the most powerful of its type in the history of the world. In the Western European parliamentary democracies powerful labor unions were able to organize and gain considerable economic and political influence. While they never displaced the capitalists from power, they were able to force more sharing of the wealth (literally). In the United States, the industrial labor union movement flourished briefly during the New Deal. But it never was able to form a labor party and it was always under assault from major sectors of the owning class virtually from the day after the passage of the national law that legalized collective bargaining in 1935.

And while the Democratic Party did represent some interests of the non-owners, the working class, both industrial and agricultural, for a brief time during the New Deal, for the most part since that time the workers and the farmers have been on their own (as is well known among more alert citizens).

Consistent with its unstoppable dynamic, in the United States the owning class, what we now refer to as the Corporate Power, has been intent on ever-expanding its ownership, ever-expanding its wealth and ever-expanding its control of the political process, in the process sweeping off the table and under the rug the few crumbs that the working class had gained during the time of Franklin Roosevelt and (pre-Vietnam War) Lyndon Johnson. Now, how did they do this? They could not possibly run openly on their true party platform of increasing concentration of wealth, further destruction of the trade union movement, ever-continuing deregulation of the economy and the environment, and so on and so forth.

And so, they decided to turn to the Religious Right as, at first, a convenient cover.

As illustrated in this book, from the time of Reagan, the Republican Party increasingly and deliberately used the Religious Right in the United States for its own political purposes. It happens that just at the time I was writing this Afterword, according to Salon.com of August 5, 2012, "a veteran Republican says that the religious right has taken over, and turned his party into anti-intellectual nuts." (That person is one Mike Lofgren [3].) Indeed, the Republican Party became the Republican Religious Right precisely for the reason outlined just above. As for the process they used, it is indeed based on "The 15% Solution," a term which, as I document in Chapter 1, I did not make up. It was designed specifically as an electoral strategy to keep the Republican Party in power. The massive voter minority-youth-"other" voter suppression campaign of the Republican Party during the 2012 Presidential election was a product of the "The 15% Solution."

Thus the Rightward Imperative for the Republicans, as described in the book and again as can be observed on an on-going basis in the United States. The so-called "Tea Party," the well-funded, hardly "grass-roots" set of organizations, is nothing more, or less, than a product of it. As of 2012 within the Republican Party it was being ever more closely merged with the Religious

Right. What I projected in the New American Republics was the ultimate outcome of the Rightward Imperative. That there would be no full-blown, effective, well-funded and well-organized national political opposition to all of this, as projected in the book, has also come to pass, at least as of this writing.

The Next Developments in Capitalism

In the book I did not deal with was what was happening to capitalism at the same time.

The present form of capitalism (as 2012), especially in the United States and the United Kingdom was eerily predicted by a now rather obscure Russian political scientist, Vladimir Ilyich Ulyanov (actually better known as Lenin) (4):

> "(1) the concentration of production and capital has developed to such a high stage that it has created monopolies which play a decisive role in economic life; (2) the merging of bank capital with industrial capital, and the creation, on the basis of this "finance capital", of a financial oligarchy; (3) the export of capital as distinguished from the export of commodities acquires exceptional importance; (4) the formation of international monopolist capitalist associations which share the world among themselves, and (5) the territorial division of the whole world among the biggest capitalist powers is completed. Imperialism is capitalism at that stage of development at which the dominance of monopolies and finance capital is established; in which the export of capital has acquired pronounced importance; in which the division of the world among the international trusts has begun, in which the division of all territories of the globe among the biggest capitalist powers has been completed."

Amazing stuff, is it not? What Lenin could not foresee from the vantage point of 1916 when he wrote this was the role that technological development itself would play in the now ever more rapidly accelerating separation of workers from the work that was going on ("the alienation of labor from capital" first described by Marx, that is, in the advanced capitalist countries the declining employment opportunities for manual workers). After all, capitalism, in the U.S. at least, focuses more-and-more on, as Lenin predicted, making profit from trading pieces of paper, "finance capital," than from making and selling goods and services. All of these factors led, among other things, to the ever-growing gap between the ultra-rich and everyone else, aided by their control of the government and powerful accomplice and enabler, the mainstream media, and resulting taxation/spending processes and priorities, and the parallel development of a more complex form of what I called in the book the "Resource Based Economy."

In the book, as you know well, all of this leads to fascism and The New American Republics. In reality, in this country it will indeed very likely lead to the imposition of some form of authoritarianism, although hopefully not quite as harsh as that of the NAR. And so it is capitalism and its natural outcomes, its inseparable dynamic that drives the United States towards some form of what is predicted for it, through the political dominance of the Republican Religious Right and its increasing control of state power. In the book, indeed I did not deal with the centrality of the nature of capitalism in driving the predicted outcomes.

The Looming Disaster: The Outcomes of Global Warming

As noted above, what I also did not deal with in the book, partly because while one could see global warming coming at the time (and I did mention it, although very briefly) one could not predict how powerful the global warming denial movement would become, and also how quickly the increasingly disastrous outcomes of global warming would be upon us. Again, I will deal only very briefly with the issue here. The most important point is that capitalism is proving itself simply incapable of dealing with the looming disaster. Why? First and foremost because it is capitalism's and the capitalists' singular drive for profit that has produced the looming disaster. The science has been well-known for at least 25 years. But the most critical elements in preventing or at least ameliorating it would very significantly reduce the profits of major elements of the modern world-wide economy, particularly of the extractive industries as well as of major users of carbon-based fuels.

Do you really think that the Koch Brothers and Exxon-Mobil (as examples) don't know that a) global warming is real and b) that human-produced carbon emissions bear the major responsibility for it? People like Sean Hannity and Rush Limbaugh—assuming they're not outright hypocrites (also, of course, a possibility)—are likely so dumb and poorly educated that they probably really do believe the myth they spew that "global warming is a hoax," just as many people in the United States actually believe that the Theory of Evolution is a hoax and that the world came into existence just as is described in the Judeo-Christian creation narrative. (That there are many other creation narratives existing around the world, ranging from that of the Hindus to that of the New Zealand Maori, none of which has any more scientific validity than theirs, is of no matter.) But the Kochs and the people who run one of the world's most profitable enterprises, Exxon-Mobil, are no dummies. If they were dumb they wouldn't be so incredibly successful in what they do.

They know. And they don't care, any more than the owners of the tobacco companies who knew, according to internal documents *from the 1950s* unearthed during the discovery process secondary to the major suits against the tobacco industry in the late 1990s, that smoking causes disease, terminal disease at that, cared. Profits come first and the devil take the hindmost, even if in the case of global warming the "hindmost" is, potentially, our species as we know it along with many others, as well as "civilization," at least as the term is currently defined. As for the extractive industries in particular, the owners are so now-profit-oriented that they don't even care that someday the fossil fuels they extract will eventually run out and there will be no more profit in that realm of human activity anyway.

A Future Socialist Revolution?

And so, one must come to the conclusion that because of capitalism's solitary focus on profits and profit-making, the only possible solution to global warming, climate change, and the preservation of the species (plural), and the creation of a truly civilized human society is some form of socialism — its historical, logical and philosophical antithesis

I will not deal with the issue of how that might come about and what form it might/should take here. Obviously I did not deal with the issue in my very brief description in the book of the Second Civil War. When (and that is "when," not "if") the latter occurs, either before or after the imposition of an authoritarian/fascist government by the Republican Religious Right and its successors, there would surely be an internal struggle within the Movement for the Restoration of Constitutional Democracy or whatever its real-life equivalent would be, over what the result of victory would mean, exactly.

(This is exactly what happened to the forces of the Republic during the Spanish Civil War, 1936-39. It happens that the Republican forces lost, not because of that struggle but because of the overwhelming intervention by Nazi Germany and Fascist Italy on the side of the Spanish fascist rebels, as well as the failure (perhaps far more correct would be to call it betrayal) of the so-called "Western Democracies" to provide even arms to the elected Spanish Republican government. It also happens that Dr. Edward K. Barsky, an important childhood mentor of mine, one of the dedicatees of this book, was at one time the Commander of the Medical Unit for the whole of the International Brigade of volunteers who came to fight on the side of the Republic. [See also Chapter 19.])

Would the outcome of the Second Civil War, were the Resistance, the MRCD, to win, be some sort of Western

European style (mis-named social democracy) "social capitalism" or "national interest capitalism?" Or would there be a full-blown socialist revolution? That is impossible to predict and I will not deal with the subject further here, either. Except to say that in fact I do not expect the next socialist revolution to begin in the United States. Because of the power of historical memory, modern socialism is much more likely to come about first through a Second Russian Revolution or a Second Chinese Revolution than a first U.S. one. Such monumental events would also have enormous repercussions in the United States, of course. Whether for good or ill—at least in the short term— no one can predict for sure.

And so, my friends, I must truly leave you now. I cannot say that I hope you enjoyed the book, for it is about some truly awful reality and then an even-worse projected history. I can say that I do hope that you learned something from my efforts, and if so that you will be able to put that learning to some good use.

Steven Jonas, MD
August 28, 2012

References:

1. "Countries Look to Robot Armies for Border Defense," aolnews.com/tech/article/countries-look-to-robot-armies-for-border-defense, 10/20/2010.

2. Jonas, S., "Is Homophobia Curable," The Greanville Post, http://www.greanvillepost.com/2012/06/14/is-homophobia-curable/

3. Lofgren, Mike, *The Party Is Over: How Republicans Went Crazy, Democrats Became Useless, and the Middle Class Got Shafted*, New York: Viking Adult, 2012.

4. Lenin, V.I., from *Imperialism, the Highest Stage of Capitalism*, http://www.marxists.org/archive/lenin/works/1916/imp-hsc/ch07.htm#definition

5. McKibben, B., "Global Warming's Terrifying New Math," *Rolling Stone*, July 19, 2012, http://www.rollingstone.com/politics/news/global-warmings-terrifying-new-math-20120719. See also, http://www.postcarbon.org/person/36202-bill-mckibben.

Appendices

APPENDIX I
The Constitution of the Old United States of America

As it stood on the day of the Declaration of Peace
and the establishment of the New American Republics
July 4, 2011

and

The Declaration of Independence, July 4, 1776 (abridged)

Note: Those sections of the original U.S. Constitution adopted in 1789 that were rendered inoperative by one amendment or another before the adoption of the 30th (Preserve America) Amendment in 2002 have been omitted. All other provisions, including those subsequently altered by Amendments 30-34, are included. The texts of the 18th and 21st ("Prohibition" and its repeal), 28th (Balanced Budget, with loopholes), and 29th (Congressional Term Limits), amendments have also been omitted.

Preamble

We the people of the United States, in order to form a more perfect Union, establish justice, insure domestic tranquility, provide for the common defence, promote the general welfare, and secure the blessings of liberty to ourselves and our posterity, do ordain and establish this Constitution for the United States of America.

ARTICLE I

Section 1. All legislative powers herein granted shall be vested in a Congress of the United States, which shall consist of a Senate and House of Representatives.

Section 2. The House of Representatives shall be composed of members chosen every second year by the people of the several States, and the electors in each State shall have the qualifications requisite for electors of the most numerous branch of the State legislature.

No person shall be a Representative who shall not have attained the age of twenty-five years, and been seven years a citizen of the United States, and who shall not, when elected, be an inhabitant of that State in which he shall be chosen.

The actual enumeration shall be made within three years after the first meeting of the Congress of the United States, and within every subsequent term of ten years, in such manner as they shall by law direct.

(Author's Note: Section 2, following the first two paragraphs, was amended by the Fourteenth Amendment, Section 2).

Section 3. The Senate of the United States shall be composed of two Senators from each State, elected by the people thereof, for six years; and each Senator shall have one vote. The electors in each State shall have the qualifications requisite for electors of the most numerous branch of the State legislatures.

When vacancies happen in the representation of any State in the Senate, the executive authority of such State shall issue writs of election to fill such vacancies; Provided, That the legislature of any State may empower the executive thereof to make temporary appointments until the people fill the vacancies by election as the legislature may direct.

This amendment shall not be so construed as to affect the election or term of any Senator chosen before it becomes valid as a part of the Constitution.

Immediately after they shall be assembled in consequence of the first election, they shall be divided as equally as may be into three classes. The seats of the Senators of the first class shall be vacated at the expiration of the second year, of the second class at the expiration of the fourth year, and the third class at the expiration of the sixth year, so that one-third may be chosen every second year; and if vacancies happen by resignation, or otherwise, during the recess of the legislature of any State, the Executive thereof may make temporary appointments until the next meeting of the legislature, which shall then fill such vacancies.

No person shall be a Senator who shall not have attained the age of thirty years, and been nine years a citizen of the United States, and who shall not, when elected, be an inhabitant of that State for which he shall be chosen.

The Vice President of the United States shall be President of the Senate, but shall have no vote, unless they be equally divided.

The Senate shall choose their other officers, and also a President *pro tempore*, in the absence of the Vice President, or when he shall exercise the office of President of the United States.

The Senate shall have the sole power to try all impeachments. When sitting for that purpose, they shall be on oath or affirmation. When the President of the United States is tried, the Chief Justice shall preside: And no person shall be convicted without the concurrence of two thirds of the members present.

Judgment in cases of impeachment shall not extend further than to removal from office, and disqualification to hold and enjoy any office of honor, trust or profit under the United States: but the party convicted shall nevertheless be liable and subject to indictment, trial, judgment and punishment, according to Law.

(Author's Note: this section was modified by AMENDMENT XVII, adopted May 31, 1913.)

Section 4. The times, places and manner of holding elections for Senators and Representatives, shall be prescribed in each State by the legislature thereof; but the Congress may at any time by law make or alter such regulations, except as to the places of choosing Senators.

(Author's Note: this section was modified by AMENDMENT XX, Section 2.)

The Congress shall assemble at least once in every year, and such meeting shall begin at noon on the 3rd day of January, unless they shall by law appoint a different day.

Section 5. Each House shall be the judge of the elections, returns and qualifications of its own members, and a majority of each shall constitute a quorum to do business; but a smaller number may adjourn from day to day, and may be authorized to compel the attendance of absent members, in such manner, and under such penalties as each House may provide.

Each House may determine the rules of its proceedings, punish its members for disorderly behavior, and, with the concurrence of two thirds, expel a member.

Each House shall keep a Journal of its proceedings, and from time to time publish the same, excepting such parts as may in their judgment require secrecy; and the yeas and nays of the members of either House on any question shall, at the desire of one fifth of those present, be entered on the Journal.

Neither House, during the session of Congress, shall, without the consent of the other, adjourn for more than three days, nor to any other place than that in which the two Houses shall be sitting.

Section 6. The Senators and Representatives shall receive a compensation for their services, to be ascertained by law, and paid out of the Treasury of the United States. They shall in all cases, except treason, felony and breach of the peace, be privileged from arrest during their attendance at the session of their respective Houses, and in going to and returning from the same; and for any speech or debate in either House, they shall not be questioned in any other place.

No Senator or Representative shall, during the time for which he was elected, be appointed to any civil office under the authority of the United States, which shall have been created, or the emoluments whereof shall have been increased during such time; and no person holding any office under the

United States, shall be a member of either House during his continuance in office.

Section 7. All bills for raising revenue shall originate in the House of Representatives; but the Senate may propose or concur with amendments as on other bills.

Every bill which shall have passed the House of Representatives and the Senate, shall, before it becomes a law, be presented to the President of the United States; If he approve he shall sign it, but if not he shall return it, with his objections to that House in which it shall have originated, who shall enter the objections at large on their Journal, and proceed to reconsider it. If after such reconsideration two thirds of that House shall agree to pass the bill, it shall be sent, together with the objections, to the other House, by which it shall likewise be reconsidered, and if approved by two thirds of that House, it shall become a law. But in all such cases the votes of both Houses shall be determined by yeas and nays, and the names of the persons voting for and against the bill shall be entered on the journal of each House respectively. If any bill shall not be returned by the President within ten days (Sundays excepted) after it shall have been presented to him, the same shall be a law, in like manner as if he had signed it, unless the Congress by their adjournment prevent its return, in which case it shall not be a law.

Every order, resolution, or vote to which the concurrence of the Senate and House of Representatives may be necessary (except on a question of adjournment) shall be presented to the President of the United States; and before the same shall take effect, shall be approved by him, or being disapproved by him, shall be repassed by two thirds of the Senate and House of Representatives, according to the rules and limitations prescribed in the case of a bill.

Section 8. The Congress shall have power to lay and collect taxes, duties, imposts and excises, to pay the debts and provide for the common defense and general welfare of the United

States; but all duties, imposts and excises shall be uniform throughout the United States;

To borrow money on the credit of the United States;

To regulate commerce with foreign nations, and among the several States, and with the Indian tribes;

To establish an uniform rules of naturalization, and uniform laws on the subject of bankruptcies throughout the United States;

To coin money, regulate the value thereof, and of foreign coin, and fix the standard of weights and measures;

To provide for the punishment of counterfeiting the securities and current coin of the United States;

To establish post offices and post roads;

To promote the progress of science and useful arts, by securing for limited times to authors and inventors the exclusive rights to their respective writings and discoveries;

To constitute tribunals inferior to the Supreme Court;

To define and punish piracies and felonies committed on the high seas, and offences against the law of nations;

To declare war, grant letters of marque and reprisal, and make rules concerning captures on land and water;

To raise and support armies, but no appropriation of money to that use shall be for a longer term than two years;

To provide and maintain a Navy;

To make rules for the government and regulation of the land and naval Forces;

To provide for calling forth the militia to execute the laws of the Union, suppress insurrections and repel invasions;

To provide for organizing, arming, and disciplining, the militia, and for governing such part of them as may be employed in the service of the United States, reserving to the States respectively, the appointment of the officers, and the authority of training the militia according to the discipline prescribed by Congress;

To exercise exclusive legislation in all cases whatsoever, over such district (not exceeding ten miles square) as may, by cession of particular States, and the acceptance of Congress, become the seat of the government of the United states, and to exercise like authority over all places purchased by the consent of the legislature of the State in which the same shall be, for the erection of forts, magazines, arsenals, dockyards, and other needful buildings; And

To make all laws which shall be necessary and proper for carrying into execution the foregoing powers, and all other powers vested by this Constitution in the government of the United States, or in any department or officer thereof.

Section 9. The migration or importation of such persons as any of the States now existing shall think proper to admit, shall not be prohibited by the Congress prior to the year one thousand eight hundred and eight, but a tax or duty may be imposed on such importation, not exceeding ten dollars for each person.

The privilege of the writ of Habeas Corpus shall not be suspended, unless when in cases of rebellion or invasion the public safety may require it.

No bill of attainder or ex post facto law shall be passed.

No capitation, or other direct, tax shall be laid, unless in proportion to the census or enumeration herein before directed to be taken.

No tax or duty shall be laid on articles exported from any State.

No preference shall be given by any regulation of commerce or revenue to the ports of one State over those of another: nor shall vessels bound to, or from, one State, be obliged to enter, clear, or pay duties in another.

No money shall be drawn from the Treasury, but in consequence of appropriations made by law; and a regular statement and account of the receipts and expenditures of all public money shall be published from time to time.

No title of nobility shall be granted by the United States: And no person holding any office of profit or trust under them, shall, without the consent of the Congress, accept of any present, emolument, office, or title, of any kind whatever, from any king, prince, or foreign State.

Section 10. No State shall enter into any treaty, alliance, or confederation; grant letters of marque and reprisal; coin money, emit bills of credit; make any thing but gold and silver coin a tender in payment of debts; pass any bill of attainder, ex post facto law, or law impairing the obligation of contracts, or grant any title of nobility.

No State shall, without the consent of the Congress, lay any imposts of duties on imports or exports, except what may be absolutely necessary for executing its inspection laws: and the net product of all duties and imposts, laid by any State on imports or exports, shall be for the use of the Treasury of the United States; and all such laws shall be subject to the revision and control of the Congress.

No State shall, without the consent of Congress, lay any duty of tonnage, keep troops, or ships of war in time of peace, enter into any agreement or compact with another State, or with a foreign power, or engage in war, unless actually invaded, or in such imminent danger as will not admit of delay.

ARTICLE II

Section 1. The executive Power shall be vested in a President of the United States of America. He shall hold his Office during the Term of four Years, and, together with the Vice President, chosen for the same Term, be elected, as follows:

Each State shall appoint, in such Manner as the Legislature thereof may direct, a Number of Electors, equal to the whole Number of Senators and Representatives to which the State may be entitled in the Congress: but no Senator or Representative, or Person holding an Office of Trust or Profit under the United States, shall be appointed an Elector.

(Author's Note: This section below was modified by AMENDMENT XII.)

The Electors shall meet in their respective States, and vote by Ballot for two Persons, of whom one at least shall not be an Inhabitant of the same State with themselves. And they shall make a List of all the Persons voted for, and of the Number of Votes for each; which List they shall sign and certify, and transmit sealed to the Seat of the Government of the United States, directed to the President of the Senate. The President of the Senate shall, in the Presence of the Senate and House of Representatives, open all the Certificates, and the Votes shall then be counted. The Person having the greatest Number of Votes shall be the President, if such Number be a Majority of the whole Number of Electors appointed; and if there be more than one who have such Majority, and have an equal Number of Votes, then the House of Representatives shall immediately choose by Ballot one of them for President; and if no Person have a Majority, then from the five highest on the List the said House shall in like Manner choose the President. But in choosing the President, the Votes shall be taken by States, the Representation from each State having one Vote; a quorum for this purpose shall consist of a Member or Members from two thirds of the States, and a Majority of all the States shall be necessary to a Choice. In every Case, after the Choice of the President, the Person having the greatest Number of Votes of the Electors shall be the Vice President. But if there should remain two or more who have equal Votes, the Senate shall choose from them by Ballot the Vice President.

The Congress may determine the time of choosing the electors, and the day on which they shall give their votes; which day shall be the same throughout the United States.

No person except a natural born citizen, or a citizen of the United States, at the time of the adoption of this Constitution, shall be eligible to the office of President; neither shall any person be eligible to that office who shall not have attained to the age of thirty-five years, and been fourteen years a resident within the United States.

In case of the removal of the President from office, or of his death, resignation, or inability to discharge the powers and duties of the said office, the same shall devolve on the Vice President and the Congress may by law provide for the case of removal, death, resignation, or inability, both of the President and Vice President, declaring what officer shall then act as President, and such officer shall act accordingly, until the disability be removed, or a President shall be elected.

The President shall, at stated times, receive for his services, a compensation, which shall neither be increased nor diminished during the period for which he shall have been elected, and he shall not receive within that period any other emolument from the United States, or any of them.

Before he enter on the execution of his office, he shall take the following oath or affirmation: "I do solemnly swear (or affirm) that I will faithfully execute the office of President of the United States, and will to the best of my ability, preserve, protect and defend the Constitution of the United States."

Section 2. The President shall be Commander in Chief of the Army and Navy of the United States, and of the militia of the several States, when called into the actual service of the United States; he may require the opinion, in writing, of the principal officer in each of the executive departments, upon any subject relating to the duties of their respective offices, and he shall have power to grant reprieves and pardons for offenses against the United States, except in cases of impeachment.

He shall have power, by and with the advice and consent of the Senate, to make treaties, provided two thirds of the Senators present concur; and he shall nominate, and by and with the advice and consent of the Senate, shall appoint Ambassadors, other public Ministers and Consuls, Judges of the Supreme Court, and all other Officers of the United States, whose appointments are not herein otherwise provided for, and which shall be established by law: but the Congress may by law vest the appointment of such inferior Officers, as they think proper, in the President alone, in the Courts of law, or in the heads of departments.

The President shall have power to fill up all vacancies that may happen during the recess of the Senate, by granting commissions which shall expire at the end of their next session.

Section 3. He shall from time to time give to the Congress information of the State of the Union, and recommend to their consideration such measures as he shall judge necessary and expedient; he may, on extraordinary occasions, convene both Houses, or either of them, and in case of disagreement between them, with respect to the time of adjournment, he may adjourn them to such time as he shall receive Ambassadors and other public Ministers; he shall take care that the laws be faithfully executed, and shall commission all the officers of the United States.

Section 4. The President, Vice President and all civil officers of the United States, shall be removed from office on impeachment for, and conviction of, treason, bribery, or other high crimes and misdemeanors.

ARTICLE III.

Section 1. The judicial Power of the United States shall be vested in one supreme Court, and in such inferior Courts as the Congress may from time to time ordain and establish. The Judges, both of the supreme and inferior Courts, shall hold their Offices during good Behaviour, and shall, at stated Times, receive for their Services a Compensation, which shall not be diminished during their Continuance in Office.

Section 2. The judicial Power shall extend to all Cases, in Law and Equity, arising under this Constitution, the Laws of the United States, and Treaties made, or which shall be made, under their Authority; to all Cases affecting Ambassadors, other public Ministers and Consuls; to all Cases of admiralty and maritime Jurisdiction;--to Controversies to which the United States shall be a Party; to Controversies between two or more States; between a State and Citizens of another State, between Citizens of different States; between Citizens of the same State claiming Lands under Grants of different States, and between a State, or the Citizens thereof, and foreign States, Citizens or Subjects.

In all Cases affecting Ambassadors, other public Ministers and Consuls, and those in which a State shall be Party, the supreme Court shall have original Jurisdiction. In all the other Cases before mentioned, the supreme Court shall have appellate Jurisdiction, both as to Law and Fact, with such Exceptions, and under such Regulations as the Congress shall make.

The Trial of all Crimes, except in Cases of Impeachment, shall be by Jury; and such Trial shall be held in the State where the said Crimes shall have been committed; but when not committed within any State, the Trial shall be at such Place or Places as the Congress may by Law have directed.

Section 3. Treason against the United States, shall consist only in levying War against them, or in adhering to their Enemies, giving them Aid and Comfort. No Person shall be convicted of Treason unless on the Testimony of two Witnesses to the same overt Act, or on Confession in open Court.

The Congress shall have Power to declare the Punishment of Treason, but no Attainder of Treason shall work Corruption of Blood, or Forfeiture except during the Life of the Person attainted.

ARTICLE IV.

Section 1. Full Faith and Credit shall be given in each State to the public Acts, Records, and judicial Proceedings of every other State. And the Congress may by general Laws prescribe the Manner in which such Acts, Records and Proceedings shall be proved, and the Effect thereof.

Section 2. The Citizens of each State shall be entitled to all Privileges and Immunities of Citizens in the several States.

A Person charged in any State with Treason, Felony, or other Crime, who shall flee from Justice, and be found in another State, shall on Demand of the executive Authority of the State from which he fled, be delivered up, to be removed to the State having Jurisdiction of the Crime.

(Author's note: The following clause, in the original, was rendered moot by the passage of the XIIIth Amendment, which itself, under the NAR, was subsequently repealed by the XXXIVth Amendment.)

No Person held to Service or Labour in one State, under the Laws thereof, escaping into another, shall, in Consequence of any Law or Regulation therein, be discharged from such Service or Labour, but shall be delivered up on Claim of the Party to whom such Service or Labour may be due.

Section 3. New States may be admitted by the Congress into this Union; but no new State shall be formed or erected within the Jurisdiction of any other State; nor any State be formed by the Junction of two or more States, or Parts of States, without the Consent of the Legislatures of the States concerned as well as of the Congress.

The Congress shall have Power to dispose of and make all needful Rules and Regulations respecting the Territory or other Property belonging to the United States; and nothing in this Constitution shall be so construed as to Prejudice any Claims of the United States, or of any particular State.

Section 4. The United States shall guarantee to every State in this Union a Republican Form of Government, and shall protect each of them against Invasion; and on Application of the Legislature, or of the Executive (when the Legislature cannot be convened), against domestic Violence.

ARTICLE V

The Congress, whenever two thirds of both Houses shall deem it necessary, shall propose amendments to this Constitution, or, on the application of the legislatures of two thirds of the several States, shall call a convention for proposing amendments, which, in either case, shall be valid to all intents and purposes, as part of this Constitution, when ratified by the legislatures of three fourths of the several States, or by conventions in three fourths thereof, as the one or the other mode of ratification may be proposed by the Congress; provided that no amendment which may be made prior to the year one thousand eight hundred and eight shall in any manner affect the first and fourth clauses in the ninth section of the first article; and that no State, without its consent, shall be deprived of its equal suffrage in the Senate.

ARTICLE VI

All debts contracted and engagements entered into, before the adoption of this Constitution, shall be as valid against the United States under this Constitution, as under the Confederation.

This Constitution, and the laws of the United States which shall be made in pursuance thereof; and all treaties made, or which shall be made, under the authority of the United States, shall be the supreme law of the land; and the judges in every State shall be bound thereby, any thing in the Constitution or laws of any State to the contrary notwithstanding.

The Senators and Representatives before mentioned, and the members of the several State legislatures, and all executive and judicial officers, both of the United States and of the several States, shall be bound by oath or affirmation, to support this Constitution; but no religious test shall ever be required as a qualification to any office or public trust under the United States.

ARTICLE VII

The ratification of the conventions of nine States, shall be sufficient for the establishment of this Constitution between the States so ratifying the same.

DONE in convention by the unanimous consent of the States present the seventeenth day of September in the Year of our Lord one thousand seven hundred and eighty seven, and of the independence of the United States of America the twelfth.

Amendments to the Constitution. (First ten amendments adopted June 15, 1790)

AMENDMENT I

Congress shall make no law respecting an establishment of religion, or prohibiting the free exercise thereof; or abridging the freedom of speech, or of the press; or the right of the people peaceably to assemble, and to petition the Government for a redress of grievances.

AMENDMENT II

A well regulated militia, being necessary to the security of a free State, the right of the people to keep and bear arms, shall not be infringed.

AMENDMENT III

No soldier shall, in time of peace be quartered in any house, without the consent of the owner, nor in time of war, but in a manner to be prescribed by law.

AMENDMENT IV

The right of the people to be secure in their persons, houses, papers, and effects, against unreasonable searches and seizures, shall not be violated, and no warrants shall issue, but upon probable cause, supported by oath or affirmation, and particularly describing the place to be searched, and the persons or things to be seized.

AMENDMENT V

No person shall be held to answer for a capital, or otherwise infamous crime, unless on a presentment or indictment of a grand jury, except in cases arising in the land or naval forces, or in the militia, when in actual service in time of war or public danger; nor shall any person be subject for the same offence to be twice put in jeopardy of life or limb; nor shall be compelled in any criminal case to be a witness against himself, nor be deprived of life, liberty, or property, without due process of law; nor shall private property be taken for public use, without just compensation.

AMENDMENT VI

In all criminal prosecutions, the accused shall enjoy the right to a speedy and public trial, by an impartial jury of the State and district wherein the crime shall have been committed, which district shall have been previously ascertained by law, and to be informed of the nature and cause of the accusation; to be confronted with the witnesses against him; to have compulsory process for obtaining witnesses in his favor, and to have the assistance of counsel for his defence.

AMENDMENT VII

In Suits at common law, where the value in controversy shall exceed twenty dollars, the right of trial by jury shall be preserved, and no fact tried by a jury, shall be otherwise re-examined in any Court of the United States, than according to the rules of the common law.

AMENDMENT VIII

Excessive bail shall not be required, nor excessive fines imposed, nor cruel and unusual punishments inflicted.

AMENDMENT IX

The enumeration in the Constitution, of certain rights, shall not be construed to deny or disparage others retained by the people.

AMENDMENT X

The powers not delegated to the United States by the Constitution, nor prohibited by it to the States, are reserved to the States respectively, or to the people.

AMENDMENT XI

(Adopted January 8, 1798)

The judicial power of the United States shall not be construed to extend to any suit in law or equity, commenced or prosecuted against one of the United States by citizens of another State, or by citizens or subjects of any foreign State.

AMENDMENT XII

(Adopted September 25, 1804)

The electors shall meet in their respective states, and vote by ballot for President and Vice President, one of whom, at least, shall not be an inhabitant of the same state with themselves; they shall name in their ballots the person voted for as President, and in distinct ballots the person voted for as Vice President, and they shall make distinct lists of all persons voted for as President, and of all persons voted for as Vice President, and of the number of votes for each, which lists they shall sign and certify, and transmit sealed to the seat of the government of the United State, directed to the President of the Senate; the President of the Senate shall, in the presence of the Senate and House of Representatives, open all the certificates and the votes shall then be counted; the person having the greatest number of votes for President, shall be the President, if such number be a majority of the whole number of electors appointed; and if no person have such majority, then from the persons having the highest numbers not exceeding three on the list of those voted for as President, the House of Representatives shall choose immediately, by ballot, the President. But in choosing the President, the votes shall be taken by states, the representation from each state having one vote; a quorum for this purpose shall consist of a member or members from two-thirds of the states, and a majority of all the states shall be necessary to a choice. And if the House of Representatives shall not choose a President whenever the right of choice shall devolve upon them, before the fourth day of March next following, then the Vice President shall act as President, as in the case of the death or other constitutional disability of the President. The person having the greatest number of votes as Vice President, shall be the Vice President, if such number be a majority of the whole number of electors appointed, and if no person have a majority, then from the two highest numbers on the list, the Senate shall choose the Vice President; a quorum for the purpose shall consist of two-thirds of the whole number of Senators, and a majority of the whole number shall be necessary to a choice. But no person constitutionally ineligible to the office of President shall be eligible to that of Vice President of the United States.

AMENDMENT XIII
(Adopted December 18, 1865)
Section 1. Neither slavery nor involuntary servitude, nor confinement to a particular place or geographic location, except as a punishment for crime whereof the party shall have been duly convicted, shall exist within the United States, or any place subject to their jurisdiction.

Section 2. Congress shall have power to enforce this article by appropriate legislation.

AMENDMENT XIV
(Adopted July 21, 1868)
Section 1. All persons born or naturalized in the United States, and subject to the jurisdiction thereof, are citizens of the United States and of the State wherein they reside. No State shall make or enforce any law which shall abridge the privileges or immunities of citizens of the United States; nor shall any State deprive any person of life, liberty, or property, without due process of law; nor deny to any person within its jurisdiction the equal protection of the laws.

Section 2. Representatives shall be apportioned among the several States according to their respective numbers, counting the whole number of persons in each State, excluding Indians not taxed. But when the right to vote at any election for the choice of electors for President and Vice President of the United States, Representatives in Congress, the Executive and Judicial officers of a State, or the members of the Legislature thereof, is denied to any of the male inhabitants of each State, being twenty-one years of age, and citizens of the United States, or in any way abridged, except for participation in rebellion, or other crime, the basis of representation therein shall be reduced in the proportion which the number of such male citizens shall bear to the whole number of male citizens twenty-one years of age in such State.

Section 3. No person shall be a Senator or Representative in Congress, or elector of President and Vice President, or hold any office, civil or military, under the United States, or under any State, who, having previously taken an oath, as a member of Congress, or as an officer of the United States, or as a member of any State legislature, or as an executive or judicial officer of any State, to support the Constitution of the United States, shall have engaged in insurrection or rebellion against the same, or given aid or comfort to the enemies thereof. But Congress may by a vote of two-thirds of each House, remove such disability.

Section 4. The validity of the public debt of the United States, authorized by law, including debts incurred for payment of pensions and bounties for services in suppressing insurrection or rebellion, shall not be questioned. But neither the United States nor any State shall assume or pay any debt or obligation incurred in aid or insurrection or rebellion against the United States, or any claim for the loss or emancipation of any slave; but all such debts, obligations and claims shall be held illegal and void.

Section 5. The Congress shall have power to enforce, by appropriate legislation, the provisions of this article.

AMENDMENT XV

(Adopted March 30, 1870)

Section 1. The right of citizens of the United States to vote shall not be denied or abridged by the United States or by any State on account of race, color, or previous condition of servitude.

Section 2. The Congress shall have power to enforce this article by appropriate legislation.

AMENDMENT XVI

(Adopted February 25, 1913)

The Congress shall have power to lay and collect taxes on incomes, from whatever source derived, without apportionment among the several States, and without regard to any census or enumeration.

AMENDMENT XVII

Adopted May 31, 1913)

The Senate of the United States shall be composed of two Senators from each State, elected by the people thereof, for six years; and each Senator shall have one vote. The electors in each State shall have the qualifications requisite for electors of the most numerous branch of the State legislatures.

When vacancies happen in the representation of any State in the Senate, the executive authority of such State shall issue writs of election to fill such vacancies; Provided, That the legislature of any State may empower the executive thereof to make temporary appointments until the people fill the vacancies by election as the legislature may direct.

This amendment shall not be so construed as to affect the election or term of any Senator chosen before it becomes valid as a part of the Constitution.

(Author's Note: The amendments pertaining to the establishment and disestablishment of the prohibitions relating to alcoholic beverages have been omitted.)

AMENDMENT XIX

(Adopted August 26, 1920)

The right of citizens of the United States to vote shall not be denied or abridged by the United States or by any State on account of sex.

Congress shall have power to enforce this article by appropriate legislation.

AMENDMENT XX

(Adopted January 23, 1933)

Section 1. The terms of the President and Vice President shall end at noon on the 20th day of January, and the terms of Senators and Representatives at noon on the 3rd day of January, of the years in which such terms would have ended if this article had not been ratified; and the terms of their successors shall then begin.

Section 2. The Congress shall assemble at least once in every year, and such meeting shall begin at noon on the 3rd day of January, unless they shall by law appoint a different day.

Section 3. If, at the time fixed for the beginning of the term of the President, the President elect shall have died, the Vice President elect shall become President. If a President shall not have been chosen before the time fixed for the beginning of his term, or if the President elect shall have failed to qualify, then the Vice President elect shall act a President until a President shall have qualified; and the Congress may by law provide for the case wherein neither a President elect nor a Vice President elect shall have qualified, declaring who shall then act as President, or the manner in which one who is to act shall be selected, and such person shall act accordingly until a President or Vice President shall have qualified.

Section 4. The Congress may by law provide for the case of the death of any of the persons from whom the House of

Representatives may choose a President whenever the right of choice shall have devolved upon them, and for the case of the death of any of the persons from whom the Senate may choose a Vice President whenever the right of choice shall have devolved upon them.

AMENDMENT XXII

(Adopted 1951)

Limits any individual to no more than two elected terms as President (text omitted).

AMENDMENT XXIII

(Adopted March 29, 1961)

Section 1. The District constituting the seat of Government of the United States shall appoint in such manner as the Congress may direct: A number of electors of President and Vice President equal to the whole number of Senators and Representatives in Congress to which the District would be entitled if it were a State, but in no event more than the least populous State; they shall be in addition to those appointed by the States, but they shall be considered, for the purposes of the election of President and Vice President, to be electors appointed by a State; and they shall meet in the District and perform such duties as provided by the twelfth articles of amendment.

Section 2. The Congress shall have power to enforce this article by appropriate legislation.

AMENDMENT XXIV

(Adopted January 23, 1964)

Section 1. The right of citizens of the United States to vote in any primary or other election for President or Vice President, for electors for President or Vice President, or for Senator or Representative in Congress, shall not be denied or abridged by the United States or any State by reason of failure to pay any poll tax or other tax.

Section 2. The Congress shall have power to enforce this article by appropriate legislation.

AMENDMENT XXV

(Adopted February 10, 1965)

Section 1. In case of the removal of the President from office or of his death or resignation, the Vice President shall become President.

Section 2. Whenever there is a vacancy in the office of the Vice President, the President shall nominate a Vice President who shall take office upon confirmation by a majority vote of both houses of Congress.

Section 3. Whenever the President transmits to the President *pro tempore* of the Senate and the Speaker of the House of Representatives his written declaration that he is unable to discharge the powers and duties of his office, and until he transmits to them a written declaration to the contrary, such powers and duties shall be discharged by the Vice President as Acting President.

Section 4. Whenever the Vice President and a majority of either the principal officers of the executive departments or of such other body as Congress may by law provide, transmit to the President *pro tempore* of the Senate and the Speaker of the House of Representatives their written declaration that the President is unable to discharge the powers and duties of his office, the Vice President shall immediately assume the powers and duties of the office as Acting President.

Thereafter, when the President transmits to the President *pro tempore* of the Senate and the Speaker of the House of Representatives his written declaration that no inability exists, he shall resume the powers and duties of his office unless the Vice President and a majority of either the principal officers of the executive department or of such other body as Congress may by law provide, transmit within four days to the President *pro tempore* of the Senate and the Speaker of the House of Representatives their written declaration that the President is unable to discharge the powers and duties of his office. Thereupon Congress shall decide the issue, assembling within forty-eight hours for that purpose if not in session. If the Congress, within twenty-one days after receipt of the latter written declaration, or, if Congress is not is session, within twenty-one days after Congress is required to assemble, determines by two-thirds vote of both houses that the President is unable to discharge the powers and duties of his office, the Vice President shall continue to discharge the same as Acting President; otherwise, the President shall resume the powers and duties of his office.

AMENDMENT XXVI
(Adopted July 1, 1971)
Section 1. The right of citizens of the United States, who are 18 years of age or older, to vote shall not be denied or abridged by the United States or any state on account of age.

Section 2. The Congress shall have the power to enforce this article by appropriate legislation.

AMENDMENT XXVII
(Adopted May 7, 1992)
No law varying the compensation for the services of the Senators and Representatives, shall take effect, until an election of Representatives shall have intervened.

AMENDMENT XXVIII
(Adopted April 15, 1999)
Balanced Budget Amendment (with loopholes); text omitted.

AMENDMENT XXIX
(Adopted April 1, 2000)
Congressional Term Limits Amendment; text omitted.

AMENDMENT XXX ("Preserve America")

(Adopted February 2, 2002)

Commencing on the day following ratification of this amendment, no person not at that time a citizen of the United States may in the future become a citizen unless at least one parent of that person is a citizen of the United States.

AMENDMENT XXXI ("Morality")

(Adopted March 25, 2005)

Section 1. Life begins at the moment of conception; the unborn child has a fundamental individual right to life which cannot be infringed by any person, or public or private agency or organization; the fifth and fourteenth amendments to this Constitution apply equally to all persons, born and unborn; any artificial interference with unborn life is murder.

Section 2. No educational institution may teach any approach to any aspect of human sexuality, outside of marriage, other than abstinence.

Section 3. Engaging in sexual relations with persons of the same sex is a matter of choice; no provision of this Constitution may be deemed to provide preferential status in the civil or criminal law at the Federal, state, or local level to any person or group of persons based on their chosen sexual choice or preference.

Section 4. Neither the Federal government nor any state or local government may make any provision for support, financial or otherwise, of persons not supporting themselves, outside of an institution expressly provided for that purpose.

Section 5. The 16th Amendment is repealed. Within five years of ratification of this Amendment, Congress is required to repeal any and all statutes providing for the levy of either individual or corporate income taxes.

AMENDMENT XXXII ("Balancing")
(Adopted October 12, 2006)
Section 1. Commencing on the first day of the next fiscal year following the date of ratification of this Amendment, separate Federal budget accounts shall be established for the maintenance of the national defense, for the payment of interest on the national debt, and for the general operations of the Federal government.

Section 2. The 28th Amendment to the Constitution of the United States is hereby repealed.

Section 3. Commencing on the first day of the next fiscal year following the date of ratification of this Amendment, any budget adopted by the Congress under which funds are appropriated for the support of any general operations, activity, or functions of the Federal government must show a surplus of income over expenditures of at least one dollar.

Section 4. No tax, fee, or other charge levied for the purpose of supporting any general operations, activities, or functions of the Federal government may be increased without the approval of two-thirds of the members of each House of Congress.

Section 5. Every item in the Federal budget for the support of general operations shall be considered to have been presented separately to the President and be subject to the procedural provisions of Article 1, Section 7, of this Constitution.

Section 6. In addition to the powers enumerated in Article 2, Sections 2 and 3 of this Constitution, the President shall have the authority to declare a "special national emergency." To take effect, any such declaration must be approved by a simple majority of the members voting of each House of Congress. During any such special national emergency, the President shall have the authority to rule by decree for a period of sixty days. This authority may be renewed by the President unless it is rescinded by a vote of two-thirds of the membership of each House of Congress. Any Presidential decree made under the provisions of this Amendment may be nullified by a vote of two-thirds of the membership of each House of Congress.

Section 7. The Fourth Amendment to the Constitution of the United States is hereby repealed.

AMENDMENT XXXIII ("Supremacy")

(Adopted August 8, 2007)

Section 1. Article 6 of this Constitution in its entirety is amended to read as follows:

This constitution, and the laws of the United States which shall be made pursuant thereto shall be the supreme law of the land, except when the President, or the Congress by a majority vote of the members voting of both houses, shall declare the Law of God to be superior to it. Article 1 section 7 of this constitution shall apply to any Congressional decision in this matter. Congress may overturn a Presidential decision in this matter by a two-thirds vote of the membership in both houses.

All Federal judges and the judges in every state shall be bound by the provisions of this amendment, any thing in the constitution or laws of any state to the contrary notwithstanding. No Federal or state court may judge any act or action taken under this Amendment for its constitutionality.

The senators and representatives beforementioned, and the members of the several state legislatures, and all executive and judicial officers, both of the United States and of the several states, shall be bound by oath or affirmation, to support this constitution; religious tests may be required as a qualification to any office or public trust under the United States.

Section 2. Neither Congress, nor any Federal court, nor any state or local government or other agency supported by tax revenues may prohibit organized or voluntary prayer or other reasonable religious devotion in any public educational institution.

AMENDMENT XXXIV ("Original Intent")
(Adopted April 12, 2010)
The thirteenth, fourteenth, and fifteenth amendments to the Constitution of the United States are hereby repealed.

Author's Note: For the U.S. Constitution as it truly stood on June 5, 2012, without "amendments XXVIII - XXXIV," see: http://www.archives.gov/exhibits/charters/constitution_transcript.html

THE DECLARATION OF INDEPENDENCE OF THE UNITED STATES OF AMERICA
July 4, 1776 (Abridged)
When in the Course of human events, it becomes necessary for one people to dissolve the political bands which have connected them with another, and to assume among the Powers of the earth, the separate and equal station to which the Laws of Nature and of Nature's God entitle them, a decent respect to the opinions of mankind requires that they should declare the causes that impel them to the separation.

We hold these truths to be self-evident, that all men are created equal, that they are endowed by their Creator with certain unalienable Rights, that among these are Life, Liberty, and the pursuit of Happiness. —That to secure these rights, Governments are instituted among men, deriving their just powers from the consent of the governed, —That whenever any Form of Government becomes destructive of these ends, it is the Right of the People to alter or abolish it, and institute new Government, laying its foundation on such principles and organizing its powers in such form, as to them shall seem most likely to effect their Safety and Happiness. …

When a long train of abuses and usurpations, pursuing invariably the same Object evinces a design to reduce them under absolute Despotism, it is their right, it is their duty, to throw off such Government, and to provide new Guards for their future security.

Such has been the patient suffering of these Colonies; and

such is now the necessity which constrains them to alter their former Systems of Government. The history of the present King of Great Britain is a history of repeated injuries and usurpations, all having in direct object the establishment of an absolute Tyranny over these States. To prove this, let Facts be submitted to a candid world.

[Author's Note: Then there is the list of particulars, here omitted].

We, therefore, the Representatives of the United States of America, in General Congress, Assembled, appealing to the Supreme Judge of the world for the rectitude of our intentions, do, in the Name, and by the authority of the good People of these Colonies, solemnly publish and declare, That these United Colonies are, and of Right ought to be Free and Independent States; that they are Absolved from all Allegiance to the British Crown, and that all political connection between them and the State of Great Britain, is and ought to be totally dissolved; and that as Free and Independent States, they have full Power to levy War, conclude Peace, contract Alliances, establish Commerce, and to do all other Acts and Things which Independent States may of Right do. And for the support of this Declaration, with the firm reliance on the Protection of Divine Providence, we mutually pledge to each other our Lives, our Fortunes, and our sacred Honor.

APPENDIX II
The Nature of Fascism and Its Precursors
Dino Louis
1998

Author's Commentary on the Dino Louis text

In our time (2048), when describing the economic and political system which existed throughout the period 2001-2023, first in the old United States and then in the New American Republics, the words "fascist" and "fascism" are generally used. However, it should be understood that, with few exceptions, the Right Wing Reactionary leadership in both the old United States and the New American Republics vehemently denied that they were fascists, and strongly shied away from ever using the term to describe themselves or any of their activities.

Even at the height of the NAR's racist oppression of the non-white peoples of the Second, Third, and Fourth Republics, and violent repression of dissent and resistance within the White Republic itself, even at the time of the most extreme concentration of power in the hands of the Executive Branch of the NAR and the substitution of the rule of men for the rule of law, and even with the perpetuation of one-party (ACNP) government, the Right pursued the fiction that it was following the precepts of Democracy and was the protector of traditional American freedoms.

Even after it had used the amendment process in the most grotesque way to make the original U.S. Constitution a mere shadow of its original self, the Right-Wing Reactionaries claimed that they were doing nothing more than protecting the traditional "American way of life." And they shunned the use of the term "fascism" at the risk of alienating some of their strongest, and most violent, supporters from the Far Right, groups and organizations that proudly labeled themselves "Fascist" and "Nazi."

But the ACNP leadership persisted in this policy to the very end. It was the natural outgrowth of a fashion broadly used by Right-Wing Reaction during the Transition Era, of racists claiming they were not racists, anti-Semites claiming they were not anti-Semitic, misogynists claiming they were not anti-female, xenophobes claiming they were not xenophobic, and homophobes claiming they were not homophobic.

It was a peculiar tactic bred of a time just before the commencement of the Transition Era in 1980 when in fact prejudice of most kinds was considered by most people to be nasty stuff. The tactic served a very useful purpose for the Right-Wing Reactionaries because many of their opponents were drawn into useless, distracting, no-win "yes-you-are, no-I'm-not" arguments, rather than discussing and exposing the true policies and desired social outcomes advocated by the Right-Wing forces, regardless of how they characterized themselves.

In our time, the phrase "if it looks like a duck, walks like a duck, and quacks like a duck, it's a duck" characterizes the approach of most historians to the study of the period 1980-2022. Thus we use the terms "racist," "anti-Semite," "homophobe" and "fascist," regardless of whether or not the Right-Wingers of the time accepted them as appropriate to describe themselves. But nevertheless, it is important to define terms. To do this, I once again draw upon the work of Dino Louis, and present his essay, "On the Nature of Fascism and Its Precursors," written in 1998.

A Definition of Fascism

(the text from here onwards is that of Dino Louis)

Fascism is a political, social, and economic system that has the following baker's dozen plus one of major defining characteristics:

1. There is complete executive branch control of government policy and action. There is no independent judicial or legislative branch of government.
2. There is no constitution recognized by all political forces as having an authority beyond that claimed, stated, and exerted by the government in power, to which that government is subject. The rule of men, not law, is supreme.
3. There is only one political party, and no mass organizations of any kind other than those approved by the government are permitted.
4. Government establishes and enforces the rules of "right" thinking, "right" action, and "right" religious devotion.
5. Racism, homophobia, misogynism, and national chauvinism are major factors in national politics and policy-making. Religious authoritarianism may be part of the package.
6. There is no recognition of inherent personal rights. Only the government can grant "rights." Any "rights" granted by the government may be diminished or removed by it from any individual or group at any time without prior notice, explanation, or judicial review. Thus, there is no presumed freedom of speech, press, religion, or even belief, automatically accompanying citizenship. There are no inherent or presumed protections against any violations of personal liberty committed by law-enforcement or other government agencies.
7. Official and unofficial force, internal terror, and routine torture of captured opponents are major means of governmental control.
8. There are few or no employee rights or protections, including the right of workers to bargain collectively. Only government-approved labor unions or associations are permitted to exist, and that approval may be removed at any time, without prior notice.
9. All communications media are government-owned or otherwise government-controlled.
10. All entertainment, music, art, and organized sport is controlled by the government.

11. There may or may not be a single charismatic leader in charge of the government, i.e., a "dictator."
12. The economy is based on capitalism, with tight central control of the distribution of resources among the producers, and strict limitations on the free market for labor (as noted above).
13. The fascist takeover of the government of a major power always leads to foreign war, sooner or later.
14. Built as it is on terror, repression, and an ultimately fictional/ delusional representation of historical, political, and economic reality, fascism is inherently unstable and always carries with it the seeds of its own destruction. To date, such seeds have always sprouted within a relatively short historical period of time.

The Economic Precursors of Fascism in the United States

Fascism does not arise when things are going well in a country. It arises only when a capitalist country faces either (a) a significant threat of left-wing takeover of the government or (b) a socio/ economic crisis with which the conventional democratically elected government is unable to effectively deal. It is likely that within the next few years the United States will face scenario (b).

As is well known, the United States' economy is in decline. Public and private debt is at all-time highs, as is the foreign trade deficit. Deindustrialization is occurring at an accelerating pace, as are the export of investment capital for productive resources and the resulting permanent loss of manufacturing jobs. There is an accelerating dis-accumulation of labor around productive resources, as the latest technological revolution proceeds apace.

The national economic infrastructure is decaying, as government investment in it is at an all-time low compared to that of other developed countries. The country faces enormous costs for the clean-up of previous private and governmental degradation of the environment. Finally, and this is a critical precursor to fascism: the "free market," currently glorified by the Right as the solution to every problem from health care to incarceration, from education to poverty, has been allowed to run rampant on a field of utter individualism.

These developments have taken place in the context of a pattern of imperial rise and decline observed in a number of countries over the past 500 years brilliantly analyzed by the Yale University historian Paul Kennedy over ten years ago now (1987). Prof. Kennedy described a pattern of overseas expansion/military expenditures, unwillingness to self-tax, dependence on borrowing, the creation of an ever-expanding national debt, all leading eventually to financial, political and diplomatic disaster. This is the pattern being followed almost to the letter by the U.S. at the present time.

There is serious social dislocation as well. Due primarily to capital disinvestment, many central cities are dying. At the other end of the geographical spectrum, the institution of the family farm is dying as well, with formerly self-employed farmers becoming rural wage-workers. The impact of global warming on water supply, agriculture, and weather patterns is beginning to become evident, with no national program to respond to it in sight. The education and health care delivery systems are failing. The supply of affordable housing is decreasing and the incidence of homelessness, even among intact families, is increasing. Racism and homophobia are on the rise, both in the thoughts and actions of many.

Economic Decay Leading to Political Change

Given the underlying gradual disintegration of the economic base of American life as we know it, domestic dissatisfaction and unrest are on the increase. Presently, many of the country's economic decision-makers support attempts to moderate the economic decline by liberal democratic means and policies. However, no U.S. government, not even a "liberal" one of the Clinton variety, has been able to effectively deal with the underlying cause of US economic decline: a fundamentally flawed capital investment policy.

To do that would first require recognizing the *fact* that the market for capital investment is different than the one for the production, distribution, and sale of goods and services. A "free" market for the latter, if properly maintained, has many obvious benefits to consumers in terms of price, availability and quality.

A "free" market for capital investment policy on the other hand leads to the situation which intensified during the Reagan-Bush era: increasing capital export; increasing use of new capital to buy existing productive resources, not create new ones; increasing use of capital for speculative purposes and investment in non-productive resources such as real estate; the increasing tendency of companies to use new capital to buy non-related businesses, rather than investing in expansion of their own.

Second, to be effective, the Administration would have to actively intervene in that market, through what is usually called "industrial policy," following the example of the world's two most successful economies, those of Germany and Japan. Even if it wanted to do this, however, no U.S. Administration would ever be able to get such a program through Congress, whether Republican- or Democratic-controlled. (Just consider what happened to President Clinton's very modest 1993 "stimulus package" and his much more ambitious, but still basically conservative health care reform proposals in the 103rd Congress.)

The economic policies that Clinton-type governments attempt to implement (not always with success) are: modestly raising taxes on those who can afford to pay; changing tax and fiscal policy to encourage worker retraining and technological development; strengthening the educational system; reforming welfare to put some of its beneficiaries to work; modest investment in rebuilding the infrastructure; cleaning up the environment; 'civilian conversion' in the armaments industry; and so forth. Such reforms, even if implemented, however, will not be able to solve the basic underlying economic problem: the shortage and diversion of domestic private investment capital.

(The primary function of the export of investment capital to cheap labor markets is to boost the profitability of that capital. But it has a secondary function as well: to attempt to maintain for some period of time the relative standard of living of U.S. workers, as their *per capita* incomes fall, by providing for them a plethora of relatively inexpensive consumer goods such as electronic products and clothing.)

People cannot "be put back to work" if there are no jobs to put them to work in. Even if people are properly trained and retrained, they cannot "work at good jobs" if there are no good jobs to work at. Infrastructure rebuilding and environmental repair does provide jobs, but not permanent ones, and again, as with military spending, new productive capacity is not created directly. On top of all this are, of course, the intensification of technological change, increase in automation, and the decline in the need for human labor input.

It is likely that the present downward trends in employment security and incomes will continue and intensify. A highly likely outcome of all this is increasing domestic unrest. This will eventually be expressed in more than the random violence of the 1992 L.A. and 1997 Houston riots. And it will eventually occur in certain highly oppressed white communities as well as black ones, as among the Appalachian coal-miners, and possibly even among such other remnants of the once-powerful American labor movement such as the auto workers or the steel workers, which have at least a family memory, if not an actual one, of what resistance in the face of misery was like.

(From the end of the Second World War onwards, the once powerful American trade union movement has gradually been destroyed. Among the signal events in this process was the ban on communists in union leadership provided for by the so-called "Taft-Hartley" Act of 1947. Whatever else might be said about them, it was U.S. communists who provided the most militant and effective trade-union leadership during the heady organizing days of the 1930s.)

(At the other end of the downward spiral of the power of

organized labor in the old U.S. was the firing of the striking air traffic controllers by President Reagan in 1981. The legal use of permanent scabs that gradually spread following this event sealed the doom of American organized labor. By the 1990s, workers who had once routinely demanded better wages, shorter hours, and improved working conditions, have been reduced to begging their employers just to let them hold onto their jobs, even if that means taking less in pay and benefits.)

In this context, if the economic decision-makers follow the pattern followed in many other countries at many other times, eventually, to remain in control of the economy and their assets, they will abandon liberal democratic attempts at reform and turn to the use of government as a repressive force. They will also use racism to re-split the black and white forceful rebellion against the declining standard of living. (Both the use of physical force and of political racism are prime features of fascist government, of course.) Indeed, during the twentieth century, a frequent national response to economic decline and increasing social unrest in a country with a democratic form of government has been a fascist takeover, through either constitutional or extra-constitutional means.

The Advent of Fascism in the United States

It thus can be postulated that fascism, as defined above, will come to the United States, perhaps as soon as during the next five years or so. As civil unrest and violent disorder spreads, given that there is no organized Left in the United States, the situation will be blamed on many factors: the blacks, the gays, the foreigners, the "liberals in Congress, the courts, and [if applicable], the White House," the media, "permissiveness," the "cultural elite/children of the 60s," taxation, and so forth.

Since it is none of the above but rather their own policies which will bring the country to its highly disrupted state, in their quest to re-establish law and order, the economic decision-makers will have no choice but to turn to fascism. The next question is, "how will that happen, by force or by political means?"

In the political arena, the "respectability" of racial politics (as shown by the German Nazi experience, an important historical precursor of fascist politics), was restored by the Reaganite-Bushists in the 1980s. Fascist-type thinking, as defined at the outset of this article, is already prominent in mainstream American politics. It was prominently featured in the speech-making at the 1992 Republican National Convention, in the 1992 Republican Party Platform and the 1994 Republican "Contract on America," in the political campaigns of various Republican and independent candidates. It will not be necessary for some new fascist party to gain respectability first, and credibility second. Its precursor already exists.

Proto-Fascist Politics

In this scenario, there will be an ever-intensifying tendency for Right-Wing politicians to propose solutions to the problems facing the country in the simplistic terms the country came to know so well during the Presidency of Ronald Reagan. As has been the pattern of every Republican Administration since that of Richard Nixon, these answers will increasingly focus on solutions which require/facilitate the concentration of governmental power in the hands of the executive branch (Lind), and invariably will involve limitations upon individual freedom and liberty. Increasingly heard will be calls for "law and order" on the one hand and punishment/separation/quarantine of the "perpetrators" on the other.

Increasingly (as is already happening), the media will be accused of fanning the flames of civil unrest simply by reporting on it (and to a limited extent on its true causes). The judiciary will more and more be described as favoring the "victims of crime," and of irrelevance. Into this mix will step the "direct problem-solvers," for whom the public has been prepared for some years.

They will promise to: "fix things," "in place of government, put God back into American life," "establish order," "get Congress out of the way of the people, make the Courts responsive, and bring the media under control."

Doing so, they promise, will "restore law and order and revive American greatness." Without saying in so many words what they are planning to do, at the end of this politico-historical process once in power the forces promoting this line will have created a fascist state. One can only hope that warnings such as this, which I have made on more than one occasion in the past and which sadly have attracted little attention, are heeded before it is too late.

Author's Note: Obviously, Louis' repeated warnings, and those of others at the time as well, were not heeded. If they had been, this book would never have existed. And that would have been a good thing.

References:

Kennedy, P., *The Rise and Fall of the Great Powers: Economic Change and Military Conflict from 1500 to 2000*, New York: Random House, 1987.

Lind, M., "The Out-of-Control Presidency," *The New Republic*, August 14, 1995, p. 18.

APPENDIX III
The Gradual Assault on Democratic Institutions
Dino Louis
1995

Author's Commentary

This Appendix consists of sketches and notes by Dino Louis. Apparently they were made for a planned essay on the gradual assault by the Right-Wing Reactionaries on the institutions that functioned to protect constitutional democracy in the old U.S. from both the threat and reality of a fascist takeover, among other things. The material was all dated from the second half of 1995. Louis apparently never completed the essay for which he put down these jottings, and there is no evidence that he ever published anything like it. Unfortunately, as we now know all too well, Louis' analysis did play out, for the most part, in historical terms.

To correctly place the thought represented in this Appendix in its historical context, recall that most historians now consider the Transition Era to have begun with the election of Ronald Reagan to the Presidency of the old U.S. in 1980. Recall too that as noted previously, some historians, this one included, consider that the Fascist Period as a whole began with Pine's election in the year 2000.

But most historians, this one included, also agree that *full-blown* fascism did not appear until the NAR was established in 2011. The historians' quibble, and it is a quibble, is over whether the Transition Era and Fascist Period overlapped or were sharply demarcated. I don't get into that issue. The important point is that this material was written at a time about halfway down the historical pathway from traditional American Constitutional democracy to full-blown fascism.

Most of the material is fragmentary (although some more attention is paid to the term limits issue than to others). Nevertheless, it is hoped that Louis' ideas on the subject will help the modern reader better understand the insidious process of "democracy destruction" that was already well underway at the time of this writing. It was appreciated by relatively few of his contemporaries. As noted by Louis, whether consciously or unconsciously, Right-Wing Reaction was already clearly out to destroy what it viewed as the three impediments to its eventually seizing completely untrammeled Executive Branch power, that is establishing by definition a fascist state. The three impediments as they saw them were: an independent federal judiciary, a Congress with power, and the independent media.

The reader should note that earlier in the same year he wrote down these thoughts, Louis had written a full essay on the results of the elections of 1994, describing them as a "prescription for fascism." That essay is reproduced in this book as Chapter 1. And three years later, Louis wrote a full essay on the nature of fascism and its economic precursors, reproduced in this book as Appendix II.

The reader may also note with interest that Louis makes no direct reference to the thinking reflected in the sketches reproduced here in either the prior or the subsequent essay. That occurrence remains unexplained. He may simply have not thought these thoughts at the time he wrote the earlier piece, although it is safe to say that the thinking reflected in these notes may have been stimulated by the book review by John Gray from which Louis has quoted at length in it.

As to the subsequent essay, the thinking described here is reflected in it only indirectly and in passing. Whether this indicates that he changed his mind on the analysis presented here, forgot it, or simply didn't think it important enough to include in the later work, can only be a matter for speculation.

However, once again we can say, with the advantage of historical hindsight, that this analysis was right on the money, whether down the road Louis himself thought it to be of value or not.

The Gradual Assault on the Institutions Protective of Democracy (Sketches and notes by Dino Louis)

I. The Establishment of Fascism and the Barriers to It

The establishment of fascism requires, among other things a dictatorship. That means, a la Nazi Germany, that even if there is a parliament, the executive branch is in full de facto control of the government. In our country, there are three principal institutional barriers to the establishment of the supremacy of the Executive Branch. Two are the other two Constitutional branches of government: the Federal Courts and the Congress.

The third is non-governmental: the press, which of course we now take to include all of those electronic and non-electronic means of communication of news and analysis known as "the media." But while the media are non-governmental, they are recognized by the Constitution: their freedom from Federal government legal intervention is protected by the First Amendment. Thus it can be said that in a sense the three major barriers to the development of Executive Branch dictatorship are built into the Constitution. This should come as no surprise, given the experience the Founding Fathers had with George III.

The Courts and the Congress present barriers to the expansion of Executive Branch power by carrying out their Constitutionally-mandated authority powers to "check and balance" the actions of the third branch (as well as in turn being "checked and balanced" by it and each other). The media do so by freely reporting to the people on what all branches of the Federal government are doing, and also engaging in analysis and advocacy.

Together the three institutions can function to keep a rapacious Executive Branch (and under the Republicans, the

Executive Branch has grown ever more rapacious) under control. Recall GHW Bush's line from sometime early in his Presidency [note to myself: will have to find that REF]. When asked about how he was planning to work with the Congress, he replied, "who needs Congress?"

II. The Republican Party and the Establishment of Executive Branch Dominance

The Republican Party has been the champion of Executive Branch dominance of the Federal government since the Nixon Presidency. That's why, I think, the Right-Wing Reactionaries are out to destroy or at least neutralize/render impotent each of the three institutions protecting constitutional democracy. It is now becoming apparent that since the election of Reagan, the Republican Party has been on a campaign to progressively eliminate, or at least destroy the independence of each one.

A. The Courts

1. "Impeach Earl Warren," the campaign of Jerry Ford back in the 60s, when he was just Minority Leader in the House. Reacting to a Supreme Court (the Warren Court) that for the first time took seriously its responsibilities for protecting the rights of individuals under the Constitution.
2. Nixon's jousts with the Courts during Watergate. His Supreme Court appointments reflecting a 19th century view of the Court as the protector of big business and the powers of government against the rights of the people.
3. Reagan weighs in with a vengeance in the character of his appointments and attempted appointments. Bork and his view that if a personal right isn't specifically spelled out in the Constitution it doesn't exist. In saying that, Bork of course completely ignores the existence of the Ninth Amendment. It happens to say that: "the enumeration in the constitution of certain rights shall not be construed to deny or disparage others retained by the people." Bork disposes of that impediment to the justifiability of his

thinking by labeling the Ninth nothing but an "inkblot" on the Constitution (Barnett).

4. More insidious than the appointments, however, is the well-orchestrated anti-Court campaign from within and without the government that gathered intensity throughout the 80s and with a very strong assist from Limbaugh and his minions on talk radio that is just roaring along now. It's fascinating. A listener to almost any randomly chosen 10-minute stretch of Limbaugh's rantings will hear him attack each of these *institutions*, the Courts, the Congress, and the media, just during that span of time. It's a major part of his major message: "they're all no good. The only thing we need is one of *our own*" (and all his supporters know what that means) "in the White House."

   That's the campaign to destroy the public trust in the Federal Courts by incessantly braying the lie that by carrying out their duties to review the actions of the other two branches of government, at the Federal, and through the 14th Amendment the state, levels, for their constitutionality, they have arrogated legislative powers to themselves. It's a classic Republican ploy, when the Supreme Court hands down a decision they don't like, not to argue the substance of the case but rather to accuse the Court of "judicial legislation."

   They also yelp incessantly about "judicial self-restraint," but never bring it up when one of their own, like Antonin Scalia, advocates overturning a settled precedent that he happens not to like. Who cares about *stare decisis*, anyway?

5. Hack, hack, hack. That's what they're doing. It's like that Jesse Helms move of 1991 to remove from the Supreme Court the power to review legislation concerning prayer in the public schools. Thank God, that got nowhere. But I think that their ultimate goal is just to get the court out of the way.

6. The intimidation of Bill Clinton in his court appointments, by this campaign.

B. The Congress

1. The Republicans just love to blame everything that's wrong with the country on the Congress, especially the "Democrat Congress." In the 90s they love to do nothing better than pretend that they had nothing to do with the Federal government in the 70s and 80s, that they did not hold the Presidency for all but four years between 1968 and 1992. (Of course, when Ronald Reagan in particular was President, they loved to say everything was just wonderful, even while his policies were running those huge deficits, and give him all the credit for it.) No, it's all the fault of that Congress.

   And even after they won control of the Congress last year, they had a hard time giving up the line. Limbaugh, for example, still told people that Congress was bad, because it was taking away their independence and telling them what to do (March 1, 1995, at about 12:40PM EST). And this is a Republican Congress he helped to elect. So what's the implication of all that?

2. The Republicans have adopted several strategies designed to undermine Congressional power.

   a. Destroy the Public's Trust

   One is to destroy public trust in the institution, by lying/distorting if necessary. For example, the House "banking scandal" back in 1992. Many House members overdrew their accounts in the special office called a "bank" (it wasn't really one, because it had no general banking functions such as loan-making) in which their paychecks were automatically deposited. As I recall, not one House member failed to eventually make the money good, usually when their paycheck came in. The Republicans and their minions presented this as a "check-kiting" scheme. It was, of course, nothing of the sort.

   b. Shift the Constitutional Balance of Power

   Another is to undermine its constitutionally mandated powers, by such measures as the line item veto. That measure would drastically shift the balance of power over spending money to the Executive Branch.

c. Amateurism in the Congress

They love to talk about having "the people" "take back" "their government." To that end, they promote amateurism in the Congress, using the "oh, anyone can do this job" to further denigrate the institution. Of course, amateurism is just what is needed at the top of this ever more complex country of ours. But if there are only amateurs in the Congress while there are professionals in the Executive Branch, who do you think is going to control things? This amateurism bit is just another ploy to concentrate power in the Executive Branch, which they expect to win back control of in 1996, of course.

d. Control by the "Special Interests"

Another is to complain, long and loud, about how moneyed interests and lobbyists control the Congress (which more and more they do do these days). The Republicans usually refer to such influences, however, not as moneyed interests and lobbyists, but as the "special interests." It was Reagan who had attached that term to agencies representing the interests of labor, various minorities, and environmental preservation. Such agencies have in fact relatively little influence on the workings of the Federal government. (Proof of that statement? Just look at how poorly the interests of such groups have fared, even under Clinton.) But a public which thinks that 15% of the Federal budget goes to foreign aid (it's less than 1.5%) is easily confused and/or misled.

It is, of course, the Republicans who are most beholden to the corporate and financial interests which shower the Congress with campaign contributions (and other perks when possible), and who also make sure that no legislation is ever passed that is designed either to reduce the power and influence of lobbyists (first by just exposing them to public scrutiny), or to remove the power of the private purse from participation in the public's elections.

e. Undermine the Democratic Process

Another "undermining strategy" is to give Congressional minorities control of lawmaking, undermining the democratic process there. The three-fifths rule for raising the Federal deficit offered as part of the "Balanced Budget" amendment which failed to pass earlier this year would have done that. So too would have the provision many of the famous 1994 "Freshman Class" of Republicans in the House wanted, to require a three-fifths vote in both Houses for raising taxes.

Note that I haven't been talking much about anti-democracy here. But that theme is part and parcel of the whole strategy to get the American public in line with untrammeled Executive Branch decision-making (the essence of fascism). We seem to be moving in the direction of the Hitlerian "Ja vote."

To hell with representative, deliberative, democracy. Let's substitute the hot button, simplistic, Initiative and Referendum method of legislating and even of amending the constitution in certain states. Let's for example remove from the people in local communities the right to democratically enact ordinances protecting the civil rights of homosexuals and call it democracy. That's what the so-called "Amendment 2," adopted through Initiative and Referendum, did in Colorado.

Let's put legislation into the Constitution, with a "Balanced Budget" amendment, limiting the ability of any Congress in the future to democratically decide to increase the Federal deficit or (horrors) increase taxes.

Let's elect Presidents, like Ross Perot, who claim to "know the will of the American people" intuitively, just like the Spanish dictator Generalissimo Francisco Franco (like Sen. Joe McCarthy, a hero of Pat Buchanan's father) claimed to "embody the soul of Spain."

f. Term Limits

And finally there is term limits, the ultimate anti-democracy/weaken-the-Congress weapon. It was originally designed to facilitate Republican takeover of the Congress and the State legislatures, and enhance the "amateurism-in-government" (read "in the Legislative Branch") movement. It's ironic that those goals were achieved at the national and many states levels through the use of the democratic process: as of the opening of the 104th Congress in 1995, close to 190 of 435 House members were at the beginning of either their first or second terms.

The term limit movement had begun back in the 1980s (Town of Brookhaven; Woodruff). The ostensible reasons for the movement were to (Kamber): break up the lock that special interests have on today's Congress; produce legislatures that are truly responsive to the people; reduce the powers, perquisites and fundraising advantages of incumbency that make elections inherently unfair; stop institutional corruption; infuse legislatures with new talent and fresh ideas; enhance democracy because most voters favor them. It was claimed that the term-limits movement was bi-partisan.

In a thorough analysis, my good friend Vic Kamber showed that, contrary to the latter claim, the term limit movement, especially as it was applied to the United States Congress, was almost entirely a creature of the Republican Party and their allies in a variety of reactionary political organizations.

As to the substantive claims, none hold water. The only way to deal with the lock that the moneyed interests and the lobbyists do have on Congress today and make the Congress "truly responsive to the people" is to enact meaningful campaign finance and lobbying reforms, something the Republicans are wholly opposed to. (And why not? For example, no two Congress people are more beholden to special interests than Newton Gingrich in the House [drug and health care companies] and Phil Gramm in the Senate [Texas banks, corporations, "investment advisors," and S&Ls] [Sherrill].) Term limits would just provide a revolving door for a stream of Right-Wing

Reactionary candidates who could raise big campaign bucks from the Right-Wing moneyed interests.

As noted, in 1994 the Republicans themselves showed how just effectively using the democratic process itself can bring a limit to anyone's term. Even that useless old evergreen Tom Foley got it in the last election. There is absolutely no provable direct connection between corruption and either long-time Congressional membership or newness to the institution. Both the new *and* the old can be corrupted, and are, from time to time. New legislators may bring new ideas, but they are not necessarily ones that will benefit the country as a whole in the long run. Just look at Gingrich's "Contract on America," so avidly supported by the "Freshman Class" (*Author's Note: That was the group of Right-Wing Reactionary Representatives newly elected in 1994*).

Finally, "enhance democracy" by permitting those people voting at one point in time to deny democratic choices to the people as a whole at any other points in time in the future? Ha. Voting by itself doesn't guarantee democracy. It's how the voting is done. Just because the mass of voters like an idea, doesn't make it a democratic one. Term limits remove the *democratic* right of any voter to pick the representative of his or her choice, just because that representative has run out of terms. That's undemocratic.

Hitler's dictatorial powers were voted to him in 1933 under the so-called "Enabling Act" by the democratically elected German Reichstag (Davidowicz). (Nazi state terror had already begun, both inside and outside the parliament by the time that vote was taken. But the original elections that brought Hitler to power as a minority Chancellor were constitutional and democratic. And it should be noted that the non-Nazi elected Right-Wing members of the Reichstag were perfectly happy to vote for Hitler's gang, even though it was already clear that it would use violence as a major weapon of governing.)

Hitler's dictatorial powers were then confirmed to him a couple of times in national votes where the choices were "yes," for him, or "no," against. There was always voting in the Soviet Union—for one slate of candidates. Did those events mean that Nazi Germany and the Soviet Union were democratic?

No. The term limits movement is just part of the anti-democracy, anti-Congress strategy being pursued by the Republicans. Nothing more. Nothing less.

C. The Media

Creating the myths of the "predominant liberal media," and the "voiceless conservative masses." Using the dominant reactionary talk radio to control political discussion in the U.S., all the while pretending that Right-Wing arm doesn't exist and there is no "fairness." Actually, there is no "fairness," but not in the sense the Right talks about it. True liberals have very little exposure on either political radio or television. And when they are permitted to appear, unlike the reactionaries who appear uncontested on all the electronic media all of the time, they are almost always presented in a "politically balanced" setting.

As for the print media, except when they from time to time just present some embarrassing facts, like the proportion of American children growing up in poverty, or get into political exposes, the "mainstream media" are hardly hotbeds of liberalism. But the Right continues to characterize them that way.

Bash, bash, bash. Knock 'em down. Undermine them. Destroy the public trust in them, just as the public trust in the Congress and the Courts is being destroyed. That's the third protector of democracy in America on its way to biting the dust.

It's fascinating. Of course, the Republicans attack the *President* all the time. But they never attack the institution of the Presidency like they attack the *institutions* of the

Congress, the Courts, and the free media. That really does give the game away, doesn't it?

Author's Note: At this point, Louis appears to have stopped writing on this subject. Whether something else grabbed his attention at the time or he simply ran out of gas, we'll never know.

References:

Barnett, R.E., *The Rights Retained by the People*, Fairfax, VA: George Mason University, 1989.

Davidowicz, L.S., *The War Against the Jews: 1933-45*, New York: Holt, Rinehart, and Winston, 1975, Part I, p. 51.

Kamber, V., "The Term Limitations Movement," *The O'Leary/Kamber Report*, 1211 Connecticut Ave. NW, Washington, DC, 20036, Vol. 6, Issue 1, Fall 1991, pp. 12.

Sherrill, R., "The Phil Gramm File," *The Nation*, March 6, 1995, p. 301.

Town of Brookhaven, New York, "Town Report Update," August, 1993.

Woodruff, J., "1991 U.S. Taxpayer Opinion Poll," 6137 Lincoln Road, P.O. Box 11839, Alexandria, VA 22312.

APPENDIX IV
On Morality and the Uses of the Law
Dino Louis
1992

[Author's Note: For a related Louis essay, actually predating this one, see Appendix V.]

Definitions

"Moral," the dictionary tells us, means (Webster's):

"1. of, pertaining to, or concerned with right conduct or the distinction between right and wrong. 2. concerned with the principles or rules of right conduct; … 4. founded on the fundamental principles of right conduct rather than on legalities, enactment or custom: moral rights; moral obligations. …

"Morality" means (Webster's):

"1. conformity to the rules of right conduct; … 4. a doctrine or system of morals. …"

These definitions and their differing interpretations provide some of the explanation for the never-ending struggles in this country over just what is "moral thought and behavior," and the closely related question on the proper role of government in private decision making on matters of personal thought and conduct. From shortly after the founding of the Massachusetts Bay Colony, in this land there have been two strongly held schools of thought on these questions. The first can be called the Fundamentalist, legal-prescription/legal-proscription school, the second the Jeffersonian, civil-libertarian, freedom-centered school. The Fundamentalists in particular have held great political power and influence from time to time.

The members of that school have always had a strong foundation in one or more (Christian, often Fundamentalist) religious denominations. They hold that there is a clearly defined set of "rules of right conduct" based in their particular religious theory, that they know with certainty what those rules are, and that the rules are absolute. Further, "morality" means "conformity to the rules" as those rules have been laid out by themselves, for everyone, religious adherents and non-adherents alike.

The Fundamentalists allow no deviation from their interpretation of what is moral, so sure are they that their interpretation is the right one for everyone, in absolute terms. They are particularly concerned with those parts of the definitions of moral and morality which pertain to sex and sexual behavior.

A major feature of the Fundamentalists' position on morality and moral behavior is their heavy reliance on the use of the criminal law for the propagation and enforcement of their views among the population. The failure of the religious forces to effectively sell their product through their own large markets, the churches, religious publications, and the religious and Right-Wing media, lead them to demand that their prescripts and proscripts be given the force of law.

Although the Fundamentalists are considered to be very strong in this country, and they are, politically, actually their position indicates moral weakness, not strength. (Unfortunately, no one in the opposition to the Fundamentalists seems to recognize that fact.) In one sense, their position is a reflection of a deep-seated (and well-founded) fear that without the force of the law behind them, relatively few people would listen. It is unfortunate for all Americans that the Fundamentalists do not have more confidence either in their teachings or the American people.

Thus in reality the Fundamentalists put little faith (if I may use that word) in the value of exhortation, persuasion, reason, education, and example. They seem to have little faith themselves that the latter tools will be effective in achieving their goals.

To the extent that the Fundamentalists are forced to rely on the criminal law to enforce their views on personal thoughts and behaviors, to that extent is the fundamental weakness of their positions and their lack of confidence in their ability to change peoples' thoughts and behaviors by moral suasion revealed.

Thomas Jefferson presented the civil-libertarian response to the Fundamentalist position in his famous "Bill for Establishing Religious Freedom" in Virginia (1779):

> "Well aware that Almighty God hath created the mind free; that all attempts to influence it by temporal punishments or burdens, or by civil incapacitations, tend only to beget habits of hypocrisy and meanness, … that the impious presumption of legislators and rulers, civil as well as ecclesiastical, who, being themselves but fallible and uninspired men, have assumed dominion over the faith of others, setting up their own opinions and modes of thinking as the only true and infallible, and as such endeavoring to impose them on others, … that our civil rights have no dependence on our religious opinions, …
>
> "Be it therefore enacted by the General Assembly … that all men shall be free to profess, and by argument to maintain, their opinions in matters of religion, and that the same shall in nowise diminish, enlarge, or affect their civil capacities."

In certain contexts, the Fundamentalists deny that they are dealing with religious matters. In those cases they like to frame the issues in such terms as "promoting family values." But the concerns of the Fundamentalists are religious matters, fundamentally. How do we know this? First, most often those who raise the issues are religious figures themselves, or are closely associated with religious denominations. Second, and more significant, the Fundamentalists usually characterize as a "sin" the behavior to which they want to apply the criminal sanction, whether that behavior is to have an abortion, to live as a homosexual, or to view/hear art the Fundamentalists describe as "objectionable." Therefore, the behavior must be punished/protected against. "Sin," of course, is a religious, not a secular concept. Third, in dealing with human behaviors they find objectionable, they often invoke "God's law" as the justification for imposing a criminal penalty on those behaviors.

Conceptual Conflict

There are three aspects of the Fundamentalist approach to morals and morality that lead to the development of the second school of moral thought in America, so eloquently espoused by Jefferson. It has stood in opposition to the first school since Roger Williams broke away from the Massachusetts Bay Colony to found the Rhode Island Colony in 1636.

Absolute Moral Values. The first zone of disagreement between the two schools is that, while there may be some "fundamental principles of right conduct" laid down somewhere, there is, in political and moral fact, no general agreement as to what they all are. If asked, each of us could come up with a list. But the lists would differ, even among people who consider themselves to be quite moral.

Take murder, for example, a violation of one provision of one of the most basic components of Western Society's basic moral code, the Ten Commandments, to wit: "Thou shalt not kill." Written in absolute terms, is it not? Well, it happens that there are some generally agreed-to exceptions to the rule, like "except in self-defense," or "except when your country's leaders tell you it's in the national interest." And, "except when a person has been found guilty of committing one of a list of crimes."

Further modifying this particular "fundamental principle" are differences among people concerning the exceptions. While virtually everyone would kill in self-defense, a significant number will not do so in war, considering it to be immoral. An even larger number oppose capital punishment, considering it to be immoral. What appears on first glance to be a "fundamental principle" of Judeo-Christian morality turns out to be not so fundamental after all. It is subject to modification. And among thoroughly responsible people there are strongly held differences over what modifications are moral.

The Role of the Law in the Management of Morality. The second difference between the two schools is their view of the relationship between the law and morality. The Fundamentalist school ignores that part of the definition of moral that says that it is "founded on the fundamental principles of right conduct rather than on legalities, enactment or custom. …" They apparently feel that without the force of law, few if any persons would follow their precepts (and thus they make them into prescripts).

This reliance on the criminal law to enforce a particular position on moral questions is nothing new in American history. For example, at the time of the Scopes "monkey trial" in the 1920s, the Springfield *Republican* noted that William Jennings Bryan, the defender of Tennessee's law against teaching evolution in the public schools, was (Greene):

> "… seeking to use the powers of government as a fortified line bristling with the terrorism of the criminal courts, and the threat of criminal penalties, as a defense for his fundamentalism."

Now, there certainly is a list of behaviors which almost everyone agrees is immoral: murder, (other than in self-defense, war, and for many, capital punishment), rape, robbery, burglary, embezzlement, fraud, and so forth. Society endorses the view that these particular acts are immoral by using the force of law to support it. But in the minds of many members of society, the list of immoral behaviors subject to *legal* penalty is, and should be, relatively short. This is because people's lists of "fundamental principles" differ so markedly.

Further, given that morality is by definition not based in "legalities," the Jeffersonian view as reflected in the Bill of

Rights is that thought and behavior on moral questions should be intruded upon by the law only exceptionally, in terms of the list agreed to by almost everyone, described above. It may be fairly concluded that the Jeffersonian view is that even if there is somewhere some absolute set of "fundamental principles" governing thought and behavior, no one knows yet what it is. Further, the Fundamentalists' view of precisely what it is carries no more weight than anyone else's, and there are and can be perfectly legitimate differences of opinion on that question.

Morality and Dumbness. In the Fundamentalist view people are basically dumb. That is, on matters ranging from deciding which movies to see, to choosing which books to read, to looking at "sexually provocative" works of art, ("dirty" and "obscene," are two other favorite words the Fundamentalists use to describe written, visual, or auditory materials they don't happen to like or find personally offensive), to choosing which recreational mood-altering drugs to use, people will invariably make the "wrong" choice. People simply cannot be trusted to do the right thing (however that is defined). Of course, it is the Fundamentalists who define right and wrong in that context. Then they go on to demand that the law be used to prevent people from getting access to materials the Fundamentalists find objectionable. In some cases they also advocate punishing those who produce/create the stuff, and/or punishing users just for using.

The civil-libertarian view is that most people are basically smart. Most of the time they will behave in ways which are fundamentally healthy and positive *for them*, *if*, (and that's a big if), they are given appropriate information about dangers, if any, and they are not subject to continued promotion of negative behaviors, (e.g., pro-drug use tobacco and alcohol advertising; pro-gambling advertising [both public and private].)

With accurate information about, let us say, the sexual content of certain movies, most people will make the choice to view or not to view that will work well for them. If people were not subject to the overwhelming barrage of pro-drug advertising that they are in this country, there would be much less drug use. In those countries in which it is widely available, sex education does work to, for example, reduce the spread of venereal disease and teenage pregnancy. In the civil-libertarian view, most people can perfectly well decide on their own what television and radio programs they want to watch/listen to and want their children to watch/listen to, if they simply have an idea of what's in the program.

As an example of the latter proposition, a garden variety morning drive-time radio show like WFAN/New York's "Imus in the Morning." The show features an egomaniacal, nasty, sexist, short-tempered, politically-reactionary host who loves to engage in personal put-downs, high school locker-room scatological humor, and discussions of the breast size and dating behavior of the (invariably female) announcers of the show's traffic report. He is surrounded primarily by a group of sycophantic yes men who egg him on in his transparent *double entendre*, painfully unfunny, pseudo-sexual shtick (certainly "objectionable" to many a Fundamentalist).

The only voice of sanity is a long-suffering sports announcer, who, as the butt of an unending series of lame barbs emanating from the host's foul mouth, must either get paid very well or be unable to find another job. But do Americans need someone to tell them whether or not they can listen to this show? No. Obviously any intelligent person will simply choose, on their own, not to.

Taking this line of analysis a bit further, most people can decide on their own whether or not a photography exhibition with a couple of homo-erotic photos in it is for them or not. Most people viewing an exhibition of art of the American Frontier can decide whether or not they agree with a museum guide text that interprets that art as glorifying Western imperialism, male chauvinism, and racism. They don't need some Senator from Alaska (Thomas) making that choice for them. Of course, the spread of information and the idea that people, especially children, can make their own choices based on accurate scientific, historical, and cultural information is abhorrent to the Fundamentalists.

Moral Questions and the Constitution

The civil-libertarian view on morality is, of course, supported by the approach to the matter embodied in the Declaration of Independence and the Constitution. In the Declaration, Jefferson put forth the concept of "unalienable Rights," "*among which* are life, liberty, and the pursuit of happiness." Further, Jefferson noted, "it is to *secure these Rights* that Governments are instituted among men" (emphasis added both times). According to Jefferson, and presumably all those men who took their lives in their hands and signed the Declaration of Independence, that is what governments are for: "to secure these rights."

Our Constitution in its Preamble calls upon the Federal government to "secure the Blessings of Liberty to ourselves and our posterity." And then in the Bill of Rights, the Constitution proscribes specific Federal legal action dealing with speech, religion, the press, and assembly. Through its protection of un-enumerated rights in the Ninth Amendment, the Constitution proscribes government activity in many areas of sexual conduct that so concern the Fundamentalists.

It is important to remember that the Constitution is very specific in listing what the government *can* do vis-a-vis personal rights (and expansive when it comes to government's powers to regulate the economy). There is no basis in the plain language of the Constitution for the Borkist view that government can do anything it wants to limit personal rights, as long as such action is not specifically prohibited (and for him the prohibited list is minuscule). Nor is there any basis for the Borkist view that unless a personal right is specifically mentioned in the Constitution, it doesn't exist (Abrams). That view flies in the face of both the Declaration and the Constitution, especially the Ninth Amendment. (No wonder Judge Bork characterized the latter in terms of an "inkblot" [Barnett]. It just doesn't happen to fit with his authoritarian, Fundamentalist, anti-Constitutionalist view of what government should be all about.)

For a majority of Americans, the Constitution and the Declaration mean that the law should stay completely out of regulating their personal thoughts and for the most part out of regulating their behaviors, as long as those do not infringe upon the rights of others. Most Americans also agree that the law should also stay out of the determination of the composition of lists of moral principles, except to the extent that most people agree that certain behaviors should be curtailed by the rule of law because such behaviors impinge directly on the rights of others.

The Role of the Law Inside the Family

Much of the current Right-Wing program on matters of conscience, and on matters of liberty and freedom of choice, focuses on children and the family. Thus, minors should not be able to get abortions without parental consent and children should not have access to pornography or "obscene" materials. Their programs to deny certain kinds of health services to certain people and deny access to certain materials to everyone is based on the premise that the family should be involved in making decisions in the named matters.

In terms of definition, "pornography" is a technical term, usually referring to visual, written, or aural material designed to stimulate sexual interest and arousal. It must be recognized, however, that "obscenity" is something that exists only in the eye of the beholder. The Supreme Court has recognized this principle in the "community standards" rule.

I think that most would agree that the family should be involved in decision making about, for instance, rules to be applied to the sexual behavior of the children at a given age. The disagreement comes over how this involvement should be achieved. The Fundamentalists would accomplish this end by law enforcement. They want to put the criminal justice system to stand *in loco parentis*. They want to interject the police and the courts into the most private precincts of family life.

Certainly, many teenage girls who become pregnant and want an abortion already go to their parents for advice, counsel, support, and assistance. They, for the most part, are in families that are strong, without any need to depend upon the law as a crutch. There are a few seven-year-olds who somehow get the money and get out to the record store to buy the latest recording of *2 Live Crew*, family preferences to the contrary notwithstanding. But there are not too many of those.

In cases in which the girl doesn't go to her parents or the seven-year-old does buy the recording without his/her parents knowing, one must say that there is a breakdown, a weakness, in the family structure and intra-family communications. The civil-libertarian position on dealing with this problem is that law enforcement is an entirely inappropriate, in most cases ineffective, measure to deal with the problem.

Actually, the Fundamentalist position on these matters is one that would weaken, not strengthen, the family structure. To the extent that the law relieves families of the obligation and necessity to talk about and establish family rules for dealing with subjects like sex, abortion, obscenity, and morality, to that extent the family structure is weakened.

The criminal law has little place inside the family except for dealing with intra-family violence, sexual abuse, and theft. Nor should laws be enacted to deal with intra-family problems that exist on a small scale (how many seven-year-olds actually do get out to the store, with the money, to buy the latest tape that some professional "moralist" has labeled as "dirty"),—laws that would deprive millions of adults of their Constitutional rights. On the other hand, the development of educational and other support programs which will strengthen the family structure so that socially productive choices can be made on these issues should be strongly supported.

Morality and American Values

What in the Fundamentalist position on morality and the law that is not consistent with the American values reflected in the Declaration and the Constitution, is not that they hold particular positions on abortion, sexual preference, obscenity or the like. Nor is the content of those positions (i.e., abortion is wrong, homosexuality is wrong, the visual depiction of sexual intercourse is wrong) not consistent with American values.

Under the Constitution, the Fundamentalists are fully entitled to hold their views, to express themselves freely on them, and to attempt without the use of force to educate/persuade others to agree with them and act accordingly. However, under the Constitution, the governmental means for implementing the American dream expressed in the Declaration of Independence, no one is entitled to enforce upon others their particular views on morals and morality by the use of the law, except in such limited matters as "Thou shalt not kill (with exceptions)."

References:

Abrams, F., Foreword to R.E. Barnett, ed., *The Rights Retained by the People: The History and Meaning of the Ninth Amendment*, Fairfax, VA: George Mason University Press, 1989, (for the Cato Institute), p. viii.

Barnett, R.E., "Introduction: James Madison's Ninth Amendment," in R.E., Barnett, ed., *The Rights Retained by the People: The History and Meaning of the Ninth Amendment*, Fairfax, VA: George Mason University Press, 1989, (for the Cato Institute), p. 1.

Greene, L., *The Era of Wonderful Nonsense*, New York: 1939, p. 152.

Jefferson, T., "An Act for Establishing Religious Freedom, passed in the Assembly of Virginia in the beginning of the year 1786," reprinted in Koch, A., and Peden, W., *The Life and Selected Writings of Thomas Jefferson*, New York: The Modern Library, 1944, 1972 (Random House), p. 311, 1779.

Thomas, E., "Time to Circle the Wagons," *Newsweek*, 5/27/91, p. 70.

Webster's Encyclopedic Unabridged Dictionary of the English Language, Portland House: New York, 1989.

APPENDIX V
On Poverty, Sin, Regulation, and Freedom
Dino Louis
1991

Regulation and Ideology

A basic theme of the Declaration of Independence, to which I have consistently referred in my work, is that all men are created equal and endowed by their creator with certain unalienable rights. This theme holds that the primary motivator of human behavior is the fulfillment of these rights. A second basic theme is that the role of government is "to secure these rights," that is, to aid our citizens in that endeavour. Under the U.S. Constitution, the Federal government has powers provided by the General Welfare clause, the interstate commerce clause, and a variety of other provisions which project it into specific economic activities.

The views of the Right-Wing, Republican, Religious, and Other to the contrary notwithstanding, other Constitutional clauses, to say nothing of the Bill of Rights, specifically preclude the government from interfering with any person's freedom to make individual choices on such matters as speech and religion. It is thus clear that the Founding Fathers held that the role of government is to protect freedom, liberty, and rights of personal conscience of each individual, while regulating economic activity for the benefit of all.

However, there is abroad in the land another line of thinking on the proper role of government. It is not as clearly articulated as the one defined by the Declaration and the Constitution. Nevertheless, as stated by the Donald Wildmons and the Phyllis Schlafleys, the George H.W. Bushes and the Jesse Helmses, the

Pat Buchanans and the Pat Robertsons, it is understandable enough. This view holds that the primary role of government is to deal with sin, as sin is defined by the holders of this position.

In this view, the role of government thus becomes to protect people from being exposed to "sinful things," like homo-erotic art or "dirty words" in popular music, and punish them by criminal sanctions if they commit a sin, like taking a currently illegal mood-altering recreational drug. It is up to the government, of course, to determine just which personal behaviors are "sinful." In practice, that determination varies over time. Its logic, if any, escapes simple understanding. At the same time, the holders of this view of the role of government would have our side largely ignore the Constitution's prescription for action in the economic realm.

This essay presents the case for the position that the values of personal freedom and unalienable rights should be the principal motors of national policy. This philosophy stands in direct opposition to the one that holds that the prevention of sin and punishment for it should be the principal motors of national policy. Representing the two major ideological camps in the United States, they can be termed the Constitutionalist and the Religious Fundamentalist.

Interpretation of Our Founding Documents

The contrasting positions of the Constitutionalists and the Religious Fundamentalists on all questions of policy are epitomized by their answers to the two major domestic policy questions with which this country is currently, sometimes violently, wrestling:

1. How are economic benefits and burdens to be distributed among the people? (In other words, what is the role of government, representing the people as a whole, in regulating economic behavior and in evening out inequality of economic opportunity?)
2. Just what is meant by the term "personal freedom"?

> (In other words, what is the role of government, if any, representing the people as a whole, in controlling the thought processes and regulating the personal behaviors of individuals?)

The Right is fond of saying that one of their primary goals is to "end government regulation," to "get government off your back." In fact, they are not against government regulation across the board. They may want to get government off your back but they also want to get it into your mind and into your bedroom. Only the Libertarians take a reasonably consistent stand against government regulation of all kinds of human activity (like the Reaganite/Bushists ignoring the Constitution on this question, but from the other end of the spectrum). The Religious Fundamentalists are actually in favor of a great deal of government regulation of: freedom of choice in the outcome of pregnancy; prayer in school; sexual preference and conduct; artistic expression; the use as well as the sale of recreational mood-altering drugs.

Thus there is little disagreement on the question of *whether* government should regulate human behavior. Rather, as noted above, the disagreement concerns only *what* should be regulated. The Constitutionalists favor active government regulation of economic behavior with minimal regulation of personal behavior in matters of conscience. In contrast, the Religious Fundamentalists (and other Rightists as well) favor a great deal of personal behavior regulation with limited regulation of the economy (Brownstein). And that regulation focuses on protecting wealth and the economic power of the already wealthy.

Thus, while the Religious Fundamentalists *say* they are against governmental regulation of economic activity, they are in fact against the regulation of only *certain kinds* of economic activity. For example, they are in favor of *de*regulation of, for example, capital investment policy, bank practices, transportation and energy policy, environmental pollution and destructive activities, industrial working conditions, micro and macro health and safety.

However, they are certainly for the regulation of, for example, the national monetary system through the Federal Reserve Bank (to control their bugaboo of monetary inflation), the setting of interest rates by the Federal Reserve and the Treasury, the macro operations of the financial markets, the operations of trade unions (to decrease their power wherever possible), strikes by public employees, secondary boycotts, the retention of seniority rights by striking workers, freely negotiated minority set-asides and affirmative action programs, and taxation policy to further benefit the wealthy and the large corporations. As I have noted before, one prominent outcome of the Right-Wing/Reaganite approach to Federal government regulation of the economy is the redistribution of wealth from the poor to the rich (Phillips).

But, the question must be asked, which approach embodies true American values? The Declaration of Independence (and the military action taken pursuant to it) established this nation and laid out the rationale for its independent existence. Its plain language can be taken as our guide to what American values are. The Declaration says that men "are endowed by their Creator with certain unalienable rights, that among these are life, liberty, and the pursuit of happiness," and that "to secure these rights, Governments are instituted among men." That's the primary function of government: securing the rights to life, liberty and the pursuit of happiness.

Thus, pursuant to the Declaration, the function of government is not to make everybody happy, but to provide everybody with the opportunity to pursue happiness. Among other things, happiness requires a reasonable economic standard of living. Standard of living is the part of the state of mind and being which constitute happiness that government can reasonably address. Therefore, government's function in relation to the pursuit of happiness is to be found primarily in the economic realm. That function focuses principally upon the achievement of a reasonably level economic playing field.

On the other hand, according to the Declaration it is not a function of American government to tell people what to think, what to believe in, what to feel, what to like and dislike. Rather, it is to ensure people that they can make free choices in these various areas of human thought and endeavour, assuming that by doing so they are not actively harming anyone else. The Preamble to the Constitution, and the Bill of Rights, confirm this view. Constitutionalists are in tune with both the letter and the spirit of our founding documents. Despite their prattle about "patriotism," the Right stands squarely opposed to both the letter and the spirit of our founding documents.

The Philosophical Basis of the Contrasting Views on Government Regulation

At the heart of the dispute on regulation of the economy and redistribution of the fruits of production is a question which has riven Western capitalist societies since the establishment of the Elizabethan Poor Laws in late 16th century England: Is poverty the fault of the poor or, worse yet, a sign of punishment for sin, or is it primarily the product of social and economic factors beyond the control of the individual? The Religious Fundamentalists and their political allies, powerful forces in our society, firmly hold to the view that poverty is the fault of the poor. According to this view it is appropriate to attempt to help the poor through private charity. The latter recognizes the poor's state of "less eligibility," as the 19th century English Poor Law "reformers" put it. (The "less eligibility" concept is indeed based on the view that poverty is the fault of the poor. Since the poor are at fault for their poverty, they are "less eligible" to receive/benefit from a variety of the good things that life has to offer to those who are not poor and therefore not culpable.) However, this view holds, any government regulation of and intervention in the economy, for the purpose of dealing with poverty, not based upon the view that the poor are either at fault for their poverty or being punished for some personal bad act, is in no way justifiable.

Furthermore, any government attempts to redistribute income and the fruits of production from the rich to the middle class and the poor constitute an entirely inappropriate interference with the natural order of things (although, as pointed out above, transfers of wealth upwards are just fine).

The progressive, Constitutionalist, view is that sin plays little, if any, role in determining social and economic standing. For most people, social and economic standing are much more related to opportunity, geography, training, education, social class of parents, race, available employment, and so forth. Likewise, Constitutionalists tend not to view personal behaviors in terms of sin. Thus, government has a very limited role in "protecting people from temptation." Likewise, engaging in such behaviors should be punished, in the Constitutionalists' view, only when they result in palpable harm to others.

These contrasting views raise an interesting question: Why is it that many of those who would leave thought and personal behavior only loosely regulated by government generally favor regulation of the economy, while most of those who want an unregulated economy desire closely regulated thought and personal behavior?

There is surely no simple answer to this question. But part of it is to be found in the will of the wealthy to have as little interference as possible in their economic lives. And the Right's concomitant interest in limiting personal liberty can be found in part in an examination of the relationship between poverty and sin, as it is seen by those who hold that poverty is the fault of the poor.

Poverty and Sin

In the view of those who hold that poverty and sin are interconnected, there are two possible causes of poverty. One, a person is poor because he is weak, weakness is a sin, and poverty is a physical representation of his/her inadequacy. Further, poverty is the punishment for the sin of weakness. A second explanation is that whether strong or weak, a person is or becomes poor through having sinned in some other area of life and is being economically punished for that infraction.

Certainly the concept of sin is central to the thinking of many Rightists. They cast so many domestic and foreign policy issues in moral terms, in the formulations of "right" and "wrong," "good" and "bad." To do the wrong thing is to sin; to do what's right is only to free one of sin (rather than doing the right thing for its own sake). Just listen to William Bennett, Reagan's Secretary of Education, Bush's first "Drug Czar," on the nature of the drug problem (Morley; Weinraub):

- "The drug crisis is a crisis of authority."
- "Drugs obliterate morals, values, character, our relations with each other and our relation to God."
- "Drug use, we say, is wrong."

And who can forget that President Bush, having run through oil, jobs, and "naked aggression will not stand," as reasons for engaging in the Gulf War, finally cast it as a moral crusade against "wrong" (1991).

The Regulation of Sin

Given that the problem is sin and sinning, one solution is punishment. This way of thinking, for example, underlies the Bush/Bennett "Drug War." In this kind of thinking, fault and sinning are equated. Therefore, in dealing with economic issues, it becomes appropriate for the poor to be punished for being poor. An unregulated economy certainly accomplishes that desired outcome.

Another solution to the problem of sin and sinning is to protect the susceptibles from temptation. The Religious Fundamentalists regard thoughts and personal behaviors like viewing pornography, having an abortion, or being homosexual, as sinful. History has shown clearly that for the most part such behaviors will go unpunished, in this life at least, unless government does the punishing.

Furthermore, many people will engage in such activities, if only given the opportunity to do so. Therefore, according to the Religious Fundamentalists, and their Rightist political allies, to protect society from these sins government should vigorously protect people against the temptation to engage in them. This is best accomplished, so the thinking goes, by curtailing or prohibiting the supply of the offending agent. If sin is indeed the enemy, its progenitors must either be actively protected against or banished.

Hence, from the Rightist perspective, government has only two regulatory functions: protecting people from, or punishing them for engaging in, sins of personal thoughts and behaviors. Both are related to the role of low economic status as a punishment for and reflection of a sinful state of being. Thus government should do nothing to interfere with the punishment of the economically sinful by the economy itself. However, government *should* actively punish those who are *personally* sinful, (as the Religious Fundamentalists define sin, of course: gambling and drinking alcoholic beverages are okay for most of them, sexual intercourse except for the purpose of reproduction is not). Government should also attempt to actively prevent any citizen from being exposed to the temptation to sinful personal behavior.

The Clash of Philosophies

Sin and dealing with it is certainly the central focus of many religions in this country, especially the Religious Fundamentalist sects on the Right. Thus it is no accident that separation of church and state, established and guaranteed by our Constitution is a major Right-Wing target. If the Religious Fundamentalists can breach this barrier, then they will indeed be able to employ fully the regulatory power of government to fight their battle against sin. Under Constitutionalism, the power of government is not to be used to fight theological battles.

Religious Fundamentalism and Constitutionalism thus reflect two strongly held, gut-level positions, based on very different philosophies of life. They are not easily reconciled by rational argument. In the 19th century the principal policy question the country faced concerned one aspect of the Declaration and the Bill of Rights: Did they apply to Negro slaves?

Today the questions are even broader:

- What is the true meaning of the Declaration of Independence, the Preamble to the Constitution, and the Bill of Rights, spelling out as they do the purpose and functions of our government?
- Do the provisions of these documents apply to all the people of the land, regardless of social class, ethnicity, sexual identity, or ideology?
- What is the appropriate role for the government in dealing with poverty and personal freedom?

One must wonder if the current struggle over poverty and personal freedom, sin and the role of government, is the slavery issue of the next century. In 1820, Thomas Jefferson described the debate on the Missouri Compromise and its implications for the future of the Union as a "firebell in the night" (Garrity and Gay), warning of future bloody conflict in the United States over the issue of slavery. Is the present debate over poverty and personal freedom that firebell for us? Has the firebell indeed rung? Do we face a Second American Civil War?

I hope that we do not. I believe that it is possible for us to resolve our differences peacefully. But to do this, I believe that some progressive overarching political philosophy is essential. And central to that philosophy would be the concept that sin and its punishment are not appropriate symbols of either the American dream or the American way.

Government Regulation of Economic Activity

Turning to the issue of government regulation of economic activity, it is vitally important to note that it is an activity primarily *reactive* to circumstance. It is not a *proactive* Government function, as the Rightists would have us believe. It is a *response* to the activities of groups or individuals who attempt to unbalance the economic playing field or take certain actions that, say, pollute the environment, thereby significantly endangering the health and safety of others. In almost all cases, regulation of an economic activity is implemented for one of two reasons.

First, one or more of the groups affected by the activity feels that left unregulated, such activity would harm their interest(s). Second, it can be determined by a responsible agency based on scientific and historical evidence that if left unregulated such activity would produce a negative outcome for some significant number of people.

For a case in point, consider a neighborhood next to a toxic waste disposal company's plant. Regulation does not come first. The economic activity that in one way or another infringes on the rights or interests of others comes first. Regulation is then invoked to respond to that situation. Government regulation is thus often something to be desired or wished for. It would be much better and much cheaper for all concerned if individuals and corporations did not take actions infringing upon the rights and interests of others to the extent that government is forced to step in. Unfortunately, many individuals and corporations take such actions and regulation becomes necessary to protect the interests of the negatively affected parties in an effective way.

Because of the nature of economic activity, for better or for worse some kind of regulation is often necessary. This is true in health services, in maintaining a safe environment, in industrial production, in financial activity, and so forth. To make the *process* of regulation the focus of attention rather than *why* it is needed distorts reality. It diverts attention from real problems. If such problems did not occur, there would be no need to regulate the activities which cause them. But life in the United States, at least at present, is not like that.

For example, take the health care industry. It operated in a generally unregulated state until the late 60s. When left alone, it concentrated on acute care, ignored health promotion, built too many hospital beds, trained too many specialists, maldistributed its resources, did not achieve reasonable standards of quality, and became very, very expensive. If hospitals when left to their own devices did not build too many beds, there would be no need to regulate hospital bed construction. But they did build too many beds, as demonstrated, for example, in a classic study by the Institute of Medicine (1976). It happens that uncontrolled health care capital formation, of which hospital construction is a major part, has been a principal driver of health care costs (Bentkoven). Since direct government operation of the health care delivery system is not desirable in our country, the only alternative is regulation.

If chemical companies when left to their own devices did not dispose of hazardous wastes in ways that cause people to get sick, there would be no need to regulate hazardous waste disposal. But hazardous wastes are unsafely dumped, as attested to frequently in the media these days. If automobile companies built cars with engines that did not pollute air, there would be no need to regulate automobile exhaust emissions. If automobile companies on their own had put in all those safety devices which have made cars safer, there would have been no need to adopt national safety standards. But they did not volunteer to make their cars safer. Thus, regulation is a fact of life, necessary to achieving and maintaining balance between the various contending forces and interests in our society, and, as stated in the Preamble to the Constitution, to "promote the General Welfare."

Now, in most cases the bad results produced by unregulated activity are no more the product of evil intent on the part of their creators than are the regulations the opponents of regulation find so odious. (The major exception to the "no evil intent" finding is probably the financial industry.) Both bad outcomes and regulation are brought about by enterprises which did not think about the consequences of their actions outside of their own spheres of activity. Further, they did not take the concerns of others into account. But this should not be viewed as a question of morality. Nor should regulation.

Regulation is neither "good" nor "bad" on its own merits. It is what it is used *for* that determines its social utility, determines whether or not it is consistent with basic American values. Many Americans seem to have a reflex negative reaction when "government regulation" is mentioned in *general* terms. This appears to be a conditioned reflex carefully nurtured over the years by the Reaganite/Bushists and more generally by the Republicans. If only the government would stop interfering, they say, all our problems would be solved. It is those nasty and mean-spirited bureaucrats who are the source of all our troubles, they say.

Never mind the real problems that they are trying to tackle. Never mind the fact that most of the problems arose before government regulation was developed to deal with them, that regulation came on the scene precisely because there were problems that had to be dealt with. But don't confuse them with facts. Just get rid of regulation, substitute the "free market" and all will be well.

But when it comes down to specifics, to events and problems occurring in people's own neighborhoods and experience, many people sing a different tune. Think of such problems as:

- Toxic waste removal
- Solid waste disposal
- Nuclear electrical generating plant safety and waste disposal
- Nuclear weapons facilities waste disposal
- Ocean dumping
- Employee safety and health
- Health services quality
- Consumer product safety
- Consumer fraud protection
- Pure food and drug supply
- Safety in housing
- Security of bank deposits
- Fraud in financial and real property investment

- Preservation of price competition
- Transportation safety

In dealing with specific problems, the closer they are to home, literally and figuratively, the more most people want regulation, not its elimination.

Regulation and Freedom

Paradoxically, regulation is one of the mechanisms which we Americans have developed to keep our economy and society as free as it is. Regulation doesn't mean control and doesn't mean ownership. It means precisely what it says: regulation, that is: causing to operate in a smooth, predictable manner. In our society, the ownership of productive enterprises is almost entirely in private hands. While this pattern of ownership has produced many benefits for the American people, it has also created certain problems for us. These problems result from many different economic activities that produce profits for those who undertake them and benefits in terms of the production of useful goods and services. At the same time it can produce certain harmful outcomes.

For example, the indiscriminate chopping down of trees anywhere they are found can produce profits for the lumber companies, jobs for the lumberjacks, economic prosperity for the timber regions, and beautiful new wooden homes. At the same time, it can eventually result in the total elimination of the natural resource, loss of recreational opportunities, destruction of wildlife, disappearance of natural beauty, the disappearance of other industries (e.g., salmon fishing), and ultimately the loss of jobs and the industry itself. Thus there are interests to be balanced.

The Rightists tell us that the best way to balance interests is through the functioning of an entirely unregulated "free market." They fondly hark back to the 19th century, a time of virtually unregulated economic activity and industrialization. During that time, the U.S. experienced unprecedented economic growth. But from the early 19th century until the 1930s Great Depression, there was also an unending cycle of economic boom and bust. This cycle often produced very hard conditions for workers.

Too, when left alone, industry after industry wreaked havoc on its environment in the form of stinking rivers, foul air, and unsanitary living conditions for many workers. Modern-day parallels can be found in Eastern Europe where there was no countervailing regulatory power to rein in aggressive but narrowly focused and uncaring factory managers. In this country, these negative outcomes, slowly lead to the enactment of measures designed to control them and correct obvious social and economic imbalances.

But regulation has never been aimed at doing away with the "free market." If anything, regulation has attempted to preserve it. The impetus to limit the free market comes from within the economic system itself, in the form of the creation of monopolies. Most early government regulation in this country was aimed not at destroying the "free market" but at trying to preserve some semblance of it. For when left alone, industry after industry moves in the direction of monopoly. In fact, it was none other than John D. Rockefeller who in the 19th century said (Martin): "The day of combination is here to stay. Individualism has gone, never to return."

The trend to "combination" continues to this very day. The boom of consolidation and takeover in many major industries that occurred during the Reagan era has been a major feature of the unregulated "free market." Left to its own devices the "free market" actually moves inexorably towards fewer and fewer competitors. Where there were once many tens of U.S. automobile companies, there are now only three. There are only seven major airlines still in existence. After GE bought RCA, there was only one large domestic producer of consumer electronics left. It is no coincidence that the Anti-Trust Division of the Justice Department was gutted by the supposedly pro-"free market" Reagan Administration.

Public regulation of private economic activity aims to level the playing field, ensure economic competition in price, quantity, and quality of goods and services, and prevent damage to the environment and the interests of workers and consumers. In one sense, monopoly is a form of private regulation of economic activity, with the owners accountable to no one. Monopoly, as Mr. Rockefeller told us, is the natural consequence of unregulated free market activity. In most cases, it benefits the owners much more than it does the consumers or the workers. The only true alternatives to a regulated economy, then, are private monopoly or public monopoly, that is government ownership of economic enterprises. We certainly don't want the latter. So if we don't want the former either, we must go with a regulated market.

A Progressive Model for the Regulation of Economic Activity

The Regulatory Process

None of this is to say that the present regulatory process is perfect. Far from it, in fact. Several major problems can be identified. Government regulation follows the only model available when it began: that used in private industry at the time. Private industry internal regulation focused principally on cost control and the prevention of theft of time and product. By and large, it did not focus on program outcomes. The monitoring of program structures and processes was used as its principal approach. Regulation focused on how things were done rather than what they are done for and how good the outcomes are. (Only recently has the Japanese approach to internal regulation, which does focus on the quality of the product, started to make its way into American industry.) The majority of U.S. government regulating has followed the earlier model.

However, a great deal of government regulation has as its objective the achievement of social utility and balance. It faces identified problems of substance. Thus, in reality regulation is primarily concerned with program outcomes, even though most of its rules address program process. To solve the problems, to produce new results, government regulation should be reformed to focus on program outcomes.

Let us once again take as an example the health services industry. Most regulation in health services is designed to count things and people, prescribe minimum or maximum spaces, specify personnel qualifications, require minimum standards for materials, set reimbursement rates, define organizational structures, and so on. But patients are interested in outcomes: do I get better, how fast, any complications?

And so, instead of focusing on process, health care regulations could begin by setting out health and health care program objectives. They could then offer a variety of mechanisms to guide and assist the providers in achieving those objectives. Objectives could be stated in terms of improved access, more equitable distribution of services, more primary care, emphasis on prevention, reduced patient waiting time, improved provider-patient communication, reduced costs, goal-oriented research, needs-based educational programs, and certainly, improved health status for the people.

Logically, therefore, government regulation of the health care industry should be changed to the extent possible from the private enterprise mode of program process regulation to program outcome regulations. While program process regulation can easily produce rigidity and limitations in options for change, program outcome regulation would allow for creativity, flexibility, and concentration on program-solving. In this approach, desired goals and objectives are established and the regulatees are given broad latitude to choose among the available means of achieving them. An excellent example of this kind of regulation was the draft *National Guidelines for Health Planning* (USDHEW), issued in the last days of the Carter Administration [1980] and quickly rescinded by the Reagan Administration. It was a progressive and flexible form of planning, by objective.

Planning

Planning is the opposite side of the coin of regulation. There is a natural American aversion to planning, because it appears to interfere with personal freedom. However, to retain our position as a leading power we must begin planning now to deal with capital investment, the crumbling infrastructure, and degradation/depredation of the environment. Environmental issues can be well used politically to illustrate the need to introduce serious planning and make it respectable. Local examples to which people relate personally should be used to sell the concept. And of course, the success of the Gulf War was repeatedly laid to the extremely detailed planning which went into the military operations before they were actually carried out.

The Goals of Regulation

As pointed out above, the principal goal of regulation is to achieve social and economic balance in an otherwise free society. This approach to regulation of economic activity is based on the role of government as prescribed in the Preamble to the Constitution. Government regulation of economic activity should be used to the extent necessary to "insure domestic tranquility," to "promote the general Welfare" and as otherwise needed to achieve its goals. Regulation of the economy should be used as necessary to maintain a level playing field, to assure safety, promote healthy competition, and conserve and redevelop both economic and natural resources.

References:

Bentkoven, J., et al, "Development of an Evaluation Methodology for Use in Assessing Data Available to the Certificate-of-Need and Health Planning Program," Washington, D.C.: National Technical Information Service, 1982.

Brownstein, R., *Selecting a President*, Washington, DC: Public Citizen, 1980, pp. 94-96, 99-100.

Bush, G. H. W., "Address to the National Religious Broadcasters Convention," Washington, DC: The White House, January 28, 1991.

Garrity, J.A. and Gay, P. (Eds): *The Columbia History of the World*, New York: Harper and Row, 1981; pp. 897, 898.

Institute of Medicine, *A Policy Statement: Controlling the Supply of Hospital Beds*, Washington, D.C.: National Academy of Sciences. October, 1976.

Martin, D., "The Singular Power of a Giant Called Exxon," *The New York Times*, May 9, 1982, Business p. 1.

Morley, J., "Contradictions of Cocaine Capitalism, *The Nation*, October 2, 1989.

Phillips, K., *The Politics of Rich and Poor*, New York: Random House, 1990.

USDHEW: U.S. Department of Health, Education, and Welfare, *National Guidelines for Health Planning* (Draft). Washington, DC: Health Resources Administration, 1979.

Weinraub, B., "President Offers Strategy," *The New York Times*, September 6, 1989, pp. 1, B7.

APPENDIX VI
"Scientific" Racism and *The Bell Curve*
Dino Louis
1995

Author's Commentary

Like Appendix III, this one consists of sketches and notes by Dino Louis. They were apparently made for a planned essay on the development of "scientific" racism by the Right-Wing Reactionaries during the late Transition Era. The notes were made following the publication of a book called *The Bell Curve* by two self-styled academics, Richard J. Herrnstein and Charles Murray (1994). Herrnstein, because of his repeatedly discredited attempts to use what he and a very small coterie of like-minded academics called "science" to prove racist theories, and Murray because he had no independent academic standing of any kind beyond his Right-Wing Reactionary foundation funding, in fact had no standing in the general social science academic community of the time.

In their book, they attempted to prove that the lower "Intelligence Quotient" levels ("IQ" was a primitive measure of human intelligence long since discarded as a tool for serious study) found by some researchers among "blacks" as compared with "whites" in the old U.S. were produced by genetic differences between the two groups (Browne). They then went on to argue that since "blacks" were genetically inferior to "whites," it didn't make any sense for the latter to spend any money trying to bring the former up to either educational or economic speed.

(One detail always ignored by racists, whether of the scientific or non-scientific variety, was exactly how skin color could be used to define anyone into groups. First of all, it was a given that there was a very wide range of skin color in any of the "races" as the racists defined them. Some "blacks" had lighter skin tones than some "whites." But that made no difference to the racists' group assignments. Furthermore, in any one individual whether "white" or "black," skin tone often changed over time in response to such factors as sun exposure, weathering, or ageing. But such facts, as was so often the case, failed to confuse the analysis of any dedicated racist, whether of the scientific or the non-scientific variety.)

The material which Louis put together, apparently in the first half of 1995, consists primarily of quotes from articles that he intended to use for his analysis, plus a few jottings of his own. Louis apparently never completed the essay for which he gathered these quotes, and there is no evidence that he ever published anything like it. Nevertheless, the reader should find the material useful in understanding what came to happen to the old U.S. in its later years.

"Scientific" racism had a long history in the white Western world, linked with the names of such discredited "scientists" as Jensen and Shockley, Galton and Pearson, Osborn and Davenport (Chase). Its "scientific" base had been on more than one occasion shown to be patently false, as for example in the lengthy book by Allan Chase entitled *The Legacy of Malthus: The Social Costs of the New Scientific Racism* (1977). Chase summarized the general theory of "scientific" racism well in the Preface to his book (p. xv):

> "Scientific racism is, essentially, the perversion of scientific and historical facts to create the myth of two distinct races of humankind. The first of these 'races' is, in all countries, a small elite whose members are healthy, wealthy (generally by inheritance), and educable. The other 'race' consists of the far larger populations of the world who are vulnerable, poor or non-wealthy, and allegedly uneducable by virtue of hereditarily inferior brains.
>
> "In the teachings of scientific racism, most of the

> human race's physiological ailments, anatomical defects, behavioral disorders and—above all else—the complex of socio-economic afflictions called poverty are classified as being caused by the inferior hereditary or genetic endowments of people and races. Historically, these core pseudo-genetic myths … have provided … 'scientific' rationales for doing nothing or next to nothing about the prevention of scores of well-understood impediments to proper physical and mental development. …
>
> "Coupled, as it often is and has been, with much older forms of gut racism based on religious, racial, and ethnic bigotry, scientific racism invariably exacerbates the already agonizing traumas … for all minorities from Auschwitz and Belfast to Boston and Birmingham (AL). Nevertheless, bigotry is not one of the functions of scientific racism; it is merely a later adjunct in the furtherance of the basic socioeconomic functions of scientific racism."

And, one might add, its political functions as well.

In the old U.S., the political forces that were supported by "scientific" racism eventually went on to carry the theory to its logical conclusion and form the NAR. "Scientific" racism itself became the basis of all "science" in the NAR: ideology clearly and completely replaced observation and experimentation. (In that, it was much like the "genetics" of Tofim Lysenko in the Stalinist Soviet Union.) During the run-up to the establishment of the NAR, data that didn't fit theory was simply ignored, as in, for example: "creation science," "Holocaust revisionism," "Wise Use environmentalism," the "social science" of Right-Wing Reactionary "welfare reform."

It is ironic that the complete devotion of the Hagueites of the NAR to "scientific" racism would hold the seeds of their eventual downfall. As pointed out in Chapter 17, so committed were they to the idea that blacks were genetically less intelligent than whites that once the NAR came into existence, they disregarded all the intelligence being gathered from the "Negro

Republic:" first, that the blacks were building self-sufficient communities; second, that they were making scientific advances in such areas as hydroponics and the generation of solar power; third, when it eventually happened, that they were building an effective, pan-racial resistance movement.

But let us see, primarily in the words of sources that Louis would have used if he had ever gotten around to writing his planned essay, what the "scientific" racism of the late Transition Era was all about.

On "Scientific" Racism: Some Notes (by Dino Louis)

Jim Naureckas, editor of *FAIR: EXTRA!*, has put this matter of the Murray/Herrnstein book very well (1995, p. 12):

> "When *The New Republic*[1] devoted almost an entire issue 10/31/94[2] , to a debate with the authors of *The Bell Curve*, editor Andrew Sullivan justified the decision by writing, 'The notion that there might be resilient *ethnic* differences in intelligence is not, we believe, an inherently *racist* belief [emphasis added].'
>
> "In fact, the idea that some races are inherently inferior to others is the definition of racism. What *The New Republic* was saying—along with other media outlets that prominently and respectfully considered the thesis ... is that racism is a respectable intellectual position, and had a legitimate place in the national debate on race. ..."

Naureckas pointed out that columnists in the *Washington Post*[3] and *Newsweek*[4] treated the Herrnstein/Murray material

1. *Author's Note:* a self-styled "neo-liberal," truly center-right political magazine of the time.

2. *Author's Note:* appropriately, Halloween.

3. *Author's Note:* the one major daily newspaper in the nation's capital.

4. *Author's Note:* a right-wing weekly newsmagazine

as "mainstream," even while Murray himself was telling *The New York Times* that "some of the things we read to do this work, we literally hide when we're on planes and trains." Not so "mainstream" after all, it would seem.

Naureckas went on to point out that Murray was right, on that point. Nearly all the "research" they cited to support their claims on the relationship between race and IQ was paid for by the Pioneer Fund, characterized by the London *Sunday Telegraph*, hardly a left-wing rag itself, as a "neo-Nazi organization closely integrated with the far right in American politics."

One of the leading Pioneer Fund "researchers" on whose work Herrnstein and Murray rely heavily is one Richard Lynn, a professor of psychology at Ulster University (in Northern Ireland) who once said:

> "What is called for here is not genocide, the killing off of the population of incompetent cultures. But we do need to think realistically in terms of 'phasing out' of such peoples. ... Evolutionary progress means the extinction of the less competent. To think otherwise is mere sentimentality."

The assertion that there is a black-white IQ gap at all (hardly supported by all research on the subject), and that it cannot be closed by any human efforts, is supported by the "research" of another group of Pioneer Fund beneficiaries.

Naureckas points out that Herrnstein and Murray, not wanting to be confused by facts, simply ignore the findings of social scientists like Jane Mercer that when IQ differences are found, they wash out if the data are adjusted for socioeconomic variables. But, Naureckas points out, the writings of Arthur Jensen, thoroughly discredited in the 70s by the work of Allan Chase among others, appear frequently in their footnotes. And Naureckas goes on with much more evidence of the use by Herrnstein/Murray of biased, pseudo-scientific sources.

Although according to Naureckas that well-known social

scientist Pat Buchanan reflected that "'I think a lot of the data are indisputable,'" Naureckas concluded that "*The Bell Curve* does indeed tell closet racists that they aren't bigots, and makes them feel better by saying that their prejudices are grounded in science."

The New York Times editorialized (1994): "At its best, the Herrnstein-Murray story is an unconvincing reading of murky evidence. At its worst it is perniciously and purposely incendiary."

The National Rainbow Coalition[5] was more direct (1994):

> "Murrayism is racism. … *The Bell Curve* … is a new book with an old theme—white racial superiority. … We define racism in four basic ways, and in a particular order: the first being as a *systematic philosophy* that defines one race as superior and another race as inferior. In fact, Murray says Asians are the most superior race.[6] The second, *prejudice* (i.e., prejudging individuals on the basis of group stereotypes); the third, *behavior* (i.e., actions, such as castrations and lynchings); and fourth, *institutional* (i.e., where the legal, social, economic and political structures produce racist results even though, to the casual eye, it may appear to be the result of 'neutral' or 'natural' causes or developments), all flow and follow logically and naturally from the first. …
>
> "Murray's *Bell Curve* is neither logically, biologically nor theoretically sound. Murray's 'white logic' leads to the following illogic: 'While on the one hand,' he says, 'Black people are inherently intellectually inferior,' on the other these intellectually inferior blacks are taking *advantage* of intellectually *superior* whites by taking their slots in school and at work because of government mandated affirmative action programs; and by taking their political slots because of the Voting Rights Act."

5. *Author's Note:* a prominent Black political organization of the time.

6. *Author's Note:* try selling *that* one in California between 1850 and 1950!

In other words, if Blacks are so dumb, how could they have achieved what they have achieved, even if their achievements are limited.

Jim Holt (1994) has raised a number of important scientific issues. Among them, he points out that:

> "The human species most likely arose only a hundred thousand years or so ago--the day before yesterday in evolutionary time. That means that any differences among the races must have emerged since then. Superficial adaptations like skin color can evolve very quickly, in a matter of several thousand years. Changes in brain structure and capacity take far longer—on the order of hundreds of thousands of years. Moreover, there is no evidence for such changes since Homo sapiens first appeared on the fossil record. *Innate differences in intelligence among the races have simply not had enough time to evolve* [emphasis added].
>
> "Second, genetic diversity among the races is minuscule. Molecular biologists can now examine genes in different geographical populations. What they have found is that the overwhelming majority of the variation observed—more than 85 percent—is among individuals *within the same race* [emphasis added]. ... [b]iologically speaking, a person's color reveals very little indeed about what's beneath his skin."

This conclusion is based on 50 years of research in population genetics. A principal finding of the definitive work in the field, the book *The History and Geography of Human Genes* by Luca Cavalli-Sforza, Paolo Menozzi, and Alberto Piazza is that (Subramanian): "Once genes for surface traits such as coloration and stature are discounted, the human races are remarkably alike under the skin. The variation among individuals is much greater than differences among groups. In fact, the diversity among individuals is so enormous that the whole concept of race becomes meaningless at the genetic level. The authors say there is 'no scientific basis' for theories touting the genetic superiority of any population over another."

The newspaper columnist Robert Reno commented on Herrnstein/Murray's use of psychometry (a now discarded field that was about as much a science as were alchemy and phrenology) (1994):

> "(1.) The 'science' of psychometry—the measurement of mental abilities—has a lengthy and somewhat disreputable history. The ideas that even modern IQ tests have reached some state-of-the-art infallibility is ridiculous. (2.) The slop Murray has served up is not only unappetizing but warmed over. Proving the inferiority of races has for 100 years been the mischief of self-promoting scholars as credentialed as Murray and as squalid as the louts who churned out the 'science' behind Dr. Goebbels' loathsome ravings. Giving Murray an 'A' for originality—or even guts—is an offense to their infamy. (3.) There is a convincing body of scientific literature suggesting Murray is simply wrong, is practicing bad genetics, that interracial differences in IQ scores are really explained by such factors as pre- and post-natal experiences."

The columnist E.J. Dionne is slightly more polite about the matter (1994):

> "[There] is a recurring pattern in American history. Whenever the social reformers are seen as failing, along come allegedly new theories about how the quest for greater fairness or justice or equality is really hopeless because people and groups are, from birth, so different. The social reformer is dismissed as a naive meddler in some grand 'natural' process that sorts people out all by itself. … The implicit argument of the book is that if

> genes are so important to intelligence and intelligence is so important to success, then many of the efforts made over the past several decades to improve people's life chances were mostly a waste of time. … Herrnstein and Murray themselves say that estimates of whether IQ is inheritable range from 40 to 80 percent. This is science? … The Herrnstein/Murray book is not a 'scientific' book, but a political argument offered by skilled polemicists aimed at defeating egalitarians."

Bob Herbert, a columnist in *The New York Times*, got back to bluntness (1994):

> "Mr. Murray fancies himself a social scientist, an odd choice of profession for someone who would have us believe he was so sociologically ignorant as a teenager that he didn't recognize any racial implications when he and friends burned a cross on a hill in his hometown of Newton, Iowa. In a *New York Times Magazine* article by Jason De Parle, Mr. Murray described the cross-burning as 'dumb.' But he insisted, 'It never crossed our minds that this had any larger significance.' Oh no, of course not. … *The Bell Curve* [is] … an ugly stunt. Mr. Murray can protest all he wants, his book is just a genteel way of calling somebody a nigger."

As to the positive power of intervention for helping people with lower IQs that according to Herrnstein/Murray does not exist, Richard Nesbitt, a Distinguished Professor of Psychology at the University of Michigan, summarized at length the voluminous evidence to the contrary. He concluded by saying (1994):

> "[I]n truth, the genetic basis for IQ differences between the races is not much discussed by social scientists because few believe the evidence has sufficient credibility

> to make it worth talking about. By contrast, the issue of alterability is much discussed by social scientists because new successes are being discovered all the time."

An extensive bibliography of criticism and critique of *The Bell Curve* was published in the *Poverty and Race* newsletter (1995). It should prove to be very helpful, as will the Special Issue of *Discover* magazine, "The Science of Race" (November, 1994).

In the end, the scientific research shows that there is simply no basis in fact for work of the likes of Herrnstein and Murray—there is not even a gene for race much less a race-linked gene that confers different levels of intelligence on members of different "races." One wonders, however, if there is not a gene for racism. The trait clearly runs in families, in regions, and among people of common ancestry. It is clearly associated with certain socioeconomically-based individual interests that are linked among both families and homogeneous social groupings. It is also indicative of a diminished level of intelligence. Perhaps Herrnstein and Murray are right after all.

References:

Browne, M.W., "What Is Intelligence, and Who Has It?" [a review of *The Bell Curve* along with two other racist books], *The New York Times Book Review*, October 16, 1994, p. 3.

Chase, A., *The Legacy of Malthus: The Social Costs of the New Scientific Racism*, New York: Knopf, 1977.

Dionne, E.J., "Saying Genes Rule Lives Is a Cop-Out for Society," *Newsday*, October 20, 1994.

Herbert, B., "Throwing a Curve," *The New York Times*, October 26, 1994.

Herrnstein, R.J. and Murray, C., *The Bell Curve*, New York: The Free Press, 1994.

Holt, J., "Anti-Social Science?" *The New York Times*, October 19, 1994.

National Rainbow Coalition, "Murrayism is Racism," *JaxFax*, Vol. II, Issue 43, 10/27/94.

Naureckas, J., "Racism Resurgent: How Media Let *The Bell Curve*'s Pseudo Science Define the Agenda on Race," *FAIR: EXTRA!*, Jan./Feb. 1995, p. 12.

Nesbitt, R., "Warning! Dangerous Curves Ahead," *Newsday*, October 23, 1994.

The New York Times, "The Bell 'Curve' Agenda," October 24, 1994.

Poverty and Race, "Anti-Murrayiana," Vol. 4, No. 1, January/February 1995, p. 18.

Reno, R., "'Bell Curve' Just Gives Ammo to Garbage Carriers," *Newsday*, October 26, 1994.

Subramanian, S., "The Story in Our Genes," *Time*, January 16, 1995, p. 54.

APPENDIX VII
The Constitution of the Re-United States of America
May 5, 2023

Preamble

We the people of the Re-United States, with faith in our humanity and ability to work together within the democratic process, in order to form a more perfect Union, banish the disease of racism, create respect for the dignity and individuality of each human being, establish justice, implement true multiculturalism, insure domestic tranquility, promote the general welfare, protect our environment, provide for the common defence, recognize the essentiality of interdependence and community to individual and species survival, and secure the blessings of freedom and liberty to ourselves and our posterity, do ordain and reestablish this Constitution for the United States of America.

ARTICLE I

Section 1. Pursuant to carrying out the responsibilities of the Federal government as stated by the Preamble to this Constitution, all legislative powers herein granted shall be vested in a Congress of the United States, which shall consist of a Senate and House of Representatives.[1]

No person shall be a member of the Executive Branch of the Federal government, a Senator or Representative in Congress, a judge at the Federal, state or local level, or hold

1. *Author's Note:* the Preamble, largely ignored by politicians, policymakers, and historians of all stripes in the old United States, was explicitly incorporated into the sections of the reestablished Constitution that described the legislative, executive, and judicial branches of the Federal government.

any office, civil or military, under the Re-United States or any State or local government thereof, who held an office of any kind at the Federal, state or local or any other organizational level under that regime known as the "New American Republics." But Congress may by a vote of two-thirds of each House, remove such disability.[2]

The Congress shall assemble at least once in every year, and such meeting shall begin at noon on the 3rd day of January, unless that day be a Saturday or a Sunday, in which case the Congress shall assemble on January 5th or 4th respectively.[3]

The terms of Senators and Representatives shall end at noon on the day of Congressional assembly in the odd-numbered years; and the terms of their successors shall then begin, except as otherwise provided for in the next two Sections.

Section 2. The House of Representatives shall be composed of 435 members chosen every second even-numbered year by the people of the several States, except that should the first national election of the Re-United States be held in an odd-numbered year, the first term of each elected Representative shall be for three years. The electors in each State shall have the qualifications requisite for electors of the most numerous branch of the State legislature.

No person shall be a Representative who shall not have attained to the age of twenty-five years, and been seven years a citizen of the United States, and who shall not, when elected, be an inhabitant of that State in which she/he shall be chosen.

The 435 seats in the House of Representatives shall be distributed among the several states in proportion by population

2. *Author's Note:* this paragraph is a reworking of Amendment XIV, Section 2, of the old Constitution. Among other things, it clearly established the Federal government's authority over the composition of the State and local governments. As elsewhere in the Constitution, with the creation of the system of direct election for President/Vice President, the former reference to "electors" was deleted.

3. *Author's Note:* this provision incorporated a slightly modified version of Section 2 of the old XXth Amendment.

as determined by the Federal census. They shall be elected from districts having reasonably symmetrical geographical boundaries.[4]

A provisional distribution of House seats by State shall be made by the convention that drafted this Constitution. The next following enumeration of House seats by State shall be made according to the best national census data available at the time within one year after the first meeting of the Congress of the Re-United States, to be revised in proportion to population as of January third of the first initial decade year (e.g., 2030) after the ratification of this Constitution, and subsequently every ten years, in such manner as the Congress shall by law direct.

Section 3. The Senate of the United States shall be composed of 153 members, distributed in proportion by population among the States, all Senators to be elected at large within each State, no State to have fewer than one Senator. The term of office shall be six years. The electors in each State shall have the qualifications requisite for electors of the most numerous branch of the State legislatures. The States shall provide for cumulative voting for the Senate seats.[5]

When vacancies occur in the representation of any State in the Senate, the executive authority of such State shall issue writs of election to fill such vacancies; provided, that the

---

4. *Author's Note:* the latter sentence was inserted in an attempt to deal with the old political practice of "gerrymandering," named after an early nineteenth century governor of Massachusetts, Elbridge Gerry, who, if he was not the first to draw odd-shaped legislative districts to meet electoral needs, was certainly an early prominent practitioner of the art.

5. *Author's Note:* the Senate as a separate, longer-term, hopefully more deliberative institution was preserved. But representation by State in it was made proportional to population, and with the adoption of cumulative voting, some provision for proportional representation within each state was made. The number 153 provided that two-thirds of the seats in the Senate would, assuming that Hawaii and Alaska voted to rejoin the Union, be awarded to the states in proportion to their relative populations, and that the Federal District would have one Senate seat (see Section 8, on the Federal District).

legislature of any State may empower the executive thereof to make temporary appointments until the people fill the vacancies by election as the legislature may direct.[6]

Immediately after they shall be assembled in consequence of the first election, the Senators shall be divided as equally as may be into three classes. The seats of the Senators of the first class shall be vacated at the expiration of the second year (except that should the first national election of the Re-United States be held in an odd-numbered year, the first class shall serve for three years), of the second class two years following the expiration of the first term of the first class, and the third class four years following the expiration of the first term of the first class, so that, after any adjustments in the term lengths of the first elected Senators made so that national elections will be held in odd-numbered years, one-third will be chosen every second year.

No person shall be a Senator who shall not have attained the age of thirty years, and been nine years a citizen of the United States, and who shall not, when elected, be an inhabitant of that State for which she or he shall be chosen.

The Vice President of the United States shall be President of the Senate, but shall have no vote, unless they be equally divided.

The Senate shall choose their other officers, and also a President *pro tempore*, in the absence of the Vice President, or when she or he shall exercise the office of President of the United States.

The Senate shall have the sole power to try all impeachments. When sitting for that purpose, they shall be on oath or affirmation. When the President of the United States is tried, the Chief Justice shall preside; and no person shall be convicted without the concurrence of two-thirds of the members present.

Judgment in cases of impeachment shall not extend further than to removal from office, and disqualification to hold and enjoy any office of honor, trust or profit under the United

6. *Author's Note:* the first two paragraphs of this Section incorporate in part the XVIIth Amendment to the old Constitution.

States; but the party convicted shall nevertheless be liable and subject to indictment, trial, judgment and punishment, according to Law.

Section 4. The times, places and manner of holding elections for Senators and Representatives, shall be prescribed in each State by the legislature thereof, except as otherwise provided herein; but unless contrary to the explicit provisions of this Constitution, the Congress may at any time by law make or alter such regulations, except as to the composition of each House and the mode of elections, and except that the national elections for members of the Congress and the President/Vice President shall take place on the first Tuesday in November in the designated years.[7]

Section 5. Each House shall be the judge of the elections, returns and qualifications of its own members, and a majority of each shall constitute a quorum to do business; but a smaller number may adjourn from day to day, and may be authorized to compel the attendance of absent members, in such manner, and under such penalties as each House may provide.

Each House may determine the rules of its proceedings, punish its members for disorderly behavior, and, with the concurrence of two-thirds, expel a member, except that no rule requiring more than a majority vote for the passage of any measure may be adopted, except as explicitly provided for in this Constitution.[8]

Each House shall keep a Journal of its proceedings, and from time to time publish the same, excepting such parts as may in their judgment require secrecy; and the yeas and nays

7. *Author's Note:* this provision was designed to retain the old national "Election Day," by specification.

8. *Author's note:* this provision was designed to prevent the reinstitution of the "filibuster rule" in the Senate, under which a minority could prevent a matter from coming to a vote, and to prevent the passage of any "3/5ths" rule for tax increases or any similar anti-democratic measures.

of the members of either House on any question shall, at the desire of one fifth of those present, be entered on the Journal.

Neither House, during the session of Congress, shall, without the consent of the other, adjourn for more than three days, nor to any other place than that in which the two Houses shall be sitting.

Section 6. The Senators and Representatives shall receive a compensation for their services, to be ascertained by law, and paid out of the Treasury of the United States. They shall in all cases, except treason, felony and breach of the peace, be privileged from arrest during their attendance at the session of their respective Houses, and in going to and returning from the same; and for any speech or debate in either House, they shall not be questioned in any other place.

No Senator or Representative shall, during the time for which she or he was elected, be appointed to any civil office under the authority of the United States, which shall have been created, or the emoluments whereof shall have been increased during such time; and no person holding any office under the United States, shall be a member of either House during his/her continuance in office.

No law, varying the compensation for the services of the Senators and Representatives, shall take effect until an election of Representatives shall have intervened.[9]

All elections, Federal, State, and local, are to be publicly financed, under law as Congress shall establish. Private contributions to election campaigns shall be permitted, but not to an amount greater than 20% of the public financing provided, either for any one candidate, or collectively for the candidates of any one party or other political organization that exists for the purpose, among others, of electing candidates to office, or for the general political activities of any political

9. *Author's Note:* this paragraph incorporated the XXVIIth Amendment to the Constitution of the old United States.

party or other political organization that exists for the purpose, among others, of electing candidates to office. No political contributions of any kind, for any purpose, over $1000.00 (adjusted annually by the average national Consumer Price Index) may be made, by any individual or private organization. No Political Action Committees or similar organizations representing private corporations, trade associations, or trade unions are permitted to make political contributions of any kind.

All representatives of private interests seeking to influence governmental actions at the Federal, State, and local level must register publicly, under law(s) to be established by the Congress. The registration statement must at a minimum include the interests, firms, and/or agencies represented by the representative(s), the specific law(s) and regulations that are of concern to them, and must be renewed annually.[10]

Section 7. All bills for raising revenue shall originate in the House of Representatives; but the Senate may propose or concur with amendments as on other bills.

Every bill which shall have passed the House of Representatives and the Senate, shall, before it becomes a law, be presented to the President of the United States; if he or she approves, he or she shall sign it, but if not it shall be returned with the objections, to that House in which it shall have originated, which shall enter the objections at large on their Journal, and proceed to reconsider it. If after such reconsideration two-thirds of that House shall agree to pass the bill, it shall be sent, together with the objections, to the other House, by which it shall likewise be reconsidered, and if approved by two-thirds of that House, it shall become a law. But in all such cases the votes of both Houses shall be determined by yeas and nays, and the names of the persons voting for and

10. *Author's Note:* the practice of buying the votes of Senators and Representatives through the medium of political campaign contributions had accelerated during the Transition Era. For the most part, before the onset of the Fascist Period attempts to institute significant "campaign finance" and "lobbying" reforms failed, while the practices at which such reform attempts were aimed played a major role in the onset of fascism. Thus the reforms were put directly into the Restored Constitution.

against the bill shall be entered on the Journal of each House respectively. If any bill shall not be returned by the President within ten days (Sundays excepted) after it shall have been presented to him, the same shall be a law, in like manner as if she or he had signed it, unless the Congress by their adjournment prevents its return, in which case it shall not be a law.

Every order, resolution, or vote to which the concurrence of the Senate and House of Representatives may be necessary (except on a question of adjournment) shall be presented to the President of the United States; and before the same shall take effect, shall be approved by him or her, or being disapproved by him or her, shall be repassed by two-thirds of the Senate and House of Representatives, according to the rules and limitations prescribed in the case of a bill.

Section 8. The Congress shall have power to enact legislation under the provisions of this Constitution, designed to carry out the substantive responsibilities of the Federal government as set forth in the Preamble to this Constitution, as well as in all the Sections of this Constitution.[11]

To establish an economic policy based on the following principles: the market for capital investment decisions will be socially based while the market for the production, distribution, and sale of goods and services will be both socially and privately based; the primary form of production will be for use; the establishment of equality of economic opportunity, the elimination of poverty, and the maintenance of a reasonable differential in both income and wealth between the richest and poorest members of society will be a primary objective; the restoration,

11. *Author's Note:* this provision made explicit what was implicit and largely ignored in the old U.S. Given its Preamble, "We the people of the United States, in order to form a more perfect Union, establish justice, insure domestic tranquility, provide for the common defence, promote the general welfare, and secure the blessings of liberty to ourselves and our posterity, do ordain and establish this Constitution for the United States of America," even the old U.S. Constitution provided for a powerful Federal government with wide-ranging authority and responsibilities, given only the political will and ability to make it so.

protection and renewal of the environment, and the use of natural resources so as to support sustainable growth will be a fundamental principle guiding all economic activity.

To lay and collect taxes, including taxes on incomes, from whatever source derived, without apportionment among the several States, and without regard to any census or enumeration[12]; duties; imposts and excises; to pay the debts and provide for the common defense and general welfare of the United States; but all duties, imposts and excises shall be uniform throughout the United States;

To borrow money on the credit of the United States;

To regulate commerce with foreign nations and among the several States[13];

To establish uniform laws on the subject of bankruptcies throughout the United States;

To coin money, regulate the value thereof, and of foreign coin, and fix the standard of weights and measures;

To provide for the punishment of counterfeiting the securities and current coin of the United States;

To establish post offices and post roads;

To establish uniform rules of national citizenship and naturalization[14];

To promote the progress of science and the arts, such

---

12. *Author's Note:* this phrase incorporated the XVIth amendment from the old Constitution and eliminated the provision located at this point in the old Constitution requiring enumeration for the laying of taxes.

13. *Author's Note:* the phrase from the old Constitution "and with the Indian tribes" was deleted here, for obvious reasons.

14. *Author's Note:* the concept of national citizenship did not appear in the original body of the old Constitution. Although contrary to the position taken increasingly during the late Transition Era and the Fascist Period by such spokesmen for Right-Wing Reaction as Supreme Court Justice Clarence Thomas that national citizenship did not exist, it was, as it happened, established in the old Constitution by the language of the Preamble, of Article I, Sections 2 and 3, and of Section 1 of the XIVth Amendment. However, that concept, of national citizenship, was not widely recognized as having been so established. It was explicitly set forth in this Constitution.

promotion to include but not be limited to the securing for limited times to authors and inventors the exclusive rights to their respective writings and discoveries[15];

To constitute tribunals inferior to the Supreme Court;

To define and punish piracies and felonies committed on the high seas, and offences against the law of nations;

To declare war, and make rules concerning captures on land and water[16];

To raise and support armies, but no appropriation of money to that use shall be for a longer term than two years;

To provide and maintain a Navy and an Air Force[17];

To make rules for the government and regulation of the armed Forces;

To provide for calling forth the militia to execute the laws of the Union, suppress insurrections and repel invasions;

To provide for organizing, arming, and disciplining, the militia, and for governing such part of them as may be employed in the service of the United States, reserving to the States respectively, the appointment of the officers, and the authority of training the militia according to the discipline prescribed by Congress;

To establish a Federal District on the geographic site of the former District of Columbia that shall be the seat of the government of the Re-United States, the inhabitants of such District to be entitled to such full, voting representation in the House of Representatives and one seat in the Senate, as if the District were a State[18];

---

15. *Author's Note:* this clause was expanded to explicitly create a role for the Federal government in support of the arts and the sciences.

16. *Author's Note:* the anachronistic "grant letters of marque and reprisal" was deleted.

17. *Author's Note:* there of course was no Air Force in 1787.

18. *Author's Note:* this provision created full Federal representation for the residents of the Capitol district without also creating the complex intergovernmental relations problems that outright statehood would have created; the old XXIIIrd Amendment was made moot.

To exercise authority over all other Federal lands throughout the Re-United States, which shall consist at a minimum of those territories belonging to the Federal government before 1997[19], whether they be national parks, national forests, wilderness areas, or wetlands, and in addition reclaimed devastated areas, or other lands as determined by law to be suitable and necessary subjects of Federal ownership, as well as forts, magazines, arsenals, dockyards, or other needful Federal buildings and lands[20];

To actively pursue the elimination of racism from the political, social, and economic spheres of national life[21];

To make all laws which shall be necessary and proper for carrying into execution the foregoing powers, and all other powers vested by this Constitution in the government of the United States, or in any department or officer thereof.

Section 9.[22] The privilege of the writ of *Habeas Corpus* at the Federal, state, and local levels shall not be suspended, unless when in cases of rebellion or invasion the public safety may require it.[23]

19. *Author's Note:* at which time the divestiture process that eventually had led to the passage of the "Natural Resources Access Act" of 2013 under the regime of the New American Republics had begun.

20. *Author's Note:* this provision placed the institution of Federal land ownership in the Constitution, explicitly overturned a major piece of NAR legislation–the single most important act leading the way to the creation of the "Resource Based Economy" that was so directly linked to the NAR's final, precipitous economic decline–and Constitutionally established the environmentally or militarily destroyed "devastated areas" as subject to Federal ownership and protection.

21. *Author's Note:* with the new economic structure clause with which the new Article I, Section 8 began, this anti-racism provision formed explicitly progressive "bookends" for the description of the responsibility and authority of the Congress and the national government.

22. *Author's Note:* the clause in the old Constitution that at this point referred to the African slave trade was eliminated.

23. *Author's Note:* as with many provisions of the restored Constitution, its authority was explicitly extended to cover the actions of government at all levels, in this case on the writ of *habeas corpus.*

No bill of attainder, ex post facto law, or law providing for discrimination on the basis of race, creed, color, national origin, gender, or gender identity, in accommodations, facilities, agencies, or institutions that are public, or private but available or open to or serving the public, shall be passed by Congress, or any State or local government.[24]

No tax or duty shall be laid on articles exported from any State.

No preference shall be given by any regulation of commerce or revenue to the ports of one State over those of another: nor shall vessels bound to, or from, one State, be obliged to enter, clear, or pay duties in another.

No money shall be drawn from the Treasury, but in consequence of appropriations made by law; and a regular statement and account of the receipts and expenditures of all public money shall be published from time to time.

And no person holding any office of profit or trust under them, shall, without the consent of the Congress, accept of any present, emolument, office, or title, of any kind whatever, from any king, prince, or foreign State.

Section 10. No State shall enter into any treaty, alliance, or confederation[25]; coin money, emit bills of credit; pass any bill of attainder, ex post facto law, or law impairing the obligation of contracts, or grant any title of nobility; or attempt to limit Federal statutory authority or its implementation in any manner, except as otherwise explicitly provided for by this Constitution.[26]

---

24. *Author's Note:* Note in addition to the general anti-racism provision of Article I, Section 8, the specific non-discrimination clause located here, reinforced later in this document by various provisions of the new Article VIII, covering Rights and Liberties. After a civil war fought over issues of race, sex, and class, in which the oppressor white male group representing the Corporate Power had lost, badly, this clause was now put in to protect white males as much as anybody.

25. *Author's Note:* the old provisions on granting letters of marque and reprisal and using only gold and silver coin in payment of debts were eliminated.

26. *Author's Note:* this last provision was aimed at the so-called "Chenoweth Amendment" of 1999, a Federal law that permitted the States to limit the authority ➤

No State shall, without the consent of the Congress, lay any imposts of duties on imports or exports, except what may be absolutely necessary for executing its inspection laws: and the net product of all duties and imposts, laid by any State on imports or exports, shall be for the use of the Treasury of the United States; and all such laws shall be subject to the revision and control of the Congress.

No State shall, without the consent of Congress, lay any duty of tonnage, keep troops, or ships or aircraft of war in time of peace, enter into any agreement or compact with another State, or with a foreign power, or engage in war, unless actually invaded, or in such imminent danger as will not admit of delay.

ARTICLE II

Section 1. Pursuant to carrying out the responsibilities of the Federal government as stated by the Preamble to this Constitution, the executive power shall be vested in a President of the United States of America. She or he shall hold his/her office during the term of four years, and, together with the Vice President who shall stand for election with him or her as a tandem, shall be elected by popular vote, as follows:

Election of the President/Vice President shall require the votes of 50% of those voting plus one. If in an election there shall be three or more President/Vice President entries, and if none of them shall receive 50% of the vote plus one, there then shall be a runoff election as between the two President/Vice President entries receiving the highest number of votes in the first-round balloting, the winner to be the entry receiving the highest number of votes in the second-round balloting.[27]

of Federal officials to carry out Federal law if local officials objected to such actions. It was named for its sponsor, Congresswoman Helen Chenoweth of Idaho, nicknamed by some during the late Transition Era as the "Militias' Mom."

27. *Author's Note:* the old Electoral College system was thus replaced by a direct election system with a guarantee that there could not be a President elected by a minority of the popular vote. Among other things, this provision made the XIIth Amendment to the old Constitution moot, and eliminated the possibility that the ➤

No person except a natural born citizen, or a citizen of the United States at the time of the adoption of this Constitution, shall be eligible to the office of President; neither shall any person be eligible to that office who shall not have attained to the age of thirty-five years, and been fourteen years a resident within the United States.

In case of the removal of the President from office, or of his/her death, or resignation, or inability to discharge the powers and duties of the said office (see Section 5 of this article), the same shall devolve on the Vice President and the Congress may by law provide for the case of removal, death, resignation, or inability, both of the President and Vice President, declaring what officer shall then act as President, and such officer shall act accordingly, until the disability be removed, or a new President shall be elected.

The President shall, at stated times, receive for his/her services a compensation, which shall neither be increased nor diminished during the period for which she or he shall have been elected, and she or he shall not receive within that period any other emolument from the United States, or any of them.

Before she or he enters on the execution of his/her office, she or he shall take the following oath or affirmation: "I do solemnly swear (or affirm) that I will faithfully execute the office of President of the Re-United States, and will to the best of my ability, preserve, protect and defend the Constitution of the Re-United States."

The terms of the President and Vice President shall begin at noon on the 20th day of the month of January next following upon their election and shall conclude four years later, at which time the terms of their successors shall then begin.[28]

---

outcome of a Presidential election, other than in the circumstance of the deaths of both the President-elect and the Vice President-elect, could be determined by the House of Representatives, as was the case under the old Constitution.

28. *Author's Note:* this provision incorporated part of the XXth Amendment to the old Constitution.

Section 2. The President shall be Commander in Chief of the Army, Navy, and Air Force of the United States, and of the militia of the several States, when called into the actual service of the United States; she or he may require the opinion, in writing, of the principal officer in each of the executive departments, upon any subject relating to the duties of their respective offices, and she or he shall have power to grant reprieves and pardons for offenses against the United States, except in cases of impeachment and crimes against the Constitution[29].

She or he shall have the power, by and with the advice and consent of the Senate, to make treaties, provided a simple majority of the Senators present concur[30]; and she or he shall nominate, and by and with the advice and consent of the Senate, shall appoint Ambassadors, other public Ministers and Consuls, Judges of the Supreme Court, and all other Officers of the United States, whose appointments are not herein otherwise provided for, and which shall be established by law. But the Congress may by law vest the appointment of such inferior Officers, as they think proper, in the President alone, in the Courts of law, or in the heads of departments.

The President shall have power to fill up all vacancies that may happen during the recess of the Senate, by granting commissions which shall expire at the end of their next session.

Section 3. She or he shall in January of each year, within four weeks of the convening of the Congress that year, give to the Congress information of the State of the Union, and recommend to their consideration such measures as she or he shall judge necessary and expedient[31]; she or he may, on extraordinary

29. *Author's Note:* see Article III, Section 3.

30. *Author's Note:* this provision replaced the old, sclerotic, two-thirds rule.

31. *Author's Note:* taking advantage of the lack of specificity of the old Constitution on the timing of the State of the Union Addresses, Presidents in the very late Transition Era and the Fascist Period skipped it altogether, thereby avoiding the necessity of giving the Congress, much less the nation, any information on exactly what it was they were doing.

occasions, convene both Houses, or either of them, and in case of disagreement between them, with respect to the time of adjournment, she or he may adjourn them to such time as she or he shall receive Ambassadors and other public Ministers; she or he shall take care that the laws be faithfully executed, and shall commission all the officers of the United States.

Section 4. The President, Vice President and all civil officers of the United States, shall be removed from office on impeachment for, and conviction of, treason, bribery, or other high crimes and misdemeanors.

Section 5. If, at the time fixed for the beginning of the term of the President, the President-elect shall have died, the Vice President-elect shall become President. Except as otherwise provided for in this Constitution, if a President shall not have been chosen before the time fixed for the beginning of his/her term, or if the President-elect shall have failed to qualify, then the Vice President-elect shall act a President until a President shall have qualified; and the Congress may by law provide for the case wherein neither a President-elect nor a Vice President-elect shall have qualified, declaring who shall then act as President, or the manner in which one who is to act shall be selected, and such person shall act accordingly until a President or Vice President shall have qualified[32].

The Congress may by law provide for the case of the death of any of the persons from whom the House of Representatives may choose a President whenever the right of choice shall have devolved upon them, and for the case of the death of any of the persons from whom the Senate may choose a Vice President whenever the right of choice shall have devolved upon them.[33]

32. *Author's Note:* this provision incorporated Section 3 of the XXth Amendment of the old Constitution.

33. *Author's Note:* this provision incorporated Section 4 of the XXth Amendment of the old Constitution. The following four paragraphs incorporated the XXVth.

Whenever there is a vacancy in the office of the Vice President, the President shall nominate a Vice President who shall take office upon confirmation by a majority vote of both houses of Congress.

Whenever the President transmits to the President *pro tempore* of the Senate and the Speaker of the House of Representatives his/her written declaration that she or he is unable to discharge the powers and duties of his/her office, and until she or he transmits to them a written declaration to the contrary, such powers and duties shall be discharged by the Vice President as Acting President.

Whenever the Vice President and a majority of either the principal officers of the executive departments or of such other body as Congress may by law provide, transmit to the President *pro tempore* of the Senate and the Speaker of the House of Representatives their written declaration that the President is unable to discharge the powers and duties of his/her office, the Vice President shall immediately assume the powers and duties of the office as Acting President. Thereafter, when the President transmits to the President *pro tempore* of the Senate and the Speaker of the House of Representatives his/her written declaration that no inability exists, she or he shall resume the powers and duties of his/her office unless the Vice President and a majority of either the principal officers of the executive department or of such other body as Congress may by law provide, transmit within four days to the President *pro tempore* of the Senate and the Speaker of the House of Representatives their written declaration that the President is unable to discharge the powers and duties of his/her office. Thereupon Congress shall decide the issue, assembling within forty-eight hours for that purpose if not in session. If the Congress, within twenty-one days after receipt of the latter written declaration, or, if Congress is not is session, within twenty-one days after Congress is required to assemble, determines by two-thirds vote of both houses that the President is unable to discharge the powers and duties of his/her office, the Vice President shall continue to discharge the same as Acting President; otherwise, the President shall resume the powers and duties of his/her office.

ARTICLE III

Section 1. Pursuant to carrying out the responsibilities of the Federal government as stated by the Preamble to this Constitution, the judicial power of the United States shall be vested in one Supreme Court, one level of subordinate appellate Courts, and one level of trial Courts, under law and regulation to be provided for by the Congress[34]. The Judges, both of the Supreme and inferior Courts, shall hold their offices during good behavior, and shall, at stated times, receive for their services, a compensation, which shall not be diminished during their continuance in office.

The Supreme Court shall have the power and authority of judicial review of the Constitutionality of actions of the other two branches of the Federal government, and of the actions of all branches of the State and local governments. All such branches shall be required to follow the decision of the Court in Constitutional matters.[35]

Section 2. The judicial power shall extend to all cases, in law and equity, arising under this Constitution, the laws of the United States, and treaties made, or which shall be made, under their authority; to all cases affecting Ambassadors, other public Ministers and Consuls; to all cases of admiralty and maritime jurisdiction; to controversies to which the United States shall be a party; to controversies between two or more States; between

34. *Author's Note:* this provision was designed to prevent the reformation of such institutions as the "Drug Courts" and "Life Preservation Courts" of the late Transition Era and Fascist Period.

35. *Author's Note:* this provision put into the Constitution the principle of judicial review developed in the early 19th century by Chief Justice John Marshall and his colleagues. That principle had been accepted and followed by all branches of government at all jurisdictional levels, until the Supreme Court removed from itself the judicial review power, in *Anderson v. Board of Education* (2003, see Chapter 5).

citizens of different States, between citizens of the same State claiming lands under grants of different States.[36]

In all cases affecting Ambassadors, other public Ministers and Consuls, and those in which a State shall be party, the Supreme Court shall have original jurisdiction. In all the other cases before mentioned, the Supreme Court shall have appellate jurisdiction, both as to law and fact, with such exceptions, and under such regulations as the Congress shall make.

The trial of all crimes, except in cases of impeachment, shall be by jury; and such trial shall be held in the State where the said crimes shall have been committed; but when not committed within any State, the trial shall be at such place or places as the Congress may by law have directed.[37]

Section 3. Treason against the United States, shall consist only in levying war against them, or in adhering to their enemies, giving them aid and comfort. No person shall be convicted of treason unless on the testimony of two witnesses to the same overt act, or on confession in open court. The legal category "Crimes Against the Constitution" shall be defined by Congress, but it shall be applied only to acts performed by officers, employees, and other self-declared representatives of that regime known as the "New American Republics," from the time of its establishment to the time of its dissolution.

The Congress shall have power to declare the punishment of treason, but no attainder of treason shall work corruption of blood, or forfeiture except during the life of the person attainted.

Section 4. Any decision handed down by the Supreme Court of the former United States before May 13, 2003 may be referred to as precedent for decisions of the Supreme Court of the Re-United

36. *Author's Note:* this section takes into account the XIth Amendment of the old Constitution.

37. *Author's Note:* this provision was modified in the old Constitution by the VIth and VIIth Amendments, incorporated into this Constitution as Sections 6 and 7 respectively of the new Article VIII

States, or any other Federal State, or local court; no decision handed down by the Supreme Court of the former United States or that regime known as the "New American Republics" on or after May 13, 2003 may be referred to as precedent by the Supreme Court of the Re-United States, or any other Federal, State, or local court.[38]

ARTICLE IV

Section 1. Full faith and credit shall be given in each State to the public acts, records, and judicial proceedings of every other State. And the Congress may by general laws prescribe the manner in which such acts, records and proceedings shall be proved, and the effect thereof.

Section 2. The citizens of each State shall be entitled to all privileges and immunities of citizens in the several States.

A person charged in any State with treason, felony, or other crime, who shall flee from justice, and be found in another state, shall on demand of the executive authority of the State from which she or he fled, be delivered up to be removed to the State having jurisdiction of the crime.[39]

Section 3. New States may be admitted by the Congress into this Union; but no new State shall be formed or erected within the jurisdiction of any other State; nor any State be formed by the junction of two or more States, or parts of States, without the consent of the legislatures of the States concerned as well as of the Congress.

The Congress shall have power to dispose of and make all needful rules and regulations respecting the territory or other property belonging to the United States; and nothing in this Constitution shall be so construed as to prejudice any claims of the United States, or of any particular State.

38. *Author's Note:* May 13, 2003 was the date of the decision in *Anderson v. Board of Education.*

39. *Author's Note:* the paragraph of this Section of the old Constitution referring to escaped slaves had of course become moot.

Section 4. The United States shall guarantee to every State in this Union a republican form of government, and shall protect each of them against invasion; and on application of the legislature, or of the Executive (when the legislature cannot be convened) against domestic violence.

ARTICLE V

The Congress, whenever two thirds of both Houses shall deem it necessary, shall propose amendments to this Constitution, or, on the application of the legislatures of two-thirds of the several States, shall call a convention for proposing amendments, which, in either case, shall be valid to all intents and purposes, as part of this Constitution, when ratified by the legislatures of three-fourths of the several States, or by conventions in three-fourths thereof, as the one or the other mode of ratification may be proposed by the Congress.[40]

ARTICLE VI

All debts contracted and engagements entered into, by the old United States of America as well as by the regime of the "New American Republics," before the adoption of this Constitution, shall be as valid against the Re-United States under this Constitution.[41]

This Constitution, and the laws of the Re-United States which shall be made in pursuance thereof; and all treaties made, or which shall be made, under the authority of the United States shall be the supreme law of the land; no officer or judge of any Federal,

40. *Author's Note:* the slavery-specific clauses of this Article in the old Constitution had become moot. It is interesting to note that even though fascism had been first brought to the old United States by entirely legal means, especially the process of Constitutional amendment, the authors of the new Constitution were willing to put every one of its provisions at risk of future amendment. They thus put their faith in the renewal of the democratic process in the Re-United States as the primary bulwark against any future "Constitutional" reimposition of fascism. That faith has so far been fully rewarded.

41. *Author's Note:* this provision recognized the debt obligation undertaken by the Movement for the Restoration of Constitutional Democracy's National Leadership Council to the East Asian Confederation, as a consideration to the latter for their intervention in the Second Civil War on the side of the MRCD.

State, or local government may use as authority for any decision or policy any other "higher law," such as the "Law of God," the "Law of the Bible," or "Natural Law," for example[42]; and the judges in every State shall be bound thereby, any thing in the Constitution or laws of any State to the contrary notwithstanding. Nothing in this clause shall be taken to mean that scientific data or evidence or moral/ethical positions may not be offered in support of any decision made under or policy referred to in this clause.

The Senators and Representatives before mentioned, and the members of the several State legislatures, and all executive and judicial officers, both of the United States and of the several States, shall be bound by oath or affirmation, to support this Constitution; but no religious test shall be required as a qualification to any office or public trust under the United States.[43]

ARTICLE VII

The ratification of the conventions of thirty-three States[44], shall be sufficient for the establishment of this Constitution between the States so ratifying the same.

ARTICLE VIII[45]

Section 1. Congress shall make no law respecting an establishment of religion, or prohibiting the free exercise thereof, or causing

42. *Author's Note:* this provision was intended to make it clear that the old "Supremacy Amendment" (see Chapter 9) that had enabled the placement of the "Law of God" above the Constitution itself was revoked, explicitly.

43. *Author's Note:* this paragraph restored the status quo ante the adoption of the "Supremacy Amendment".

44. *Author's Note:* this is the same percentage of 48 states that the original number required for ratification of the old Constitution was of 13 states, it being unclear at the time of adoption of the new Constitution whether either Hawaii or Alaska would rejoin the Union; the Federal District was to have no role in ratification.

45. *Author's Note:* This new Article covered Rights and Liberties. In any cases of conflict with the old Bill of Rights, the original First Ten Amendments to the Constitution, the latter was amended to conform to the new, expanded list. Further, an attempt was made to remove ambiguities from the Bill of Rights, which became Sections 1-10 of this Article.

any breach in the wall of separation that stands between church and state; or abridging the freedom of speech, or of the press; or the right of the people peaceably to assemble, and to petition the Government for a redress of grievances. Freedom of speech and expression does not extend to the creation in another person of the apprehension of imminent physical harm.[46]

[The subsequent language in this Section is taken from language of the "Declaration of Rights" of the Treaty of Paris (1990) adopted by an international organization called the Conference on Security and Cooperation in Europe. This treaty was signed, ironically, by President George H.W. Bush. But it was never submitted to the old U.S. Senate for ratification (Bush, G. H. W.; "Charter of Paris"). Some of the language is redundant with that found in other Sections of this Article, but in the shadow of the horrors of American fascism and its prelude, the drafters wanted to be certain that the basic rights and freedoms would be clearly protected by the Constitution.]

Human rights and fundamental freedoms are the birthright of all citizens of the Re-United States of America, are inalienable and are guaranteed by law.

Without discrimination, every individual has the right to:

- Freedom of thought, conscience and religion or belief;
- Freedom of expression;
- Freedom of association and peaceful assembly;

No citizen of the United States of America will be:

- Subject to arbitrary arrest or detention;
- Subject to torture or other cruel, inhuman or degrading treatment or punishment;

Every citizen of the United States has the right:

- To know and act upon his/her rights.

46. *Author's Note:* this first paragraph, of course, is primarily the original "First Amendment" of the old Constitution. However, the "Wall of Separation" between Church and State fully implicit in the old Constitution was made fully explicit in this one. To prevent the exploitation of the right of free speech by the forces of hatred and division, as happened to an increasing extent during the Transition Era and of course the Fascist Period, a free speech limitation incorporating the English Common Law Intentional Tort of Assault was added to this Section.

The Congress shall have power to enforce this or any other Section of this Article by appropriate legislation.

Section 2. Each State may raise a well regulated militia, under the direction of the State government, for such purposes as it may assign; under such regulation as the Federal government may decide upon, private ownership of firearms may be permitted.[47]

Section 3. No soldier shall, in time of peace be quartered in any house, without the consent of the owner, nor in time of war, but in a manner to be prescribed by law.

Section 4. The right of the people to be secure in their persons, houses, papers, and effects, against unreasonable searches and seizures, shall not be violated, and no warrants shall issue, but upon probable cause, supported by oath or affirmation, and particularly describing the place to be searched, and the persons or things to be seized.

Section 5.[48] No person shall be held by Federal, state, or local government to answer for a capital, or otherwise infamous crime, unless on a presentment or indictment of a grand jury, except in cases arising in the land, air, or naval forces, or in the militia, when in actual service in time of war or public danger; nor shall any person be subject for the same offence to be twice put in jeopardy of life or limb; nor shall be compelled in any criminal case to be a witness against him/herself, nor be deprived of life, liberty, or property, without

47. *Author's Note:* this paragraph clarified the original intent of the old Constitution that indeed the Second Amendment applied strictly to state militias, not the private ownership of firearms, and also explicitly provided for government-regulated ownership of same.

48. *Author's Note:* this section combined the Vth with the complementary parts of the XIVth Amendments to the old Constitution.

due process of law; nor deny to any person within its jurisdiction the equal protection of the laws; nor shall private property be taken for public use, without just compensation, as that just compensation may be determined by Congress, fully taking into account the interests of both the nation and the immediate affected community as well as the private property owner.[49]

All persons born or naturalized in the United States, and subject to the jurisdiction thereof, are citizens of the United States and of the State wherein they reside. No State shall make or enforce any law which shall abridge the privileges or immunities of citizens of the United States;[50]

Section 6. In all criminal prosecutions, the accused shall enjoy the right to a speedy and public trial, by an impartial jury of the State and district wherein the crime shall have been committed, which district shall have been previously ascertained by law, and to be informed of the nature and cause of the accusation; to be confronted with the witnesses against him; to have compulsory process for obtaining witnesses in his/her favor, and to have the assistance of counsel for his/her defence.

Section 7. In suits at common law, where the value in controversy shall exceed twenty thousand dollars, the right of trial by jury shall be preserved, and no fact tried by a jury shall be otherwise reexamined in any Court of the United States, than according to the rules of the common law.

Section 8. Excessive bail shall not be required, nor excessive fines imposed, nor cruel and unusual punishments inflicted.

49. *Author's Note:* so much for the highly contentious promoter of selfishness, the old "takings clause" as it was interpreted by the greedy and selfish Right-Wing Reactionaries.

50. *Author's Note:* this paragraph of Article 8, Section 5 is taken from part of Section 1 of the old XIVth Amendment. The post First Civil War Section 2 of the XIVth had become moot. Section 3 of the XIVth (eligibility for office) was superseded by Article I Section 1 of this Constitution. Section 4 (debt obligation) was superseded by the first paragraph of Article VI of this Constitution.

Except for crimes against the Constitution committed prior to July 4th, 2023, the use of the death penalty by any level of government jurisdiction is prohibited.[51]

Section 9. The enumeration in the Constitution, of certain rights, shall not be construed to deny or disparage others retained by the people.

Section 10. The powers not delegated to the United States by the Constitution, nor prohibited by it to the States, are reserved to the States respectively, or to the people.[52]

Section 11. Equality of rights under the law shall not be denied or abridged by the United States or by any state on account of sex. The right of citizens of the United States to vote shall not be denied or abridged by the United States or by any State on account of sex.[53]

Section 12. A woman's right to choose the outcome of any pregnancy shall not be interfered with by law at any level of jurisdiction, until the time in fetal development of entirely independent viability shall be reached. The exercise of that right, free from interference by any person, organization, or governmental authority shall be protected under the law.

Section 13. No disability or discrimination may be attached to any person on account of gender preference, identity, or

---

51. *Author's Note:* thus with one, political, exception, the death penalty was outlawed.

52. *Author's Note:* all the provisions of the old XIth (judicial power definition) and XIIth (electoral college voting system modifications) Amendments had either become moot or were included elsewhere in this Constitution, as noted above.

53. *Author's Note:* this section combines the old XIXth (female suffrage) Amendment with the language of the "Equal Rights Amendment" that was passed by Congress before the onset of the Transition Era but, after an intense Right-Wing Reactionary campaign, falling short by one state of the requirement in the Old Constitution for ratification.

orientation in any public accommodation, facility, or institution, public or private employment, or educational institution receiving public support. Equal access to the benefits and requirements of the civil law may not be denied to any person on account of gender preference, identity, or orientation.

Section 14. Neither slavery nor involuntary servitude, nor confinement to a particular place or geographic location, except as a punishment for crime whereof the party shall have been duly convicted, shall exist within the United States, or any place subject to their jurisdiction. Congress shall have power to enforce this article by appropriate legislation.[54]

Section 15. The right of citizens of the United States to vote shall not be denied or abridged by the United States or by any State on account of race, color, or previous condition of servitude. The Congress shall have power to enforce this article by appropriate legislation.[55]

Section 16. The right of citizens of the United States to vote in any primary or other election for President or Vice President,

---

54. *Author's Note:* this is the old XIIIth Amendment, herein expanded to cover such crimes against humanity as the Second Holocaust. The anti-Confederacy provisions of the XIVth either became moot or were incorporated elsewhere, as noted.

55. *Author's Note:* this is the old XVth Amendment. The old XVIth (income tax provision) was incorporated into Article I, Section 8 of this Constitution. The XVIIth (referring to the procedures for electing Senators), and the XVIIIth and XXIst Amendments (alcoholic beverage sale prohibition and its repeal) had become moot. The relevant provisions of the XXth (Presidential election procedures modification) Amendment were incorporated into Articles I and II of this Constitution; the provision concerning Congressional election of the President had become moot, pursuant to the second paragraph of Article I Section 1. The Restoration Convention chose not to enact term limits of any kind, concluding that no matter how the provision might be couched and for what purpose, they would be anti-democratic. Thus the XXIInd and XXIXth Amendments were ignored. The matter of the XXIIIrd Amendment, concerning the rights of residents of the Federal District, was addressed by Article I, Section 8 of this Constitution. All of the other Transition Era/Fascist Period Amendments were of course dropped.

for electors for President or Vice President, or for Senator or Representative in Congress, shall not be denied or abridged by the United States or any State by reason of failure to pay any poll tax or other tax. Registration for voting shall be granted on the presentation of printed or electronic proof of residence in the respective voting district.[56]

Section 17. The right of citizens of the United States, who are 18 years of age or older, to vote shall not be denied or abridged by the United States or any state on account of age.[57]

DONE in convention by the unanimous consent of the States present the fifth day of May in the Year of our Lord two thousand and twenty three, and of the restoration of Constitutional democracy in the Re-United States of America, the first.

References:

Bush, G. H. W., "CSCE: Putting Principle into Practice," *U.S. Dept. of State Dispatch*, Vol. 1, No. 13, Nov. 26, 1990.

"Charter of Paris," signed, November 21, 1990; excerpts printed, *The New York Times*, Nov. 22, 1991; U.S. Dept. of State, "CSCE at a Glance: Fact Sheet," September, 1990.

56. *Author's Note:* this is the old XXIVth Amendment. The XXVth (Presidential disability) Amendment was incorporated into Article II of this Constitution.

57. *Author's Note:* this is the old XXVIth Amendment. The XXVIIth (Congressional pay-increase rules) Amendment was incorporated into Article I, Section 6, of this Constitution.

DISCLAIMER

In this book, the use of quotations from the writings, speeches, or sayings of any real person, living or dead, or real organization, institution, or agency, should in no way be taken and is not to be taken, directly, indirectly, explicitly or implicitly, to mean that any such individual, organization, institution, or agency would agree with, support, endorse, implement, or associate themselves with, in any way, form or manner, whether in present time or at some time in the future, any of the real or fictional and/or historically projected actions, legislative, executive, judicial, or other, initiatives, acts, deeds, thoughts, or actions of any kind, by any of the characters, movements, governmental or non-governmental bodies, agencies, groups, or associations, real or fictional, appearing or described in this book. Nor should it be taken that there is any implication, indication, or insinuation that any thought or action of any real person would in any way lead to any of the fictional future events, happenings, or outcomes described in this book, whether involving real or fictional persons or characters. Furthermore, any similarity between any of the fictional characters in this book and any real person, living or dead, is purely coincidental.

ABOUT THE AUTHOR

Steven Jonas, MD, MPH is a Professor of Preventive Medicine at Stony Brook University (NY). He is a Fellow of: the New York Academy of Sciences (elected), the American College of Preventive Medicine, the New York Academy of Medicine, the American Public Health Association, and the Royal Society of Medicine (London). He is the author/co-author/editor/co-editor of over 30 books and has published numerous articles and reviews in both the academic and the lay literature, on health policy, health and wellness, and athletics. On the political side, he is a Senior Editor, Politics, for *The Greanville Post* (http://www.greanvillepost.com/); Editorial Director and a Contributing Author for *The Political Junkies for Progressive Democracy* webmagazine (http://thepoliticaljunkies.org/); a Columnist for *BuzzFlash@Truthout* (http://www.buzzflash.com, http://www.truth-out.org/), a "Trusted Author" for *Op-Ed News* (http://www.opednews.com/); and a Contributor to *The Planetary Movement* (http://www.planetarymovement.org/), as well as several other progressive webmagazines. He is also a 30-plus year triathlete and a certified ski instructor.

CPSIA information can be obtained
at www.ICGtesting.com
Printed in the USA
FSHW021432230220
67318FS

9 780984 026340